I0702768

"E. Pluribus Unum"
…From Many, One."

A Novel

MARVIN V. BLAKE
(Author of "Why")

E. Pluribus Unum
Copyright © 2023 Marvin V. Blake

All rights reserved. No part of this book may be used or reproduced by any means, graphic, electronic, or mechanical, including photocopying, recording, taping or by any information storage retrieval system without the written permission of the author except in the case of brief quotations embodied in critical articles and reviews.

Because of the dynamic nature of the Internet, any web addresses or links contained in this book may have changed since publication and may no longer be valid. The views expressed in this work are solely those of the author and do not necessarily reflect the views of the publisher, and the publisher hereby disclaims any responsibility for them.

Library of Congress Control Number: 2023915139
Paperback: 979-8-9886071-5-1

Contents

"You have to be carefully taught."

—Oscar Hammerstien II

****

"It is easier to build Strong Children, than to repair broken men."

—Frederick Douglass

****

*"The Ultimate tragedy is not the oppression and cruelty by the
bad people, but the silence over that by the good people."*

—Martin Luther King, Jr.

****

*"They made us many promises, more than I can remember. But they
kept but one-they promised to take our land...and they took it."*

—Chief Red Cloud

****

With the exception of historical figures, all characters
in this novel are fictitious, and any resemblance to
living persons, present or past, is coincidental.

For...Linda

Linda Ogburn Blake

CHAPTER 1

Manassas Virginia (The Woods) - July 29, 1861

The distinctive alien, man-made sounds, of clumsy rustling movement in the thick underbrush, abruptly suspended the foraging for food by the numerous small, nocturnal, woodland animals that inhabited the forest.

Jason Billings, a runaway slave, the former manservant of a recently killed in action, officer of the army of the Confederate States of America, continued his relentless pursuit for freedom, steadily plodding through the dense forests of the northern Virginia country-side.

It had been six days since the death of his Master, Lieutenant Jesse Billings, who was mortally wounded and died, at the battle of Bull Run.

In his frantic efforts to avoid captivity, Jason had been hiding during the day, and traveling by night, using the North Star as his celestial navigational guide.

His last fixed-gaze at the heavens had revealed, brilliant panoply of stars that were now steadily, gradually, growing dimmer.

When he looked to his right, he noticed that at the horizon, the sky was beginning to change from purplish-black, to a light azure blue, nature's inevitable sentinel, heralding the rapidly approaching rising of the sun, the dawning of a new day.

Jason stopped to check his bearings. In the early morning light, he no longer had the North Star as a beacon.

He knew that his best chance of avoiding accidentally circling back toward the Confederate lines, that it was absolutely essential that he continue moving in a northeasterly direction.

Not being familiar with the dense woods of North-Eastern Virginia, there was a distinct possibility that he could become disoriented, confused, and inadvertently find himself right back were he started, behind the Confederate lines.

Jason realized that with the rising of the sun, he would soon be bereft of his celestial compass, the North Star, to guide him.

Without conscientiously realizing what he was doing, Jason as was his ritualistic habit—began to scratch at one of the two, long ago healed, and jagged twin scars, just below his rib gage, on each side of his torso.

He was now actively looking for an appropriate spot to rest. A location that would offer concealment, as well as a modicum of reasonable shade, that would provide relief from the relentless oppressive heat and humidity, of Virginia's mid-summer sun.

Jason was acutely aware of the necessity to avoid being spotted during daylight hours. The risk of being captured by the "*Slave-catchers*", white men — who for a cash bounty — made their living by capturing, and returning runaway slaves to their owners, was an ever-present danger during daylight hours.

The growth of this lucrative occupation, "Slave-Catcher", exploded following the 1850 United States Congress' passage of the Fugitive Slave Act.

As he moved deeper into the forest, Jason spotted a large fallen tree. Upon inspection he was pleased to find that through decay, the interior of the huge tree, was to a large extent, hollow.

Using his hands and several tree branches as entrenching tools, the runaway slave was able to scoop-out enough dead and decaying wood, to allow him to uncomfortably, slip inside this natural shelter.

Hungry and exhausted, Jason reached into the pocket of his gray Confederate Officer's breeches hand-me-downs, given to him by his recently killed-in-action, deceased, Master, Lieutenant Jesse Billings.

The pockets of the gray uniform pants were stained nearly Union blue, from the wild berries that the twenty-six-year-old fugitive slave, had been constantly stuffing into the pockets of his pants, during his desperate northern odyssey, his flight for freedom.

After he learned of Lieutenant Billings' death during the fighting at the first significant land battle of the civil war, the battle of Bull Run, Jason had made an impromptu, spontaneous, decision to run, to escape.

As he made his way through the woods, Jason's thoughts were of his mother, and of his brilliant, precocious, sister Mandy, who he would be leaving behind, trapped and enslaved, at the Rosewood Plantation.

Jason thought it ironic that one of his sister's favorite expressions, "*Carpe Diem*", cease the day, "*run*" this unexpected opportunity to escape slavery, was his, here and now.

Jason had not hesitated. When the opportunity arose, he had fled, making his way to freedom in the North.

****

His plan was simple. He would make his way to the Union Army lines. Once there he intended to join the ranks of Mr. Lincoln's Army of liberation, the Army of the United States of America.

More than anything, Jason yearned to be free. To be a free man, free to pursue the lofty goals that had been continuously read to him by his sister Mandy.

Those majestic, soaring, inspirational words penned by Thomas Jefferson; "Life, liberty, and the pursuit of happiness." Words boldly and proudly stated in the country's founding document, the Declaration of Independence.

In addition to his pursuit of these lofty sentiments, Jason was also committed to what for him was the noblest of all aspirations; Jason Billings wanted to free his mother and sister. He wanted to kill rebs.

To kill his life-long oppressors; to kill the white devils that had raped and killed his aunt Sadie, the aunt that he would never know; the white devils who sold his grandmother, raped his mother and countless other black women.

His reason for living, his mission, his long latent suppressed —more twenty-six years gestation—, motivation had finally surfaced.

Jason Billings wanted to kill the white men who were fighting to maintain the system, the South's *"Peculiar Institution"* Slavery, the legalized, sanctioned by law, practice of human bondage.

He specifically and especially, wanted to kill his biological father, Lucas Prentiss, the white overseer at the Rosewood Plantation.

Additionally, Jason wanted to kill Henry Billings, the Master of Virginia's Rosewood plantation. Henry Billings was the white man who had repeatedly raped his mother.

Henry Billings the white man who had impregnated his mother; who had then ignored and humiliated the product of his routine sexual assaults, Jason's sister Mandy.

Jason wanted to kill Henry Billings, the white man, who as did so many white slave owners, had enslaved his own biological daughter, Jason's sister Mandy.

Jason Billings was obsessed with his desire to kill Henry Billings, the Master of the Rosewood Plantation, the white man who he held to be directly responsible for his, and his family's life of enslavement.

Jason was determined and resolute. He had expanded his hatred and made his life's mission, the killing of any man that supported, condoned or fought for the preservation and the expansion of the political system, and the twisted ideology that held him, his family, and millions of black men, women, and children, in a state of perpetual bondage… Slavery.

Jason was eager to fight to free, and to liberate his mother and sister from the shackles of human bondage.

His mother Ruth and his sister Mandy were his only family, the family that he had been forced to leave behind. His family still held in bondage, slaves toiling on Virginia's Rosewood plantation.

****

Jason sat hunched and cramped, surrounded by a cacophony of woodland sounds, within the cool confines of the hollow log. He ignored the pins and needles "tingling", sensation in his cramped feet.

The forest was awash with the soothing wild melodious, symphony of a multitude of chirping birds, mixed with the incessant buzzing of millions of insects, and the noise made by small animals scurrying among the twigs and fallen leafs that covered the ground.

Jason was finding it increasingly difficult to keep his eyelids, which were steadily growing heavier and heavier, from closing.

Gradually the combination of the heat and the humidity trapped in the interior of the log, and Jason's fatigue, had the sedative effect of lulling the runaway slave into a fitful, dream filled, sleep.

Images and memories of his beloved mother Ruth, and of his beautiful, brilliant younger sister Mandy, who he loved and adored, continuously flitted across Jason's mind.

At the age of thirteen, Jason's mother Ruth had been an innocent, vibrant, beautiful, young, innocent girl. Ruth had just crossed the threshold from being a child, to that of becoming a young woman.

Thirteen-year-old Ruth, Jason's mother, had been raped, forced to submit to the carnal lust of Lucas Prentess, Rosewood Plantation's white overseer.

Jason was the spawn of the overseer's continuous frequent, forced sexual encounters with the helpless thirteen-year-old slave girl, Jason's mother, Ruth.

****

Jason awoke with a start. He heard the distinctive sound of what he thought was multiple boots crunching twigs and debris, in the undergrowth, boots that were stealthily approaching his hiding place.

He felt as if the sounds of his heart thumping, would surely give him away. His immediate thought was, "*Slave-Catchers*"!

Jason held his breath. Despite his efforts to do so, he could not suppress the roaring in his ears, the noise of his uncontrollably, rapidly beating heart.

He felt as if his heart was about to explode from within his chest.

The runaway slave was unarmed. Except for his hands, he was totally defenseless.

Jason could do nothing but hold his breath, hoping that the slave-catchers would pass by, that they would not discover him hiding in the hollow log.

Suddenly Jason felt the log being lifted up off of the ground. He and the log were being violently shaken. Unceremoniously, Jason tumbled from the hollow log, onto the ground.

"Well looka here…looka here!" Jason lay sprawled, face down on the ground.

Instinctively, largely due to having lived his entire life as a submissive slave, Jason kept his head lowered; his eyes were fixed upon three pairs of scuffed army boots that filled his line of vision.

"Get up off your black-ass boy. What the hell is you doing hiding in that ole rotten log?"

Jason's initial thought was that of fear and terror. Despite the fact that slaves were not allowed to be members of the Confederate Army, it was well known that slaves were routinely purchased, borrowed, or conscripted by the Confederate Army, from their white owners.

The army of the Confederate States of America forced the slaves to perform menial labor. The slaves dug latrines, and entrenchments. They felled trees, they built bomb shelters, reinforced the outer-walls of the forts. The black slaves built the quarters for the rebel officers and men; they did the soldiers' laundry.

Some of the conscripted slaves served as domestic servants, attending to the needs of officers, officers who frequently also happened to be their slave's Masters, their owners.

While the slaves were not members of the Confederate Army, if a slave ran away from the army, if he were to be captured by the Confederates soldiers, the runaway slave could and often would, be shoot for desertion.

"Look at me boy…what the hell are you doing hiding in that log?"

Jason slowly raised his head. As his eyes moved from the ground to take in the faces of the soldiers, he had noticed that the trousers of the three soldiers surrounding him were not gray; instead their trousers were light blue in color.

A broad grin rapidly spread across Jason's face when he realized, that these soldiers were not rebels.

Neither soldiers of the confederate army, nor had mercenary civilian slave-catchers, been the ones who had discovered his hiding place.

Instead the very people that had found him were the people that he had been seeking. These men were his liberators. They were Yankee soldiers.

These men were members of the Union Army.

****

Jason struggled to his feet. While still bent-over, his head bowed, he interlaced his fingers and clasped his hands onto the top of his head.

The shortest of the three infantrymen, a scrawny acne faced eighteen-year-old Private from New Hampshire, by the name of Mickey, kicked Jason squarely in the seat of his pants.

"Cat gotcha tongue boy? Watcha doing boy…you spying for the Rebs ain't cha?"

Jason spun around to confront the soldier that had delivered the kick. As he turned, he was struck in the stomach with the butt of a rifle wielded by a pimply, pockmarked face "farm-boy", turned New Hampshire Volunteer Private soldier.

The impact of the blow forced Jason to his knees. The third soldier, a stocky grizzled bearded man, who appeared to be in his late thirties or early forties, with three strips on each arm of the sleeves of his shirt, spat a thin stream of tobacco juice to the ground.

The older soldier, the soldier that Jason immediately identified as the man in charge, Sergeant Stanley Crawford reached down and grabbed Jason's elbow. He glared at the two privates; "You knuckle heads hold on there."

"Give the nigger a chance to speak. Who are you boy…whatcha doing in these woods?"

Jason, gingerly holding his bruised ribs, gasped; "My name is Jason Billings. I ran away from the rebel army. I want to join you. I want to join the Union Army. I want to fight with you to free my mother and my sister. To free my people."

The private with the pimply, pockmarked face snorted; "Now don't that beat all. This fancy talking buck thinks we fighting the Johnny Rebs to free the niggers."

The sergeant struck Jason's face with a vicious backhand slap. "Don't you lie to me boy. Ain't no such thing as niggers in the rebel army."

"Them Johnny rebs may be stupid sheep-fuckers, but they sure as hell ain't dumb enuff to be putting no guns, in the hands of you nigger bucks."

Sergeant Crawford leaned down, and roughly grabbed Jason by the shirt. He spit a stream of brown tobacco juice, which narrowly missed Jason's face.

"Listen-up boy, the Union Army ain't fighting this war to free you darkies."

"Me, Jonas and Mickey here, we're down here fighting to teach these pig-fucking rebs a lesson."

"We gotta teach these rebs that they ain't gonna get away with attacking and killing Union sojers, like they went and done last April, at Fort Sumpta."

"They can't go around claiming that the 'lection was rigged. They can't keep on spouting secess-crap, splitting up the Union, just cause Ole Abe Lincoln, fair and square, done been elected President."

"Nigger I'm gonna ask you just one last time…who the hell are you and whatcha doing in these woods?"

Jason slowly rose to his full 6' 2" height. He towered above the three Union soldiers. Each of the soldiers pointed his rifle at the abdomen of the tall, slender, muscular, black man.

Rubbing his sleeve over his still bleeding split lip, Jason looked directly at the Sergeant; "My name is Jason Billings. I was in the camp of the Confederate Army's, Brigadier General, Thomas Jackson's camp, during the recent battle at Bull Run."

"I was there as the personal slave of a Confederate Army officer, lieutenant Jesse Billings who was killed during the fighting."

"During the confusion following the battle, especially with the death of my Master, amid the wild celebrations, and with no one paying attention to me, I seized the opportunity to run, to attempt to escape. I've been looking for the Union Army…I want to join your ranks. I want to fight the rebels."

Without warning, the burly sergeant struck Jason in the temple with the butt of his rifle. Jason sank to his knees, and collapsed. He lay dazed, limp, sprawled, semi-conscientious on the ground.

Sergeant Crawford turned to the two privates, "tie um up boys. We'll turn him over to the captain."

The sergeant casually spit a stream of tobacco juice toward the feet of the runaway slave.

"If there's one thing I just can't abide, it's a lying, smart-assed, uppity-nigger."

****

Captain Daniel Clarke, the commanding officer of Company 'C' of the 5th New Hampshire Volunteer Infantry, sat alone in his tent, totally absorbed, staring at the regimental orders, sprawled before him on his desk.

Captain Clarke was leaning on his elbows, glancing first at his orders, and then studying one of the several maps, that cluttered his desk.

Deep lines furrowed his forehead as he concentrated, mulling over the numerous squiggly lines, denoting the many streams, hills, valleys and forests, that separated *Washington City,* the nation's capital, from the thousands of victorious rebel soldiers that had recently routed the Union forces at Bull Run.

At yesterday morning's meeting with his junior officers, Colonel John H. Baxter, the Commanding Officer of New Hampshire's 5th Volunteers, had ardently, emphatically stressed the absolute necessity to establish and to maintain a defensive perimeter between the *Union's Capital,* and the recently victorious Confederate forces, that were under the command of Brigadier General P.G.T. Beauregard.

Captain Clarke threw his dividers onto the map. He sat back in his chair and began to slowly, methodically, message his temples.

The captain sighed, took a deep breath, and exclaimed; "how in the hell did I get here."

****

CHAPTER 2

Prior to the April 12, 1861Confederate States of America's firing on Fort Sumter, marking the commencement of hostilities between the North and South, Daniel Clarke had been an academician, an educator, and a scholar.

Daniel Clarke, Ph.D., a Harvard College graduate, was currently an Assistant Professor of History, at New Hampshire's Dartmouth College.

Dr. Clarke, "*Dapper Dan*", as he had affectionately been nicknamed by a few close friends— because of his penchant for wearing fashionable men's clothing apparel— was in every sense of the word, a truly dedicated scholar.

Dr. Clarke was an avid, astute student of United States, and World History.

Intellectually, he had always held a fascination, admiration, a sense of pride for his young nation's role in inspiring the old world, to question, to reject, and to replace totalitarian forms of government ruled by despots, with his country's radically new, representative republic-democratic, form of government.

As a youth growing up, and attending school in southern Hanover New Hampshire, young Daniel remembered how he had been in awe, and how surprised he had been, when he first learned a little of the 18th century history, of his hometown.

Daniel vividly remembered—when as a ten-year-old seated in Hanover's little schoolhouse his being taught the history of Dartmouth College.

Daniel and his fellow, all white classmates, were taught how the state's preeminent repository of knowledge and academia, Dartmouth College, had been initially created to educate the youth of New Hampshire's indigenous, Indian Tribes.

During his formative years, Daniel had been raised in a homogeneous, all- white community. The town's populace consisted wholly, of the children and the grand children, of European immigrants.

Although he and his childhood friends had never actually seen an Indian, through the local newspapers, they knew of the existence of supposedly hordes of wild Indians, savages that plundered and ravaged the land, west of the Mississippi River.

Daniel fervently believed that the words penned by Thomas Jefferson in the nation's founding document, the Declaration of Independence—

"We hold these truths to be self-evident, that all men are created equal, that they are endowed by their Creator with certain unalienable Rights, that among these are Life, Liberty, and the pursuit of Happiness" —; to be among the most prophetic, and inspirational words, that man had ever written.

The fact that his forbearers, the 18th century white men of the then New Hampshire Colony, believed that *even primitive* Indians, were capable of being educated, that they could be taught to read and to write, was to Daniel Clarke, enlightened validation of his strongly held conviction, his moral steadfast belief in the innate intelligence, and the humanity of all mankind.

As to the moral and political question of slavery, that had divided and now split the nation, Daniel Clarke was a true believer, and an avid outspoken, advocate of the inherent equality of man…of all men.

Captain Daniel Clarke, Commanding Officer Company "C" of the 5th New Hampshire Volunteer Infantry was a devout, morally committed, abolitionist.

****

Captain Clarke, annoyed by the noisy commotion-taking place directly outside of his shelter, turned his head toward the entrance of his tent. "What's going on out there? Who's making that racket?"

He opened the flap of the tent and saw three soldiers, a sergeant and two privates kicking and prodding with their rifles, a bound man, whose hands were tied behind his back.

Captain Clarke's stare intensified as he scrutinized the distraught, stumbling captive. The man was a Negro.

The stocky sergeant and the two privates snapped to attention.

The sergeant saluted. Captain Clarke, his gaze fixed upon the captive, with a fleck of his fingers to his forehead, casually returned the salute. "What's this commotion all about… what do we have here sergeant?"

"Captain, we found this-here nigger in the woods, hiding in a hollow log."

"Claims that he's a runaway slave. Says he was the slave of some reb officer that got his self killed in the big fight last week…says his name's Jason something or nother."

Captain Clarke noticing that the two privates were still standing at rigid attention, mumbled, "You men can stand easy."

As he walked over to have a closer look at the black-man kneeling in the dirt before him, his hands tied securely behind his back, the Captain asked; "What do you make of his story sergeant, do you believe him?"

Sergeant Crawford began to vigorously, shake his head; "No sir Cap'n I don't."

Captain Clarke's eyes shifted from the captive to the sergeant. He raised a quizzical eyebrow; "You say that with such an air of convection and certainty. Why so sergeant?"

Sergeant Crawford turned his back and spit a thin stream of tobacco juice to the ground. Sheepishly he wiped his mouth with the sleeve of his shirt.

"Scouse me sir…reason I don't believe him is 'cause, this here boy don't talk like no nigger that I've ever hear'd talk."

"He claims that he's aiming ta make his way north, and to join up with us, the Union Army."

Captain Clarke remained silent; his eyes fixed upon the sergeant. When the Captain did not speak, Sergeant Crawford continued; "Cap'n, this boy just don't sound like a nigger… sir."

Captain Clarke raised an eyebrow; "and exactly how should… using your distasteful words sergeant, how do you think a nigger should sound?"

Sergeant Crawford, sensing that he had annoyed the captain, quickly responded.

"Oh, he's got that slow irritating southern-rebel drawl alright, but that aside Cap'n, he talks, his words — no offense Cap'n — sounds more like yourn than any nigger, free or slave, that I've ever heared."

The sergeant's diatribe peeked the Captain's intellectual curiosity. He stepped back toward his tent; "you men, bring the prisoner into my tent."

The two privates, followed by Sergeant Crawford, dragged Jason into the tent of "C" Company's Commanding Officer.

When Jason attempted to stand, the privates unceremoniously, pushed him to his knees. Captain Clarke sat at his desk. He drew his large Navy Colt pistol from its holster, and placed it conspicuously onto the table.

The Captain inserted the forefinger of his right hand inside the trigger guard, the circular metal loop that surrounded the trigger, of the heavy pistol.

"Sergeant, I want to talk to the prisoner, alone. Untie his hands."

Private Jenkins, the taller of the two privates, unsheathed a lethal looking Bowie Knife, and cut the rope that bound Jason's wrists behind his back.

After the three soldiers exited the tent, Captain Clarke cleared his throat; "There's no need for you to knell like that." He lifted the pistol from the table and rested it on his left knee.

"Make yourself comfortable."

Jason managed to maneuver his legs in such a way that instead of his weight being supported on his knees, he was now seated, his legs beneath him, squatting on the wooden floorboards of the tent.

****

Jason sat gingerly rubbing his wrists. The ropes that had bound his arms behind his back had cut off the circulation to his hands.

His head snapped up in response to the Captain's question; "Who the hell are you and what were you doing hiding in the woods?"

Jason carefully, cautiously began to stand. He froze when the army officer deftly lifted the huge pistol from his knee, and leveled the weapon at his head.

Captain Clarke, in a calm measured voice, said; "I did not give you permission to stand."

Bent over caught between and betwixt being seated and his assuming an erect upright posture, Jason froze in place; "I apologize sir, do I have your permission to stand?"

The Captain made an affirmative upward motion with his pistol. Jason stood.

For the first time, Captain Clarke had the opportunity to actually see and to appraise the physicality of the tall, imposing, fugitive slave.

Daniel Clarke, Ph.D., college professor's assessment—not necessarily that of Captain Daniel Clarke, Commanding Officer Company "C" of the 5th New Hampshire Volunteer Infantry—, was that the man standing proudly before him, was strikingly handsome, and exuded an undeniable air of intelligence, and of shear masculinity.

The tall, lean, muscular man standing before him, reminded him of the bronze statues that he had frequently seen on display, in the New York and Boston museums. Artist's depictions, probably white artists', sculptures of aboriginal African Warriors, hunting in the grassy savannahs of the "*Dark Continent.*"

What he found to be particularly striking was the fugitive slave's stance, his posture, and his demeanor.

The way that the man carried himself was to the Captain, similar to that of a well-trained soldier, a disciplined professional standing at attention before an officer of superior rank.

This black-man's bearings and demeanor were in stark contrast to the subservient posture he had witnessed in the few free Negroes, that he had encountered.

Jason spoke; "Sir I am a fugitive ex-slave. My name is Jason Billings."

Inexplicably, the black-man paused, hesitated then in a steely voice, he continued.

"Correction sir, my slave name was Billings, the family surname of my former slave masters."

"As of this very instant, this moment Sir, I reject the name Billings. My name is now Jason, …the name given to me by my mother. My surname henceforth is Ruth, the Christian name given to my mother by her mother."

"Sir, … my name is Jason Ruth."

It is my understanding that according to the laws of Virginia, I am now the legal property of Mr. Henry Billings, the father of my deceased former master, Lieutenant Jesse Billings, of the Army of Nothern Virginia."

"As I told your men when they discovered me in the hollowed-out, dead tree, I was recently, prior to and during last month's battle at Manassas, sorry Sir, the battle at Bull Run, a slave in the camp of the Confederate Army, attending to the needs of my master Lieutenant Billings, the heir to Virginia's Rosewood plantation."

"It was shortly after the conclusion of the fighting, while in the camp of the Confederates, that I learned that my former master, Lieutenant Billings was *KIA,* killed in action on the field of battle."

"For months, prior to that battle, I had been looking for an opportunity to escape. However, my being constantly at the beck and call of my master, Lieutenant Billings, the opportunity for me to attempt an escape, did not present itself."

"That night, after their victory at Bull-Run, as the Confederates celebrated, and because of my no longer having a master to attend to, I realized that the time for my escape was ripe. I ran. By escaping, as defined by the Confederate state of Virginia, a fugitive slave.

"I was hiding from slave-catchers and the rebel army, when your men stumbled upon me asleep, resting in a hollowed-out tree."

"Sir, I wish to join you. I want to join the Union Army. I want to fight with you to abolish slavery."

"It is my intention to fight to free my mother and my sister. To bare arms in this fight to free my people."

"For nearly two weeks, I've been making my way north toward the capital, toward Washington City. Mostly I hide during the day, and follow the North Star at night."

Captain Clarke slowly lowered the pistol. His initial thought, after listening, hearing, and digesting the black-man's "*speech*", was that now he was beginning to understand Sergeant Crawford's skepticism.

He recalled that the sergeant's response to his inquiry, as to why the sergeant did not believe, the black captive's story, had been; *"Cap'n reason I don't believe him is 'cause, this here boy don't talk like no nigger that I've ever before, hear'd talk."*

This Negro, this fugitive slave, this man that stood proudly and defiantly before him, did not in any way shape or form, resemble or fit the stereotypic image of the stupid, ignorant, illiterate, sub-human, Southern slave.

Daniel Clarke's absolute, long held belief and his perception, of the slave's living in squalor, dejected like beaten animals under the South's "Peculiar Institution" Slavery, was momentarily shaken.

The contrast, the dichotomy between his long-held image, engraved in his mind, recently reinforced by Harriet Beecher Stowe's novel, the image of the subservient, illiterate, "shuffling" black-slave, and this well-spoken fugitive-slave, couldn't have been have been more striking.

Daniel had been led to believe that the very foundation, the bedrock of the south's ability to enslave and to subjugate four million Negroes, was to keep the slaves illiterate, ignorant and uninformed.

The man standing before him, most assuredly did not fit that description.

This tall, erect, impressive man appeared to be the total antithesis of the lifelong image that he had envisioned of the docile, helpless, illiterate, subservient Negro-slave.

Captain Clarke pointed his pistol toward a chair. He nodded his head indicating that Jason should take a seat. The Captain was intrigued.

His intellectual curiosity had been aroused. Captain Clarke's…no more precisely… *Daniel Clarke, Ph.D., Professor of American and World History, Dartmouth College,* unquenchable, thirst for knowledge, had been stimulated.

****

CHAPTER 3

Before the war, on numerous occasions Daniel had had the opportunity to hear the soaring brilliant, elegant, orations of a learned Negro, a former escaped slave, the renowned spokesman for the emancipation of his enslaved people, Mr. Frederick Douglass.

This aberration now seated in his tent, this tall, statuesque, black-man, who claimed to be an escaped slave, a human being who had been ostensibly, for his entire life, been treated like chattel. If the man was telling the truth, this was the first apparently literate slave, that Captain Clarke had ever, encountered.

The former college professor quickly reasoned that his initial assumption, that is…this articulate black-man was indeed, truly literate, might not be necessarily true.

Daniel knew from experience that eloquent diction and elocution, did not necessarily equate with literacy, and certainly did not guarantee intelligence.

Captain Clarke extended the barrel of the pistol to touch a packet of documents lying on the table. With the barrel of the gun, he pushed the packet toward the black-man.

Withdrawing the pistol from the documents, the Captain in a firm authoritative voice commanded; "Read."

The black-man seated before him, picked-up the packet. He stared in silence for several minutes at the papers.

Just as the captain was about to conclude that the black-man though well spoken and articulate, was not actually literate that he could not actually read and write, the black man began to speak.…

> *"Captain Daniel Clark, Commanding Officer Company C — 5th New Hampshire Volunteer Infantry."* **"SECRET"**

The captain hastily extended his hand toward the black-man; "that's enough…give those classified documents back to me."

As the captive, the black-man was about to open the packet; the captain pointed his pistol at the prisoner. The black-man's hand dropped from the packet. With steady fingers and obvious trepidation, he tentatively handed the packet to the captain.

Without breaking eye contact with the black-man, Captain Clarke accepted the packet, and stuffed the documents into the front pocket of his uniform blouse.

"Okay mister, you've got my attention, I'm all ears. Once again, who the hell are you? Where did you come from and what were you doing snooping around in these woods?"

Jason, no longer staring down the barrel of that ominous pistol, let out a deep breath; "Sir as I told those men that apprehended me, my name…my slave name was Jason Billings. I have now taken, of my own volition, in your presence, the name Jason Ruth."

"I am an escaped slave making my way north to Washington City. I was being held in bondage, in the confederate army camp of General Thomas Jackson."

"My former master, Lieutenant Jessie Billings, one of General Jackson's junior officers, was killed in action, during the recent fighting at Manassas."

Captain Clarke's reaction to the slave's language, the syntax, the words, and his apparent at least, superficial military knowledge of the rebel forces that had routed General McDowell's Union Army, just eight days ago at Bull Run, was immediate and intense.

In addition to stimulating his intellectual curiosity, his brief hurried, military training, now lead the recently commissioned brevet-captain, to recognize the potential value of this fugitive slave, to the success and to the safety of his command, the soldiers of Company 'C'.

While Jason was not the first runaway slave that had made his way to Union lines following the commencement of hostilities between the Confederate and the Union Armies, he was in fact, the first runaway slave that had made contact with the state of New Hampshire's Volunteer Infantry.

Having heard rumors of scores of fugitive slaves that had escaped to Washington City during these early days of fighting, Captain Clarke had been led to believe that the runaways seeking sanctuary and protection were gaggles of helpless, wretched, ignorant, souls.

****

It was the common understanding and the belief of the Union Army's Officer Corps, that the only value that these runaway slaves could possibly contribute to the war effort, whether for the Confederate Army, or for the Union Army, would be as menial laborers.

Captain Daniel Clarke, the Commanding Officer Company 'C' of the 5th New Hampshire Volunteer Infantry, had almost instantly recognized, that the imposing, well-spoken, fugitive slave that was now seated at his desk had the potential of becoming a valuable, military asset.

Captain Clarke rose from his chair, walked over and pulled aside the flap that covered the entrance to his tent and bellowed; "Sergeant Crawford."

The sergeant, who had remained on guard outside the Captain's tent, instantly entered the tent. "Yes sir, Captain what do you want me to do with this here nigger?"

The captain glared at his sergeant; "Sergeant, I find that particular word… "*Nigger*", that you men seem to bandy around so loosely, to be offensive."

"Please refrain from using that distasteful, vile, epithet in my presence"

He turned and looked directly into the alert brown eyes, of the fugitive slave; "This gentleman…what was your name?" "Jason sir, my name is Jason Ruth."

Captain Daniel Clarke turned his head to face the sergeant; "Sergeant Crawford, have someone bring lunch for me and for my guest."

"Mr. Jason Ruth and I will be dining together here in my tent."

Sergeant Crawford snapped to attention; "Yes sir." He saluted, spun on his heels, and exited the tent.

****

CHAPTER 4

By the flickering light of old battered kerosene lamp, the two men, one a white Union Army Officer, the other a black fugitive slave, sat quietly eating. Each man was surreptitiously taking stock of the other.

Daniel Clarke, the abolitionist, College Professor/Captain in the Union Army, was fascinated with the black man… this apparent aberration seated across from him.

As for Jason, his thoughts were of survival. Now that he had made contact with the Union lines, what next?

Which of his multiple personas should he display? Jason instinctively knew that the white man, who sat across from him, could be pivotal in the success or the failure, of his fulfilling his lifelong repressed obsession.

Jason Ruth wanted white men to pay, to atone for the centuries of pain and misery that they had inflicted on his people. Jason felt that the currency, the price of his freedom, should be paid in the spilling of the white man's blood.

Jason intended to kill as many white southern slaveholders, and their supporters, as was humanly possible.

He sensed in this white officer, sympathy as well as empathy, for his plight as a runaway slave.

Jason suspected, reasoned, that this Captain's abolitionist sympathies were similar to those that he suspected, were held by that white Yankee schoolteacher, who back on the plantation, had taught his sister Mandy, to read and to write.

Before Jason could speak, Captain Clarke, abruptly pushed his chair back, rose and walked to the entrance of the tent. He opened the flap and called out; "Corporal of the guard!"

A burly, clean-shaven soldier, armed with a long rifle, to which was affixed an ominously, deadly looking steel appendage, appeared as if from thin air.

The soldier stood at attention, his rifle held rigidly before him, bisecting his body in the military position of present arms. "Sir?" Captain Clarke pointed toward Jason; "Secure this prisoner for the night."

The captain turned to address Jason; "We'll talk again in the morning."

Jason was surprised by the sudden change in the captain's demeanor. Silently Jason chided himself, for letting his guard-down.

Perhaps he had misread the captain. After all, Yankee or not, the Captain was still a white man.

The soldier tied Jason's hands behind his back, grabbed him by the shoulder, and roughly ushered him from the Company Commander's tent.

****

Jason was roughly pushed to the dirt floor, of what he surmised was a storage tent. He was forced to lie on his stomach, while the soldier, with a length of rope, tied his legs together. Without uttering a word, the soldier extinguished the single lantern, and left the tent.

Jason rolled over onto his back. Lying in the dark on the dirt floor, Jason tried to relive in his mind this, his first encounter with the Union Army.

The mannerisms, the attitudes, of the three Yankee soldiers that had found him hiding in the hollow tree, Jason realized, were surprisingly similar, nearly identical to that of the Confederate soldiers from whom he had so recently escaped.

A familiar phrase came to mind; *"Po White Trash."* This was the less than flattering slur, the phrase that the slaves living at his former home, the slave community of Rosewood Plantation, secretively whispered among themselves.
Jason smiled as he wryly reminisced, reflecting upon how the slaves, who under their breath would mutter the denigrating, pejorative, words, *"Po white trash",* how those black-slaves before mumbling that phrase, made sure, that they were well outside of the hearing of those so-called *"Po white trash"* individuals.

Despite their plight in life, despite their abject poverty and their ignorance, they, the *"Po White Trash",* were, ___**WHITE**___.

"Poor White Trash" those were the words frequently used by Henry Billings, the Master of Rosewood, when he would derisively dismiss, and describe those whites that he euphemistically referred to as being *"economically challenged"*. Those whites, the *"Poor White Trash"*, that segment of the white population, who did not have the financial means, to purchase black-slaves.

The three *"Po White Trash"* soldiers, who had pulled him from the log, had quickly dispelled any illusions that Jason may have been harboring, as to the attitudes of white Northerners toward blacks.

Jason had wanted to believe that the Yankees, the Northern white men fighting against the men in gray, the Confederates, the slave masters that had held him in bondage, that the Northern white men, were the enlightened liberators that he, for all his life, had prayed and hoped for.

The Yankee officer, Captain Daniel Clarke, was to Jason, proving to be a major disappointment. Jason was beginning to bemoan the fact that he had foolishly, let his guard down.

Initially slowly, grudgingly, gradually, during the course of their lengthy dialogue, Jason had actually begun to trust the white man, the Yankee Captain.

When the captain had abruptly summoned the armed soldier, and then ordered the soldier to; "Secure this prisoner for the night", Jason had been abruptly, jolted back to reality.

He admonished himself for dropping his guard, for his weakness, for allowing himself to almost, trust a white man.

> Jason pledged to himself that he would not make that mistake again. He sat with his back braced against a barrel; his hands and legs securely tied before him.

> Clumsily do to the fact that his hands were bound together, Jason was finding it awkward to scratch the two childhood, long-since healed scars, just beneath his rib cage.

The camp was filled with the ambient noise, the muffled background sounds that are present in any large encampment of men.

The noise, coupled with the affects of the first full meal that he had had, since leaving the Confederate lines, instead of being an irritant, began to lull Jason into a drowsy state of somnolence, of semi-conscientiousness.

Jason began to think of, and to reminisce and expound, upon his early childhood as a child, as a *"pickaninny"*, growing up on Virginia's Rosewood Plantation.

A dull ache in his abdomen, from the butt of the soldier's rifle, coupled with his having eating, a real meal, for the first time in over a week, resulted in his head, slowly falling to his chest.

> Jason drifted off into a fitful, dream filled sleep.

CHAPTER 5

Rosewood Plantation Essex County Virginia – 1844

Eight-year-old Jason lay fidgeting, tossing and turning on his crumbled, cornhusk mattress, the tall slender, strapping, physically awkward slave boy, was restlessly, fitfully tossing and turning lying uncomfortably, his arms and legs tangled in his sweat-soaked bedding.

The harder he tried to will himself to sleep, the more stubbornly, the sought-after sleep, eluded him.

The young boy was desperately, valiantly attempting to fall asleep. To turn off, to mute his mind, and dull his senses, before the inevitable, nightly arrival of the **WHITE MAN**, their master, to his mother's bed.

The nearly uninterrupted twelve hours of back-breaking, physical labor that he had just expended, tending to the plantation's endless rows of cotton plants, had resulted in Jason's body feeling as if every muscle, every bone in his body, was wracked with pain.

The young slave boy's body—still the developing body of a child—, ached from head to foot.

Despite the physical discomfort that he was experiencing, by far the most excruciating pain being felt by the adolescent slave-boy, was the numbing, humiliating, pernicious, eroding pain, to his mental psyche.

The pain he was forced to endure each night, when because of the paucity of space, that was afforded by the cramped slave cabin, he was despite his revulsion, being forced to listen to the sounds made by the two adults — his mother and the white Massa —, as they *"rassl'd in da bed"*, on the other side of the thin, semi-transparent, sheet that bisected the cabin.

He could not block-out the loud, disturbing, sounds being made, on the other side of the sheet. In his mind, he pictured the white master, brutally ravaging and violating his beloved mother, Ruth.

Each night, when *"da Massa come ta visit"*, Jason would find himself resorting to biting his lip, to keep from screaming.

His prepubescent body would tremble, as he fought the urge to give in to the rage, to give vent to his burning desire to stop the huge white man from hurting his mother… to kill the white *Massa* who habitually, nightly, tortured his mother.

Jason was determined to obey his mother, to keep his promise to her. He struggled to concentrate, to will himself to remember and to obey his mother's pleading, tearful words; *"chile yose is ta jus be stil. We be da prop-o-tee of da Massa. He can do wha he want wid us."*

     "Ain't nuthin you can do bout it, ceptin ta gits da boof of us, kilt!"

Jason would lie passively in bed, just inches away from the two copulating, writhing bodies, separated by the flimsy sheet.

He would stuff the bed coverings into his mouth to stifle his silent screams of protest, his anguish, as the white man, the Master committed, nightly sexual degradation, and humiliation against his *"helpless"*, mother.

Abandoning his futile efforts to fall asleep, Jason's thoughts would return to his mother's tearful instructions; *"Dun matta what da Massa be do'n ta me, dun you mak no noise, dun ya maks a soun."*

Jason bewildered, confused had pleaded; *"but mama what if Massa Henry be hertin' you?*

His mother had placed both of her hands on her son's shoulders and looked directly into his eyes; *"It dun't matta wha da Massa be duin' ta me. Ise his pro-po-tee, we's boff his pro-po-tee. Evry nigger on da place be his pro-po-tee."*

After the first few weeks of the Master's nightly visits, Jason began to become increasingly aware of, and at first, startled by the change in his mother's vocal responses to the Master's sexual assaults.

In the beginning his mother had lain silently on her bed, while the white man, the Master violated her.

Occasionally Jason would hear his mother utter an involuntary moan as the white man, their Master, pushed and shoved, *"rutted like an ole hound, humpin' som bitch dog in heat"*, while hurting his mother.

By the end of the third week of the *Massa's* nightly visits, while Jason would lay awake, agitated, groaning, helplessly gritting his teeth, he began to notice what to him, was an alarming change in his mother's responses, to the *Massa's* predictable, nocturnal visits.

In addition to what Jason had perceived were the now familiar groans of pain and discomfort uttered by his mother, as she squirmed and bucked under the *Massa's* ghostly pale white body, Jason began to notice a distinct change in the frequency, and the tenor of her moans and groans.

His mother's unintelligible, moans and groans, were beginning to more and more, sound like words of encouragement and passion.

Increasingly, the no longer muffled sounds emanating from his mother's bed, had changed. The volume and the intensity of the groans and moans had escalated.

His mother's initially suppressed utterances of pain and discomfort had changed.

For some unknown reason, that his young adolescent mind could not fathom, the sounds emanating from his mother's bed had now become her urgent expressions of encouragement, and of pleasure.

****

Jason's beautiful, loving mother Ruth, at the age of fourteen as had befallen most of the plantation's young black female slaves —, had as a routine fact of plantation life, been deflowered, *"broken-in"*.

Unfettered sexual access to the plantation's black females was a universally accepted and understood, added incentive, a bonus, an important fringe benefit, an additional means of compensation, for recruiting and retaining, white overseers on southern plantations.

It was thought by most within the Rosewood Plantation's slave community, that the white man, *"da Obeerseer"*, Lucas Prentiss was the man who had sired Ruth's first *"high Yella" youn'n"*, her son Jason.

To Lucas' chagrin and disappointment, the beautiful caramel colored teenage slave girl Ruth, his favorite piece of black *"pootang"*, had caught the eye of Henry Billings, the plantation's Master.

This unfortunate turn of events had sent a clear signal to the white overseer, as well as to every other male, both white and black on the Rosewood Plantation.

The slave girl Ruth, for all males, white or black, was now officially and literally, *"hands off."*

****

During *Masssa Henry's'* nightly visits to his mother's bed, young Jason would concentrate on pretending to be asleep. As he lay listening to the sounds of their coupling, he had become increasingly confused.

Where in the beginning of the *Massa's* visits, he had heard from his mother, groans of pain and discomfort; now the *prepubescent slave boy,* did not know what to make of the throaty declarations that were spewing forth from her lips.

> *"Oh Massa dat feel soo good; dat it, dat it, right dere; ahh, ahh, feel sooo good; Massa you is so hard."*

These words now being shouted by his mother, were the same *"dirty"* words that the slave boys routinely banded around when they disparaged, whispered and talked about the black slave girls that had been referred to in the slave community as, *"loose wimmin, easy-gals, hors and bad-gals."*

<hr>

E. Pluribus Unum

Jason would flinch and recoil when he heard *Massa* Henry's voice; "Damn right it's good– I'm coming – I'm coming – Ahhhh, Oh Shiiit! And then the child would hear nothing but silence — interrupted by muffled sounds of heavy breathing.

> Jason found himself dealing with a perplexing paradox. How could it be?

> Was it possible that his beloved mother, the one person that the young boy worshipped, respected, and revered above all others, could actually be enjoying; *"doin da nasstee, let alon doin da nastee wid da white Massa."*

Working from sun-up to sun down hoeing and picking in the endless rows of cotton was slowly but inexorably, beginning to take its toll on the young slave boy's body, as well as his spirit.

Ruth was one of the few fortunate slaves that were not forced to work in the fields.

Ruth had become an accomplished seamstress. In addition to her skills with a needle and thread, Ruth also served as the personal maid for the Mistress of Rosewood, Margaret *"Peggy"* Billings, and as the wet nurse for Mistress Margaret's infant daughter, Rebecca.

On one especially hot and humid evening, after an especially harsh, brutal day in the fields, under the relentless whip of the overseer, Jason sore and bone-weary, entered the slave cabin, lay down on his bed and almost instantly fell asleep.

When Ruth, with her two-year-old baby girl Mandy, asleep in her arms, returned to the cabin she found Jason sprawled across his bed.

The seven-year-old boy's back bore the marks of multiple blows from the overseer's lash.

Ruth gasped at the ugly wilts that crisscrossed her son's lacerated back.

Reflexively, involuntarily giving vent to her feeling of frustration and hopelessness, she squeezed her sleeping infant to her breast.

Baby Mandy startled, awoke and began to cry. Ruth stood almost perfectly still, petrified, transfixed. She relaxed the arm holding the baby.

She balled up her fists, and placed the knuckle of the index finger of her right hand into her mouth. The knuckle muted the low, piteous moans that rumbled through, and shook her body.

Ruth slowly pulled the sheet that divided the cabin. She sat on her bed, tears streaming down her cheeks, gently rocking her daughter. And prepared for the nocturnal visit of Henry Billings, Master of Rosewood

That evening, with her little boy lying exhausted, only a few feet away, oozing blood from the wounds on his back; *"he be whipped ta da bone"*, as she lay under Henry, Ruth decided to do everything that she could, she would perform every sexual act that she knew, or had heard of, to satisfy and to please *da Massa*.

Henry lay spent, wrung-out. Still cupping and kneading one of Ruth's heaving, perfectly formed caramel colored breast. He was exhausted, completely sexually, satisfied.

Henry's head was reeling; he thought; "my god, that was the wildest, most intense, the best sex that I've ever… ever experienced."

****

CHAPTER 6

As they lay in the damp bed, basking in the "after-glow" of mutual sexual release, Ruth despite her lifelong commitment to quiet passive acceptance and subservience, summoned up all of her courage and blurted out; "Massa Henry, ma lil boy Jason he be plum tuckered out a sore. Massa Lucas, he be layin da lash hevy ta my boy's back."

For what to Ruth felt like an eternity, Henry just stared at her. A wide-eyed expression of disbelief and incredulity covered his face.

Henry was taken aback. This was the first time in his life that he had heard one of his black slaves, albeit this his breathtakingly beautiful, mahogany, diminutive, bed wench, question the whipping of a slave by the white Overseer.

Ruth's body language suggested that she anticipated and expected to be struck by the *Massa!*

Henry broke eye contact with the beautiful slave — his property that now lay quivering beside him. He slowly shook his head from side to side and looked away.

Henry sat up, his legs hanging over the side of the bed. He put on his pants, his shirt, and his shoes and without uttering a word, left the slave-cabin.

Three days later, on yet another extremely hot, sultry night following the Massa's usual hurried departure from his mother's bed, Ruth pulled back the dividing sheet and tiptoed over to her sleeping son.

The tension that Jason always felt when the *Massa visited* had dissipated from the young boy's, physically exhausted body.
As Jason finally relaxed and was about to fall asleep, his mother came over to his bed, bent down and gently whispered in her son's ear; *"In da monin' yose is ta sta ner da Big House an play wid youn Massa Jessy. Yo'se gotta memba boy, yong Massa be ya Massa. Yose ise ta do what evva he wonts yose ta do."*

****

Ruth sat at the kitchen table drinking coffee with her best friend Fannie, the Big House Cook. Ruth and Fannie routinely, began the day, the thirty minutes or so before the sun rose, sipping coffee and sharing gossip.

Ruth confided in her best friend Fannie, *"Da white Jesus done heered my prayas. I got down onst my knees an ast him dat my boy Jason be tooken from da fields. Da lawd done heered my prayas. Glory bee Fannie, dey been done took my boy outta da fields."*

Fannie reached for a bowl of freshly picked peas. As if they had a mind of there own, her nimble fingers began to busily separate the peas from their pods.

Ruth did not notice the faint smile that began at the corner of her friend's mouth.

Fannie, as did everyone else on the plantation, knew that *"da Massa had token Ruth fo his bed wench."*

Fannie blew on her steaming hot coffee, and muttered under her breath, but definitely intended to be heard; *"I rekon dat da white Jesus ain't da onest white man you dun been on yo knees befo."*

Ruth chuckled; she knew that her friend was not being snide, nor was she being vindictive. She was merely acknowledging, *"The way it was…a way for black females to survive… living enslaved, under the rule of white-men."*

Both Ruth and Fannie knew as did every slave woman, every slave mother, in the entire slave community knew and adhered to; *"Ya duzz what ya has ta do, to keep ya chilrens saaf."*

****

CHAPTER 7

Jesse Billings was the hyperactive, precocious six-year-old son of Henry and Margaret Billings.

Everyone living at Rosewood knew without a doubt, that the still plump — lingering residual baby fat —, cherubic faced little boy Jesse Billings, was the spoiled, pampered heir; the future Master of the Rosewood Plantation.

Jesse's early schooling, his learning of the ABC's, was mostly at the knee of his mother Peggy. Peggy Billings' primary teaching aid had been a set of wooden blocks that bore on each of its four sides, both in upper and lower case, the letters of the alphabet.

The blocks were supplemented by Peggy's reading to her son, from her collection of the classic fairy-tales.

At bedtime, Peggy would tuck Jesse into bed, and read to him; usually one of the Brothers Grimm's - Fairy Tales, until the tyke, fell asleep.

Jesse had soon become bored and began to turn up his nose, fidget and squirm, when the adults, his mother and/or his father, repeatedly attempted to read to him, from the classic, "Once Upon A Time – European derived, Fairy Tales."

Young Jesse had been blessed with a vivid, and a very active imagination.

While still a toddler, Jesse had listened to his father, and his father's best friend and lawyer Luis Frazier, discuss the expansion of what they referred to as the spreading of "civilization", across the continent.

Jesse had over the course of his childhood years, gradually developed a fascination with the tales of the opening of the vast, still untamed Wild West.

The little boy was thrilled when his father Henry, or his *Uncle Looey*, Luis Frazier, the family's attorney, and Henry's best friend, would read to him the heroic exploits, and the escapades of the fearless white, trailblazing, frontiersmen.

Little six-year-old Jesse would beg and tearfully plead with his role models, the two adult white men, his father and his father's best friend *Uncle Looey*, to read to him the exciting adventures of the rugged mountain-men, the early western pioneers.

Young Jesse's preference, that he had made abundantly clear to his parents, was that he be read exclusively, adventure-stories, tales of the heroic, courageous white-frontiersmen, the men who were the vanguard, who were conquering, the wilderness, bringing civilization, to the wild, wild, west.

Both Henry and Luis would relentlessly, continually, emphasize to the impressionable boy, that the civilizing, the taming of the west, could not be achieved without the conquest and the elimination of the west's cowardly, indolent, lazy, ignorant, natives… the barbaric, savage, wild Indians.

Young Jesse had been indoctrinated, brought up to believe that the country's glorious future, its crowning accomplishment would be the achievement of its' "Manifest Destiny", the expansion of the United States, from the Atlantic Ocean, to the Pacific Ocean.

And that the achieving of this goal, would require the elimination, the extinction, of the murderous, heathen savages, the vile, uncivilized red men, the indigenous American aboriginals, the Native Americans, who for centuries, had inhabited the vast lands west of the Mississippi River.

Jesse spent his playtime acting out, recreating as best he could, the many adventures of his fictional *"Dime-Novel"* hero, the to him, bigger than life character, "Buckskin Bob".

Absolutely central to the young Slave-Master's imaginary fantasies, was the absolute necessity that he, that is that his alter ego (*Buckskin Bob), own and ride, a trusty loyal stead, his faithful horse "Blackey"*.

Little Jesse had pleaded with his father to give him one of the plantation's many horses.

Jesse's Mother Peggy, had insisted that at six, plumb little Jesse was not physically, nor was he emotionally ready to own, let alone ride by himself, a horse.

She would frequently lament; "Henry he's just a baby." He's far to young, too little to be riding a pony, not to mention riding a horse."

Henry thought that he had come up with the perfect solution. He and Peggy had recently been having frequent, lengthy, sometimes heated, discussions about their little boy's increasingly obvious loneliness.

Jesse's loneliness was undoubtedly due to the total lack of there being, other white children on the plantation, for the young *Massa* to interact with. Jesse had no childhood peers. Other than his annoying little sister, Rebecca, there were no other white children on the plantation. Jesse was alone. He had no one to play with, no one to socialize with.

Peggy seeing how bored and forlorn her little boy was becoming, seeing how he wistfully looked at the little black children as they romped around, playing in the dirt that made up the streets of the slave village, Peggy had begun to in earnest, look for a solution for her son's loneliness.

Henry had suggested to Peggy, that they assign one of the young, pre-teen slave boys, to attend to Jesse's needs. He reasoned that the older boy would be an attendant, a companion, and would be in a position to if you will, "baby sit" the six-year-old Jesse.

At first Peggy had rejected Henry's suggestion that young Jesse, at the tender age of six, literally have dominion over his own personal slave.

However, after weeks of silently observing her six-year-old son's pathetically sorrowful, longingly wistful face, as he watched the slave children at play, Peggy reluctantly, decided to allow Jesse to play with the young slave children.

Peggy asked Henry to give orders to the overseer Lucas Prentiss, instructing him to tell the mothers of slave children, the five and six-year olds, that their future Master, young Jesse would be playing with them.

Despite the five and six-year-old slave children initially adhering to their mother's instructions, after two weeks of *Massa Jesse* frolicking amidst and among them, *Massa* Jesse was accepted and treated by the children as just another member of the group.

Jesse was viewed and received by the group as just another six-year-old playmate. This despite the slave mother's almost daily, firm warnings and admonition to their children; *"Wha eva yu do or da white chile, Massa Jesse do ta yu, don't back talk or sass da youn Massa!"*

****

On yet still another, in a slew of especially hot and steamy mornings, following a particularly heavy mid-summer thunderstorm, which produced a sudden deluge of rain, that turned the dirt streets into rivulets of mud, the previously benign, young Jesse's previously tranquil, situation had abruptly changed.

The playgroup of five and six-year-olds comprised of a total of eight, seven black slave boys, and Jesse where gleefully playing, wallowing in the warm mud.

A group of three of the boys, that included Jesse, began to deftly construct a miniature mud-house. The structure, though simplistic and crudely, childishly designed, bore a vague resemblance to the "Big House."

The most striking feature of the miniature house of mud was the three-tier design.

The intent of the trio of young builders, which included one white — although now that he was entirely covered with mud, *two black slave boys, and* one white, temporarily black boy —, was to construct a multi-tiered structure.

The columns to support the second floor of the mud house were being put into place, when a barrage of huge mud-balls that had been thrown by two of the non-participating boys struck and caused the collapse of the mud-house.

Jesse and his two fellow builders were stunned. Before they could vent words of protest. The three builders were being pelted with mud-balls, thrown by the five little boys, the boys that had not participated in building the mud-house.

The three mud sculpturers retaliated. Mud balls, thrown by each of the eight boys, filled the air.

Lightnen' a lanky swift six, nearly seven-year-old, waded up a mud ball and with amazing velocity, and unfortunately very little accuracy, threw his mud ball at the chubby legs of mud-covered Jesse.

Jesse, who had thrown several mud balls during the free-for-all melee, was busily preparing to launch his fourth mud-missile, suddenly yelped in pain.

The mud ball thrown by *Lightnen'*, hit Jesse, flush on his chin. Jesse clutched his chin, and fell to the ground.

Fannie the Big House cook, who had witnessed the boys frolicking in the mud, dropped the bucket of water that she was carrying and ran to the aide of the young Massa.

Fannie hurriedly sloshed through the muck and picked the young *Massa* up from the mud. Jesse whimpering was momentarily dazed, stunned, and confused. The little boy clung to Fannie's apron. Jesse was not seriously hurt.

Fannie roughly, grabbed *Lightnen*, the child who had thrown the mud ball that had struck Jesse, by the scruff of his neck. *"Chile is yu done loss yu mine?"*

The frightened little slave boy was squirming in Fannie's firm grip. When he looked up into Fannie's frantic eyes, and saw naked fear and horror, the mortified and frightened little boy began to sob, to cry uncontrollably.

"Ise sawry Miz Fannie. I jus throw in' mud lik evree bodi else." Jesse, who still clung to Fannie's apron, continued to whimper.

****

After hastily entering the kitchen, with the young *Massa* still clinging to her apron, in her haste to clean and to examine Jesse's face, Fannie gently sat the little boy on the large wooden table that she used to clean and cut vegetables.

Fannie was judiciously, carefully, attempting to access the extent of the injury to the young *Massa*'s sunburned chin. Fannie gently, tenderly, washed Jesse's face with a warm towel. Jesse's cheek was bruised and slightly swollen.

After she had removed a layer of mud from the little boy's face, Fannie let out a reverent, audible, sigh of relief.

"Prase da lawd. I thanks ya Jesus." Fannie spoke soothingly. *"Yose alrite Massa Jesse. Da skin ain't eben been broke."*

Jesse was sporting a small purplish bruise on his left cheek. Fannie was gingerly holding the little boy's face firmly in her left hand, while with the warm towel, she continued removing mud from the little boy's neck and hands.

****

Peggy, closely followed by her Maid/Seamstress Ruth, rushed into the kitchen. Fannie's back was toward Peggy. "Fannie, where is he? Where's my baby?

Jesse peeked out from behind Fannie. Although he was covered in mud, his face was remarkably clean. Peggy noticed a small purplish, bruise on her son's left cheek.

The little boy had a huge smile on his face, and a large oatmeal cookie in is hand. "Mommy, look at this big cookie Fannie gave me."

Fannie, in her haste and in her state of panic and apprehension, had forgotten that she had sent one of the Jesse's playmates, to fetch the Mistress with instructions to; *"Tell da mistress data young massa Jesse be hurt."*

Peggy visibly overcome with relief, placed her silk handkerchief to her mouth, and meekly lowered herself onto one of the kitchen chairs.

Ruth hurried over to the caste-iron stove, removed the teakettle and poured a cup of tea for her mistress. She placed the teacup on the table and discretely, went to stand behind Mistress Peggy.

Fannie lifted Jesse from the table, and placed him on the floor. Jesse, cookie in hand and a large smile spreading across his face, ran to the welcoming, open arms of his mother.

The entire slave community had been on pins and needles. They were all apprehensive, frightened, stunned.

The rumor, like wild-fire, had quickly spread throughout the slave community; One of their own *chilin*, the laundry woman, Suzy's boy, little six-year-old, almost seven, *Lightnen;* *"dun bust Massa Jesse in da haid wida rock."*

****

CHAPTER 8

Henry lay sprawled across the couple's huge, four-poster, and canopied bed.

Peggy was seated at her vanity, rubbing her hands and arms with a lemony, scented lotion.

She gazed into the large mirror, setting atop her vanity, and spoke to her husband, who was casually reclining on their canopied bed; "Henry, when that boy came running up the stairs shouting; "*Missy Margret come quick, Massa Jesse be hurt.*"

"I almost fainted. I tell you Henry; I have never been so frightened in my entire life."

Henry propped himself up on an elbow; "Now Sugar it was just a small bruise. As a matter of fact, Jesse was really proud of his little *wound.*"

"You know what honey? After you put him to bed, and I finished reading to him from one of his favorite frontier tales, Jesse looked up at me, rubbed his chin and said; "Daddy it'll take more than a stray arrow from them wild Injuns to hurt *Buckskin Bob.*"

Henry now sitting upright, supported his weight leaning on his right elbow. "The question now is what are we gonna do about that little pickaninny that hit Jesse with the rock?"

Peggy turned to face her husband; "Henry what do you mean, what are we going to do about that little pickaninny? We both know that it was just an accident. They were little boys playing in the mud. There's no reason, no need to do anything."

Henry removed his legs from the bedspread; both of his feet were now planted firmly on the floor. "Sugar we both know that it was an accident, that they were all throwing mud-balls. In truth anyone in that group could have been hit."

"But honey the truth of the matter is that the one who threw the mud-ball, is a black boy. The boy that was hit by the mud-ball, is a white boy."

"Here in the South, regardless of their age or of the circumstances, it has never been, nor will it ever be acceptable, permissible, for a black to strike a white person."

"That little black pickinney that threw the rock has got to be punished."

Peggy placed the jar of beauty-cream that she had been holding in her hand, onto her dressing table. "Henry that's absurd. You can't be seriously suggesting that we should whip a six-year-old child?"

Henry held up his hand palm facing outward, toward his wife; "Now hold it right there, that's just it. That's the problem honey.

That was a little black bastard that threw the rock, and I chose the word bastard, not necessarily as an epithet, but as a statement of fact, that hit our son."

"Since we don't allow our niggers to marry, we avoid problems, histrionics, that some planters who allow their slaves to marry, encounter when either a husband or a wife is sold. Not to mention that our insistence of enforcing the practice of encouraging the black wenches to lay with multiple, randy, bucks is profitable. The more they rut, the more pickaninnies are dropped. The more black pickaninnies, the more salable slaves for us."

"I guess you could say that, literally speaking, when you correctly apply the meaning of the word bastard, then all of Rosewood's pickaninies, are actually, little black bastards."

Peggy turned back to her dressing table. She replaced the cork into the open jar of hand cream. "Henry, you know that I detest that kind of language. I find your flagrant, loose usage of those words, "randy bucks and wenches", to be vulgar and offensive."

Henry was contrite; "Forgive me Sugar, I apologize for my intemperate choice of words. I was merely attempting to make a point."

"Where was I… oh yeah, I was making a point. We can't treat that little pickaninny like we would a white kid, a real six-year-old child.

The one that threw the rock as well as every last one of those little black bastards, are not children. They are slaves, our slaves, our property."

Henry rose from the bed, he walked over to his wife and gently, reassuring, placed his hand on her shoulder. "Of course, we won't publicly whip the little nigger"

"Instead of the lash, we'll have his mammy publicly give him a good hard spanking, say fifteen good solid whacks with a paddle, on his little black behind."

"We'll have the punishment administered by his mammy, during the Sunday services, that they hold at that shack, that the niggers call a church."

"Sugar, you must never forget, that as a matter of fact, and strategically, we the white people of Rosewood, are outnumbered twenty-five to one by our niggers."

"What you may now see as innocent, cute little five-year-old pickaninies, in ten, fifteen years, are going to grow up to be big strong nigger-bucks. Black bucks capable of committing all kinds of atrocities."

"The public spanking will teach, and reinforce for all of the darkies, young and old alike, a vitally important lesson. That, By God, no nigger is ever justified in striking a white person!"

"Our very survival as a civilized society is dependent upon the nigger's absolute acceptance, belief and adherence to that basic, omnipotent law of nature."

Peggy placed her hand over that of her husband's. With a sigh, which Henry correctly interpreted as her acceptance and her agreement with his proposed plan of action, she turned and looked into her husband's eyes.

"Henry I've been thinking. I've given it a great deal of thought. I've decided that you were right."

Henry was momentarily confused. He gave his wife a quizzical look.

"I'm ready to reconsider your suggestion, your idea to have one of the older slave boys attend to Jesse's needs. The older slave boy can play with Jesse while watching over him, protecting him, keeping him safe."

Inwardly Henry smiled to himself. From out of the blue, as if sent from heaven, a solution.

Serendipity, Jesse's little accident, had opened a way for him to accommodate the wishes of both of the women in his life, his cherished, beloved, adored white wife Peggy, and his compliant, subservient, obedient black "bed-wench", Ruth.

The very next day Ruth's son Jason's, daily laboring in the cotton fields under the relentlessly scorching mid-summer Virginia Sun, and the persistent bite of the overseer's whip, was miraculously, unexpectedly, and inexplicably ended.

From that day forth, young six-year-old Jesse Billings, the heir to Virginia's Rosewood Plantation, would then, — and for the entirety of his relatively short-life — be attended to, and would be obediently and faithfully served by Jason, the *"high yella"* son of, caramel colored Ruth, his father's beautiful bed wench.

****

Of the many demeaning things that Jason was obligated to submit to as Jesse's slave-playmate and protector, by far the most humiliating and most demeaning to his young psyche, not to mention his permanently scarred torso, was when, *"da youn Massa"* insisted that he, serve as "Buckskin Bob's (*da youn Massa's*), trusty steed, "Blacky."

Initially, when reenacting *"The Adventures of Buckskin Bob"*, young *Massa Jesse,* would have Jason get down on his hands and knees.

Jesse — *Buckskin Bob (Massa Jesse)* — would order *"Blacky"* the Wonder Horse (eight-year-old Jason),* to get down on his hands and knees in the dirt. *Buckskin Bob (Massa Jesse)* would then climb up onto the slave-boy's back.

The pudgy little white boy, arms clasped around *"Blacky's* neck, found it difficult to stay on the back of the black slave-boy, as they clumsily scurried in the dirt, chasing the wicked, savage, Red Skins.

Henry, after having observed his now happy and contented six-year-old son and heir, continually tumble from *"Blacky's"* back, came up with what he thought, was a plausible, workable remedy to the problem.

****

CHAPTER 9

Atlas, the plantation's, gigantic 6'4", 250 lb., black as mid-night, heavily-muscled, Blacksmith/Leather Craftsman, stood deferentially behind *Massa* Henry.

Henry Billings, himself a large man at 6' 0", 185 lb, along with his slave Atlas, stood in the shadows, watching little Jesse (*Buckskin Bob*), scurrying around, playing in the dirt, astride his trusty steed, *(Blacky)* Jason.

The two adult men, one the tall white Master, the other a massive behemoth, a giant slave, were both concentrating, studiously watching the boys play.

Henry puffed on the small cigar that he held firmly between his lips. He removed the cigar from his mouth, and blew out a small stream of grayish-blue smoke. Then using the cigar as an extension of his hand, he pointed towards the boys.

The slave-boy Jason was helping his *Massa*, six-year-old Jesse up from the dirt. *Massa* Jesse, having nothing to hold onto other than Jason's shirt collar, had once again fallen off of the back of his trusty steed "*Blacky*", the wonder horse.

Gesticulating with his cigar, Henry spoke; "See that there Atlas, Jesse keeps sliding off of that nigger-boy's back. I want you to make Jesse, a little saddle, cinch, stirrups, bridle, bit and all, so that *Massa* Jesse can control "*Blacky*." So he won't keep sliding, off the back of his pretend horse.

Twelve days later, Atlas presented Henry with Jesse's beautifully hand-tooled, miniature leather saddle.

Henry, with a stern expression, inspected the saddle. He pulled and buckled the cinch; he examined the miniature oak-wood stirrups that were securely attached, to the mini-saddle's, two six by six-inch fenders.

With a broad smile of satisfaction, Henry turned and the patted Atlas on his broad back; "Now that there is a fine-looking little saddle. Any one of our pickaninies, would be proud to have this saddle, strapped to his back"

Henry picked up the saddle and carried it to the house. He stood at the foot of the stair, rested the saddle on the banister and called to his wife; "Peggy are you up there? I've got something that I want you to see."

Peggy was seated at her desk. With a firm dainty hand, she had just completed the printing of a list of items that she intended to have Atlas hand to Mr. Wilson, the proprietor of the town's mercantile store, when he went to town for supplies.

"What is it dear? I'm finishing up here at my desk." Henry, dragging his permanently stiff right leg, followed by Rufus his manservant, who was carrying the saddle, climbed the stairs.

After motioning to Rufus that he should remain in the hall, Henry entered Peggy's sitting room.

"Honey you know how you've been worried sick, and how you've been so upset about Jesse's many scrapes and skinned knees from his playing; acting out the adventures of "Buckskin Bob?""

"Most of those scrapes and skinned knees, happen when Jesse, or as our little boy would prefer that I say, when "Buckskin Bob", falls off of the back of that nigger-boy that he rides."

Peggy's curiosity was aroused; "Yes darling, I know and we both know and remember, how unhappy our little boy was before we made Ruth's boy Jason, Jesse's playmate."

Henry opened the door; "Sugar I think I've solved the problem." He stuck his head into the hallway; "Rufus bring it in here."

Rufus, holding the miniature-saddle in both hands, shuffled into the room. Peggy, whose elbows were on her desk, had been resting her head on her "steepled" hands; she rose to her feet; "What in the world…?"

Rufus placed the miniature saddle onto the back of an empty chair. Peggy moved from behind her desk, and walked over to examine the tiny saddle.

Margaret (Peggy) Billings, who enjoyed a well-deserved reputation as one of Essex County's most prominent and cultured, patrons of the arts, moved from behind her desk.

She walked over to Rufus and slowly, meticulously began to examine, what appeared to her to be the smallest saddle that she had ever seen.

Peggy proceeded to delicately run her hands over the soft hand-tooled, engraved leather, over the saddle horn, over the pommel. She caressed the elegant, saddle- skirt, with its soft white cotton-fleece padding.

With a look of unmistakable admiration and wonder in her eyes, Peggy clasped Henry's hand and proclaimed; "This leather mini-saddle is one of the most breathtakingly, beautiful, exquisite, "*Works-of- Art*", that I have ever seen."

****

That same evening, following a late supper in the cabin that he shared with his woman Fannie, Atlas sat brooding, bent over the table, holding his head in his huge hands.

Fannie, having finished washing the dishes and tucking her son Pee Wee into bed, poured herself a cup of coffee and joined Atlas at the table.

Noticing her man's sullen mood, his furrowed brow, and the pulsating vein that rhythmically throbbed in his forehead, as he slurped hot coffee from his mug, Fannie wearily with a sigh sank into the chair opposite Atlas at the table.

"What's bothr'n ya man? Yu been sitin der slumped ova dat tabul lookin lik yu done loss ya bes fren."

Atlas sat back in his chair. To Fannie, the large mug that the big man held in his trembling hand resembled one of the baby cups that she had seen the little white girls play with.

Atlas placed his coffee mug onto the table. *"Fannie ise dun dun sumpin bad, real bad."*

Fannie was alarmed. It was not at all like Atlas to be in such a foul mood. The giant of a man was known and respected throughout the slave community, for his even-minded temperament, his ready smile, and his gentle, mild manner.

Fannie put her warm strong hand over the huge, callused, black-hand of the big man. *"Atlas, what's da mata wid ya? "Ya can tell me…talk ta me."*

Atlas huge shoulders shuddered. Fannie released his hand. *"Let me getcha sum mo coffee."*

Fannie returned to the table. She placed the steaming mug of coffee in front of Atlas. Ignoring the steam that was rising from his mug, Atlas took a long gulp of the scalding, hot drink, wiped his mouth with the back of his hand, and then he morosely, sullenly, slumped back in his chair.

Fannie returned to her seat. She once again took the big man's hands in her's, and stared pleadingly into his eyes. *"Lawd ah-mightee man, wha ya dun gone an dun?*

Atlas told Fannie of Henry's instructions, two weeks ago, that he make a saddle, to be used by young *Massa* Jesse.

He told of how he and the *Massa* had stood watching the two little boys, young *Massa* Jesse, and Ruth's *high yella* boy Jason, playing in the dirt.

He told Fannie how Ruth's boy would get down in the dirt on his hands and knees. How chubby little *Massa* Jesse would climb up on the slave-boy's back, and attempt to ride the boy like he was a horse.

Atlas told Fannie, how *Massa* Jesse, despite his hanging on with all his might, hugging his *"Wonder Horse-Blacky"* (Ruth's boy Jason), around his neck, how the chubby little *Massa,* would invariably slide off of *Blacky's* back.
Atlas said that *Massa* Henry had told Atlas that a saddle was needed to prevent the young *Massa* Jesse, from falling off of his *pretend* horse.

Fannie, listening intently to Atlas, was dumbfounded, confused. She could not comprehend why the big man was so upset?

Was he upset because little *Massa* Jesse and Ruth's boy were playing at riding horses? That just didn't make sense.

Little kids had been playing that game forever. As far back as she could remember, children at play, especially little children, would often sit on the backs of one-another, mimicking grown-ups riding horses.

True enough, she thought, she had never seen, nor had she ever heard of a child putting a real saddle, on the back of one of their playmates.

Atlas went on to tell Fannie, of how he had created a miniature saddle, by meticulously copying, with painstaking attention to detail, *Massa* Henry's favorite saddle. The saddle that the *Massa* no longer used following the accident, *"when he come ta be a cripple, afta he dun brokin his leg."*

He placed his hands over his eyes, and began to whimper; *"Oh lawd what ise I dun gone an dun ta dat chile?"*

Fannie was confused, thus far, as far as she could tell; Atlas had dutifully, diligently, complied with *Massa* Henry's orders.

"Atlas wha fo is ya whinin'? It soun ta me lik ya dun dun wha da Massa dun tol ya ta do."

"Fannie yu dunt unnerstan. I ast da Massa why…"

Abruptly Fannie sprang from her chair exclaiming, *"Sweet Jesus."* She smelled smoke, something was burning, and smoke was seeping out from the corners of the large brick oven.

In her attempt to console Atlas, Fannie had completely forgotten that two trays of rolls were baking, more accurately; two trays of rolls were burning in the oven.

Fannie dropped Atlas' hands, and rushed over to the oven. She grabbed a towel, pulled open the door of the oven, and removed the charred, burnt, smoldering rolls.

While Fannie was busy cleaning up the mess, Atlas' mind wandered, drifted back to the day when *Massa* Henry gave him the specifications for Jesse's saddle

Massa Henry's instructions were that he should make a practical, functional saddle, a saddle that would fit the back of *"Blackey"*, and would accommodate the body of a 30 to 40 pound six-year-old little boy.

That saddle had to snuggly fit around the frame of Ruth's skinny 50 to 55-pound boy, Jason.

Initially Atlas had been at a loss as to how to proceed. After hours of contemplation, Atlas decided to use *Massa* Henry's dusty, hardly ever used, custom made saddle, as his template.

Henry's father, Artimas Billings an avid horseman, had passed on to his son before his death, a custom-made "Western" style saddle, that he had had made to his demanding specifications, by a fancy Yankee saddle- maker.

The saddle had been made in Delaware, and had been transported, overland to Rosewood.

Fannie returned to the table. She playfully, with her open-hand, slapped the back of Atlas' head. With feigned annoyance she sat across from Atlas, and sarcastically stated; *"Ise wants ta thank ya for helpin me wid dem burnt rolls."*

Atlas resumed his narrative. He told Fannie of how, when he first showed *Massa* Henry the completed miniature- saddle; *"Da Massa looked lik he thought I dun good. Den da Massa ast me, wher da sterups?"*

"I hoed boff my hands ta gatha lik dis." Atlas spread his hands apart, approximately 10 inches. *"I say ta da Massa, wont no need fo sterups. Yung Massa Jesse can eezy, frum off da grund, thro he leg cross Jason and da saddle."*

Fannie was still confused. Up to this point, as far as she could tell, Atlas' actions and his explanations were in compliance with *Massa* Henry's orders.

"Atlas wha fo ya whinin'? It still soun ta me lik ya dun wha da Massa dun tol ya ta do."

"Fannie ya dunt unnerstan. I ast da Massa why duz he wants sterups on da saddle.

"Massa says dat da sterups ain't fo ta get on, da dere fo Yung Massa Jesse ta stay in da saddle. And fo him ta make blacky move fasta"

Atlas' face was once again contorted into anguished folds. He began to wring his hands together.

He placed the knuckles of the index fingers of both hands into his eye sockets, and began to piteously lament; *"Oh lawd wha ise I dun gone an dun ta dat po chile?"*

Fannie saw the anguish in Atlas' face. She decided that it was best that she not interrupt. She had never before seen Atlas this upset.

Fannie thought it best that for now, she would just listen. She would concentrate; listen to what her man was saying. Let him; *"get shed uh what was bothern' him."*

Atlas removed his knuckles from his red-rimmed eyes; *"When Ise bout ta cut da wood fo da sterups, Massa Henry come ta da stabul wid the predest pair of lil cowboy boots dat Ise eva dun seed."*

The big man's voice seemed to rise an octave; *"Dem boots be da same leather as ise da saddle. Den Massa Henry hands me a long piece uh da leather. He tol me ta mak ah bridle an a bit fo "Blacky's" mouf. Oh lawd wha ise I dun dun...?"*

Fannie showing remarkable restraint remained silent. She rose from her chair and loving, as though the behemoth sobbing before her was a small child, she walked over to Atlas and hugged him to her bosom.

Atlas managed to compose himself. He looked up into Fannie's questioning brown eyes; *"Boof a dem fancee lil boots got dem ah sharp metal spur on da back."*

"Fannie, Massa Jesse gonna ride Roof's boy, like he be a mule. Lik he be ah animal. Da yung massa gonna kick, an kick, an kick dat po boy wid dem sharp as ah knife, metal spurs. Dem spurs gonna cut Roof's boy sumpin awful."

With tears flowing down his cheeks, Atlas pleaded with Fannie; *"Pleese Fannie, tell yo fren Roof, dat her boy dat yung Massa Jesse be ridin lik a hoss, tell ha dat Big-Atlas be wantin ta to talk wid her. I wants ta tell her Ise sawry, I wants ta beg her ta forgive me"*

****

E. Pluribus Unum

CHAPTER 10

Manassas Creek Virginia: July 30, 1861

(Bivouac location - Company "C" New Hampshire 5th Volunteer Infantry

The toe of a soldier's boot, nudging Jason below his left armpit, caused the exhausted runaway, to groggily stir. A tin cup of water, and a tin plate filled with runny eggs, grits, fatback, and a piece of corn bread, lay on the dirt floor, between Jason's out-stretched legs.

Jason recognized the ruddy face of the private, that the sergeant last night had called Mickey. Mickey was the pimply-faced soldier that yesterday, had discovered him hiding in the hollow tree.

Mickey threw a dirty, heavily encrusted with dried egg yoke, wooden spoon onto the plate. He did not remove the ropes that were securely tied around Jason's ankles and his wrists.

Jason, with both hands tied together, managed to lift the cup of water to his parched lips. He thirstily drank the water, and placed the cup on the dirt floor. He ignored the filthy wooden spoon and instead, using the corn bread as a utensil, eagerly scooped the food into his mouth.

Private Mickey Slade, watched with interest as the professed runaway slave gulped down his food. He had thought that the slave would use the dirty spoon, or if not the spoon, that he would use his fingers as eating utensils, to eat his meal.

Mickey was grudgingly, slightly impressed, when the slave improvised.

The runaway-slave had examined and discarded the filthy wooden spoon. Instead of the filthy spoon, or his fingers, the slave had used, as an eating utensil, the cornbread, which he used as a scoop and as a sponge.

Jason struggled to his feet. During his time as Jesse Billings' slave-valet at the Virginia's Military Academy, and as Lieutenant Jesse Billings' slave-orderly at the Confederate camp, Jason had been exposed to and had become acquainted with the stratification, the deference due and accorded to soldiers, of differing ranks in the military.

He knew by looking at the soldier's uniform, its simplicity, the lack of markings and/or insignia, that the man standing before him was a private in the Union Army. A ranking that Jason had come to equate among these white soldiers, as being analogous to that of the *"black field-hand"*, in his former life, as a slave on the Rosewood Plantation.

Despite this knowledge, or more precisely, because of this knowledge— that this pimply-faced soldier holding the menacing rifle, occupied the very bottom rung of the army's chain-of-command and of its social ladder—, Jason instinctively decided to address the soldier as "Sir."

"Excuse me *Sir*, before we go to see the Captain, I would like your permission to relief myself."

Before joining the Army, Mickey Slade had lived his entire life in the poorest, the slum section, of the city of Hanover New Hampshire.

Hanover, his hometown, was almost entirely devoid of blacks. Mickey had literally, never before held a conversation with a black, a free black or a slave.

Mickey was momentarily confused and astonished. This was the first time that he had ever been addressed by anyone, in civilian life or in the army, as "*Sir.*"

All of his life Mickey had been led to believe that blacks, especially black slaves, were stupid, ignorant creatures.

Contrary to his preconceived beliefs, Mickey thought that the way this smart-assed nigger spoke, didn't sound at all like the nigger dialects that he had used, and had heard used, by his fellow soldiers.

This nigger talked better than he did. This *coon,* talked like an officer.

Private Slade stood mute, dumbfounded. Jason realizing that the soldier was confused, quickly changed the idiomatic tenor of his speech; *"Suh, I'se needs ta taks me a leak."*

Mickey's face turned a beet shade of red. Who the hell does this nigger think he is? He pointed his rifle at Jason's stomach. "Nigger I don't know what you're up to. My orders are to bring you to the Capn', afta you eat."

"Now get your black ass ta moving, before I run you through with this here pig-sticker."

Jason admonished himself. How could he have been so careless, so trusting, so naive?

He had forgotten the fundamental precept, the philosophy of human societal existence and survival, repeatedly told to him by his sister Mandy.

Jason instantly realized that he had made a mistake. He chided himself, for forgetting a fundamental axiom for survival, when dealing with *"Po White-Trash"*, never let them think that you're mocking them."

Despite Mandy being his younger sister, Jason readily acknowledged the fact that his sister… his teacher, had managed to attain a highly developed level of education and degree of literacy, far superior to his.

This fact was undoubtedly a consequence of his sister Mandy's special relationship, with the Billings' children's tutor, Eleanor Leary.

Eleanor Leary was the young, idealistic, Yankee college-educated schoolteacher that had been brought to Rosewood, to teach the Billings children, Rebecca and Jesse—Jason's former Master, literature, mathematics, and the classics.

Jason remembered having once, innocently asked his sister; *"Mandy...why* do the whites treat us like animals?"

Mandy's response had been to share with her brother, the words of the one and only white woman that she had grown to love, respect, and revere, Miss Eleanor Leary.

Mandy told her older brother of the time that Miss Leary had shared with her, her white Irish-immigrant father's favorite racist-slur.

After her family had arrived in America, and when he could not find work, her father had told of the *slew of anti-Irish signs that he had encountered, proclaiming; "Irish, and Niggers, need not apply".*

Miss Leary told of how, as the family sat huddled together, cold and hungry, her father, Sean O'Leary, the son and grandson of itinerant potato farmers, all born and raised in Downy Court, Ireland, would quote to his impoverished family, what was to him, the comforting refrain;

"Well, at least we ain't niggers."

Jason remembered how after hours of discussion and contemplation, Mandy had been able to finally, make him understand.

The point of her repeating this, what Mandy had initially thought to be an insensitive insult, what Miss Leary had actually been doing, was sharing with a black-slave girl, on a cotton plantation in the slave holding state of Virginia, her own white-catholic-immigrant's life experiences, that underscored, and reinforced, what she had earlier taught her two brilliant students, the white girl Rebecca, and the black girl Mandy.

Jason remembered his sister's saying that Miss Leary had previously ended a Sociology-Lecture, by closing with this sentence;

"It appeared to be true, that within almost all societies, the different stratified layers of that society, each layer of the society, found someone or some group, within that society, to "look down" upon.

In essence to lend stability and acceptance of their plight, the group members especially those who thought of themselves as the downtrodden—, ascribed to the mantra;

"That no matter how bad things are, you should take comfort in the fact, that they could be worse."

Miss Leary had translated her father's favorite, seemingly racist-slur, for Mandy; *"At least we ain't niggers",* into poor white trash jargon that to them meant; "No matter how bad they *(The White Ruling Class),* treats us, *"At least we (poor whites), ain't niggers."*

****

With the point of his bayonet just inches from Jason's spine, Private Slade marched the runaway slave to the entrance of Captain Clarke's tent.

Private Slade gestured, with a nod of his head that the prisoner, should stand at the side of the tent.

Private Slade pulled the tent's flap aside and with a slight stammer, which manifest itself when the private was nervous or frightened, announced; "Pri…pri…private Michael Slade, with the nig…nigra prisoner, reporting as ordered sir."

Captain Clarke responded; "bring the prisoner in private."

Private Slade motioned for Jason to enter the tent. A shove in the back by the butt of the private's rifle, propelled Jason into the tent.

Despite the increasing brightness of the new day, provided by the rising sun, the interior of the tent was dimly illuminated. A lite oil lamp sat in the center of the captain's desk.

Jason quickly noted that there were five occupants in the tent. Captain Clarke was seated at the desk. On each side of the Captain was an armed soldier.

Seated on the floor, hands tied behind their backs, were three blacks. Two black men, and who to Jason, appeared to be a young, teenaged black girl.

Jason quickly scrutinized and assessed the bound men. Both of the men, as was the girl were endowed with what his sister Mandy, would have described as typical "Negroid", phenotypic features.

They each had very dark, nearly black skin, a flat *"bow-tie"* nose, kinky-hair, and thick bulbous lips. Both Jason, and Private Mickey Slade, were momentarily, stunned by the undeniable attractiveness, of the young girl.

Jason immediately concluded that more than likely, the three blacks were runaway slaves, more precisely; that they were all, including the girl, runaway "field-hands", slaves that worked almost exclusively in the fields, planting, caring for, and harvesting the crops, primarily the cotton.

The two men, as was the girl, were obviously, what the white overseers called "prime-stock." They were all well muscled, typical "field-hand", slaves.

Captain Clarke acknowledged Jason's presence by indicating that he should stand next to him. The captain pointed to the three blacks seated on the floor.

"Early this morning one of our perimeter guards caught these three attempting to sneak into the mess tent." He scowled, made a menacing face and said; "I've half a mind to have them taken out into the woods and shot as rebel spies."

The three dejected slaves stared in horror at the captain. Their faces reflected apprehension and stark, naked, fear.

The older slave clasped his bound hands together, and raised them towards the heavens, as if in prayer and plaintively moaned; *"Pleees Massa dun whup us, dun kilt us. We ain't rebs. We jus got da hungrys. We be jus, lookin fo sumpin ta eat."*

The younger man began to moan and to weep; *"Oh lawdy dey fixin ta whup us, gwine ta peel da skin rite offa us black backs!"*

Captain Daniel Clarke, Ph.D., Associate Professor of History at Dartmouth College, was confused.

This rapid cascade of sounds, which he assumed were English words, heavily encased in a harsh southern accent, was to the captain's ears, incoherent, and practically incomprehensible.

Though it was obvious that the two men were attempting to communicate with him, he simply could not understand what the black men were saying.

In civilian life, as an avowed abolitionist, Daniel Clarke had attended various rallies, meetings and lectures, advancing *"the cause"*, the abolition of slavery.

On numerous occasions Daniel had met and held intelligent, often lengthy conversations, with freemen of color.

Those gentlemen's—freemen of color—, command of the English language, their vocabulary and their diction, had been precise, and impeccable.

Dr. Clarke was of course very familiar with Harriet Beecher Stowe's 1852 hugely popular novel, "Uncle Tom's Cabin."

During the course of his reading the novel, Daniel had to admit, that he had been forced to slowly, and to methodically read, and re-read Mrs. Stowe's depiction of the slave's dialect.

Daniel had been able to understand Mrs. Stowe's presentation of the slave- dialect, by putting what he perceived as the *mangled English* words, into context, with Mrs. Stowe's story line, the novels plot, and the overall surrounding narrative.

Daniel's fictional, literary exposure—*"Uncle Tom's Cabin"*—, to the Southern black-slave's dialect, their words, their diction, was not at all that similar to the speech patterns of the few freemen of color, the educated blacks, that he had encountered in his world of academia, or through his abolitionist activities.

This was especially evident, when in his mind; he contrasted the gibberish spewing forth from these pathetic slaves, with the soaring, inspirational orations of that most celebrated and famous "Freeman of Color", Mr. Frederick Douglass.

The torrent of unintelligible sounds, the obvious pleadings of the two black-slaves at his feet, was to the Union Officer, incoherent, undecipherable, sounds of hysteria.

Captain Clarke looked from the two wretched slaves, to the tall statuesque black-man standing beside him; "I believe last night you said that your name is Jason…correct?"

Jason nodded his head. Sergeant Crawford, with brown tobacco juice spittle, embedded in his scraggily beard, stepped in front of Jason and without warning or an utterance, buried his fist into Jason's mid-section.

"Boy, you speak up when the Capn' talking to you. Ya hear?" Jason doubled over, the wind knocked from him, more startled than actually hurt.

Captain Clarke reproachfully looked at the sergeant; "That's enough sergeant."

He then quizzically, expectantly, turned his attention to Jason. Jason straightened and resumed his posture; "Yes sir my slave name, I believe, because of my Slave Master's surname, would be Jason Billings. My mother's name is Ruth."

Jason then, snapped to Attention. A posture that he had seen the cadets at VMI, and more recently the Confederate Soldiers, assume. Attention a stance that Jason equated with a posture assumed, and appropriate for the discussing of serious matters.

Jason standing at rigid attention, looking down at the captain from his full six foot, two inches, in a booming voice proclaimed, "Sir, my name is Jason Ruth."

Captain Clarke, briskly ordered the sergeant to remove the ropes that were securely tied around Jason's wrists. He pointed to the three cowering slaves seated on the floor.

"I don't understand what they're saying. Putting aside the obvious fact, that they're hungry, and although I think that I recognize a mispronounced word here and there, I have not been able to put those garbled words into meaningful, coherent, sentences."

After vigorously rubbing each of his chafed wrists, Jason kneeled down, and sank to the floor.

He firmly but gently, placed his hands onto the shoulder of the adult male slave.

Speaking in what Jason and his sister called *"nigger talk"*, the universal slave colloquial dialect, he was able to easily calm down, and to allay, the fear and the apprehension of the three cowering slaves.

The older of the two male fugitive slaves stated that they, the three of them, were a family, a father and his two teenage children.

"Ise be Buford. Dis here muh boy Curtus, an he sista Pumkin. Deys be muh chilrens. We'se be da probty ah Massa Cyrus Jones. We's all be wok'n in da massas' cotin feels."

> *"Massa Cyrus tret us prit nah good. He be ah good massa. Oniest whup me an mah boy ifn he feels we not wukin' fas enuf."*

> *"Da Massa an da white oberseer nevah befo whup da gal. Dey boff ah dem, liks ta tak turns ta pesta Pumkin."*

> *"Massa dun sooed off, boff my chilrens mudda's."*

The father explained that his decision that they run, had been made when he heard, via the slave grapevine, that their Master was planning to sell his daughter, *"inta da sportin' life."*

Jason gave the slave's shoulder a reassuring squeeze. He stood, faced the Captain, and briefly, succinctly repeated, in concise and precise, grammatically correct English, the older slave's narration.

The captain for the first time, let his eyes methodically, thoroughly, examine the strikingly beautiful, trembling young black girl.

Once again, the captain thought of the bronze statues, depicting the regal, beautiful, ebony, Nubian princesses, that he had seen in exhibits, in the New York, and the Boston museums.

Captain Clarke turned and gave an order to the company's 1st sergeant; "Sergeant Crawford, stand the girl up."

Before the sergeant could comply, eager, young, Private Michael Slade, a soldier regarded by his fellow soldiers as being lazy, lacking initiative, was lifting the terrified female-slave, to her feet.

Later that night when *"lazy-ass"* Mickey, retold the incident to his squad-mates, of when he lifted the girl, by placing his hands under her armpits, how he had managed to "cop a good feel" of the "softest and firmest, perky little tities yall could ever imagine squeezing".

The captain examined the trembling female-slave. This time he looked beyond and discounted, the filthy rags and the girl's dirty face.

Standing before him, being supported by the *"wandering"* hands of the acne-pocked faced private, was a strikingly, beautiful, young female.

Daniel's eyes made a quick assessment of the obviously frightened, cowering black girl. The girl was of average height, approximately five feet, five inches tall.

She was in every sense of the word, truly black. Daniel had a fleeting thought, the complexion of her skin, reminded him of the color of the black-ebony keys on his mother's pianoforte.

The girl's facial features were typical of those that the captain had come to associate, with what he had come to perceive of, as being typical Negroid features.

Her nose was broad and flat, with flaring, widespread nostrils. Her lips were thick and full. Her hair was short and coarse. The texture of her hair was kinky, nappy woolly.

Captain Daniel Clarke remembered thinking that; the black girl standing, trembling before him, was truly beautiful.

The girl, whose name the tall, obviously literate slave Jason, translated as being Pumpkin, stood demurely, head lowered, eyes cast downward, fixed on the floor of the tent
Although Daniel had not received formal training as a professional soldier, he immediately saw and appreciated the potential value— the gathering of military intelligence— that could be gleaned from these people, the local inhabitants of the countryside, these runaway slaves.

Following the unexpected, catastrophic, defeat and the panicky retreat of the Union Army at the Battle of Bull Run, Captain Clarke had been given orders to prevent, or to at least slow-down, what many high ranking, both civilian and military officials thought would be, the rebels anticipated invasion of Washington city, the nation's capital.

Captain Clarke's company had been hastily dispatched without providing the commanding officer, with vital information, to face the enemy.

The captain had only a rough estimation of the rebel's strength. He did not know if he would be facing infantry, cavalry, or both.

He was totally ignorant as to the terrain, the natural fortifications, of the surrounding area.

Captain Clarke was bereft of any military intelligence relevant to his hastily issued, rearguard orders.

Captain Clarke returned his attention to Jason, and in a voice dripping with feigned respect, spoke; "Will now…Mr. Jason Ruth, would you be so kind as to ask these men a few questions for me?"

Jason eyes traveled from the Captain's to the two slaves seated on the floor.

Jason swallowed and cleared his throat. "Captain Clarke, I would be honored to assist you, by accepting your offer of employment, if that is your intent."

"If I am not to be accepted as a soldier in your army, alternatively, it would be my honor, to be your employee, to work for you as your interpreter.

To work for you, and with you… to work as a freeman of color."

****

E. Pluribus Unum

CHAPTER 11

Washington City - August 12, 1861; Command Tent - Commanding Officer of New Hampshire's 5th Volunteers

Following the completion Company "C's" assignment, to serve as a forward element of armed forces, protecting the capital from imminent invasion, by rebel forces, after the rebel's victory at Bull-Run, Captain Clarke made a formal request, for a meeting with Colonel John Baxter, his regimental commander.

Lieutenant Alexander Jensen, the young aide to Colonel John H. Baxter, exited the tent of the regimental commanding officer. Captain Clarke, who had been standing relaxed, in the shade of a large, leafy tree, smoking a small cigar, stepped toward the junior officer.

Lieutenant Jensen approached the captain, stopped thirty inches from his superior officer, and snapped to attention. He stood rigid, his feet together at a forty-five-degree angle, and saluted; "Captain Clarke, the Colonel will see you now."

Captain Clarke dropped his cigar to the ground. With his right foot, he stepped on the still smoldering cigar, and ground it into the dirt.

The captain casually, haphazardly, returned the Lieutenant's salute. He straightened his uniform tunic, walked over to the tent, and knocked on the slab of wood, engraved with the words; "Colonel J.H. Baxter, Regimental Commander."

The single word neither whispered, nor was it shouted— "Enter", which could only be interpreted as a command, to be obeyed, ushered forth from the confines of the tent.

Colonel John H. Baxter was a career army officer. He was a graduate of the United States Military Academy (West Point).

In 1846, as a young cavalry officer, Colonel Baxter had fought gallantly and bravely, during the war with Mexico, along with many of his now fellow, senior Union, and Confederate Army Officers.

Seated behind the large but simple wooden desk, was at first glance, a rather ordinary, non-distinct, looking man in his late forties, or possibly his early fifties.

John H. Baxter was a man of average height, approximately 5'8" tall. He weighed one hundred and fifty pounds, yet when he stood, John Baxter, because of his self- assurance and military bearing, gave the impression of
a physically, imposing man.

Despite his own self-assurance and confidence, Captain Clarke, inexplicably felt in awe, and slightly intimidated when in the presence of Colonel John H. Baxter, this decorated, distinguished, career Army officer, his commanding officer.

Captain Clarke stood at "Attention", two steps directly in front of the Colonel's desk. He saluted and announced; "Captain Clarke, "A" Company, 2nd Battalion, Sir".

Colonel Baxter continued his reading of an official looking document. He looked up, saluted, and greeted the Captain; "Good evening Daniel. Please, stand at ease."

In deference to, and because of his respect and admiration of the Colonel, instead of relaxing his posture to the extent of "*Standing-At-Ease*", Daniel, instead, in one continuance motion, spread his feet apart, approximately 18" and clasped his hands behind, and in the small of his back.

This, the military posture of "*Parade Rest*", while less formal then the position of "*Attention*", was thought by Daniel to be at this time, far more appropriate, than the informal position of "*Standing-At-Ease.*"

Colonel Baxter removed the quill from his inkwell, and scribbled his name to the bottom of the document that he had been reading. The Colonel replaced the quill into the inkwell.

He pointed to a vacant chair; "Please, Daniel, be seated." Captain Clarke, as instructed… ordered, sat in one of the two vacant chairs in the Colonel's tent.

Colonel Baxter leaned back in his chair, placed his hands behind his head, and in a commanding military voice, spoke; "Captain Clarke, I haven't had the opportunity to commend you and your company, for the manner and the results, of your recent two weeks in the field."

"Major Anderson, my Executive Officer, briefed me as to your extensive, thorough reconnaissance, which enabled me in-turn, to confidently report to General McClellan, that the rebel forces have withdrawn, and no longer pose an immediate threat to the capital."

Daniel seated in one of the chairs, facing the Colonel's desk, despite the Colonel's words of praise and the Colonel's conciliatory tone, the Captain sat stiffly in his chair, feet planted firmly on the floor, his hands held the brim of his Officer's Kepi Cap, in his lap.

Captain Clarke's back was ramrod straight. Colonel Baxter made a mental note, that though seated, his subordinate was seated at "*Attention.*"

Colonel Baxter noting his subordinate's discomfort, opened the conversation; "You wanted to speak with me?"

Daniel cleared his throat; "Sir, I would like to discuss with you, Mr. Jason Ruth." Noticing the momentary look of confusion on the Colonel's face, he hurriedly continued.

"Sir, Jason Ruth is the highly literate Negro, that my men discovered hiding in the forest, in a hollow tree. The fugitive-slave, Jason Ruth claimed to be a runaway slave, whose wish was to join us, and to assist in our fight to free his people."

"Mr. Ruth claims, that he had been the slave, of a Confederate Officer. That officer being the son of Henry Billings, a wealthy planter, the owner of Richmond Virginia's, Rosewood Plantation.

"Jason…I beg your pardon Sir, the runaway slave Jason Ruth, had most recently been the slave-valet of one of the Confederate officers, a Lieutenant—Captain Clarke paused while he retrieved a slip of paper from his tunic—, a Lieutenant Jesse Billings, who was killed during the recent unfortunate, skirmish at Bull Run."

Colonel Baxter interrupted, "I believe that you wrote in your formal report, that the runaway slave stated, that his goal was that of joining the Union Army.

"That his desire was to—the colonel picked-up a sheet of paper from his desk, and began to read— "to join the army and fight to free his people".

"If that is the reason for this meeting, if you are asking for my permission for this runaway slave to join the Union Army, I'm afraid the answer is an emphatic, resounding <u>No</u>. Your request is denied."

"I believe that you stated that the runaway's name is Jason, and that this Jason stated, that his reason for joining the army, is to "free his people".

"That reason, to "free his people", captain, is not the official mission, nor is it the goal of the United States Army."

"The mistaken belief, that this war is being fought to "free the slaves", is a gross misconception on his part. The purpose for the Union Army fighting this war, is absolutely not to free the "darkies".

"President Lincoln, our Commander-In-Chief, has made it abundantly, and crystal clear, that the mission of the United States Army, in fighting this war, is to restore the Union."

The colonel paused…as if he wanted to give Daniel time to digest his words.

Then he continued: "Moreover captain, there is in effect, a 1792 Federal Law that prohibits Negroes and Mulattoes from serving in the United States Army."

"If we were to enlist black, runaway slaves into the Army, it would result in our breaking federal law."

"Our reason for our fighting this war, as unequivocally stated by the Commander-In-Chief, is for the restoration of the Union."

For the first time, Daniel's respect and admiration of Colonel Baxter, was severely shaken.

Daniel Clarke, Ph.D., the abolitionist, had found the Colonel's cavalier, dismissive, use of the pejorative term "darkies", to be extremely offensive.

However, Captain Daniel Clarke, the soldier, realized and understood that military protocol and military law, did not permit or allow from him, any overt objection or critique, on his part, of his superior officer's choice of words.

Colonel Baxter noticed that the Captain appeared to relax in his chair. The Colonel erroneously attributed the Captain's change in posture, to the junior officer feeling more comfortable, in his presence.

The Colonel's assumption that Captain Clarke's, now noticeably more relaxed posture, was buttressed, when the captain asked from him, and was granted by him, permission to speak.

"Sir, as noted in my report, in addition to Jason Ruth, there were three other runaway slaves, who found their way to our lines. Though those three were not attempting to join the Union Army, they were at least refugees, seeking our protection, seeking, if you will, political-asylum."

"Sir, I think it's safe to say, that during our prosecution of this war, especially as we move deeper into the South, capturing rebel territory, we can anticipate that hundreds, thousands, or maybe even tens of thousands of runaway slaves, will seek refuge within our lines."

"Colonel, when I began to question the three members of this slave family, runaways that were asking for our protection, quite frankly sir, I was finding it extremely difficult to understand what they were saying."

Colonel Baxter leaned forward, and planted his elbows firmly on his desk.

Captain Clarke, seeing the confusion, the perplexed questioning look, in the Colonel's expression, quickly resumed his narrative.

"Colonel, quite frankly, I estimate that out of every twenty words that the runaways said, I was lucky if I recognized, not to mention understood, maybe three or four. Needless to say, I was having a great deal of difficulty deciphering, understanding, besides their obvious asking for food, what they wanted."

Daniel had recognized that at least thus far, the Colonel had shown little, or no concern, for the slaves' inability to communicate, their "wants" to the Captain.

Captain Clarke quickly shifted his point of emphasis. "Colonel, after having the previous night, talked and interrogated, the runaway slave, Jason Ruth, I came to the belief, that the indigenous slave populations, could prove to be an invaluable source for us, of military intelligence."

Daniel was studiously watching the Colonel's facial expressions. The Regimental Commander's look of boredom and disinterest was slowly changing.

The Captain thought; now I've got his attention. Daniel pressed on; "As stated in my report, the original strength of Company "F" of the rebel forces attached to General Thomas Jackson's Rebel Brigade, of Virginia infantry, at full strength had consisted of 160 men.

After the battle at Bull Run, as stipulated in my report, the Confederate's Company "F's" strength, had been reduced to 94 effectives. Additionally, I learned that General Jackson's Brigade, had been ordered back to Richmond."

"This information was communicated to me by the aforementioned fugitive slave, Jason Ruth, who I noted in my report, had been serving as the personal slave for one of the Rebel Officers, who had been killed during the battle at Bull-Run."

"In addition to the fugitive-slave Jason providing us with this important Intel, I found out that Mr. Ruth is extremely, literate. He can read and write, and for our intents and purposes, Mr. Ruth is bilingual."

Although Colonel Baxter had received an excellent education at West Point, he did regret that the academy had not offered classes, teaching a foreign language.

Colonel Baxter was astonished. Before he could ask, Captain Clarke continued; "Our runaway slave, Jason Ruth, is fluent in English, as well as being fluent in what he called— his words Sir—, he is also fluent in *"nigger-talk."*

"The fugitive-slave Jason was able to immediately, on the spot, in real-time, instantaneously, translate, again his word Sir, "nigger-talk", the almost, at least to me, unintelligible words of the three slaves that we encountered, into concise, grammatically perfect, English."

"Colonel, because the 1792 Federal Law expressly prohibits Negroes and Mulattoes, from serving in the United States Army, I am requesting permission to hire the fugitive-slave Jason Ruth, in the capacity of Scout and Interpreter."

Colonel Baxter, a true Connecticut Yankee, was a devout, loyal believer in, and defender of the Union.

Nonetheless, as did many white Northerners, John Baxter was also a man who believed in the superiority of the White Man, and consequently, the innate inferiority of the Negro.

Still, despite his belief in the inferiority of the black-man, a belief that had been drummed into his head since childhood, Colonel Baxter instantly appreciated and saw the logic, and the potential military intelligence significance, of the Captain's statements.

As a senior field-grade Union Officer, one rumored to be being seriously considered for promotion to Brigadier General, Colonel Baxter had been briefed, and made aware, by both political and military leaders, of the possibility, the problem, of encountering vast numbers of runaway slaves.

Many high-ranking officials, both in the army and in the civilian government, referred to, and thought of these runaway slaves, as being "Contraband", goods and property, used by the confederates, in the furtherance their ability to fight the war.

The Colonel almost immediately, instinctively, appreciated the military advantage of obtaining vital, tactical, strategic, and logistical military information, from the runaway slaves.

He reasoned that the potential quantity, and the presumed quality, of valuable information about rebel activity, would be exponentially increasing, as the numbers of fugitive slaves, seeking refuge behind Union lines, increased.

Captain Clarke's formerly relaxed posture had disappeared. He now sat uncomfortably, stiffly, awaiting a response from the Colonel.

Colonel Baxter removed a sheet of official looking, plain paper, from a desk drawer, and began to write; "Captain, I have no objection to our employing the runaway slave", he looked up at Daniel, … "Jason Ruth, is that correct?"

Before the Captain could respond, Colonel Baxter continued, … "I believe you suggested, as a Scout/Interpreter."

Colonel Baxter folded the sheet of paper, reached across his desk, and handed the document to his subordinate. "Give this to the Quartermaster."

Captain Clarke stood at Attention, and saluted. Colonel Baxter returned the salute.

The Captain executed an about-face, and proceeded to leave. When the Captain reached the door of the tent, Colonel Baxter remarked; "Good job Daniel, well-done"

His hand on the doorknob, Captain Clarke turned; "Thank you Sir."

Daniel opened and read the folded sheet of paper:

August 12, 1861

5th New Hampshire Volunteer Infantry

I hereby authorize the hiring of the fugitive slave, Jason Ruth, as a Scout/Interpreter for the 5th New Hampshire Volunteer Infantry.

The fugitive slave, Jason Ruth will be supervised by, and report directly to; Captain Daniel Clarke, Company 'C' Commander of the 5th New Hampshire Volunteer Infantry.

The fugitive slave, Jason Ruth is to be compensated at the rate of sixteen dollars per month ($16.00/Mo.)

John H. Baxter

Colonel John H. Baxter, Commanding Officer, New Hampshire 5th Volunteers

****

CHAPTER 12

Regimental Headquarters - New Hampshire's 5ᵗʰ Volunteers May 15, 1862 (1700 hrs)

Jason's duties as the "*de-facto*", "regimental clerk", gave him ready access to the dispatches, correspondence and communiqués between, the numerous Union forces prosecuting the war effort.

In addition to the plans for the movement of troops and equipment, Jason was also privy to the written, war-related thoughts and policies of the Union-Army's generals, and the Washington politicians.

Unfortunately, the majority of his time was spent attending to the routine, mundane "scutt-work", generated by the 5ᵗʰ New Hampshire Infantry Regiment.

Today, Jason's day, had been an exceptionally busy one. Most of his day had been spent reviewing and correcting, the sick call lists, submitted to headquarters, by the numerous companies that made up the regiment.

As he finished correcting Company "A" clerk's, spelling of the ailment that had excused Pvt. Norman Jackson from two days of duty — a severe case of the "*crewp*", to a severe case of croup—, as he was about to leave for the day, when Jason was abruptly stopped, by Lieutenant Gregory Sharp.

Lieutenant Sharp was a twenty-one-year-old, farm boy, who had just been assigned to regimental headquarters, as a Junior Aide to Colonel Baxter.

"Ruth, this dispatch just arrived for the Colonel. Before you leave, get it decoded, and hand-deliver it to the Colonel's aide."

Jason took the dispatch from the Lieutenants outstretched hand. His first thought was, "damn, if I had left a minute earlier, or if Lieutenant Sharp had come a minute later, I'd be on my way for an evening of fun, with one of the doxies over at the "Contraband Saloon."

Jason sat back in his chair and carefully unfolded, and began to decode the regimental dispatch:

Jason reacquired his seat. As if by rote, reading but not really absorbing the words, he began to copy the communiqué.

After having copied nearly eight paragraphs of the document, he abruptly stopped.

With a slight trembling of his hands, and with a pronounced, noticeably intensified look of deep concentration on his brow, he placed his quill into the inkwell, and he began to slowly, reread the entire official, military communiqué.

Date: May 21, 1862

FROM:

Rear Admiral Samuel Francis DuPont, Commander South Atlantic Blockading Squadron

TO:

Major General George B. McClellan, Commander, Army of The Potomac

SUBJECT:

The commandeering of the C.S.S. **Planter,** *a 1ˢᵗ Class, Coastwise armed steamer"*

The ships ordinance consisted of a 32-pound pivot gun; a 24-pound howitzer, and four artillery pieces, including approximately 200 rounds of ammunition, intended for delivery to a Confederate fort.

The above referenced vessel was attached to the command of Roswell Ripley, Brig. General, CSA.

On May 13, 1862, at approximately 0300 hours, The CSS Planter, flying the South Carolina and Confederate flags, sailed past Southern Wharf, towards the fleet of Union ships, blockading the entrance to, and the exit from, Charleston Harbor.

The course set by the ship's captain passed within easy range of the batteries of five (5) Confederate Harbor Forts.

As the Planter approached each of the Confederate Forts in their path, CSS Planter was challenged. Each challenge was met by the ship captain's correct display of the appropriate Confederate Navy signals.

At 0430 hours, the CSS Planter sailed past Fort Sumter. Once out of the range of the fort's cannon, the captain lowered the Palmetto and Rebel flags, and hoisted in their stead, a white bed-sheet.

The CSS Planter then set a course straight for the Union Navy fleet.
Lieutenant J. Frederick Nickels, of the USS. Onward, spotted the Planter, flying the improvised "white-flag."

As the steamer came near, and under the stern of the USS Onward, one of the CSS Planter's Colored crewmen stepped forward, and shouted, 'Good morning, sir! I've brought you some of the old United States guns, sir!'"
After "boarding" the Confederate War Ship, hauling down the flag of truce, and hoisting the American ensign" Lieutenant Nickels transferred the CSS Planter to his commander, Captain E.G. Parrott of the USS Augusta.

E. Pluribus Unum

In addition to a Confederate naval vessel, Robert Smalls, the highly intelligent twenty-two-year old escaped slave "Contraband", presented Admiral DuPont with, Confederate code books, maps of mines and torpedoes that had been laid in the Charleston Harbor.

The remarkable, seamanship, bravery, and intelligence, displayed by this runaway black slave— "Contraband"— Robert Smalls, successfully leading a small band of seven black slave crew members, past five heavily fortified Confederate harbor forts, underscores the potential value to the Union, of allowing black slaves— "Contraband"— to enlist, and to serve in, the Armed forces of the United States.

JE Callahan, Ensign, USN

JE Callahan

For and by direction of RADM, SF DuPont, Commanding Officer, South Atlantic Blockading Squadron

Jason, who had been leaning over the desk, intently reading and rereading the military dispatch, slumped back in his chair.

The furrows in his brow had disappeared. Jason carefully, slowly, as if he were holding the *"Holy Grail"*, placed the document on the desk, and with a barely perceptible sigh, he slowly exhaled.

****

CHAPTER 13

Salisbury Maryland, 1860

Gregory Sharp was born and raised on a tobacco farm, in Salisbury Maryland, one of the largest towns located on the flat, rich, fertile, plains of Maryland's Eastern Shore.

The young Lieutenant's home state Maryland, a slave-holding state, was one of the four Border States, that geographically, and philosophically, divided North from South.

Control of the Border States that divided the states that had remained loyal to the Union, from those states that had seceded and were in open rebellion against the Union, were considered by both the North and the South, as crucial.

President Abraham Lincoln, the Commander-In-Chief of the Armed Forces of the United States of America, was obsessed, and rightfully so, with the need to keep the Border States, with their large segments of fanatical, pro-slavery, and their anti-slavery citizenries, in the Union.

The principal city of Maryland's Eastern Shore, Salisbury Maryland, is located adjacent to, and east, of the Chesapeake Bay.

During the summer months, Salisbury's climate can be accurately characterized, as being hot and humid, subtropical weather, an ideal climate, for the cultivation, and the growth, of tobacco plants.

The two economic engines that had, during the 18th and 19th centuries, fueled the growth and the prosperity of the city of Salisbury, were the tobacco trade, which in turn, was dependant on the slave trade, for the availability and the provision of slave-labor.

The onset of the civil war had split the loyalties of the Salisbury community. Many families, including those members of Kenneth Sharps' family, had split loyalties.

The sustained economic health, of Maryland's Eastern Shore, was dependent upon its principal cash crop, tobacco. And the planting, cultivating, and harvesting of the tobacco plants, were in turn, dependent upon the ready availability of slave labor.

These pragmatic, economic facts, coupled with two centuries of their living in a society, a culture that sanctioned and promulgated human bondage, contributed to the fact that more than 90% of the Salisbury population was sympathetic to the Confederacy.

Before the war, the absolute minimum requisite manpower needed, to make a success of the Sharp family's small farm, had been provided by Gregory's father Kenneth Sharp, and his three sons; Matthew the oldest, Anthony the middle son, the youngest son Gregory, and the family's three male, black slaves.

The success of the Sharp's tobacco farm was dependent upon the fulltime labor in the tobacco fields, of the farm's seven adult men. Seven men, the four white owners and their three black slaves, working in concert, side by side, in the Sharp family's, 12 acre, hot, humid, tobacco fields.

Gregory's mother Rowena had died in 1840, as a consequence of the tragic, difficult delivery of her youngest son, Gregory.

Beulah, the family's solitary female slave, had been *"tendin ta da Miztress"*, Rowena during the deliveries of all three of her sons.

The delivery of the first two boys had been relatively easy, uneventful.

Rowena's third delivery began, as had the previous two. Beulah, who had no reason to anticipate trouble, was surprised, shocked, and unprepared when what she had thought would be an easy, uneventful, delivery of the third child, had instead, turned into a tragic disaster.

Rowena's third delivery began, as had the previous two.

Beulah, had first become mildly alarmed when she had first noticed that the mistress's *"honey pot"*, was not opening, like it had for the other babies.

Beulah was pleading, encouraging the Mistress *"ta push, ta push"*. With her hands, while her Mistress was screaming, Beulah attempted to open *"da gates ah da honey pot"*, to her surprise, the after-birth was expelled from the *"da gates ah da honey pot"*, followed by a copious amount of blood and tissue, which in turn, was followed by the head and the body of the baby.

The bleeding had become a trickle. Beulah washed and cleaned the Mistress' *"honey-pot"*, and packed it with clean, absorbent, linen.

Beulah cleaned the infant, and then presented him to his mother. Rowena had smiled, and then weakly, exhausted, had laid her head back onto the pillow to rest.

Fifteen minutes later, when she went to check-in on *"da Miztress"*, Beulah found Rowena semi-conscience, laying in a pool of her own blood.

Beulah would never forget those feelings of helplessness, then hopelessness that she had felt, as despite every thing that she could do, she watched as the life drained from her mistress' eyes.

Beulah was committed. Even though she realized her mistress was beyond hearing her, she had promised *"Miztress Rowena"*, that she would *"tak kar of, an rase da baby boy."*

Although Gregory had been born into a life, a world, devoid of females, despite the fact that he would never know his birth-mother; as Beulah held the screaming, squirming, tiny white infant in her arms, Beulah, the Sharp family's lone black female slave, swore; *"ta da sweet baby Jesus"*, that she would do everything that she could, to be a substitute mother, *"fo dis po chile"*, for this helpless, innocent one, her beloved mistress' baby.

****

In mid-April of 1861, immediately following the bombardment and the subsequent surrender, of Fort Sumter—the federal fort located at the mouth of the South Carolina's Charleston River, by Confederate forces, under the command of Brigadier General P. G. T. Beauregard—, the sentiments and the prevailing sympathies of most of the Salisbury residents, had been overwhelmingly in support of the Confederacy.

Every one of the male members of the Sharp's family, with the exception of young Gregory, were fervently and enthusiastically in support of the Confederate siege and the artillery attacks, on Fort Sumter.

****

After an exhausting day, twelve hours, from sunup to sundown of working in the fields, the four white men, that comprised 57% of the Sharp farm's work-force, would sit down, at their segregated table, to eat a hearty meal, prepared by the family's female slave, Beulah.

Inevitably, the main topic of dinner conversation at the Sharp's dinner table—having supplanted talk about the progress of the tobacco crop—was the taking of Fort Sumter, by the Confederate Army.

The prevailing topic of conversation, would center on the vague, not clearly understood, issue of "States Rights."

Kenneth the widowed father, and his eldest sons Matthew and Anthony, were adamant supporters of "States Rights", especially the state laws that supported and upheld the legalized practice of human bondage, slavery.

Gregory, the youngest member of the Sharp family, neither supported, nor did he condone, the South's *"Peculiar Institution"*, *Slavery.*

Unlike his father and his brothers, Gregory had been nurtured and raised, solely by a black slave.

While it was true that many of his friends and acquaintances had been raised, even suckled by a black *"mammy"*, the difference was that all of those friends had had, as a part of their lives, their white mothers.

The one and only female, that Gregory had lovingly ever known, for the entire twenty years of his life, was the one person who had always been there, for him to turn to, Beulah his black-slave, Beulah his surrogate mother.

The one female in his life who would comfort him when as a toddler, he had a *"boo boo"*. The only person, who he could comfortably confide in, could tell of his nightmares, when he dreamed of the monsters that lived under his bed.

The woman who when he was a child growing up, would for no particular reason, give him a cookie and hug him to her breast, was Beulah, his *"black-slave"*, Beulah his surrogate mother.

Beulah, the only mother that he had ever known, was by virtue of her birth, a black slave.

"States Rights", to Gregory was merely a code word; a euphemism used by the politicians, to dignify and to justify the South's *"Peculiar Institution"*, Slavery.

Gregory could not and would not support a political philosophy that condemned Beulah, his black mother, the Sharp family's female *"black-slave"*, to a future of perpetual, and eternal, enslavement.

In the Sharp family household, Gregory the youngest son, who was also the family's business manager, who at an early age had shown an aptitude for numbers and logic, was the sole member of the family whose sympathies, and loyalties, were with the Union.

Despite his political beliefs, which definitely, emphatically, supported the abolition of slavery, Gregory while working in the fields with his father, his brothers and side by side with the family's three male slaves, Gregory too, as did his father and his brothers, referred to their fellow workers, their three adult male slaves, as *"boy"*.

****

CHAPTER 14

Washington City - New Hampshire's
5th Volunteers - August 1862

Jason had been thrilled, inspired by the daring and heroic actions of Robert Smalls, a black-man who as was he, been classified by the United States government, as being "*Contraband*", gave him hope.

His goal, his ambition to join the Union Army, to kill the white devils that had raped and killed his aunt; to kill the white devils who had sold his grandmother, raped his mother, that ambition was still alive, lingering and smoldering, etched deeply into his consciousness.

It had been nine weeks, more than two months, since his hopes of being allowed to enlist in the army, had been bolstered by his reading of the exploits of his fellow ex-slave, "*Contraband*", Robert Smalls.

Nine weeks had passed since he had read and had become aware, that the subject of blacks enlisting in the Union Army, was being discussed, or at least contemplated, at the highest echelons of the military's "Officer Corps."

More than two months of his daily, of methodically, meticulously scanning the dispatches for an announcement. Nine long weeks, since he had seen the bright flame of hope, begin to dim like the faint flickering light of a forgotten, dying campfire.

And then it happened.

****

CHAPTER 15

Washington City - March 16, 1863; Command Tent - Commanding Officer of New Hampshire's 5ᵗʰ Volunteers (1730 hrs)

Jason was both excited and elated, when Major Anderson, the regiment's Executive Officer, assigned him the task of transcribing the Regimental Commander, Colonel Baxter's, detailed plan for the regiment's compliance and implementation, of a recently received directive:

"Compliance with and enactment of, the "Second Confiscation and Militia Act of 1862.""

The directive was from the office of the Secretary of War, Edwin M. Stanton. The Secretary of war was well known by the Union Army's Officer Corps, as being a staunch advocate for the recruitment and the enlistment of *"Colored"* soldiers.

Jason sat at his desk, stunned. For the third time, he once again focused his attention upon the verbiage, of what he considered the most salient section of the newly passed law, the "Second Confiscation and Militia Act of 1862."

He reread for the third time, section twelve, and the section of the law that he had underscored. The section that he had concluded, that at least on paper, "Freed the slaves whose masters, were serving in the Confederate Army".

SEC. 12. *And be it further enacted, That the President be, and he is hereby, authorized to receive into the service of the United States, for the purpose of constructing intrenchments, or performing camp service or any other labor, or **any military or naval service for which they may be found competent, persons of African descent**, and such persons shall be enrolled and organized under such regulations, not inconsistent with the Constitution and laws, as the President may prescribe.*
Jason had spent the last fourteen months working as a civilian. His official listing was that of a "Contraband Scout/Interpreter", employed by the Union Army.

While his ability to read and write, and his analytic skills, had enabled him to earn a decent salary— sixteen dollars per month —, in reality he was categorized exactly the same, as were the black ex-slave women, who did the camp's laundry.

Jason resented the fact that the army had classified him as being "Contraband". More precisely, Jason resented being held to, and being listed, as non-combatant, "Contraband."

Over the past year, through his Army salary, and coupled with the small but steady, few dollars he had won playing poker at the "*Contraband Saloon*", minus the ten dollars per month that he spent for female companionship, Jason had amassed over $250.

Immediately after having read "The Second Confiscation and Militia Act", Jason began to make plans.

Jason Ruth, "Contraband Scout/Interpreter", informed Major Anderson of his intent to resign his lucrative civilian position ($16.00/month), in order to fulfill his dream, his burning desire to achieve his goal, of fighting against the Confederacy, by enlisting as an infantryman, in the Union Army.

His plan was to pack his belongings and to travel north, to Boston Massachusetts.

Once he arrived in Boston, he planned to enlist as a recruit, in the newly formed, Massachusetts 54th Infantry.

CHAPTER 16

Boston Massachusetts - Boston Commons, March 11, 1863

Jason sat eating his lunch on one of the many benches, situated in the city's sprawling park.

In an effort to save money, Jason had hopped a Baltimore & Ohio freight train, hauling coal, whose destination fortunately for him, he had learned, was Boston Massachusetts.

Jason pulled the rolled-up sock from his pocket, and carefully counted the crumbled "*greenbacks.*" Despite his frugality, his funds had dwindled down to sixty-three dollars.

Despite his ardent fervor to join the Union Army, Jason had allowed himself to become sidetracked by the wondrous sights of this huge Northern Metropolis.

While eating a delicious sandwich that he had purchased from an immigrant, Italian pushcart vendor, he was leisurely browsing through a discarded, February 16, 1863 copy of the Boston Journal; Jason's eyes were drawn to and riveted upon, an announcement:

<u>TO COLORED MEN</u>

54th

REGIMENT!

MASSACHUSETTS VOLUNTEERS
—OF—

→AFRICAN DESCENT!

$100 BOUNTY

At the expiration of the term of service.

Pay, $13 a month!

State aid to families:

Recruiting office

→Corner, Cambridge & North Russell St., Boston

Lt. J.W. APPLETON, Recruiting Officer

Jason slowly, meticulously, reread the notice. He suppressed a satisfying burp, and declared;
"Okay, today's the day."

****

Jason, his battered suitcase in-hand, approached a well-dressed, elderly black man. The man leaning on a cane, made of rich mahogany wood, wore a well-tailored suit, and a black, stovepipe hat.

Jason removed his Union Army forage cap, and politely addressed the black man, using the words, idioms, and inflictions that he had always used, when speaking to elderly, "black-folks."

> *"Scuse me Uncle, can yos help me? Ise lookin' fo, dis here streets. I wonts ta go ta da cona ah Cambrige an Nof Rusell St."*

The elderly black man removed the pince-nez spectacles from the bridge of his nose and glared at Jason. And in a crisp, clipped, resonant, New England-Yankee voice, declared;

"Young man, I don't know you, and furthermore, I can unequivocally assure you, that by no stretch of the imagination, am I your uncle!"

Jason was stunned, speechless. He was flabbergasted. This was the first time that he had actually, with his own ears, heard a black man speak, elegant, flawlessly, grammatically, correct English.

As a boy growing up, living in slavery, he and his sister Mandy had been blatantly, guilty of breaking one of the South's fundamental laws, the law that prohibited, the teaching to… or for slaves to learn, to read and write.
On several occasions, Mandy had shared with him, the essays, and several of the magnificent, eloquent speeches which had been purported to have been penned and delivered, by the fabled ex-slave, abolitionist, Frederick Douglass.

It was said that Mr. Douglas, as had Jason, was an ex-slave, who had escaped slavery, for freedom in the North.

Although Jason did believe— especially when Mandy, during the course of the delivery of her didactic lessons to him, had actually utilized correct English grammar —, that there were literate black people, still, somehow in the recesses of his mind, Jason had always harbored lingering doubts, about the literacy, the "myth", of the actual existence, of prominent, well-spoken and educated, black men.

The eloquence and loquaciousness of the black man standing in front of him, had the effect of immediately, there and then, dispelling, those doubts.

Without uttering another word, the black "gentleman", reached for the newspaper that Jason held in is hand, and began to read the announcement:

<u>**TO COLORED MEN**</u>

54ᵗʰ

REGIMENT!

MASSACHUSETTS VOLUNTEERS

—OF—

→AFRICAN DESCENT!

$100 BOUNTY

At the expiration of the term of service.

Pay, $13 a month!

State aid to families:

Recruiting office

→Cor, Cambridge & North Russell Sts, Boston

Lieut. J.W. APPLETON, Recruiting Officer

After having swiftly read the recruitment notice, the elderly black man neatly folded the paper, and returned it to Jason.

Jason immediately noticed a discernible change in the black man's body language, in the black man's demeanor.

The elderly black man, in a gesture clearly meant to be reassuring, placed his hand on Jason's shoulder, "Please forgive me young man. I do you an injustice."

"Am I correct in assuming, after having read that recruitment notice, that you are interested in joining the fight to liberate the colored man? Is my assessment of your intent correct?"

Still speechless, Jason affirmed the black man's conclusion, by nodding his head.

The elderly black man took a deep breath. "I admire, respect and celebrate any man, especially any black man, who is eager and willing to risk his life to eradicate, the enslavement of our people."

"While I am obviously of African Descent, through no action or achievement under my control, as fate would have it, I was fortunate to have been born the son of black parents, who happened to live in the North, and who also happened to be Free."

"For my entire adult life, I have lived the relatively comfortable life of a "Colored Professional.""

"Living in my segregated community, being respected by the "Free blacks, and being tolerated by the white man."

"Meanwhile, all of my enslaved black brothers and sisters were living, if you can call it living, more apt I would think, enduring and surviving as best they could under the whip, in the slave states, of the so-called Confederate States of America."

"I too and my family, though certainly not nearly to the degree of my southern brethren, the black slaves laboring on the plantations in the South, have suffered under the systemic, deplorable, dehumanizing, segregationist policies and practices prevalent, in all of the geographic sections of our country."

Jason sat motionless, mute as if he were transfixed, as he listened to the simplistic, yet soaring oratory, of the distinguished black man.

The elderly black man, noticing the confused look on the young man's face, hesitated, then resumed; "Forgive my ramblings, as my wife keeps constantly reminding me, I talk, entirely, too much."

"You asked of me, a simple question. Again, I ask for you to forgive me."

When I spoke, my tone of voice, the verbiage, and my condescending attitude, was entirely unnecessary and uncalled for."

 "I sincerely apologize. If I am to be truly forthcoming young man, I must confess to my being both envious, and jealous of you."

Although his curiosity was beginning to be aroused, Jason remained silent.

The elderly black gentleman continued; "Quite frankly young man, I envy your youth, your physical strength, and your vitality."

"Most of all I envy the fact that at this moment in time, in history, once again through no action or achievement under yours or my control, you young man, and not I, have the opportunity, to actually take up arms, and to join in the fight for our people's freedom."

There ensued an awkward moment of silence. Neither man spoke.

The elderly man removed his *"spectacles",* from his eyes, and with a strikingly stark-white handkerchief that he had removed from his vest-pocket, rubbed the lenses.

He sighed, reset the glasses onto the bridge of his nose, looked directly at Jason and spoke; "I believe you were asking me, for directions?"

Jason took a deep breath; "Forgive me sir. Your apology is quite unnecessary. It is I, who owe you an apology."

"Instead of my approaching you as a gentleman of breeding and intellect that you obviously are, I, because you are a black man, spoke to you in the voice and the vernacular, that I have always used when speaking to fellow-blacks."

Now it was the elderly gentleman's turn to stand dumbstruck, speechless, his mouth open, gaping in astonishment and wonder. His eyes narrowed as he quickly regained his composure; "Young man, please come, sit with me for a moment."

Jason followed the impressive, articulate, black man to a nearby park bench.

"First, let me apologize for my initially, rude, response to your query".

"Quoting the words of my dear wife, Paula; I'm beginning to act like a doddering, crotchety, old man".

"I would like to formally introduce myself. My name is Charles William Blake. If you prefer, you, as did my mother, as do my close friends and family, call me *"Charlie-Willie"*.

"I am a teacher. For the past twenty-two years, I have dedicated my life to the provision of quality education, for the black children of Boston."

****

Jason sat in silence, respectfully waiting for Mr. Blake, *"Charlie-Willie",* to continue.

"For more than two decades, I have taught English Grammar and English Literature, to the colored children of Boston, at the Abiel Smith School for Colored Children."

"Not until this very moment, other than by a few valedictorians, graduates of our school, have I had the pleasure of hearing a young black man, extemporaneously, speak as clearly and succinctly, as do you."

"May I ask your name? I would very much like to know to whom I am speaking."

Although he was curious, and intrigued by Mr. Charles William Blake,
Jason had decided, that rather than expending valuable daylight talking to this man, albeit this fascinating erudite, black man, it was far more important to him, that he locate the recruitment site, and that he enlist in the Union Army.

Carefully choosing his words, he responded; "My name is Jason Ruth. I was born and grew up as a slave, on a large Virginia cotton plantation.

I escaped from slavery. I've traveled north to Boston, in order to join the newly commissioned, Massachusetts 54th Infantry Regiment."

Charles was immediately conscious, and aware of the lack of detail, and the brevity of the young man's response.

When it had become obvious to him that there was far more to this young black stranger, this young black man that he had pre-judged— there it was again (prejudice), the word that had plagued Charles Blake for his entire life.

The professor had always considered the compound word "pre-judgment", as being the root, the very essence, synonymous with the very definition, of prejudice.

Prejudice! The one word, that if you eliminated economic factors, *the word* that Professor Charles *"Willie"* Blake, believed was the bedrock, the foundation that supported and encouraged the abysmal treatment of blacks in America.

When the slightly disheveled, young black man had approached him, even before the young man spoke, and then began speaking in the street vernacular of so many of the illiterate, uneducated, blacks who roamed the streets looking for work, Charles had instinctively, almost automatically pre-judged, and aloofly regarded the young black man, with contempt and distain.

Now Professor *"Charlie-Willie Blake"*, quite frankly, felt ashamed. He realized that he, a man who abhorred and railed against prejudice, that he had pre-judged this young man.

He had unwittingly succumbed to the dominant white society's *"knee-jerk"*, dissent into racial prejudice.

Charles was shaken. *"Prejudice"*, that was the pernicious, ubiquitous practice that he so abhorred. That ugly word *"Prejudice"*, pre-judgement, which had plagued him his entire life.

It was ironic that he, Professor Charles William Blake, had rushed to judgment, and thus mistakenly categorized, this young man, as being idle, illiterate, ignorant, black *"riff-raff."*

Charles's burning intellectual curiosity, had been acutely aroused. What exactly had this well-spoken young man said, what was his name… oh yes Jason, Jason Ruth.

Noting the youth's impatience, the way that he was impatiently tracking the passage of time, by constantly looking at the position of the sun in the sky, it was obvious to the professor that Jason was anxious to be on his way.

Charles decided against pursuing a discourse of questioning, which very well might have quenched his burning intellectual curiosity.

"Young man, I can deduce from your squirming and fidgeting that you're anxious to complete your mission… to be on your way."

As Jason was about to protest, the distinguished professor, raised his hand; "No need to apologize, I too, if I were a young man, would be, as they say, *"chomping-at-the-bit"*, eager to fight to free our people."

"After having read the recruitment notice, before I had had the opportunity, and might I add, the distinct privilege, of speaking with you, I had intended to merely as a matter of convenience to myself, direct you to the address listed in that notice."

"That I will not do."

Now Jason was both annoyed and surprised. He was about to verbally "lash-out" and rebuke this pompous black man; this man who due to the man's obvious had initially been impressed him.

Jason was now beginning associate with this man, the derogatory term, the insulting term, that he had heard flippantly, banded around the slave community, *"House-nigger."*

"*House-nigger*", was the label frequently applied to one of those slaves, almost universally a "*high-yella*", complexioned haughty-taughty, black slave of privilege.

"*House-niggers*", slaves who worked in the "*Massa's*" Big House; "house-niggers" were those slaves that ate the "white-folk" food; slaves who were exempt from toiling in the fields from sunup to sundown; slaves who did not have to live in constant fear, the anticipatory fear of at any moment, feeling the excruciating, painful-bite of the overseer's whip.

"*House-niggers*", slaves that ascribed to, and gave credence and adherence to, the divisive code, the credo, that served to divide and stratify, the slave community;

> *"If yo's white, yu's allrite"*
> *"If yo's brown, yu's can stik around"*
> *"If yo's black, yu's gotta git back"*

Before Jason could react to the professor's declaration, his refusal to extend to him, the simple courtesy of answering, of giving direction, Charles elaborated.

"The address listed in the newspaper, is for but one of the locations designated as a site, for the recruitment of "Colored" men to enlist in the 54th Massachusetts Infantry.

"You, my young friend, are indeed an extremely lucky, a fortunate young man. Of all of the strangers that you could have asked for direction, you asked me. It's serendipity." Jason, are you acquainted with the word serendipity?"

Jason shook his head from side to side, and uttered one word, "No."

Charles nodded. "Many people who are familiar with the English noun, the word, serendipity, define it and interpret it, employing its most simplistic definition, that is; "to by luck, find something of value."

"I personally, reserve my use of the word "*Serendipitous*", the adjective form of the noun serendipity, to denote, not only the luck of discovery, but to ascribe to the one experiencing the "*luck*" of discovery, his or her having the ability, the talent, to use that discovery, to accomplish good."

By now, Jason was not only annoyed and confused; he was becoming increasingly, impatient.

Seeing that he was about to lose his audience, the black educator, continued.

"Forgive me young man…Jason. As I explained to you earlier, I once again, as my astute wife Paula, constantly admonishes and reminds me, rightfully so, I must confess, I have a tendency to be a bit loquacious."

"*I* talk entirely, too much."

"It just so happens that this week, this day, you are in luck. Serendipity has smiled upon you."

"Today, three of the country's most respected, eloquent, erudite and influential, abolitionists, Wendell Phillips, Sojourner Truth, and Frederick Douglass, will be assisting, in the Union Army's efforts to recruit Colored men, for the 54th Massachusetts Infantry, at the "African Meeting House", our "Joy Street Church.""

Despite the fact that he was pressed for time, Jason reluctantly, somewhat sheepishly, confessed to the professor, that of the three names that he obviously assumed that Jason was familiar with, Frederick Douglass was the only name that he recognized.

Charles being now, fully conscience of the young man's impatience, his eagerness to be on his way, was delighted to see in this young stranger, a definite, intellectual curiosity.

Instead of answering, what he imagined would logically be Jason's next unspoken question
— *"Who are Wendell Phillips, and Sojourner Truth"*,
the professor decided not to further delay the young man.

Instead, he would allow Jason to discover for himself, the identity and the accomplishments of Wendell Phillips, and Sojourner Truth.

****

Following the directions given him by Professor Blake, Jason was able to easily find Boston's Joy Street Church, which was serving as a temporary recruiting center, for the Massachusetts 54th Infantry Regiment.

A rather short, corpulent, very dark-skinned black man, wearing a dark blue suit, greeted Jason at the door of the church. Suspended from the black man's neck was small silver cross, dangling from a thin silver chain.

"Sir, can I be of assistance?"

****

Jason remembered fleetingly thinking, contrasting, the quiet, reserved, speaking voice, the dignity, of this particular black clergyman, with the "fire and brimstone" the soaring rhetoric, of the southern cotton plantation's black *"Slave-Preachers."*

The slave preacher was usually an intelligent verbose man, with an innate or acquired, oratory gift, that rivaled that of the white politicians, and the professional stage actors.

The slave preacher was a well-respected, member of the slave community. His slave -societal status was on par with that of the slave-artisans, those slaves who possessed unique skills; the blacksmith, the conjure-medicine woman.

The slave preacher officiated at baptisms, at weddings *(Jump-da-broom),* and at funerals. He ministered to the sick and the infirmed. He shepherded the souls of the oppressed slaves.

The Slave-Owners allowed, encouraged, and sponsored; the Sunday sermons delivered to the slaves by the *"Slave-Preachers."*

Supposedly, the slave preacher's function was to promote Christianity among the *"African heathens"*, the black slaves.

In reality, at least from the perspective of the white slave-owners, the primary function of the slave-preacher was that of pacification of the black masses.

The slave preacher was of immense value to the slave owners. His sermons and preachings, tended to validate and justify, the enslavement of the black peoples.

The slave preacher's constant admonitions to the slaves to have patience, to be obedient, to be passive, his predilection for, and emphasis of quoting selected biblical passages such as *"the meek shall inherit the earth"*, were messages that in effect, justified slavery, and that encouraged the slaves to accept their earthly-plight.

After all, typically at the end of his sermon, the preacher would proclaim words to the effect that; "Be patient, suffer in silence, for all would be well in the afterlife."

> *"On dat Great Getting'up Moanin";*

> *"In de uppa room wid my Lawd."*

The Slave-Owners allowed, encouraged, and sponsored, the Sunday sermons delivered to the slaves, by the *"Slave-Preachers."*

In reality, at least from the perspective of the white Slave-Masters, the primary function of the slave-preacher was that of pacification.

To justify to the slave, that he accepts his preordained station in life, that of enslavement for him and for his progeny, into perpetuity.

The white clergy, in league with the white owners of the slaves, feed to the slave preachers, *"cherry-picked"*, biblical passages, e.g., *Genesis 1:27 "God created man in his own image";* *Genesis 9:25 "Cursed be Canaan. Let him become the lowest slave to his brothers; Romans 13:1 "Let everyone be subject to the governing authorities...have been established by God".*

The white slave owners provided the slave preachers, propaganda materials.
Material such as hand-held fans with the purported image of a "white, blond haired, blue eyed Jesus", were prevalent among the slaves.

The picture of the "white, blond haired, blue eyed Jesus", that the slaves religiously hung on the walls of their dirt-floor cabins, was the last face that the pious slaves saw at night, and the first face that they saw in the morning.

The image that bore the profile of a white man, with long straight-flowing brownish-blond hair, clear blue eyes, the picture that the slave preachers assured their black congregations, was the face of their savior, the face of Jesus, the Son of God.

This was the image—the image of the messiah, the face of a white man, with long straight-flowing brownish-blond hair, and clear blue eyes, gazing reverently at the heavens.

This image overtly and subliminally, reinforced in the slave's mind, when the slave, each morning, looked into his mirror, the image reinforced the message, that the Southern slave-owners, with the often-unwitting help, of the "*Slave Preacher*" incessantly drilled into the slave's head.

Punctuating and emphasizing, in the mind of the slave, the perceived fact, that they were different, that they, black the man, was not created in the image of God. The Slave Preacher, some knowingly, most inadvertently, helped propagate the message, that the black man was different, that the black men were indeed, inferior.

The definitive "*cherry picked*" biblical passage that the so-called pious Evangelical-Christian Southerner referenced to justify slavery was
Genesis 9:25; "*Cursed be Canaan. Let him become the lowest slave to his brothers.*"

The Slave-Owners were the southern white-ruling class, the wealthy titans of the southern agricultural industry. By and large, the Slave-Owners were the men who owned, the tremendously profitable, large cotton, tobacco, and sugar plantations.

The legally sanctioned and codified practice of "Human Bondage" slavery provided the white plantation owners, with an enormous, invaluable pool of free labor.

Although the insatiable demand for cotton by the North, and from foreign countries, ensured the plantation owners, substantial profits, by eliminating the cost of labor, through the utilization of slave labor, the plantation owners enormous profits, ballooned into tremendously huge profits.

In addition to the vast monetary savings realized by the plantation owners, i.e., eliminating the cost of the labor, for the planting, for the cultivating, and for the harvesting of their cash crops, the plantation owner's legal ownership of their human property, an estimated four million black slaves, men, women, and children, property whose average value was between $500.00 to $800.00, per slave, represented to the plantation owners, an additional 2 to 3.2 billion dollars in collective wealth.

The plantation owners skillfully, masterfully used the slave-preachers as propaganda agents. The black slave-preachers, unwittingly and sometimes from a few unscrupulous scoundrels, willfully served as a buffer, between the white-slave owners, and their black-slaves.

The failed attempt, by the abolitionist John Brown, in 1859, to incite a slave uprising in Virginia, was fresh and constantly on the minds of the slave-owners.

John Brown's failed mission was to "*liberate*" guns from the federal armory at Harpers Ferry, Virginia, and to arm the slaves. His goal was to lead an army of armed slaves in an insurrection, against their white masters.

The thought of armed black men, giving vent to centuries of suppressed hatred and rage, against their white-oppressors, was an ever present, constant, fear that haunted the slave-holding South.

The black slave-preacher was an effective means, an agent to quell unrest among the slaves. His sermons were instrumental in mollifying the slaves. Persuading the slaves, to meekly accept the "*message*", the white man's interpretation of "*da words in da bibil...*"

The slave-preacher's constant admonitions to the slaves was; *"to have patience, to be obedient, to remain docile and passive"*.

The black slave-preacher's quoted, and emphasized selected biblical passages, such as *"the meek shall inherit the earth; he who lives by the sword, shall die by the sword"*, *"obey the governing authorities"*, were messages that in affect, justified slavery, and that encouraged the slaves to accept, without resistance, their plight, their life of perpetual bondage, on Earth.

Typically, at the end of his sermon, the slave-preacher would close with words such as;

"Yall bees patient hear me. Yu's gotta sufffa in silence. One day, one day we alls be goin ta da promiseland."

Which would be followed with the soulful singing, of poignant hymns:

"Swing lo sweet chriot...comin fo ta carry me home"
"Swingin lo sweet chriot...comin fo ta carry me home"

"I looks ova Jorden...an what did I see...comin fo ta carry me home...ah band of angels comin fo me...comin fo ta carry me home"

"We gonna ride da chariot in da monin lawd"

"We gett'n ready fo da judgemen day...My lawd, My lawd"

Jason remembered his mother Ruth's, and for that matter the entire slave-community's, absolute belief in the slave-preacher's melodious, sonorous, lyrical, mollifying words.

The slave-preachers promised that their reward, for passively enduring this life of back-breaking, tedious labor; the degradation and humiliation, that their *"Hell on Earth"*, their life of "Human Bondage", would be rewarded with eventual prosperity, salvation, and eternal-life in the after-life.

****

The pastor of the Joy Street Church led Jason to a staircase that descended down one flight, into the church's basement.

The basement was a surprisingly large, well-lit, cool and airy room. Three of the four walls, had two 18" x 36" screened windows, that were each held open with a stick, that created an eyelevel view, of the ground above.

Periodically, a pleasant, cooling breeze lazily moved the white lace curtains, which covered the windows in the northeast corner of the room.

Three white union soldiers, all three sergeants, were seated behind a four-foot long wooden table. The recruiting sergeant, who was seated at the center of the table, wore on each of the sleeves of his uniform, the six interlocking chevrons of a Sergeant Major.

The two soldiers who sat flanking the sergeant major, each wore on their blue-uniform sleeves, three inverted chevrons that identified them as sergeants.

In front of each of the white non-commissioned officers, was a line of black men, attempting to enlist in the Massachusetts 54th Infantry Regiment.

To Jason the middle line of potential enlistees, the line that he had chosen, was moving at a snail's pace. Jason glanced at the two young men in the outer lines, who had been even with him, when he had chosen the center line.

Both of those black men, fellow recruits, were appreciably closer to the white soldiers seated at the long table

For some reason, the movement of the line, reminded Jason of the lines he had stood in as a slave, when picking cotton on the Virginia Plantation.

During harvest-time, the status-line between household slaves and field hands would frequently become blurred.

During the harvest, slaves who ordinarily did not work in the fields, the house-slaves and the craftsmen, found themselves working, side by side, picking cotton, with their perceived, socially inferior, black-brethren, the field hands.

Jason recalled the sense of urgency that gripped the plantation during cotton-harvest time.

For the slave community, harvest-time was an event that obliterated the line between the *"high-yella"* house-slaves and the mostly,*" black as midnight"* field hands.

The time that nature allotted, between the ripening, and the picking of the cotton-boll, was exceedingly short.

At the end of the day, after literally *"slaving"*, twelve, hours in the field, Rosewood's eighty-three slaves, men women and children, after separating by hand, thousands of bolls of cotton, from tens of thousands cotton plants, would line up, in multiple lines, to have each of their cotton leaden sacks, weighed by the overseer.

Jason chuckled to himself, as he stood in the slowly moving line of young black men, here at the "Joy Street Church", eager to join the Union Army.

He thought of an apropos descriptive phrase that he had frequently encountered, when decoding Union Navy communiqués, when he worked for the army as a "Contraband Scout/Interpreter", *"All Hands-On-Deck!"*

After standing in line for twenty minutes, finally his progress—when he had joined the center line, he had been behind thirteen black men—, had advanced to the point where he found himself behind, but two men.

Jason's eyes were drawn to a small group of people, engaged in conversation at the foot of the stairs.

The black clergyman, was shaking the hand of a tall, light-skinned *"Colored man."* The man's head was covered with a salt and pepper blend of semi-woolly, semi-straight, hair.

The distinguished looking black gentleman had a booming, commanding, baritone voice.

Jason instantly recognized the man. He knew, from photographs that had been shown to him by Captain Clarke, the Union Army Officer, who had hired him as a civilian "Contraband Scout/Interpreter", the identity of the imposing distinguished looking, black man.

Jason knew, from a daguerreotype image that Captain Clarke had shown him, that the man standing no more than a dozen feet from him, was the celebrated abolitionist, and champion of women's rights, a man that he could personally relate to, the runaway, ex-slave, Frederick Douglass.

Just as he was about to sacrifice, abandon his place in the line, and approach Mr. Douglass, he was startled by a loud irritating voice that broke into his reverie; "Well boy-yo, are you deaf and dumb? Are you here to join up, or are you gonna just stand there gaping with your mouth open, looking like a fish outta water?"

Jason's eyes were immediately drawn to the pale blue eyes of the grizzled, white soldier, seated at the center of the long table.

The soldier appeared to be in his late thirties, or early forties. He had a ruddy, reddish complexion, mutton-chop, symmetrical sideburns that extended to his jaw-line and a bulbous nose, lined with a web of blue varicose veins.

The obviously impatient soldier spoke with that peculiar "Yankee" accent that had been described to Jason as being an "Irish-brogue."

A speech pattern that Jason had heard spoken by a few of the New Hampshire's 5[ths], enlisted men, and by most of Boston's working-class men.

The lilting tone was a strikingly distinct dialect that Jason surmised, was associated with that of, first-generation Irish immigrants.

From his time spent with the Union Army, as a "Contraband Scout/-Interpreter", Jason was aware of the fact that the man addressing him, the grizzled, white soldier, was a Sergeant Major. The highest enlisted rank in the Union Army.

The sergeant major pushed a single sheet of paper, an enlistment contract forward. He dipped a quill into an inkwell, and on a scrap piece of paper, scribbled an "X."

One of the Union Army's, senior non-commissioned officers, extended the quill to Jason, pointed his index finger to the bottom of the enlistment contract, and barked; "Okay boy-yo, make your mark here."

Jason took the proffered writing implement, from the sergeant's hand and with a confidant steady hand, signed his name; *Jason Ruth.*

The soldier seated beside the sergeant major chuckled, "well whatta you know sergeant major, appears to me that what you got there, is one of them educated nigras."

The sergeant major grunted. "Take a seat over there boy-yo." He pointed to a long bench that was occupied by at least, fifteen young black men.

As he walked toward the black men that he assumed where his fellow recruits, Jason's eyes returned the spot where he had last seen the Joy Street Church pastor, and Mr. Frederick Douglass.

The space at the foot of the stairs, that had just moments ago, been occupied by the pastor and the celebrated, world renowned, black-abolitionist, was now empty.

****

CHAPTER 17

CAMP MEIGS, Readville, Massachusetts (May 4th, 1863)

Because of the enthusiastic, rapid, response, to the Union's strident clarion; "Call To Arms", by black-men from all over New England, from New York, from Pennsylvania, even free blacks from such distant locales as Canada, and the Caribbean Islands, answered the call.

The fact that the number of potential recruits, far exceeded the original quota, which was to enlist a thousand black-men into the 54th, the
Massachusetts Surgeon-General, administered to the black recruits, a meticulously rigid, thorough, medical examination.

It was said to be the opinion of the Surgeon General, that the black men who passed the 54ths strenuous medical examination, were the healthiest, and most robust group of men to have ever, been mustered into the service of the United States.

Jason lay resting on the dirt floor, in his extremely limited, small corner of the canvas tent, which he shared with three of his fellow recruits. The four tent mates were all privates, in the Massachusetts 54th Infantry Regiment.

Although he, for the past year, had lived and worked in a Union Army camp, as a civilian *"Contraband Scout/Interpreter"*, Jason was not at all prepared for the rigid, Spartan-like, training regime, of this particular Union Army "basic training-camp."

During his time spent as a civilian "Contraband Scout/Interpreter", for the New Hampshire 5th Infantry Volunteers, Jason had been privy to practically all levels of Union Army communications, including those correspondence pertaining to the proposed establishment of, "Regiments of African- American Soldiers."

On the topic of blacks serving in the army, the prevailing, recurring theme of the *"military-chatter"* had been, that if and when *"colored"* soldiers were allowed to serve, their service would be limited to a "Non-Combat" role.

The *"colored"* soldier's service would be restricted to that of *"hard-labor"*, and to performing menial tasks.

In essence it was perceived by the majority of the Union Army Officer Corps, that the *"black soldier's service* in the United States Military, would be essentially identical to how he always served the white-man, either as an unpaid laborer (slave) in the South, or as a minimum wage laborer, a *"freeman-of-color"*, in the North.

Fortunately for Jason, and his fellow black-recruits, black men who had enlisted specifically, and explicitly to fight, to remove the yoke of slavery from the necks of the black populace, fortunately for them, there were a few prominent, powerful white politicians, and abolitionists.

Men like Massachusetts' Governor, John A. Andrews, who established the Massachusetts 54th, had envisioned for the *colored soldier*, the opportunity for the black man to fight for his freedom and the abolition of slavery.

These powerful white men, were determined to do everything within their power, to ensure that the Massachusetts 54th, if given the chance, would be combat-ready, well trained, and prepared to fight.

Governor Andrews had combed the state, twisted some arms, and was able to provide for the 54th, his state's fledgling black regiment, some of the state's finest, battle-tested white officers.

The governor had persuaded one of Massachusetts "native sons", Captain Robert Gould Shaw, a veteran of the recent Union victory at Sharpsburg Maryland, the battle of Antietam, to serve as the Massachusetts 54th, Commanding Officer.

Because he was now the Commanding Officer of an infantry regiment, Captain Shaw was promoted to the rank of Colonel.

Colonel Shaw and his handpicked cadre of white commissioned officers, with the assistance of several white non-commissioned officers, were committed and dedicated, to the training of the black soldiers of the 54[th.]

Colonel Shaw was convinced that, if given the opportunity, under his guidance and leadership, the men of the Massachusetts 54th, would prove themselves in combat.

****

Headquarters of the 32nd Regiment Massachusetts Volunteer Infantry (April 1863)

The Presidential Executive Order (Lincoln's Emancipation Proclamation), which in addition to "freeing the slaves", had also nullified the 1792 law that prohibited African Americans, from serving in the Union Army.

Following President Lincoln's issuance of the Emancipation Proclamation, which provided for the president, the political capital for the formation of a Combat Regiment of *"Colored"* soldiers, an unanticipated problem for the Union Army immediately surfaced.

It had been stipulated by the Secretary of War, Edwin M. Stanton, that Black regiments were to be comprised solely of black enlisted men, led by white officers.

Subsequently the creation of the "*All Black*" Massachusetts 54th Volunteer Infantry, was by definition, and as a result of the Army's past practices, lacking an essential component, a vital component, necessary for the success of any army.

As a result of its'—by law, exclusion of blacks in the military—, in the United States Army, there were no battle-hardened, seasoned *black non-commissioned officers.*

Black combat veterans, men who would have had led, and held troops together, in combat.

There were no black sergeants and corporals (*non-commissioned officers*), who had seen, experienced and survived, the horrors of war. No black corporals, no black sergeants that combat veteran soldiers would say, were men who "*had seen, the Elephant.*"

In its infancy, in the critical formative months of its existence, the fledgling, "*All Black*" Massachusetts 54th Volunteer Infantry, was in desperate need of combat-seasoned, non-commissioned officers.

Non-coms, needed to train the black soldiers.

****

Sergeant Major Donovan, and his two fellow white sergeants were, all three, veteran "non-commissioned officers", whose permanent assignment was the 32nd Regiment Massachusetts Volunteer Infantry Battallion.

The three combat-tested white, non-commissioned officers, had been stunned, when they had been issued temporary duty "*TAD*" orders, which essentially placed the three battle-hardened non-coms, "*on loan*" to the
newly created, all black infantry regiment, the Massachusetts 54th.

As he inventoried and packed his gear, Sergeant Major Sean Patrick Donovan, vividly recalled his and his fellow sergeants reaction, when Colonel Prescott, the Commanding Officer of the 32nd Regiment, Massachusetts Volunteer Infantry Battalion, summoned the three non-coms to his office, and apologetically, handed them their TAD orders:

From: Headquarters United States Army of the Potomac

Special Temporary Assignment of Duty (TAD) April 5, 1863

To: Colonel Robert T. Prescott, Commanding Officer of the 32nd Regiment, Massachusetts Volunteer Infantry Battalion

Subj: Temporary detachment; your command, the below listed NCOs.

---

1)   Sergeant Major, Patrick Sean Donovan;

2)   Sergeant Heinrich George Schmidt;

3)   Sergeant William James Fitzgerald

The above-named SGTS. are to be relieved of duty (your command) effective 0001 hours, May 2nd, 1863, and are ordered to report to Fort Meig, Massachusetts, not later than 0900 hours May11th, 1863, to enter upon a fixed period of TAD in connection with the training of "Colored" infantry of the Mass 54th.

This assignment is in response to an identified critical lack of NCOs, with combat service, needed to train recruits of the Mass 54th.

The exigencies of the Army making this necessary, the above-named NCOs are not authorized delay en route leave.

"Upon the completion of the "Basic Training" of the colored soldiers, and prior to the deployment of the Massachusetts 54th Volunteer Infantry;"

1) Sergeant Major, Patrick Sean Donovan; 2) Sergeant Heinrich George Schmidt; and 3) Sergeant William James Fitzgerald are authorized one hundred twenty hours (five days), furlough.

On the sixth day following the deployment of the 54th, the three white non-commissioned officers; 1) Sergeant Major, Patrick Sean Donovan; 2) Sergeant Heinrich George Schmidt; and 3) Sergeant William James Fitzgerald, prior to 2400 hours of the sixth day, the above referenced NCOs, are hereby ordered to report back for duty, with to the 32nd Regiment Massachusetts Volunteer Infantry Battalion."

Michael E. Flood
Brigadier General, US Army
Adjutant General

By Direction;

After having read, then reread the orders, the Sergeant Major concluded that apparently, some rear echelon desk-jockey, some paper-pusher in the War Department, for reasons known only to them and to God, had selected these three white sergeants, all combat veterans, for "Temporary Duty", "TAD" assignments to train, and to prepare, the black recruits of the Massachusetts 54th, for combat.

After more than twenty-five years of service in the army, the Sergeant Major had received more than his fair share of stupid "rotten" orders.

These orders—to try to convert a bunch of niggers, jungle-bunnies, into combat soldiers—were among the worst, the stupidest damn-orders, that he had ever received.

He and the other two 32nd non-com's, sole consolation was that their orders had emphatically stipulated that, under **NO** circumstance, were they, nor were the 54th's white-officers or the black enlisted men of the 54th, to consider the three sergeants (NCOs), as being members of the Massachusetts 54th Volunteer Infantry.

As he secured the third duffel bag that held his belongings, Sergeant Major Sean Patrick Donavon, sighed and lamented; "*Alas…orders is orders.*"

****

CHAPTER 18

CAMP MEIGS, Readville, Massachusetts (May 7th, 1863)

When the three white non-commissioned officers (NCOs) arrived to fulfill their *"TAD"* assignment at Camp Meig, they were far from impressed by what they saw.

After reporting in, they were led to the "White Non-Commissioned Officers" barracks, by three of the poorest excuses for soldiers, that the three battle-hardened combat veterans collectively, had ever seen.

The three blacks, the so-called *black-soldiers*, were dressed in various assortments, and combinations, of civilian attire.

Sgt. Schmidt, in a thick pronounced German accent, asked the black man, actually the black boy, who was carrying his baggage, a boy who appeared to be no more then in his teen's; "Why are you soldiers, not in uniform?"

The black boy-soldier's answer; *"Suh dey ain't dun givin' us dem pretty blew suits yet"*, served to reinforce the three non-coms, pre-conceived assessment of the blacks' fitness, to serve in the army.

Sgt Fitzgerald snorted and in a lilting voice that bespoke of his Irish heritage, asked; "And what might your name be, boy-you? And where do you hail from?"

"Ise be James Smith, but ever body, days calls me "Jimbo." Ise a runna. I dun run away from bein' a slave in Ten-na-see."

Sgt Schmidt turned his attention to the black man carrying the belongings of the senior non-commissioned Officer, the Sergeant Major, and asked; "And you "Pops", what's your name…and where do you hail from?"

This black man, in stark-contrast to *"Jimbo's"* age, appeared to be almost middle-aged.

"Sir, my name is John Maxwell. I am a Freeman of color. I was born and raised in Boston Massachusetts."

Jason Ruth, the third black soldier in civilian clothing carrying the white non-coms' belongings, remained silent.

To Jason's relief, just before the sergeants probing questions would have inevitably turned to him, the group reached the wooden building that had been designated as the billet, for "White Non-Commissioned Officers."

Sgt Schmidt held the door ajar, as the three baggage-laden, black soldiers, whose *"Uniform of The Day"*, was apparently civilian attire, carried the sergeants' personal luggage, into their quarters.

The senior non-com, Sergeant Major Donovan, with a wave of his hand, and a curt dismissive gesture, dismissed the three black soldiers.

****

The interior of the small NCO cottage was laid-out roughly, in the shape of an "L". Three-fourths of the area of the room, the long arm of the "L", was designated for the living spaces, of the two junior non-coms, Sergeants Schmidt and Fitzgerald.

The short arm of the "L" was walled off. Admittance into this sequestered section of the room was through a separate, locked, door.

The relatively large room within a room, behind the door, was the living space for the senior white, non-commissioned officer, Sergeant Major, Patrick Sean Donovan.

The rank of Sergeant Major entitled him to, and he had earned, the right to the privacy, of his sequestered quarters.

Sergeant Major Donovan especially relished and appreciated the quiet, atmosphere, and the seclusion that his room afforded him, and the option, to either eat his meals alone, or if he so choose, to socialize, and to strategize, with his two, fellow white non-coms.

While he at first had chosen, to eat his meals alone in his room, by the second week of training, the Sergeant Major had come to appreciate the advantages, and the practicality, of his eating with his subordinate NCOs.

Sergeant Major Donovan had quickly come to realize, that the informal, relaxed convivial, environment, created by his eating with his subordinate non-coms, facilitated his ability to obtain from them, their candid, unfiltered, accurate, reports and assessments, of the training of the black recruits

The Sergeant Major routinely used the few hours, after evening-chow, and before Taps, as a forum for the white non-coms, to assess and to report on the progress of the training, of this battalion of, what the white non-coms referred to as, their black *"Jungle Bunnies."*

During meals, or as casual conversation, during or after-dinner rounds of poker, the three sergeants, would share anecdotes—some hilarious, some pathetic, most illuminating—, of the black-recruits progress, or more to the point, especially during that first week, the black-recruits, lack thereof.

On one such occasion, Sgt Schmidt, the stub of a cigar clenched between his teeth, was doubled over with laughter.

When between guffaws of laughter, he was able to control himself, he said; "I remember the first time that I tried to "drill", those *black-birds*."

"After I finely got them "Coons" to line-up in a straight line, I says to 'um…clear as a bell mind you… I says to 'um, "Compnee…Right…Face.""

"Two of them boys, one in the center, the other on the end, turns left; them two "monkeys" practically kisses the "burr-headed Nigger" next to um."

Sgt Fitzgerald had roared with laughter. "What did you do Willy? Sgt Schmidt stood. "I pulled both of those idiots out of the line, stands 'um side by side, and I says to 'um…what the fuck do you think you're doing?"

"I says to um…I don't know what you pansies are use to doing back there on them plantations, but in this man's army, men don't kiss each other."

"Men don't kiss men!"

"Don't you idiots know your **_RIGHT_** from your **_LEFT!_**" "Them two turds just stood there, wide-eyed, staring into space."

"I walked up to the boy nearest me. I stuck my face about two inches from his and shouted; "When I ask you a question boy…I want an answer. Do you hear me boy?!"

"Yes Suh Ise hears yu Suh. Da answer Suh be dat my Mama, she dun learn'd me rite from wrong. But Suh, ain't nobody eva dun learn'd me, my Rite from my Leff, Suh"

Sgt. Fitzgerald had been overcome with laughter. He began to cough, as he choked on the hot coffee that he had been drinking. Hot coffee had dribbled down his chin.

The flustered white non-com, exclaimed; "Shit." With the edge of his shirtsleeve, Sgt Fitzgerald hastily wiped the hot liquid from his chin.

After regaining his composure, Sgt. Fitzgerald decided to share with the group, what he considered, one of his more enlightened experiences, with the black recruits."

"Do you lads remember that dumb-coon, that kid, carried our gear to this place?"

When no one answered, the sergeant continued; "I think he said that his name was Jimbo. Well that's neither here nor there…where was I?"

"Oh ya…I was showing the "Jungle Bunnies", how to breakdown, then to reassemble, their rifles."

"Well this one dumb burr-head…Jimbo, kept asking questions. Mind you, I have to admit, most of his questions were pretty good."

"What bothered me was that that boy, no matter how many times I told him not to call his weapon a gun, that coon kept it up, he keeps on calling his rifle, his gun."

"I got so pissed off, that I made the boy stand at attention, holding his rifle at port-arms, in front of the platoon."

"I went over and stood, maybe a foot away from that dumb-ass black recruit, snatched the rifle from his hands, and shoved the weapon, five or six inches from his stupid face;

"You stupid burr-head coon. I pushed the rifle back into the jungle bunny's hands. Repeat afta me. "This is my **RIFLE**."

That scared shit-less coon stuttered;"

"Diss, be's my rifle";

"Then I grabbed the black boy's crotch and squeezed; not too hard mind you, just hard enough to get his absolute attention. "And this…boyo?"

Sgt. Fitzgerald could no longer contain himself, he chuckled…I added with just a smidgen of pressure with my hand…and what's this boy?"

"What's this?"

"I swear…that black boy was turning white. He muttered"

"Dass my dick sergeant"

"Wrong boy…let's call this, this here… I increased the pressure on his crotch…this here is your **GUN**. Got It?"

"Yes sergent dat bee's my gun."

"I grabbed hold of the boy's rifle with my right hand, and with my face six inches from his, I shouted;

"This is your **RIFLE**, then I grabbed, with my left hand, and squeezed his crotch…And this boyo… this is your **GUN**."

"I let go of his sack and again grabbed hold of the rifle, pushed it into his chest and shouted, **_THIS_** is for **_KILLING_**, then I let go the rifle, and again grabbed his crotch, squeezed a little and shouted, and **_THIS_**, boy-yo, this is for **_FUN_**!

Sgt. Schmidt, along with Sgt. Major Donavan, all three noncoms being very familiar with that little *"teaching limerick"*, laughed heartily along with Sgt. Fitzgerald.

Sergeant Major Donovan looked at his pocket watch. He stood, and tossed his cards face down on the table.

"Gentlemen, it looks like we've still got a hell of a lot of work to do."

"Reveille's at 0500. I want the company ready to move out at 0545.

The Sergeant Major then turned and walked over to, and opened the door to his small room. With his back to his fellow white-NCOs, he turned his head and emphatically, resolutely said, "Good night."

****

Chapter 19

CAMP MEIGS, Readville, Massachusetts (May 11ᵗʰ, 1863)

Jason's day had begun at 05:00, when he and his tent-mates were rudely awakened, by the shrill, blaring sound of reveille, hideously blown by the company bugler.

Before they could react to the strident, clarion call of the bugle, before the recruits could remove the cobwebs and wipe the sleep from their eyes, Sgt, Henry Smith formerly (*Heinrich Schmidt*), burst into the tent.

"All right you liver-lipped, burr headed maggots…get them black rusty hands off your cocks, and grab your socks. I want all of you maggots
in full field-packs, with your rifles, on the drill-field in fifteen minutes."

"Move it…move it maggots, move it!!"
****

Freddie Gilliam, a twenty-two-year-old, agile light brown-skinned young man, who had grown up on the teeming streets of New York City's black ghettoes, deftly extricated himself from the confines of his woolen, army issue blanket.

After his arrest, and his speedy conviction for theft (pick-pocketing), the presiding judge had given "*Fast-Hands-Freddy*", the option; five years imprisonment, or immediate enlistment, for the duration of the war, in the Union Army (Colored Troops).

Freddie, assuming that their was no way that the "*Offays*" in the army would give a nigger a gun, and put him up front "*where he could get his black-ass kilt*", choose to "join-up", to enlist in the Massachusetts 54ᵗʰ Infantry Regiment.

"Damn, sometimes I could swear dat dat peckerwood, "*Paddy*", sergeant's got eyes in da back ah his head."

With his foot, Freddie nudged the man across from him, lying on the dirt floor, of the small communal tent. "Time ta get yo black-ass up and at um, Young Blood…time ta Rise and shine."

The young man…a mere teen-ageer, James (*Jimbo*), Smith, was a sixteen-year-old runaway slave from a Tennessee cotton plantation.

After the sale of Jimbo's mother and his three year-old-sister, by their— for the most part benevolent master, to a Maryland tobacco planter, to pay off a gambling debt, Jimbo had run off the plantation… he had escaped.

Young James' primary goal, his mission in life, was to find his mother and sister; to earn enough money to purchase his mother and sister, and for them to reunite as a *"free-black-family."*

By using his wits, and with the help of white Quakers, members of *"the Underground Railroad"*, Jimbo had "over shot" Maryland, were he had hoped to find his family, and had made his way to, and found employment in the anthracite coalmines, of North/Eastern Pennsylvania.

For the entirety of his life as a slave, Jimbo had not had need for *"book-learnin'*, numbers and such." Now for the first time in his young life, he was actually being paid "real money", for his labor.

Although he couldn't *"cipher"*, Jimbo was acutely aware of the fact, that at his meager salary of 50 cents per day, it would be virtually impossible, for him to amass enough money to purchase the freedom of his mother and sister.

When on January 1, 1863, President Lincoln issued his Executive Order, the "Emancipation Proclamation", Jimbo's initial thought upon hearing of the presidential decree was, *"Praise da lawd, jubilation day dun come!"*

When it was explained to him that the "Emancipation Proclamation", stipulated, that only those slaves being held in states that were in rebellion — The Confederate States of America —, against the Union, that only the slaves in "Rebel" states, *"Shall be then, thenceforward, and forever be free"*, Jimbo's euphoria had quickly turned, into heart-wrenching disappointment.

Jimbo's mother and sister were enslaved in the state of Maryland.
Maryland, Delaware, Kentucky, and Missouri, were the four slave-holding Border States that had remained in the Union.
The historic "Emancipation Proclamation" would not mean freedom for Jimbo's mother and sister.
One of his fellow miners, a white man —though due to the layers of black coal-dust, that covered all of the men who worked underground in the mines, it was sometimes difficult to discern between black and white men —, told Jimbo of the formation of the Massachusetts 54th Infantry Regiment (Coloreds).

Although Jimbo was illiterate, and almost completely ignorant of the ways of the world outside of life in the slave community, and the Pennsylvania coalmines, Jimbo was by no stretch-of-the imagination, stupid.
In fact, Jimbo had been blessed with an impressive amount of common sense, and innate intelligence.
As his fingers, unconscientiously caressed the handkerchief, that contained the meager amount of coins and paper currency that he had manage to accumulate, Jimbo's mind had begun to race.
Despite his inability to read or to write, and his not being able to properly *"cipher"*, Jimbo had rapidly come to conclude that, while it was unlikely that he would ever amass enough money to purchase his family's freedom—he held no illusions of saving-up enough from the ten dollar per month army pay—, Jimbo reasoned that if he enlisted…by his joining the Union Army, it was conceivable that the Yankees, instead of giving him enough dollars,

would give him hundreds, possibly even thousands of *"Yankee-bullets"*, that he could use, to help free his family.

With the sixty-three dollars and seventy-five cents that he had managed to save, Jimbo bought a train ticket to Boston Massachusetts.

****

John Maxwell, was a thirty-two year old free black man, who for ten years, had raised and supported his family, which consisted of John, his wife Ellie, and their two sons, ten year old Grady, and six year old Douglas, by working long hours, as a janitor and stock-boy, at a Boston, mercantile store.

John's income, supplemented by that of his wife Ellie's earnings as a chambermaid at the Beacon Hill Hotel, provided a relative modicum of stability and security, for the Maxwell family.

Ellie would never forget the exact date (February 16th, 1863), and the exact time (7:20 PM), when John, sitting at the kitchen table sipping coffee, showed her the recruitment notice imploring men of color to join the Massachusetts 54th Infantry.

After reading the call to arms, Ellie had been immediately struck with an intense, overpowering sense of foreboding, and near paralyzing fear.

Although at the time, he gave no observable indication, Ellie knew that her man, John Maxwell would answer the call to arms.

Her husband, the father of their two sons', young black boys, who would god-willing, grow-up to become two fine black men, John, in order to ensure his and Ellie's sons' future as freemen, would attempt to enlist.

At the age of thirty-two, John Maxwell, was the oldest of the 54th's black recruits.

As so often happens, age is associated with wisdom. Hence to no one's surprise, the white, regimental Senior Non-Commissioned Officer (TAD), Sergeant Major Patrick Sean Donovan, had assigned to John Maxwell, the thirty-two-year-old recruit, now referred to by his fellow black soldiers, as *"Pappy"*, the unofficial designation of acting squad leader.

****

After ten hours of marching, drilling and rifle practice, the exhausted recruits of Company "A" was dismissed.

Jason sat alone, in the back of the squad's tent, watching and listening to the cacophony of noise, being made by his fellow, black recruits, the members of Company "A."

Freddie Gilliam, the slick, street-wise con-artist, from the streets of New York City, was attempting to find soldiers interested, Freddie's words, *"interested in partakin' in a lil game of chance."*

Freddie rattled the dice in his right hand; *"Okay boys, I knows you aint got much money, seeing as how we all been waiting fo that foist ten dollar pay, from dis here army."*

"Tell you what, you can bet wid money ifin you got any, or if you aint got money, wid pieces of paper. In Harlem, we calls dem pieces of papers I.O.U.ˢ."

Two men, whose faces were familiar to Jason, but whose names he couldn't remember, ambled over, accepting Freddie's invitation.

Freddie looked directly at Jimbo, *"Say Young Blood...how about you. You interested in making yooself some easy money?*

Jimbo shook his head; *"Naw Mista Freddy...aint got no money ta gamble. Ise savin' my money."*

Freddie, having set his sights, on a group of men who had seemed to be receptive to his invitation to "*shot-craps*", abruptly stopped.

He turned and stared at Jimbo.

Freddie placed his hand on Jimbo's shoulder, pivoted and in a loud mocking voice, shouted; *"Yall hear dat? Did you hear what dis nigga said?"*

"What's dat you said nigga? Freddie, in a tone of voice meant to be mocking, mimicking, Jimbo's, derisively repeated Jimbo's statement;

"Ise savin' my money."

An uneasy silence fell over the campsite. It seemed that all of the men within the sound of Freddie's voice, had fallen silent, listening… waiting.

Waiting to see what was happening.

Freddie, wiping spittle from his lips, looked directly at Jimbo and incredulously, repeated *"Ise savin' my money?"*

"Savin' your money...savin' your money for what nigga? For da future?

"You thinks, you gots a future niggah?"

Freddie looked away from Jimbo. Freddie's facade, his carefree, wise guy, demeanor, had vanished.

"You thinks, you gots a future"? He turned his gaze from Jimbo toward the men milling around.

His eyes surveyed the silent black men.

"You thinks, any of us gots a future? You're wrong boy. Ain't none of us got no future, not a real future in dis war, not in dis here country."

"You thinks cuz dat Massa Linkum, sitting in dat great-big white house, dat we dun bilt fo him, done finally let us join dis army, so's dat we can fight to free da black man?"

Freddie, in a series of challenging short-thrusts, with the index finger of his right hand, repeatedly poked Jimbo's chest with his finger.

Jimbo took several tentative, steps backward and in a plaintive, hurt voice, pleaded with Freddie; *"Cut dat out Mista Freddy."*

Freddie, ignoring Jimbo's words, continued; *"Huh…huh…huh, does you think dat niggah? "Niggah you bes be believn' …he din't."*

"Truff be told, is dat "Massa" Linkum dun let us join up cause, white folks in da Noff be tired a seein' der white boys dying in dis here war. Dey wants ta give dem rebel cannons, some black boys for target practice…some black meat ta blow-up…ta blow ta kingdom-come"

"Oh dey won't, get us <u>ALL</u> kilt. Too many niggahs for dat ta happen. Some of us will live. But afta we dun wid dis here war, none of us black-folks, in dis country, will be free, really free."

"Word on da streets is dat afta dis war, Massa Lincoln wants ta ship all our black asses back ta Afrika. Ta Afrika, can you believe it?"

"What da fuck does I know bout Afrika?" What does any of yall knows bout Afrika? I aint neva been ta no Afrika"

"I don't know bout you, but I'm here ta tell ya, I ain't gonna be sent ta no Afrika. I ain't fixing ta have my black ass, eaten-up by no damn lions."

Freddie, realizing that everyone within earshot was intently listening, stopped talking and reverted back to his more comfortable persona.

He abruptly stood, rattled the dice held in his hand and jubilantly exclaimed; *"Okay boys who wants ta win some moo…ney?"*

****

Jason had been surprised, astonished, and a bit humbled, by the depth, and the sincerity of Freddie's diatribe.

This was the second time, since his arrival in Boston, that he had unwittingly, misjudged… pre-judged, the sensibility, the depth of conviction, and the intelligence of a fellow black man.

In each instance; first the elderly black gentleman, the academician, who he had addressed as *"Uncle"*; then Freddie Gilliam, the black "city slicker, con-man", a member of his squad, who had just, probably, unwittingly, revealed himself as being a man with deeply held political beliefs.

Jason internalized what he had just heard, had witnessed. His thoughts reverted back to his sister Mandy's two favorite admonishments to him:

"Jason of all the wonderful things that Miss Leary taught me, which I in turn have tried to teach you, I want you to always remember these two facts-of- life; "first, that all men are created (born), equal…and secondly, do not pre-judge, be he black, or white, red, brown or, yellow…don't pre-judge your fellow man."

Jason remembered how his extraordinarily intelligent little sister would underscore the white Yankee teacher's words; "Miss Leary would always end her *sociological* pronouncements, with these words of wisdom… that to avoid being afflicted with blind-prejudice, by reminding me that it was just plain foolish, to judge the content of a book, solely by its cover."

****

Drill, drill, drill, and then drill, drill, drill some more. Assemble, load, aim, and fire their antique muzzle-loading rifles, followed by hours of bayonet practice. Parry, thrust, Again and again and again.

That was the daily ritual fostered on the black-recruits, by the three battles hardened, white, NCOs.

Although he at first had been reluctant to admit it (albeit-to-himself), Sergeant Major Donovan was beginning to develop a genuine sense of pride and respect, for this…his, "nigger-army."

In fact, while he, and his two fellow TAD, white non-coms had at first flippantly, referred to the black men of the Massachusetts 54th, as the "nigger-army", the Sergeant Major had come to now dismiss and reject, that demeaning, pejorative, sobriquet.

These men's transformation from that of a rag-tag, gaggle of undisciplined civilians, to disciplined soldiers, in just three short weeks, had been remarkable.

Since his first enlistment in the United States Army in 1838, some twenty-five years ago, eight years before the Mexican war, Sergeant Major Sean Patrick Donovan, had seen and trained hundreds, possibly thousands of recruits, all of them to a man, had been white men.

The progress of the recruits of the 54th, during their basic training, for their short time in the Army, replete with the social-baggage of being black, that they carried on their backs, to the Sgt. Maj., was remarkable.

In fact, the Sergeant Major, would rate this group of recruits as being as well prepared, combat ready, as any that he had trained.

In Sergeant Major Donovan's opinion, there remained but one important element needed, in order for Massachusetts 54th to become a "crack" combat unit.

E. Pluribus Unum

As did any successful, disciplined, combat unit, going all the way back to the Roman Legions, the 54th needed a corps of good, steady, non-commissioned-officers (NCOs).

It had been four weeks since he had reported for duty (TDA), to the 54[th's] Executive Officer, Lieutenant Colonel Norwood Penrose Hallowell.

For the first time since he had been ordered to the 54th, Sergeant Major Donovan, regretted the fact that his orders sending him to train the black soldiers were a Temporary Duty Assignment (TAD) orders.

Although he loathed the fact that he could not—nor would he if pressed, have admitted it out loud—if he had been given a direct order, the Sergeant Major would not have minded… would have in fact secretly welcomed, the opportunity to lead these black soldiers…*"his"* black soldiers, into battle.
Sergeant Major Donovan, shook his head, let out a barely audible sigh, and softly mumbled… "Alas, orders— is orders."

****

Pvt. John (*Pappy*) Maxwell, Pappy, when asked by Sergeant Major Donavan to become platoon Sergeant, had at first expressed doubts about his ability to led troops.

Pappy was acutely aware of the fact that his age, but probably more importantly, because of his status in the 54th, as a Northern-born, literate, free-black man, had resulted in creating a chasm, between him, and a large segment of the 54th's recruits.

He had reasoned that at his "advanced" age of thirty-two, contrasted against the barely post-adolescent age of twenty, the average age of the recruits—, would be an obstacle, one that would most likely; separate him from the much younger recruits.

The Sergeant Major had responded to Pappy's doubts, by pointing out to then Pvt. Maxwell, that in his more than twenty odd years in "this man's army"—the Sergeant Major's had been serving in the U.S, Army for twenty-five years, much of it spent training "raw" recruits—, how he had come to appreciate, that in addition to leadership, the new young recruits, needed, and tended to respond to a disciplinarian, a *"father-figure"*, to help them transition from civilian, to military life.

He assured Pappy, that the age difference between the Platoon Sergeant and the recruits, was far from being a liability, but was instead, an asset.

The Sergeant Major, for what Pappy thought would be his last words about the appointment, spoke; "Listen-up Maxwell: "When the shit hits the fan…when the bullets start flying, them boys ain't gonna be looking for a pal to lead them."

"They don't need a Sgt. who's gonna be their buddy, they don't need a Sgt. to wipe their butts, what they're gonna need is a Sgt to kick their asses…to keep them alive."

Pvt. John "Pappy" Maxwell, thanked the Sergeant Major for the offer and with a considerable amount of trepidation, and with the approval of Colonel Shaw, accepted his promotion, to the rank of "buck" Sergeant.

****

The vast majority of the recruits of the 54th were either ex-slaves, who by Southern custom and Southern law, were forbidden to learn to read and to write; and free-born blacks, whose opportunities for achieving literacy, in the de facto, segregated North, was actually, extremely limited.

Sgt. Maxwell welcomed and quite frankly unabashedly, solicited, the assistance and the friendship of Pvt. Jason Ruth.

Weeks before, Sergeant Major Donovan had recommended, to the 54th commanding officer, Colonel Shaw, the promotion of Pvt. John Maxwell to the rank of Sergeant, "Pappy" had been becoming increasingly impressed by the literacy, and even more so, the intelligence, and the unexpected, military experience and knowledge, of Pvt. Jason Ruth.

Because they shared the same communal tent, Pappy had had enumerable opportunities to observe how Jason carried himself, and to listen to the way the strikingly handsome, tall recruit, adapted to and blended in, with the divergent multiple cliques of recruits.

Pappy had been fascinated by Jason's ability to instantly, seemingly without effort, to adapt his speech patterns, to match the words, the cadence and his dialect, in accordance to the speech patterns of those, to whom he was engaged in conversation.

Pappy had listened to exchanges between Jason and Freddie Gilliam, the street-wise New York, "hustler", which if he hadn't known otherwise, would have led you to believe that the two men, had both been raised, together in the slums, in the streets of the urban ghettoes.

Conversely, Pappy had heard a "different" Jason, talking one-on-one, with "Jimbo" Smith, the illiterate ex-slave.

Jason's grammatically correct speaking voice, his dialect, and his manner of speech, had automatically, reverted to that of a southern slave, an illiterate slave, forced to labor in the fields of the Southern plantations.

The subservient speech of an illiterate black slave, toiling in the hot Sun, in the fields of a Southern Cotton Plantation, laboring under the watchful eye of the malevolent, white "Massa."

Sgt. Maxwell was impressed with, and in awe of Jason's uncanny ability, to seamlessly, spontaneously, adapt his speech patterns, to conform with that of the group to whom he was conversing.

Pappy remembered a recent pivotal, enlightening, conversation that he had had with Pvt. Jason Ruth. When he then, (Pvt. John *"Pappy"* Maxwell), after listening to and witnessing three such exchanges between Jason, and three recruits from totally-disparate backgrounds, had casually asked Jason; "How do you do it?"

E. Pluribus Unum

For several awkward seconds, Jason had stared in silence, his eyes, quizzically examining "Pappy's."

"How do I do it? Do what? Forgive me Pappy; you'll have to be a little bit more specific. I'm having trouble deciphering, defining, "IT." What exactly is the antecedent of your pronoun "IT"?"

"Pappy" spread his arms in exasperation and exclaimed; that, that right there. What you just did."

"One minute talking with Jimbo, you sound like an illiterate, ignorant "field-hand. Then when you're talking to me or to—he looked around and spotted Pvt. Joseph Atkins, a former Canadian teacher who the men naturally had come to refer to as "the professor"—, or when you talk with the professor".

"That…that there, switching from, …the way you speak when talking to the "Professor", and the next minute…the very next minute…, the way you speak when you talk to Freddie or to "Jimbo".

"How, and why do you, so automatically, fluently, change your manner of speaking? That is precisely, what I'm referring to. That is the "antecedent" for my use of the pronoun "IT".

Jason continued to stare at Pappy. He shrugged his shoulders. "I'll gladly answer your two-part how and why, question. First, I will answer the "<u>How</u>."

"It's a long story, and I won't bore you with the details. As I've shared with you before, I was blessed with having a brilliant, little sister, Mandy.

"In addition to my sister Mandy teaching me to read and to write, she, as did my mother, and the entire "slave-community", especially the slave mothers, taught the children, all of the little black slaves, so much more, than grammatically correct English."

"They taught us how to survive"! "As to the <u>WHY</u>, why do I use different words and speech patterns when speaking to different groups of people, you might say that it's an almost automatic, involuntary, defensive-survival mechanism, that's almost universally used, in some degree, by slaves."

"Unless you've been a slave, trying from day-to-day…to survive in the white-man's world, it's difficult…damn near impossible, to explain."

Jason, paused...deep in thought.

Pappy thought that Jason's now, apparently being at a loss for words, had the effect of underscoring the ex-slaves last sentence.

Jason continued; "It's a habit…a survival tactic, that has become second nature to me. In essence slaves, attempting to avoid harsh often inhumane, corporal punishment, or to at least lessen its severity, will say; Jason paused before continuing; *"dey says wha eva da Massa wonts ta hear…howsum eva "da Man", da Massa, he wonts ta hear it."*

In addition to Sgt. John "Pappy" Maxwell recognition of his inability, to relate with the company's ex-slaves, he knew that he was also woefully ignorant, and lacking, when it came to his knowledge and understanding, of military tactics.

The fact that Jason Ruth was literate, as too, were a few others, Pvt. Atkins, the "professor" came to mind—while the vast majority of the black recruits could neither read nor write—was a contributing factor, it was not the only factor that had led to Sgt. "Pappy Maxwell's" high opinion of Pvt. Jason Ruth's, leadership potential.

****

Pappy recalled having been especially impressed, when during their many conversations as privates, Jason had shared with him the work that he had performed for more than a year, as a salaried; "Scout/Interpreter for the 5th New Hampshire Volunteer Infantry Regiment."

Pappy had been fascinated, when Jason told him of the contents of many of the telegraph cables, that he had transcribed for the, 5th New Hampshire Volunteer Infantry's, Commanding Officer.

The communications had been from general, to general and between other high-ranking officers. The communiqués had been in the form of hand delivered dispatches, and telegraph cables, that had in detail, described the planned movements of Union and rebel troops.

Jason had spoke of battle plans, and how in "real-time", while battles were being fought, he an escaped slave, had been privy to the thinking of the Senior Officer Corps of the Union Army.

At first, Sgt. "Pappy" Maxwell assumed that his age was the reason, the motivating factor that led to some of the black recruits behind his back—, referring to him as *"Uncle",* Sgt. Maxwell.

It was only after he heard a few disgruntled black soldiers, ex-slaves, bitterly, reminiscing about their former life in bondage on the plantation, that Sgt. "Pappy" Maxwell came to appreciate another, far less respectful meaning for the ex-slaves seemingly innocuous use of the avuncular word, *"Uncle."*

The black recruits (ex-slaves), would be derisively speaking of those physically-fit, sycophantic young slaves…young male slaves who, regardless of the circumstances, never-ever, had a critical or a harsh word to say about the *"white-Massa".*

On the plantation, and now those who were no longer on the plantation, these, passive, acquiescent, black men were often saddled with and contemptuously labeled as *"Uncle Toms."*

Sgt. Maxwell, while not a military, "born-leader-of-men", had in fact, been born with the innate intelligence, to recognize his strengths, but far more importantly, Sgt. Maxwell had the good sense, to recognize his weaknesses.

Following his unexpected promotion to "buck" Sergeant, "Pappy" Maxwell, had quickly come to conclude, that if he were to have any chance of becoming a successful platoon sergeant, he needed to find a way to bridge the chasm, to find a way and means, of communicating with all of the recruits.

Sgt. Maxwell needed an ally, a conduit, a "go-between"; one of their own someone that the black recruits would respect and would listen to. A black soldier who could, and had, *"walked the walk",* and could literally, *"talk the talk".*

He needed a black man who could bridge the gaping social divide, that existed between the black recruits, between the recruits who were black*" free men",* black men who had been born free, black men who, under United States law, had lived their entire lives, as free men—, as opposed to that segment of black recruits, the *ex-slaves* who were relegated, by their fellow recruits, the black *free men,* to the "inferior" status and distinction, of being black, *free**D**men."*

Black *free men* versus… literally, versus black, *freed men.* An insidious subtle but divisive, social distinction, that was conducive to the creation of a social caste system, in the black community, as well is in the Massachusetts 54th Infantry Regiment.

The black recruits, men who had escaped slavery, the *"black free**D**men",* who if not for this war, these men would be considered by U.S. law, as being "Fugitive-slaves" felons, subject to arrest, in every state and territory, of the United States of America, be it North, South, East or West, subject to arrest and *"deportation"*, being returned to their owners, and once again, enslaved.

Sgt. John Maxwell was convinced, and managed to convince Sergeant Major Donavon, that Pvt. Jason Ruth, "fit-the-bill", and was most assuredly, that man, the black man who could literally speak to and for, the black soldiers of the Massachusetts 54[th.]

Both the white Sergeant Major, and the recently promoted, black, buck-sergeant, agreed that Pvt. Jason Ruth was the man who could bridge the gap between the black recruits. Those who were born freemen, and the black recruits the ex-slaves, the free**D**men, and could unite the black men of the 54th.

Upon the pleadings of Sgt. "Pappy" Maxwell and the recommendation of Sergeant Major Donavon, to Colonel Shaw, the 54th's commanding officer, Pvt. Jason Ruth was promoted to the rank of corporal; and designated squad leader of the 1st squad, 1st platoon, of the 54th's, Company "A".

✹ ✹ ✹ ✹ ✹ ✹ ✹

In a loud, booming, clear voice, that resonated with undeniable authority, Sergeant Major Patrick Sean Donovan, barked the order; ***"Comp…Nee, TEN …HUT."***

Instantly, as if by magic, five rows of soldiers, each row comprised of twenty black men, in unison, as one body, snapped to attention.

As he looked at each of the expressionless, black faces that stared, seemingly unseeing, straight ahead, the Sgt. Major noted with satisfaction, that none of the black faces that the Sergeant Major, menacingly glared at, acknowledged his stare.

Not a single soldier flinched. They all stared straight ahead.

Sergeant Major Donovan, the grizzled combat veteran of the war against Mexico, and numerous battles in this current civil war, suppressed a smile of pride, of satisfaction, and accomplishment, of a job well done.

The Sergeant Major inwardly mused to himself, the only thing that this company of Union soldiers had in common with that rag-tagged mob of illiterate, undisciplined recruits, that he had helped to recruit and train, more than a month ago, was their "black faces."

The precisely aligned, disciplined rows of black-soldiers standing before him, were a far cry from the bedraggled mass of — in his words — "*scraggly jigga-boos*", that he had recruited, and sworn in, just a scant five weeks earlier.

After slowly walking up and down the five rows of the rigid, motionless ranks of soldiers, where each soldier stood tall, heels together, feet spread apart at a thirty-degree angle; the ground supported the butt of each soldier's rifle.

Each rifle muzzle was stationary, immobile, fixed in place, held by the soldier's right hand, beside the soldier's right leg. One hundred rifle muzzles pointed upward, perpendicular aimed toward the sky.

Sergeant Major Donovan, now standing at the center of the first row, trumpeted a single command; "***Comp-nee…PARAAADE… REST***"!

As one, the five symmetrical rows, the one hundred black-soldiers of the 54[th's] "A" Company, simultaneously, with their right leg anchored in place, took one step to their left, while at the same time, snapping their left hand to the midline of their backs. At the same time, each soldier fully extended the hand of their right arm, which was firmly around the barrel of their rifles.

The butts of the one hundred rifles remained in place, on the ground.

The Sergeant Major silently, surveyed the soldiers for a full moment. His alert pale blue eyes had not detected, any extraneous movement within the ranks.

The response, by each of the black-soldiers to his orders, had been in perfect synchronization with those of his fellow soldiers, to his left, and to his right.

"Sergeant Maxwell." "*Pappy*" Maxwell, who was the first soldier in the first row, snapped to attention and responded.

"Yes Sir."

Sergeant Major Donovan barked; "Front and center."

As "*Pappy*" stood at attention before the Sergeant Major, in a firm low voice, discernable only to "*Pappy*", Sgt. Major Donovan gave instructions;

"Okay boy-yoo. Now they're all yours. Tak'um out twenty miles and back."

"Double time for five miles, rifles held at port-arms. Then regular march the next five miles. Giv'em a ten-minute break, then repeat the pace for the last ten miles."

"Take a twenty-minute break. When you return to camp, let's just say I would be a bit pissed-off, if you were not moving at the pace of double time."

"Needless to say boy-yoo, I expect that every piece of equipment that goes out, from rifles to shoelaces, is brought back, and returned to inventory."

"Pappy" (Sgt Maxwell), executed a perfect "about face", and in a firm, loud and clear voice barked; ***"Comp-nee "A", Ten…Hut." "Leff…Face;" "Comp-nee…Port…Arms!" "By column of two's; Double time…Haarch."***

The 1st and 2nd rows of United States soldiers moved out at a trot; they were immediately followed by the 3rd, 4th, and 5th rows.

****

Sergeant Major Donovan, walking swiftly, enroute to the white NCO quarters, noticed to his left, Colonel Robert Shaw, the 54th's Commanding Officer, having an animated, heated discussion with his adjutant, and the regiment's Executive Officer, Lieutenant Colonel Norwood Hallowell.

As the Sergeant Major came within hearing distance of the two officers, Colonel Shaw abruptly, interrupted his conversation, and summoned his senior non-com; "Sergeant Major, a moment please."

The Sergeant Major turned and approached the Colonel. He stopped approximately thirty inches from the Colonel, assumed the military posture of Attention, saluted and spoke: "Sir?".

Colonel Shaw returned the salute. "Stand at ease Sergeant Major. What a stroke of luck. I was just about to send for you. Colonel Hallowell and I were discussing the status, your progress, in the training of the troops."

"We were about to take our discussion inside to my office. Please join us."

Colonel Shaw's office was an 18' x 30' room. In the center of the room was a small desk.

On the wall, directly behind the desk, was a Daguerreotype-photograph of Abraham Lincoln, the 16th President of the United States of America, the Commander-In-Chief of the Union's Armed Forces,

Standing upright on the floor, in two bronze base stands, flanking Colonel Shaw's desk, were two large flags.

Two feet behind, and to the right-shoulder of the seated Colonel Shaw, was the flag of the United States of America. Equidistance from the Colonel's left shoulder, stood the newly created Regimental Colors, the battle flag of the Massachusetts 54th.

Two wicker-chairs were strategically positioned, facing the colonel's desk.

Colonel Shaw waved his hand, pointing in the direction of the two unoccupied chairs facing his desk; "Gentlemen, please be seated."

Lieutenant Colonel Hallowell sat. Sergeant Major Donovan remained standing. He had once again, assumed the military posture of "*Attention*."

Having spent twenty-eight years in the Army, unless he was given a direct order, the Sergeant Major considered it a breech of military protocol, for him, an enlisted man, to be seated in the presence of his commanding officer.

The Sergeant Major remained standing at "Attention."

Colonel Shaw looked up from the papers that he had been shuffling on his desk. "Sergeant Major, you have my permission, please take a seat."

Sergeant Major Donovan, still standing at "Attention", spoke; "With all due respect sir, in my twenty-eight years in the army, while on duty, I have never sat in the presence of my Commanding and Executive Officers."

While he himself, was not a career soldier, Colonel Shaw did admire and respect those professional officers and enlisted men, who were.

Rather than making the "old war-horse", Sergeant Major Donovan uncomfortable, the colonel acknowledged the Sgt. Major's sentiments by nodding his head; "Very well then, Sergeant Major, you may stand
"*At Ease*."

In response to that command, the Sergeant Major, his right leg anchored, took a short step, horizontally extending his left leg thirty inches, while he simultaneously, clasped both of his hands, into the mid-line of his back.

Although the position assumed by the Sergeant Major was not "*At Ease*", was instead that of "*Parade Rest*", Colonel Shaw reasoned that absent a direct order, this position of semi-"*Attention*" was the closest to "*At-Ease*", that the Sergeant Major would assume.

"Sergeant Major, Colonel Hallowell and I have been discussing your remarkable progress in the training of the men." "

From our perspective, the job that you and Sgts. Schmidt and Fitzgerald, have accomplished, transforming this disparate group of civilians—tradesmen, dock-workers, farmers, even former slaves, into soldiers, is nothing short of…well nothing short of being a stellar, miraculous, achievement."

The Sergeant Major flinched. Both Colonel Shaw, as was Lieutenant Colonel Hallowell, were momentarily startled by the Sergeant Major's reaction to the Commanding Officer's compliment.

Seeing the officer's confusion, in an effort to explain his involuntary response to Colonel Shaw's words of praise, the Sergeant Major requested permission to speak freely.

"Sir, when me and my fellow "*Prod*", Sergeant Fitzgerald, along with that "*Kraut*" Sergeant Heinrich, when the three of us all serving with the Massachusetts 32nd, received "*TAD*'s", to this *Nigger*… pardon Sir, to this Colored Regiment, the three of us, independently and collectively, thought that we were getting the royal-shaft."

The Sergeant Major paused. When there was no reaction from either of the two officers, he took a deep breath and continued.

"Everyone, at least to me it seemed like nearly everyone, in the 32nd, officers and men alike, were of the mind that the forming of a Combat Regiment made up of *Niggers*… again I beg your pardon Sir, I meant to say a Combat Regiment made up of *Coloreds* to fight the *Rebs*, was just another Washington political stunt, doomed for failure."

"I still vividly recall the first time when I stood in front of that raggedy bunch of "*Spades*." Sorry Sir, when I stood in front of that group of *Coons, Niggers, Jiggy-boos, Tar-babies*, those are just a few of the names that we…uh regular white soldiers, routinely called black people."

"I mean Sir, living up here in the North, most of us have been around, and seen a few uppity free-*Niggers*. *Niggers* that could read and write…that could read and write, almost as good as a white man could."

"Most of us, grudgingly giv' um credit for that. Even though a lot of the men still swear that them…reading and writing, is some kind of parlor trick. Like teaching a bird… a parrot to talk, or training a monkey to bang little cymbals together, and beg."

"Honestly Sir, when we first heard that they were recruiting blacks for an all Colored Combat Regiment, most of the lads thought that very few if any, of the blacks would join-up."

"And then if they did, that any those boys, would be sluggards, bums, who joined-up not to fight, but to get "three hots and a cot", and to get paid, fifteen dollars a month."

The Sergeant Major continued; "Hell sir, it wasn't as if the men didn't appreciate the fact that having black soldiers would be helpful. Somebody's
got to dig the latrines, cut down the trees and such, but *Niggers* actually fighting, shooting, bayoneting, clubbing men to death, men who are trying their damndest, to do the same to you, will Sir, none of us thought that the blacks were capable…that they were suited for or, up to it."

Hell colonel, some of those boys didn't even know their right from their left, those feelings, that the mob standing…mostly slouching, before me, was an inferior species, not men, certainly not soldiers. I, myself, thought them to be, a gaggle of sub-humans."

"Then Sir, gradually as each day passed, and I got to know the men. Got to know and appreciate the talent and the character of a *"Pappy", beg pardon Sir, you know him as* Sgt. Maxwell, when I began to recognized the suppressed but undeniable, leadership potential of that boy, Jason Ruth, that's when I began to think of these black-recruits, as Union Soldiers."

"As to how they will actually perform in combat Sir, that remains to be seen."

However, Sir, if I were a betting man, and I am, or a drinking man, which I am, I'd be willing to bet a bottle of good Irish Whiskey, that if the 54th actually sees combat, they will acquit themselves well."

Smiles began to spread across the faces of both Colonel Shaw and Lt. Colonel Hallowell.

Colonel Shaw picked up a document from his desk. He flourished the document in the air. "Gentlemen, these are official orders from the War Department."

"The 54th has been ordered—the colonel began to read the document —, to break camp and to board the troop-transport, De Molay.

"The 54th's destination is Beaufort, South Carolina."

Colonel Shaw reached into the bottom drawer of his desk. He stood, his right hand behind his back, not visible to either Sgt. Maj. Donovan or to Lt. Col. Hallowell.

Colonel Shaw said; "Sgt. Major, you are dismissed. The Sgt. Maj. snapped to *Attention,* saluted, executed a precise *about-face*, and took two steps toward the door.

Colonel Shaw spoke; "Sgt Major." As the Sgt Major turned with a quizzical look on his face, Colonel Shaw, with his right hand, nonchalantly, tossed an oblong object, in the direction of the Senior Non-Com.

The Sgt Major deftly, reflexively, with his left hand, caught the missile. It was a dark brown bottle. He read the label;

"O'Rielly's 150 Proof Pure Irish Whiskey."

Without uttering a word, the Sergeant Major, opened the door, and left the office of Colonel Robert Gould Shaw, Commanding Officer, of the Massachusetts 54th Volunteer Infantry Regiment.

****

CHAPTER 20

Boston Massachusetts - May 28, 1863 (Boston Common - 0900 Hrs)

The more than one thousand enlisted black soldiers, and their thirty-seven white officers, the soldiers of Massachusetts 54th Infantry Regiment, each man attired in his dress blue uniform, stood fidgeting, awaiting the order to step-out, to march, to parade, flags and banners unfurled, before the citizens and the impressive number of assembled, state, local, and federal politicians and dignitaries.

Before his deployment, each and every man of the 54th had been made aware of the Confederate president, Jefferson Davis' draconian order that stated:

> *If captured, black soldiers, would not be treated as prisoners of war, as were captured white Union soldiers. The black soldiers would instead be sold into slavery. And their white officers would be executed.*

Instead of instilling fear that would result in mass desertions by the 54th's black soldiers and their white officers—which was the motive for the issuance of order—, the Confederate's directive had the effect of inspiring the regiment.

In spite of, and to a large extent because of, the *death sentence placed upon the heads of—captured in battle—,* black soldiers and their white officers, the full complement the Massachusetts 54th Infantry Regiment, stood at the ready, their heads held high.

Colonel Shaw seated ramrod straight in his saddle, a look of satisfaction and pride etched upon his face, raised his ceremonial sword. As he rotated the polished sword, it caught and reflected the brilliant sunlight.

In response to his signal, the regiment's appropriate field grade and company level officers, gave the command:

"Men of the Massachusetts 54th, ***ATTEN…HUT.***"

In unison, the men of the 54th, snapped to attention. *"**Fowaard…March!**"*

****

The men of the Massachusetts 54th Infantry Regiment marched through the streets of Boston to a tremendous outpouring of cheers, with a few scattered jeers, and a smattering of racial slurs.

The more than one thousand strong regiment, to a man— marched sharply, heads held high—to the docks of Boston, and boarded the Union Navy's troop transport, *"De Molay."*

The troop transport's destination was into the heart of "Rebel Country."

On route to the first state that had fired on Union troops and had led the secession of states from the Union. The men of the 54th's, destination was, the coast of South Carolina.

For many of the soldiers of the 54th, especially for the black soldiers, this sea-voyage was their first. This was the black men's first time aboard a ship, a ship sailing upon the waters of the, often turbulent, Atlantic Ocean.

In preparation for the regiment's deployment, Colonel Shaw had advised the 54th's company commanders, to communicate to the men through their non-coms, the possibility that they might experience some discomfort, *"sea-sickness"*

Pvt. James *"Jimbo"* Smith's smooth ebony colored face had turned an ashy gray.

Jimbo was having difficulty holding-down the remnants of the three eggs, the home fried potatoes, and the four pancakes, smothered with thick maple syrup, that he had enjoyed this morning for breakfast.

Jimbo like many of his fellow recruits had at breakfast, indulged themselves by "wolfing-down", attacking their last meal at Fort Meigs, before the 54th's shipped out.

"Lawdy my belly feels lik I'se been tryn ta ride a wild stumpin mule. I'se feeling liks I'se gonna die."

Pvt. Freddie Gilliam, feeling more than a bit quezzy himself, in an attempt to mask his own discomfort, placed his hand on Jimbo's abdomen;

*"Would yall listen ta dis niggah moanin' and groanin'. "Boy ya thinks dis rockin' boat hurts your tummy, just wait till one ah dem "ofay" white-cracker Rebs, skewers you like a pig on a spit, wid his bay-**OO** -net?"*

When the transport, packed with the men of the 54th and their equipment; the ship's crew, and their animals, when the ship crested a huge wave, then plunged down, toward, what to Jimbo, seemed like the bottom of the Earth, Jimbo grimaced, trying with all of his will power, to refrain from spewing out, the mouth full of bile that was trying to gush forth from between his tightly clenched teeth.

Freddie Gilliam's teasing of Jimbo, was relentless.

"Hey now niggah, I bet bout now, you thinkin' which ah dese is betta."

"Drownin in dis here ocean… or being ripped open by a reb bay-oo-net, from here," Freddie placed his finger on Jimbo's throat, and dragged it down the to Jimbo's scrotum; *"ta here."*

"Or maybe u're black-ass being captured by dose crackers, mos likly bein'tortured…and den sold back, a slave ta pick cotton on some peckerwood ofay's plantation."

Jimbo swatted Freddie's finger from his body.

Freddie's teasing had been a distraction. His hazing had had a therapeutic effect, on Jimbo's bout of seasickness. Jimbo's mind, instead of focusing on the motion of the ship, had been diverted.

Jimbo was now concentrating on, and grappling with defending himself from Freddie's verbal assault.

"Cut dat out Mista Freedy. Leff me be"!

Corporal Jason Ruth had been assigned as squad leader of one of the ten men squads of Company 'A." Cpr. Ruth was the *"titular"* leader of the 1st squad, 1st platoon, of the 54th's, Company "A."
The men that comprised the 1st squad, the men that Jason led were:

1) James (*Jimbo*) Smith ; 2) Freddie Gilliam; 3) Joseph Atkins (*The Professor*) the former Canadian School Teacher; 4) John Mills; 5) Homer Jackson; 6) William (*Billy*) Sinclair; 7) Lucious Clay; 8) Leroy (*LEEE…ROY*) Franks; 9) Curtis Smith (*Smitty*); and the squad leader; 10) Cpr. Jason Ruth

****

CHAPTER 21

Hilton Head, South Carolina, June 1863.

During the first weeks on the island, the activities of black men of the 54th were strictly confined to that, of performing monotonous, menial labor.

The black soldiers were relegated to chopping-down trees, repairing roads, painting the officers' quarters, policing the grounds (*picking up litter*), shoveling and discarding, literally; tons of *horse-shit*, were among the routine duties, assigned to the black soldiers.

On this particularly hot, humid balmy day, Sgt Maxwell had assigned to Jason's squad the task of cleaning the stables and currying the officer's horses.

Freddie Gilliam, shirtless, a yellow bandana tied around his forehead, which was saturated with sweat mingled with dirt, was methodically shoveling horse manure onto a tarp.

Freddie threw his shovel to the ground at the feet of Pvt. Joseph Atkins, and exclaimed; *"This shit stinks!"*
Pvt. Atkins (*the Professor*), nimbly jumped over Freddie's discarded shovel.

"For once Gilliam, I am in total agreement with you. Not only do I agree that this—he pointed with his shovel—this excrement literally stinks, I'm beginning to think that my enlisting in the Union Army, stinks."

"I left Canada and joined the 54th with the belief that I could fight, for the dignity and the freedom of the black man."

Freddie put his hands on his hips and glared at Pvt Atkins. *What da fuck you talkin' bout niggah?"* Freddie turned around and spoke to the rest of his fellow 1st squad mates.

"Can yall believe it. Dis nigger is up to his eyeballs in horse-shit, an he still talkn dat high falottin "edjacated... niggah, bull-shit."

Jason, who was in total agreement with both the professor's, as well as with Freddie's sentiments—which he felt were one and the same, stepped in—; *"Alright you guys...knock it off."*

"We all, every last one of us, including Freddie, we all...all of us joined-up to fight, to kill Rebs. Sergeant Maxwell tells me that Colonel Shaw has been constantly, repeatedly, petitioning General Hunter, asking for permission to let the 54th fight, as he put it, "To give us the opportunity to engage the enemy".

William (*Willy*) Sinclair, a cobbler's helper, whose primary job as a civilian had been to shine the customer's shoes after they had been repaired, gave a derisive laugh; *"I ain't com here fo no damn engagement. I don't wanna kiss they pale, lily-white behinds, I joined dis here army, ta kill me sum of dem ofay-crackers"!*

"Jason looked at his men, some of whom returned his gaze with a puzzled, expression, as if they were trying to understand. Without missing a beat, Jason resumed, his voice adjusting to and emulating the speech pattern of his men... *"Colonel Shaw keeps askin da man, da genral, ta let us fight dem reb-crackas dat been whipping and rapin our yunguns, our sisters, our mother's... our womenfolk."*
"Sergeant Maxwell...Pappy says it's just a matta of time. We'll get our chance ta fight."

"Now get back to work. I don't care if it's one shovel full, or if it's ten wagon loads full of horse shit. Lets' act like soldiers, follow orders and not give them any excuse, for not letting us fight."

****

CHAPTER 22

Hilton Head, South Carolina, Office of the Commanding Officer- Massachusetts 54th - June 8, 1863.

Colonel Shaw was seated at his desk, his back to the door, his eyes transfixed, focused, staring at the map affixed to the wall.

The colonel was calmly rolling a long, fat, aromatic cigar, back and forth, between the thumb and forefinger of his left hand.

The colonel held a champagne glass in his right hand. On his desk was an open bottle of wine.

There was loud knock on his closed door. Colonel Shaw swiveled his chair around, facing the door. The colonel cleared his throat, and in a somewhat high-pitched, yet unmistakably commanding voice uttered a single word; "Enter."

Lt. Colonel Norwood Penros Hallowell, the 54^{ths} Executive Officer, stepped into the office.

"Rob...you sent for me? What's wrong?"

Colonel Shaw placed his glass on the desk. "Colonel Hallowell, you are to stand at attention, when addressing your Commanding Officer."

Lt. Colonel Hallowell, immediately "snapped-to." "Yes Sir, Lieutenant Colonel Hallowell, reporting as ordered, Sir.

Colonel Shaw rose, picked up a sheet of paper from the top of his desk, walked around the desk, and handed the paper to his second-in-command.

Lt. Colonel Hallowell, swiftly read the paper:

<u>X Corps U.S. Army Department of the South</u>

June 7, 1863

To: Colonel Robert Shaw, Commanding Officer, Massachusetts 54th Volunteer Infantry.

From: Brigadier General Charles Harken

Subj: Field Orders

The officers and men of the 54th, are to augment the 2nd South Carolina Volunteers (Colored), under the command of Colonel James Montgomery.

1) The combined forces of the 2nd South Carolina Volunteers (Colored), and the Massachusetts 54th, are to proceed to the town of Darien, Georgia; 2) They are to capture and/or destroy any and all rebel combatants encountered; 3) They are to capture and/or to destroy arms and supplies, e.g. mounts, food, forage, that can be used by the enemy.
a.   The combined forces of the 2nd South Carolina Volunteers (African Descent), and of the Massachusetts 54th, are under the command of Colonel James Montgomery.
b.   Colonel Robert Shaw is 2nd in command of the combined forces; The 2nd South Carolina Volunteers (African Descent), and The Massachusetts 54th

Anthony F. Seward
Colonel, U.S. Army
Adjutant General

By Direction;
Major General, David Hunter
Commanding Gen. X Corps., U.S. Army Department of the South

Lt. Colonel Hallowell looked up from the orders, to the face of his commanding officer.

An expression of satisfaction, of joy, bordering on glee, had spread across Colonel Shaw's face.
"Pen" — Lt. Colonel Norwood Penrose Hallowell, who for as long as he could remember, had been known to his friends, as "Pen" —, it's finally happening, it's come at last." The two soldiers clasped each other's shoulders.

The time has come to show the combat readiness of the 54th.

Colonel Shaw retraced his steps, reached into the side drawer of his desk, and removed a tin-cup. He removed the cork and poured a generous amount of amber liquid from the neck, of his last bottle of "O'Rielly's 150 Proof Pure Irish Whiskey."

Colonel Robert Gould Shaw, the Commanding Officer of the Massachusetts 54th, and his Executive Officer, Lieutenant Colonel Norwood Penrose Hallowell, raised their drinks into the air; without prompting, in unison they exclaimed; "To the 54th".

CHAPTER 23

THE OUTSKIRTS OF DARIEN
GEORGIA - *June 11, 1863*

Jason, as were the entire column of soldiers who had two hours ago been marching, was now walking. The brisk, sharp, military cadence bellowed by the NCO's, had ceased sometime after the first ninety-minutes of marching.

The men of Company "A", despite being fatigued, had managed to maintain a semblance of the three abreast formation, at the front of the 54th's, lead column.

Colonel Shaw sat erect, at the head of the column, leaning forward in his saddle.

Lt. Colonel Hallowell, astride a large chestnut gelding, reigned in his mount beside the 54th's commanding officer. The two white officer's horses', as if they had practiced the maneuver, synchronized their military-gait, walking forward, in-step, side-by-side.
Lt. Colonel Hallowell, leaned across his saddle; "Colonel, has Colonel Montgomery made known to you exactly what, he wants us to do when we enter Darien?"

Colonel Shaw leaned over, "He has not changed his original instructions. The 2nd South Carolina troops will lead the attack. The 54th are to be held in reserve."

One of Colonel Montgomery's 2nd South Carolina (*Contraband),* white junior officers, reigned up beside the Massachusetts 54th's two senior officers.

The lieutenant's hand touched the bill of his cap*;* Colonel Shaw returned the salute. "Sir, Colonel Montgomery sends his compliments. The colonel instructed me to inform you that our forward reconnaissance revealed that the town is at best, lightly defended.

Although there were no signs of entrenched enemy troops, the Colonel anticipates that there still remains the real threat, of significant resistance from snipers, and from rebel, civilian-partisans.

Colonel Montgomery wants you to bring your troops the 54th, forward to join his, 2nd South Carolina troopers.

The lieutenant saluted, and without waiting for his salute to be returned, wheeled his horse around, and galloped back, toward their intended objective, the little town of Darien Georgia.

Colonel Shaw, glanced at his Executive Officer; "Okay *"Pen"*, this is what we've been training for.

"I'll ride ahead and meet with Colonel Montgomery. You are to relay to the officers, and to our non-coms, Colonel Montgomery's orders."

"I want the 54th to join me at the front, within twenty minutes."

Colonel Shaw turned his horse's head in the direction of the still lingering cloud of dust that had been raised by the 2nd South Carolina's messenger, and hurried forward.

****

The two "*Full Bird*" Colonels —both regimental commanders of recently commissioned Union Army Regiments "Colored" —, stood in a clearing, fifty yards removed from the ranks of Colonel Montgomery's, 2nd South Carolina Infantry Regiment.

The two senior Union Army officers were immersed in what appeared to be a heated, contentious, discussion. Colonel Shaw handed back the field glasses to the ranking officer, Colonel James Montgomery.

"With all due respect Colonel Montgomery, I don't see any threat or any signs of activity that warrants our attacking and torching the town. The only signs of activity that I observed were two matronly looking white women, and two male Negroes.

Colonel Montgomery raised the field glasses to his eyes; "I'll tell you what I see Colonel."

He swept the glasses from one end of the thoroughfare, to the other, of what they had both described as being the town's "*Main Street*."

"I see two white women and two old black field-hands. The white women give aid and comfort to any "Johnny-Reb" that happens by, or who may be lurking, armed and hiding."

"As for those two slaves they, by planting, hoeing, and harvesting the crops that feed the Rebs, they are thereby feeding and sustaining the rebellion."
Colonel Montgomery lowered his field glasses. For a fleeting second, Colonel Shaw thought that he saw reflected in the man's eyes, the fiery fanatical eyes of a zealot.

"Shaw, it is our duty…our calling, to do all that we can do to stop, to end the ungodly practice of slavery. We were sent here, at this moment, by God, we are here as God's instrument to strike a righteous blow toward ending the institution of human bondage."

"If indeed we find no resistance, we will confiscate any and all *contraband;* we will put to the torch in this town, every last house, shop, building, and edifice."

Colonel Shaw, himself an avid abolitionist, saw in Colonel Montgomery's eyes, the "*fanatical-fire*", that he had once seen radiating from the eyes of the martyred abolitionist, John Brown.

In a calm, controlled voice, Colonel Robert Gould Shaw—the son of Francis George Shaw, and Sarah Blake Shaw, both prominent, renowned, supporters of the emancipation of slaves, and the abolition of slavery—, spoke; "Colonel Montgomery, I too abhor slavery; I too fight to abolish slavery and to reunite the Union. However, I do not subscribe to making war on the innocent, civilian populations, by destroying their homes, and their fields."

Colonel Montgomery deliberately, methodically hung his field glasses around his neck. He then looked directly at his subordinate officer, Colonel Shaw.
"Colonel Shaw I will take a company of the 2nd South Carolina to the eastern end of …he pointed his finger, "Main Street." You will take a company of the 54th to the western edge of "Main Street." I will fire my pistol twice, into the air in rapid succession. You are then to order your soldiers to proceed to remove from stores and homes; furniture, food and any materials, that could be used by the enemy."

"After such materials, "contraband", has been loaded into our wagons, the buildings, shops and homes are to be set to the torch."

If you refuse to fully comply, and to execute my orders, I will have you placed under arrest, for failure to follow lawful orders, from your superior officer, while engaged in combat with the enemy. You will face a court martial to answer the charges of insubordination, and of treason."
"Colonel Shaw, do you understand?"

Colonel Shaw snapped to attention…saluted and responded; "Yes Sir."

****

After having been briefed by Lieutenant Pierce, the Company's 1st Platoon Lieutenant, Sergeant "Pappy" Maxwell, had been, with some degree of urgency, looking for Jason. Pappy stopped one of the soldiers assigned to Jason's squad, Pvt. Homer Jackson. *"Jackson, have you seen Corporal. Ruth?"*

Pvt. Jackson, who was busy adjusting the straps of his knapsack, looked up, *"Yeah Sarge… last time I seed him, he was ova dere."* He pointed in the direction of a group of men checking their equipment.

Pappy hurried over to Jason. Jason was off to the side, having an animated discussion with *"the Professor"*.

Jason was shaking his head; "I don't agree. I don't think that the reason they refer to General McClellan as *"Little Napoleon"* is not necessarily because of his military acuity. I think the nickname came about because as was Napoleon, General McClellan too, is short and, because of the way our *"Lil Mac"* poises in those pictures."

The Professor looked puzzled; "What pictures?"

Jason shrugged; "you know those *"by Brady"*, daguerreotypes.

"The ones were General McClellan always has his right hand between the buttons of his uniform tunic. That's the way General… *"Emperor"*, Napoleon Bonaparte poised for his official portraits"

"Seems to me that General McClellan tends to think of himself, as the second coming of General…*Emperor* Napolcon."
Pappy interrupted. In a crisp, no nonsense tone, he placed his hand on Jason's shoulder and spun him around. "Corporal Ruth, a moment please."

Without a word, Jason stepped away from *"the Professor"*.
Taking his cue from *"Pappy's"*, urgent tone, Jason responded to his friend, who at this moment was obviously functioning as his Sergeant, employing formal, military protocol.

"You wanted to speak to me sergeant?"

"Colonel Shaw wants two of our squads, twenty of the 54th's soldiers, to join a like number of the Carolina 2nd's, to secure the town.

Colonels Montgomery and Shaw will personally led the combined forces.

Your squad, and a squad from Company "C" have been chosen. Gather your men, gear-up, and report back here in ten minutes.

Jason, spurred on by the surge of adrenaline coursing through his body, hurried to assemble his squad, and to give them *"the word."*

This was it. Combat!

At last, this was his chance, his chance to fight the evil men who for selfish economic reasons, espoused and promoted the doctrine of "White Supremacy".
A bigoted doctrine that Jason believed to be the false moral justification, espoused and promoted by the wealthy Southern planters, the Confederate Aristocracy.

His chance to fight those evil men, who would kill and maim in many cases, there own kinsmen, who would kill northern relatives, their own family members, in order to defend, maintain, and to perpetuate their Southern way of life, to defend and to perpetuate White Supremacy; to perpetuate slavery.

This was his chance to fight the evil men who were tenaciously fighting to keep him, his mother, his sister…his people, forever enslaved.

Sergeant Maxwell, Corporal Ruth, and the men of the 1st squad, of the 1st platoon of the Massachusetts 54th's Company "A", reported to Colonels Montgomery and Shaw.

Per his Commanding officer's orders, Sergeant Maxwell ordered Jason's ten-man squad to "form-up", and to join the ten men of the 54th's Company "D's", 1st squad.

The twenty-two black soldiers and their two white officers, fell-in, and were aligned behind the twenty-three men of Colonel Montgomery's 2nd South Carolina Volunteers.

Jason and Sergeant Maxwell were a short distance removed from their men. Pappy— although they were well out of the earshot of the men—, leaned over and in a subdued voice asked; "Jason…are they ready?"
Jason took a deep breath. He was stoic, resolute; exhibiting confidence and perhaps a little bravado; Jason shook his head in the affirmative. "Pappy the men are sharp; they're well trained." In a voice exuding confidence; "as to if they're ready, if they're ready for combat…hell if I'm ready for combat…I guess we'll know for sure when they, …when we come under fire."

"Sarge, I was wondering." Jason hesitated. Pappy stared intently at Jason, waiting for him to continue. Jason spoke softly…almost whispering," the 54th and the South Carolina's combined strength is over fifteen hundred men. Why are we attacking a Confederate Town with only twenty soldiers?"

"Word" is the town is either deserted, or it's lightly defended. For whatever reason, Colonel Montgomery, feels that twenty soldiers can easily do the job. Besides since the Colonels will be in front, fully exposed leading the men, I guess their confident that we won't come under heavy fire."

"Jason still not quite fully satisfied, asked; "Sarge, what exactly is the job…what's our mission statement?"

Sergeant Maxwell smirked. "I asked Lieutenant Pierce that very question. He said that our job is to do, whatever Colonel Shaw orders us to do."

The combined force, guns cocked and at the ready, led by their commanding officers, rode slowly, methodically, from opposite ends, toward the center of the little town's "*Main-street.*"

The only movement…the only sign of life that Jason saw was that of two middle-aged white women, one dressed in a frayed blue dress, while the other wore a drab brown frock.

Two black men, who to Jason, appeared to be physically in their prime, were holding packages with one arm, and ropes controlling four skinny mongrel, dogs, with their other hand. Jason quickly concluded, that the black-field hands, were the white women's' slaves.

The four yapping and barking dogs were being restrained two apiece—, by the two burly slaves.

One of the dogs broke the frayed rope that had been restraining him, and dashed, barking and growling, toward Colonel Montgomery's mount.

The colonel's horse reared up on his hind legs, his front hooves thrashing at the air. Colonel Montgomery calmly, fired his pistol at the charging dog. The bullet from his heavy Navy Colt, struck the cur, just above his left shoulder.

The dog yelped and fell whinnying piteously, into the cloud of dust. The hoofs of the Colonel's horse's forelegs crashed down, shattering the bones of the mongrel's left hip.

The white women in the blue dress ran screaming, into the street. "You filthy Yankee scum, you killed my dog!"

Colonel Montgomery, glared at the woman; "watch your mouth you…you Jezebel-harlot… you white slut."

Colonel Montgomery turned his attention to the two-black slave; "You there… you can drop those packages in the street, and come with us. You're free, you're no longer slaves."

The two slaves looked at each other. They were both obviously confused. Then the taller of the two spoke; *"We sur- noff thanks yah suh…but we dun giv awr promise tah Massa Wilbut an ta Massa Reginall, dat we be takin care ah da place, whil dey off to da war."*

Colonel Montgomery gave the two black men a disgusted look; "Whether you like it or not, now you're freemen, that means that you can work for nothing for this…this white-trash, or you can choose, instead to work for wages."

"But the one thing you can't be anymore, thanks to President Lincoln, you can't be a slave."

Colonel Montgomery turned his attention to one of his junior officers, "Lieutenant Sims, remove any, and all things of value, from the stores and the houses of these rebel traitors."

"Every thing that we can't carry, I want stacked in the middle of the street. I want the contraband and the buildings…all of the buildings including the houses, put to the torch."

"Colonel Shaw, you wanted to see action…well here it is. So far, how do you like it?"

Colonel Shaw, who sat his horse, and was speechless, dumbstruck, as the men of the 2nd Carolina (*African Descent*), commenced shattering the doors and windows of the buildings, stripping and the looting the stores and houses.

Colonel Montgomery shouted to Colonel Shaw; Colonel Shaw, order the men of the 54th, your men, to follow the example sit by my troops."

"I want everything, all the contraband that we can carry, loaded onto the wagons. Anything that we can't carry is to be brought to the center of this street, and put to the torch."
When Colonel Shaw hesitated, Colonel Montgomery, with that fanatical gleam in his eyes, in a loud clear, resonant voice, a voice that he clearly intended to be heard by others witnesses perhaps, shouted, "Colonel Shaw…those are my orders, my ***DIRECT ORDERS*** to you."

"Colonel Shaw, do you intend to carry-out my orders?"
Colonel Shaw once again sat-up, ramrod rigid in his saddle. He saluted and in a firm voice responded by answering… "Yes Sir."

****

CHAPTER 24

Hilton Head, South Carolina, Massachusetts 54th - Bivouac Company A 1st Platoon *June 13, 1863.*

Billy Sinclair sat despondent, his elbows on the little makeshift table that sat in the middle of the tent. His pained, dejected, expression made him look as if he was carrying the weight of the world on his shoulders. Billy was slouched over, holding his head in his hands.

In contrast, Freddie Gilliam, pacing back and forth in the rear of the 1st squads' tent, was a bundle of animated, gleeful energy.

"Did yall see how Colonel Mongomery put dem white-trash wimmen in their place? Man, when he called that white bitch a slut, and din he tol us ta burn dat town down, I swear I felt so good, got so excited, I almost peed my pants."

Billy jumped up and shouted. *"Shut your filthy mouth Freddie, dose white ladies won't hurtin' nobody. What wud you ah dun, iffin somebody dun gone an shot u're dawg? Colonel Mongomery he dun kilt her dawg!"*

Freddie turned, and pointed his finger at Billy. *"Will looka here...did yall hear dis nigger? He be stickin' up fo dat white woman. Dat white woman who'd, widout givin it a second thought, would hav his black-ass whupped, maybe even strung-up fo looking da wrong way at her."*

"Well niggah, I'll tell you what I woodn't a dun, I'de sho nuff not gone runnin', an cussin' at no white man, who had a smokin' gun in his hand."

Freddie turned facing the rest of the squad; *"I may not have the book- learnin' dat Pappy, da Professur, and Corporal Ruth has got, but I sur as hell gotta cnuff sense not to go runnin' an cussin at ah white man wid a gun in his hand, ova no flea-bitten dawg."*

At the mention of his name—more precisely, his nickname—, Pvt. Joseph Atkins (*the Professor*), gave way to a repressed impulse, and joined the discussion.

"I don't know about the rest of you guys, but I sure as heck didn't enlist in the 54th, to harass harmless women, or to burn down towns depriving its inhabitants, the women and children, of food and shelter"

Freddie smirking, derisively, sarcastically responded; *"Well la-de-dah.*

If dat don't beat all. Watta we got here? Look who dun decided ta talk wid us po, dum, ignorant, niggers."

"Just what da fuck…scuse me, just what da <u>HECK</u> did you join up fo… Prooo-fes-ur?"

Without giving Pvt. Atkins a chance to respond, Freddie continued his rant.

"Well Mista edjacated Neee-grow, I'll tell you why I joined-up, I joined up to keep my black-ass from bein' locked up in som stinkin jail. I figured dat gettin' paid ta shovel shit fo da army, is a hel- uv- a- lot betta, din shovelin' shit fo free… fo da white man."

Freddie fixed the *"Professor"*, with a withering, challenging, stare. *"Well mista high fahlotting, Neee-grow… is you gonna answer me?"*

Pvt. Atkins, who during his time with the 54th, had for the most part, kept his personal history, and his political opinions to himself, regretted having allowed himself, to be drawn into this discussion.

He felt trapped.
Freddie, thinking that the "Professor's" silence denoted weakness, continued to goad the soft-spoken, articulate, black man. *"What's da matter Neee-grow, cat gotcha tongue?"*

When the "Professor" didn't answer, Freddie turned his back on the soldier and declared; *"Jus lik I thought. You jus one ah dem free-foo-rain, Neee-grows dat thinks dey betta din us. Yall act like yall Shit-Don't-Stink."*

Pvt. Atkins shrugged his shoulders, and recalling an expression that one of his instructors at Montreal's McGill College, an Englishman, a visiting scholar, often used before reluctantly committing himself to a course of action: *"In for a Schilling…In for a Pound."*

Pvt. Joseph Atkins (*the Professor*) decided that this time, this one time, he would answer *"Fast-Freddie Gilliam"*.

In a solemn, calm, steady voice, Pvt. Joseph Atkins began to speak. "My parents were slaves on a tobacco plantation in this country. The plantation was in Dorchester County, on Maryland's Eastern Shore.

"My parents, as did their parents, as did their parents parents, had labored for centuries, for more than eleven-generations, my family had literally, "slaved" under the blazing sun, in Maryland's tobacco fields."

Pvt. Atkins paused, he wanted to give the squad a chance to understand and to appreciate, his personal lineage, his family's history under the yoke of tyranny, living…surviving under Slavery, the South's *"Peculiar Institution"*, the legalized practice of Human Bondage.

The "Professor's" fellow soldiers, the men of the 1st squad including Pvt. Frederick Gilliam, sat silently listening. The professor had their undivided attention.

Jason, who had only minutes earlier, resisted his impulse to step-in and put an end to this rapidly escalating, acrimonious, situation, too was mesmerized, deeply, viscerally, impressed by Pvt. Atkins narrative.

Jason eyes scanned over the men of his squad. They were all, intently listening to the "Professor."

"When I was seven years old, just about ready to join my father in the fields, a former Dorchester slave, a black woman whose name was…whose name is Harriet Tubman, an escaped slave who because of the Fugitive Slave Act, was a wanted felon, at her own peril, returned to Maryland, and helped my family escape."
"*Moses*", that's the name they called Miss Tubman; she led my family north to freedom. Miss Tubman and her white "Underground Rail Road" friends, led my mother, my father, my thirteen-year-old sister Sally, and me…Harriet Tubman, "*Moses*", led my family to freedom, to "*the promise land*", she led us all the way to Canada."

"It was when I was in my senior year at college, when I heard, for the first time, that the United States was forming an infantry regiment of Northern black soldiers. I quit school. I left McGill College. And for the first time, since I was seven, I have returned to the land of my birth, the land of my ancestors, the United States of America."

"While I, by no means think that I possess the courage, or the faith of a "*Moses*", a Harriet Tubman, I promised God that if I was given the chance, that I would do all that I could, to fight for the freedom of all of my black brothers and sisters, down here, in the land of my birth, here in the United States of America."

Freddie, attempting to hide his embarrassment, sheepishly broke the awkward silence that ensued.

"*Hey man, I dint know. I'm sorry dat I called you "foo-rain". I din't know.*"

Freddie made a circle; waving his arm encompassing all of the men in the tent. "*Did any of you guys know dat da "professor" was born a slave in dis here country?*"

No one answered. "*See Professor, till jus now, nobody know'd dat bout you.*"

Jason slipped out of the tent. He scanned his surroundings, looking for Sgt. Maxwell.

He was anxious to share with "Pappy", the news. The news of how unwittingly, Pvt. "*Fast Freddie*" Gilliam, by teasing the "*Professor*", had united the 1st squad, and possibly the entirety of Massachusetts 54th's, Company "A."

****

BOOK II

CHAPTER 25

Richmond Virginia – April 17, 1866
(Law Office of Luis Frazier, Esq.)

Luis Frazier, Esq., the well respected, distinguished, attorney/ businessman, sat at his desk, hunched over an impressive stack of legal documents.

By far the most striking physical feature of Luis Frazier, Esq.'s outward appearance, of his persona, was reflected in the intensity of his penetrating, piercing, steely blue eyes.

When he was pleased or if amused, Luis' eyes would sparkle and would give one the impression that they were looking into a soothing, tranquil, deep blue pool of still water. However, when he was angered, Luis' eyes would smolder, cloud-over, and darken. When that occurred, those who knew Luis well, learned to read the warnings, and to give the attorney plenty of *"room"*.

His dark smoldering blue eyes were indicators of trouble. His eyes could accurately be perceived as *"beacons, harbingers"*, alerting one to the probability of rapidly approaching, tumultuous events.

During the majority of his personal and professional life, Luis had been described frequently, as a rather short, portly, rotund gentleman.

Now one year after the assassination of Abraham Lincoln, one year following four disastrous, devastating, years, colloquially referred to by Richmond's despondent, defeated citizenry as; *"The War for Southern Independence"*, Luis was now, more accurately being characterized, as a stately gentleman, of medium height, weight, and stature.

As Luis often proclaimed — tongue in-cheek —, when speaking half in jest to Rebecca, his beautiful twenty-year-old ward; "The only good thing that came as a result of the recent hostilities, was my shedding of sixty pounds of extraneous, ugly fat."

All of his life, Luis had been a devout, adamant supporter and proponent of the South's — codified in law —, *"Peculiar Institution"*, Slavery, the legal practice of human bondage.

In the South and especially in the city of Richmond Virginia, before and during the first few years of the relatively short-lived rise and fall of the Confederate States of America, even amid the confusion and the turmoil of defeat, Luis Frazier, Esq., had been held by the city's *"movers and shakers"*, in the highest esteem.

Almost to a man, those men who would wield the power, men who would come to occupy the highest political echelons of the Confederate Government, those men, admired and respected Luis Frazier.

That steadfast perception, that of Luis' being a true believer, an ardent supporter and proponent of slavery, began to slowly, gradually change, after his best friend Henry Billings' daughter Rebecca, had unexpectedly, miraculously, re-entered his life.

****

Luis and his now deceased best friend, Henry Billings, the former owner and Master of Rosewood, one of Virginia's most successful cotton plantations, Luis Frazier and his friend Henry Billings, were both men who had been regarded and acknowledged, as having been staunch, loyal supporters of the Confederacy.

In addition to having been Henry Billings' best friend, Luis was also his— the Billings family's—, attorney, and business manager.

In the immediate aftermath of Abraham Lincoln's election as the 16th president of the United States, both Luis and Henry had correctly surmised, concluded, that civil war, between the North and the South, was imminent.

In response to the political climate in the country, Henry Billings, the owner and Master of Rosewood, one of Virginia's most successful cotton plantations, had given Louis Frazier, Esq., explicit instructions to his best friend and business manager, to liquidate, to divest, to remove all of the Billings family's substantial holdings from Northern banks, businesses, and establishments.

Following financial divestiture, Luis had been instructed, by his friend to invest Henry's considerable fortune into banks and war related enterprises, such as iron foundries and munitions factories, that were located in the South.

All of the substantial Billings' assets were to be redirected and restricted to enterprises geographically located well south, of the Mason -Dixon Line.

In the two years following Luis' removal of the Billings family's funds from Northern banks and financial institutions, Henry and his best friend, Lawyer/Business Manager, Luis Frazier, invested heavily in support of the Confederacy.

At Henry's insistence, Luis on his behalf had purchased for Rosewood, approximately, $250,000 worth of Confederate War Bonds.

The bonds were backed and guaranteed, by the full faith and credit of the now defeated and defunct, Confederate States of America.

In addition to the war bonds, Henry had actively and enthusiastically supported the Confederate cause, through multiple, investments in various Southern manufacturing and munitions plants.

By the fall of 1862, Henry's patriotic investments in "The Confederacy and the Cause" were being considered, in "neutral" financial circles, as investment, financial, failures.

Although the Confederate Treasury, continued to taut the strength and solvency of its bonds and currency, it had become increasingly clear that the South's strategic goal of conducting a swift short war, with the North suing for peace, was not in fact, realistic.

Fortunately for his best friend, Luis' innate business sense and acuity, tempered his heart felt patriotic zeal, for the financial solvency and stability, of the Confederacy.

Unbeknownst to Henry, Luis had sequestered, withheld, and converted $50,000 of Rosewood's assets, into gold coins.

As Luis would later explain to his best friend, through the use of a series of clichés; "You should never put all of your eggs into one basket. And you should always have a solid Plan "B" to — if need be, fallback on".

Luis was fond of reminding Henry of his own — Henry's often quoted —, favorite axiom. "By all means, one should hope for the best outcome, but more importantly, one should always, always — have a solid contingency — plan, for the worst."

Luis and Henry's contingency plan was to take advantage of the passage of Lincoln's Homestead Act, the law that made ex-slaves eligible for grants of free land west of the Mississippi River.

A vitally important stipulation of the Homestead Act, was that the individual awarded the grant, must live and farm the land for a minimum of five contiguous years.

Henry's black ex-slave Ruth — who for more than two decades, had clandestinely shared her bed and her body with Henry, and was the mother of Henry's mulatto — daughter Mandy, had enthusiastically agreed to allow Luis to file, in her name, the application for a 160 acres tract of land, in the Lost Springs, Kansas.

Ruth — the former slave, now a free woman of color — had agreed to Henry's plan to have her move, to travel, with him and his daughter Rebecca, to start over, to rebuild his beloved Rosewood, in the west.

To Henry's chagrin, utter surprise, and consternation, his former slave and paramour, meek, docile, Ruth, had placed a condition, an ultimatum, for her participation in Luis and Henry's "Plan B." Ruth had insisted that her teenage daughter, Mandy be included as a member of their emigrant group.

Once again Luis smiled, chuckled as he inevitably did, as he recalled Henry's incredulity, when he repeated, as best he could, in her slave's dialect, Ruth's exact words;

"Massa Henry, Ise wanna go wid yu an Miztress Bekka. Ise luv dat chile lik she be my own. Mandy be my chile Massa an if Ise truly free, I aint gone no-wer wid-out my chile, Mandy."

As he reclined in his swivel chair, for a fleeting moment thinking back, reminiscing, Luis once again experienced the heart-wrenching anguish and grief that he had felt, almost three years ago, after reading the letter sent by Samuel Smith, the wagon master of the Billing's, ill-fated wagon train.

April 4th, 1863

Dear Mr. Frazier,

It is my painful duty to inform you of a tragedy that has befallen the Henry Billings family, traveling, with my wagon train, under my guidance and protection.

Mr. Billings and his daughter's governess, a Negress by the name of Ruth, were attacked and killed by a war party of hostile Indians.

Your friend Mr. Henry Billings fought and dyed bravely, attempting to protect his daughter, Miss Rebecca Billings.

I truly regret informing you that Miss Rebecca Billings, and her Negress servant, Mandy, were abducted by the heathens.

A posse of men, led by me, followed the Indians, until we lost their trail, and were forced to abandon our search and rescue efforts.

With my deepest sympathy,

Sincerely,
Sam Adams. Smith
Captain Samuel A. Smith, Wagon Master

CHAPTER 26

Richmond Virginia - December 27, 1863 – Home of Luis and Delilah- Ann Frazier

Luis Frazier and his rather homely, pedestrian, looking wife Delilah, were about to conclude their evening meal.

Delilah was a twenty-eight-year-old, tall, slender, plan, yet to many, still an oddly attractive woman, daintily dabbed at the corner of her mouth with a fine linen napkin.

She picked up— between her thumb and index finger— a delicate silver bell, which had been strategically placed near her right hand. Delilah, ever so gently, rang the bell.

Luis, who was seated at the end of the eight-foot dinning room table, barely heard the almost inaudible tingle, the sound of the bell.

Within seconds, Simon, one of three black slaves owned by Luis and Delilah Frazier, was at Delilah's side.

Despite having witnessed Simon's rapid response to being summoned innumerable times, Luis still, could not help but marvel at what he considered to be, the old slave's truly remarkable hearing, and agility.

Following his receipt of notification of the death of his best friend and protégé, Henry Billings, and the abduction by wild, savage Comanche Indians, of Henry's daughter Rebecca, Luis had been inexorably, steadily, slowly drifting into fits of melancholy, and depression.

The Billings family; Henry, his wife Margaret (Peggy), their son Jesse, and their daughter Rebecca, had over the years, become regarded, thought of by Luis, as his extended family, his adoptive family.

It was during a particularly severe bout of loneliness that Luis—thanks to the neighborhood's matronly spinster, who was covertly, behind her back, referred to as "*the old maid*" Delilah Cooper—, was pulled from his self-inflected, deep, dark, abyss, of loneliness and despair.

****

After a brief courtship, Luis motivated more so from a sense of despair, rather than from love and/or affection, Luis Frazier, Esq., and Delilah Copper, were wed.

The breathless entrance of Maybelline, the family's cook, interrupted Luis brief revere. *"Massa Frasa, suh, dars ah genelman an ah lady at da doo askn fo yu."*

Luis, who had been expecting his law clerk, James Alexander, to drop off a draft of a recently concluded deposition, neatly, meticulously, folded his napkin and placed it onto the lace-covered table.

Luis pushed his chair back from the table. He raised his eyes and looked fleetingly at his wife; "That would be James and his wife Gloria. Please excuse me my dear."

As he left the dining room, he entered the parlor, which was awash with the soft glow from the strategically placed candles adorning the eight-foot high Christmas tree, standing majestically in the corner of the room.

Standing at the entrance to the room, was a tall angular man. With his right hand, the man was unbuttoning a heavy sheepskin coat. In his left hand he held a wide brimmed hat.

The brim of the man's hat was folded in the style that reminded Luis, of the headwear worn by westerners, the predominant characters depicted in the "Dime Novels" that he had given, so many years ago, to a very young, Jesse Billings.

Standing off to the side, behind the tall stranger, as if mesmerized by the huge evergreen tree, gazing with wonder, her face in profile, was a young woman.

Luis' initial impression of the woman was that she was young, she was neither tall, nor could she be described as short.

When she untied and removed her bonnet, the combined light given off by the burning, softly crackling, Yule log in the parlor's large hearth, and the light from the candles hanging from the Christmas tree, revealed her long, shoulder length tresses of reddish-blond hair.

As the woman turned to face Luis, the flickering light from the hearth, illuminated the two dimples recessed in her cheeks, and highlighted the young women's brilliant, crystal-clear, blue eyes.

Luis heart began to race. He placed his hand on his chest, and in a reverent whisper, he softly murmured; "Rebecca…?"

Then with growing, increasing conviction, the volume and intensity of his voice increased. "Becky, Becky, it's really you, oh my God, Becky, it is you.

Rebecca took a tentative step toward Luis. Luis rushed over to Rebecca and scooped her up into his arms.

****

Captain Samuel Smith, his wide-brimmed, high crowned Cowboy hat held tightly in his hand, remained standing motionless, in the vestibule.

Sam Smith's mind fleetingly reviewed the multitude of things that he had seen and experienced in his previous life as a seafarer, the years that he had spent living as a frontier's man with and among the Cheyenne Indians, combined with the past six years that he had shepherded scores of wagon trains, with hundreds of emigrants, across the continent.

During none of his many life adventures and experiences, had Sam Smith witnessed the degree of unbridled joy and happiness, flowing from… being so openly displayed, by this man, Luis Frazier.

This polished, erudite, accomplished scholarly man, who stood, unashamedly weeping with joy, the man that he presumed to be Rebecca Billings' Protector, her Benefactor, and Sam's correspondent, was the honorable Mr. Luis Frazier, Esq.

Sam Smith, the rugged frontiers' man, a man whose outlook on life had been forged from a vast and extensive, potpourri of life's experiences, stood perfectly still, speechless, dumbstruck.

****

CHAPTER 27

Samuel A. Smith – Seaman, Frontiersman, Wagon Train-Master

Samuel Smith, a man who had sailed and challenged the mighty Pacific Ocean. The rugged frontiers' man, who had fought and lived with the wild untamed, plains Indians.

Both Sam Smith and Luis Frazier had for nearly a year, been haunted, living with almost identical feelings of guilt. Guilt brought on, stoked and feed by the death of Henry Billings, and the abduction and captivity by the Comanche, of Henry's beloved daughter, Rebecca.

Samuel Smith, seafarer, frontiers-man, Wagon Master, and Luis Frazier, Esq., were two men with totally, diametrically, different backgrounds.

In 1826, at the tender age of eight, young Samuel had been orphaned and left alone in the world. A drunken sailor that she had been servicing had killed his mother Lilly, one of New York City's many water front prostitutes.

For four years, following his mother's death, young Samuel had survived on the docks, living by his wits.

Sam begged, he stole, and frequently to survive, he was force to sell the only thing of value that he owned, he sold his body.

It was one of Sam's sexual patrons, a young, handsomely rugged looking, merchant-ship's officer, who had suggested that Sam join him at sea, as his cabin boy.

The offer that guaranteed "three hots *(meals)* and a cot", had been to the desperate waif, a Godsend.

It was after three months at sea, during their first voyage as shipmates, when Sam's benefactor, the lecherous, ship's officer, mysteriously, while fulfilling his turn at the mid-watch, lost his balance and *"fell-overboard"*.

Sam's benefactor, his former client, was officially listed in the ship's log as, "Man Overboard - Lost at sea."

After years of sailing, plying the waters off the North American Pacific Coast, from San Diego to San Francisco, Sam had become increasingly fascinated with the panoply of dense, seemingly virgin, vegetation, and the abundance of wild-life, clearly visible from aboard ship.

Sam remembered having thought, "Oh my God, so this is what heaven looks like." It was then and there that Sam decided to quit, to abandon his life at sea.

Sam intended to spend the remainder of his — still very young life —, exploring and enjoying the land, the vast untamed wilderness of the North American Continent.

For the next 16 years, Sam lived his life, as a mountain man, trapping beaver, and living off the land. The last ten years Sam lived with and among the Cheyenne Indians.

It was following the massacre and mutilation of his Cheyenne wife and his two Cheyenne sons, during a raid by a Pawnee war party that Sam had decided to leave the world of the Cheyenne.

"Sails Big Canoe", the name given to Sam by the Cheyenne, returned to the world of the "Hair-mouths" as, Captain Sam Smith, Santa Fe Trail - Wagon-Master.

****

It was while serving as the Wagon Master of that ill-fated twenty-seven wagon, procession which included the Billings party, that Sam had let his desire for expedience — just five more miles —, overcome his duty, his responsibility to the protect, to ensure the safety of the settlers under his charge.

To this day, he lamented over and over in his mind, "I should have never left them alone.

Sam had left the Billings Party, Henry Billings, his daughter Rebecca, Rebecca's black Lady's Maid, Ruth, and Ruth's daughter, Mandy, the party's muleskinner Mr. Bruce Logan, and that big Swede fellow, the "Good Samaritan", alone to fix that damn busted wagon wheel."

Captain Smith would forever be plagued with guilt, anguish and remorse.

To this day, Captain Smith could not rid his mind of the horrific images that he saw at the scene of the massacre.

The mutilated bodies, of the men with their genitals stuffed into their mouths. The disfigurement, the cutting off of her breasts, that the Indians had inflicted on Ruth, the black woman, who for more than twenty years, had been Henry Billings mistress.

But most of all, Captain Smith, could not stop thinking of that pretty little blond white girl, and her servant, the cute little black girl, taken captive by the savages.

He was well aware of the brutality, the humiliation, and the frequent torture that the Indians routinely, reigned-down upon their captives.

Captain Smith knew from personal observation that female captives —including white female captives — were enslaved, and were routinely, and repeatedly raped by the warriors.

****

Chapter 28

Richmond Virginia - Home of Luis and Delilah Ann Frazier – January, 1864

Luis' feelings of guilt for Rebecca's captivity by hostile savages, stemmed from the professional and personal advice that he had given his best friend, Henry Billings.

Unable to raise, in a short period of time, the exorbitant amount of money demanded by unscrupulous scalawags, to prevent foreclosure on the Rosewood plantation, Luis had helped his best friend and protégé, Henry Billings, devise and implement, what they had called, "Plan B."

He was absolutely convinced that his advice and consul were instrumental in Henry's decision to emigrate, to take his family across the continent, through hostile, Indian Territory.

"Plan B", was the plan, the scheme, that Luis and Henry had concocted for, the Billings'; *"Resurrection"* of the Rosewood Plantation, on land west of the Mississippi River, given to Henry, by the Yankee Government.

Luis had suggested to Henry that he use his more than twenty year extra martial relationship, with his black slave Ruth, his *"side-piece"*, mistress, to take advantage of President Lincoln's "Homestead Act."

Through the simple act of granting Ruth the black slave-woman, with whom Henry had had a continuing twenty-two year sexual relationship her freedom, and on his behalf, have Luis his attorney and business manager, in her the *"freed slave"* Ruth Billings' name—, apply to the Yankee Government for a 160-Acre land grant.

The plan was that after five years, Henry Billings would buy the land from the *"free-woman of color,* Miss Ruth Billings. By that time, the passage of five years, Henry employing his vast knowledge of agriculture, and using his considerable resources, Rosewood would have been resurrected, in Lost Springs Kansas.

Had he not made Henry aware of the Yankee's passing of the "Homestead Act", and had he not suggested, and devised "Plan B", Luis fervently believed that his best friend, and his best friend's daughter, would still be alive.

And that this beautiful young girl—who now with the passage of time and life experiences, had most definitely become a woman—, this young woman who now stood before him, who he had held and rocked in his arms when she was an infant, who he had loved and cherished as if she were his own child, Rebecca Billings, would not have experienced the unspeakable horrors, that she had endured, and survived over the past year.

✱✱✱✱✱✱✱

Luis, his arm around her shoulder, escorted Rebecca to the long goose-down, stuffed sofa, facing the crackling Yule log in the large hearth.

The eight-foot evergreen, Christmas tree stood standing, as if it were a majestic sentinel, guarding the blazing Yule log.

The tree was trimmed with strings of cranberry garland. Strands of strung popcorn encircled the tree, and strategically placed miniature wax candles, illuminated the tree, and the room.

Rebecca's eyes began to well up with tears. Despite all of her resolve not to weep, not to show any semblance, any hint of shame, or weakness, silent tears cascaded down her cheeks.

It was at that very moment, in this family holiday setting, that Rebecca let herself truly believe, and fully accept that she was indeed safe, that she had returned from the nightmarish hell of living as a captive, a slave of primitive, savage, Indians.

Rebecca's prayers had been answered. She had been delivered, returned to the white world, the civilized world of white society.

Luis assisting Rebecca with the removal of her coat was aware of a slight shiver, a trembling of her shoulders, at Rebecca's futile attempt to suppress, or at least to conceal, her emotions.

As her coat slide from her shoulders, Luis could not help but notice the obvious swelling, the distention, of Rebecca's abdomen.

It was at that moment, as Luis stared at Rebecca in bewilderment and confusion, that his wife Delilah Anne entered the parlor.

Delilah Anne quickly with one glance took in the tableau before her and without thinking, blurted-out; *"Why Luis—that girl's pregnant!"*

✱✱✱✱✱✱✱✱✱✱✱✱✱

Chapter 29

Richmond Virginia –Home of Luis and Delilah Ann Frazier 1864

To her surprise and dismay, Rebecca had found it awkward and surprisingly, oddly, difficult to reenter the "white world." A world, a lifestyle, that she had longed for, pined for, every minute, every hour, every day, of the nearly a year that she was being held captive by the Comanche.

Following her return to the "white world", Rebecca's collective experiences with her white brethren, had gradually forced her to conclude, and to accept, that life for her in the "white world", would never be the same.

Instead of her being welcomed as one who had had the courage to endure, and to escape her nightmare. One who had survived, the ordeal of a years' captivity as a slave of the Comanche, she was instead being criticized, ostracized, blamed, and shamed, for having had the temerity to survive, to have lived, to have returned to the "white world."

To Rebecca, this "white world", this world of white privilege, to which she had been born, this society, built upon the backs of black slaves, people who themselves and their descendants would by law, in perpetuity, be enslaved, this "white world" now to her, seemed to be, somehow distasteful and repugnant.

When she and her sister Mandy, her former black slave, had been taken prisoner by the Comanche, for the first time in her young pampered life, Rebecca had actually experienced the humiliation, the degradation, of being treated as if she were less than human.

In the land of the Comanche, Rebecca and Mandy, her former slave, sisters who were born three days apart, fathered by the same white man, Henry Billings, Master of the Rosewood Plantation, were now truly equals.

Both sisters one white, the other black, were slaves of the Comanche.

As slaves, they were both treated as if they were property, chattel, horses or dogs, owned by their masters and mistresses. The masters that they had all of their lives, been taught were savage, barbarians; the vicious, red-skinned Indians.

On many occasions following her repatriation, during the night Rebecca, as she lay safe in Luis and Delilah's house, on the silk sheets, spread across her canopied bed, tossing and turning, she would stare at the ceiling, attempting to by sheer will-power, will herself to sleep.

Invariably being unable to fall asleep, Rebecca's mind would wander.

She would reluctantly relive and recall, the time that she and her sister Mandy were held captive, slaves of the Comanche.

Rebecca would involuntarily shake and tremble, as she relived in her mind the incessant, frequent, beatings rained down upon her by her principal antagonist, her Comanche master's grandmother, an old practically toothless squaw, known to the "People" as *"Hen's Teeth."*

****

Rebecca and Mandy had been the sole survivors, when their disabled wagon was attacked by a group of marauding, bloodthirsty, Tonkawa Indians.

Henry Billings, Rebecca and Mandy's father, and Mandy's mother Ruth, the Billings' recently manumitted slave, were both slaughtered and mutilated, by the Tonkawa.

While fleeing from the Tonkawa attack, the two sisters, Rebecca and Mandy were captured by a small Comanche scouting party, a group consisting of three Comanche warriors.

Stone Fist, one of the three Comanche warriors, who captured or as the girls would later discover, rescued the sisters, was for his bravery and tenacity in the battle against the Tonkawa, awarded the white captive, Rebecca.

Among the numerous tribes of plains Indians, Stone Fist was well known and regarded as one of the fiercest, and the most lethal, of the Comanche warriors.

For centuries those warriors that owned slaves captured in battle, could do as they pleased, with his captive slaves. Rebecca Billings, formerly of Virginia's grandiose, Rosewood Plantation, was the property of Stone Fist.

Running Eagle, Stone Fist's confidant and closest friend, the young brave who had been the leader of the Comanche scouting party, took Rebecca's black sister, Rebecca's former slave, Mandy.

After having been herself a slave, treated as a slave for six months, Rebecca had slowly come to question, and to finally reject a lifetime of prejudice, and self-serving economic propaganda.

For sixteen years, she had absorbed from her parents, her peers, and from her religious leaders, pious reasoning for the *"moral-acceptance "of human bondage,* had been drilled into her head. Rebecca had been misled, by a society, a culture, attempting to defend and to justify the South's *"peculiar-institution"*, slavery.

Rebecca Elizabeth Billings had been born, the only daughter of Henry and Margaret Billings, the Master and Mistress of Virginia's, renowned, enormously successful, Rosewood Cotton Plantation.

For her entire life, as a female member of the *"Planter"* class, she had been lavished with love, pampered, and treated as befits one who is symbolic, of the perceived image of Southern femininity.

At the age of fourteen, on the brink of the transition from girlhood, to that of a young woman, Rebecca Billings exuded an aura of beauty, innocence, and chastity.

Young Rebecca Billings was the epitome of the white, Southern Belle.

Rebecca had lived the sheltered and pampered life, of a delicate daughter of the Southern Aristocracy.

The environment in which Rebecca was raised, was one that surrounded, enveloped her, and exposed her to the beliefs, the values and the teachings espoused by her religious leaders, her family, her friends, and by her slave holding neighbors, whose wealth and prosperity was dependent upon their ready access to slave labor.

Slave labor, the "free" labor that provided the intense, backbreaking labor that supported the Plantation society, of the agrarian South.

Miss Eleanor Leary, the tutor hired by Henry Billings to teach his children the "Classics", had taught Rebecca, and unbeknownst to Henry, had taught Rebecca's slave Mandy, the history of slavery as it had existed and was practiced, by the ancient Roman and Greek civilizations.

Miss Leary had explained that while these European, white civilizations, would enslave enemies captured as a result of armed conflict, the captured slaves were given the opportunity in time, to gain their freedom.

And once free, the former slaves were allowed to assimilate, and to become accepted as citizens in that society.

Rebecca had, over time, to a large extent, come to attribute the sanctioned, lawful, practice of enslaving blacks by whites—with the black slaves having no chance for freedom and assimilation into the white society—, to the readily observable, physical differences between the black slaves, and their white masters.

The masters were the ruling class, the descendants of white, Europeans who had immigrated to America. While the slaves consisted of blacks, who either themselves or their parents, had been uprooted from their African-Homeland; chained and shackled below the decks of filthy slave ships, and transported, for sale, to the American South.

When she was a five-year-old child, growing up in the constant company of her, likewise five-year-old slave playmate Mandy, Rebecca had innocently asked her mother; "Mother… why can't Mandy and her brother Jason, sit with us when you teach me my 'ABC's'?

She had been told — actually she had been lectured, by her mother and by her father; by the family, and by her friends —, that; "They're not like us. They don't look like us. They don't talk like us. They are inferior creatures, sub-humans. They will never be our equals. They can never be your friends. They are our property!"

****

To the people living in the South, one of the most devastating and insidious affects of the onset of the Civil War was the steady, spiraling, downward trend, of the Southern economy.

The rapid rising of the rate of inflation, with the concomitant devaluation of Confederate currency, did not portend well for the stability, and the viability of the Confederacy.

The loss of his son and his wife, and the nefarious business activities of "scalawags", engaged in dubious transactions that threatened his claim to ownership of his home, were instrumental factors that had led to Henry Billings' decision, to leave Rosewood.

His decision to abandon his family's Rosewood Plantation, and to relocate himself and his daughter, to the vast, "free", fertile, virgin lands, west of the Mississippi River.

Prior to her father's decision to immigrate to the west, Rebecca—with one notable exception, that being her personal slave Mandy —, Rebecca had tacitly come to believe in the racial superiority of whites, and the innately, inherent, inferiority, of blacks.

These basic core beliefs that had been constantly drilled into her head served as the bedrock, the foundation for her life-long acceptance and support of the South's "peculiar-institution", the legalized enslavement of blacks.

Now after her personal ordeal, after having been herself, made a slave, of losing her independence, after having loss her right to free choice, for the first time, Rebecca had come to question her core beliefs.

Rebecca had been converted.

Rebecca was now of the belief that prejudice and bigotry, were corrosive and damaging, even to her people, white people.

She had come to believe that, human bondage was insidiously, morally damaging and would eventually be detrimental, to the lives of those whites, who sanctioned defended, championed, and advocated for the preservation and the expansion, of the South's source of free labor, the enslavement of persons of African descent.

Rebecca vividly recalled, those quiet serene nights on the vast, empty prairie, under the ever-vigilant eyes of the three Comanche warriors, when she and her black sister Pretty Buffalo Hair (*Mandy*), quietly talked.

As they sat alone, apart from the three warriors — who were returning her to her white world—, she and her black sister, would sit, staring at the heavens.

Two solitary figures, sisters adrift on the endless, treeless-prairie, staring at the black sky dotted, with its countless, thousands, millions, of bright stars, Rebecca remembered discussing, with her sister, her evolving, and heartfelt negative feelings, her doubts about the morality, of the practice of slavery.

Once—with the help of her sister Pretty Buffalo Hair (Mandy), who had chosen to remain with, and to become a Comanche—when after she had successfully escaped from her-bondage, when she had been returned to the "white-world", Rebecca once, and only once, had questioned the depth of her "conversion". Her conversion from having been a life-long proponent of slavery, to one who now, believed in the total abolition of slavery.

Was her change of attitude a matter of true moral, conviction? Or was her conversion merely a matter of expedience, of shear desperation?

Had she truly, really, sincerely, rejected her heritage, or was she, even if sub-conscientiously, merely pandering to *Pretty Buffalo Hair* (Mandy), in order to gain her black sister's assistance in helping her to escape from the Comanche?

Rebecca had herself, for eight months, been a slave of the Comanche.

After her life as a slave of the Comanche, for what to her had been an interminable eight months, Rebecca had slowly come to question, and to finally, to reject sixteen years, a lifetime of prejudice, and propaganda, that had been drilled into her head, defending and justifying the South's "peculiar-institution", slavery.

After countless hours of sleepless reflection, laying on these luxurious… oh so soft, silk sheets, in "Uncle Luis's and Aunt Delilah's townhouse, tossing and turning, attempting to find a comfortable position for her expanding abdomen, Rebecca had eventually, finally, with absolute certainty and convection, come to believe, and to accept the truth, to her, an absolute truth.

That slavery is evil, vile, and morally corrupt. Slavery should be abolished!

****

Chapter 30

Richmond Virginia - March, 1864

Delilah had at first, been shocked, and appalled when that crude frontiers'- man Captain Samuel Smith, a little more than four months earlier, had shown up unexpected, on their doorstep. Shown up with "that white-squaw", Rebecca Billings, in tow.

"That white-squaw" was the pejorative, derogatory, term that Delilah and her sisters, Beatrice and Cynthia, routinely used when they were alone, and they were discussing Rebecca.

Delilah's youngest sister Cynthia had been stunned when Delilah had first informed her and Beatrice, of Rebecca's existence; Apoplectic when she was told that Rebecca had arrived in a state of advanced pregnancy.

And simply mortified when Delilah spoke of Luis's determination to have "that fallen-woman", "that white-squaw", who he called his niece, live with them, as a member his and Delilah's, and by extension, Cynthia and Beatrice's families.

It was at the beginning of the second week of Rebecca's stay with the Frazier's', that after two weeks of virtual seclusion, a distraught Rebecca, had finally, reluctant and timidly, sought out Luis, and asked "*Uncle Looey*", for his assistance, for his advice.

Luis was sitting, sipping brandy and puffing on an aromatic cheroot. A thin haze of white smoke wafted slowly toward the ceiling.

While reading the news, of the Confederate Army's latest exploits in their prosecution of the war, he had been fixated, engrossed with a brief, strikingly, succinct, paragraph.

A deep furrow appeared, and intensified in his forehead, as he read the lead article, on the front page of the Richmond Gazette:

NEGRO SOLDIERS CAPTURED

Four Yankee negro soldiers, captured in James City County, were brought to this city yesterday, and delivered at the Libby Prison.
The four negroes, where then placed into the solitary cells of the Yankee officers.
This is a taste of negro equality, we fancy; the said Yankee officers will not fancy overmuch.

Luis' initial reaction to the article, was an exacerbation, an amplification of the intensity, of the rage that he, and the vast majority of his Southern compatriots had felt, when on July 17, 1862, the Yankee Congress passed that abominable piece of legislation the; "Second Confiscation and Militia Act."

Luis's facial muscles contracted. A scowl of displeasure swept over his face. Luis recalled the angry, righteous, indignation, and the torrent of invectives, and blasphemous, words that he and his cohorts had heaped upon the Yankee Congress, during their weekly poker game.

The Confiscation and Militia Act served to formally free those slaves, whose masters were serving in the Confederate Army. The freed slaves were now being classified by the Union, as being, "*Contraband* of War."

Luis recalled that as early as mid 1862, Confederate military and civilian government officials, had been increasingly, becoming alarmed, at the numbers of slaves — now officially called by the Yankees, "contraband" —, runaways, attempting to join the Union Army.

The "contraband-soldiers, were being used by the Yankees, as laborers. They dug entrenchments, cooked and cleaned for the white troops. They transported munitions, the "contrabands", thus far the contrabands, had not been allowed to fight in combat.

The prohibition against fighting, the killing of white southerners, was not due to a sense of morale propriety.

Luis as did the Confederate General Staff, knew that the reason, that the black soldiers, were not being committed to combat, was because of political considerations.

Those in positions of power, both in the North and in the South, knew that the reason for President Lincoln's reluctance to *"Pull the cork from the bottle"*, *"To unleash the hounds of hell"*, that is the unleashing of the armed black soldier, to fight against his former white master, was not due to feelings of racial superiority, nor was it due to racial loyalty, held by *"That Black-Baboon"* sitting in the White House, Abraham Lincoln.

Those in power, on both sides of the war, knew that Lincoln was afraid that the mere thought — that of black men, killing white men —, would lead Maryland, Delaware, Kentucky, and Missouri, the four border states that had remained loyal to the Union, to secede, and to join with, and to fight for the Confederacy.

Luis recalled that fateful day last year, when in May of 1863, when the Union Government officially announced the establishment of the Bureau of Colored Troops.

Due to the failure of the Union army to achieve significant victories in the East, and to the declining morale, and recruitment of soldiers in the North, President Abraham Lincoln had finally decided to allow blacks to enlist as combat soldiers, in the Union Army.

He recalled having thought at the time, that Lincoln had finally, done the unthinkable.

Lincoln, a white man, had signed a law that legalized and encouraged blacks to bear arms, to fight, to kill, white men. Lincoln had *"Pulled the cork from the bottle"*; Abraham Lincoln had indeed, unleashed the hounds of hell!

Slowly as he began to evaluate the subtlety and the irony of the reporter's prose, the furrows of annoyance itched into Luis's forehead, began to gradually dissipate.

Luis reread the last sentence of the article. He especially, appreciated the sarcasm of the last sentence:

"This is a taste of negro equality, we fancy, the said Yankee officers will not fancy overmuch."

His clinched facial muscles relaxed. A wry smile, replaced the previous scow of displeasure.

Luis rolled his cigar between the thumb and forefinger of his right hand, and softly mumbled; "Let's see how long it takes those damn Yankee officers, being forced to live in those cramped cells with those filthy Nigras, before they come to their senses and change their minds, about white men and blacks, being equal."

****

Rebecca tentatively, timidly, knocked on the doorframe. Luis with a look of annoyance raised his eyes. Rebecca stood, head bowed, her hands demurely clasped together.

When Luis realized that it was Rebecca seeking his attention, a broad smile spread across his face.

Luis placed his cigar in the ashtray on the coffee table, folded his newspaper, and enthusiastically waved his arm; "Rebecca, please, please come in…have a seat."

Luis stood, he waved his hand pointing toward one of the easy chairs indicating that the now very pregnant Rebecca, be seated.

Rebecca slowly eased herself into the chair to which, Luis was pointing.

Luis stood, picked up the crystal decanter of still cool spring water sitting on the table, and filled two glasses.

He walked over to Rebecca, and handed her one of the glasses. Luis then picked-up, and repositioned the rooms vacant chair, next to Rebecca.

He was cautiously, pleased, and delighted that Rebecca appeared to be ready to talk, to break out from her self-imposed isolation.

To the best of his knowledge, the fact that Rebecca was pregnant, and in all likelihood, had been impregnated by a wild Indian, had not been a topic discussed by Rebecca with anyone, certainly not with him.

Rebecca, held the glass to her lips, and sipped the now tepid water. It was apparent to Luis that she was extremely uncomfortable.

In an attempt to put her at ease, Luis too, sipped from his glass. He did not speak. He did not press her. Luis had concluded that when Rebecca was ready to talk about her horrific ordeal, she would.

After a moment of uncomfortable silence, Rebecca slowly, carefully, sat her glass down on the carpet beside her chair. She continued to hold in her hand, the cloth napkin that Luis had wrapped around her water glass.

Rebecca remained silent, nervously twisting the napkin that she held in her hands. Her eyes were fixed on the wall directly behind Luis's head.

Luis sat motionless, upright in his chair, patiently, attentive, waiting for Rebecca to speak.

Rebecca lowered her gaze. Her eyes met those of her benefactor, her savior, Luis Frazier, her father's best friend, her very own *"Uncle Looey."*

"Mandy and I, were witness to the slaughter and the mutilation, by those godless, wild, cannibalistic, savages, of our father Henry, and Mandy's mother Ruth."

Luis was momentarily taken aback, stunned, when Rebecca, either un- intentionally, or purposefully, acknowledged that Henry Billings was both her, and the black slave girl Mandy's, father.

Although the widespread practice of white male slave masters — more often than not, by force—, having had routine, frequent, sexual relations with their black female slaves, was a well known *"secret"*, the acknowledgement of offspring, that resulted from these sexual encounters, was strictly taboo.

The physical similarity between the two girls, one white the other black; their striking resemblance to Henry, including the distinctive, delightful dimples in their cheeks, over the years had led many a visitor to the Rosewood Plantation, to discretely speculate as to who was the beautiful slave girl's, biological father.

To acknowledge the children of these liaisons was most definitely not, in accordance with the norms of *"polite"*, Southern society.

Luis, as Henry Billings' best friend and confidant, had for years; been aware that Henry was the slave girl Mandy's, father.

Luis vividly remembered one particular evening, when he and Henry were relaxing, smoking cigars and drinking bourbon, Henry had confided in him.

On that particular occasion, in Luis's office, sharing smooth aged whiskey with his closest friend, Henry's normal reserve, had led to a loosening of his tongue.

Since Henry had broached the subject, Luis had decided to, finally throw caution to the wind, to once again ask out-right.

Spurred on by curiosity and having had consumed a considerable amount of fine Kentucky bourbon, Luis cautiously inquired as to the parentage, of Henry's daughter's perpetual playmate and companion, the beautiful, obviously, mulatto slave girl Mandy. Mandy who was an exact, darker version of Henry's beautiful blond, blue-eyed daughter, Rebecca.

"You know Luis, I'm only human. Over the years, like any healthy white man, I've had the urge to sample some "*dark meat*." But during all of those years, I've only lain with one slave."

Henry poured himself another drink and had chuckled, "I know what you're thinking. I've owned hundreds of fine "high yellow", mahogany-brown, and ebony, black as night, wenches. It's hard to believe, but it's true, that I've had only one."

"For more than twenty years—other than with the love of my live, my beloved, wife Margaret—, Ruth, the mother of the black slave girl Mandy, is the only woman, white or black, that I've had sexual relations with."

Henry glanced at his friend. He noted the look of skepticism in Luis's blue eyes. Henry placed his right hand on Luis's shoulder, and gave a gentle, yet firm squeezed.

"It's true that Ruth was the only one. But it's also true that the slave Ruth and I, for more than twenty years, at least five times a week, we fucked like bunnies."

When Luis, himself a little unsteady, asked if by chance Henry's twenty-year dalliance with the slave woman, what was her name…?"

"Henry had burped and answered, "Ruth, her name is Ruth. Henry had reached for the crystal liquor decanter, and in slurred inebriated — for him rather crude language —, confessed that he, was the "sire", the "contributor, the ejaculator of the sperm", that had "*come*", to result in the birth of the slave girl, Mandy.

****

Rebecca's audible sigh jolted Luis from his reverie. Rebecca took a deep breath, and then continued.

"While daddy and our guide Mr. Logan, were changing the splintered wagon wheel, he had asked that Mandy and I, lead the horses to water."

"We had recently, no more than twenty minutes earlier, crossed a small stream. The stream was approximately a quarter mile from our crippled wagon."

"When we first heard those terrifying screams from the attacking Indians, Mandy and I were petrified, paralyzed with fear. My immediate instinctive response was to run back to the wagon. Mandy grabbed my arm and dragged me toward the horses, she was shouting; "run Becky, run."

"One of our horses, daddy's stallion, had broken loose and fled onto the prairie. Mandy swung up onto the back of the horse that had not bolted. I thought that she was going to abandon me. Instead she turned and rode back for me."

"Riding double, we fled. Just when I was beginning to think that we had escaped, I heard the sound of horses galloping behind us. Sobbing and clinging to Mandy's waist, I looked over my shoulder and saw three, half naked savages, their bodies streaked with black and red paint, about to overtake us.”

“Instead of stopping us, the three painted demons, wildly kicking their horses, raced by. The three demons from hell, who had killed my father and Mandy’s mother, were themselves being chased by three, screaming, half naked, Indians.”

“Mandy frantically turned the head of our horse, away from the flight of the fleeing painted demons, and their pursuers”

“Both Mandy and I were unabashedly crying, when we were overtaken by the three Indians, who had been in pursuit of the painted savages.”

Rebecca began to tremble. Luis rose from his chair bent down and gently placed his arms around the distraught young woman, the girl — now clearly a young woman — that he had known and cherished, since her birth.

For several moments, Rebecca remained with her head cradled against Luis’s shoulder, crying softly

Finally, she raised her head. Rebecca accepted the large linen, men’s handkerchief that Luis handed her, and wiped her red-rimmed eyes.

She looked up into the now stormy, blue eyes of her benefactor; “He raped me Uncle Luis! Stone Fist raped me, over and over.

Again, and again, and again *Uncle Looey*, that beast that animal, Stone Fist, raped me!” Rebecca and her “*Uncle Looey*” sat in silence. She sat silently weeping, her shoulders heaving, her head resting in his lap. Luis sat, enraged, on the arm of the chair. They were both, silently, sobbing.

****

After several minutes, Rebecca clumsily, struggled to her feet. Luis clasped her hands in his and assisted her. She returned the handkerchief to Luis, and with both hands, massaged her swollen belly.

“Uncle Luis, what am I to do? As Aunt Delilah pointed out, two weeks ago, upon my arrival, I’m pregnant. Not only am I pregnant, I’m carrying the spawn of a Comanche warrior. Stone Fist, the one being on this Earth, that I hate above all others.”

Rebecca placed her hands over her eyes, and took a deep, cleansing breath. Slowly she slid her hands from her eyes, placed them under her chin, and cupped her face.

With tears, once again welling-up in her eyes, in a piteous, pleading voice she again asked; “What am I to do? I’m carrying a monster, a barbaric, heathen savage.”

“*Uncle Looey*, what am I to do?” Stoically, she wiped a tear from her eye, and calmly, resolutely, in a clear, determined voice, asked;

E. Pluribus Unum

"What can I do?"

Luis' heart went out to Rebecca. This beautiful young woman, his niece, this child Luis had caught, and mentally made note of Rebecca's at first referring to him as "Uncle Luis, then under heightening stress, reverting to *"Uncle Looey—*, was his responsibility.

Luis knew that until the day he died, he would always feel an unrelenting sense of guilt for the death of Rebecca's father, and consequently, guilt for Rebecca's suffering at the hands of those savages.

After all, he was the one who had concocted, "Plan-B", and had suggested that Henry use, pervert, Lincoln's Homestead Act, to swindle the Yankees out of 160 acres, of prime, virgin, farmland.

If not for his ego, his supposedly superior knowledge of, and ability to manipulate the law, Henry Billings would have never taken his family into hostile Indian Territory.

Luis placed his hands onto Rebecca's shoulders, and looked deeply into her eyes. Although the whites of her eyes were red-rimmed, the irises were crystal clear, bright blue.

He saw in Rebecca's eyes, strength and determination. Luis gently squeezed her shoulders and in a sympathetic, yet firm voice spoke; "You and I, tomorrow, together, we'll go see Doctor Sawyer."

****

Chapter 31

Richmond Virginia – Office of Theodore Sawyer, M.D. - March 1864

Dr. Theodore Sawyer had served as the principal, physician for the people of Richmond, and its surrounding counties, for almost a half century.

In 1859, after forty-five years of delivering babies, setting broken bones, and seeing to the health of the populace, Dr. Theodore P. Sawyer looked forward, with a great deal of anticipation, to retiring.

After finding and training, Dr. Reginald Jacobs, a qualified potential young replacement, Dr. Sawyer had felt, as did the community, that he had more than earned, the right to relax, to retire.   To as he put it, just go fishing!

Dr. Sawyer had planned to spend the rest of his life, his golden years, in blissful freedom. A life devoid of urgent, unpredictable, summonses, day and night, to attend to the ailments of the community.

In retirement, Dr. Sawyer had had every intention of living a life of blissful leisure. Free to commune exclusively with nature, and to spend his time, matching wits with the fishes that inhabited the James River.

Dr. Sawyer had looked forward to at last… to removing the hand carved wooden shingle, suspended over the door to his office:

Dr. Theodore P. Sawyer, MD

And replacing it with a a far less distinguished shingle, that simply read:

GONE FISHING

Unfortunately, the onset of the war between the North and South, had thrown a wrench into Dr. Sawyer's plans.

After a mere two and a half years as Dr. Sawyer's replacement, young Reginald Jacobs, MD, the young twenty-eight-year-old physician, whom Dr. Sawyer had meticulously, handpicked and trained as his successor, abruptly, spoiled Theodore P. Sawyer, MD's plans, for a long blissful, retirement.

Shortly following the South's decisive July 16, 1861 victory, at Bull Run, in a moment of youthful zeal and patriotism, young Reginald Jacobs, MD, had on a whim, without having given prior advanced notice, joined the Confederate Army.

Dr. Sawyer—who quite frankly was becoming increasingly, maddeningly bored spending his days fishing—, abandoned his fishing pole, and eagerly returned to the practice of medicine.

****

At the conclusion of his physical examination of his patient, Dr. Sawyer, instructed Rebecca to get dressed, and to join him in his office.

Rebecca, now fully clothed, knocked on the frame of the adjoining door, which separated the examining room, from the doctor's office.

The doctor was seated at his desk, quill in hand, writing notes on a sheet of paper. To his right was a door which lead to his living room, which Rebecca had noted when she and Luis arrived, served as the doctor's waiting room.

On the wall behind his desk was a framed copy of his medical degree. Two wooden shelves, that housed numerous medical textbooks, framed the framed, medical diploma.

Rebecca sat nervously, waiting for Dr. Sawyer to speak. As he continued to write, her eyes roamed around the small office. She was able to read the old English script on his framed diploma:

THE TRUSTEES OF
UNIVERSITY OF PENNSYLVANIA
SCHOOL OF MEDICINE

CONFER UPON

Theodore P. Sawyer

THE DEGREE OF

Doctor of Medicine
MAY TWENTY-FIFTH EIGHTEEN HUNDRED AND NINE

****

Dr. Sawyer placed his quill in the inkwell. He folded his hands on his desk. "Welcome Home Rebecca. I can't begin to describe to you, how delighted I was to here the news of your safe return."

Rebecca blushed. "Thank you, doctor. If I might, I would like to ask of you, a small favor."

Dr. Sawyer sat back in his chair. "Of course." Rebecca leaned forward in her chair; "I would very much appreciate having my Uncle Luis join us."

Dr. Sawyer admonished himself for his lack of sensibility. The beautiful young woman seated before him was, understandably frightened, fragile.

He as had everyone in Richmond, had heard of the massacre, almost a year ago, that had befallen the Henry Billings party, at the hands of brutal, savage, Indians, during the Billings' attempt to settle on open, fertile virgin land, west of the Mississippi River.

Dr. Sawyer recalled the elation that he had felt, when just a short two weeks ago, there occurred, what many had called *"The Christmas Miracle."*

Rebecca Billings was rescued, returned to civilization, into the care of Luis Frazier, Henry Billings' best friend, and Luis's wife, Delilah.

Dr. Sawyer stood, and walked around his desk. He gently took Rebecca's hands in his; "As you wish. Of course, my dear, I have no objection to Mr. Frazier's joining us."

He released Rebecca's hands, walked over to the door that led to his waiting room; "Mr. Frazier—, Luis, who had been glancing at a copy of the newspaper, with concern clearly visible on his face, looked up.

In addition to Luis, there were ten other people seated in the waiting room. Dr. Sawyer, seeing the look of alarm on Luis's face, smiled.

Dr. Sawyer, with the door held slightly ajar, gestured; "Mr. Frazier, if you please…"

Luis somewhat mollified by the doctor's smile, recovered his equanimity. He folded and placed the newspaper, on his now vacant chair, and entered Dr. Sawyer's office.

Dr. Sawyer pointed to the unoccupied chair, next to Rebecca. Rebecca and Luis's chairs were approximately a foot apart.

Rebecca reached for her uncle's hand, as Dr. Sawyer seated himself behind his desk.

"First, Mr. Frazier, am I correct in my assumption that you are Rebecca's uncle?"

Before Luis could answer, Rebecca interjected; "Uncle Luis and I, are not related by blood. However, I have known Uncle Luis for the entirety of my life.

He is, …was my father's closest friend. He is the only one, he and Aunt Delilah, they are the only family that I have."

Luis reached into the breast pocket of his waistcoat, and produced, what appeared to the doctor, to be a legal document.

Dr. Sawyer reached for his wire-rimmed spectacles. He looped the wires around his ears, leaned over his desk, and slowly, meticulously, and began to read the officious, legalistic-looking, document:

The Last Will and Testament of Henry Billings:

I Henry Artimas Billings, being of full age, and of sound mind and memory, hereby make publish and declare this instrument to be my Last Will and Testament, hereby revoking all prior Wills and Codicils.

Item I

I have one living child, and heir, Rebecca Elizabeth Billings, who as of the date of execution of this, my Last Will and Testament, has reached the age of sixteen.

Item II

Real Property and Monetary Assets

I bequeath all of my assets; capital, bonds; ownership, interest in any and all real property and real estate to my one and only surviving child, Rebecca Elizabeth Billings.

I here by bequeath any and all of my monetary assets to interest to my one and only surviving child, Rebecca Elizabeth Billings.

Item III

Executor of My Estate:

I appoint Mr. Luis Frazier, Esq., my closest friend and business associate, as Executor of my estate, and if my death precedes her reaching her majority, her 21st birth date, Luis Frazier, as the legal guardian of my only surviving child, Rebecca Elizabeth Billings.

IN WITNESS WHEREOF:

I have here unto set my hand to this, my Last Will and Testament.

The 10th day of March, in the year of our lord, 1863

Henry Billings   *Dated: March 10, 1863*
City: Richmond: State: Virginia: Nation: CSA

Signature 1st Witness Signature 2nd Witness

---

*Luis Frazier*___ **Dated: March 10, 1863** *Ralph Williams*___ **Dated: March 10, 1863**
City: Richmond: State: Virginia: Nation: CSA City:
Richmond: State: Virginia: Nation: CSA

Satisfied that Luis Frazier, was in fact Rebecca's legal guardian, and had both a moral and a legal right to be present; the doctor removed his glasses, and sat back in his chair.

Dr. Sawyer sat forward, placed his elbows on the desk, and interlaced the fingers of his right and left hand together.

He pointed the index finger of his right hand at Rebecca's swollen abdomen, and spoke directly to Luis; "Mr. Frazier, other than the obvious fact that she's pregnant, and that in itself speaks of her being a healthy female, considering the ordeal that she has so recently experienced, Rebecca is in remarkably good health."

Rebecca disengaged her hand from Luis. She firmly set her feet on the floor and straightened her back.

It was obvious to both Dr. Sawyer and to Luis, that Rebecca was gathering her thoughts… that she was carefully gathering her thoughts, searching, attempting to find the right words before speaking.

After a brief, but awkward moment of silence, Dr. Sawyer spoke; "Rebecca, would you like to speak?"

Rebecca took a deep breath; "I cannot bear the thought of giving birth to a savage heathen. Each time that this thing… this monster inside my belly kicks, I become faint, lightheaded."

A single tear trickled down her cheek. Rebecca wiped the solitary tear from her face.

Luis reached for her hand. Instead of taking his reassuring proffered hand, Rebecca folded her hands in her lap. In a firm steely voice, she proclaimed: "I do not, want to give birth, to Stone Fist's papoose!"

Although Dr. Sawyer had concluded that Rebecca's pregnancy, was most likely due to her having been violated during her long period of captivity by the Comanche, he had been momentarily confused and surprised by Rebecca's vehement, emphatic statement; "I do not want to give birth to Stone Fist's papoose!"

Seeing the brief flicker of confusion in the doctor's eyes, Luis quickly explained that the savage, who had continually, raped Rebecca, was an especially brutal Comanche warrior, whose name was Stone Fist.

Rebecca looked from Luis to Dr. Sawyer. Dr. Sawyer met Rebecca's sorrowful, pleading eyes.

The doctor — over the course of his more than fifty years of practicing medicine —, had seen on many occasions, that same pleading, imploring expression, on the faces of countless, desperate women, who had found themselves forced to live with an unwanted pregnancy.

                                                                 E. Pluribus Unum

Dr. Sawyer frowned. His mind began to race; *"She's going to ask me to abort her unborn child"*.

Dr. Theodore Sawyer, as were most of his fellow physicians, was adamantly opposed to abortion.

However, unlike many of his medical colleagues, whose opposition to abortion was based primarily upon economic interests, Dr. Sawyer's objections were based purely upon his belief, in the sanctity and the preservation of human life.

It was well known, that one of the prevailing, driving forces behind the medical community's opposition to abortion, was by many, motivated by a significant number of physicians' attempts, to eliminate the practice of midwifery.

Midwives, women who delivered babies, frequently attended to the "female-needs", of women who could not afford the services of a physician.
It was a well-known fact that Midwives charged considerably less for their services, than that charged by the doctors. Midwives performed abortions.
Most physicians thought of Midwifery as being a threat to their economic power, as well as being a threat to their social standing and prestige.

Dr. Sawyer's objections to abortion however, were based purely upon his belief, in the sanctity and the preservation of human life.

Dr. Sawyer was by no means under the illusion that, his refusal, or for that matter, the unlikely refusal of all doctors to perform abortions, would end the practice of terminating unwanted pregnancies.

> He was not naïve. Dr. Sawyer was well aware and knew — throughout history, probably since the beginning of time — that females; girls, and women have always sought ways to end unwanted pregnancies.

He was also cognizant of the fact that unfortunately, far too many of the females, out of desperation, attempting to terminate unwanted pregnancies, resorted to crude, often dangerous, lethal methods.

All to often, Dr. Sawyer had been hastily summoned, in desperate attempts, to save the lives of usually, often hopelessly hemorrhaging, moribund, females, suffering the tragic after-effects of "botched" abortions.

Botched abortions induced by the insertion of foreign objects, such as knitting needles, coat hangers; iron spokes from broken wagon wheels, into the vagina and the uterus.

Botched abortions induced by douching with caustic solutions such as lye diluted with vinegar. Taking by mouth, strong drugs and/or toxic herbal-plant extracts.

The moral and professional underpinning, the foundation of Theodore Sawyer's belief system, was his steadfast adherence to, and his belief in two sacred doctrines; the *"Golden Rule"*, and the physician's *"Hippocratic Oath."*

The "Golden Rule", the Judeo-Christian tenet to; "Do unto others as you would have them, do unto you."

And his pledge to *"First, Do No Harm."* Words contained in the "Hippocratic Oath", the pledge that he had sworn to, upon his graduation from medical school.

Dr. Sawyer's professional ethics were steadfastly based upon his sworn commitment, his promise, to *"First, Do No Harm."*

Dr. Sawyer's professional life, indeed his entire life, was based upon his commitment to life. To live by two sacred promises, that he *"Do unto others as he would have them, do unto him."* And his sacred pledge as a physician, his promise to *"First, do no harm."*

****

The one and only benefit that Dr. Sawyer could ascribe to his brief retirement, other then his few fishing sorties, was that paradoxically, his time away from practicing medicine, had given him the opportunity, the time to make himself familiar with the rapidly changing, face of medicine.

He was amazed at how far behind, how out of date; he was in keeping abreast of the relatively recent explosion of scientific knowledge.

In Europe, the work of Luis Pasteur, the French Chemist and Microbiologist; the contributions of Germany's Robert Koch, and closer to home, the work of a young American physician, a Boston Yankee, Horatio Robinson Storer.

Dr. Storer had been one of the first physicians, to establish a medical practice that concentrated exclusively, on the medical needs of women.

Young Dr. Storer was definitely making his mark in medicine. Dr. Storer had gained fame and recognition, as being the first surgeon to remove the uterus of a human, pregnant female.

Horatio Robinson Storer, M.D., was acknowledged by the medical community, as having been the physician responsible for the creation of the medical specialty, Gynecology.

In addition to his recognized by his colleagues, acclaimed knowledge and skill as a physician and surgeon, Dr. Storer was especially admired by Dr. Sawyer, for his staunch advocacy, his heralded role as one of the leaders of the movement currently sweeping the country; *"The Physicians Crusade Against Abortion."*

The Physicians Crusade Against Abortion was the national movement, which led to the passage of strict, anti-abortion laws, in most of the states, states both in the North, and in the South.

Throughout his long, dedicated career, to the dismay of his colleagues, and of his social peers, Dr. Theodore Sawyer had steadfastly lived by, and clung to his personal and professional, beliefs.

He did not, and would not perform non-medically indicated, abortions.

Dr. Sawyer had adamantly, refused to participate in the lucrative, 1850's common practice, of performing abortions for the wealthy Protestant gentry.

During his more than fifty years as a practicing physician, Dr. Sawyer had performed but three abortions. In each of the three cases, the patients and the circumstances met either one or more, of his absolute criteria for terminating a pregnancy:

1. The pregnant female had not experienced "Quickening"; movement of the fetus.
2. If during a difficult delivery, failure to terminate the pregnancy, would lead to the death of the mother.
3   The female had been raped, and/or her pregnancy was the result of incest.

Fortunately for his conscience, of the three abortions that he had performed in the past, each procedure had met one or more of his self-imposed criteria, which satisfied his participation in performing an abortion.
Abortion was to Dr. Sawyer, if not medically indicated, considered an abhorrent, loathsome, medical procedure.

Rebecca's vehement, animated proclamation to Dr. Sawyer; "I do not want to give birth to Stone Fist's papoose!", had taken Luis completely by surprise.

When Rebecca had asked him to accompany her, for her appointment to meet with Dr. Sawyer, Luis's initial impression was, that the meeting was to access Rebecca's general health.

It was now clear to him, and he was convinced, that Dr. Sawyer understood, that Rebecca was about to ask the doctor to perform an abortion.

Luis's initial instinctive reaction was to think; "I am an attorney, an officer of the court. I can be disbarred for having prior knowledge of the intent to commit a criminal act, and not bringing it to the attention of the authorities."

He took one look at Rebecca, and his apprehension, was immediately replaced with a feeling of shame and guilt.

Dr. Sawyer sat back in his chair. "Rebecca are you asking me to assist you in terminating your pregnancy, to perform an abortion? You do realize that to seek out, and then to have an abortion, is illegal?"

Rebecca remained quiet Luis seeing Rebecca's uneasiness, turned to face Dr. Sawyer.

"Dammit man, I am an Attorney-at-Law, a member of the Virginia State Bar. As such, I am well versed with, and cognizant of the law."

"As Rebecca's guardian as well as her attorney, it was I, not her that in light of the *extraordinary,* extenuating circumstances which resulted in her being impregnated, that I suggested that she consider having an abortion."

Rebecca was surprised and grateful for the lie. She raised her eyes and once again reached for and held Luis' hand tightly in hers.

Dr. Sawyer's eyes met and locked with the unwavering, bright blue eyes
of Richmond's best-known litigator, the widely respected, and formidable attorney, the esteemed Mr. Luis Frazier, Esq.

Looking into the attorney/guardian's eyes, Dr, Sawyer observed, what he considered, an interesting physiological, phenomenon. The intensity of the color of the irises of Mr. Frazier's previously tranquil, bright blue eyes, was slowly changing.

The attorney's eyes were darkening, smoldering, clouding over.

"Mr. Frazier in addition to the fact that abortion is against the law, I as a physician, and more importantly, as a God-Fearing man, have deeply held, serious moral and ethical objections, to abortion."

"First and foremost, as a human being, and secondarily as a doctor, I abhor the taking of a human life. I have spent my entire professional-life, attempting to save and to preserve human-life."

"When I completed medical school I, as did all of my fellow medical school graduates, took an oath. The Hippocratic oath, to above all else, to "Do no Harm.""

"Believe me, I am acutely aware of, and completely sympathetic to Rebecca's plight".

"However, if I were to even consider performing an abortion, my patient would have to not be, *"Quick with child"*. Both Rebecca and Luis stared at the doctor. They were obviously confused.

"Dr. Sawyer explained; "to be quick with child", is an archaic expression, dating back to antiquity, to the ancient Greek and Roman civilizations".

"It simply means that the pregnant female, has felt the fetus kick, felt the fetus move."

"The, physicians of that era, and even now, concluded that the movement, the "*quickening*", indicated that a developed, viable fetus was present."

"The movement, the kicking, the "*quickening*", attaches a right to life, to the fetus."

"Despite my deeply held, moral convictions, my conscientious objections
to abortion, I must confess that during my career, with great trepidation, I have performed three abortions."

"In each instance, each of my patients met at least one or more, of the three absolute criteria, for me to even consider, terminating a pregnancy".

"I will consider performing the abortion if; the pregnancy was due to rape and/or incest; or if during the course of the pregnancy, or during the delivery, failure to terminate the pregnancy would lead to the death of the mother".

"However, Sir, I reaffirm. I will absolutely not, consider performing an abortion, if the pregnant female, my patient, has experienced any sign of *"Quickening"*. That is activity, the movement of a live baby."

Dr. Sawyer stood and moved to sit on the corner of his desk. He leaned over, his head no more than fifteen inches from Rebecca's face.

"Rebecca, during the physical examination, by your own admission, you have over an extended period of time, on multiple occasions, felt the baby move. In my professional opinion, you are well into the third trimester of this pregnancy."

"I will not terminate this pregnancy. Furthermore, my moral convictions not withstanding, as your doctor, I must advice you of the medical risks to you, associated with a third trimester abortion."

"The risk to the mother, …to you of life-threatening complications, most notably, that of uncontrolled bleeding, is greatly increased."

"Rebecca, I delivered you. I have been your doctor all of your young life."

"I would very much like to remain your doctor. I want to attend to you through the remainder of this pregnancy. I would be honored if you decide to allow me to deliver this baby."

"And after he or she is born, if it is your wish, I will do every thing in my power, to assist you in placing the baby, into an appropriate home."

"It's possible that we, you me, and your guardian, Mr. Frazier, that we can place the child in an appropriate home."

"Richmond has a few orphanages for coloreds."

****

Chapter 32

Richmond Virginia - Home of Elijah
and Carolyn Simpson 1831

During the course of his wife, Carolyn's pregnancy, Elijah Simpson had been elated. The anticipation, the prospect of soon having a son and heir, was to him, exciting and most exhilarating.

That he sires a male child, was an essential, a necessary component of Elijah's grandiose plans for the future governance of his beloved Virginia, and potentially, the governance of the United States.

While Elijah Simpson was acknowledged by those men who sat in the seat of power in Virginia's political circles, as one of the must powerful, influential men in local and state politics, to his neighbors, Mr. Elijah Simpson, Attorney at Law, was an unassuming, friendly, moderately, successful lawyer.

The name Elijah Simpson, to local, county, and state Virginia officials, both elected and appointed, was synonymous with the words; "Power Broker- King-Maker."

While Elijah was content, even preferring to wield his massive political power from behind the scenes, it had always been his latent, unspoken desire, his intent, to use his considerable political power and influence, to
making his, yet unborn son, the first Simpson, to hold the office of Governor of the great state of Virginia.

And then ultimately, with his assistance, his son, his protégé, after the completion of his successful gubernatorial stint, his son and heir, could with his help, conceivably, be elected to the Presidency of the United States.

After all, the state of Virginia was considered by most of the nation, as being the birthplace, and breeding-ground, of United States Presidents.

Carolyn upon seeing the disappointment in here husband's eyes, gently placed her hand on his cheek and whispered, "Elijah, I know you had your heart sit on a boy. Darling, don't despair."

"We're both young and healthy. We have lots of time, for having lots of babies.

Elijah, the next one will be a boy; I promise, just you wait and see. You'll have your son."

Despite the couple's robust efforts, four years past before Carolyn was able, with a broad smile covering her face, share the good news with Elijah.

Carolyn had happily announced that she was once again, with child.

Elijah's hopes for an heir were once again dashed. The couple's second child to exit Carolyn's womb, was a beautiful, pink, nearly bald — a few wispy strands of brown Hair —, brown eyed, baby girl.

Though Elijah was devastated, he took comfort and solace in his wife's optimistic, encouraging words, "We're both young and healthy. We have lots of time, we'll have lots of babies"

Elijah, as he did when confronted with a particularly vexing, stubborn, business problem, resolved to "plow" ahead, until he ultimately, managed to correct the deficiency.

Whenever Delilah Anne, his four-year-old daughter, tearfully came to him for assistance when she had not been able to accomplish a task, Elijah would wipe away the tears from her eyes; "Sweetheart, you've got to keep at it till you eventually, get it right!"

Elijah lived by and was a staunch proponent and practitioner of his favorite cliché; "If at first you don't succeed, try, try, try again."

Following the birth of the couple's second daughter Beatrice, Elijah, anxious to "try, try, try again", almost on a daily bases, sought out their family doctor, and his good friend Dr. Theodore Sawyer.

Inevitably, at some point in their conversations, Elijah would literally plead with the good doctor, seeking his permission to "resume normal marital relations", with Carolyn. Elijah Simpson was eager and determined to father a son.

Elijah, who loved his wife deeply and dearly, was elated when Dr. Sawyer, finally assured him that, "the resumption of husband and wife relations, between he and Carolyn, was once again permissible."

That the couple, Elijah and Carolyn Simpson, was absolutely fertile was never in doubt. Predictably, and not in the least bit unexpected, ten and a half months following Elijah and Carolyn's resumption of "normal" marital relations, Carolyn once again had gone into labor.

As he had previously done twice in the past, when Carolyn, his very pregnant wife informed him; "Elijah, it's time, the baby's coming", Elijah had dispatched his house slave Minnie, "to fetch Dr. Sawyer."

As he had done twice before, while awaiting the anticipated birth of his *"son"*, Elijah paced nervously, in the downstairs parlor.

Twenty minutes after Dr. Sawyer' arrival, Elijah's stood gazing up the stairwell. He heard his house slave Minnie's frightened, panicky, laments; *"Oh lawd, oh lawd, I ain't neba seed so much blood befo."*

Elijah ran up the steps. Taking them two at a time. Minnie, her arms loaded with clean white towels, collided with her Master.

Without uttering a word of apology, she rushed past Elijah and into the bedroom that he shared with his wife, his beloved Carolyn.

Carolyn lay motionless on the bed. Her face was a pale, white, ghostly mask, devoid of color. The sole semblance of color was the bluish, cyanotic hue of her lips.

Blood soaked towels were everywhere. The beige carpet that covered the floor was a bright crimson red.

As Elijah rushed to his wife's side, Dr. Sawyer, with the thumb of his right hand, was gently lowering the lids of Carolyn's wide-open, lifeless eyes.

Carolyn's death — while giving birth to their youngest daughter — had resulted in the development, the creation of a deep, impenetrable, chasm between Elijah and his three daughters.

Despite the fact that his conscience mind and intellect — being continually reinforced by the solicitous words of Dr. Sawyer —, understood and accepted, that Carolyn's death was no one's fault, that it had been "an act of God", sub-conscientiously, Elijah could not rid himself of persistent feelings of guilt.

****

Chapter 33

Delilah Anne-Simpson –
Richmond Virginia – 1839

Delilah Anne Simpson, was the eldest daughter of Elijah Simpson, Esq.

Elijah Simpson was the most powerful, influential, and prominent member of Richmond's powerful, Democratic Party.

Of his three children, all females to Elijah's everlasting chagrin — Delilah, his first born, was by far his favorite.

When Delilah Anne was born, Elijah — despite his most valiant efforts —, Elijah could not hide from his wife, his disappointment, his regret that the infant was not male.

When his seemingly always cheerful, *"pleasingly-plumb"* wife Carolyn, had first presented to Elijah, their firstborn, their newborn baby girl, Carolyn had immediately sensed and seen in her husband's eyes, his disappointment.

The smile on Elijah's face had slowly faded, following the proud father's lifting of the flap of the tiny blanket, covering the infant. He beamed as he counted five fingers on both tiny hands; and five toes on each chubby foot.

Abruptly Elijah's facial expression changed. All of the anticipated appendages were present and accounted for, with the notable exception of one, the absence of a penis.

Carolyn had presented Elijah with a healthy, beautiful, healthy, daughter.

Chronologically, Delilah Anne was merely three years older than her sister Beatrice, and five years senior to her youngest sister, Cynthia.

Because of their father's misplaced, misguided, but strong and genuine, feelings of guilt; feelings that he associated with, his unrelenting, insatiable desire for a male heir, Elijah had unwittingly, abdicated his parental responsibility, to rear his three girls.

Delilah Anne had grown up as not only the big sister, Delilah Anne, due to their father's benign-neglect, had been forced to assume the mantle of surrogate mother, and father, for her younger sisters.

Delilah Anne, at the tender age of eight, due to the death of her mother, and her father's subsequent guilt-ridden grief, had been forced to grow-up quickly, to become an adult.

Delilah Anne vaguely remembered the time, before the birth of her sister Cynthia, when her mother and father, would play games with her, would each night, before she fell asleep, read fairy-tales to her and her younger sister Beatrice.

She remembered, when her sister Cynthia was born, how suddenly and horribly, things changed. She remembered how her father had changed, become morose, cold, and indifferent towards her and to her sisters.

Following the death of his beloved wife Carolyn, to him his daughter Delilah Anne, the sparkling, laughing child that Elijah had playfully bounced on his knee, had ceased to exist.

Because of her father's deepening depression, his neglect and withdrawal from the children following her mother's death, Delilah Ann had stepped in to fill the void. Delilah Ann sacrificed her youth, to raise her sisters.

Delilah Anne's admirable devotion and commitment to raising her younger siblings, had in terms of her, Delilah's personal life, exacted an exorbitant cost.

****

Under "big" sister Delilah Anne's guidance, Elijah Simpson's two youngest girls had blossomed into two beautiful, debutantes, delicate, fragile flowers, of Richmond's social society.

Delilah Anne's selfless commitment to ensure the success of her two teenage sisters' successful, "*coming-out*", had been at the cost of her own youth.

Delilah Anne had been deprived of having a normal childhood.

Delilah Anne's life had been devoid of that all-important phase in a young women's development, especially in the development and maturation, of the young white women, of the Antebellum-Southern Aristocracy.

She had been deprived of experiencing that period in her maturation, when the social functions, the courting rituals, that transitioned white females-of - quality, from adolescence, to young adult women.

In large part, thanks to her maternalistic guidance, help and devotion, Delilah Anne's sisters, Beatrice and Cynthia, had both married well.

Beatrice had married Raymond Jefferson, a successful planter, and became the Mistress of Sycamore Palms, a large, sprawling, cotton plantation, just south of Richmond.

Cynthia — in the autumn of 1861, shortly after the commencement of hostilities between the Union and the newly formed, Confederate States of America —, had been wooed by, and eventually wed to, a well-to-do middle aged Richmond widower, the honorable Lawrence F. Pinckney, a circuit-judge, known to be active and extremely influential, in Richmond politics.

E. Pluribus Unum

With the two younger sisters successfully married, and now no longer a part of Elijah Simpson's household, Delilah Anne had come to the realization that in her efforts, her dedication, to successfully raise her sisters, to ensure that they married well, how that selfless-effort, had adversely affected her life.

Delilah Anne could not help feeling that she had sacrificed, forfeited, loss her opportunity to have a happy married life of her own.

With just herself and her father left to occupy their spacious house, Delilah Anne was saddled with the unenviable task of taking care of her father, of serving as her father's companion, his social secretary, and of being Elijah Simpson's official, and unofficial hostess.

Delilah Anne felt that any chance that she may have had for a normal life, a husband and children of her own, had passed her by.

She accepted the fact that she would, in all likelihood, live out her life as a spinster. And thanks to her penchant and weakness for chocolates, as an overweight, chubby old maid.

As each day, each week, each month, each year passed, Delilah Anne had become increasingly resentful, bitter, and petulant.

There were times when she lay brooding, alone—as usual—in her bed, that she fiercely, and passionately, resented her father. She resented her sisters. She resented and chastised herself for having sacrificed her happiness, her life, to ensure the happiness of her sisters.

Delilah Anne would spend many lonely nights lying in bed, hugging her pillow to her breasts, pretending that she was being embraced by a handsome lover, while she rhythmically, slowly, squeezed, caressed and stroked the sensitive fleshy, pea-size nodule, at the apex of her vagina.

Delilah Anne was resigned. She had gradually come to believe that by her decision to devote her life to the rearing of her sisters, that she had forfeited her chance for happiness, her chance at becoming a wife and mother.

Following Cynthia's marriage, Delilah Anne's life had evolved into a routine that consisted of her assisting her father, by serving as his secretary, his hostess. And by her inability to resist satisfying her unquenchable appetite for the taste of sweet, delicious, creamy, chocolates.

****

Chapter 34

Richmond Virginia - Home of Elijah Simpson and his Daughter – Elijah Anne- June, 1863

It was during one of her father's frequent, interminable, political dinner parties, that Elijah formally introduced Delilah Anne to the highly regarded, and respected Richmond lawyer, Mr. Luis Frazier, Esq.

Luis Frazier was most often described at first glance, as being a rather short corpulent "fidgety", Southern Gentleman.

Despite Luis' expanding girth, which undoubtedly contributed to his propensity to copiously perspire, Luis was a man of boundless energy, who seemed to be in constant motion.

Luis' most distinctive feature was his eyes. He had the most penetrating, piercing blue eyes.

When he was pleased or amused about something, his eyes would sparkle — many said —, would give one the impression that they were looking into a soothing, tranquil pool of blue-pristine water. However, when he became angry or resolute, Luis' eyes would smolder, cloud over, and darken.

Although she had never met the renowned, Mr. Frazier, Delilah was well aware of the lawyer's stellar reputation as an extremely talented, intelligent, and shrewd attorney.

It was said by those who had had dealings with Mr. Frazier, "caution, beware", if those penetrating, piercing, bright blue eyes of his start to cloud over, to smolder, one should tread lightly,"

This warning referred to the involuntary reaction, of Luis' autonomic nervous system.

A *"tell"*, a quirk known to his poker playing friends, and to a few of his adversaries. When he became angry, Luis' normally tranquil, clear blue eyes took on a hue, reminiscent of the transformation of a calm blue-sky, prior to the onslaught of the fury of a violent thunderstorm.

When her father introduced Delilah to the renowned lawyer, she looked deeply into eyes. Delilah had been disappointed, and a little confused.

Delilah's initial impression of Mr. Luis Frazier, stemmed from what she saw — or more to the point —, what she did not see in his eyes.

Based upon what she had heard, and had been led to believe, while the man who smiled and lightly held her hand in his somewhat moist palm, was as he had been described, short, and corpulent, his eyes which supposedly were so expressive, and were said to be his most striking feature, Delilah found his eyes to be blank, and devoid of expression.

Luis Frazier's eyes did not convey either tranquility or turmoil.

Delilah's assessment of the eyes of Luis Frazier was, that his eyes were lifeless, cold, … dead.

****

Following the dinner party, after the guests had departed, Delilah Anne gave her father—her less than flattering—first impression of the man that he had lavishly praised and categorized as, "A Rising Star in Richmond Politics."

When asked by Elijah to elaborate, Delilah Anne recounted her in-depth appraisal of Luis Frazier.

"Father, based upon what I had heard from you, and from overhearing conversations between you and your many business associates, I was disappointed. I was not at all impressed with Mr. Frazier"

"Although we talked but briefly, I found him to be somewhat of a dullard. He did not appear to be at all interested in politics, or for that matter, it seemed as though he was not the least bit concerned about our recent military set-backs at the hands of the Yankees."

"In point of fact, when two gentlemen who were lamenting, the second failure of our own General "Bobby" Lee to defeat the Yankees in their own fields in the North, **when he invaded** Gettysburg Pennsylvania, Mr. Frazier declined to express his feelings, or to put forth an opinion."

"Mr. Frazier merely shrugged his shoulders, and without commenting, walked away."

"When I had the opportunity to look into Mr. Frazier's eyes, instead of my catching a glimpse his vaunted intelligence, or indeed any hint of emotion, I literally saw nothing."

"Frankly his eyes reminded me of that expression one might say, when looking into the eyes of a dead fish."

At first Elijah was stunned, bewildered at his daughter's professed, initial impression of Luis Frazier.

Then slowly, as if he had just experienced an epiphany, Elijah walked over and began to rummage through the clutter of papers piled high on his desk.

He retrieved from the bottom of the stack of papers, two worn, *dog-eared,* documents.

Without preamble, he handed the documents, one at a time, to Delilah Anne.

With a confused look on her face, Delilah read the first sheet of paper, which was clearly a copy of an original:

April 4ᵗʰ, 1863

Dear Mr. Frazier,

It is my painful duty to inform you of a tragedy that has befallen the Henry Billings family, traveling, with my wagon train, under my guidance and protection.

Mr. Billings and his daughter's governess, a Negress by the name of Ruth, were attacked and killed by a war party of hostile Indians.

Your friend Mr. Henry Billings, fought and dyed bravely, attempting to protect his daughter, Miss Rebecca Billings.

I truly regret informing you that Miss Rebecca Billings, and her Negress servant, Mandy, were abducted by the heathens.

A posse of men, led by me, followed the Indians, until we lost their trail, and were forced to abandon our search and rescue efforts.

With my deepest sympathy,

Sincerely,
Sam Adams Smith
Captain Samuel A. Smith, Wagon Master

After having read that document, with an inquisitive look, Delilah Anne reached for the second document, a parchment.

Wordlessly, Elijah handed her the second missive. She began to read:

REWARD OF $10, 000 DOLLARS
FOR THE SAFE RETURN OF MISS REBECCA ELIZABETH BILLINGS

On April 4ᵗʰ, 1863, a white female by the name of Rebecca Billings and her Negress servant, known as Mandy, were abducted, from a wagon train, being guided by the famous pathfinder, Captain Sam Smith.

The wagon of the Billings family, having experienced a broken wheel, was temporarily separated from Captain Smith's wagon train. While three men were working to repair the wheel, the Billings' wagon was attacked by a band of marauding savages.

The adults, Mr. Henry Billings, Mr. Bruce Logan, and Mr. *Lars Johansson*, from a neighboring wagon, were tortured, and butchered.

Miss Rebecca Billings (Becky) is:

Height – 5' 4"
Weight – 98 to 100 pounds
Hair – Blond
Eyes – Blue

CONTACT:

Mr. Luis Frazier, Esq. C/O Central Post Office,
Richmond Virginia

$10, 000 DOLLAR- REWARD

As Delilah Anne read and then reread the documents, Elijah forced himself, for the first time, in a very long time, to really look at his daughter, with what he hoped, was an unbiased, critically, discerning eye.

The stern woman, his eldest daughter, who stood before him was a little stout, plumb, plain looking woman; a woman who was rapidly approaching middle age.

Elijah felt as if his mind was racing a mile a minute. What had happened to his daughter? What had happened to that happy, always smiling, little girl; his and Carolyn's, first born?

Was this stark transformation that he clearly saw for the first time, at this very moment, was this Delilah Anne, his fault?

Had his decades long dismissive attitude toward his children, been responsible for Delilah's apparent lack of empathy?

Was his abdication in the rearing of the girls, his leaving their upbringing to Delilah Anne; his decades of misguided, irrational blaming of the kids, for them being somehow, responsible for their mother's death, were these, his transgressions the molders of Delilah Anne's character?

Delilah Anne had made a snap judgment of Luis Frazier. She had failed to see and to recognize that the man was depressed, that he was racked with grief, guilt and sorrow.

That Luis Frazier's state of mind, his grief, was strikingly similar to that which he, Elijah her father, had carried for decades, following the death, of her mother, his beloved and cherished wife, Carolyn.

Elijah pointed to an easy chair. Delilah Anne attempted to hand the papers to her father. He waved his hand, dismissively, which at least delayed her attempt to return to him, the two documents.

It was widely known, among the elite, by those in power, in the city of Richmond, the Capital city of the Confederate States of America, that just six months earlier, Luis Frazier, the prominent attorney's best friend, Henry Billings, had been massacred by savage Indians.

And that during the Indian attack, Henry's only surviving child, his daughter Rebecca, had been captured and enslaved, by those same, vicious, heathen, barbaric, savages.

****

Delilah Ann with her hands demurely folded in her lap, as her father had indicated, sat primly, awaiting her father's comments.

It was widely rumored and/or, at least suspected and admired by most of Richmond's "*Movers and Shakers*", that Henry Billing's scheme to obtain 160 acres of prime, virgin farmland free, from the Yankees, was concocted by one, Mr. Luis Frazier, Esq.

That particular plan was predicated upon Luis and Henry's successfully, circumventing, and manipulating the Union's 1862 Homestead Act.

In order to lay claim to the free land; 1) One must have not ever, taken up arms against the U.S. government; 2) You must be a man or woman (including freed slaves), at least 21 years of age; 3) You must agree to live on and farm the land for at least five contiguous years."

This meant that the official claimant, Ruth Billings, Henry Billing's former slave and concubine…Henry Billings, daughter Rebecca, and Ruth's teenage daughter, Mandy, would emigrate together, to lands west of the Mississippi River.

Hence, the Billing's party, consisting of; an adult white man; a black female (former slave), and two teenage girls, one white, the other black, joined a westward bound wagon train, their destination, Lost Springs Kansas.

In order for the wagon train to reach, Lost Spring Kansas and its' final destination, Sante Fe New Mexico, the wagon train would travel south-west, via the Sante Fe Trail, through hostile, "Indian Territory."

Elijah leaned across his desk, picked up and removed the stopper from the crystal decanter of water that stood in the corner of the desk, and filled two glasses.

With water glass in hand, he walked from behind his desk, and handed the glass of water to Delilah Anne.

He returned to set in his chair, behind the desk. Elijah waited until his daughter had sipped the water, then dabbing at the corners of her mouth with her handkerchief, placed the water glass on the desk.

Elijah removed a small cigar from the humidor situated on the far-right hand corner of his desk.

E. Pluribus Unum

He slowly, meticulously lit the cheroot, and blew a stream of aromatic gray smoke into the air.

"Delilah, I was a bit surprised and somewhat confused by your initial impression of Luis Frazier. I was particularly put-off by your less than flattering comments."

"Until recently, to be more precise, until four months ago… ―, he paused and pointed to the letter on his desk before Luis received that letter from Captain Smith, Luis Frazier had been an energetic, brilliant lawyer.

Luis was held in the highest esteem by the political and social elites, of Richmond's society."

"It was after his receipt of that letter informing him of the horrific death of his best friend, and the abduction of his friend's daughter by savages, a child that he has known for the entirety of her life, a child that Luis cherished, that Luis' demeanor, indeed some have said, as do I, it seems as though, his whole personae has changed.

Delilah Anne sat rigid, attentive, listening to her father's words. Elijah, in a soft, yet distinctly audible voice, told of the deep friendship that had existed between Luis Frazier, Richmond's most prominent, successful attorney/ businessman, and his best friend, Henry Billings, one of Richmond's most highly-regarded members of the South's slave holding, aristocracy.

Elijah reminded Delilah Anne of the steady decline and the state of disrepair, of Henry Billings' renowned, Rosewood Plantation, following the seizure of the property by the Old Dominion Reality Inc., a cadre of greedy, local, despicable, opportunistic, scalawags.

Elijah shared with his eldest daughter, in detail the brilliant, yet simple plan that Luis had devised and had helped to implement.

The "scheme" that had allowed Luis' friend Henry Billings, to avoid bankruptcy and financial ruin, while providing for Henry the prospect, and the means, for the rebuilding his beloved Rosewood Plantation, west of the Mississippi River.

Elijah told of how Luis had suggested, the plan, and how Luis had given the plan his strongest support, and encouragement.

Elijah told of how the plan, Luis' idea… Luis' plan, had led to the migration of Henry Billings and his daughter Rebecca, from their home in Richmond, to uncivilized lands across the Mississippi River, across the North American Continent.

The Billings party had traveled by covered wagon over the vast open-plains, through the wilderness, passing through hostile Indian Territory.

Louis' plan… his plan, his grand scheme that had ultimately resulted in the horrific death of his best friend; and God only knows, what humiliation and degradation may have befallen his best friend's daughter, Rebecca.

Sweet, innocent, Rebecca, who before she had learned to walk and to talk, her *"Uncle Louey"*, had bounced on his knee, and had read fairy tales to, it was because of Luis Frazier's ingenious plan, that *"Little Becky"*, was either dead, or now God forbid, in the hands of the savages.

Elijah told his daughter of the crippling, all consuming, mentally paralyzing, guilt that had enveloped Luis.

He told of Luis' rapid decent into a state of severe melancholy.

Delilah Anne had sat intrigued, captivated by her father's words. Shrewdly she thought, perhaps she had been a bit hasty, in her cavalier, assessment of the renowned, Mr. Luis Frazier, Esq.

Delilah Anne intuitively realized that Mr. Luis Frazier just might represent her last chance. This could very well be, her last opportunity to avoid living the rest of her life, as an aging, lonely, old maid-spinster.

She rationalized that the onset of Luis Frazier's depression, his melancholy state of mind, was obviously associated with his receipt of news of the Indian attack. The massacre that had resulted in the tragic demise of the Billings family.

Her quick, analytical, mind concluded that conceivably, by her lending an understanding sympathetic ear to Luis' feelings of loss and guilt, concomitant with her rebuilding his sense of self-worth, that in time, she could insert herself into his life.

Delilah was confident that, Luis Frazier's depression could be reversed.

Delilah Anne set about carefully, surreptitiously, inserting a sympathetic, pleasant, positive element into Luis' life. She was confident, that over time, Luis could be made to shed his morbid feelings of guilt.

And by her creating for him a crutch, a lifeline, namely one Miss Delilah- Anne Simpson, Luis Frazier just might be susceptible and receptive, again over time, to her innocently insinuated, hints and thoughts of matrimony.

It was toward the end of a prolonged two-week stint of a particularly severe period of depression and guilt, that for the first time in his life, Luis actually contemplated suicide.

Luis would sit at his desk for hours, attempting to work but unable to concentrate. Despite his efforts to the contrary, his mind would wonder.

Luis' mind would invariably drift off to happier times. He would reminisce, recalling, reliving the wonderful times that he had spent with the Billings family.

He thought of the time that he had spent at the Rosewood Plantation. Time spent with his best friend Henry, Henry's wife Peggy, and their two beautiful children, Jesse and Rebecca.

In his reverie he envisioned once again, himself laughing, sipping whiskey and smoking cigars with Henry. Of reading Dime Novels of the wild, untamed frontier, to wide-eyed Jesse.

And of the bubbly little Rebecca, emitting squeals of laughter, her sparkling blue eyes twinkling, her blonde pigtails flying as he bounced her on his knee.

Luis's smile would invariably gradually change, to that of abject horror, as the serene, tranquil daydream morphed into his recurring nightmare.

****

In his vivid imagination, Luis saw his friend Henry Billings being butchered, by legions of howling, red devils.

He heard Henry's plaintive, helpless, screams as he was being scalped. He heard the anguished screams of pain when his friend was being mutilated, being castrated, by hordes of those godless red savages.

In his mind he envisioned Henry's daughter, sweet, little, innocent, defenseless, Rebecca, his Goddaughter, being brutalized, dragged by the hair, her beautiful blonde hair; dragged to who knows where, and being subjected to only God knows what.

Fortunately, before his depression could totally overwhelm his sanity, Luis was paid a visit by Elijah Simpson, and his matronly, spinster daughter Delilah Anne.

Delilah Anne Simpson was exceedingly familiar with, and well versed at recognizing the signs and symptoms displayed by men afflicted with, and suffering from severe depression.

Delilah Anne had spent the better part of her life, protecting her sisters as well as protecting her father, from his— Elijah's —, irrational behavior, his inappropriate actions, triggered by his guilt, resulting from his frequent bouts of manic depression.

The inappropriate, flagrant often-hurtful words that frequently tumbled from their father's lips, she knew were triggered by guilt. Guilt that fueled and feed, Elijah's frequent debilitating episodes, of manic depression.

The persistent, pernicious, guilt that plagued Elijah stemmed from his blaming himself for his wife Carolyn's death, during childbirth. An all consuming, overwhelming guilt that Elijah had borne, since the untimely death of his wife, Delilah Anne's mother, during the birth of his youngest child, Cynthia.

On numerous occasions, Delilah Anne had overheard her father moaning… "It's my fault…I shouldn't have pushed her…been so insistent."

Delilah Anne knew that he was referring to the constant, unrelenting, pressure, that her father had placed upon her mother. Elijah's all-consuming desire, his obsession, that Carolyn bear him a son.

Thanks to the timely intervention of his patron Elijah Simpson's, matronly spinster *"Old Maid"* daughter, Luis Frazier, Esq. was pulled from the deep, dark, abyss, of loneliness and despair.

Delilah Anne had spent the better part of her life, protecting her sisters as well as protecting her father, from his, — Elijah's —, irrational behavior, his inappropriate actions, triggered by guilt, resulting from his frequent bouts of manic-depression.

As she had hoped, as a result of her sympathetic, attentive, listening and her ministering to Luis' rambling rants, during his sporadic bouts of manic depression, Luis had come to more and more, look to her, as a necessary stabilizing element in his life.

Delilah Anne's ultimate goal, her plan was to trade her current position as her father, Elijah Simpson's surrogate wife, his *"Old-Maid"* daughter and hostess, for the much more desirable, socially acceptable and prestigious role of, being the wife of one of, if not the most talented attorney, in Richmond, the capital city of the Confederate States of America.

Delilah Anne reasoned that her marriage to Luis Frazier would be beneficial to all. She would finally shed the horrible, demeaning, mantle of "Old-Maid"; Luis' would regain his mental stability, and once again reclaim his position at the top of Richmond's legal community; and lastly, Elijah Simpson — her father — would in Luis, finally have the son that he had wished for, for lo these many years.

****

As she had hoped, as a result of her sympathetic, attentive, tactics, her listening and her ministering to Luis' rambling rants, during his sporadic bouts of manic depression, Luis had come to more and more, look to Delilah Anne, as a necessary stabilizing element in his life.

Delilah Anne's plan, her ultimate goal, was to trade her current position, that of being her father, Elijah Simpson's *"Old-Maid"* daughter and hostess, for the much more prestigious and socially accepted title, of Mrs. Luis Frazier,
the wife of one of, if not the preeminent legal mind, in the Confederate States of America.

As she had planned, Delilah Anne slowly, methodically, managed to insert herself, as a steady, calming influence in Luis' life.

To the delight of his professional peers, Luis' unpredictable, inopportune, outbursts, during business conferences, his mood-swings, abruptly ceased.

As she had hoped for and anticipated, Luis had gradually, slowly but inexorably, developed an appreciation, and a dependency, upon Miss Delilah Anne Simpson.

On September 15, 1863, in a quiet civil ceremony, Luis Frazier and Delilah Anne Simpson were married.

****

Shortly following their marriage, slowly but surely, Delilah had been for the most part, successful in her efforts to extricate Luis from his deepening state of depression, from his frequent mood swings, from his slow, gradual descent into the abyss.

An important strategic component of her plan to rehabilitate, to salvage Luis' prominence, his reputation as a talented attorney, was for Delilah, to persuade her father, to shift the locale, the site of the coveted, weekly, Elijah Simpson, poker game.

Elijah was a staunch advocate and believer in the old adage; "Keep your friends close; and your enemies closer." His adherence to this sentiment had influenced Elijah's decision to create a weekly-poker game, with a few of his political cronies, allies as well as a few of his political foes.

By design, the site of Elijah Simpson's *"Poker-Night"*, was the home of Elijah Simpson.

For years Delilah had assisted her father, by acting as the hostess, of Friday's *"Poker-Night"*.

Delilah requested of her father, that he relocate the weekly gathering, from the home of Elijah Simpson and his eldest daughter, the then Delilah Anne Simpson, to her new domicile, the home of Luis Frazier, Esq., and his wife, Mrs. Delilah Anne Frazier.

Her most persuasive — she thought —, logical argument for the change in venue of *"Poker-Night"*, was that although she was no longer Elijah's hostess, she could still, continue to be the *"Poker-Night"* hostess, if the weekly poker game was moved, to the home of Delilah Anne and Luis Frazier.

Elijah fully appreciated Delilah's contribution to the success of *"Poker-Night"*. He immediately and pragmatically, saw the wisdom of his daughter's suggestion.

The weekly poker game was moved to the Frazier's home.

****

Almost immediately, following the relocation of *"Poker Night"*, Delilah Anne, began to notice marked improvement in Luis' demeanor.

For Delilah Anne, in addition to the uplifting of her husband's spirits, a definite, unanticipated bonus of the poker-nights was that invariably, following the completion of the games, Luis would wordlessly, without fan-fare, present to her his winnings. Winnings that more often than not, were quite substantial.

When Delilah had nonchalantly asked her husband about his apparently, remarkable skill as a poker player, he had chuckled; "My dear, there's nothing magical or remarkable about it. My success is merely due to the fact, that as an effective litigator, I have developed a keen sensitivity, and a   heightened awareness of, the mannerisms displayed by individuals, who find themselves in stressful circumstances."

Her curiosity aroused, and knowing that Luis would elaborate, Delilah had remained silent, waiting for her husband to continue.

"I'll give you an example. Your father, my esteemed father-in-law, Richmond's pre-eminent political "King-Maker", Elijah Simpson", when engaged in poker, has a very slight, easy to miss, but telltale weakness."

Delilah's interest, continued to increase. Try as she might, she could not think of a single weakness — associated with business —, that she could attribute to her father.

"To our local, elected and/or appointed county and state officials, the name Elijah Simpson, is synonymous with such words and phrases as; "Brilliant; Power- Broker; King-Maker; Master-Manipulator.""

"Your father is regarded as an unflinching man of cunning and strength. He is perceived of, and rightfully so, as being a shrewd, stoic, man, the consummate, dealmaker."

"Indeed, these laudatory superlatives, often employed to describe Elijah, are for the most part, accurate and justified. Yet rarely, if ever, will the brilliant, shrewd, stoic, Elijah Simpson, best me at poker."

Delilah Anne now intrigued, actually fascinated, asked; "Luis, what makes you so confident? What leads you to so confidently, and adamantly believe, that you can consistently, best Papa at cards?"

Luis took a deep breath; Elijah Simpson, the shrewd, implacable, stoic "Power Broker, when engaged in the game of poker, has a telltale weakness."

"When Elijah is dealt a hand of cards, Luis — seeing the confused expression on his wife's face — paused and began to explain to Delilah, a few rudimentary rules of "draw-poker.""

"Each player is initially dealt five cards. The players are in-turn, allowed to either wager, or to fold."

Delilah was once again perplexed. "Luis, I don't fully understand. Of course, I understand the meaning of the term "wager", however, the meaning of the alternative action, the term "fold", in this context, eludes me."

Luis smiled; "Forgive me my dear. In the context of poker, the meaning of the word, the term, "to fold", is to quit, to withdraw."

"Since it is not my intent at this time, to teach to you, the game of poker, I will forgo most of the minutia, and get directly to the point."

"Those players that wager, are given the option to hold… that is to keep the original five cards dealt them, or they are allowed to replace, by discarding, that is by trading, as many as three cards. This, the player may choose to do, in an effort to improve his, that is the player's hand."

"When your father improves his poker-hand, his left eyebrow, slightly, almost imperceptibly rises, followed by his shuffling of his cards."

"Elijah is not alone among our regulars, to manifest a tell-tale indicator of success or failure. Similarly, if our esteemed mayor, the honorable Joseph Snyder, improves his hand, his honor the Mayor, absent-mindedly strokes his chin whiskers."

"My ability to detect and to correctly interpret these idiosyncrasies, clues if you will, recognizing these tell-tale signs, gives me a decisive advantage.

"Observation and the correct analysis of human behavior, contribute to my skill, my success at poker."

                                                  E. Pluribus Unum

****

His "*Tell*", Luis' involuntary physiologic response, which Delilah knew was a reliable predictor of her husband's mood, was beginning to be slowly displayed by her husband.

Seated at the dining room table, directly across from Luis, Delilah saw the transformation, the change in her husband's normally bright blue eyes.

If his usually bright blue eyes were to suddenly cloud over, to become dark and smoldering, the change was more often than not, a predictor of Luis' rapidly developing displeasure and disdain.

Delilah sensed that she was in danger of stoking and possibly incurring, her husband's, ire.

Luis reached for his brandy snifter. He slowly, gently swirled, sloshed, the amber fluid in the goblet; "Delilah, did I hear you correctly? When you were referring to Becky, were your words… "She and her child, have been living with us", were those your words?"

Delilah was stunned. She hesitated before attempting to formulate a reply. That Luis was agitated, and was becoming increasingly annoyed, was unmistakable. Luis, in what Delilah thought was an extremely stern voice and manner, continued.

"Becky and Henry Billings, Jr., Little-Hank, are members of this family, members of our, family. It's offensive to my ears to hear you, my beloved wife, refer to Becky and Little-Hank in a derisive, dismissive tone as; "she and her child, have been living with us."

"Our Home is Rebecca's home. And as long as I have a home, Rebecca and Henry, Jr., will have a home. Rebecca and Little-Hank will always be welcome to live in my home."

"Now if you would be so kind as to excuse me, I will retire to the confines of my study. There I will avail myself of yet, another brandy, and one of my, as you so succinctly opined, my "smelly" cigars."

Luis rose from his chair, picked up the decanter of brandy, and left the dining room.

****

Delilah Anne remained seated. Why had Luis found her perfectly innocent, truthful words, to be so offensive?

What exactly, had she said, what had caused this sudden change in Luis' demeanor? Furtively, frantically Delilah Anne concentrated, attempting to recall her exact words.

Reluctantly she conceded; "Rebecca is a beautiful, twenty-one-year old, young woman in the prime of her life. It's been four years since she was delivered from the savages. More than three years since she and her child have been living with us…I think that the time has come for Rebecca to begin to build a life of her own."

"I think that the time has come for Rebecca to begin to build a life of her own."

Delilah Anne found herself more and more, when thinking, inserting small tidbits of Luis's "poker-terminology", words and expressions that Luis would use, when explaining the meaning of the vernacular of poker.

Poker meanings for common English words, such as the term; He has a "Tell."

"Thinking metaphorically, Delilah wondered if perhaps she had prematurely, "Revealed her hand."

****

Chapter 35

Richmond Virginia –Home of Luis and Delilah Ann Frazier February –1865

Delilah sat relaxed, in the parlor, with her sisters, Beatrice and Cynthia. Her sisters' children, Clayton, age eight, and five-year-old Seymour, Beatrice's two boys, and Cynthia's two girls, Clara age four, and Annabelle, age two, were nosily playing in the rear of the huge room.

Hattie, the ebony cook, entered the parlor. The robust, matronly slave was carrying young Henry, Jr., the son of Luis and Delilah's purported "niece", Rebecca Billings.

"Scuse me Mistres Lilah, Mistres Bekka dun gone ta da oface wid da Masta. I be thinkn' dat da baby could play wid da uda chilrens."

Cynthia frowned, clenched her jaw, and flashed a withering glance toward her sister and confidant, Beatrice. Beatrice attuned to, and seeing her sister's discomfort, placed the china cup that she had been holding, onto its matching saucer on the table.

Hattie stood silently, rocking the baby. She felt the inexplicable tension that had suddenly swept over the room. Just twenty minutes earlier, when she served tea and crackers to the three sisters, the mood in the room had been warm, light, bordering on festive.

Delilah, tea cup in hand, looked up at the black slave; "Hattie, now is not a good time, Henry, Jr., seems to be cranky. Why don't you take him upstairs for his nap?"

Hank, who had just recently, tentatively, taken his first steps, turned his head in response to the sounds of the children playing, in the back of the room. Henry, Jr., began to squeal and to squirm in Hattie's arms.

Although he had not quite mastered ambulating efficiently on two limbs, his locomotion expertise on all four of his limbs, that is crawling, was well developed. *"Play, play,... down... put me-down."*

Delilah, placed her cup and saucer on the table, turned, and in a stern voce, addressed the slave; "Hattie did you hear me? I want you to take Henry, Jr. upstairs at once, now! It's time for the *papoose's* nap."

Hattie cradled the now crying, wailing little boy to her amble bosom; *"Hush now chile. It be bout time fo yu nap. Yu got plenny time ta be playn' wid dem uda chilrens."* Hattie turned, and swiftly left the room.

As the sounds of the upset, crying child, receded, Beatrice was the first to speak; "Thank you Delilah. I declare, frankly I don't know how you can put up with these…your living conditions."

"How in the world you manage to live in the same house with that harlot, that "White-Squaw" Rebecca Billings, and her little half-breed, brat, is beyond the scope of my Christian apprehension."

Cynthia chimed in; "Can you imagine…the nerve of that black wench, that nigger, thinking that we would allow our children, to mingle, to play with that beastly-little savage, Rebecca's wild, half-breed red- skinned, bastard?"

Beatrice had been nodding her head signifying her agreement, as Cynthia continued her diatribe.

"When my husband, the judge, first informed me of the latest conflict between whites and the red-skinned savages…you all have heard of that unpleasant incident that occurred last November?" She looked in turn from one sister to the other.

"That skirmish between those Yankee soldiers, way out west, with an encampment of hostile savage Indians, that included their women and children, my initial reaction was one of shock and regret."

Beatrice interrupted; "Cynthia are you referring to that glorious victory by Colonel Chivington, over hundreds hostile savages, camped beside some godforsaken, water hole in the Colorado Territory?"

Before Cynthia could respond, Delilah joined in the conversation; "Oh yes, Luis and I discussed the story when it was reprinted in the Richmond Gazette. I believe the incident occurred at some mud-hole called "Sand Creek.""

Cynthia, not wanting to give up her role as the principal purveyor of what she considered especially "juicy", current events, picked up the narrative; "Sand Creek", that's correct. Although I truly despise Yankee soldiers—at least until recently—, for the most part, their soldiers are civilized, white men."

"To no respectable southerner's surprise, those awful bleeding-heart Yankee Abolitionists, are characterizing that Yankee Colonel Chivington's fabulous victory, over those red savages, as a massacre. Honestly, can you imagine, white, God fearing Christians, believing such nonsense?"

Delilah answered her sister; "At first, when Luis told me of the incident in Colorado, I must admit that I too— as I believe was Cynthia's reaction, at first—, could not understand the need of Colonel Chivington, to kill the Indian women and their children."

"Now after having heard the Sand Creek incident, being discussed by Luis and father's poker-playing cronies, I must admit to having reexamined my position, as to the shooting of the Indian women and children."

Cynthia and Beatrice looked quizzically at their older sister, anxiously awaiting her amplification of her thoughts.

Delilah took a deep breath, and continued; "You all remember Mr. Saunders the banker?"

Beatrice interjected; "Oh yes, that disgusting short, bald man who loves to "accidentally", brush up against the bosoms of young girls."

Cynthia could not at first, place the name Mr. Saunders. However, following her sister's anecdotal comments, and her description of the man, she began to rapidly nod her head, acknowledging her familiarity with the name, and the man.

Delilah resumed; "In any event, during a recent poker-night, when the men were discussing the battle at Sand Creek, I overheard, and paused to reflect on Mr. Saunders' stated position, when the issue of the killing of the Indian women and children became the topic of discussion."

"Mr. Archibald Saunders' statement, while not at all eloquent, and certainly by no means Christian, gave me pause. His comment had a ring of truth, despite his crude phraseology."

Both Beatrice and Cynthia were now giving their older sister Delilah, their undivided attention. They were obviously both, eager to hear the banker's thoughts, in regard to the killing at Sand Creek, of helpless, defenseless, Indian women and children.

Delilah reached for the porcelain teapot, and refilled her cup. She delicately sipped, the still uncomfortably hot beverage, placed the cup in its saucer, and continued; "Mr. Saunders actually lauded and supported, the soldiers killing of the Indian women and Children. His exact words were; "You can not think of those savages, as people."

"The so called innocent Indian women and children should be thought of as *breeders*. And as Colonel Chivington refers to the brats, the so-called children, should be thought of as *nits*."

"The women—*breeders*—, who spew forth the children— *nits* — who as we all know, turn into *lice*. "Lice, barbaric heathen warriors, that rape, torture and kill us. Who kill real people; real white men; real white women; and real white children."

Delilah watched the faces of her sisters as they mulled over the vitriolic words, of Mr. Archibald Saunders, the perverted banker, trying to gauge their reaction.

Both Beatrice and Cynthia were nodding their heads, signifying their concurrence and agreement, with the slimy Mr. Saunders.

Delilah delivered the "*Coup de gras*", "Papa, with his remarkable memory, gave credence to Colonel Chivington's philosophy, by quoting the Colonel's exact words as they appeared in a Colorado newspaper:

"Damn any man who sympathizes with Indians! ... I have come to kill Indians, and believe it is right and honorable to use any means under God's heaven to kill Indians. ... Kill and scalp all, big and little; nits make lice."

The three sisters sat silently for a moment, each woman enmeshed, in her own bigoted thoughts.

Delilah picked up the silver bell that sat on the table, adjacent to the teapot. With a delicate, dainty flexing of her wrist, she rang the bell. Almost instantly, Hattie appeared. *"Yessm?"*

"Hattie, please refill the teapot, and if we have any left, bring another plate of crackers."

Cynthia lifted the fragile, delicate china teapot, and refilled her porcelain teacup. She then reached for a cookie, and took a small bite. Annabelle,
Cynthia's two-year-old daughter, was at her feet, tugging at her skirt, attempting to gain her mother's attention.

Cynthia picked up her little chubby, pink-cheeked, blue-eyed child, and lovingly began to lavish kisses upon the little girl's cheeks. While holding her child in her arms, she glanced at her sister and in an exasperated voice asked; "What in the world was your nigger-woman, what's her name… Hattie, thinking?"

Following Cynthia's daughter's return to play with the other children, Delilah, partially in answer to what Cynthia had believed was a rhetorical question, and introduced a new topic for discussion.

"Last year when Lincoln, that baboon in the Yankee White House, issued that ridiculous paper, that the Yankees assert sets our slaves free, our darkies have become increasingly difficult to handle."

Beatrice closed her eyes, her lips pressed tightly together. She appeared to be concentrating. "For the life of me ladies, I can't remember what that document that you're referring to, was called."

Cynthia blurted out; "My husband, the judge, says that the document in question, is in fact, merely a pseudo-legal proclamation, a presidential Executive Order."

"A lawless, desperate act by the Yankee president to encourage our slaves to abandon their homes, to runaway, and to incite, and participate in slave insurrections'."

"The judge calls the document of which we speak, Abraham Lincoln's, Emancipation Proclamation", a blatant unconstitutional overreaching of Executive Power.

Delilah interjected; "I've heard daddy and Luis, when talking to their friends during their weekly poker games, refer to their concerns about the troubling, changing, attitudes, of our slaves."

"In the past three months', as the slaves begin to hear about that damn proclamation, we are experiencing an alarming increase in the number of runaway slaves."

Why just last week, three of Mayor Snyder's slaves, ran away. Just took off, presumably running toward the Yankees."

The consensus of daddy's poker buddies, those influential gentlemen, is that as more and more of the slaves are made aware of the prevailing provision of the proclamation, that is; those slaves within the Confederate States,
"are forever free", that the darkies that don't runaway, will become increasingly, agitated, belligerent, dangerous."

"In the words of the banker, that loathsome little, perverted man, Archibald Saunders; "The Natives…that's my euphemism, by which I of course, mean the word that he used, *"the niggers"*, are indeed, becoming Restless."

****

Chapter 36

Richmond Virginia (1867) – Law Office of Luis Frazier, Esq.)

Despite the passage of time, more than four years, Luis could still feel tears began to well-up in his eyes, when to his surprise, he was suddenly nearly unseated, by thirty pounds of the cutest, most energetic, swirling, whirling, dervish, his three-year-old nephew, Henry Billings, II.

While Luis was precariously, attempting to regain his balance, his beautiful, blond haired, blue eyed, ward, little Henry's mother, Rebecca entered his inner office.

"Uncle Luis, have you seen the baby? It's time for his nap. One minute he was playing in the outer office, I turned for just a second, to shut the door, when I looked back, he had vanished."

Luis looked between his legs, there below his desk, seated on the floor, in the "U" shaped cut-out space that usually housed his legs, looking up and grinning from ear to ear, was his three-year-old nephew, Henry Luis Billings, II, "Little-Hank".

Luis turned toward Rebecca, folded his arms, placed his left hand under his chin, and with the index finger of his right hand pointed to the grinning, giggling, tyke, kneeling beneath his desk.

Rebecca immediately picked up on the twinkle, the merriment, emitting from Luis' eyes.

As soon as Little-Hank, had learned to stand upright, unassisted, the toddler had abandoned crawling.

For young Hank, his discovery of the much faster, efficient, and surprisingly *"fun"*, means of locomotion, walking, then running, was essential for the playing of his favorite game, the ancient— but to baby Hank—, new game of Hide and Go-Seek.

Rebecca nodded her head, acknowledging to "Uncle Louey", that she understood. That she was aware that her hyperactive son was hiding beneath the desk.

"Oh dear, it seems as though I've lost my baby, my little boy." Rebecca sat down in one of the two office chairs. She put her hands over her face and began to whimper, in the most piteous voice that she could muster; *"Oh dear, oh dear, what am I to do. I've lost my little boy."*

Luis glanced down at his nephew. Little-Hank upon hearing his mother's anguished words hastily crawled out from under the desk.

The childish grin that only moments ago, had lit up the child's face, had been replaced with a look of genuine pain and horror.

The little boy's face was contorted. "Mommie don't cry. I'm here Momma. Please don't cry."

Rebecca realizing that her little ruse may have gone to far, stood and with a broad smile spreading across her face, opened her arms, welcoming the unconditional, loving, welcoming, embrace of her son.

After promising Rebecca that he would be home in time for dinner, mother and son—his ward/niece Rebecca, and her son Henry Jr.—, left the office,

Luis, with a weary sigh of contentment, straightened the voluminous pile of papers, strewn across his desk.

Luis wearily moved from his chair, to the small sofa aligning the wall. His intent was to relax for a moment, before closing the office.

He closed his eyes, and with an audible sigh, relaxed his aching muscles.

Although his intent had been to sit for just a moment, his mind began to drift. Luis thought of how his life had dramatically changed.

How he now, as if by magic, had an extended family, his wife Delilah, Rebecca, little Hank, and Delilah's sisters.

****

Chapter 37

Richmond Virginia (Reconstruction - August, 1867) Home of Luis Frazier, Esq - Attorney-at-Law

Little Henry Luis Billings, II, burst into the kitchen of his home. The impressive three story, brick town-house, owned by Mr. and Mrs. Luis Frazier, Esq., Little-Hank's *"Uncle Looey"* and *"Auntie Lilah."*

Hattie Mae Smith, the Frazier's robust, full-breasted, ebony, *colored* cook, and her husband Willie James Smith, whose slender, wiry frame was in stark contrast to Hattie Mae's bulk, although his skin pigmentation nearly matched that of his wife's, were both seated at the kitchen table.

"Hattie, momentarily startled by the toddler's energetic arrival, placed her steaming coffee cup onto the table. *"Lansakes chile, dun yus eva walk, or duz yus eva jus stan still? Yu so fidgety, it be lik yu got ants in yur pants."*

Mr. and Mrs. Willie James Smith, were paid employees of the Frazier's.

Hattie's employment was as the family's cook, and Willie as the Frazier's butler, and Luis' personal valet.

Mr. and Mrs. Willie James Smith, because of their positions as employees of Luis Frazier, Esq., were two very visible examples of, those *"Nigras'"* now receiving paid-wages.

The pro-slavery segments of the defeated Confederacy ascribed the paying of wages for *"Nigra"* labor, as being the primary destabilizing factor, which was destroying the Southern economy.

****

Luis, Delilah, and Rebecca were sipping coffee, following the completion of one of Hattie's scrumptious, delicious, dinners. Rebecca folded and placed her napkin on the table. *"Uncle Looey* and Aunt Delilah, please excuse me. I want to tuck the baby in, and I promised to read him, a bed-time story."

Luis began to rise. He placed his napkin on the chair, and slid his chair from beneath the table. Delilah spoke; "Luis instead of retiring to your study, for your ritualistic snifter of brandy, and the smoking of one of those god-awful, smelly cigars, please sit and chat with me for a while."

Luis leaned over and reacquired his napkin. He placed it on the table, and sat.

Luis turned to Willie, who was in the process of clearing the china and silverware from the table; "Willie, instead of having my brandy in the study, I'll have it here." He turned to his wife; "My dear, would you care to join me, in a brandy?"

"Luis, you know that I don't imbibe strong spirits. Willie please, just bring brandy for one. In deference to Mrs. Frazier, tonight we'll forgo the cigar."

"Yassuh Mr. Luis…I'll be bac d'rectly." With that, Willie, both arms overloaded with dining accoutrements, left the dining room.

Luis sat back in his chair. His arms were folded across his chest. Luis gave his full attention to his wife.

"Delilah, to what do I owe this unexpected, but entirely welcome, invitation to, as you say, sit and chat?"

Delilah sat primly, erect, her back pressed firmly against the back of her chair. She took a deep breath. "Luis I am beginning to have some serious concerns regarding Rebecca."

Just as Luis was about to reply, Willie, carrying a silver tray, entered the room. A crystal decanter, half filled with an amber colored liquid, flanked by a large brandy snifter, was balanced on the tray.

Wordlessly, Willie poured the brown, aromatic, liquid into the snifter. *"Will that be all suh?"*

Luis picked-up the snifter, swirled the liquor around in the goblet, and took a sip. He gave an appreciative sigh of appreciation. "Ahh… that's excellent brandy."

Luis placed his drink on the coaster that Willie had placed before him. "Thank you, Willie. Yes, that will be all."

Willie stepped away from the table. *"Yes suh. Good nite suh."* He turned and faced Delilah; *"Good nite miztress…* he caught himself, and softly muttered…*good nite mam."* Willie pivoted and left the dining room.

"Forgive me my dear…what were you saying…oh yes…it sounded as if you have concerns about Rebecca?   I don't quite understand. What exactly is the nature, the bases, of your disquieting, apprehension? As far as I can tell, Becky seems to be perfectly happy, she's in good health, and she's obviously devoted to Little-Hank."

Delilah, with an exasperated look of solemn impatience on her face, in a whiney voice, uncharacteristically, exclaimed; "That's precisely the point Luis. Don't you see, Rebecca's entire life now consists of, and is dedicated to her son… to Henry, Jr."

"Rebecca is a beautiful, twenty-one-year old, young woman in the prime of her life. It's been four years since she escaped from the savages. More than three years since she and her child have been living with us."

Rebecca is a strikingly attractive young woman, with a substantial, equally attractive dowry. She should have a bevy of beaux's, sniffing around her, while seeking from you, your permission, to pay court."

Delilah took a deep breath; "I think that the time has come for Rebecca to begin to build a life of her own."

While she was speaking, Delilah had been intently staring into Luis's expressive, blue eyes, searching his face, looking for telltale signs of agreement, and more importantly, for signs of annoyance.

Delilah, more than anyone, was acutely aware of her husband's, sudden, sometimes volatile, mood changes.

****

Chapter 38

Richmond Virginia (Reconstruction - August, 1867)

The military campaigns, the bloody, armed hostilities, of the Civil War had ended two years earlier, when on April 9th, 1865, General Robert E. Lee, surrendered the Confederate Army of Northern Virginia, to the Union's General Ulysses S. Grant, in the rural town of Appomattox Court House, Virginia.

In the hallowed halls of the United States Congress, the political battles between the liberal, and the conservative members of the nation's legislative branch of government, continued to rage.

The Radical Republicans, led by Congressman Thaddeus Stevens of Pennsylvania, were committed, determined to punish those rebels, who had for more than four long years, tenaciously fought to maintain the Southern slavocracy.

On March 2, 1867, Congress, led by Radical Republicans, brought Reconstruction to Richmond Virginia, the former capital of the relatively, short lived, self-proclaimed, Confederate States of America.

Ironically, Congress in acknowledging Richmond's former status as the Confederate capital—the political center of the recent rebellion, in essence, the South's number one city—, designated Virginia; Military District Number One.

In an attempt to counter the Radical Republicans, President Andrew Johnson appointed Major General John M. Schofield, as Commander, of Military District One.

****

BOOK III

Chapter 39

The City of Chester, Virginia
(Freedmen's Bureau – August 1867)

The distinguished, handsome, surprisingly young, colored soldier, dressed in Union Army blues, with three light blue strips, chevrons pointed downward, set below three blue interconnected arches, on each sleeve of his uniform tunic, sat hunched over a pile of official looking papers.

Sergeant Major, Jason Ruth sat pensively, lost in thought, at his small desk, located on the first level of the offices of the Chester Virginia, Freedmen's Bureau, located just outside of the city of Richmond.

Despite his door being closed, the steady cacophony of noise coming from the communal spaces that surrounded his little enclave, was making it difficult for Jason to concentrate.

The six colored soldiers under his immediate supervision, two corporals and four privates as was he, were all soldiers, temporarily detached from Company "C", 1st Platoon, of the Union Army's XXV Corp.

The small detachment of Union soldiers, were presently engaged in trying to maintain control of the increasingly growing number of restless, hungry, emancipated ex-slaves. Men who for the first time in their lives—at least by the Government—, were referred to as *__Men__*, free-*__Men__*-of-color.

The crowd was comprised almost entirely of unemployed, ex-slaves, who were seeking assistance from the new Freedmen's Bureau. An agency created in Washington City, by the congress', Radical Republicans, whose mission was to help in the transition of the former-slaves, into free men.

Sergeant Ruth was lost in thought. His mind fleetingly reflected upon how radically, things had change, in such a relatively short period of time.

It had been a little more than two years, since the rebel's General Robert E. Lee, had surrendered, to the Union's General Ulysses S. Grant.

General Lee's surrendering of the Army of Northern Virginia was the historical event that marked the end of the Civil War. Lee's surrender marked the death null, for the Confederate States of America.

General Lee's surrender had served as the seminal, definitive, event that had solidified and emphatically, declared the end of legalized slavery, on the North American Continent.

The Sergeant Major still found it difficult to believe, and hard to accept the fact that at the age of thirty-two, that he, a former slave, was one of the highest ranking, non-commissioned officers, serving in the United States Army.

Jason Billings, former runaway slave, was now Sergeant Major Jason Ruth. He had been sent by the United States Army, to assist his kinsmen, the more than four million former slaves; adjust to a life of freedom.

Sergeant Major Ruth was the second in command, of this small army detachment.

The Sergeant Major was subordinate only to Lieutenant Andrew Price, a recently commissioned, young white "*shave-tail*" officer, who let everyone who would listen, know, how much he regretted, not having seen action, in the recently concluded war.

Lieutenant Price, the young white officer officially in command, and Sergeant Major, Jason Ruth, the former runaway slave, was the United States Army's representatives, in charge of the Chester, Virginia Federal Office, of the newly created Freedmen's Bureau, a government agency created to assist in the transition of a life of slavery, to a life of freedom.

Sergeant Major Ruth closed the folder and placed it into the middle drawer of the desk. He reached into the pocket of his uniform trousers and removed a small, skeleton key.
The Sergeant stood and locked the drawer. He straightened his back, squared his shoulders, and left the office.

****

Chapter 40

Regimental Headquarters - New Hampshire's 5ᵗʰ Volunteers August 13, 1861

Jason's original, official army designator, that of being a "Contraband-Scout/Interpreter", had been at best, only partly accurate.

When Captain Clarke gave him the good news, Jason had initially welcomed and embraced the designator "Scout." He was thrilled at the prospect of for the first time in his life, being actually paid for his labor.

While there was merit in the army's designation of Jason's position as an Interpreter, to his disappointment, the word "Scout", proved to be a complete misnomer.

In his capacity as a "Scout/Interpreter", Jason had envisioned himself as being a solitary armed combatant; looking for, locating, engaging, and killing, confederate soldiers. Killing the white man.

Killing the men that had enslaved, and now the men who fought, to keep his people, enslaved.

Jason's fervent desire was to kill the men who sympathized, sanctioned, and justified the actions of those white devils, his former Master, Henry Billings, the Master of the nearby Rosewood Plantation. And the despised white man, Lucas Prentiss, Jason's biological father, the overseer of Rosewood.

Jason was fully cognizant of the fact, that his simplistic, assessment of the duties of a *"Scout"*, was in actuality, an almost exact replication of the prevailing theme of the old *"Dime Novels"*, that served as the back-drop, which depicted the "Adventures of Buckskin Bob, against the "Savage Redskins", that his young *"Massa"* Jesse Billings, had emulated, as a child.

The prevailing theme of those *"Dime Novels"*, those fictitious tales, that promulgated the alleged superiority of the white man over the red man, that inspired the games, that as a boy, he and his young *Massa* Jesse Billings, had played, Massa Jesse as (*Buckskin Bob*), and Jason would serve his Massa, in the role of *"Blackey,* Buckskin Bob's trusty stead.

Now working for the Union Army as a "Scout/Interpreter", initially in his mind, Jason's imaginary recasting of those childish games, Jason had envisioned himself as being the vengeful Union Army Scout, with the Confederate Soldiers being analogous to those *"Savage Red Skins"*.

****

Chapter 41

Regimental Headquarters - New Hampshire's 5th Volunteers November 7, 1861

Captain Clarke, in an effort to take advantage of, and to utilize Jason's demonstrated literacy, and his apparent above average intellect, had assigned to Jason, the duties of a civilian, "Adjunct-Company Clerk."

Once it became known to his fellow officers, that Captain Clarke had under his command, an exceptionally literate *"Contraband"*, a runaway slave, for all intents and purposes Jason ceased to be working exclusively, for Captain Clarke.

Within weeks, to Captain Clarke's chagrin, word of, and examples of the exceptional high quality of the work of his, *"Literate Contraband"*, eventually came to the attention of the cadre of field-grade, and senior officers, at regimental headquarters.

Instead of his being eventually sent into the field, instead of being given the opportunity to fulfill his life-long, repressed desire—that is to *"kill the white man"*—, Jason Ruth, the Contraband - "Scout/Interpreter", who had been functioning as a Company Clerk, was officially reassigned to regimental headquarters, as a civilian, Adjunct Regimental Clerk.

While Captain Clarke had been vehemently opposed to Jason's transfer, he was fully aware that his military rank, and his status as the commanding officer of Company 'C' of the 5th New Hampshire Volunteer Infantry, precluded his giving vent to, or submitting, an official objection.

Captain Clarke was fully attuned to and familiar with, the reality and the exercising, of the ageless military adage **RHIP**; "Rank Has Its Privileges."

Despite Jason's disappointment of not being armed and sent into the field to fight, he adapted well, to the passive, relatively sedentary life of, a behind the lines, Regimental Clerk.

Jason eagerly accepted the challenge, the opportunity to openly, utilized his here-to-fore, clandestine skills, reading, writing, and problem solving, skills that he had been taught, in defiance of Southern Law, by his sister Mandy.

For the first time in his life, Jason's suppressed intellect was being unleashed, finally being, fully liberated.

Jason's eager, thirsty young mind, sopped up information, similar to the way a sponge absorbs water.

During his life as a slave, it had been imperative, for his safety and the safety of his mother and sister, that he keep secret, his ability to read and to write.

On the plantation, the bulk of the reading material that Jason had been exposed to during his enslavement, were the books and pamphlets, that Rebecca Billings, the young white Mistress of the Rosewood Plantation, gave to her playmate, Mandy, Jason's sister.

When Jason had inadvertently, discovered, accidentally stumbled upon his sister Mandy, *"reading."* At first, he had thought that his sister was *"play-acting",* pretending to understand the squiggly characters in the book, that she was pretending to be reading.

When he had initially asked Mandy; *"Wud dat yu do'n Mandy? Duz yu knos wud dat means?"* Jason had fully expected that his sister would laugh and would respond by confessing that she was *"jus funnin'."*

Instead Mandy, startled, had slammed the book shut. *"Jay, wer ya com frum? Wu fo yu do'n spy'n on me?"*

Jason had been surprised, by the accusatory tone in his little sister's voice. Mandy had always, shown difference to him.

She had always held him in awe. Mandy had always, both figuratively and literally, looked up to her "Big Brother."

When she saw the hurt in her big brother's eyes, Mandy was instantly ashamed of her response, at her outburst.

Then and there, Mandy made a momentous, potentially dangerous, decision. She opened the book, and in a calm, steady, deliberate, voice, began to read:

"We hold these truths to be self-evident, that all men are created equal, that they are endowed by their Creator with certain unalienable rights, that among these are life, liberty and the pursuit of happiness."

A look of astonishment, surprise, and absolute incredulity, spread across Jason's face. *"Mandy wud dat yu sayn'? Is yu funnin' me...is dem relly da words in dat der book?"*

Mandy had slowly, reverently, closed the book. And in a voice and inflection that Jason had come to associate with, *"rich white foks talkn'"*, Mandy had answered; "Those Jason, are the exact words as they are written in this book."

 "That Jason, is real, ***POWER***. " As Mistress Rebecca and I have been taught by Miss Eleanor Leary, and that we unabashedly believe that; "Knowledge is indeed, ***POWER!***"

Now in his role as an adjunct regimental clerk, to his delight, Jason was being inundated with voluminous stacks of reading material. Of particular interest to him, were the military dispatches.

The military dispatches introduced Jason to the formal language, and the thought processes, of the officers. He began to get a sense of the thought processes of the men who gave the orders to other men, to attack...to retreat...to kill, or be killed.

Jason began to understand the thought processes of those men, who he had come to believe, held the real power, the men that comprised the Union Army's Officer Corps.

****

Chapter 42

Richmond Virginia (Home of Luis and Delilah Frazier) - August, 1867)

Rebecca's life revolved around her son Henry Billings, II. In her relatively short life-time, twenty-one years, *which constituted* some 7,665 days, two of those days, would for her, be forever indelibly, seared into her mind.

The first was that fateful day on the western prairie, when the savage, cannibalistic, Tonkawa Indians, murdered, mutilated, and butchered, her father.

The other was *March 10, 1864, the day that Henry Billings, II, her son, little "Hank", was born.*

When Dr. Sawyer had adamantly refused to assist her, in terminating her unwanted pregnancy, a pregnancy that the doctor knew, had resulted from her being repeatedly raped by, a savage Indian, Rebecca had been inconsolable, devastated.

Despite her pleadings, and despite the fact that her unwanted pregnancy, actually met one of the doctor's professed, restrictive, criteria for his terminating a pregnancy, that being rape, Dr. Sawyer had, because of the advanced stage of her pregnancy, had refused to reconsider his decision, not to terminate her pregnancy.

When Rebecca and her guardian Luis, had pressed him, by pointing out that Rebecca's having been raped, met his criteria, Dr. Sawyer had countered, by reminding them that his examination, had determined that Rebecca was in the third trimester of her pregnancy.

He went on to emphatically— Luis thought, dramatically—, point out, that an abortion, at this late stage in her pregnancy, would put Rebecca's life in danger.

Both Rebecca and Luis had reluctantly, been forced to accept the doctor's rational, and the finality of his decision.

Rebecca vividly remembered, the discomfort, the excruciating pain that she had experienced throughout her prolonged, period of labor.

She recalled her feelings of resentment and her anger. She remembered her resolve, and her determination, to immediately; when this was over, to have her guardian, take *"IT"*, to the orphanage for "Coloreds."

****

The formerly, spasmodic, ephemeral, bouts of discomfort, had now been replaced by an unrelenting, intense pain.

As she squeezed her maid Hattie's hand, and tried to comply with
Dr. Sawyer's calm yet urgently, repeated instructions to "push".

Rebecca recalled her feelings of exultation and relief, when her final "push", had resulted in the passage of the unwanted *"creature"*, from her body.

She remembered her reaction to the sound of crying. She remembered her reaction when Hattie brought the kicking, crying, writhing *"creature"*, to her bed.

Rebecca remembered her reaction to Hattie's words; "*Miz Becca dis here be yur son.*"

She remembered the promise that she had made to herself. Her promise to loath the spawn of that barbaric savage, Stone Fist, the Comanche warrior that had over, and over, and over again, raped her.

She remembered listening to the incessant wailing, emanating from the squirming, and twitching, little bundle in Hattie's lap.
She remembered how she had, refused to look at *"IT."* She remembered Hattie, sitting in the corner, rocking and shushing that… that, *"creature"*.

Rebecca remembered Hattie's soft brown eyes, staring at her, welling-up with silent tears, those eyes, pleading, with her, imploring her.

She remembered when Hattie walked over to the bed and opened the blanket.

She remembered when she—filled with loathing—, first looked at *"IT."*

She remembered how suddenly, and unexpectedly; her heart had begun to race.

She remembered, when she first saw the ruddy, dimpled cheeks, the full-head of jet-black hair, how instantly her determination, to loath *"IT"*, had somehow, miraculously melted, dissolved, vanished.

She remembered her joy, her feeling of exaltation, when *__"he"__* gripped and squeezed her finger.

She remembered how thrilled she was when she looked into his large, innocent, black, obsidian, colored eyes.

She remembered the over-whelming joy that she felt, as she looked down at, the lively, contented, beautiful baby, nursing at her breast.

She remembered that that, was when she ceased to think of the bundle as an *"IT."*

She remembered the exact moment that she came to realize, that she loved this tiny being, with every fiber of her being.

With all of her heart, Rebecca Billings truly loved this tiny miracle.

Rebecca Elizabeth Billings, loved her *"SON."*

****

Chapter 43

Richmond Virginia - Home of Luis
and Delilah Frazier - August, 1867)
(Bed Room of Henry Billings, II)

"Please, Mommy, please. Just one more story Mommy…*puleeease.*

Rebecca pulled the bed covers up and gently tucked them under her son's chin.

She made and exaggerated, exasperated face. She smiled; "Henry it's time for you to go to sleep".

Goldie Locks and The Three Bears had been tonight's second, *pu-leeease*, mommy, story.

Rebecca gently kissed her son's forehead, cupped her hand around the chimney of the lamp, and gently blew.

The light from the full moon, filtered through the curtains, softly illuminating the room.

As she left the room, Rebecca glanced over her shoulder. Little-Hank was lying on his side, fast asleep, hugging his favorite "Teddy bear."

With her hand on the doorknob, Rebecca hesitated. She stood immobile, listening. Aunt Delilah, her voice modulated, but slightly elevated, for some reason, kept repeating her name.

"Luis I am truly perplexed. Whenever I speak to you of Rebecca's isolation, her failure, to meet people, to socialize, with young people her own age, why do you inevitably, become combative, defensive?"

Luis was slowly shaking his head from side to side. Meticulously and deliberately, he folded his latest edition of the Richmond Gazette.

For weeks, Delilah's number one topic of discussion, had been a continuous, endless, series of criticism, directed towards Rebecca and her son, Little-Hank.

Intellectually, Luis understood why his wife was annoyed. Hell, any woman would be upset at having a grown woman, a stranger, and her child, suddenly insert themselves into her household, into her family.

Conceptually, that fact not withstanding, Luis found the tenor and the tone of Delilah's comments, to be somewhat disconcerting.

His annoyance stemmed from the fact that during his and Delilah's courtship, and subsequently after their marriage, he had often discussed with her, and confided in her, the depth of his and Henry Billings, Rebecca 's father's, life-long friendship.

Luis had shared with Delilah, his grief and the pernicious, all consuming, oppressive, remorse and feelings of guilt, which had plagued him, following his friend's untimely, tragic death.

Luis was aware of, and sympathetic to, the unsettling upheaval, and turmoil, that Rebecca's, unexpected arrival at their doorstep, must have introduced into Delilah's life.

Luis struggled to focus. He once again willed himself to listen, to concentrate on the words pouring forth from Delilah's shrill voice.

"Rebecca is a strikingly attractive young woman, who incidentally, as we are both aware, just happens to possess a substantial, equally attractive, dowry."

Despite the fact that, intellectually he could empathize with and to a degree understand the cause for Delilah's frequent, festering sour moods, nonetheless, Luis was becoming increasingly annoyed with what he considered to be her lack of understanding, and her constant, persistent, nagging.

Delilah's voice, droned on; "It is not my intention to be crude, tactless, or hateful. However, Luis, at the risk of incurring your displeasure, by constantly repeating myself, I feel compelled to point out that, Rebecca should be inundated with dozens of potential suitors."

"Luis, as her surrogate father, you should be busy, sifting through the cards of those young men, who should be seeking your permission to call on Rebecca."

Delilah took a deep breath; "Luis this is our home! I think that it's high time for Rebecca, to begin to build a life of her own. She should be building a life for herself, as well as a life and a future, for her son."

Delilah's assessment of Luis's mood was correct. Luis was indeed, becoming increasingly, annoyed.

Despite his growing annoyance at his wife's words, and his resentment of her only slightly veiled veneer of jealousy, Luis knew that there was definitely, more than a degree of validity in Delilah's diatribe.

Delilah sat quietly, anxiously awaiting her husband's response. Luis took a deep breath, clasped his hands together, forming a steeple. He began to speak; "I apologize my dear for being so insensitive. There is a great deal of truth to your thoughts, your feelings, and your words."

Delilah, with an involuntary audible sigh of relief, relaxed. She took her husband's hands into her own, and gazed deeply into his eyes. She once again marveled at the clarity, the calm, soothing tranquility, of his sparkling blue eyes.

His eyes, bereft of any hint of resentment, reassured her. She felt confidant that this time, she had not "over-played her hand."

Luis gently, reassuringly, squeezed her hands. "I am forced to concede, that your characterization of my behavior and attitude towards Becky is for the most part, accurate."

"Admittedly, I have turned a "blind-eye", to her increasingly isolationistic tendencies. But in my defense, considering all that she has gone through, and my actions that contributed to the tragedy, I ask you, can you honestly blame me?"

"Four years ago, when Rebecca came to us, she was all alone in the world, a child, with a child, growing in her womb.

In addition to the joy and relief that I felt at her safety and deliverance, I selfishly, also felt the weight, the burden of the tremendous sense of guilt, that I had been carrying, being lifted from my shoulders."

"There standing before us was the daughter of my best friend, whose untimely death, as well as the capture, torture and rape of his daughter, and her subsequent pregnancy, I felt was due, to a great extent, to my enormous ego."

"After all, it was I, the acclaimed by so many, brilliant Luis Frazier, Esq. who concocted the scheme, the plan.

The plan that would have Lincoln's Yankee Government, through our manipulation of the 1862 Homestead Act, unbeknownst to them, give free and clear, 160 acres of virgin, fertile land, to Henry Billings, a wealthy, slave owning, fanatically, staunch supporter of the Confederacy."

"It was because of me, that my best friend sought out and joined, that ill- fated wagon train. It was because of me that those savages, murdered and mutilated Henry's body. It was because of me that Becky was captured, tortured, and raped by that barbaric savage that to this day, continues to plague her, the savage that she calls, "Stone Fist."

"It was because of me that that sweet little innocent child was subjected to what we can only imagine, must have been a living Hell!"

"I say this in an obvious attempt to justify my negligence. I owe Rebecca and Little-Hank, much more than just a roof over their heads. A sanctum in which she uses to hibernate, secluded from society, from the rest of the world."

"What I owe Rebecca and Little-Hank, is the opportunity for them to have long, prosperous, and happy lives."

"That is a sacred debt that I owe to my friend Henry Billings, the man that I loved as if he were my brother. The man who lost his life, following my advice that he relocate his family, in the West."

Luis picked up his newspaper; he leaned over and gently kissed Delilah's forehead.

"I will speak to Rebecca. Encourage her to make friends, to socialize with young people. I'll point out to her that while her self imposed isolationism may seem to be safe, comfortable, and satisfying, it is in fact unhealthy and not at all fair to Little-Hank."

"Rebecca has to re-assimilate, reclaim for herself, and for her child, her birthright. She needs to regain and reclaim her rightful place, as a Southern lady of breeding."

****

Chapter 44

Richmond Virginia -"Le Grand Vieux Manoir"
Restaurant, 7:30 PM (September 1867)

Rebecca was uncomfortable, ill at ease. She was seated at the table of one of the few remaining, respectable, Richmond eating establishments.

Her beautiful long blonde hair was parted in the center, and gathered into two symmetrically bejeweled chignons, at the nape of her neck.

Rebecca was resplendent, wearing a fashionable, blue chiffon evening gown.

The uncomfortable dress billowed out, at least two feet from her legs, which were snugly; encased in a frilly pair of, lace pantalets.

Rebecca remembered wryly thinking—while Hattie was encouraging her to hold her breathe, as she pulled at the laces of the corset—, that the steel frame of the crinoline cage, that supported the gown, was more restrictive than any of the rawhide thongs, that the Comanche had used to restrain her, during the time that she had been held a captive-slave.

Rebecca's escort, a pale, pasty complexioned, rather stocky man of medium height, with the beginnings of a receding hairline, was seated directly across from her at the intimate, yet spacious dinner table.

Her "date" appeared to be engrossed in deep thought, as he perused the items listed on the large menu.

Delilah's younger sister Cynthia had introduced Rebecca to her dinner companion, Mr. Horace Stapleton, Esq.

Mr. Stapleton before he joined the prestigious law firm of Luis Frazier, Esq., and Associates, had held the position of law clerk and protégé, for the Honorable Judge Lawrence F. Pinckney, Cynthia's husband.

Cynthia had reluctantly acquiesced to the pleadings of her sister Delilah, to invite Mr. Stapleton to attend a small birthday celebration at her home.

The celebration was being given in honor of their father, Elijah Simpson's, 65th birthday.

Although Mr. Horace Stapleton, Esq. had thought it odd when his mentor Judge Pinckney, had practically ordered him to come to the gathering alone, Horace Stapleton—in addition to his being an accomplished, ambitious, young lawyer—, Horace was an equally accomplished, and opportunistic, sycophant.

With out a moment's hesitation, Horace, always anxious to please the judge, his mentor, an established, influential politician, had compelled him to comply with the judge's wishes. Horace had eagerly accepted the invitation.

As she sat starring, her eyes transfixed on the shiny, thinning, and prematurely balding pate in the center of her escort's head, Rebecca's mind began to drift.

She vividly recalled the rather unpleasant, tense "*talk*", two weeks earlier that she and Uncle Luis had shared.

Their frank "*Heart-to-Heart*", talk had occurred shortly after she had finished reading, the third of the now requisite, three bedtime stories to her son, and she had finally been able to tuck the covers up under Little-Hank's chin, and kiss him goodnight.

While propped up in her bed, absent-mindedly rereading her favorite, play, Shakespeare's Romeo and Juliet, she had heard a gentle, but firm knocking on the door of her bedroom.

Rebecca had placed a bookmark in the large tome; "The Collected Works of William Shakespeare", and closed the book. She pulled her bed-sheet under her chin. "Yes…who's there?"

"It's me Becky, Uncle Luis. I saw your light under the door. If its not inconvenient, I would like to speak with you. May I come in?"

****

Rebecca was convinced that it was Delilah who had convinced Uncle Luis, that quote; "It was time that she ended her self-imposed cloistered existence".

"That it was time for Rebecca to reenter Richmond Society, to make a life for her and her son."

The fact that she had lived a year as a captive-slave of the Indians; that she had been repeatedly raped; that she had subsequently, given birth to her son Henry II, her beautiful baby, that society so cavalierly referred to as a "half-breed", to infer and to suggest that these events would not be an issue, Rebecca knew, as she suspected, Uncle Luis knew, was absurd, and absolutely ludicrous.

Though she had initially taken umbrage with his words, his presumptive criticism and his intrusion into her chosen lifestyle, eventually Rebecca had grudgingly, relented.

She had promised her uncle that she would at least give consideration, to the salient points that he had raised, that they had both agreed, were valid.

After considerable soul searching and introspection, Rebecca had reluctantly allowed herself to give credence to at least, a modicum of Luis' assertions.

Although she still dismissed Luis', or as she was convinced more than likely, Aunt Delilah's assertion, that she could nonchalantly, smoothly, as if nothing had happened, reenter Southern Society, Rebecca in an effort to please Luis, had with considerable trepidation, reluctantly accepted, Mr. Horace Stapleton's unexpected invitation to dinner.

****

Chapter 45

Richmond Virginia – September 1867 – Restaurant "Le Grand Vieux Manoir", 7:39 PM

Rebecca's mind was pulled from its' revelry, by the high-pitched voice of her dinner-date.

"Although one cannot seriously expect the cuisine here, to be on a par with that of the Parisians, still I've been led to believe that it's quite good."

Horace lifted his head from the menu; "I've been told that the escargot, in this establishment, is extraordinary, delicious."

Before the war, on several occasions, as an adolescent, and as a young pre-teenaged girl, Rebecca had accompanied her father on business trips to Richmond.

Unbeknownst to Horace this was not the first time that she had dined at this particular French Restaurant.

Despite the hardships that had befallen most of Richmond, the city's renowned French Restaurant; "*Le Grand Vieux Manoir*", had managed to survive and remarkably, appeared to be thriving.

When she and her escort had entered the restaurant, and were being shown to their table, Rebecca had been acutely aware of a subtle, but definitely discernable change in the atmosphere, in the ambience of the trendy, upscale, eating establishment.

Horace too, had been cognizant of the effect that their entrance, had evoked from the other diners. He had given a great deal of thought to his choice of an appropriate restaurant. Horace had carefully, meticulously, weighed his options.

While he was not one who was prone to participate, or to necessarily believe in malicious gossip, he was however, conscious of, and acutely attuned to, the power of public opinion, most especially, the detrimental affect that pernicious gossip and innuendo, could have on his burgeoning political career.

Horace's initial inclination, as to where he and the "*white-squaw*", should dine, had been to choose a secluded, small, out of the way restaurant.

A spot where it was unlikely that he would be recognized by his friends and acquaintances, the people of breeding and influence, in Richmond Society.

After thoroughly weighing the pros and the cons of his decision, Horace had decided that it was in his best interest, that he not offend, either his mentor, the esteemed Judge Pinckney, nor would it be wise of him to risk offending the *"white-squaw's"*, guardian, the well connected, extremely successful, powerful, attorney and entrepreneur, Mr. Luis Frazier, Esq., who just happened to be, his new employer.

Besides, he reasoned, as distasteful as being seen in the company of the *"white-squaw"*, might be, there was always a case to be made for what he hoped some might perceive of, as his act of tolerance and courage.

After all, not many gentlemen would have had the courage, to be seen in public, with Rebecca Billings, the white woman, who for nearly a year, had been a captive-slave, subjected to the carnal cravings and lust, of the Godless, heathen, Comanche Indians.

Inwardly Horace smiled at the possibility of his being perceived as; The magnanimous Horace Stapleton, who in the face of public –opinion, and at the risk of his reputation, had escorted to dinner, the notorious Rebecca Billings, the woman being blithely referred to in polite society, as being that debauched, permanently soiled, fallen harlot.

Horace placed the menu onto the table. Alerting the hovering waiter that he was ready to order.

Attempting to attract the waiter's attention, Horace raised his hand and snapped his fingers; *"Garcon si vous plai."* Instantly, the waiter was at the table. *"Oui monsieur?"*

Horace with a definite air of sophistication, began to speak; *"I would like to order si vous plai. Dos escargots with…uh garlic sauce and those cheesy potatoes, et un bottle of chardonnay por favor."*

While Horace was considered by his colleagues to be an erudite, highly educated man of letters, he—as did many of his contemporaries—did not have a great deal of respect for, nor did he value the culture, of non-American, foreign cultures.

Horace, as did most of the post Civil War politicians, North and South, viewed the Atlantic and the Pacific Oceans, as God given and an intended, welcome natural barriers, that surrounded, isolated and insulated America, from the world; From the *"Others."*

In the minds of the populace, the oceans were thought of as vast, infinite, bodies of water. As God given physical barriers that encouraged, and indeed legitimized, overwhelming support, for the popular, political sentiment and foreign policy, proudly acknowledged and proclaimed as "Nativist-American Isolationism."

President George Washington, the country's first president, and revered as Virginia's favorite son, in his 1796 Farewell Address to the new fledgling nation some seventy-one years earlier, has advised that we should avoid foreign entanglements.

This sage advice still resonated, and served as the template for the nation's foreign policy.

In Virginia, with the notable exception of the Confederacy's recent unsuccessful attempts to forge alliances with European powers during their failed rebellion, the sage, sanguine advice of President Washington, remained sacrosanct.

If his fellow diners, the patrons of *"Le Grand Vieux Manoir"*, had noticed how horribly Horace had mangled the French language, it was apparent that his lack of command of French, had in no way diminished their general perception that, Horace Stapleton Esq.'s, was a sophisticated, up and coming, leading pillar of the new, Southern society.

The confused waiter a recent English-speaking immigrant from Lyon France—, not fully understanding the gentleman's dinner order, remained at the table, staring quizzically, at Horace.

Reflexively, without thinking, Rebecca spoke; *"Neus tenons deux orders d'escargots en sauce a l'ail et deux pommes de terre augratin, et une bouteille de chardonnay s'il vous plait."*

The waiter turned toward Rebecca, *"Tres bien madamselle"*, with a flourish, he picked up the menus and departed.

Rebecca's eyes met Horace's weak, reproachful, accusatory watery gaze. Instantly realizing that her spontaneous display of fluency in French, had somehow embarrassed Horace, Rebecca hastily explained.

"When I was a young girl, I believe that I had just celebrated my thirteenth birthday, my mother — who had home-schooled me my entire life, realizing that she had reached her limit, in terms of expanding and broadening my understanding of the world, and being fully cognizant of my seemingly unquenchable thirst for knowledge —, convinced my father to hire a tutor."

"Daddy, while he reluctantly agreed, was adamant that the tutor—who would be spending hours, many of them alone with his "Little princess", be a refined, cultured, Southern Lady."

"As you can appreciate, finding a highly educated "Southern Lady", who mother insisted, be a graduate from an accredited institution of higher learning, was a daunting task."

Horace, who had been attentively listening, raised a disapproving eyebrow, at that comment. A comment that he perceived as Rebecca's inference, that Southern Ladies lacked the intelligence to earn a college degree.

Rebecca seeing Horace's displeasure, hastily clarified. "As you are aware, our southern society, encourages females, to during our formative years, concentrate on preparing ourselves to be Southern Ladies."
"We're taught the basics, reading writing and rudimentary arithmetic."

"Science, mathematics, and studying other world-cultures, in our society, are reserved for southern men."

"Fortunately, father was able to obtain the services of the most marvelous teacher, a recent college graduate, to tutor me and my older brother Jesse.

Her name was Miss Eleanor Leary. She was from Nebraska, a Yankee, educated at Illinois' Oberlin College. Miss Leary was responsible for opening-up a whole new world for me, for Jesse, and for Mandy."

Realizing that she had inadvertently made a mistake, by mentioning the name of Mandy, her former slave, her black sister, Rebecca, without taking a breath hastily continued.

"Miss Leary taught us history, mathematics, and my favorites, the old-world classics. She made us aware of and familiar with, the rudimentary grammar and the vocabulary, of a few of what she called, the "Romance" languages, English, French, and Spanish."

Horace, his mouth agape, sat silently stunned. He was surprised, and genuinely impressed with the extent of Rebecca's education and her, apparent sophistication.

Horace, as did practically everyone in Richmond, and indeed almost everyone in all the surrounding countryside, knew of the torrid, scandalous tale of Rebecca Billings.
The purveyors of gossip, especially scandalous, "juicy" gossip, had heard of, heralded and embellished, the tale of the former Mistress of Rosewood Plantation's, capture by heathen savages.

While these couriers of malicious gossip, knew of Rebecca's heroic escape and rescue, after having survived nearly a year of "unspeakable", treatment at the hands of wild, heathen, barbaric, Indians, the gossip inevitably centered around Rebecca's subsequently, having given birth to a dark, swarthy complexioned "half-breed."

When Horace's former-employer, Judge Pinckney, had asked him to, as a personal favor, to take Luis Frazier, his friend and colleague's niece, the *"white squaw"* to dinner, he had reluctantly agreed.

In addition to having his mentor Judge Pinckney, in his debt, Horace had expected to, after spending a boring evening with a semi-illiterate tart, A fallen woman as it were, Horace fully intended after dinner, "to have his way with the slut, the *"white squaw."*

Horace had been taken aback, stunned and impressed by Rebecca's obvious intelligence, her breeding and with the extent of her education.

During Rebecca's explanation as to how she had learned to speak French, Horace remembered her frequent, almost reverent, mentioning of the name Mandy. Exactly who was this Mandy?

He dismissed the thought by presuming that "Mandy" had been a fellow student from a neighboring plantation.

Horace, as did most of the Richmond populace, was familiar with the pedigree of the Billings' family.

It was common knowledge that during the antebellum era, at the height of its prominence, the fabulously wealthy Billings' family, was comprised of four individuals; the master of the renowned Rosewood Plantation, Henry Billings, his wife Margaret, and the couples two children, a son, Jesse, and their daughter, Rebecca.

Horace was shocked, and confused, when in response to his innocent question, "who is Mandy, Rebecca explained that Mandy, was her life-long playmate and companion. That Mandy had been one of the Plantation's black slaves.

Horace's confusion was due to the fact that until recently, more precisely, not until the end of the war, Southern Law, had strictly prohibited the teaching of slaves to read and write.

Violation of that bedrock law, was not only a serious breech of "civilized" behavior, the teaching of a black slave to read and write, was regarded by Southern society as being an odious, vile, felony that endangered the lives of all white citizens.

It was understood at all levels of Southern Society, that strict adherence to, and enforcement of this universally held Southern law, was essential, for the preservation of slavery.

Believing that he had misunderstood Rebecca, and before he could ask for clarification, Horace's train-of-thought, was abruptly and rudely interrupted.

A steady drone of uneasy whispering and mutterings was emanating from, many of white patrons of the restaurant.

****

Chapter 46

Richmond Virginia – September 1867 - *"Le Grand Vieux Manoir"* Restaurant - 7:50 PM

Rebecca too was aware of, and had reacted to, the palpable change, in the ambient background noise, that now permeated the restaurant.

Where the initial reaction to her and Horace's entrance into *"Le Grand Vieux Manoir"*, had caused a momentary disturbance, a rumbling of uneasy disquieting, apprehension in the room, now for some reason, there had first been a moment of unnatural silence, a quietude which had been immediately followed by a cacophony of fevered chatter.

Curious as to what was causing the commotion, Rebecca turned her head.

Being seated by the maitre d' at a table, on the far side of the room, was a tall, strikingly handsome, Negro soldier. The young man wore the dress blue uniform of a Sergeant Major, actively serving in the Army of the United States of America.

The dashing soldier was holding the chair for his dinner companion, a tall, slender, dark-skinned black woman, in a smartly tailored, beautiful white-lace evening-dress, which contrasted with, and highlighted, and complimented, her beautiful ebony complexion.

Rebecca's first reaction at the sight of the young couple was that of cultural shock and surprise.

Despite her having, for nearly a year, lived as a captive-slave, among the Comanche; despite her genuine deep-seated, and unconditional love for her black sister Mandy; despite the life altering events that she had experienced; Rebecca, still had deeply embedded in the subconscious recesses of her mind, deep down, at her the core of her being, Rebecca was still a Southern White Aristocrat; still a daughter of her upbringing in the Slave Holding South.

As a product of the Southern Aristocracy, having been raised, reared, and indoctrinated in a culture that endorsed, supported and advocated the inferiority of blacks, Rebecca had been for a moment, actually a few seconds, stunned at the sight, the reality of the sight of a black couple, being seated and served, in a white eating establishment.

****

The American Civil War, a war that the recently defeated, vanquished Southerners referred to as, the "The War for Independence, or more commonly, "The War Between The States", had been a vicious, unrelenting blood bath, which had resulted in the maiming and the deaths, of hundreds of thousands of Americans.

The American Civil War, a horrific conflagration that had often pitted friend against friend, cousin against cousin, and even brother against brother.

It had been two years since the end of the American Civil War.

The Civil War had been a sustained condoned, *"civilized"*, fratricide.

The Civil War, that had been fought and won by the North, had been fought, in order to restore the Union, and to abolish slavery.

Rebecca fully understood and appreciated the fact that, the southern society that had for centuries, legally, enslaved blacks, that had enslaved her black sister Mandy, no longer existed.

And it was most definitely true, that during this time, this period of time immediately following the Confederacy's ignominious defeat, by the Armed Forces of the United States, that life in the South had, and continued to undergo, what many in the South considered *cataclysmic,* drastic changes.

It was patently obvious, that during this time, when the former rebellious Southern states, were seeking re-admittance into the Union—during this so-called period of Reconstruction—, the Radical Republicans in the United States Congress, had forced upon the Southern populace, here-to-fore unthinkable social and political changes.

One of the *egregious* changes — that the die-hard rebels, vowed would only be temporary— was the sight, in Southern society, of blacks and whites integrating, eating together, as equals, in the same restaurant.

****

After having watched the entry, and the seating of the black couple, into *"Le Grand Vieux Manoir"* Restaurant, Rebecca returned her gaze to her dinner-companion.

"Rebecca was genuinely shocked by the stark hostile expression, the undisguised, disdain, bordering on hatred, that she saw in Horace Stapleton's eyes.

Horace muttered behind clinched teeth; "look at those uppity-niggers.

"My God…the world has gone insane, completely mad. "I apologize Rebecca."

Rebecca followed Horace's gaze. The strikingly handsome, tall, black soldier, with a broad smile on his face, was now seated across from his dinner companion.

The handsome young couple was in an animated discussion, smiling at each other, holding hands on top of the table, obviously enjoying one another's company.

Rebecca turned her attention to Horace. And with an earnest look of bewilderment, she remarked; "Mr. Stapleton, I am certain that I would gladly accept your apology, if in fact sir, I knew why you feel the need to   apologize?"

Horace unfolded his napkin, and placed it in his lap. "I was apologizing for having remained seated, having remained silent, when those…those *Nigras* were allowed to be seated in this establishment."

"Although externally, at least I hope that is the case, I appear to have remained calm, I assure you that within, I am enraged at this indignity."

"If it were not for the fact that we, that is Judge Pinckney and I, are dealing with that blood-thirsty Yankee-Republican Congress, attempting to rewrite our state constitution, I would insist that those two "jungle bunnies", be immediately removed from these premises."

"Can you believe the nerve of that slimy "coon" sergeant? Look at him, decked-out in that outlandishly, grotesque, blue uniform. Strutting in here like a peacock, who instead of displaying his feathered plumage, is blatantly brandishing those rows of bright shinny medals."

"Ten to one, the only action that nigger ever saw during the war, was the shining of the officer's boots, and the only weapon that he shouldered, was the shovel he wielded to dig the white Yankee-officers' latrines."

As the waiter uncorked a bottle of chardonnay, and handed the cork to Horace for his olfactory examination and approval, despite her resolve not to impolitely stare at the black-couple, Horace's cynical comments, led Rebecca to once again discreetly, surreptitiously, scrutinize the black soldier.

Rebecca's ordeal of having been forced to live among the Comanche, to somehow survive; to survive even as a slave, in a nomadic, hunting-warring society that glorifies bravery, masculinity, and courage in battle, had bestowed upon her the acquired ability, through concerted observation, to separate the true warrior, from the pretender.

While living as a captive slave of the Comanche, Rebecca had developed an eerily, uncanny ability, to almost instantly discern between those young men — the braves who were seeking recognition as warriors — between those who would succeed, and those who would fail.

She could invariably tell, which of the braves would gain the tribal honor, of being proclaimed and recognized as defenders and protectors of the *"People"*, which of the young men would be accorded the ultimate honor, of becoming a Comanche Warriors.

Her thorough but brief, assessment of the bearings, the confidence, and mannerisms exuded by the dignified, tall, black soldier, led her to almost instantly conclude, that the distinguished looking soldier that Horace had so cavalierly dismissed as a pretender in uniform, that the black sergeant, was in all probability, in every sense of the word, entitled to the appellation, that of being a true warrior.

So intense was her concentration, that Rebecca only vaguely recalled hearing Horace asking the waiter; "Exactly who is that Nigra…and why do you allow his kind to sit and eat in this restaurant with decent, respectable, white people?"

She clearly, distinctly, heard the waiter's response; "That gentleman monsieur, is Sergeant Major, Ruth. I believe that the Sergeant Major, is the soldier in charge of the Chester, Virginia Federal Office of the Freedmen's Bureau."

As she reluctantly, refocused her attention back to Horace, Rebecca experienced a vaguely strange, nagging, yet persistent sensation.

Although she could not explain it, could not put her finger on it, Rebecca could not help thinking that the soldier's face was familiar, that she had seen the dashingly, handsome, Sergeant Major before.

****

Chapter 47

Richmond Virginia – September 1867 - "Le Grand Vieux Manoir" Restaurant - 8:55 PM

Although the outward display of animosity shown by their fellow white diners, had for the most part, ceased, Horace's displeasure at what he continually referred to as; "the nerve of those… those uppity niggers", continued unabated.

No matter how hard she tried, how adroitly and skillfully, Rebecca attempted to redirect the conversation, Horace would not be deterred.

Horace continued to relentlessly, inject his, trite, racist, invectives, into what could have been, and should have been, a polite dinner, conversation.

"Just stop and think about its Rebecca. A couple of years ago, instead of sitting at that table, preening like a peacock, giving orders to a white man, even that white man—nodding his head in the direction of their waiter—, who is clearly a limp-wristed sissy, just a few years ago, that "Uppity Nigger" would be bowing, scraping, and serving food to his betters, the white people."

The once nasty, festering, ugly, and repugnant, background noise, that had initially been directed toward Rebecca, which had then abruptly shifted to the black couple, eventually subsided, to be replaced by the amorphous sounds, the tidbits of multiple conversations, that pervaded most of the popular eating establishments.

Rebecca, sat quietly, outwardly, politely, listening to Horace's inane prattle, his endless racial vindictive-slurs decided, that finally…finally, she had had enough.

She had sat patiently, listening to this pompous, full-of-himself, pampered "blowhard", pre-judge, denigrate and belittle a complete stranger, a man that he had obviously, never met.

Frustrated and annoyed, Rebecca began to experience intense, feelings of loss, of guilt, and of shame. Although she saw his lips moving, and heard the noise coming from his mouth, Rebecca managed to "tune" her dinner companion, Horace Stapleton, Esq., out

Wistfully she began to recall, the not so long ago, numerous long conversations, *that she and her black sister Mandy had had, while lying under the vast panoply of stars blanketing the skies of the* endless western-prairie.

She remembered how she and her black sister Mandy had lain at night forlorn, adrift in a vast ocean of gently rippling, knee-high grass, nostalgically, gazing at the stars; reverently marveling at the vastness, the majesty, and the glorious wonder, of the universe.

She remembered her's and Mandy's vow; that if they were ever able to escape from the Comanche, and return to civilization, that they would together, do everything that they could, to abolish all forms of human-bondage.

As she sat stoically enduring the company of this blatantly racist bigot, reluctantly, Rebecca forced her mind to refocus, to return to the present.

Rebecca reasoned that her living in the oppressive, stifling, atmosphere of racial prejudice, that permeated post-Civil War, Richmond Virginia, she could not help but ponder the living conditions, the senseless hatred and prejudices, that she and her half-Comanche son, would have to face.

Rebecca had promised her aunt and uncle, that on this dinner-date, which they had so painstakingly arranged, that she would make a genuine, concerted effort to behave—or more precisely, she had promised to adhere to, Aunt Delilah's exact, precise words, which were to, *"please comport yourself in a manner befitting, a well breed Southern Lady."*

Rebecca methodically, carefully, placed her knife and fork onto her plate, next to her barely touched entrée.

Calling upon her ability to project the appearance of patience and restraint, essential attributes that she had developed, in order to survive captivity and enslavement by the Comanche, Rebecca folded her napkin and placed it on the table.

 "Mr. Stapleton, it is my turn to extend an apology to you. I am afraid that I have been suddenly beset with a dreadful headache. Would you please be so kind as to take me home?"

Horace incorrectly attributing the onset of Rebecca's headache, to having been caused by the presence of those two *"Nigras"*, — who in defiance of all that is decent and proper—, were being allowed to dine in the Restaurant, hastily rose.

"Of course, my dear. I fully understand."

Until the black couple had arrived at the restaurant, Horace had been thinking of Rebecca as the *"white-squaw"*, *white trash, a fallen woman without morals, with whom he fully intended this evening, to use to satisfy his "manly-needs."*

Now as a Southern Gentleman, faced with the responsibility of speaking up, of defending and preserving the southern way-of-life; in a voice meant to be heard throughout the restaurant, Horace exclaimed; "Any well-breed Southern Lady would become ill, would feel uncomfortable dining with *"Nigras."*

"Please my dear…please excuse my insensitivity; I appreciate your patience and your indulgence."

Lowering his voice, Horace mumbled; "Your, errr… shall we say, the onset of your headache, is perfectly understandable."

"I can see how, after all that you've been through, you having been forced to live among those wild, heathen, Indians, and now being forced to dine socially, with these *"freed Nigras"*, would be troubling, as well as being upsetting."

Remembering her promise, to behave, *"to comport yourself in a manner befitting, a well breed Southern Lady"*, without uttering a word, Rebecca pushed her chair backward, and rose from the table.

As if by magic, the waiter appeared with Rebecca's cloak, and discreetly presented Horace with the bill. Horace reached into his coat for his billfold, extracted several bank notes, crumbled them in his hand, and tossed them onto the table.

 "He then draped the wrap around Rebecca's shoulders, and proceeded to usher her toward the exit.

Immediately to their left were two tables, which had been placed together, in an effort to accommodate the seating of two young white couples.

As they were picking their way, squeezing between the tables, moving toward the door, Rebecca clearly and distinctly over-heard the conversation being held between the two white female patrons, of the co-joined tables, two typical representatives of what remained of the so called cadre of "well breed, Southern white ladies."

The *"ladies"* were sipping coffee. One of the women leaned over and in a strident, nasal voice—that was obviously meant to be heard by those patrons in and even beyond, their immediate vicinity—, "I don't know which is more disgusting, eating with uppity niggers, or having to dine with a despoiled, white-squaw slut."

Rebecca gave Horace, a quick, furtive glance. Although it would have been virtually impossible for him not to have heard those vile, misogynistic, and racist comments, Horace did not react. He continued, seemingly oblivious to the insults, to walk toward the door. Horace's demeanor had not change.

As Horace held the door open for her, Rebecca thought that she noticed that a slight, almost imperceptible smile that had formed, at the corners of her escort's mouth.

****

Chapter 48

Sergeant Major Jason Ruth, and his date, Miss Maureen Montgomery, were seated, engrossed in conversation. Jason had been telling Maureen of his history, living as a slave here, in Richmond Virginia.

Jason told Maureen of the elation he had felt, when he had received orders, posting him to Richmond Virginia's Freedmen's Bureau.

Jason confided in Maureen, telling her of his disappointment, his abject misery, upon his hearing that, in 1864, three years past, the Rosewood Plantation—"lock stock and barrel"—, had been sold by Henry Billings, to the an outfit, a shady outfit, the Old Dominion Reality, Inc, which had subsequently ceased to exist.

Hence Henry Billings, the owner of his mother and sister, had sold the plantation, sold all of the slaves, with the exception of Jason's mother, Ruth, and his sister Mandy.

Henry Billings, his daughter Rebecca, Jason's mother Ruth, and his sister Mandy, had immigrated to unknown lands, west of the Mississippi River.

Jason and Maureen were seated but three tables distant, from a table occupied by the two verbose, and annoyingly, rude couples.

They had both clearly heard the crude racist comments, being directed at them, and at the distraught, white couple, who were in the process of leaving the restaurant.

Maureen had gasped, and impulsively, quickly placed her napkin over her mouth. Unfortunately, her attempt to mute her involuntary sound of anguish was not successful.

Jason's initial, visceral response, to the racial slurs, and to Maureen's discomfort, was that of anger.

Utilizing a skill that he had developed prior to engaging the rebels in battle, he was able to successfully suppress, his instinctive impulsive, reflexive, desire to seek immediate retribution, for these and a lifetime of verbal and physical abuse, by the "white man."

For the entire evening, though unsaid but by implicit, mutual consent, both he and Maureen had ignored the nasty comments, both subdued and overt, that had greeted, and continued, following their entrance into the trendy,
"Le Grand Vieux Manoir" restaurant.

Their tactic of ignoring and not responding to the hecklers, appeared to have been successful.

During the course of their meal, as time passed, the intensity, and the volume of the barrage of ugly insults, had diminished, and had gradually subsided.

In deference to Maureen, and completely contrary to his hot-blooded, smoldering emotions, through sheer will-power, Jason had managed to initially, remain composed, calm, and stoically quiet

Despite his best efforts to remain calm, the gruel, snide comments directed towards him and Maureen, and apparently at the vaguely familiar, departing white woman, had caused a familiar white-hot flash of anger, to shot through his body.

Jason's nostrils had flared; the pupils of his eyes had contracted. He felt his heart pounding in his chest, accelerating and redirecting, the flow of blood, from his digestive tract, to his arms, to his clenched fists.

These autonomic nervous system changes, in his body's physiology, were not at all, unfamiliar to Jason.

The effect was the recurrence of those all-to-familiar sensations, those feelings surging through his body, which served to amplify his primordial *"fight or flight"* response.

Jason's proclivity for instinctively making the right chose between those two options, *"fight or flight"*, had ultimately culminated in his transformation, from being an obedient, docile, slave, to that of becoming a professional soldier, a combat veteran, and by extension, a freedman, who just happened to be, a trained, lethal, proficient, killer of men.

Jason was on the verge of succumbing to the blinding rages that he had felt, just prior to, and during combat. The blinding rage that he had felt before he would calmly, and methodically, charge into the midst of the enemy. Forays that had resulted in his shooting, stabbing, slashing and killing, scores of rebel soldiers.

As he began to rise from his chair — Maureen, in an attempt to restrain him, placed her hand firmly on his arm, and pleaded; "Jason, Jason…don't… please don't."

"That's exactly how they want you to react. To be goaded into a rash response, that only reinforces their wicked pre-conceptions, their blind, baseless, stereotypic prejudices, that we are beneath them, that we are impulsive, uncivilized, unthinking, animals."

Jason looked down into Maureen's pleading, beautiful, expressive, dark mahogany, brown eyes.

As suddenly as his anger had manifest, the act of his looking into her sorrowful, pleading, desperate eyes, had just as quickly, caused his anger to dissipate.

Jason forced himself to relax. He slowly, reluctantly., eased himself back into his chair.

Jason picked up his napkin, and slowly, methodically, spread it across his lap. "Thanks Mo."

"*Mo*" was the affectionate nickname that at some now forgotten, magically, intimate moment, during the course of their first date, he had spontaneously begun to call her.

Maureen had at first thought of Sergeant Major Jason Ruth, as being pompous and presumptuous.

She remembered having thought; "He has some nerve. Supplanting my perfectly lovely feminine name Maureen, given to me by my mother, with a harsh one-syllable utterance, "*Mo*"!

By the end of that first, delightful, perfectly charming evening, Maureen had come to accept and to indeed, anticipate and enjoy, the sound of "*Mo*", as it frequently, playfully, flowed from his incredibly, handsome mouth, framed by the neatly trimmed mustache, of the dashing Sergeant Major.

 "Mo, you're absolutely correct. Sometimes despite the fact that I should by now know better, occasionally some racist white "*cracker*", says or does something, that tends to push my buttons, causing me to fly off the handle."

"Believe me, once again Mo, I truly appreciate your Herculean, or should I say "*Herculisa*", efforts to protect me from myself."

"It's becoming increasingly difficult for me to restrain myself."

"I have to keep reminding myself that as the highest ranking, "*colored*" noncommissioned officer of the U. S. Army in Richmond, not to mention my being the second in command, of the United States Military Detachment, assigned to Richmond's Freedmen's Bureau, I have a duty and a responsibility to comport myself, in a manner that befits my rank and my position."

Maureen reached for, and gently squeezed Jason's hands. Jason noticed the softening, as well as a distinct twinkle of amusement, reflected in Maureen's eyes.

"Okay Mo, I'll bite…why are you smiling? What's so funny?

While still holding his hands, Maureen in a voice that was an exaggerated, very poor attempt to impersonate Jason's, spoke;

"*My dear…it's becoming increasingly difficult for me to restrain myself. After all, I am the highest ranking, colored noncommissioned officer in Richmond, indeed in the whole-wide world.*"

Maureen, contorted her face, cleared her throat, put her fists on both sides of her torso, puffed out her chest, and in the absolute lowest vocal registry that her vocal cords would allow, made a guttural, grumbling, sound;

"*Harrumph … It is my solemn duty and my responsibility to comport myself, in a manner that befits my esteemed rank and position.*"

A broad, self-deprecating grin, spread across Jason's face. They both broke out in spiels of laughter. When they were finally able to regain control, they smiled at each other, and sipped their coffee.

The white patrons of the *"Le Grand Vieux Manoir"* restaurant, who had been intently anticipating and awaiting, the reaction, the response by the tall soldier and his *"lady"*, were at first surprised, then disappointed.

The black couple's response…laughter, was to say the least, to most of the diners, unexpected, and somewhat annoying.

Many of the restaurant's white-patrons, found the black-couple's ability to remain calm, ignoring the insults, extremely disappointing.

When it became obvious that the hoped-for conflagration would not be forthcoming, most of the patrons, including the solitary black-couple, resumed their evening out, enjoying the superb French cuisine, of *"Le Grand Vieux Manoir.*

****

Chapter 49

Maureen Marie Montgomery

Maureen Marie Montgomery was one of the many educated free-blacks, who had left their relatively safe haven in the North, and answered the clarion call of her fellow free-blacks, that black freemen and women, should help.

At the urging of respected, and even revered, men and women, men and women of conscience; Frederick Douglass, Harriet Taubman, Sojourner Truth, who with many other abolitionists, heeded the call of the American Missionary Association, for black and white educators, to go South.

When she was asked, Maureen Montgomery, a free-black born in New York City, reared and educated in Chicago Illinois, had literally jumped at the chance to join the crusade, to go South, and to help educate the millions of illiterate freedmen, the emancipated ex-slaves.

Maureen was the daughter of Gabriel and Winifred Montgomery.

Maureen's father Gabriel (*Shaika*), born to Africa's Mandinka tribe, and Maureen's mother Winifred *(Nieghesha)*, a tribal member of the Ivory Coast, had in the summer of 1825, been abducted, stolen from their West African homeland, enslaved, and transported to the "New World."

Shaika, Maureen's father, and his father, and his parents, parents…*for as long as the old ones could remember*, were all of West African descent.

Nieghesha, Maureen's mother's lineage, her ancestral tribal allegiance, was to her West African homeland, the Ivory Coast.

In the summer of 1825, *Shaika* and *Nieghesha*—born enemies from two warring South African tribes—, had both been stolen, wrested away from their two distinctly different cultures, by white slavers.

The two teenagers were each snatched from their families, their homelands, and placed in chains aboard a Spanish slave-ship.

****

The slave ship's cargo-manifest listed; six hundred-fifty "Negro slaves"; Four hundred twenty-five males; two hundred twenty-five females.

The slaver had "*taken-on*" its human-cargo at four ports, stretched along the South African coastline.

Maureen's parents, who were then total strangers, had been born members of two distinctly different, hostile to each other, West African tribes.

The West Africa Mandinkas, and the Ivory Coast had for centuries, been constantly at war with each other.

The human black-cargo were cramped, practically immobile, lying head-to-foot, packed in like sardines, on layered shelves, below deck of the slave-ship.

A clinging, putrid odor, a foul miasma, saturated with the fetid smell of human excrement, and sour vomit, permeated the slaves' berthing area, the ship's cargo-hold.

Shaika and *Nieghesha* were forced to endure the horror that millions of black-slaves, before and after them had and would experience, the humiliation of being *"packed-like-fish"*, in the hold, below the decks of slave-ships; —, forced to make, and endure, the *"middle passage."*

Shaika's and Nieghesha's, Maureen's future parents, each separately, at the same time, on the very same slave-ship in shackles, were brutally separated from their homeland, and transported across the Atlantic Ocean, to the "New World."

The Spanish slaver set sail from the west coast of Africa, carrying Maureen's future parents *Shaika* and *Nieghesha;* destination, the British West Indies.

****

Maureen's Parents – Slaves In Jamaica 1825 - 1828

Shaika, the Mandinka warrior, and *Nieghesha* the young maiden from the Ivory Coast, two "natural-enemies", were sold to the same white, Jamaican Sugar-Cane Planter, Jacob Montgomery.

Within weeks of their purchase, Jacob Montgomery changed *Shaika's* and *Nieghesha's* *"Afrikan"* names, to what he considered lest threatening, and by far, more easily pronounced Anglicized names, to that of Gabriel and Winifred Montgomery.

Gabriel and Winifred, both displaced teenagers, labored, day after day, week after week, month after month, side by side under the blazing-hot tropical sun, in the Jamaican sugar cane fields.

Although the white overseers rarely noticed Gabriel and Winifred's little displays of affection, their fellow slaves, especially the female slaves, were aware and approved of, the fact that the two *"Afrikans"* were smitten.

Whenever circumstances and the opportunity allowed, Gabriel and Winifred would clandestinely manage to touch, to fleetingly hold hands, and to exchange lovelorn glances.

E. Pluribus Unum

Sex among slaves for the express purpose of increasing the wealth of the plantation owners, was an accepted practice, a facet of "animal husbandry", which the slave owners regarded no differently than that, of the breeding of cows, pigs or horses.

As in the breeding of four legged-stock, the breeding of slaves i.e., the mating of male and female, for the explicit purpose of increasing his "stock", his property assets, was to be solely at the desecration of the slave-owner.

Emotional displays of affection, or romantic entanglements, between male and female slaves, especially while they were laboring in the sugar-cane fields, were strictly forbidden.

Eventually after having received numerous lashings from the overseer's whip the sting of the whip had been invariably followed by the sneering curt admonishment; "you two dumb-assed niggers better stop touchin' each other, stead of chopping cane" —, Gabriel and Winifred were separated.

It seemed only fitting and proper to "Massa Jacob's" slaves, most of who had been born into slavery, and were generations removed from their African roots, that the two strange "*Afrikans*", would and should, be together.

Two months following their being separated, and three years after their abduction from Africa, Gabriel and Winifred, with the help and the encouragement of their religious-abolitionist benefactors, together literally hand-in-hand, managed to run… to escape.

Those same abolitionists arranged and stood as witnesses, at Gabriel and Winifred's wedding.

And with the support and assistance of Christian missionary abolitionists, the two fugitive slaves, were whisked away—once again on sailing ships—from slavery in Jamaica—, ostensibly to freedom, in the northern, United States.

****

The young couple set foot on American soil, landing in New York City, February 3, 1828.

Gabriel and Winifred found the adjustment to the hustle and bustle of city-life, to be both difficult and confusing.

Gabriel because of his imposing, muscular physique, and his readily demonstrable physical strength, was able to easily find steady work as a laborer on the docks of New York City's Harbor; Winifred worked as a self-employed laundress.

Neither Gabriel, nor was Winifred, strangers to demanding, physically exhausting, hard work.

For the most part in the United States, black-slaves, men and women who had managed to escape the South's "*Peculiar Institution*", by making their way to the North, particularly those that sought refuge in New York City, had managed to meld, to blend in, with the black masses; the black freemen, and escaped slaves, the teeming hordes, living in New York's black ghettoes.

The fact that for their entire lives as slaves in the *"New World"*, Gabriel and Winifred had only experienced life, laboring in the fields of a sugar-cane plantation, was not the only impediment for their failure to assimilate into the black community.

Indeed, as were they, a sizeable segment of Manhattan's, north of 100th street (*Harlem's*), population, was comprised of black men and women who had escaped slavery from sugar-cane plantations, albeit, those from America, escaping from the sugar-cane plantations of South Carolina, Mississippi, and Louisiana.

Despite Gabriel and Winifred's shared life experiences with this segment of the Harlem populace—they too had been slaves who had for years, lived, toiled and eventually escaped from the backbreaking labor on a sugar-cane plantation—, Gabriel and Winifred were in fact, ***"DIFFERENT."***

Unfortunately, in addition to the handicaps of being black and illiterate, Gabriel and Winifred carried with them—as soon as they opened their mouths to speak—an easily, immediately, detectable trait, that identified them as being ***"DIFFERENT."***

Gabriel and Winifred's melodic, singsong manner of speaking, made them stand out, marked the two of them, as ***"DIFFERENT."***

Indeed, if they—those to whom Gabriel and Winifred spoke…if they would take the time to listen closely, to concentrate, they would have realized that the Jamaicans were actually speaking—or as some described it—singing beautiful, melodically accented English.

However, among the black inhabitants of Harlem, eager to establish social superiority over someone… anyone, Gabriel and Winifred Montgomery were labeled, *"caste"*, as being foreign, of being alien, of being ***"DIFFERENT."***

This placed the newlyweds at a decidedly distinct, social disadvantage.

In the summer of 1837, Winifred Montgomery gave birth to the couple's only child, a bright, precocious, beautiful baby girl, whom they named, Maureen Marie Montgomery.
In the ensuing years, despite of, and in part, because of, the family's being socially ostracized by their Harlem neighbors, economically, Gabriel, and Winifred, managed to prosper.

In 1840, three years after the birth of Maureen, the industrious, hard-working couple, who by ghetto standards were relatively financially well off, Gabriel and Winifred non-the-less, made the decision, for their daughter's sake, to provide their gifted, loquacious, daughter, the opportunity that she have a better life. Gabriel and Winifred decided to leave New York City.

Maureen's parents reasoned that if they, when they were frightened teenagers, had had the courage to escape slavery in the sugar-cane fields of Jamaica, now it was only fitting that they once again, for the sake of their daughter, muster-up the courage to move, to relocate, to start anew.

Gabriel, and Winifred mutually, together, decided to move to a section of the country where their daughter would have a chance to thrive and to realize her full potential, regardless of the color of her skin.

It was only fitting that once again motivated by love, this time the love of their daughter, that Gabriel and Winifred, would have the courage to move again, essentially to their next, "new world".

This time, not across an ocean, not across a sea; this time they would move across the American Continent, in order to make a better life for their only child, their daughter Maureen.

After finally, jointly, together, reaching that decision, on the night before their departure from Harlem, Gabriel, holding his wife's hands in his, lovingly gazed into Winifred's eyes and reverently uttered, in his melodic baritone voice…

"—Dat gurl Maureen…our daughta, she gonna be somdin'"

****

Chapter 50

Richmond Virginia, Jefferson Street   Sept 27, 1867 11:00 PM
Maureen's Basement-Apartment

Jason took the keys from Maureen's hand and deftly opened the door of her modest apartment.

Immediately to the left of the side door of the neat two-story residence, was a narrow wooden door that opened to a wooden staircase that led down to Maureen's basement apartment.

The interior of the apartment was noticeably cooler than that of the still mucky, *"Indian Summer"*, humid, sticky-air above ground.

Jason's initial impression of the small below ground apartment had been, though the space was extremely limited, Maureen had made the scant available space, neat, comfortable, and surprisingly utilitarian.

When Jason had first been invited to visit, he had been less than impressed by the room's 8 by 12-foot, allotment of available floor space.

The height from floor to ceiling was 6½ feet. Jason's height, his head practically touching the ceiling of her apartment, had inspired Maureen to playfully label Jason with the sobriquet, Sergeant Major *"Gulliver."*

Noticing how Maureen had laughed, and had appeared to derive immense pleasure from repeating his new nick-name; Sergeant Major *"Gulliver"*, Jason had asked; "Okay Mo, I'll bite, what's so funny…what's the significance, of the word Gulliver?"

Maureen had walked over to her bookshelves, and after perusing the spines of a small, but impressive collection of books, selected a green embossed, book.

She walked over to Jason, kissed him on his forehead, then she handed him, the leather-bound tome.

"After you read the first few chapters of this early 18th century classic—by the way one of my favorite books—, the answer to your question, the reason for my calling you Sergeant Major Gulliver, I promise you, will become obvious.

Jason accepted and quickly read the title of the book.

He casually placed the book on the table, and redirected his full attention, to the inspection of Maureen's living quarters.

Perhaps due to his height, the fact that he had to stoop, to avoid bumping his head on one of the four wooden beams, that supported the basement's ceiling, Jason was experiencing mild, claustrophobia.

Thankfully the room's single window, set in the wall opposite the sofa, had helped to somewhat alleviate, Jason's "closed-in" feeling.

Midway, on the wall opposite the steps, excavated, carved out of the brick-wall, facing the sofa, was a recessed niche, which housed a cast-iron, pot-bellied stove, with duct-work, a cylindrical chimney, disappeared into the ceiling.

Maureen had cleverly furnished the apartment with furniture and fixtures that served multiple functions.

A small table, with two wicker chairs, occupied the corner of the east wall.

The wall opposite the steps, served as the backdrop for a sturdy, Victorian style, brown sofa.

The sofa consisted of two down-stuffed cushions, encased in a wooden-frame supported by twin, 3-foot-high solid oak, armrests.

A two shelved bookcase, five-feet high, sat at the center of one of the walls.

On the wall opposite the bookcase, were two 1½' x 2' brown leather hassocks.

Four wheel-castors, each with rubber brake pads, had been attached at each corner, on the bottom of the hassocks.

On his third visit to Maureen's cellar-apartment, Jason came to appreciate the purpose of the hassock's wheels.

The mobile hassocks, served dual functions. During the day they sat stationary, against the wall. The dual hassocks provided extra seating.

Jason thought it curious that attached to the sides of the hassocks, were two hooks.

He deduced that apparently at night, one or both of the hassocks were rolled over perpendicular to, and then attached, to the sofa.

Tonight, after their intriguing dinner date at *"Le Grand Vieux Manoir"*, that previously all-white, swank French restaurant, as was their want, they were more-or-less seated, but actually reclining on one of the hassocks, engaged in heavy necking.

Instead of reluctantly stopping Jason's wandering hands as they caressed and explored her body, as she had on each of his two previous visits to her apartment, this time Maureen's moans and sighs had markedly intensified.

Maureen abruptly disentangled herself from Jason's embrace. She stood on trembling legs, and with her foot, shoved the empty hassock toward the sofa.
Jason's curiosity as to the purpose of the presence of hooks attached to the hassocks was immediately resolved, when Mo leaned down and inserted one of the hooks into an eye-ring, affixed to the sofa that Jason, here-to-fore, had not noticed.

Jason jumped-up, joined Maureen, and hastily attached the remaining, dangling, hassock hook into an unoccupied eye-ring. He then pushed the second, untethered hassock to the sofa. Using the hooks, he attached the freestanding hassock, to two still unencumbered, eye-rings on the sofa.

To his delight, Jason's curiosity was satisfied. The hooked-hassocks had become extensions to the sofa, which transformed the sofa into a spacious bed.

****

Maureen's Street Basement Apt. - September 28, 1867 – 12:30 AM

Maureen lay in Jason's arms, basking in the after-glow of their lovemaking, flexing her fingers that had been gently twisting the sparse curly hair on Jason's chest.

Jason had drifted off. He had fallen asleep.

Maureen lazily moved her hand. Her fingers gently kneaded and caressed Jason's now flaccid, limp, penis.

Jason had begun to emit a rhythmic, barely audible snore. Maureen smiled when her closed hand, the hand that had been holding Jason's inert member, began to expand.

Maureen gently, caressingly, tightened her grip around Jason's now steadily, stiffening, penis.

Her final thought before she too, drifted off into a welcomed, exhausted sleep, was;

"Ah...yet another reason justifying my bestowing upon Sergeant Major Jason Ruth, his new nickname. She chuckled... the current state of his male-member, certainly validates his new nickname."

"My very own Sergeant Major "Gulliver.""

****

Chapter 51

Richmond - Sept 27, 1867 - Meeting Hall of "The South Shall Rise Again" (TSSRA) - Regional Headquarters 2200 Hrs.

Emblazoned in bold blood-red letters, on a white bedsheet that hung on the wall, was the mission statement of their organization; "The South Shall Rise Again" (TSSRA).

"We the White Knights of the Confederacy,

Pledge Our Lives, and Our Sacred Honor to

The Protection, and the Promulgation of

White Racial-Supremacy."

Following the conclusion of their weekly, always heated *"bitching"* session, where the attendees as usual, had ad nauseam, complained and bemoaned the *'Reconstruction"* policies of the Radical Republican Yankee Congress, four men, the acknowledged leaders of the Richmond branch of '*TSSRA*', had remained behind.

Sydney Savage, the 32-year-old, nominal leader of Richmond's fledgling chapter of the TSSRA, sat at the head of the rectangular, wood-table, rubbing his eyes, while he studied his cards.

Sydney had been born and raised on a small farm in Essex County, Virginia.

He was the middle child, the fourth son in an uninterrupted string of eight straight boys, before his mother, gave birth to his baby sister, Susie.

Sydney's father and mother, Lamuel and Martha Savage, in 1822, with their one-year old son William, Sydney's oldest brother, had immigrated from Liverpool England, to America, in the hope of finding a better life for the Savage family.

Ostensibly the purpose of the TSSRA leadership's remaining after the meeting, was to plan and to strategize, plots, acts of defiance and intimidation, against Yankee carpetbaggers, and their *"Freedmen"* nigger-lackeys, while indulging in smoking cigars, drinking whiskey, and playing a few hands of draw-poker.

****

A dense cloud of pungent, gray cigar smoke hung in the air, creating a semi-dense artificial fog, in the oil-lamp illuminated room.

Clouds of swirling acrid smoke irritated Sydney's eyes.

The stale smoky air, and the accumulating mounds of cigar-ash covering the floor, was a by-product of the steady shrinkage collectively, of the four cheap cigars, clenched between Sydney's teeth, and the teeth of his three scruffy companions.

Unconscientiously, Sydney accepted and rationalized, that the smoke and the ashes, were merely minor irritants that were consistent with his overall philosophy of life.

For as long as he could remember, it had been hammered into Sydney's head that *"the end —, in this case the taste and satisfaction that he derived from his cigar, more than—, justified the means."* That is the enduring of the discomfort of the smoke polluted air, and the messy accumulation of mounds of ubiquitous, cigar ashes on the floor.

As the four men were taking their seats, Rodney Baxter, one of the younger members of the clandestine, secret society, breathlessly, burst through the door.

John Henshaw (*Johnny-boy*), who was the acknowledged "hot-head" of the leadership group, in one swift motion, drew *his pistol* from his waistband.

Sydney quickly raised his hand restraining, Johnny-boy. "Hold on Johnny-boy."

"Rodney…what in hell's wrong with you boy? You could have got your dumb-ass, fool-head blown off."

Rodney leaned over, panting, attempting to catch his breath.

"Sorry Mr. Savage". Rodney, leaning over, his hands on his knees, continued to gasp.

"Finally, he was able to speak; you know that fancy foreign restaurant down on Brook Road?"

Before Sydney could respond, Rodney continued; "well sir words been spreading over the city bout a nigger-couple, that had the nerve to show-up expecting to be seated and to be served dinner, by white-folks. Can you believe it?"

"Them two coons, the black-nigger sergeant from over there at that Freedmen's office, and his black school-marm whore, just waltzed in, strutting like a couple ah black peacocks."

"And can you believe it…them limp-wrist, fancy-pants foreigners, just let um stay, sit and eat, right there in the middle of the place, with decent white-folks."

Travis Wilson, the pseudo-intellectual member of the group, whose bland unimposing physical statue and demeanor, was by far the less threatening or intimidating, of the five men seated at the table asked; "what happened Rodney, did the white patrons protest, did they object? Did they at least remove themselves from the restaurant? Did the white patrons leave en masse?"

Although he did not always understand Mr. Wilson's *"fancy words,* Rodney understood enough to began to vigorously shake his head from side-to-side, "no sir, no siree, not nary a one of those white folks got up and left."

"For all I know, them black *"jungle-bunnies"*, are still in that haughty-taughty, high-faloutin' foreign restaurant, having themselves a good ole time, acting like they as good as white-folks."

Sydney placed his right-hand onto Rodney's shoulder and firmly stirred the agitated youth, toward the door.

"Thanks for bringing this to our attention Rodney." While he did not resist and allowed himself to be pushed toward the door, Rodney swiveled his head, and looked over his shoulder at Sydney. His eyes were pleading, imploring.

"Mr. Savage, ain't we gonna do something about them niggers"?

Sidney stopped. He placed both hands on Rodney's shoulders and gently, but firmly, spun him around. "What would you have us do son"?

Rodney was momentarily confused, a bit put-off. He looked over his shoulder, at the four men seated at the table.

Three of the men sat calmly, sipping their drinks and puffing on their cigars.

Besides himself, Mr. Henshaw (Johnny-boy) was the only man in the room, who showed even an inkling of annoyance at the news of "uppity niggers" invading one of their white restaurants.

Rodney, his eyes locked, pleadingly, on Johnny-boy, blurted-out; "we could go over there, wait for them coons to leave. Then if nothing else, we could damn-well, at least scare the bee-jesus outta them niggers."

Sidney squeezed the young man's shoulders, forcing Rodney to meet his eyes; "We're not ready. We don't yet, have the numbers, the membership, nor the public sentiment."

"Have patience son. It's just a matter of time. Keep the faith. We maybe down now but… he pointed to the white bed-sheet hanging on the wall; and in a firm reverent voice, reading the bold, blood-red letters on the white besdsheet, that hung on the wall, *raised his right arm in a 45° angle and* proclaimed; "TSSRA, The South Shall Rise Again".

Sydney walked the youth to the door. Before closing the door, he repeated; "Keep the faith, TSSRA"!

After each of the five men had looked at their cards, the dealer, Franklin Hardwick, seated to Sydney's right, placed his cards face-down on the table, picked-up the deck, and grunted; "Okay gennelmen, pair of Jacks or better to open. Can anybody open"?

John Henshaw (*Johnny-boy*) threw five dollars onto the center of the table. "Open for five."

Two of the three men seated at the table, with the notable exception of Sydney, hastily threw five dollars into the *"pot."*

While everyone *"called"* Johnny-boy's bet, no one—perhaps because of Johnny-boy's exuberance—, no one raised the bet.

Sydney slowly, one card at a time methodically re-examined the cards that he'd been dealt: The deuce of spades; the Ace of diamonds; the tray of spades; the Ace of spades; and finally, the five of spades.

He rearranged the cards, placing the two aces next to each other, the Ace of diamonds on the outside, next to the Ace of spades, and the three remaining cards in ascending, numerical sequence.

With judicious deliberation, Sydney accessed the situation.

Everyone at the table knew that at a minimum, a pair of Jacks had been dealt to Johnny-boy. Thus, that Johnny-boy had opened the betting; holding an initial hand whose strength was obviously equal to/or stronger than that afforded by a pair of Jacks.

Sydney had been the only player who had not immediately called, Johnny-boy's— at least for *"Stingy"* John Henshaw—, *Johnny-boy's* extravagant wager.

Sydney concluded that everyone at the table, with the possible exception of Johnny-boy, probably held cards that either beat a pair of Jacks, as did his, pair of Aces, or they thought that they had a reasonably good chance of drawing cards, that would improve their hands, beating a pair of Jacks.

Franklin Hardwick, whose turn it was to be the dealer, looked to the man seated next to him, on his left, "how many"?

Travis Wilson, the middle-aged owner of a men's haberdashery hat store, cleared his throat, and pushed three of his cards toward Franklin; "I'll take three."

The dealer's gaze was next directed toward Mr. Edward "Eddie" Greene, the owner and proprietor of Greene's Livery; an establishment whose principle assets were listed as; ownership of seventeen prime-horses, four mules, two small freight wagons, and seven taxi-hacks.

His livery and wagon service proudly provided *"Taxis'"* at reasonable fares, to the white citizens of Richmond.

Franklin repeated his question; "how many"?

Eddie pulled a card from the end of those held in his hand, placed it face-down on the table, and pushed it toward the dealer; "I'll take one please."

Franklin dealt the card on the top of the deck, to Eddie.

Franklin turned his attention to Johnny-boy; "Cards?" Johnny-boy held his five cards, tightly to his chest; "I'm good…I'll play these."

Almost imperceptibly, Franklin raised his right eyebrow and gave Sydney, the leader of the *"Klavern"*, an anticipatory, deprecating, and quizzical glance.

"Sydney?"

Sydney examined his cards. He had quickly surmised that, based upon the number of cards retained, and those discarded by the men at the table that;

Travis Wilson, probably held a pair of face cards, most likely either queens or kings; Eddie Greene was either holding two pair, or conversely, holding four cards (multiple-suits), in numerical sequence——*possible straight*, or four random cards, of the same suit—— *possible flush.*

Sydney factored into his analysis, Johnny-boy's parsimonious history of being a rather conservative… a *"stingy"* bettor.

He reasoned that Johnny-boy, who usually at most, would bet and/or raise a dollar, and would rarely call a bet that exceeded two-dollars, must have been dealt a very strong hand.

Sydney slowly, one card at a time, methodically re-examined his cards: The deuce of spades; the Ace of spades; the Ace of diamonds; the tray of spades; and finally, the five of spades.

He rearranged the cards, placing the two aces next to each other, and the three remaining cards in numerical sequence.

Prior to the "Draw" Sydney had intended to keep his pair of aces, and to draw three cards, the allotted maximum. Sydney reasoned that by drawing three cards he could either pick up a third Ace, or at least be dealt a second pair. That was logically the smart-move.

Sydney, a man who believed in playing the percentages, for a few fleeting seconds, hesitated.

Then, impulsively, uncharacteristically, Sydney rejected the "smart-move."

Instead of holding onto his two aces and discarding three cards, he broke – up his pair of Aces, and drew one card.

By drawing one card Sydney *"gambled"* upon the far riskier prospect, of his filling an inside straight, if the card he was dealt happened to be a four.

Sydney placed his one dis-card, facedown on the table, and slid the card toward Franklin.

"I'll take one."

Franklin dealt Sydney, one card from the top of the deck.

Franklin then placed the deck of cards on the table.

He picked-up his five cards, removed a single card placed the card facedown onto the table;

"Dealer takes one."

Franklin dealt himself one card.

Impatiently, without giving Franklin the opportunity to look at his cards, or waiting to be asked by Franklin the dealer, Johnny-boy hastily threw five dollars, the maximum bet allowed, onto the stack of bills in the center of the table.

Franklin was annoyed. He retrieved the five dollars that Johnny-boy had bet, reached across the table, and handed the money to Johnny-boy.

"Wait your turn Johnny-boy." He turned toward Travis. "Your bet."

Travis threw his cards— facedown—, onto the table. "I fold. I'm out.

Franklin's attention shifted to Johnny-boy; "Your bet Johnny-boy?"

Once again, Johnny-boy threw his five dollars onto the table.

Eddie Greene, who had been absently, shuffling his cards, picked up two five-dollar bills. He threw one five-dollar bill into the pot; "see your five and raise you five.

Franklin addressed Sydney; "It's on you Syd. Cost you ten to call."

Sydney studied his cards.

Johnny-boy was becoming inpatient. "Come on Sydney, make up your mind. Are you in or out? Either fish or cut bait"!

Sydney picked-up his stack of dollar bills. With calm deliberation, he counted ten one-dollar bills and stacked them onto the table, next to his cards.

He threw the ten singles onto the table; "I'll call the ten, he then counted five additional single note bills, and threw them onto the table; "And I'll raise five."

Although *"ciphering"*, as Johnny-boy called it, was not his forte', Johnny-boy hesitated before blurting-out; "that's twenty to you Franklin."

Franklin threw his cards, facedown onto the table; "To rich for my blood."

Franklin turned to Johnny-boy. "What do you say Johnny-boy? It's on you, ten bucks to call, or fold."

Johnny-boy reached into his left pants-pocket, pulled out two wrinkled fives, and five crumbled singles. He looked directly at Sydney; "I call.

Franklin counted the money in the pot. He then proclaimed; "Pot's right."

"Okay Johnny-boy…show us what you got?"

Johnny-boy spread out his cards. "Full-House, three fours and a pair of Jacks."

Eddie grunted and exclaimed, "Shit." He spread out his cards. "I've got a straight, 5 to the 9."

A broad grin spread across Johnny-boy's face. Franklin asked, "Sydney"?

Sydney, in a calm, firm, voice replied. "I too, have a straight."

Johnny-boy, a broad, greedy grin spreading across his face, leapt from his seat, both hands extended, eagerly reaching for the money.

Sydney spread his cards on the table. "A straight-flush." Ace of Spades; Deuce of Spades; Three of Spades; Four of Spades; and the Five of Spades.

Defeated, his face crest-fallen, reflecting abject misery, Johnny-boy slumped back down into his chair.

****

Chapter 52

September 28, 1867 – Richmond Virginia, Jefferson Street - 1:35 AM

Jason's internal alarm clock caused his eyes to open. He awoke, momentarily disoriented. Maureen was lying blissfully, her bosom rhythmically rising and falling with each gentle breath. She was fast asleep, her head resting on Jason's left arm.

Gently, trying to avoid disturbing her, Jason slid to the edge of the bed, reached down to the floor, and began to grope for his trousers.

After several almost laughable, blind, futile, attempts, probing, feeling for his clothing, his fingers finally encountered and wrapped around, his uniform trousers.

As gently as he could manage, Jason attempted to extract—without waking her—, his arm from beneath Maureen's head.

Just when he thought that he had succeeded with his maneuver, Maureen began stir.

"Mmm…" noticing that Jason was in the process of putting on his trousers, she grasped his arm. "Jay what are you doing? You're not leaving, are you?"

Before Jason could answer, she continued. "This was our first time, she hesitated searching for the right words, our first time— Maureen could feel the blood rushing to her cheeks— you know…our first time… being ah intimate, together."

Maureen was not a virgin; not a stranger to the physical act that she and many others euphemistically referred to as, the act of *"making-love."*

The obligatory so called *"facts of life"* talk, had been dutifully given to her by her mother when she had, at the age of fourteen, experienced the onset, of her first menstrual cycle.

The happiness and the emotional bliss that she felt following her and Jason's *"making-love"*, was that that although she was not a virgin this, what she had experienced last night, with Jason, was in actuality the first time that she had actually *"made-love."*

After pulling the straps of his suspenders over his broad shoulders, Jason leaned over and kissed Maureen. He pointed to the shiny brass buttons on his uniform tunic. "I have to be back at the Freedmen's Bureau alert and bright-eyed, before reveille at 0600."

Then giving a remarkably accurate impersonation of the jocular words that Maureen had earlier used at dinner, Jason pushed out his chest and exclaimed; *"After all, I am the highest ranking, colored noncommissioned officer of the U.S. Army in Richmond, maybe in the whole-wide-world."*

A huge radiant grin, spread across Maureen's face. "Okay my handsome *"Sergeant-Major Gulliver'*, go, go if you must. Attend to your duties."

I guess we'll just have to have patience, wait a little while…" she raised an eyebrow, "this evening?" Without waiting for an answer, Maureen continued.

"We both have to focus and dedicate our time, in the pursuit of the greater goal. That is with the support of Federal Congressional-Reconstruction, it's our duty to promote and to secure, the assimilation, and the advancement of our people."

Jason squeezed her hand. "Mo, I just love it when the teacher in you takes over, and your speech-pattern reflexively begins to sound like that of Frederick Douglass."

"Believe me sweet-heart, there's no place I'd rather be than in your bed, loving you."

"How would it look if the man that you…yes you Maureen Marie Montgomery, you so aptly and eloquently described as, and I quote:"

"The highest ranking, colored noncommissioned officer of the U.S. Army in Richmond, maybe in the whole-wide-world", were to be AWOL?

"Alas, my love, as they say in the military, *"Duty Calls."* I really have to get going."

He opened the door, stopped looked over his shoulder, and mischievously asked; "I am invited to dinner, aren't I?"

Maureen laughing, threw a pillow at his head, and facetiously asked; *"Do's the Sun rise in the East?" Do white folks think we're all stupid?*

Jason deftly caught the pillow and tossed it back onto the bed.

"I'll see you around seven." He closed the door, and patiently waited.

He smiled when her heard the sound of Maureen lowering the solid wooden bolt into place.

He leaned against the door. Satisfied that it was secure, Jason walked over to the hitching-post and untied his horse.

****

Chapter 53

September 27, 1867 – Richmond
Virginia – Jefferson Street – *11:35 PM*

His head lowered, Johnny-boy seated astride his seven-year-old gray-mare saddle horse, was aimlessly, listlessly, plodding along through the city's streets.

Totally absorbed in self-pity, and cursing under his breath at the persistence and the extent of his bad luck, Johnny-boy was unaware of the fact that his horse— completely oblivious to human societal changes—, had strayed into the "colored" residential section of the city.

Before the War, these neat little brick houses, characteristically surrounded by white washed picket fences, had belonged to the city's middle-class, white families.

These had been the homes of Richmond's merchants, the shopkeepers, the artisans, the people who served as the bedrock, the foundation of the city's populace.

The pre-Civil War owners of these houses in general, admired their so-called "betters." The white cadre of middle-class citizens envied the aristocratic planter-class, the owners of the large plantations, that for their existence depended upon the slave labor of thousands of black slaves.

They, the white middle-class, had marveled at the flamboyant life-style of the aristocratic Planters; the grand, palatial mansions, the fine polished carriages, drawn by matched-bred horses, the powdered women, resplendent in their European imported gowns.

In contrast these same middle-class whites looked with disdain, at the whites that they considered their inferiors.

The non-slave holding white farmers who toiled on their small plots of land, eking out a subsistence. The white men who were solely dependent upon themselves and their wives and their "*brood*" of children, for the requisite labor needed to work their farms.

While Richmond's middle-class whites derisively referred to the farmers as being, "*Poor-white-trash*" they, as did the plantation owners, considered the multitude of black-slaves owned by the planters as being subhuman, little more than animals."

Subsequent to Congress' plans for post-war Reconstruction which included the creation of the Freedmen's Bureau, a steady influx of educated blacks, free-blacks from the North, had come south to assist the newly emancipated slaves, to prepare for and to adjust to being free, for life after slavery.

As the northern black "carpetbaggers" moved into the middle-class neighborhoods, the so-called "*decent whites*", moved out, relocating in Richmond's suburbs.

This societal phenomenon was referred to, by the recently transplanted northern blacks, as, "*the White-Flight*".

This section of town, with its neat brick houses, surrounded by the white-washed picket fences, the previously white middle-class neighborhood, had been transformed into what Richmond's white citizenry now derisively referred to as Richmond's, "***Uppity Black-Niggerhood***".

Johnny-boy's mood was becoming increasingly gloom. All night long during the poker game, he had been slowly, but steadily losing.

Sullenly, under his breath he mumbled; "Of all the rotten luck. I'm finally dealt a decent hand, a "*pat*" hand. A full-house, trip fours and a pair of Jacks... and I still lose."

Johnny-boy racked his brain, trying to recall the poker-hands of the men who, after the last draw, had been seated at the table.

What Johnny-boy had thought, added insult to injury was the fact that while Sydney Savage was raking-in the last "*pot*"— his "pot, scooping-up the money that should have been his—, Sidney, that smug son-of-a-bitch, had had the nerve to boast as to how he had filled his "inside" straight-flush, by drawing a four.

And then after looking at the three fours in Johnny-boy's "full-house", Sydney had chuckled; "can you beat that, not only did I draw a four, filling an inside straight, I drew the four of spades; the only four, not being held by Johnny-boy.

Johnny-boy, his head cast down looking at the cobbled street, under his breath mumbled; "If it weren't for bad-luck...I'd have no luck at all."

Lost in thought and self-pity, Johnny-boy was allowing his horse to leisurely take him home.

He looked over his shoulder at one of the neat brick houses.

Impulsively, Johnny-boy reined-in, his horse. Something was off, odd.
Something was out-of-place.

Slowly he dismounted and with the mare's reins in-hand, he cautiously walked his mount over to the house.

Johnny-boy looped the reins of his horse, over the bar of the hitching post.

The long reins attached to the bridle of a large chestnut stallion, were loosely wrapped around the hitching rail. The stallion swiveled his head, and softly expelled air from his nostrils.

Johnny-boy, in an effort to calm the stallion, placed his sweaty hand on the horse's muzzle.

Johnny-boy's trembling hand stroked the horse's flank, stopping at the leather-saddle. The dim light emanating from the first-floor windows of the house facilitated his cursory examination of the saddle.

The saddle set atop a blue blanket, edged with yellow trim. On the lower edge of the blanket were the letters, "*US.*"

Johnny-boy recoiled. He reflexively jerked his fingers from the letters *US*.

His reaction was as if his fingers had touched a red-hot branding iron.

Johnny-boy grabbed the reins of his horse, and quickly led the mare away from the neat little brick house.

Johnny-boy was confused. He had no doubt that the horse tethered to the hitching post in front of the neat little house, was the mount of a Yankee soldier. And that that soldier, was a black nigger soldier, a member of the army referred to by his fellow members of *TSSRA,* as the "*Yankee Army of Occupation.*"

He muttered under his breath; "What in blazes is a Yankee soldier, most likely a black-nigger soldier, doing in this residential section of Richmond"?

Then as if he had just been struck with sudden insight, Johnny-boy with his right hand gave a resounding slap to his forehead.

Johnny-boy reminded himself that this, the formerly white middle-class neighborhood that he had known so well before the war, had now after the war, changed with the influx of black Yankee-carpetbaggers.

The previously white middle-class neighborhood had been transformed into what his fellow bigots in the secret, fledgling-white supremacist "TSSRA", flippantly referred to as, that "Uppity Black-*Niggerhood.*"

Johnny-boy remembered how earlier that evening... how his poker game had been interrupted when that idiot Rodney Baxter, brought the news that a black couple—the nigger sergeant in charge of the soldiers assigned to the "Freedmen Bureau", and his black whore—, had shown up for dinner at that fancy French Restaurant.

Johnny-boy reasoned that since the French Restaurant in question, was a mere two miles from this community, the rider of the Yankee army horse, could very well be the same uppity-nigger, who had "*invaded*", integrated, the all-white, French Restaurant.

Johnny-boy mused to himself; "maybe, just maybe, my luck is about to change."

****

While he had earlier "*lost*" his money in a card game, following the TSSRA meeting, he reasoned that if he were to kill the uppity nigger soldier, that that just might, be a way for him to "*win*" from his fellow TSSRA bigots, their respect and admiration.

Johnny-boy rationalized that by his killing the "nigger-soldier" and his black-whore, especially killing them on the very night that they had desecrated fundamental, basic Southern values, would gain for him, the respect and admiration of his TSSRA, white supremist comrades.

On foot, Johnny-boy led his mount to a spot behind the row of brick houses. He carefully looped and then tied the horse's reins around a small mulberry-bush.

Johnny-boy keeping to the shadows, doubled back to the brick house, the house that had had the *US* Army horse, tied to its hitching post.
As he approached the house, Johnny-boy noticed that now, there was no visible light, in the windows on the first, or the second floor of the dwelling.

However, in the rear of the house, from a ground-level basement window, he saw the faint flicker of light, which he assumed was coming from an oil lamp, possibly from a candle.

Johnny-boy, on his hands and knees, crawled over to the basement window.

The window was slightly ajar, held open with a small metal rod.

Johnny-boy lay sprawled on the damp grass, peering into the dimly lit room.

On a sofa bed, directly opposite the window, Johnny-boy saw the black man and woman, their bodies glistening with perspiration, entangled on the sofa bed.

The couple was in the passionate throes of making love.

****

Johnny-boy was transfixed by the erotic tableau happening before his eyes.

From his vantage point, Johnny-boy's line-of-vision from the basement window, afforded him a "*bird's eye view*", directly between Maureen's invitingly, enticing, spread-open legs.

The bodies of the tall, lanky, yet well muscled caramel-colored black man, and the exquisitely beautiful, black-as-coal body, of the woman were moving in perfect synchronization.

Maureen's beautiful ebony face was framed by the stark white pillow, on which her head rested.

Jason—his weight supported by his hands that were placed on either side of Maureen's pillow— was intently, lovingly, gazing into Maureen's dark brown eyes.

Johnny-boy swallowed hard as he watched the big man slowly, almost teasingly, repeatedly, plunge his thick, swollen penis, into what Johnny-boy silently verbalized as the black woman's *"moist, hot, pussy."*

Maureen moaning in passionate ecstasy raised her hips, gyrating her pelvis in perfect unison, meeting each of Jason's deep, penetrating, thrusts.

Jason leaned over and covered Mo's lips with his.

Sensually, his tongue began to dart into Maureen's mouth, in sync with the deep, penetrating thrusts of his rock-hard penis, into Maureen's welcoming vagina.

For a full five minutes, Jason's engorged penis steadily descended, plunging into Maureen's welcoming vagina.

Completely beyond his control, an unanticipated physiological change overwhelmed Johnny-boy's body. Johnny-boy was experiencing a tremendous erection.

The rhythmic sucking, slapping, sensuous sounds of the lovers' bellies were increasingly arousing him, as they collided, as each thrust of the nigger-soldiers' hips, was met by the synchronized arching of the black-sluts pelvis.

Jason feeling that he was close to exploding, and not wanting this blissful sensation to end, slowly lowered himself so that the entire length of his body, completely covered Maureen.

Jason placed his arms under Maureen, hugging her, melding their bodies together.

He then deftly, in one effortless, athletic motion, rolled over. The lovers had reversed positions.

Maureen lay on top straddling him, her knees making small indentations into the mattress.

Jason lay flat on his back. His throbbing penis remained deep within the recesses of Maureen's vagina.

Maureen leaned over, flattening her ebony breasts, against Jason's chest, and hungrily kissed Jason's lips.

Jason in turn, wrapped his arms tightly around Maureen's waist, hugging her, melding their bodies together as one, while he rhythmically continued, the upward thrust of his hips.

Maureen opened her mouth and began sucking on Jason's probing tongue.

Johnny-boy shuddered. He could scarcely believe his eyes.

Jason began to slowly slide down on the bed, inch by inch, until his feet made contact with the floor.

Johnny-boy watched transfixed, as the nigger-soldier placed his hands under the black-slut's perfectly shaped, ass and effortlessly, while still locked in a passionate kiss, the Yankee-nigger soldier stood, lifting the woman, as if she were a feather, from the bed.

Maureen had instinctively locked her legs around Jason's waist, thus facilitating and intensifying the exquisite physical sensations she was experiencing from the depth of the penetration, of Jason's rock-hard penis.

After *stopping, gyrating,* brushing against and bouncing off, two walls of the small apartment—his hands all the while, firmly supporting, kneading and caressing Maureen's buttocks—, Jason deftly, managed to return the two co-joined in ecstasy lovers, to the sofa bed.

There, writhing on the rumpled bed, after a series of rapid, deep, thrusts by Jason, and the resultant exclamations of sexual gratification from Maureen, the two lovers simultaneously, convulsed, gasped, and climaxed together.

Initially when he had stumbled upon the "two niggers rutting, copulating like dogs in heat", Johnny-boy had intended to burst-in and to shoot them both while they were distracted fornicating, when they were totally vulnerable.

Johnny-boy's hastily formed plan, was to first shoot the black soldier, and then after he had had a chance, to "stick his dick into that hot black pussy", and then, and only then, after he *came, "shot his load"*, he would shoot the black-whore.

Johnny-boy stood in place, mesmerized by the erotic scene, that he had been watching.

Unfortunately, Johnny-boy's voyeurism had had an unanticipated effect on his body.

His right hand, the hand that had been holding his pistol, was now holding and stroking his penis.

Johnny-boy was unaware as to when, he had replaced in his dominant hand, the cold steel of the pistol, with the hot throbbing flesh of his penis.

Suppressing a moan of release, Johnny-boy uncontrollably, ejaculated spewing semen between the fingers of his hand, and the already damp, green grass.

Johnny-boy, on trembling legs, stood, wiped his "sticky" right hand on his trousers, picked-up his pistol from the grass, retrieved his horse and as quietly as he could manage, left.

****

<hr>

Chapter 54

(Two-Miles Distant from Maureen's Apartment)

Johnny-boy sat behind a stand of oak trees; two miles removed from Maureen's apartment.

For more than two hours, he had lingered, hidden behind trees, literally, lying in wait.

Johnny-boy had a clear line of vision of the well-traveled road.

Approximately five miles further south, the road was bisected by a secondary road, actually a recent path that lead to the barracks which housed the detachment of black soldiers, who were assigned to the "Freedmen's Bureau."

Johnny-boy knew that to return to his unit, that "coon-nigger soldier", would have to pass his way.

His simplistic plan had been "ambush"; to lay-in-wait, and using the trees for cover, to ambush the unsuspecting black soldier as the "nigger", returned to his duty station at the Freedmen's Bureau."

Johnny-boy had anticipated, had assumed that as soon as that *"nigger-buck"* had finished fucking that wench, he smirked as he remembered the apropos military jargon—, as soon as the nigger soldier had *"shot his load"*, that the black soldier would, as he himself had always, unfailingly done—, that the black soldier would have immediately "pulled on his breeches, and *skedaddled."*

Unfortunately, contrary to Johnny-boy's expectation, the black soldier had not immediately *"skedaddled"*.

****

It had been over two hours and still, the black soldier had not appeared on the road.

As he sat on the ground, propped up against the trunk of an oak tree, impatiently waiting, Johnny-boy, for what it seemed to him was the "umpteenth" time, checked and rechecked his weapons.

Once again, he removed the heavy LeMat revolver, from the waistband of his trousers, and checked the load. Satisfied, he stuck the handgun, beneath the waistband of his semen-stained, trousers.

Johnny-boy reached over and picked up his round-bore, muzzle loading, single shot musket.

Reassured that the weapon was loaded and primed, he placed the stock of the long-gun on the ground at the base of a tree, while leaning the barrel against the tree's trunk.

After having been on edge, for more than two hours, lying -in-wait, Johnny-boy's tense muscles began to relax.

He attempted to recall the details of the scene that he had just witnessed.

Though he at first was finding it difficult to separate the sensually erotic sex acts that he had witnessed, from the far less erotic, but now to him, the far more important details of what he had initially intended to be find, as a result of his "military-reconnaissance."

Johnny-boy concentrated, attempting to recall details, non-erotic details, that would help him execute this, the initial phase of his plan. His plan was to kill the black soldier.

Johnny-boy's brow furrowed, wrinkled, as he strained, forcing himself to concentrate.

What details had he noticed before and after, he had unexpectedly, become mesmerized, transfixed, watching the two niggers doing it, fucking like horny rabbits, on the bed?

Johnny-boy concentrated, straining to put aside, to ignore the uninhibited sex scenes, and to recall exactly what he had observed of *"military"* significance.

He ticked-off, on his fingers; 1) a shinny Spencer lever-action, nine-shot repeating rifle, had been propped-up against the wall; 2) The black soldier's leather gun belt and holstered colt service revolver had been draped over a chair.

Deep in thought, Johnny-boy quickly compared and contrasted his meager, old "antiquated" scavenged weapons with those of the combat veteran, black soldier.

Johnny-boy's single shot, muzzle loading long-gun, was no match for the soldier's, Spencer lever-action, nine-shot, repeating rifle.

Despite the fact that Johnny-boy was an excellent marksman, his targets had consisted of empty bottles and the occasional squirrel.

In his mind, Johnny-boy questioned, the steadiness of his aim, when shooting at a moving target.

A target that if he missed, had the potential of returning fire, especially returning fire with nine bullets in rapid succession, from that Spencer repeating rifle.

Under his breath Johnny-boy mused; "what if for some reason, my shot missed the "nigger"? "Before I can reload, that black "nigger-soldier", would be on me like stink on a shit."

While Johnny-boy had been raised to believe that "niggers" by nature, were cowards, and that one good white man, could easily outfight two or three niggers, Johnny-boy could not erase from his mind, the physically imposing image of the lean, well-muscled black soldier.

Nor could he ignore, nor could he dismiss, the implied significance of the two rows of combat medals, that hung from the tunic of the black soldier's uniform.

Although he detested and, despised the Yankee Army, Johnny-boy had come to grudgingly concede and accept, that the Yankee Army had decisively defeated his boys in Gray, his Confederate Army.

Johnny-boy had deduced that from the looks of those medals hanging from his tunic; "this particular nigger was a combat veteran who had been tested in battle, and who had more than acquitted himself well, under fire."

Johnny-boy recalled the often repeated, always inspirational words hammered into the heads of the members their fledgling white supremacist klavern, by Sydney Savage, their *"know-it-all" self-anointed* leader.

"Boys…always remember, there's more than one way ta skin a cat."

As he had been told, over and over again by the leader, "first define your objective, then pick the easiest way of achieving success."

Johnny-boy shrugged and mumbled under his breath; "hell's bells Sidney, I know my objective."

His intent was to gain the respect and admiration of the TSSRA, by killing the "uppity-nigger" soldier and his black whore.

As he lay in the damp grass, absent mindedly squeezing and massaging his semi-erect penis, Johnny-boy had an epiphany.

He reasoned that the easiest and by far less dangerous, way for him to achieve his objective of "killing" the uppity-nigger soldier, was to murder the black soldier's slut, after having "helped hisself to some of that juicy, inviting, black-pussy."

Johnny-boy was confident that when the black-slut's mutilated body was discovered, the logical conclusion by the white police would be, that she had been murdered by that uppity black nigger soldier.

Hell, according to that boy, that stupid kid—*what was his name…Rodney something or other—*, who had interrupted their card game, dozens of white people had seen the nigger soldier, and his slut, leave that fancy, foreign restaurant together.

Johnny-boy smiled. Pleased with his plan, his well thought-out, *"strategic battle-plan."*

He was convinced that based upon the circumstantial evidence that the police would find, the black US Army Sergeant, would be arrested, and hanged for murder.

And in addition to killing two uppity niggers, the scandal just might be enough to end decent white folks, having to endure the presence of armed nigger soldiers, in the streets of Richmond.

****

For more than two hours, he had lingered, hidden behind the trees, literally, lying-in-wait, wet, chilled, by the early morning dew.

With each passing moment, Johnny-boy was becoming increasingly nervous and apprehensive.

What if he had miscalculated? What if the nigger decided to spend the night with his slutty-whore?

Johnny-boy had a clear line of vision of the well-traveled road.

He instantly became alert; when in the distance he saw the outline of an approaching rider.

His heart began to race in his chest, pounding like a smithy's hammer on an anvil.

Slowly, inexorably, Johnny-boy's trigger-finger slid from the exterior of the long gun's trigger-guard, and onto the weapon's trigger.

The military-sniper—as he thought of himself— began to profusely, perspire.

With each— it seemed to him—, earsplitting heart beat, the image of the approaching rider, grew and sharpened.

****

Jason, reminiscing in the afterglow of his second date with Maureen, ignored the unexpected agitation of his huge stallion.

A gust of wind had brought to the horse, the unmistakable scent of a nearby mare. The huge stallion's nostrils flared.

The stallion snorted, his ears stood up, pointing in the direction of a scraggly, sparse stand of oak trees.

While whistling an unnamed, yet familiar tune, Jason was reliving his second date with the ebony beauty, Miss Maureen Marie Montgomery.

Miss Maureen Marie Montgomery (*Mo*), who Jason considered to be, the most intelligent, witty, and beautiful black, literally black-woman, that he had ever met, had been one of the northern "Free-born", Negro teachers, who had joined, and subsequently been sent, by the American Missionary Association, to educate the millions "Freed-men and women", in the post-Civil war South.

A broad grin spread across Jason's face, as his mind played a word game with the initials of her name, as it appeared on the official roles of the American Missionary Association; *M*iss *M*aureen *M*ontgomery.

He chuckled to himself..., *uMMM, uMMM,* Good.

In his mind, Jason replayed the events of the evening, culminating with his delicious, alone time, with Mo.

His time making love to… no more accurately, his time making love with, the exquisitely beautiful, witty, intelligent, literate, ebony teacher, who he now definitely thought of in terms of her being, his very own, *"Nubian Princess"*.

Lost in thought, reliving the wondrous events of the evening, Jason ignored the fidgety antics of his now, skittish, agitated, stallion.

When the black soldier passed, within twenty feet of him, Johnny-boy slowly let out his breath.

As the image of the soldier began to slowly recede, Johnny-boy, his hands shaking, unsteadily, lowered his weapon,

With a forced utterance of bravado, he muttered "Dammit I shouda shot and kilt that uppity-nigger."

****

Abruptly, Jason stopped whistling.

He rubbed his forehead, remembering the moment when he had accidentally bumped his head against one of the beams, supporting the ceiling of Maureen's basement apartment.

He recalled how Maureen had laughed and teasingly, referred to him as, *"Gulliver"* ...her Sergeant Major Gulliver." And how she had impishly teased him when he had asked the reason for her bestowing upon him, the nickname, *"Sergeant Major Gulliver."*

Jason reined in his horse. "I left that book; "Gulliver's Travels" on her table".

"I promised Mo that I would read that book."

Jason turned his horse around, and galloped back, toward Maureen's apartment.

****

September 28, 1867 – Maureen's Apartment – 2:50 AM

Maureen lay on her crumbled bed, wide-awake. She deliberately, had not bothered to straighten the bed, or to change the damp bed linens.

Instead, after Jason's departure, Maureen had wrapped herself in the wrinkled sheets, inhaling the smell, the intoxicating musk, languidly wallowing in Jason's distinctly, masculine aroma.

Her mind was abuzz with the implications, the possibilities, and the ramifications of what had just taken place between herself, and the dashing Sergeant Major, Jason Ruth.

Maureen Montgomery was a thirty-year-old highly educated, intellectually, emotionally, accomplished, mature, black woman.

She embraced, and would forever appreciate the fact that it was because of the courage of her parents who had escaped slavery from the Caribbean Island of Jamaica—that she was one of the fortunate—, relatively speaking, one of the few blacks who lived free, North of the Mason-Dixie line.

Of the North's population of nineteen million (19,000,000), only two hundred fifty thousand (250,000), one in a hundred, were black

While Maureen was totally committed to the abolishment of slavery, and was an ardent believer in those inspirational words, penned, nearly a century ago by Thomas Jefferson, in the nation's Declaration of Independence;

"That all men are created equal..."

Maureen as did many Northern blacks, particularly, educated, free-born blacks, who had had limited, if any exposure, with those who were actually black-slaves, *to her chagrin,* harbored an *unreasonable,* cultural prejudice, toward the more than four million people of African decent, her enslaved-brethren... black men, black women and black children, living...surviving, in bondage, in the South.

Among the things that Maureen found to be most distressing, offsetting, was what she perceived of, as the slave's *"cowardly",* subservient, docile demeanor.

Their apparent acceptance, as manifested to by their actions—especially by those former slaves, who after having found freedom in the North, continued to comport themselves as if they were an inherently inferior, dimwitted, lazy, people.

Despite her intellectual rejection of these pre-judgments, these prejudices toward blacks raised as slaves in the South, Maureen had come to realize, to acknowledge that subconsciously, at least inwardly she, as did many Northern freeborn *"Negroes",* harbored these latent, insidious, perceptions.

Jason Ruth, a black man born into slavery; a virtually self-taught, while enslaved, black man who had escaped Southern bondage, who had served, and continues to serve with honor, courage and valor in the union Army, had freed Maureen's mind of those latent prejudices.

Jason Ruth had liberated, freed, *"Emancipated"* Maureen's mind, from the gripe of those pernicious, irrational, preconceived, prejudices.

At the age of thirty in this 18th Century-Elizabethan Era, although she was relatively inexperienced, and was definitely far from being sexually sophisticated, Maureen Montgomery was not a virgin.

The first time that she, in the words of her college roommate, *"had gone all the way"*, occurred during her sophomore year at Oberlin College.

Nineteen-year-old Maureen Montgomery had been enthralled and infatuated, with an *"Older Man"*. A twenty-three-year old *"Senior"*, Howard Cabot.

To young Maureen, Howard Cabot, (a *"Senior"*, no less), —a white Connecticut, abolitionist-zealot—, was an erudite, sophisticated man of the world.

Her infatuation had gradually dissipated and had inexorably, turned to anger and resentment, after she finally came to accept, that the Connecticut Yankee's enumerable, disingenuous, excuses; as to why he avoided being seen in public with her, were his own self-serving lies.

Her second "affair" had happened a mere two-years-ago.

Her sexual partner had been a black pseudo-intellectual; a fellow teacher at the Benjamin Banneker School for Coloreds, a man who more than anyone she had ever known, was obsessed with, and manifested an exaggerated, absurd, black-on-black degree of racial prejudice.

U.S Army Sergeant Major Jason Ruth was the third man with whom Maureen had, in the words of her Oberlin College roommate, *"gone all the way."*

This was it. This time, without a doubt, Maureen Marie Montgomery was absolutely sure; she was positively certain, that she was in love.

Unable to fall asleep, still wrapped in the fragrant, Jason scented bed sheet, Maureen walked over to the kitchen table, and lit the oil lamp.

In addition to it being a platform for the preparing and the eating of meals, the table served as her desk.

She picked up the book, the copy of "Gulliver's Travels", that she had given Jason. Maureen gently placed the book onto the floor.

Maureen reached under the table, pulled out a sheet of paper, and began to write:

REPORT CARD
TO: Sergeant Major, Jason Ruth (My Sergeant Gulliver)
FROM: Miss. Maureen Marie Montgomery
DATE: September 28, 1867
SUBJECT: **SEXUAL REPORT CARD**

Sergeant Major, Jason Ruth; of his work tonight was most certainly that of an **A+**. Sergeant Major, Ruth's work was of great depth and wonderful penetration. The depth was that of such which could be felt hours after he finished. The need for New exploration was totally unnecessary as the work on the original areas was so thorough and powerfully overwhelming.

Sergeant Major, Jason Ruth also does exceptional Mouth Work which lingers after!

Maureen chuckled, folded the paper in half and placed it between the pages of the novel.
She heard the sounds of hoof beats of an approaching horse.
Maureen smiled and tightened the bed sheet surrounding, caressing, and clinging to her shoulders. "How thoughtful, my gallant Sergeant "Gulliver" has returned for his book."
Barefoot, Maureen crossed the floor to the door, and lifted the wooden board that served to lock and secure the door. She turned and walked back to the table to retrieve the book.
As the door began to swing open, with her back to the entrance, she smiled, picked up the book and asked in her sexiest, coquettish voice; "Back already?"

****

September 28, 1867 – Maureen's Apartment 4:12 AM

As he approached Maureen's basement apartment, Jason noticed that the door was slightly ajar. A sliver of light was visible between the door and the doorframe of the house.

Immediately he surmised that something was wrong.

Jason was absolutely certain that before he left, that he had checked the door, to ensure that it was bolted and secure.

With his pistol drawn and holding onto the saddle horn, he swung his right leg across the saddle, and leapt to the ground while the big horse was still in motion.

Jason swung the door wide open and rushed headlong, down the steps, rapidly sweeping his colt from side-to-side.

Maureen's naked body was grotesquely sprawled across the sofa bed. The lower portion of her right arm, her forearm palm up, at a ninety-degree angle was bent away from her body.

Jason dropped his pistol, ran to the bed and attempted to revive Maureen.

"Mo, Mo, baby open your eyes. Oh God…please, please honey open your eyes! Who did this to you? Wake up…wake-up. Please, please please, sweetheart…pleeese…

Jason sat on the bed, rocking and sobbing, cradling and holding Maureen's limp, lifeless, body.

****

Rather than going home to his farm as he had intended when he had left the poker-game, Johnny-boy decided instead, to return to the city, return to the meeting hall of the TSSRA.

He was anxious and could hardly wait to report, to boast, to tell the TSSRA's Grand Wizard, Sydney Savage, of his impromptu actions.

To report to his mentor, the details of how he had, on his own, taken the initiative, how he had devised and executed a plan to kill that uppity, Yankee-Nigger soldier, and his black whore.

A satisfied sneer spread across Johnny-boy's face as he recalled the events that had transpired when he returned to the black-whores house.

He recalled the look of shock and surprise in her eyes, the terrified expression, which had quickly turned to apprehension, then to fear, when he pushed the door open, and entered the room.

He recalled the black-sluts high pitched words; "who are you…what do you want…what are you doing here?"

Johnny-boy smiled as he remembered having answered; "Now is that any way to talk… specially after you being so nice and all…and opening the door for me?

Johnny-boy stood leering, menacingly, between the door and Maureen.

As Johnny-boy advanced toward her, Maureen with both hands, flung the book that she held in both hands, at the intruder, and darted toward the door.

Johnny-boy raised his right arm, using it as a shield, and easily managed to deflect the book.

In a display of contempt and anger, he kicked the large book back toward Maureen.

In two strides he was upon Maureen. With his right fist, he punched her in the face. He grinned at the sound of the cartilage breaking, in Maureen's nose.

With his left knee firmly planted dug into the bend of her elbow, Johnny-boy was able to immobilize her, pinning her arm down, across the top of the table. With all of his strength, Johnny-boy, using the heavy book as a hammer, smashed the book down onto Maureen's wrist.

Maureen screamed and fainted.

Staggering under her weigh, Johnny-boy failed in his attempt, to pick Maureen up.

He grunted, lowered her to the floor, grabbed her by her uninjured wrist, and dragged her across the floor, to the sofa bed.

As Johnny-boy was attempting to lift her onto the bed, Maureen began to stir.

Maureen regained conscientiousness, and in almost unbearable, excruciating pain, with her uninjured arm, lashed out, raking her fingernails across Johnny-boy's face.

Johnny-boy yelped. He reflexively released his grip on Maureen's arm. His hand went to his cheek.

He looked at his hand. His hand was streaked with his own blood.

Enraged, he delivered a series of vicious kicks to Maureen's ribs; "You black slut…you black-nigger bitch."

Johnny-boy placed his hands around Maureen's neck, and in a blind fury, began to squeeze, and squeeze, and squeeze…

Still trembling with rage, Johnny-boy suddenly relaxed his grip from around Maureen's throat.

"Damn it, I killed her too quick. Shit, now I can't make this black bitch, suck my cock. Can't force her to wrap them thick red lips around my cock…shit…damn!"

"Hell, she's still warm. I bet the way she was humping that nigger-soldier, she's probably still wet down there."

Johnny-boy spread Maureen's lifeless body on the bed and removed the sheet, now a shroud, from around her corpse. Johnny-boy lasciviously, stared at the semi-mutilated, naked remains of Maureen Marie Montgomery.

With his right hand, he began to rhythmically stroke his erect penis. Johnny-boy momentarily removed his hand from his stiff penis. He knelt on the bed and spread the legs of the corpse.

Without a moment's hesitation, Johnny-boy raped the bodily remains of, Maureen Marie Montgomery.

****

September 28, 1867 – Jefferson Street – Maureen's Apartment 4:20 AM

Gradually, after a mere seven minutes, a brief span of time that to him seemed like an eternity— Jason, consumed by unfathomable feelings of love, grief and remorse, ceased his metronome-like rocking and cradling, of Maureen's lifeless body.

Jason's overwhelming sense of loss and grief had morphed, into something far more sinister. His grief had become supplanted by an all-consuming need and desire for revenge.

The hot blood, pulsating through the veins and arteries feeding his grieving brain, was fueling one blinding thought.

Jason wanted…he needed…revenge. He needed to avenge the inhumane, cowardly, atrocities, inflected by some anonymous coward, upon Maureen.

With a calmness and deliberation, that belied, his feelings of rage, Jason gently, lovingly, lowered Maureen onto the bed.

His training as a senior non-commissioned combat officer in the United States' Army had surfaced, and now dictated and guided his actions.

Jason checked his pocket timepiece. Forty minutes had elapsed since he and Maureen had laughingly confirmed, that he would be coming to dinner, later this evening.

During that short span of time, someone, possibly more than one person, had invaded her home, tortured, raped, and murdered Maureen.

Jason took a deep, cleansing, calming, breath. He forced himself to dispassionately think, to examine the scene of the unknown enemy's, "sneak-attack."

For the first time since his discovery of her mutilated remains, Jason forced himself to, between heart-wrenching sobs, dispassionately, examine Maureen's body.

Jason lifted her fractured left arm. He observed that the motionless, dangling forearm when at rest, made a right angle with Maureen's upper arm.

He lifted her right hand and noticed that one of her neatly manicured fingernails, was broken.

Jason spread her fingers. He noticed that some sort of foreign substance—congealed blood— was lodged beneath Maureen's ~~her~~ fingernails.

Jason reached into his trousers and retrieved his pocketknife.

Furtively, his eyes quickly scanned the small room. He saw the book lying on the floor. Jason picked-up the book, opened it, and tore out a page.

He placed the paper under Maureen's right hand and with his pocketknife, scrapped the debris from beneath her fingernails.

Intermingled with the congealed blood was skin. Wrinkled, dirty, but definitely, pale white-skin.

From this evidence, he deduced that the man or the men, who had subjected Maureen to these atrocities, were white.

Jason picked the bed sheet up off of the floor, and wrapped it around Maureen's body. He gently placed Maureen's shrouded body onto the bed.

He shivered—not in response to a chill in the early pre-dawn, air—, he shivered instead, in response to a cold, deadly, wave of hatred, that flowed through his body.

Jason managed to take a deep, calming, breath.

From the meager evidence, that Mo had managed to leave, the congealed blood and the pale wrinkled skin, under her fingernails, Jason concluded that a white man, or white men, had murdered Maureen.

Once again, it was the white man, who had deprived him of someone he loved.

The first was his former owner and slave master, Henry Billings.

Henry Billings the white man who had debased his and his sister Mandy's, mother Ruth.

Henry Billings the white man who had impregnated his white wife Margaret, the Mistress of the Rosewood Plantation, and his black slave, Jason's mother Ruth, during the same week, possibly on the same day.

Henry Billings who when Jason was a boy, had literally saddled him as if he were an animal, to be ridden, spurred by his son and heir, Jesse Billings.
Henry Billings who was the biological father of his daughter, the *"White Princess"*, Rebecca Billings, and Jason's beloved black sister, Mandy.

Jason slammed shut, Maureen's door.

Jason examined the ground leading to, and away from the house. He noticed a series of four fresh clumps of horse droppings, spaced approximately twenty to fifty yards apart, in the direction leading back toward the center of Richmond.

****

September 28, 1867 – Road Leading Back To The Center Of Richmond 5:27 AM

In addition to his eagerness to report, and to subsequently bask in the anticipated praise from Simon Savage, the TSSRA's Grand Dragon, Johnny-boy was beginning to have nagging second thoughts.

Johnny-boy had in the past been the target of the mercurial disposition and temper, of his mentor and idol, Simon Savage.

The more he thought about it, the more he began to doubt the wisdom of disturbing, waking, the Grand Dragoon this early in the morning, before sunrise.

Although he was certain that his recounting of last night's incident, more specifically, his actions in the furtherance of the cause, would be well received by the Grand Dragon, one never knew how Simon Savage would respond to being awakened before the crack of dawn.

Johnny-boy decided that it would be prudent of him, to wait for sunrise.

To at least wait until he heard the crowing of the rosters, before he himself, *"crowed"* to the Grand Dragon about his most recent serendipitous, patriotic exploits.

Johnny-boy began to, with steady even pressure— to pull on the reins of his galloping mare.

Gradually the horse's forward progress slowed to a gait, then to a canter, and finally the tired mare's pace was that of a walk.

****

Aided by the light of the fading full moon, which was now giving-way to the purplish beginning traces of sunrise, Jason quickly ascertained that the tracks leading back toward the city, were made by a single rider.

Instead of spending time meticulously examining sign, tracking the single rider, Jason decided to save time. He chose to abandon tracking and instead, leapt upon the back of his huge stallion, and raced headlong along the well-traveled, primary road that lead back to the city of Richmond.

****

Johnny-boy, continuing his leisurely pace, allowed his mind to drift. A derisive smile of satisfied contentment, spread across his face.

He chuckled as he thought of how, in this one eventful night, his luck had gone from good, to bad, and then to great.

The good, when during the poker game, he was dealt a full house. The bad, when the Grand Dragon drew one card and filled an inside straight flush.

And how his luck had finally changed for the better, when he had just happened upon the nigger-soldier and his black bitch, slut.

Johnny-boy was suddenly shocked from his wistful daydreaming. He sensed impending danger.

Johnny-boy thought that he heard the distinctive sound of a rapidly approaching horse.

He furtively looked over his shoulder. Although the mare beneath him continued to plod along, for Johnny-boy, time and motion, seemed to have stopped, to be standing still.

****

As Jason crested a small hill, he spotted a lone rider, head-down, slouched in his saddle, slowly plodding along.

Jason pulled his Spencer repeating rifle from its scabbard, and dug the heels of his boots into the flanks of the stallion.

His mount leapt forward answering the command that had been driven into him, hour after hour, day after day, instilled into the horses of the U.S. Calvary (Colored). He "CHARGED"!

****

When Johnny-boy saw the black "aberration from HELL", black horse and rider, charging down toward him, his initial reaction was petrifaction.

Johnny-boy froze.

Fortunately for him his mount, the aging mare, bolted in fright as Jason's huge black stallion bore down upon them.

Johnny-boy regained his senses and frantically whipped and kicked the mare. Attempting to escape.

Jason's huge cavalry mount rapidly closed the distance. When he drew along side of the fleeing, panicky white man, and was about to sweep past him, Jason, holding the Spencer rifle in one hand, and the reins of his horse in the other, swung the barrel of the rifle backward, striking Johnny-boy in the chest.

Stunned by the blow, Johnny-boy dropped like a stone to the ground. He scrambled to his feet. In his panic to escape he had neglected to reach down and remove his rifle from the saddle scabbard.

A fatalistic sense of calm, had replaced Johnny-boy's initial panic.

Johnny-boy reached into the waistband of his trousers. His sweaty palm encountered, and surrounded the butt of his LeMat revolver.

With his left hand, he deftly removed his "sticker", a thin lethal-looking, nine-inch Italian stiletto-knife, from his left boot. Johnny-boy raised his pistol and fired at the back of the still mounted black soldier.

His horse's momentum carried Jason, an additional twenty-five yards past the spot that the white man had fallen.

As Jason leaned over preparing to dismount, he heard the sound of a pistol discharge, and the concomitant whining sound of a bullet, whizzing past his ear.

Jason crouching, jumped to the ground, and attempting to present a difficult to hit moving target, sprinted, zigzagging, toward, the white man.

Johnny-boy, now in control of his emotions, sighted down the barrel of his pistol, cocked the hammer, and squeezed the trigger. Nothing…the pistol had misfired.

His momentary calm having deserted him, Johnny-boy, stiletto-knife still clutched in his left hand, dropped the pistol, turned his back to the rapidly approaching black soldier, and began to run.

As he closed the distance between himself and the fleeing white man, Jason silently, berated himself for his not having followed, and adhered to his military training.

His actions had been antithetical to all that he had been taught, as a senior non-commissioned officer of the United States Army.

He had forfeited the element of surprise. He had allowed the enemy to gain the advantage of being stationary, "entrenched"; defending ground, as opposed to being, as he realized that he was, the more vulnerable combatant, advancing, without cover toward an armed, entrenched, enemy.

Jason at 6' 2", athletic, combat trained, soldier's body, easily overtook Johnny-boy.

When Jason tackled the panting, man, Johnny-boy began to wildly flail his arms.

Johnny-boy's "sticker", the stiletto-knife came within inches of Jason's throat.

Jason penned the arms of the squirming, exhausted, frightened man, behind his back.

Johnny-boy, attempted to "disarm" the black-soldier, by reasserting a demeanor of "White-Supremacy", that he, as a white southerner, had believed and espoused for his entire life.

"Get off-ah me nigger! Assaulting a white man! Nigger, I'll have you whipped till the meat falls off-ah your black ass, bones.

Despite his fulminating rage and hatred, his blinding fury, his contempt for this white man and for all that he stood for, Jason Billings, docile, subservient slave; ex-fugitive slave; Jason Ruth, Sergeant Major in the United States Army, hesitated.

In his mind he heard Maureen's mirthful, yet filled with pride, words; "You are the highest ranking, colored noncommissioned officer of the U.S. Army in Richmond, maybe in the whole-wide-world."

Her words had the effect of mollifying Jason's raging, primordial urge for retribution, for revenge.

Was this the right man? Was the fact that this white man was alone, on the road leading from Maureen's place; to the city; at daybreak… was this evidence…circumstantial at best, enough? Enough proof of this man's guilt?

As the man squirmed, twisting and turning under Jason's grip, the easterly light of the rising sun, illuminated three reddening, inflamed, thin scars on the white man's left cheek.

In Jason's mind, slight doubt was replaced by a certainty, by absolute **_CONVICTION!_**

With all of the force that he could muster, Jason smashed his fist into the face of the sneering white man. Again, and again, and again, sobbing and chanting; "this is for Mo, this is for Mo."

Jason pummeled Johnny-boy's face into a bloody pulp. The gory mass of blood, tissue, and broken bones, no longer resembled that of the face of a human being.

Jason stopped the pounding, only when, because of physical fatigue, he could no longer lift his arms.

Feeling alone, empty, and lost, Jason managed to stand. Wearily, without a backward glance he stumbled over to his horse.

He had missed reveille.

Sergeant Major Jason Ruth, was for the first time in his army career, was absent without leave, he was AWOL.

Jason didn't give it a second thought. He didn't care.

Jason mounted his horse, turned the stallion's head toward the northwest, and slowly, deliberately, rode off.

****

Chapter 55

Richmond Virginia – Sept 27, 1867 – Home of Horace Stapleton , Esq. 11:30 PM

Horace was in a foul mood as he fumbled with his key ring, attempting to locate the key that opened the door of his apartment. Finally finding the correct key, he opened the door and angrily threw is cloak on the sofa.

His noxious frame of mind had started when that Nigger soldier, and his black whore had brazenly entered the restaurant.

Horace's carefully crafted plans to wine, dine, and following dinner, in the secluded confines of his carriage, to fuck the "white squaw", with or without her cooperation, had been derailed, side-tracked, ruined.

Horace sat in his easy chair gently swirling, then slowly sipping from his brandy snifter. He stared dully, without actual comprehension, at the intricate, elaborately labeled bottle; "*Le Cognac de Napoleon.*"

His eyes, though a bit bleary from the night's consumption of spirits, focused on the dark amber liquid in his glass. Once again Horace lifted his snifter, and this time in one hasty gulp, emptied the glass.

He removed the globes, and extinguished the two oil lamps in his parlor. Mentally and physically exhausted, Horace went to bed.

As he lay in bed, tossing and turning, unable to fall asleep, reliving in his mind, the events of the evening, Horace began to sardonically chuckle to himself.

He mused that in large part, his past actions, his political lobbying at the state legislature, had been responsible for that 'Nigger" sergeant and his black whore, brazenly showing up at the restaurant, and spoiling his plans for the evening.

Despite his efforts, his concerted attempts to fall asleep, "to get some rest", sleep eluded him. He listlessly lay in the bed. Just as he was about to finally drift off, a series of loud poundings, reverberated from his door.

Horace frowning stood, lit the candle on his nightstand. He then glanced at the dial of his pocket watch. The time was twenty minutes past three.

Horace opened the drawer of his nightstand, and removed a small derringer pistol.

He picked up his robe from the foot of the bed, and shrugged into the loosely fitting garment. Horace placed the small caliber pistol into the pocket of his robe, and walked toward the door, muttering to himself; "Who in blazes can that be at this time of night?"

Horace lit the oil lamp on his nightstand. He glanced at the face of his pocket watch; 3:40 AM.

"Who is it…who's there?" A high-pitched, yet distinctly masculine voice answered; "It's me Mr. Stapleton; Donny…ah…Donald Hicks"

Donald Hicks was a local businessman, who during the prosecution and the conclusion of the war had concentrated the bulk of his business transactions in conformity with the slimy, treacherous, behavior that many in the Southern community ascribed to opportunistic, white Southerners.

Traitors, who during and after the war had profited, from and exploited, the plight that had befallen, so many of their white neighbors.

Donald Hicks through his shady, business activities, had earned, and deserved the derogatory pejorative, used by the southern community.

Donald Hicks was considered by most, to be truly, a deplorable "*scalawag.*"
Horace and a few other so-called upstanding pillars of Richmond 's elite, men who would never publicly socialize, associate, or be seen in the company of a Donald Hicks, had managed to substantially enrich themselves, by clandestinely assisting and aiding and abetting, Donald Hicks and his ilk.

These unprincipled men, encouraged and persuaded Northern banks to purchase dirt-cheap, vast acres of Southern farmland, former Grand Plantations, thousands of acres, often paying as little as ten cents on the dollar, of the lands actual value.

While the acquisition of rich fertile farm-land was immensely profitable, Horace, Donald Hicks, and their land grabbing associates, were acutely aware of the fact that in order for them to realize the staggering pre-Civil War profits, made by the former plantation masters, enormous wealth from the planting, growing, harvesting and the subsequent selling of "King-Cotton", it was imperative that a reliable source of cheap, — preferably free, as in "slave-labor" —, was needed.

On one occasion, while in Horace's presence, Donald Hicks had vociferously complained and cursed about the hordes of "shiftless", lazy niggers" that had sprung up in the city, "*ignorant coons*", pestering decent white-folks.

Horace recalled his having been irritated and annoyed, as he had halfheartedly listened to Donald Hicks' inane, whiney voice; "I tell you Mr. Stapleton, there oughtta be a law against it."

Startled from his usual indifferent, superficial attempt to feign interest in the "Scalawags" prattling, Horace had abruptly, interrupted.

"Just a minute Hicks, what exactly did you just say? You said something about there should be a law against *"it"*. **Against** what?"

At first Donald Hicks had seemed to be confused by Horace's questions.

As he impatiently waited for a response, Horace imagined that he could smell *"the wood burning"*, as Hicks struggled to remember his recent comments.

"Oh…what I said was that we need to do something about the gangs of *"black jungle-bunnies"*, roaming our streets."

Horace remembered thinking that, for once in his life, Donald Hicks, had inadvertently, uttered an intriguing, intelligent, thought provoking sentence.

Hundreds of former slaves who for the first time in their lives, found themselves homeless and unemployed, were roaming the city's streets.

Many of the former slaves, now *"freedmen"*, were searching for love-ones; wives and children, family members, separated, sold, torn-apart, victims of the legal, insidious, slave-trade.

One thing that practically all of the unemployed *"freedmen"* had in common was that they were looking for work.

The increasingly large groups of black men, aimlessly wandering around the streets, begging for work or for handouts, had become an annoyance and blight, to the Richmond citizenry.

Horace reasoned, and rightfully so, that through legislation collectively, they could rid the city of the increasingly growing bands of "shiftless" ex-slaves, while simultaneously solving the *"New Plantation Master's"* need for a cheap labor-force.

Thus, the scalawags, with the aid of Richmond's elite, and an embittered racist state legislature, had passed Virginia's 1866 Vagrancy Law.

****

The formal preamble of the Vagrancy Law proclaimed that;
"There hath lately been a great increase of idle and disorderly persons in some parts of this commonwealth."
There was no mistaking the fact, that this opening sentence of the law, was most assuredly exclusively directly aimed, at the ex-slaves, the black freedmen.

The law declared that any person who was thought by officers of the law (local sheriffs), to be unemployed or homeless, would be forced into employment, for up to three months, most often as farmhands; tillers, caretakers, and harvesters, of the cotton-crop, and be paid wages far below that being paid to white farmhands.

The law went on to stipulate that if the so-called vagrant ran away and was subsequently recaptured, the so-called vagrant would, for three months, be forced to work in the cotton-fields, for no wages, while shackled and forced to wear a ball and chain.

Horace remembered how following his initial reading of the new law, an involuntary broad smile had spread across his face.

He remembered nostalgically, exclaiming; "Legalized free black-labor… ah just like in the good-old days. Just like in the good-old days."

"Without firing a single shot, through the legislative process, we managed to accomplished what four years of war, with the tragic loss of a half million Southern white-boys' lives, could not accomplish. We've made Virginia, and possibly the entire South, *Great Again*."

Dejected, and weary, as Horace walked from his bedroom to the front door, a wry, derisive, smirk crossed his face. His mind fleetingly fixated on that old adage, *"be careful of what you wish for."*

Ironically, Horace recognized that in large-part, he was responsible for tonight's fiasco; responsible for the audacity of that Nigger Sergeant, all decked-out in his garishly brazen Yankee Uniform, and his black-whore spoiling his evening.
The passage of the Vagrancy Law had served as the impetus for the radical Republicans in the United States Congress, to create the Freedmens Bureau, and to send Federal troops, black Union soldiers, to protect the rights of the ex-slaves.
With his left hand on the door-knob, and his right firmly holding the derringer, in an irritated whisper he uttered; "Hicks are you alone?"
"Yes sir…it's just me." Horace opened the door. Upon verifying that Hicks was in fact alone, Horace removed his right hand from the pocket of his robe, and pointed to an easy-chair.
Donald Hicks, correctly interpreting the gesture, his hat in hand, seated himself.
"Okay Hicks, this had better be good. What in hell possessed you to come banging on my door at this ungodly-hour?"
Obviously uncomfortable, Donald Hicks took a deep, calming breath, and began to speak; "Mr. Stapleton there's been some trouble.".
Horace was genuinely confused. Although he had a clandestine, at best a tenuous relationship with Donald Hicks, their relationship by no means warranted, this late-night intrusion.
Before he could protest, Hicks hurriedly began to incoherently babble; "your lady-friend, the young woman that you had dinner with this evening, was set upon by one of my acquaintances."
Horace was totally puzzled; "Hicks, what in the hell are you talking about?"
Donald Hicks began to perspire; to squirm and to fidget uncomfortably in his seat.
In an agitated voice, Horace demanded; "How in hell could you know that tonight, I went out to dine? And why in God's name, would you know where I went, and who happened to be my dinner companion? Were you following me?"
Hicks raised his hands in protest; "No sir. What happened was purely by accident. One of my boys, Jimmy Ryan, just happened to be driving the carriage that you hailed this evening, outside that fancy French Restaurant."
"Jimmy right away, recognized you and the woman you were with. Well sir, and these are Jimmy's words, he was shocked to see you with that fallen woman, the "white-squaw." The woman that all the decent women of Richmond are talking about."

"That slut, the white woman who all those wild Indians, those red-niggers out west, captured and repeatedly screwed, passed around among them reskinned-bucks, and fucked again, and again, and again for a whole year."
"You know Sir, he was talking about the Billings woman, the one taken in by that lawyer, Mr. Frazier and his wife, the white woman who was rescued from them heathen Indians."
Horace, still annoyed, but his curiosity now having been aroused, remained seated, silent, concentrating, listening without commenting,

Hicks realizing that Horace's anger had dissipated and had been supplanted by curiosity, took a deep breath and continued; "Jimmy said that he was not at all surprised when you ordered him to stop the carriage here, at your residence".

"The lad admitted to me that he recalled having thought to himself; "well good for Mr. Stapleton, he's gonna take that whore up to his place and get hisself some of that well-broken in, white squaw pussy".

"However, Sir, the lad was a bit confused and taken-a-back, when you got out, and the woman remained in the carriage. He said that you instructed him to drive the woman to her home, to the residence of her uncle, Mr. Luis Frazier."

At that point Stevens reached into his coat pocket and removed his linen handkerchief. He nervously wiped his brow, and in a plaintive, high pitched voice, continued; "Jimmy swears to me, that he had fully intended to take the woman to the address that you gave him."

At that point Stevens hesitated. Once again beads of moisture had appeared on his forehead. He began to perspire and to squirm in his seat. Stevens nervously ran his tongue over his thin dry lips. He furtively blotted his brow with his damp handkerchief, "Sir can I please have a glass of water?"
Horace stood, walked over to the side-bar, lifted the pitcher of water, and half-filled a glass-tumbler.

Horace walked over to Stevens and thrust the glass of water toward him. Stevens accepted the proffered drink. He drained the glass, wiped his mouth with his now sodden pocket handkerchief, and sat back in his chair.

Horace returned to his seat. He stared expectantly at Donald Hicks, waiting patiently waiting for him to continue. After a full moment of uncomfortable silence, Horace impatiently blurted out; "Go on man! From the way you pounded on my door, I'm assuming that there is a lot more to this tale."

Hicks shuddered, took a deep breath, then continued; "Jimmy says that for about ten minutes they drove along in silence."

"He said that his head began to reel from the smell of the woman's perfume. He actually described to me, the effect on his body of the woman's scent, of her aroma, of the woman's perfume mixed with the scent of her body.

Again Sir, his words not mine; "*I swear to you Mr. Hicks, bumping along in the carriage, my prick rubbing up against my trousers, I suddenly had the biggest, throbbing hard-on, that I've ever had in my life.*"

"The lad says he couldn't stop thinking of how that white-squaw — once again Sir, his words not mine —, how she had spread her thighs for God only knows, how many, countless redskin bucks. Maybe here was a golden opportunity, a chance for him, Jimmy Ryan, to stick his pecker in what he called, "that fantastically, sweet smelling pussy.""

Horace leaned over, placed his elbow on the table, and lowered his head into his hand. While he was pretty sure that he knew what was coming. His only thought now was, how would this — whatever *this* was —, how would *this* affect him.

Seeing the shift in Horace's demeanor, Stevens hurriedly continued; "Jimmy pulled off of the road, snapped the reins and sped into the woods."

"When he was well beyond sight of the road, Jimmy says he stopped the carriage and jumped down to the ground. And with his left hand, through the fabric of his trousers, he was continuously squeezing his ready to burst, throbbing engorged pecker, with his right hand, he flung open the door of the carriage."

"Jimmy said that he pulled the hussy from the carriage." For an awkward moment, both Horace Stapleton and Donald Hicks, sat in complete silence.

"Jimmy said that the woman lay sprawled on the ground, clutching her bag. He remembered saying, as he pulled down his trousers; "Okay slut…now it's my turn." To his surprise, instead of cringing or attempting to flee, the woman willingly, almost demurely, extended her left-hand to him."
"When Jimmy eagerly reached for her hand, without warning the "white-squaw", let loose a blood-curdling scream (*"Aahe-hey"),* and in one swift motion, with a knife that had been concealed in her bag, practically severed Jimmy's hand, from his wrist."

"Jimmy says that at first, it had felt like she had slapped him on his wrist. When he looked down at his arm, he was shocked to see bright-red blood gushing from his forearm."

"Jimmy says that his hand was practically separated from his wrist. The hand was dangling, attached to his arm by two strands of tissue."

"He said that the woman had gathered her dress into her hands, and that she had run off in the direction of the road."

Hicks picked up his empty glass, walked over to the side-bar, removed the stopper from the crystal whiskey decanter, and filled his glass to the brim with the aromatic, dark-amber liquid, and with one continuous gulp, drained his glass.

Horace sat back in his chair. The expression on his face was that of annoyance and incredulity. He looked directly into the eyes of Donald Hicks, a man that he thought of as an opportunistic scoundrel. A pawn that was useful, yet completely expendable.
"Hicks this is a fascinating story. But I must confess, I am more than a bit, confused and annoyed".

The woman that you described…oh I forgot, how did you phrase it…in your friend Jimmy's words, you described her as a slut, a whore, the "White Squaw", why do you think the escapades of your thuggish associates with that trollop, would be of interest to me?"

Donald Hicks once again mopped his perspiring brow with his handkerchief.

"Well Mr. Stapleton, I figured that since other than Jimmy, who nobody pays any attention to or notices, you were the last person to have been seen with the Billings woman. And quite honestly, we don't know what may have befallen the woman when she fled into the woods, I felt it best that you be prepared in the event that the authorities…the police become involved.

****

Chapter 56

Richmond Virginia –Sept. 27, 1867 – Cobblestone Road Two Miles from "Le Grand Vieux Manoir", 10:15 PM

As they sat in silence, swaying with the motion of the carriage, Horace and Rebecca each, were engrossed in their own thoughts.

Rebecca, who had been gazing out the window, was surprised when after fifteen minutes, the carriage stopped. At first, Rebecca had been confused, irritated, slightly annoyed.

Unbeknownst to Rebecca, Mr. Horace Stapleton had ordered the livery driver to stop at a neat two-story house. Horace turned to Rebecca and quickly explained that the house was his home.

Before she could protest, give vent to her annoyance and apprehension, Horace quickly provided what to her at the time she considered —, a perfectly logical and rational explanation.

"Miss Billings, unfortunately the effect of the events that spoiled our evening, that precipitated your headache, to be more precise, the temerity of those "Uppity Nigras", has befallen me."

"I too have developed a splitting headache. I was wondering, since your home is located a considerable distance across town, and I on the other hand, pointing to the two-story house, live here, if you would mind if I did not…

A surge of relief coursed through her body. Rebecca raised her hand, not allowing Horace to finish the sentence. "Of course, Mr. Stapleton, and by the way, I hardily agree".

It would be foolish and quite unnecessary, for you to travel in pain, across the city, then have to turn-around, and once again traverse back across the city to this very spot, your home."

Rebecca noted, that either Horace had missed the sarcasm in her voice, or more than likely, Mr. Horace Stapleton, Esq., just didn't care.

****

For the first time that evening, Rebecca began to relax. Before, during, and after dinner, she had been pondering as to how she should, and would interact with Mr. Stapleton, at the conclusion of the evening.

Rebecca had promised her aunt Delilah, that she would be open-minded, and that she would, "give the gentleman a chance".

She had found Stapleton's racist, oafish behavior in the restaurant to be, obnoxious, and inexcusable. Rebecca had come to the conclusion that Horace Stapleton, was a dyed-in-the wool, bigot.

In deference to the feelings of her aunt and uncle Rebecca, during the latter part of the evening, had been trying to construct a civil polite way to end, before it actually began, her relationship with Horace Stapleton.

The monotonous, rhythmic, sound of the clicking of the horse's hoofs on the cobbled streets, was relaxing, hypnotic.

For the first time that evening, Rebecca felt relaxed. She was slowly giving in to drowsiness.

As her eyelids began to close, and she was about to dose off, she sensed that something had changed. Although the carriage was still in motion, the clackity clacking sound of the horse's hoofs had ceased.

Rebecca sat up in her seat and looked out the window. The carriage was no longer on the stone-cobbled street. The dirt path that they were now traversing, was surrounded by trees.

Confused, Rebecca attempted to communicate with the driver. With her hand bag, she wrapped upon the partition that separated driver from passengers.

Instead of slowing down, the driver snapped the reins, and the carriage sped forward. Careening through the foliage.
Rebecca was thrown back in her seat. At that instant she realized that she was in danger. Rebecca knew that her most dreaded, subconscious, irrational, phobia was occurring…no was reoccurring, Rebecca knew she was being abducted.

The carriage stopped. The driver jumped down from his perch and flung the door open.

The light from the bright full moon, shone through the windows of the vehicle. Rebecca's worst fears were reinforced. The driver stood before her, squinting. His left hand was squeezing the slight, yet noticeable bulge in his pants, his erection.

Inwardly, silently, she screamed; *"No not again…never, never again."* Rebecca realized that she was about to be raped.

For a brief moment, the image of the pudgy, pale middle-aged white man, was replaced by the image of the one man, that she truly feared, and hated. *"Stone Fist."*
Stone Fist, her former Comanche captor. The deadly, lethal warrior who was acknowledged and feared by both red and white men, men living on lands bordering the Comanche Hunting Grounds.
To these white-men— settlers, lawmen, soldier, and by the red men, tribes that were the ancient enemies of the Comanche—, Stone Fist was regarded as the fiercest, the most lethal, of the Comanche warriors.
The driver grabbed Rebecca by her wrist, and roughly pulled her from the carriage.

****

E. Pluribus Unum

Chapter 57

Richmond Virginia –Sept. 28, 1867 –
Home of Horace Stapleton 4:20 AM

Donald Hicks ended his *dialogue* by describing how, Jimmy had managed to wrap his damp, urine and semen, stained-drawers around his hand and his wrist, and how he somehow, had managed to drive to Doc Sawyer's house.

Horace's initial reaction was that of relief. He exhaled, and under his breath uttered a low, barely audible sigh.

His feeling of relief was predicated upon the fact, that a police investigation of the incident, was in all probability, unlikely.

As best as he could tell, the slut that he had practically been ordered to take to dinner, had not been hurt.

Horace knew that in the event of an investigation by the authorities of a white woman, being brutally attacked, the fact that last night, most of the patrons at *"Le Grand Vieux Manoir"* restaurant, including that Yankee nigger soldier and his black whore, had seen him leave with the "white-squaw."

Horace was reassured by Stapleton, that despite his injury, that *"Mick"* buffoon Jimmy Ryan, would not go to the police. Additionally, Horace believed that because of her sullied reputation as a woman of ill-repute, in all likelihood, Rebecca Billings would not report the incident to the police, or for that matter, to her uncle…. his employer, the esteemed Luis Frazier, Attorney-at-Law.

****

Chapter 58

Home of Luis and Delilah Frazier
– Sept. 28, 1867 (5:06 AM)

Hattie hurried over to the pot-bellied stove, picked-up the coffeepot and filled a mug with the now luke-warm, coffee.

With her right hand, Rebecca picked up the cup. As she raised the cup to her lips, her hand began to tremble. Luke-warm liquid spilled down the front of her dress.

Hattie rushed to her employer's side. *"Landsakes Miz Becca, what's ailing you. Yuz be as white as a bed-sheet. Thank da lawd dat coffee won't real hot."*

Rebecca raised the mug to her lips, spilling coffee down the front of her rumbled, dirt encrusted, evening dress. Hattie hurried over and with a towel, hastily blotted the coffee stain that was spreading and saturating the front of Rebecca's dress.

Rebecca surrounded the mug with both hands. She drained the mug, placed it on the table, and rose from the table.

"I'm all right Hattie. I'll be going to my room now…goodnight." When she reached the door she paused, looked over her shoulder, and in a calm composed voice spoke; "Hattie, please don't speak of this…to either my uncle or to my aunt."

Hattie lowered her head and mumbled; *"Yessum."*

Although for two whole years, she had been *"free"*, no longer a slave, now being paid wages for her labor; Hattie found that deeply embedded old habits — forty years a slave —, were hard to break.

Hattie knew that something terrible had happened to *Miz. Becca*. Something that *Massa* Luis should know.

For a brief moment she wrestled with her conscientious. Then she shrugged her shoulders and mumbled to herself; *"Gal being a slave or being free, dun mak no diffrence. Yu knows betta den ta go stickn yo nose in da white-folks bizzness."*

****

Chapter 58

Law Offices of Luis Frazier and Associates - Sept. 28, 1867 (10:20 AM)

Luis Frazier, Esq. Founding Senior Partner, of the prestigious law firm of "Luis Frazier and Associates", sat at his desk, head buried in the morning edition of the *Gazette.*

Horace Stapleton, the law-firm's senior associate, the young lawyer thought to be next in line for a junior partnership, in Richmond's largest and most prestigious law firm, knocked on the heavy, solid mahogany-stained door.

Luis snapped the paper shut and placed it on his desk and bellowed, "Enter!".

Horace pushed the door open and stepped on to the plush, wall-to-wall, ankle high, thick carpeting that covered the floor of the spacious office.

"You wanted to see me Mr. Frazier?

Luis nodded his head and pointed. His gaze was fixed upon the plush red-leather couch, situated in the recessed rear area of the office.

Horace did as directed. He walked over to the sofa, sat down and was instantly enveloped, practically submerged, in the lap of unbelievable luxury.

Luis newspaper in hand picked up one of the two chairs that faced his desk, and walked over to the sofa.

Horace had been alarmed when he was informed that the "*Boss*", had summoned him to his office. His state of apprehension led to his not noticing, and not appreciating the possible significance of the newspaper, that Luis clutched in his hand.

Horace's initial thought, after the curt non-verbal exchange, was that that *"white-squaw"* *bitch,* had told him *her uncle*, of her having been attacked last night, by that Irish lout.

Horace had rationalized that since he had not had an inkling, nor had he before the incident, had prior knowledge of the attack, that he was not at fault, and could not be held responsible for the livery driver's assaulting Rebecca.

Despite has rationalization, reluctantly Horace had come to recognized and accept the fact, that his failure to accompany and deliver the "*bitch*" safely home, might very well, be construed by Luis, as gross negligence on his part.

Luis placed his chair directly in front of his subordinate. From this vantage point, he was looking down at Horace.

If both men had been standing, Horace would have towered over his much shorter employer. However, in his current position, that of his body being literally engulfed, swallowed in the folds of the leather couch, negated any semblance of the physical supremacy that he usually enjoyed, in Luis' presence.

Luis sat in silence, glaring at his subordinate. Horace was becoming increasingly uncomfortable.

Luis broke the silence. "Well Mr. Stapleton…what do you have to say for yourself?"

Horace thought, " *Ah Oh! He called me Mr. Stapleton. He always calls me Horace. He knows! I'd best get out in front of this thing.*"

"Sir, I was horrified, and disgusted, when I heard about the trouble that had befallen your niece last night."

"Mr. Frazier I sincerely hope that Miss Billings…Rebecca, told you of the extenuating circumstances, that lead to my sending her home alone, with that degenerate Irishman."

Luis sat bolt upright in his chair. "You did what? Did I hear you correctly sir? Are you telling me that you sent Rebecca home alone? What in blazes is it that you're saying man?"

"I thought it odd that Rebecca didn't come down to breakfast this morning. Naively, I accepted my wife's suggestion that Rebecca, was resting after her long, presumably, enjoyable evening with you."

"Is she all right…was Rebecca hurt?!"

Almost immediately, Horace realized that he had committed one of "THE LAWYER'S… THE LITAGATOR'S, CARDINAL MISTAKES. "

Because of his assuming that facts were known by this third party, he had volunteered incriminating…in this case, self-incriminating, unsolicited information.

Horace took a deep calming breath; "No sir. To the best of my belief and knowledge, Miss Billings was not hurt."

"To the best of your belief and knowledge? Don't speak to me using that feckless, legalistic jargon. Answer my question!

"Explain yourself sir!"

Horace realizing that he had *"stepped into it"*, composed himself and regurgitated for Luis, the news that was brought to him, "At 3:40 AM", in the middle of night, by Donald Hicks."

As he was retelling the details of the attempted sexual assault of Rebecca by the livery-driver, Horace could not help being alarmed by the startling, mesmerizing, change in Luis' eyes.

Horace hesitated. He was momentarily confused. He had not anticipated, been prepared for Luis' reaction to his second-hand recounting of last night's events.

This was the first instance in which Horace found himself being the catalyst, the agent responsible, for the legendary darkening of Luis Frazier's eyes.

It was a well-known fact, a phenomenon, experienced at some point, by practically everyone employed at "Luis Frazier and Associates", the proclivity of the irises of the *"BOSS"* eyes, to change color, to become a barometer of Luis' anger.

Luis had the most penetrating, piercing blue eyes. When pleased with or amused by something, his eyes would sparkle, and would give one the impression that they were looking into a soothing tranquil pool of water.

However, when he became angry or annoyed, Luis' eyes would smolder and darken.

It had been said by many of those who had been the target of Luis' angry stare that; "It was akin to watching the relentless approach of a ferocious, raging, summer thunderstorm."

In addition to the disturbing transformation of the color of Luis' eyes, for the first time, Horace noticed a steady accelerated throbbing of the blood vessel aligned along Luis' temple.

Horace made a hasty decision. He decided to change tactics. He deduced that it was in his best interest, to try to placate Luis. To appeal to *"Uncle Louey's"*, paternal instincts, by emphasizing that Rebecca was not hurt, and to laud her courage by showing his admiration for how she had managed to fight back, and escape.

Horace relaxed. Apparently, his ploy had achieved the desired effect. As he looked into the eyes of his mentor, he noted that the color of Luis' eyes had lightened. Luis' eyes had returned, to pale blue.

Both Luis and Horace sat for a moment, in silence.

Luis slowly, carefully, unfolded the copy of the newspaper that he had been clutching, in his right hand.

For the first time, Horace noticed the slightly crumbled newspaper. Luis refolded the paper. He pointed the paper at Horace, as one would point a gun, at an adversary during a duel.

"Mr. Stapleton, earlier when I sent for you…when I asked you to explain yourself, I had no idea, no reason to think that you, a man that I considered a man of honor, a gentleman, would have under any circumstances, failed to have seen my niece, safely home."

"Indeed, my motive for sending for you, was to discuss with you, the headline story in this morning's *"Gazette."*

Luis pointed to the newspaper's headline story, glared at Horace and commanded; "read it."

In response to the passage by the state legislature of "Virginia's Vagrancy Act", radical Republicans in the United States Congress, have dispatched to the state's capital city, one hundred fifty, Negro Troops.

Ostensibly, the justification for sending the troops is to protect the newly emancipated colored "freedman" from unlawful as well as from, what the Congressional Republicans called, discriminatory, "lawful" persecution.

When Horace finished reading the story, he folded the newspaper and placed it on the sofa. He then sheepishly looked at Luis.

"It had been my intention to have a little sport with you, to in essence, gloat."

"As you are well aware, I had forecast that those hardheaded boys in the legislature, by passing that Vagrancy Act, would bring the wrath of those Radical Republicans in the Yankee Congress, crashing down upon us."

"My exact words to you at the time were, that passing that ill-conceived legislation would be seen by those hard-liners in the congress, as being analogous to the Yankees, as our waving a red flag in the face of an angry, enraged, bull."

Luis' semi-relaxed posture, stiffened. He moved to the edge of his chair. "Your confession, and that is exactly how I see it. Your admission of responsibility, your culpability, for a crime that you perpetrated against my niece, was to me upsetting, and completely unexpected."

"To say that I am disappointed in your behavior is a gross understatement. Your lack of chivalry…your actions which imperiled and endangered the life of Rebecca, are unforgivable and inexcusable".

Luis returned to his desk. He tugged on a cord inconspicuously situated, behind the drapes that framed his window.

Within seconds, there was a loud knock on the door. Before Luis could answer, a rather short, yet undeniably large, burly man opened the door. "You need me Mr. Frazier?"

Although he could not recall the man's name, Horace immediately recognized the stocky, physically imposing man.

It was common knowledge among the firm's eighteen lawyers and their supporting staff, that the burly, rotund, muscular man, who stood a mere five feet-seven inches, and weighed two hundred-forty pounds, was the personal body-guard of the *"Boss"*, Luis Frazier, Esq.

It was often said by many — but never while in his presence —, that Rudolf Gunther, Luis Frazier's more than competent, and unquestioning fanatically devoted, personal body-guard, was as *"wide as he was tall."*

While his eyes never wavered from glaring intently at Horace, Luis raised his hand, which Rudolf Gunther correctly interpreted, as his employer's command that he stop, listen, and not speak.

Luis in a calm, dispassionate voice, addressed Horace; "You Sir, have betrayed my trust."

"I cannot, and well not be associated with a man that I cannot trust. Mr. Gunther, whom I do trust, will escort you to your office."

Luis pulled on the thick gold chain, which was attached to the gold pocket watch in his vest

 "The time is now 11:45 AM. You have fifteen minutes to gather your belongings. At precisely 12:00 O'clock, noon, Mr. Gunther will personally escort, a concept that you apparently do not appreciate, you from the building."

"Those possessions of yours that you cannot carry, I will have sent to you."

 "You are no longer an employee of this firm."

Without uttering a word, Rudolph Gunther took two menacing steps toward Horace.

Horace hastily stood, and was ushered, for the last time, from the offices of "Luis Frazier, Esq. and Associates – Attorneys-At-Law.

****

Chapter 59

Home of Luis and Delilah Frazier
– Sept. 28, 1867 (1:10 PM)

Hattie Smith, the Frazier's cook stood quietly, concentrating, attentively, as Delilah spoke.

Delilah Frazier her employer, Mistress of the Frazier's fashionable, brick town-house, was dictating the menu for that night's, three course dinner.

"Baked ham, collard-greens, freshly shucked corn, candied yams, and mashed potatoes. And Hattie, please if it's not too late in the day, do you have time to bake a pan of that delicious corn-bread that Mister Frazier loves so much?"

"The three of us, Mister Frazier, myself, and Miss Rebecca, do so enjoy your delicious, fresh, just out of the oven, corn-bread."

"Hattie, please don't take offense. She handed a sheet of paper to Hattie.

While Delilah was slowly, methodically reading aloud, for Hattie the recipe for the dinner's first course, the French soup, *"Vichyssoise"*, both women were startled by the unexpected, raised-voice of the man of the house.

"Rebecca…Delilah, where are you? Is anyone here?"

"I'm here dear, in the kitchen."

Delilah was alarmed. For Luis to be home at 1:00 PM on a weekday, was unusual, unheard of, and quite frankly to Delilah, somewhat upsetting.

She dropped the book from which she had been reading — *"French Cuisine-for Southern Style Cooking"* —, onto the kitchen table, rose to her feet, and accompanied by the sounds of a flurry of rustling petticoats, hastily left the kitchen.

What Delilah saw when she entered Luis' den/library—her husband's body language—, was to her both alarming and disconcerting.

Luis was standing at the bar pouring himself, a generous helping of Kentucky bourbon.

Delilah stopped short; "Luis what's wrong? Are you ill? Without waiting for an answer, she hurried over to her husband, and placed her hand on his forehead.

Satisfied that Luis' was not feverish, she withdrew her hand. "Why aren't you at your office? And for heaven's sake, why are you partaking of strong spirits, when it's barely high noon?"

Instead of answering Delilah's rapid, staccato-barrage of questions, in one gulp, Luis drained his glass. With the empty tumbler in hand, in a trembling voice he turned toward Delilah; "Where's Rebecca?"

Delilah's was once again alarmed and confused. Her uneasiness was intensified.

Delilah's confusion was not due to those innocuous two words, *"Where's Rebecca?"* Her concern was due to the desperation, the fear that she had distinctly heard, in Luis' voice.

"Why…I believe she's in her room'.

Luis hastily attempted to place his empty glass onto the edge of the sidebar. The glass tumbler wobbled, then fell and shattered on the parquet floor.

"Luis what is it…your frightening me."

Luis, ignoring the broken glass, walked over to Delilah. He gently placed his hands on her shoulders, and looked into her eyes.

"I apologize my dear. It was not my intent to upset you."

Luis took Delilah's hand and guided her to the sofa. Together, they sank into the upholstered soft leather, couch.

"This morning I asked Horace Stapleton to come to my office. My reason for sending for him was a bit selfish, but I assure you, totally innocent."

"I thought myself clever, by employing a convenient subterfuge."

"I had intended to use an article in today's newspaper as a ploy, a ruse to tactfully eventually I had hoped, to get a sense of his evening-out, dining with Rebecca last night."

Delilah began to relax. She felt relieved. A coquettish smile began at the corners of her mouth.

"My aren't you the clever one. Well don't keep me waiting in suspense. What did Horace have to say?"

"What did that cad have to say? That sorry excuse for a man, for a so-called gentleman, had a hell of a lot to say."

Once again Delilah was becoming alarmed. She could not imagine what Horace could have possibly said, that would have caused Luis to swear in her presence.

Abruptly Luis stood. "After I left for the office this morning, did Rebecca come down, and join you for breakfast?"

Before Delilah could answer, Luis continued; "Have you actually seen Rebecca today?"

Before answering, Delilah paused to think. She realized that the answer to Luis' explicit question, "Have you actually seen Rebecca today?" was actually no.

Delilah realized that, as of this very moment, this instant… now today, she had not yet, seen Rebecca.

She had assumed that the reason Rebecca had not come down to breakfast was that she was overly tired, from her dinner date.

After all, last night was the first time, since she had been returned to civilization—almost three years after she had been held captive by Indians, *"loathsome, heathen-savages"—*, that Rebecca had actually gone out, socialized with one of her kind, a white-man.

Luis, growing impatient, waiting for a response, repeated his question; "Delilah today, have you actually seen Rebecca?"

Delilah refocused and after a moment of contemplation, answered; "I haven't actually, seen Rebecca today. I did however this afternoon, about an hour ago, send Hattie up to her bedroom, with a lunch tray.

Ignoring the broken glass on the floor, Luis once again revisited the sidebar.

He reached under the counter-top, picked up two glass tumblers in which, he then, poured into each glass, two-fingers of Kentucky bourbon.

He then walked back to the couch and offered Delilah one of the tumblers.

Delilah ignoring the proffered drink, demanded; "Luis I insist that you tell me this instant, what is wrong. You're clearly upset. What did Horace say?"

Luis placed both drinks on the table. Then he repeated to his wife, the morning's conversation, and the subsequent events that occurred, between himself, and Horace Stapleton, Esq., who as of 11:45 this morning, ceased to be an employee of the law firm; "Luis Frazier, Esq., and Associates, Attorneys-At-Law."

Luis walked over to the entrance of the study. For the first time, he noticed that the door to the study was ajar.

"Hattie, Hattie, please come here." While he waited for the black-cook to arrive, an ironic thought flashed across his mind.

In the *"Good Old Days"*, a mere two years past, he would never have used the word *"please",* when summoning his black-slave Hattie, the very same Hattie who was now free, and his employee.

Hattie came into the room. In contrast to her black face, her hands were covered with flour, and were artificially white.

"Yessum Masta… a means yessum Mista Frazier?"

In a stern authoritative voice, the voice that he used in court during his cross-examination of a hostile witness, Luis asked; "When you took lunch up to Miss Rebecca, was she all right?"

E. Pluribus Unum

Hattie looked bewildered. Her gaze rapidly shifted from Luis, to Delilah, then back to Luis.

"Suh, Ise dun ritely know what yu means."

Luis, attempting to put the clearly nervous black-woman at ease, softened, modulated, his tone of voice, and rephrased his question.

"Did Miss Rebecca appear to be in good-humor…was she in a good mood?"

"Well suh when I brung her da food, she be seated, starin' out da window. Ise called her name three times afore she looks at me. She ack lik she dun eben seez me."

"Laytah wen Ise dun gon bac for da tray, it ain't been touched." Miz Bekka, she be still staarin' out da windoe."

Luis and Delilah exchanged worried glances.

Despite her earlier resentment and misgiving about the wisdom of Rebecca's coming to live with them, with the passage of time, Delilah had become genuinely very fond of Rebecca, and had come to absolutely love and to adore "Little-Hank", Rebecca's son.

Delilah had evolved. She now, whole-heartedly viewed her family…the Frazier family as being comprised of Luis, herself, Rebecca, and Rebecca's son Henry Billings, III, whom she had grown to think of in terms, of his being her and Luis', grandson.

Luis broke the momentary silence by once again addressing Hattie; "What time did Miss Rebecca come home last night?"

"Did Miss Rebecca talk to you…did she tell you why she was upset?"

"No suh. She jus aks me ta promise not to tell yu and da Mistress."

Once again silence permeated the room.

Delilah broke the uncomfortable silence; "Hattie, you may return to your work of preparing dinner."

Hattie bowed her head, and mumbled; *"Yessum."*

As the recently freed former slave—now the Frazier family's gainfully employed cook—, turned to leave, Delilah stopped her.

"Hattie, *Vichyssoise* is not to be served tonight."

Once again Hattie mumbled; *"Yessum",* and left the room.

****

When they were alone, Luis asked; *"Vichyssoise*? What was that all about?"

"Before you arrived home, Hattie and I were in the kitchen planning tonight's dinner."

"Prior to her evening out, Rebecca had told me that Horace had made reservations for them at that elegant French restaurant that everyone is giving high praises, the *"Le Grand Vieux Manoir."*

"Because last night was Rebecca's first social engagement… well I thought that serving the French soup, would remind her of a pleasant evening."

"Now that obviously, would be inappropriate."

Luis nodded his head in agreement.

"Delilah, I'm worried about Rebecca. What do you think? Should we approach her? Should we go to her?"

Delilah shook his head. "No. I don't think that that would be wise."

"From what I gathered from the account told to you by Horace Stapleton of last night's events, and from Hattie's observations, we should thank God, Rebecca did not suffer any apparent physical injuries."

"I think that the best course now is for us to wait. She'll talk to us when she's ready. When she feels comfortable discussing with us, last night's horrific events."

As Hattie's husband Willie, served the evening meal, he could not help but notice a distinct difference in the usual mood in the dining room.

Earlier Hattie had told him of *"Da strange go-in-ons.* About; *"Miz Becca, scarin' da life outta me, nockin on da kitchen daw, when da Sun bout ta come-up."*

How when she carried a lunch-tray up to Miss Rebecca; *"Miz Bekka dunt eben touch da vittles; dunt eben looks at me."*

Hattie had told Willie about when she, standing outside of the library, just happened to have overheard the discussion; *"Twix Miz DeLielaa an Mista Luis."*

Almost immediately, following Willie's departure from the dining room, Luis, unable to remain silent, broke the uncomfortable, awkward silence.

He slowly placed his knife and fork beside his plate; "Rebecca earlier today, I had an opportunity to speak to Horace Stapleton.

Stapleton told me of your having been accosted last night by that thug, that cowardly livery-driver."

Rebecca, her head angled slightly, resting on her shoulder, had been with her fork, absently pushing two pieces of carrot on her plate.

It had taken several seconds for Luis' words to register.

Rebecca dropped her fork and stared directly at her uncle.

"Horace told you that I had been attacked? How did he know that I had been attacked? It all happened well after we had departed company. After he complained of a headache, and instructed the driver to drop him off at his house."

Delilah rose and hurried to sit next to Rebecca. She held Rebecca's left hand in both of hers. Before Delilah could speak, Luis answered Rebecca's question.

"Horace had a visitor last night… or should I say, earlier this morning, before dawn, from an acquaintance of his, who knew and had recently, just spoken to, your assailant."

As he spoke, Luis had been closely watching Rebecca's face. He was concerned. How would she react? He did not know what to expect, tears, sorrow, and anger, or perhaps, even rage. These emotional displays he would have understood.

Instead, the emotion that Rebecca projected, was that of cool, calm, serenity.
She appeared to be completely—eerily he thought—, composed.

Without his having to ask, Rebecca placed her knife and fork beside her plate, took a deep breath, and in a calm, quiet, and lucid voice, began to speak.

"When that disgusting, horrid man was about to attack me, a fatalistic calm and determination swept over me. My thoughts were crystal clear. In my mind, I knew and realized, and had accepted the fact that my survival, or my death, was in my hands."

Rebecca called for Hattie. When the cook entered the dining room, Rebecca spoke to her son. "Little Hank, go with Hattie, she'll get you ready for bed."

"Kiss *"Uncle Louyee"* and *"Auntie Lilah"* goodnight. I'll be up shortly, to read you a story, before tucking you in for the night".

When Hattie and her son had left the dining room, Rebecca sipped a swallow of water from her glass. Then she resumed her narrative.

"Last night was not the first time that I had experienced those thoughts, those feelings... that my survival, or my death, was in my hands."

"When I was a captive-slave of the Comanche, there was a horrid, practically toothless old woman, who constantly beat, and tormented me".

"Her name was *Hen's Teeth*. She was called Hen's Teeth because of the one yellow, decaying tooth, that remained in the front of her mouth."

"One morning, when most of the Comanche warriors had left the village in search of buffalo, one of the young teenage boys, who had not yet taken to the warpath, riding as if the devil was chasing him, at a full gallop, rode into the village straight to the lodge of the headman, Chief Old Wise One."

"The boy told of a large group—more than fifty—, Pawnee warriors, who he had observed, unseen by them, four days ride from the village."

Rebecca then explained and exclaimed, with a noticeable amount of disdain in her voice, how for generations, the Pawnee have been hated enemies of the Comanche. She stated that the two tribes, for centuries, have raided, plundered and killed each other.

Rebecca paused as she intently studied the faces of both her aunt, and uncle.

Both Luis and Delilah appeared to be fully attentive, even enraptured.

Since her deliverance from captivity, more than two years ago, this was the first time that Rebecca had talked to either of them, at length, about her life, as a captive of the Comanche.

Rebecca continued; "Chief Old Wise One immediately, sent two teenage boys, young men not yet warriors, to find, and to alert our Comanche warriors of the eminent danger to the village."

He then called for an emergency council of those twenty-three, mostly old or physically impaired men, the warriors who had remained in the village.

Rebecca continued; "Although women were not allowed at council, it was common practice—for young women and adolescent boys, to eavesdrop when important matters were being discussed."

"When the council ended, the remnants of the Comanche warriors, those who had not joined the large hunting party, began to make preparations to defend the village, to protect the women and children."

"When I asked one of the several women who were engaged in animated conversation, what was happening, I will never forget what Little Flower said to me."

Delilah interrupted; "Little Flower, who was Little Flower?"

Luis' too was curious. His eyes had not for an instant, left Rebecca's face.

During his many years—more than three decades—, as a brilliant trial attorney, Luis had developed the ability to reliably, ascertain the depth of an individual's conviction, when they were giving sworn testimony, or when they were being deposed, under oath.

During the course of Rebecca's narration, Rebecca's face had remained calmly, serene. However, when Delilah had asked; *"Who was Little Flower?"* Luis noticed a definite softening of Rebecca's features.

In a subdued, almost reverent voice, Rebecca volunteered; "Little Flower was Mandy's... my sister Mandy's, adoptive Comanche-mother."

At this point, Delilah was totally confused. She opened her mouth to speak; "Your sister? What sis …", she was stopped in mid-sentence.

Luis had raised his hand. "Delilah, I'll explain later. Rebecca, please continue."

Rebecca took a deep breath, and then she continued. "Little Flower said that the primary objective of the Pawnee raid, was to steal horses, to kill the Comanche warriors, and to capture and to enslave, Comanche women and children."

"I remember thinking, what exactly was she saying. As if she were reading my mind, Little Flower elaborated"

"Once the Pawnee have killed and scalped our warriors, they will kill the old women. They will then rape, then beat, and enslave our young women.

"I will never forget the calm, the matter of fact way that she spoke."

"Little Flower looked in turn, at each of the women. She then addressed the group."

"Some here, especially those with small children, will choose life. To live with their children as captive-slaves of the Pawnee."

"I, as will many of the women here, will fight the Pawnee, to the death."

"Little Flower with that same dispassionate tone, turned to me and said;

*"This, "**Pale Blue Wolf's Eyes**, is our way of life."*

Rebecca's throat was dry. She picked up her water glass and frowned, when she realized that the glass was practically empty.

Luis had not touched the glass of water at his place setting. He picked up his water glass, rose from his chair, walked around the table, and handed the glass of water to Rebecca.

Rebecca gratefully accepted the glass, and drank half of its contents.

Luis did not return to his chair. Instead he sat in the chair immediately across from his wife.

Rebecca dabbed at her lips with her snow-white, linen napkin, glanced at the expectant expressions on both her aunt and uncle's faces, and continued.

"For three days, the camp was a beehive of frantic, but definitely not panicky, controlled, methodical, activity. All inhabitants, men, women and children, were preparing to meet and repulse, the expected Pawnee attack."

"I was petrified. Mandy attempted to calm me by assuring me that although Chief Old Wise One's days of hunting and combat, were for him, distant memories, what the old warrior had lost in physical prowess, had been more than compensated for, by his enhanced ability for clear, strategic thinking."

"In camp, including Chief Old Wise One, there was a total of twenty-three adult men, warriors who had over the years fought to protect the *"People."*

For many years, decades for most of them, each of these warriors had, counted coup, scalped, maimed and killed the enemies of the *"People."*

Delilah was fascinated. Like everyone she knew — friends and family alike, she had, all of her life, heard stories, tales about the *"Wild Heathen Savage Indians"* that roamed the west.

To actually hear a first hand detailed account of how the savages lived, by someone who had lived among them was indeed a rare experience.

When Rebecca spoke of the savages having *"counted coup"*, Delilah thought of interrupting, of asking her to explain the term, *"counted coup."*

Delilah suppressed her impulse. Fascinated, she decided against interrupting Rebecca.

Instead, she looked at Luis, who was intently listening, concentrating, and absorbing each and every one of Rebecca's words

Rebecca's words were pouring forth, like surging pent-up water, suddenly overflowing a dam.

Over the years Luis had professionally, on many occasions, seen clients undergo this… this cleansing catharsis. The victims of atrocities, who had initially, been reluctant to speak of their traumatic experiences, who now because of some cataclysmic event, purged themselves, verbalized, let it all out.

Rebecca continued; "Of the twenty-three— tested in battle warriors, who had remained in the village, Strong Bow, was the sole warrior who had not yet seen forty winters."

The fact that Rebecca had frequently used Comanche terms and phrases — *"moons"*, *"winters"*, *"sleeps"*, *"counting coup"* —, to express herself, had not gone unnoticed and unappreciated by Luis.

"Strong Bow had *"two-moons"* past, sustained a broken leg while a member of a Comanche raiding party, against the Utes."

"Strong Bow, though not yet fully recovered, had regained the ability to walk and to run, without the aid of a large tree-branch, which he had fashioned into a crude crutch, ten *"sleeps-past."*

"Chief Old Wise One knew that the only hope for the village to survive the attack of fifty Pawnee warriors, was if his Comanche warriors returned in time, before the Pawnee assault."

"If his elite, able-bodied warriors did not return in time, Chief Old Wise One knew that the encampment would be overrun…that his people would be slaughtered."

"The venerable, battle scared chief, as did every member of his band resolved that, if help did not arrive, that they would die as they had lived. They would die Comanche. They would die fighting."

"Chief Old Wise One delegated to Strong Bow, the task of delaying the inevitable. Strong Bow would lead the Comanche defenders in the only course that would ensure the killing of at least some of the Pawnee warriors, and perhaps give the *"People"*, a little more time… perhaps allowing some to escape."

"Chief Old Wise One's instructions to Strong Bow were; *"Before they attack, while they think that we are unaware of their presence, when the Pawnee dogs creep within reach, they are to be greeted with the twang of our bows, the loosing of hundreds of arrows. The sound will echo throughout the village.*

"The flight of Comanche arrows will block out the light of Father Sun."

Rebecca ran her tongue over her now dry, parched, lips. She reached for her water glass and drank. She once again ran her tongue over her lips.

Satisfied, she placed the glass on the table, and an eerily calm monotone- voice, continued to speak.

"Little Flower, my sister Mandy, and I, were in the lodge of Gray Wolf, feathering arrows, when the Pawnee attacked."

"Two of the Pawnee warriors burst into the lodge. Little flower and Mandy were seated on buffalo robes, closest to the tepee's entrance'.

"One of the Pawnee demons swung his war-club at Little Flower's head."

"She moved her head a fraction to the right, and took the brunt of the blow on her shoulder. Little Flower fell to the ground, stunned, motionless, not moving."

"When the Pawnee leaned over Little Flower, Mandy struck. Screaming a Comanche war-cry, *"Aahe-hey… "Aahe-hey"*, she lunged at the startled warrior, plunging into his neck, the heads of the three arrows, that she held clutched tightly in her right hand."

"Two of the sharp arrow heads punctured the large pulsating vein, beneath the skin on the right side of the Pawnee warrior's neck."

"The second warrior seemingly oblivious to the presence of both Little Flower and Mandy, had swept past them toward the back of the tepee, knocking over the iron tripod that supported the kettle of buffalo sinew, submerged in the boiling water."

"I had retreated to the rear of the tepee, frantically attempting to hide under a pile of three heavy buffalo robes."

"As I lay trembling, holding my breath, beneath the heavy buffalo skins, I remember squeezing my eyes shut and praying; "Please, please, God...not again"

"The Pawnee warrior lifted and threw away, the buffalo robes, under which I had been hiding."

"The warrior reached down and grabbed me by my hair. In an utter blind panic, I flailed at the hand that was lifting me. I was completely unaware of the nine-inch, serrated, buffalo hide-skinning knife that I held, tightly clutched in my hand."

"Inexplicably, the Pawnee warrior released me. For a second, he stood frozen, silently looking at the thin trickle of blood oozing from the shallow wound that my knife had inflected upon his wrist."

"I looked down at my trembling hand. My knuckles were a ghostly white. It was then that I became for the first time, aware that I held in my hand, the nine-inch, serrated knife."

"The Pawnee ignored the shallow wound. A contemptuous grin spread across the enemy warrior's hideous face. Once again he reached for me."

"I remembered cringing, flailing away blindly with the knife."

"Then I heard a dull thud. I watched petrified, as the Pawnee warrior silently fell, facedown on one of the buffalo robes, just inches from me."

"A Comanche battle-axe was deeply embedded, buried between the Pawnee warrior's shoulder blades. The battle-axe's feathered handle protruded from his back."

"Standing over the dying Pawnee, was Stone Fist, the Comanche to whom I belonged, the man who had methodically, repeatedly raped, humiliated and dehumanized me."

"The Comanche hunting party had returned. The Comanche warriors had arrived just minutes, after the Pawnee had commenced their attack, an attack which would have surely annihilated our…the village."

"The Comanche warriors, led by our chief…I'm sorry what I meant to say was that… the Comanche warriors lead by the band's war chief, Chief Thundercloud, killed, vanquished, and drove off the surviving Pawnee warriors."

While holding and gently squeezing Rebecca's hands, Delilah looked deeply, searchingly, into *her niece's* eyes.

"How horrifying, you poor child. I can only imagine…that's not true, I can't, I just cannot begin to imagine, what you've gone through."

"I dare say, I don't think that any of us can truly appreciate, what you've been through. You must have been frightened beyond words."

Luis, as did his wife, had been listening intently, spellbound, almost transfixed, by the content and the emotional depth of Rebecca's narration.

He too had been moved. His feelings and emotions had run the gamut, from that of being horrified, to heartfelt, unbridled feelings of pride in Rebecca's demonstrable ability, to respond to a crisis, and to defend herself.

To the best of his knowledge, this was the first time that Rebecca had in detail and in depth, talked about her life, among the Comanche.

Luis remembered thinking; "Finally, for the first time, Rebecca had opened up. For the first time, she had vented, purged herself, and brought out into the open, this litany, this cauldron, of repressed, haunting malignant, memories."

In the past, Rebecca had—albeit reluctantly when she spoke to Dr. Sawyer, when she had asked for his help to terminate her pregnancy—, of having been raped by the Comanche warrior, Stone Fist.

On those rare occasions, Luis had concluded that Rebecca's motivation for speaking-out, was not her attempting to gain sympathy, but was instead a necessary means, for her to explain her pregnancy, and the subsequent birth of her son.

In addition to the inherent horror of Rebecca's dispassionate, yet riveting discourse, Luis, was now struck by the underlying irrefutable, fact that Rebecca, had to a degree, assimilated, and had bonded with her captors.

For better or for worse, Luis now had what he considered confirmation, of his latent, lingering, suspicions.

Last nights' attempted rape of Rebecca, coupled with what he had just heard from Rebecca, served to reinforce in Luis, what he had reluctantly come to believe.

He knew and accepted, that the sweet innocent Rebecca, the beautiful young woman that he had known before she had been abducted, no longer existed.

Rebecca's reaction to last night's attempted assault, emphasized to him, the fact that the time that she had spent as a captive of the Indians, had undoubtedly contributed to her ability to successfully defend herself, at least physically, defend herself, in *"White Civilized"* society.

Her life among the savages had heightened and intensified, Rebecca's "flight or fight", reflex.

Non-the-less, this confirmed knowledge, not withstanding, Luis was deeply troubled.

****

Chapter 60

For more than a week, Rebecca had been mulling over in her mind, the events of her disastrous evening-out with Horace Stapleton.

Over and over again, she had analyzed and dissected in her mind, the series of events that had transpired, during that fateful evening that had culminated in her being attacked by that coach driver.

Rebecca had racked her brain, trying to reconstruct that evening. What in the world could have led that grotesque, pale, rotund, balding middle-aged man, to abduct, and then attempt to assault and to rape her?

It had taken hours…days, of her pleading with Uncle Luis, to finally convince him not to have the carriage driver—whose name she now knew to be James *"Jimmy"* Donovan—, arrested.

Luis had been adamant, determined to have the driver; *"Brought before the bar of Justice"*, to answer for his *"outlandish criminal behavior."*

Luis had repeatedly asked himself, what to him was a rhetorical question; *"What in the world had the man been thinking?"*

Although the question was to him rhetorical, Luis had come to conclude that, *"The man must have been insane!"*

Luis rationalized that even the rowdiest low-life thug, let alone a *"simple minded teamster"*, would not dare to accost a white woman, a white lady of status, whose safety had been put in his charge.

It was only after Rebecca repeatedly, vehemently kept insisting to him that his perception of her as a *"lady of status"* differed drastically, from that of how, the citizenry of Richmond, Virginia, saw her.

Confused and a little bewildered, Luis had asked her to elucidate…to explain.

It was Rebecca's turn to take the hands of her beloved uncle in hers. She had looked deeply, pleadingly into the eyes of her guardian.

"Dearest *"Uncle Looey"*—unwittingly, she had used the term of endearment that as a child, she had lovingly called Luis—, I have absolutely no doubt that you think of me as a proper young Southern Woman, a paragon of white Southern gentility."

'Unfortunately, Uncle Luis in reality, to the vast majority of our friends and neighbors, ~~I'm~~ I am thought of as a fallen-woman, a trollop, a whore."

Luis started to object. He began to vigorously shake his head in denial. His intention was to assure her, that not everyone in Richmond was a bigot.

"No, no honey…" Rebecca raised her hand, effectively stifling Luis' weak, but well-intentioned, protestations.

Rebecca disengaged her right hand, from his and gently placed the index finger of her now freed hand, across the Luis' sputtering lips.

"It's true Uncle Luis, the vast majority of our friends and neighbors, and even to some extent to our relatives, I'm thought of as a disgraced, fallen-woman, a strumpet, a whore".

Luis began to shake his head in denial. "No, no honey…that not true"

"*Uncle Looey*, Little-Hank and I, both of us truly love you and Aunt Delilah. After all, you and Aunt Delilah are the only Grandparents that Little-Hank has ever, or will ever know."

A solitary, involuntary tear, begin to slowly trickle-down Rebecca's cheek.

Luis hastily reached into his waistcoat, removed a stark white linen handkerchief, and gently dabbed at Rebecca's cheek. He then placed the handkerchief into his niece's hand, wrapping both of his hands gently, but firmly, around hers'.

"Four years ago, when I literally, out of the blue, showed up pregnant, destitute, and alone, on your doorstep, you without a moments hesitation… you took me in."

"For that and for the love that you and Aunt Delilah have lavished upon me and Little-Hank, I will be eternally grateful."

Luis, noticing that Rebecca's voice had begun to falter, rose from the sofa on which they sat and walked over to the side bar.

He picked up a clear crystal decanter; half filled with brown Kentucky whiskey, and filled a glass. He replaced the decanter and then lifted-up a pitcher of cold spring water, and filled a second glass.

Luis returned to the sofa and handed the glass of water to Rebecca.

He raised his glass to his lips, and gulped down its fiery contents.

Rebecca in an attempt to regain her composure haltingly sipped her water.

Luis reached for, and removed the water glass, from Rebecca's hand. He placed the glass on the table.

For a brief moment, both Luis and Rebecca sat in an uncomfortable, silence.

Rebecca was the first to speak; "*White Squaw, Slut, Whore*", these are but, a few of the "*choice*" words that total strangers, not to mention our so-called friends and neighbors, and yes even a few relatives, have been calling me."

"For the most part, usually, the slurs are whispered behind my back."

"Frequently however, whether by design or by accident, those hurtful words are uttered, "*accidentally mind you*", just loud enough, for me to overhear."

While Luis found Rebecca's words to be troubling and upsetting, upon reflection he was forced to admit, if only to himself, that he was not totally surprised by her heart-wringing revelations.

For years in his heart, he had refused to believe or to acknowledge, that which he intellectually, and pragmatically knew to be true.

Luis possessed a superbly trained analytical mind. As an accomplished litigator, attorney, an officer-of-the-court, he had been conditioned…trained to accept fact above sentimentality.

Fact; Rebecca had been brutally and repeatedly raped, by naked, wild Indians, and yet she had somehow managed to survive, and to escape.

Fact; Rebecca had been impregnated by a red-skinned savage, and had given birth to a mixed-blood child.

For years Luis had been blindly resisting, failing to accept, and to acknowledge the reality and the consequences of these two blatantly, obvious facts.

Despite his love for Rebecca and his overwhelming paternalistic wish and hope that, she and Little-Hank, would eventually be accepted, and welcomed into Richmond Society, Luis knew, that this fervently hoped for, status, was unrealistic.

Despite her resolve to try, for her son's sake, to try to ignore, or to at least, to tolerate and endure the constant barrage of unspoken slights, and the whispered snide-remarks alluding to her having been defiled and tarnished, by "godless, wild Indians" —, Rebecca had gradually become convinced that, she and her "mixed-blood" son, Henry II, would never be welcome, in the post Civil War, white-world of Richmond Virginia.

Rebecca and her son whom he loved as if he were his own grandson, her mixed-blood child, they were not now, nor would they ever be welcomed into his and Delilah's, Richmond Society.

Luis was snapped out of his momentary revelry, and drawn back to the present, when Rebecca's breathlessly, spoken words registered in his mind…

"*Little-Hank and I have to move, we have to relocate, we have to leave Richmond.*"

Luis was stunned.

"Becky, I hear you… I hear you. Believe me I truly do understand. You have every right to be upset."

"I have an idea. Why don't you and Little-Hank take a little vacation? Get away from the gossip and sniping, so prevalent here in Richmond."

"I'm sure that your Aunt Delilah can arrange for you and Little-Hank to visit, to spend some time with her cousin Sheila and her husband Lawrence, at their Savannah Plantation."

Rebecca indicated her denial of his suggestion, by slowly shaking her head.

"Uncle Luis, I appreciate your suggestion. But *Uncle Looey*, I have to confess, to tell you that from the way that I, and my son have been treated, I have serious doubts as to the way we would be treated in Georgia, or for that matter how we would be treated anywhere in the South."

"I appreciate and I understand, your belief…what I know is your fervent hope, that I, an unmarried young white woman of means, and her son, would be accepted by persons living in a locale, an area other than, and far removed from Richmond."

"I honestly think that our being welcomed and accepted, would be dependent upon whether or not those Savannah residents, are aware of my past."

"I shudder to think of how they would react if…but more likely then if, of how they would react when, they became aware of the fact that for nearly a year, I had lived with, and was being constantly raped by Indians."

"That I, a genteel, God fearing, Southern Lady, had given birth to a *"mixed-blood"*… what I've heard, some say, given birth to an *"abomination"*, my son, your nephew, that some here in Richmond, derisively continue to refer to, not by his given Christian name Henry Billings II, not by his nickname Little-Hank, but by nasty, pejorative, racial invectives such as; that *"red-nigger"*, or *"the red-nigger-bastard"* of that *"white-squaw-whore's bastard-papoose."*

"Unfortunately, Uncle Looyee, neither you or can I, control the bigoted words and actions of our so called, *"civilized"* neighbors.

"Neither I, nor did my son, your nephew Henry Billings II, choose to have an Indian who raped me, a savage Comanche Warrior, be my son's father."

The likely-hood that my beautiful mixed-blood son, a *"person-of-color"*, would be accepted in Savannah, or in Atlanta, or in Charleston, or for that matter, in any community in the South, is at best, extremely remote."

"Uncle Luis, when I said that we have to leave, to relocate, I meant that we not only had to leave Virginia, Little-Hank and I, have to leave the South.

Before Luis could respond, Rebecca continued:

"Uncle Luis, do you remember Eleanor Leary?"

Luis' hesitated he squeezed his eyes shut, small wrinkle lines greased his forehead, as he concentrated, attempting to place a face, with that vaguely familiar name.

Rebecca seeing her Uncle struggling to refresh his memory, to recall the name Eleanor Leary, continued; "Miss Leary was the Yankee teacher, the tutor that daddy hired to broaden my education, to expand my knowledge of the classics."

"Miss Leary was an exceptionally, excellent teacher. But more importantly, she was a remarkable, insightful, woman."

"I remember thinking at the time, that many of the opinions and views held by Miss Leary, especially those dealing with our institution of slavery, were due to her being ignorant, of the true practices and beliefs of our Southern Society."

"Although Miss Leary never spoke of, nor did she ever disseminate or advocate, Yankee Abolitionist Propaganda, I can't help remembering something that she once, emphatically said."

> *"No one now living, or for that matter, no one who has ever lived, or in the future will ever live, has had, or will have, any control over who their birth parents would be."*

> *"What we can and should endeavor to control, is who we are and who we chose to become."*

"During our time as captive/slaves of the Comanche, when we were alone together, and I was wallowing in self-pity, lamenting over and over, Why…Why… had I been made a slave, my sister Mandy, having been a slave all of her life… Mandy would attempt to comfort and to console me, by repeating to me, Miss Leary's words.

Luis leaned forward, avidly, attentively listening. Rebecca's reference to the phrase, "Yankee Abolitionist Propaganda", had peaked his intellectual curiosity.

Rebecca resumed speaking; "Having now myself, been a "slave" of the Comanche, having literally been someone's property; having been subjected to the dictates and the whims of my "Master", I now fully understand and appreciated the many sanguine words, that Miss Leary shared with me and Mandy."

"My being forced to live in constant fear of being sold or traded by Stone Fist, my "Master" to another tribe, afraid of being summarily, permanently separated from my only family, my sister Mandy, these constant fears, profoundly influenced my thinking."

"They made me come to examine and to question the so-called morality, the values that had been drummed into my head, instilled in me as a child, as an integral component, of my Southern heritage."

"I certainly did not choose to have an Indian rape, and rape, and rape me!"

"Nor did my son, your nephew Henry Billings II, chose for his father, a heathen, savage, Comanche Warrior."

For one of the few times in his adult life, Luis was unable to find the right words, words that would alleviate Becky's pain, words that were appropriate for the circumstances.

Luis began to berate himself. He wracked his brain, searching for the right words. Instead of speaking, articulating his usual cogent thoughts and opinions, Luis Frazier, the renowned orator, found himself speechless, confined to listening.

Despite her resolve for her son's sake—, to try to ignore, or to at least, try to tolerate and endure, the constant barrage of unspoken slights, and the whispered snide-remarks and innuendoes, alluding to her having been defiled tarnished, by those "godless, savage, heathen, wild Indians, Rebecca's frustration persisted."

Luis was forced to acknowledge and accept the *"Facts"*. The absolute fact that Rebecca was convinced that, she and her "mixed-blood" son, Henry II, would never be welcome, in the post Civil War, white-world, of Richmond Virginia.

****

In a steady, calm, imploring voice, Luis began to speak.

"Becky, was it really only a mere five-years-ago, that that man…that wagon-train Master, I believe his name was Captain Smith, brought you home to us?"

Rebecca, with an affirmative nod of her head, acknowledged that the man, who had delivered her to Luis' door, had been the famous western-frontier – pathfinder, Captain Samuel Smith.

"Becky believe me, in a way, Captain Smith's bringing you to us that Christmas, was not your deliverance, it was actually my salvation, my personal deliverance."

Now it was Rebecca's turn to be confused.

Seeing the confused look in her eyes, Luis quickly explained.

"I was devastated when I received the news that the wagon train that you and your father were traveling with was attacked, and that my best friend, my life-long friend, your father, Henry Billings, had been killed."

"And that you the sweet little girl that I had bounced on my knee, that I have known since your birth, had been abducted by those red-skinned savages."

"As a result of those tragic events, I sunk into a deep, moribund, near suicidal, state of depression."

"I was immersed in, and experiencing, an overwhelming, debilitating, deep sense of guilt. After all, it was I who had devised the *"clever"* plan that had led to your father's decision to make a fresh start in the west."

"So, you see Becky, although it did not entirely rid me of my guilt and depression, having you returned, alive and healthy, delivered to our door by Captain Smith, restored my faith."

"It was to me, my Christmas miracle, and in fact, it was my deliverance."

"You and Little-Hank have made this house, this edifice, this amalgamation of stone, brick, and wood, a home, Delilah's, mine, yours', and Little-Hank's home."

Rebecca was visibly moved by her uncle's words. She was overwhelmed to have heard Luis affirm that during her captivity, that she had not been forgotten.

"Believe me *Uncle Looey*, no one more than I, could be more aware of, or appreciative of the love and support that you and Aunt Delilah have given to me and to Little-Hank."

"*Uncle Looey*, what were your words…how did you describe it?"

"*Uncle Looey*, you and Aunt Delilah have made for Little Hank and me…this amalgamation of brick and wood… our home."

"But this—to paraphrase your sentiments and your words—, this amalgamation of bigots, with their blatant and snide racial slurs and epithets, is definitely not the environment, the community in which I want to raise my son."

"*Uncle Looey*, it breaks my heart when our beautiful little boy, constantly comes to me seeking explanations. Asking questions, that I, his mother cannot adequately answer."

"What do you say when your four-year-old asks you…Mommy why did cousin Clayton call me a "*red-mongrel bastard*?" Mommy, what does that mean?"

"What do you say when your five-year-old comes home from school, bruised and battered. Having been fighting because kids taunted him; called him a *red skinned savage*, and his mother a *white-squaw, whore*."

Luis sat in abject, stunned, silence. In the span of a mere forty-minutes, once again, he found himself to be at a loss for words.

"*Uncle Looey*, I and my son Little Hank, your nephew… your *"grandson"*, have got to relocate. We have to leave Richmond; we have to leave the South."

****

Luis, emotionally deflated, slumped in his chair. There it was. Finally, it was out in the open. The words and thoughts that he had suppressed, the thoughts that he now knew, that Becky had been harboring as well, had been spoken.

Although their leaving Richmond would break his and Delilah's hearts, Luis was forced to agree with his beloved ward, his *"niece", his and Delilah's daughter* Rebecca.

Luis had been forced to accept as fact, that Rebecca's and Little-Hank's living in the South, would crush their spirit, and would ultimately, ruin their lives.

****

"Uncle Luis, I need your help. I wouldn't ask if I had another choice."

"The money that my father left me, the money that you're holding, the trust fund that you set-up for me, I need those funds."

"In order for us to relocate, to move to another section of the country, I really need those funds."

Luis reached down and opened one of his desk drawers.

"Becky, do you have any idea as to the size and scope of your holdings, the liquid assets of your trust?"

Not waiting for a response…knowing that Rebecca would realize that his question was rhetorical, Luis continued.

"During that period of time before the war, before the commencement of armed conflict, when we all knew that the war was eminent, your father, in his patriotic zeal, instructed me to invest his entire fortune exclusively, in support of the Confederate cause."

"Instead of following his instructions to the letter, without your father's approval or his knowledge, I diversified. Subsequently, your inheritance is quite substantial."

"Becky, as difficult as it is for me to accept and to admit, reluctantly I have to agree with your assessment. The prospect, here in the South, for a good
life, for you and Little-Hank, is at best, remote.

Luis through a lifetime of experiences…because of his unbridled love for Rebecca and Little-Hank, had now come to question his life-long acceptance of the self-serving, beliefs, racial prejudices, and attitudes of the Antebellum and post Civil War, Southern Society.

The Southern way of life, that he had, all of his life supported, defended, and believed in, was hostile to, and discriminated against two of the three persons, not counting his wife Delilah, that Luis truly loved, Rebecca, and her son, Henry Billings, II…Little-Hank.

For the first time, at least the first time out loud, Luis Frazier, gave voice to his changing, evolving, feelings.

"Our defeated South is reeling, licking its wounds. That we were fighting for states rights… poppy-cock…balderdash."

"The unvarnished truth is that we were fighting…we fought to defend our way of life, to retain, to preserve, and to protect the bedrock institution fundamental to of our economy, we were fighting to keep and to expand the institution of slavery."

"Slavery a concept that is an anathema to the core-beliefs laid down less than a century ago by the nation's founding fathers, penned by Thomas Jefferson, one of us, a Virginian, in the Declaration of Independence;

"We hold these truths to be self-evident, that all men are created equal."

"I believe in my heart, that the only way that we Southerners could morally permit and justify the institution of slavery, more precisely, black-slavery, was because those that we enslaved, we characterized as being less than human, as a species of "sub-humans".

"After all, …they don't, look like us."

"While our defeat at the hands of the Yankees, removed once and for all,
the legal justification for slavery, it had little to no effect, in the removing of
the spurious morality, that for centuries allowed so many of us, to accept the morally bankrupt justification, for black-slavery…that is that they're not like us, they're black, they're sub-human…they're different."

"You're right Becky. I'm afraid that whether conscientiously, or unconscientiously, in the eyes of many Southerners, you and Little-Hank,
your mixed-blood son, my nephew, who I will always think of as my grandson, will always be different."

"It breaks my heart to admit it…and I know that Delilah will be devastated, but none-the-less, I am forced to agree. You and Little-Hank, should leave the South."

****

Rebecca sat attentively, in one of the two leather chairs, facing her Uncle Luis' desk.

Luis was seated behind the desk. He was concentrating, shifting through two stacks of documents.

Luis extracted four sheets of paper from one of the stacks that he had neatly placed on the desk. He quickly read the documents. Then with a satisfied sigh, he sat back in his chair.

"Okay Honey these four sheets of paper, gives the total value and the itemized holdings in your trust."

Luis reached across his desk, extending two of the papers toward Rebecca.

Rebecca quickly glanced at the papers, before attempting to return them to her uncle.

She was momentarily confused and surprised, when Luis refused to take the proffered sheets of paper.

In a stern, all business, no nonsense tone-of-voice, Luis spoke; "Read the papers Rebecca. Make sure you read and understand each entry. If you don't understand something, anything, I'm here…to answer your questions."

Rebecca placed the papers on his desk. She smiled; "Uncle Looyee, you've read the documents, I trust you…I love you."

E. Pluribus Unum

Luis picked up the papers and once again this time, he forcefully, thrust the sheets of paper toward Rebecca.

"Miss Rebecca Elizabeth Billings, we are conducting business. In this setting, please don't address me as "Uncle Looyee." I am Luis Frazier, Esq., your attorney and financial adviser."

Rebecca was flustered. She looked at Luis, confusion and hurt in her eyes.

Luis relented.

"Becky you and Little-Hank are about to go out on your own. You're the adult."

"Your net worth, in terms of liquid assets, available funds, is currently just a little bit north, of eighty thousand dollars."

Rebecca frowned, then she began to speak; "Excuse me *Mr. Luis Frazier, Esquire,* exactly how much is "a little bit north of, eighty thousand dollars?""

Luis smiled and chuckled under his breath, "*touché*" Miss Billings."

"I applaud, respect, and I completely, whole-heartedly agree, with the delivery, the appropriateness', the inference, and the specificity of your question."

"Indeed, Miss Rebecca Billings, it has been established that, in this office, when we are discussing your financial affairs, *business* is *business*."

Both *"Uncle Looey"* and his beloved niece *"Becky"*, looked each other in the eye, and together, simultaneously, they both smiled.

Luis cleared his throat. "I apologize for my use of slang. Especially my unwittingly cavalier use of the word "***north***", a word which… to put it mildly, here in Richmond and for that matter I dare say, through-out the South, conjures up still, all-to-fresh, negative memories."

"In financial parlance, *"north of"* connotes an estimated amount, an approximation, usually slightly higher than the stated, unspecified amount."

"Becky, have you decided as to where you and Little-Hank will be relocating?"

Rebecca did not immediately answer. She hesitated, gathering her thoughts.

Luis remained silent. It was obvious to him that Rebecca's not giving an immediate response to his simple question, probably meant that to his niece, perhaps that question, was not at all, quite so simple.

Rebecca took a deep breath. "I've given a lot of thought as to where we should go. Where in this huge, unbelievably vast country, would Little-Hank have the best chance to thrive, to live up to, and to fulfill his full potential?"

"I thought first of moving up North."

Luis was surprised to hear that Rebecca was seriously considering living *"behind enemy lines"*, of relocating to live in the North. Moving to an area where the victors, the vengeful northern populace in general, hated and despised all southerners, Luis did not believe that such a move, was in her or in Little-Hank's, best interest.

As he was about to voice his objections, his doubts as to the wisdom of her relocating to the North, Rebecca resumed speaking.

"Then when I began to weigh the pros and cons of relocating to a large cosmopolitan city, such as New York, or maybe Boston, or perhaps Philadelphia, I began to rationally exam what had made me and Little-Hank here in Richmond, the targets for bigotry, blind prejudice, and hate."

Before Luis could question her apparent preference for living in a large northern metropolis, Rebecca explained.

"My rationale for living in a large city is based on my assumption that large cities, more so than small towns, tend to have more diverse populations."

"My hope is that a large diverse population will be more tolerant, will be more likely, to accept a none-white child."

"After all, the paramount reason for my contemplating moving, my making the decision to relocate, to remove myself and my son, is for the sake of my child, your grandson, Little-Hank.

"I realized that instead of getting away from the factors that lead to our being ostracized, our relocating to the North would instead introduce, yet another factor, a reason for discrimination."

Luis was impressed by her logic, her obviously well thought out reasoning.

However, when Rebecca did not explain what she meant by; "our relocating to the North would add yet another factor for discrimination", Luis simply asked.

"Becky, that other factor, I assume that you're referring to your being held as a captive slave of the Comanche. How would Yankees in New York or Boston, or for that matter Philadelphia, know that part of your past?"

"Rebecca smiled. And in a sweet syrupy voice, dripping with only a slight exaggeration of her inherent, inbred southern drawl, answered;

"Dear, dear "Uncle Looey. I'm afraid Suh, that I must inform you that unfortunately, that your assumption is incorrect."

"I am surprised that you, a Southern Gentleman, an esteemed "Officer-of-the-Court", with your vast experience of observing and studying people, would not appreciate the fact that as soon as I opened my mouth, the northern citizens could not help but to immediately, categorize me as "other".

"Eventually I suppose in time, I could change, lose or at least modify my Southern speech pattern. And perhaps eventually over time, I'd be allowed to assimilate, to become a member of the community."

"On the other hand, my son, your grandson, Henry Billings II, will forever be a person-of-color, in their eyes, *"Other"*. He can't change the color of his skin. He won't be allowed to assimilate.

In our society, people-of-color, will always be looked upon, and considered as being" Others.'""

Rebecca leaned over and held Luis' hands. She looked deeply into her guardian's tranquil blue eyes;

"Uncle Luis, I'm not naïve. I now realize through my life's experiences, that in this "White Anglo-Saxon, Judeo-Christian Country", my son because he is not white, but is instead a person-of-color, will always face discrimination."

"It was because I was helped by a woman of color, my very own sister Mandy, that I managed to escape from the Comanche, and was returned to civilization".

"When I escaped and I, returned home to you, I vehemently vowed that never, as long as I live… never would I again venture west of the Mississippi River."

"However, for my son's sake, Little-Hank and I will be relocating, crossing that great divide, the Mississippi River, making a fresh start in the West."

Rebecca lifted her finger, and added as an afterthought; "That is we will be migrating to lands, west of the Mississippi.

Our home will be in the northwest, hundreds of miles removed from the hunting grounds of Little Hank's biological father, the Comancheria, the land of the Comanche."

Although in the west, Little-Hank will still, undoubtedly, encounter bigotry, the fact that the sight of mixed-blood children, the children of white men and Indian squaws, and for that matter the children of captive white women, and Indian braves is a reality, a fact of life."

 "Some might say that "misery loves company", I say that *"Others"* find comfort, in the company of "Others.""

Luis sighed. He had listened, attentively, dispassionately weighing the strengths and the flaws in Rebecca's "oral augments."

Finally, at the conclusion of his "deliberation", Luis Frazier, Esq., respected attorney, and the loving "Uncle-Father-Grandfather" reluctantly decided to accept and to support the logic and the wisdom, of Rebecca's decision.

****

BOOK IV

Chapter 61

The Comanche - Lords of the Southern Plains (1864)

The low throaty, guttural warning growls of two mongrel dogs were quickly silenced, when the dogs chased after the fresh meat, thrown to them by one of the approaching warriors.

The Comanche raiding party led by Chief Thunder Cloud, riding single file, splashed across the narrow, muddy shallow body of water, into the provinces of Northern Mexico.

In the dead of night, guided only by the reflected light of the luminescent, bright, full-moon—a brilliant "*Comanche Moon*"—, twenty warriors, whose faces were streaked with horizontal and diagonal lines of ominous black and yellow war paint, stealthily approached the sleeping, Mexican, peasant village.

The small raiding party, with the notable exception of its leader, Chief Thunder Cloud, a veteran, experienced, warrior of scores, of battles and raids, was comprised of twenty-three warriors, all young braves who had eagerly volunteered, to follow Chief Thundercloud, the vaunted, celebrated, war chief.

The target of the raid into Northern Mexico was a peasant village, just south of the big water known to the *"People"* as, the *Kwana Kuhtsupaa*; to the white-Texans as the (The Rio Grande).

The raid, to acquire horses, scalps and captives, and to gain honors by counting coup on their adversaries through combat, was to take place across the expanse of water that the hair-mouthed white-Texans, the *"Tejanos"*, as well as the Mexicans the *"tahbay-bohs"*, called the Rio Grande.

Chief Thunder Cloud's well earned, and deserved reputation as a courageous warrior, was a man who had led many successful war-parties and raids for horses and captives, against the enemies of the Comanche, the true *"People.*

It was the belief—espoused by the band's Holy Man, "He Who Speaks To Ghosts"—, that Chief Thunder Cloud was a "chosen" warrior, one anointed by the "Great Spirit", a warrior who truly possessed strong, powerful, medicine.

For as long as the *"People"* could remember, following their acquisition, and their breeding, and domesticating of the horse, Comanche warriors had been routinely conducting bloody forays into the white man's territory, the land to the South, the land the *tejanos, and the tahbay-bohs,* called Mexico.

The low throaty, guttural warning growls of two skinny mongrel dogs had been quickly muted, when the hungry dogs pounced upon the fresh rabbit meat, thrown to them by two of the approaching Comanche warriors.

The dogs' feasted, as their lives, were quickly ended, by the piercing of their throats, by two arrows, expertly loosed by two of the advancing warriors.

Stone Fist, a stocky, well-muscled, agile young warrior silently pushed open the door of an adobe walled dwelling. He stood silently his battle-axe held tightly in his right hand—, listening to the sounds of heavy snoring, coming from the bed occupied by the Mexican peasant, and his woman.

Swiftly, noiselessly, on moccasin-encased feet, Stone Fist approached the sleeping couple. Stone Fist bent down, his face inches from the sleeping woman, and firmly placed his hand over her mouth.

The well proportioned, diminutive, woman, startled from her slumber, opened her eyes and beheld the painted, black and yellow-streaked face
Of, *"El Diablo"*, the devil.

She attempted to scream, but the ironclad grip of the calloused hand of the painted, ghastly, hideous *"demon"*, clamped across her mouth, muted the sound of her voice.

The woman was helpless, suspended in mid-air like a rag-doll, clawing at the incredibly strong left arm of the demon.

She watched as this devil incarnate, touched the flat edge of his tomahawk to the forehead of her snoring husband, *counting coup,* and exclaimed in a flat, emotionless, steely voice, *"Aahe-hey"*, ("I Claim it!").

As Stone Fist turned to leave the dwelling, the heart stopping, terrifying, primordial, blood-curdling war cry of the *Nermernuh*, split the still, sultry air.

The ancient battle cry of the Comanche *(Nermernuh)*, the, the fiercest, deadliest, horse-warriors to have ever roamed the southern plains of the North American continent, froze the hearts of the village's inhabitants.

The woman's husband abruptly bolted upright in the bed. He, as did the entire village, had heard the petrifying, frightening, ancient battle cry of the Comanche.

The terror-striken woman, being held by the huge red, yellow and black-faced demon, was now instantly, immobilized by a paralyzing fear, as her husband bolted upright, when he heard the blood curdling, terrifying ancient scream, the war-cry of the Comanche.

The Mexican peasant-farmer clumsily, in a frenzy of panic, reached under the bed, groping for his rifle.

As his clammy fingers grasped the stock of his weapon, Stone Fist, with one swift powerful blow of his battle-axe, split the man's skull in half.

Blood mixed with Gray matter, gushed from the man's bisected skull, and coalesced onto the rumbled bed coverings.

The Mexican woman's struggles ceased. Her pregnant, with-child, body went limp. Mercifully, she had fainted.

Effortlessly, as if he was lifting a child's doll, Stone Fist slung the woman across his back, and sprinted from the adobe hut.

****

Chapter 62

Comanche Encampment (Kutsueka Band) - Lodge of Gray Wolf - 1869

It had become obvious to Little Flower that her daughter Spring Blossom, during the latter stages of her second pregnancy, needed help.

Her daughter, now heavy-with-child, needed someone, a woman to assist her, in the maintaining of the lodge of Stone Fist.

Little Flower was a persistent, determined, strong advocate for her daughter.

Nightly, now for two times the fingers on her hand, after his evening meal, when her husband, Gray Wolf, Spring Blossom's father, sat by their fire, contently smoking his pipe, Little Flower would incessantly speak of how; "their with-child daughter Spring Blossom, who had adopted *"Never Still"*, their orphaned grandson—how Spring Blossom, the daughter of Gray Wolf, was struggling."

Initially Gray Wolf had not been moved by Little Flower's words. Gray Wolf, as did all the *"People"*, accepted without question the essential roles, the division of labor between Comanche, men and women.

In Comanche society, it was the role of the male to hunt, to provide food, buffalo hides for tepees and clothing; the essentials needed to shelter and protect the *"People"* from their enemies.

In addition to protecting the *"People"* from their enemies, the Comanche warrior's function was to conduct raids against their enemies, capturing and confiscating horses, weapons, valuables, and their enemy's women and young children.

Thereby weakening the enemy, while strengthening and enriching the *"People."*

Due to the inevitable loss of young men in battle, the assimilation of captive young women who could and would, give birth to future Comanche Warriors, both male and female—, thereby ensuring the survival of the *"People"*, was an accepted, essential practice.

It was the role, the duty of Comanche women, to construct the home (*the tepee*); to transport the tepee and the family's belongings across the vast expanses of the plains, as the warrior-hunters, followed the constantly migrating herds of buffalo; to skin and to cur the hides of animals brought down by the hunters; to butcher preserve and cook the meat needed for the survival of the *"People"*; to make the clothing needed for the *"People's"* survival during the cold, frigid, winters on the plains; to raise and to care for the small children.

Spring Blossom's need for assistance had been exacerbated after she and her husband Stone Fist, had fulfilled their tribal and familial duty, the adopting of the grandson of Little Flower and Gray Wolf; Spring Blossom's nephew; and the *"orphaned"* infant son of Stone Fist's life-long best friend, Running Eagle.

Spring Blossom's husband Stone Fist and her brother Running Eagle had been, for their entire lives, far more than best friends, they had been, in every sense of the word, true brothers.

Her brother Running Eagle, whose death, had been by the hands of Pretty Buffalo Hair; the black captive-slave girl, who Running Eagle had chosen to be his wife.

The black girl who had come to respect, to embrace, and to accept the life of the Comanche; the black girl who before being taken captive by Running Eagle, was in her former life, a black-slave on a Virginia cotton plantation, where she had been given, by her white Master, the Christian name, Mandy Billings.

The black girl, who had been given the name *Pretty Buffalo Hair* by her adoptive Comanche father, Gray Wolf; the black girl whose mind had been attacked by demons from the *"shadow-world"*; the black girl, *Mahn-Dee,* who under the control of evil, malevolent spirits, had slain her husband, Spring Blossom's brother, Running Eagle.

The as yet unnamed infant boy-child, Gray Wolf's grandson, was the offspring of Pretty Buffalo Hair and Spring Blossom's brother, Running Eagle, Son of Gray Wolf.

Stone Fist and Spring Blossom had assumed the responsibility of caring for, and rearing, the virtually orphaned, son of Running Eagle.

That Running Eagle's family would adopt the orphaned child was expected.

It was the way of the Comanche.

"Our daughter, who has adopted our orphaned grandson, because of her difficult first pregnancy, is struggling in her efforts to maintain the lodge of her husband, Stone Fist."

"Spring Blossom needs our help."

"I have persuaded Spring Blossom to discuss with Stone fist, the practicality of his bringing into his lodge, a second strong female."

"A woman to assist Little Flower with the skinning of the animals slain by Stone Fist; a woman to help with the preparing and cooking of the family's meals, and to help care for and raise our grandson, now her son; and to assist Spring Blossom in the care of Stone Fist's, soon to be born child."

"My husband, our children, Running Eagle and Spring Blossom, as was the plan of the Great Spirit, have for many winters, *removed themselves from* our tepee."

"Our needs are such, that I can alone, easily without assistance, maintain the lodge of Gray Wolf."

"Spring Blossom has agreed."

Gray Wolf removed the stem of his pipe from between his lips. He looked to his wife. Gray Wolf was confused.

"To what, has our daughter-Spring Blossom agreed?"
"She has agreed that the Mexican slave *"Neetah"*, that was gifted to us by Stone Fist… that *"Neetah"* and her daughter Chiquita, should be returned to the Lodge of Stone Fist."

Spring Blossom, her mother Little Flower, and most importantly her husband Stone Fist, had all agreed that the practical solution to the problem of maintaining his lodge would be for Stone Fist, to take a second wife.

It had been agreed to between the mother and daughter, that Gray Wolf's and Little Flower's Mexican slave-girl Juanita—who during this time of Spring Blossom's advancing pregnancy, had now, as had her predecessor Pale Blue Eyes (*Beeky*), Pretty Buffalo Hair's white sister—, had become the virtual nightly receptacle for Stone Fist's seed, that *"Neetah"*, would be the ideal second wife for Stone Fist.

A second wife in number and in standing, who under Spring Blossom's direction, would assist in performing the duties, of maintaining the lodge of Stone Fist.

It was during the eighth moon of her pregnancy, when it was becoming increasingly difficult for her to perform the many chores of the wife of a Comanche warrior, that Spring Blossom had reluctantly relented, and accepted the advice of her mother, Little Flower.

Spring Blossom agreed to approach her husband. To suggest to Stone Fist, that he take into their tepee, the captive Mexican woman *"Wah-Nee-tah"*, as his second wife.

It was obvious to nearly all of the band's women, that during this time, nearing the ninth moon of Spring Blossom's difficult first pregnancy, that Spring Blossom needed help to assist her, in maintaining the lodge of the band's most prolific hunter- warrior, Stone Fist.

This sentiment was amplified, reinforced, after Spring Blossom and Stone Fist fulfilled their familial duty, by adopting her orphaned infant nephew, now her son, following the unanticipated tragedy that had befallen the baby's parents.

****

Chapter 63

Comanche Encampment (Kutsueka Band) Lodge of Stone Fist – 1868

Stone Fist and his close friend and mentor, Thunder Cloud, War Chief of the Kutsueka (Buffalo-eaters) band of *Nermemuh* (the People), sat, legs crossed, cleaning their recently acquired Spencer and Henry, lever action, nine shot, repeating rifles.

The rapid firing rifles had been obtained by the War Chief, after prolonged, heated, trade negotiations, with a trio of New Mexican bandit/traders.

The War Chief had exchanged plundered livestock; horses, four times the number of fingers of both hands; the same number of cattle, plus two of four captive Mexican women, for two cases of rifles which contained twelve guns per case, and five hundred rounds of ammunition.

Stone Fist inwardly mused that his friend the great War Chief, Thunder Cloud, as usual, had struck a hard, profitable, bargain.

The rifles, and ammunition, had been distributed, one each, by the war chief, to the twenty-two warriors—excluding himself—, that he had successfully led; in the recent raid upon the Mexican Village.

Chief Thunder Cloud had struck a hard bargain.

Thunder Cloud had distributed, the rifles, one each, to the twenty warriors that had raided the sleepy Mexican Village.

As was his right as the leader of the raiding party, Chief Thunder Cloud kept for himself, two of the rifles, plus one hundred rounds of .56-56 rimfire cartridges.

The outlaw-traders, men known to the Mexican's and to the hair-mouthed *tejanos*, as *Comancheros*, were frequent, welcomed guests in Comanche encampments, welcome guests who traveled safely in the *COMANCHERÍA*, the ancient land of the Comanche.

The *COMANCHERÍA*, the vast hunting grounds of the Comanche, was the *"People's"*, conquered territory, abundant with sweet tall prairie grass, that nourished and fattened, endless herds of grazing beasts.

During most of the year, buffalo, deer, and small game, were plentiful. The terrain was awash with deep and shallow rivers, with banks that offered wood, forage, fruits, nuts and berries.

The *COMANCHERÍA encompassed* 750 X 900 square miles; bordered in the west by eastern New Mexico; to the north by south-eastern Colorado and southern Kansas; to the east by the area designated by the U.S. Government, as the *Indian Territory* (Central-Oklahoma); and to the south, the *COMANCHERÍA*, extended to within eighty miles of the bustling *tejano* village of San Antonio Texas.

The *COMANCHERÍA,* which had been fought for and defended by generation after generation of Comanche warriors, provided the *"People"* with all of the essentials needed to support, and to sustain the Comanche way of life.

In addition to providing modern weapons to be used by the *"People"* for hunting, raiding, and for the making of war on their enemies, the renegade New-Mexican bandit/traders, the *Comancheros,* as they were called by the white Texican-*tejanos,* were a vital conduit, which made available to the *"People",* especially the women, laborsaving metal utensils from the world of the white man.

Such metal implements, as cooking-pots and pans, sewing needles, butcher- knifes, which served to greatly lighten the Comanche women's oppressive workload.

As Stone Fist stared down the barrel of his new weapon, he smiled and inwardly mused that once again, his friend the war chief, Thunder Cloud, as usual, had struck a hard, profitable, bargain.

Both of the warriors were oblivious to the sounds coming from within the confines of the lodge of Stone Fist.

Stone Fist and Chief Thunder Cloud were intently concentrating, as each warrior was studiously, meticulously, in silence, dismantling and cleaning his newly acquired rifle.

Spring Blossom, the first of Stone Fist's two wives, sat quietly, directly opposite her husband, and his guest, Chief, Thunder Cloud.

Spring Blossom, the undisputed head-woman of Stone Fist's lodge, devoid of any semblance of false modesty, was nonchalantly in the process of removing her left breast, from the now relaxed lips of her satiated infant, her three moons old, second, daughter, *Moon-Glow*.

Neither Stone Fist, nor did his guest, Chief Thunder Cloud, react at the sight of Spring Blossom's casually displayed, perfectly formed breast, whose beauty was enhanced by a thin line of white milk, which served to form an ivory-halo, surrounding her still moist, erect brown nipple.

Stone Fist's second wife Juanita, her daughter of five summers Chiquita, and Spring Blossom's eldest daughter of four summers, *Winona,* was seated in the rear of the tepee.

The Mexican mother and the two small girls, were softly laughing, giggling, as they played with the family's son of nearly five winters,

The male child, who was constantly in motion, had been aptly named *"Never Still."*

Juanita, whose three-syllable name had been reduced to two syllables, first by the village children, then by everyone, to *"Neetah",* was playfully bouncing *"Never Still",* the adopted son of Stone Fist, on her knee.

Juanita had just reached her eighteenth winter, when she and her still in-utero, unborn, infant daughter Chiquita, were carried away from her sleepy little village, four summers past, by Comanche warriors, during a raid into her Mexican village.

Gray Wolf, the stately grandfather, of Stone Fist's now three small children, had, at his wife's suggestion, gifted back to Stone Fist, *"Wah-Nee-Tah"*, the captive, Mexican slave woman.

****

The volume of the usual low level, village's ambient noise, outside of the confines of the tepee, had inexplicably increased.

Stone Fist, without interrupting his work, raised his head, and spoke; *"Neetah"*, go…see what is the cause of the disturbance."

Juanita immediately placed their gurgling son into his rocking cradle, sitting on one of the numerous, thick buffalo robes, that covered the floor of the tepee. She rose and quietly left the lodge.

Stone Fist grunted and refocused, returning his full attention, to the cleaning of his rifle.

As the two warriors were reassembling their rifles, Juanita reentered the lodge. Stone Fist raised his eyes.

Although he remained silent, his second wife *Neetah,* answered Stone Fist's unspoken question; "My husband, I would speak."

Stone Fist nodded his head.

"Crooked Eye, one of the many young braves watching our herd of ponies, has entered the village, followed by…try as she might, the Comanche words that she was searching for, to describe what she had observed, alluded her.

Seeing the growing look of annoyance on the faces of her husband and his honored guest, Chief Thunder Cloud, Juanita hastily reverted to her native language; "Crooked Eye, has entered our village, followed by an… *"El negro hombre"*, who leads a pony, and two pack-mules.

Without uttering a word, Chief Thunder Cloud, and Stone Fist, rose to their feet. Both men, their rifles cradled in their arms, turned toward the entrance of the tepee.

Juanita hastily, scurried to the tepee's entrance flap, and held it open for the two warriors.

****

E. Pluribus Unum

The scene that was unfolding in the middle of the village, to Thunder Cloud, was vaguely reminiscent of a similar event that he remembered, having witnessed, only four summers past, involving his young mentee, Stone Fist,

Upon seeing the black man, his head held high, confidently riding, unafraid into the Comanche encampment, Stone Fist too, for a fleeting moment, remembered that fateful day, when he, Crooked Arrow, and his best friend Running Eagle, the father of his son, *"Never Still"*, had brought the black girl *"Mahn-dee"*, and her white sister, into the lives of *the "People."*

At that time, nearly four summers past, when the three young warriors, Stone Fist, Crooked Arrow, and the martyred warrior, Running Eagle, had triumphantly entered the village with seven captured horses, two mules, and the two captive females.

On that occasion, the three jubilant young Comanche warriors, had taken in battle, the horses, mules and the two female captives from four cowardly warriors of the *"People's* mortal enemies, the cannibalistic, Tonkawa.

One of the female-captives had been a sniffling, cowering, frightened white girl, while the black female, though obviously frightened, had stood tall…her head held high.

"Mahn-dee", the black captive-slave girl, who had been gifted by Running Eagle, to his mother Little Flower, had proven herself to be an intelligent, tireless worker, who was able to quickly adapt to, and eagerly accepted, and embraced the life of a Comanche woman.

The impressive black girl, who called herself *"Mahn-dee"*, had been adopted as the daughter of Gray Wolf and his wife, Little Flower.

Gray Wolf, because of the texture of his adopted daughter's full head of semi-straight, curly, wavy, beautiful, black hair, had given *"Mahn-dee"*, the Comanche name *"Nananisuyake Ta? Si? Woo? Tso? Yaa"*, (Pretty Buffalo Hair).

****

Crooked Eye the young warrior escorting the black-man, was still basking in the attention and the honors that he had won, on his first raid for horses and scalps.

That group of fifteen warriors, led by Stone Fist, had after a sixteen-sleeps long foray, into the land of the Pawnee, had resulted in the successful acquisition of fifty war-ponies, and six scalps, from one of the *"People's* ancient enemies.

Crooked Eye, effortlessly, nimbly, dismounted from his pony, and sprinted over to Chief Thunder Cloud, who stood next to Stone Fist, the warrior recognized by all, as the fiercest and the most lethal, of the Comanche.

"My chief, I bring word from our headman, Chief Old Wise One."

"After our guest, the black-man, has rested and eaten, when the Sun Father grows faint in the western sky, there is to be a tribal council of Chiefs and senior warriors, in the lodge of Chief Old Wise One.

<hr>

Chapter 64

The Lodge of Chief Old Wise
One 1st Council Meeting

Old Wise One's lodge was large and roomy. The red, faintly glowing embers of a small fire in the stone pit, in the center of the tepee, were still smoldering. The warriors in attendance were seated in two concentric semi-circles.

Old Wise One, He Who Speaks To Ghosts, Thunder Cloud, Gray Wolf, Stone Fist, Dull Knife, Thoughtful Man, and two additional elders, made up the inner circle.

Three feet behind, these tribal leaders, was the outer circle, which was comprised of respected warriors who had on many occasions, distinguished themselves in battle.

Old Wise One packed the band's centuries old ceremonial bone-pipe with tobacco and sumac leaves. He tamped down the blend, removed a glowing twig from the fire-pit, and lit the pipe. The old man puffed several times, the bowl of the pipe began to glow.

Old Wise One blew a stream of smoke to the East. He then passed the pipe to He Who Speaks To Ghosts, the band's shaman seated to his right, who in turn repeated the ritual, passing the pipe to, Thunder Cloud, then to Gray Wolf, then to Dull Knife, to thoughtful Man, and finally the pipe was passed to the most recent member to have gained admittance to the inner-circle, Stone Fist.

After Stone Fist repeated the ritual, and the inner-circle of warriors had all blown smoke to the four corners of Mother Earth, Stone Fist passed the ceremonial pipe to the second tier of warriors, seated in the outer circle.

After each warrior had repeated the ritual with the sacred pipe, the pipe was returned to Old Wise One, the band's Headman.

Old Wise One, with trembling hands, lifted the sacred pipe above his head. Stone Fist, the junior member of the inner-circle, rose and walked over to the Headman, who handed him the pipe.

Stone Fist turned and extended the pipe to the black-man.

The black-man gingerly, carefully, took the pipe from the strong, obviously battle-scarred hands of the most physically imposing specimen of an Indian warrior that he had ever seen.

With deliberate reference, solemnity, and respect, the black-man repeated the smoking ritual.

The black-man returned the pipe to Stone Fist, who then turned on his heel, gave the pipe to Chief Old Wise One, and resumed his seat, at the far end of the first row of warriors.

Chief Old Wise Man spoke; "Why do you, a member of the black tribe, travel through the land of the Comanche?"

While he did not understand the words that the old man spoke, the black man understood and acknowledged the deference that the assembled warriors showed the man.

He concluded that the old Indian was most likely: *"Da Boss Man."*

In a steady, measured, booming voice, the black-man, began to speak. As he spoke, he slowly, with exaggerated, emphatic motions, placed his right forearm, diagonally across his chest; *"Ise dun come here in peace."*

"My name be Britton Johnson, da white men dat da Comanches—he made a rapid backward wavy movement of the index finger of his right hand across his chest—, *da white mens dat Comanches calls tejanos, dem mens, dey calls me "Nigger Britt."*

Chief Old Wise One, unable to conceal his confusion looked to his right, to his oldest friend and advisor, the Shaman, He Who Speaks To Ghosts.

"What is the black-man saying? He makes the sign for "peace", and then he makes the sign for Comanche. The sounds that leap from his lips, before and after he does the hand talk, to my ears are harsh, and have no meaning."

Gray Wolf, a well-respected warrior, whole for thirty summers, had crossed and gone beyond the *COMANCHERÍA*, raiding and interacting with many different tribes of red men, was well versed in Sign, the universal language of the plains, rose.

"I would speak." Old Wise One nodded his permission.

Gray Wolf walked over to the black-man. He stood directly in front of the stranger and slowly, silently, with his hands, attempted to communicate with sign; "Why have you come to the land of the Comanche?"

The black-man had a quizzical, bewildered look on his face. Gray Wolf once again, employing sign, repeated his question.

"Why have you come here, to our land, the land of the Comanche?"
The black-man took a deep breath and squared his shoulders.

He first met the eyes of Gray Wolf. He then let his gaze, take in the two rows of warriors.

In his steady, measured, melodic voice, the black-man, began to speak. As he spoke, he once again, with slow deliberate, emphatic movement, placed his right forearm, diagonally across his chest, and repeated; *"Ise dun come here in peace."*

Chief Thunder Cloud stood. "I would speak." Immediately, the lodge became silent. Old Wise One looked to the war chief, and nodded his permission.

The war chief stepped forward. In a stern authoritative, commanding voice, he addressed the assembled warriors; "My fellow Comanche…do any of you speak the black-man talk?"

Deliberately and methodically, Thunder Cloud's gaze fell in turn, upon each of the warriors. No one spoke. The lodge remained silent.

Satisfied that no one understood the words of the black-man, Thunder Cloud spoke directly to the man to his right, the holy man, the Shaman, He Who Speaks To Ghosts.

"Our sister, the black woman, *Pretty Buffalo Hair*, before she was assailed and overcome by "*Evil Spirits*", demons that severely injured her mind, our sister, *Pretty Buffalo Hair*, who He Who Speaks To Ghosts, has chosen to feed and protect, spoke the black-man's words."

"Perhaps, if Chief Old Wise One agrees, our holy man, He Who Speaks To Ghosts, could persuade the black Comanche woman, *Pretty Buffalo Hair*, to listen to, and tell the council, what is being said, when the black-man speaks."

Chief Old Wise One looked quizzically at his friend, He Who Speaks To Ghosts. The Shaman gave a brisk affirming nod of his head.

Chief Old Wise One spoke. "Let it be so. When Father moon ascends in the sky, we will once again hold council."

****

E. Pluribus Unum

Chapter 65

The Lodge of He Who Speaks To Ghosts

When He Who Speaks To Ghosts, entered his lodge, the lodge that he shared with his neophyte apprentice *Pretty Buffalo Hair*, he was greeted by the familiar sound of one of those nonsensical incantations, being chanted by the afflicted, addle-brained, black woman.

Seated before him, seemingly unaware of, and completely oblivious to his presence, was the beautiful black Comanche woman, *Pretty Buffalo Hair*.

> *"Jesus luvs me...yes I know...*
> *fo da bible tells me so...*
>
> *Red, brown, yella, black,*
> *or white...we's all precious in his sight...*
>
> *Yes Jesus luvs me...yes Jesus luvs me...*
> *Yes Jesus luvs me... cuz da bible tells me so"*

In the past, on several occasions, He Who Speaks To Ghosts, had asked *Pretty Buffalo Hair*, to translate and to explain to him, the meaning of her alien incantations.

Invariably, she would merely shrug and in a flat toneless voice, she would state that the chants, the meaningless, nonsensical sounds, had somehow been planted in her mind.

Although *Pretty Buffalo Hair* had no memories of her former life, prior to her being taken in, sheltered, by He Who Speaks To Ghosts, when left alone, *Pretty Buffalo Hair* would unconscientiously hum, sing, or recite, verses that she had learned, as a child, while being rocked to sleep, on the lap of her black mother.

Pretty Buffalo Hair's fingers, were a blur as she adroitly attached eagle feathers to four of the many rattles used by the holy man, when he applied salves, administered plant elixirs, and exorcised evil, nasty, spirits from festering wounds.

He Who Speaks To Ghosts stood silently, listening, immobile, inside the entrance to the lodge.

In his mind he was comparing the facial features of the Pretty Buffalo Hair, the black woman that the "People" had adopted and accepted as Comanche, with those of the stranger, their guest, the black-man.

The holy man's brow was furrowed in deep concentration. His agile mind was comparing and contrasting, the easily recognizable physical features and characteristics between the Comanche woman, who had at one time, spoke the black-man's talk—the black-man now in their midst—; and the "Comanche", the people with whom Mandy Billings, now known to the "*People*", as Pretty Buffalo Hair, had chosen to live.

While the reddish-brown color of the woman's skin was similar to, if not exactly consistent with that of the Comanche, it was starkly different from the dark, almost black skin-color of the men that the Mexicans referred to as *"el negros."*

Neither Pretty Buffalo Hair, nor did the black-man, now a guest in their midst, have the *"People's"* high cheekbones. The shape of Pretty Buffalo Hair, and the black-man's eyes was oval.

The shape of the eyes of the *"People"*, and indeed the shape of the eyes of the *""People's"* allies the Kiowa, and of their enemies, the Utes, the Apache, the Tonkawa, the Pawnee, especially the eyes of the infants, and of the young children, were slightly slanted.

Pretty Buffalo Hair's, once beautiful, sparkling, light brown eyes, were now dull and lifeless. The color of the eyes of the *"People"*, as was the color of the eyes of this black stranger, appeared to be black.

Unlike the lips of the "People", Pretty Buffalo's lips were full, yet they were not nearly as thick and bulbous, as those of the black-man.

The lips of the Comanche, as were the lips of their allies and neighbors, the Kiowa as were the lips of their hated enemies, the Utes, the Apaches, the Pawnees, the Kickapoos, and the Tonkawa, their lips were thin.

He Who Speaks To Ghosts', smiled as he remembered his initial thought, when he had first seen the black girl's long, wavy, bouncy, beautiful, hair. He recalled having the fleeting thought; "her hair appears to be heavy."

The black woman's hair, as was the hair of the "Comanche", both males and females, was parted down the center of her head.

Two symmetrical long, heavy braids, tied with rawhide, glistening from the generous application of bear grease, rested on each of her shoulders, framing her firm breasts.

While the hair of He Who Speaks To Ghosts, indeed the hair of the native-born *"People"*, was worn in the same fashion as was that of Pretty Buffalo Hair, unlike the hair of the black Comanche woman, the texture of the native-born Comanche's hair, was straight, limp. The two braids lay placidly, without life, on their shoulders.

In contrast, when the black-man who had been seated before the tribal-council removed his hat, an event, similar to the blossoming of wild flowers, sprang from his head.

A full head of coarse, wooly, hair emerged. He Who Speaks To Ghosts, remembered thinking that the removal of his hat, had added three inches, to the black-man's height.

                                                                      E. Pluribus Unum

The shaman spoke; "Pretty Buffalo Hair, I would speak with you. Chief Old Wise One, as do all of those at council, ask for your assistance."

The strikingly handsome, black Comanche woman continued her work. She did not acknowledge He Who Speaks To Ghosts' presence.

Though he was standing but a foot behind her, it was if she had not heard the words, spoken to her by the Shaman, her mentor and benefactor.

He Who Speaks To Ghosts, walked over to the woman and gently removed an eagle feather, from her hand.

Pretty Buffalo Hair continued to stare at her empty hand. "Pretty Buffalo Hair, I have been sent by Chief Old Wise One, to seek your assistance."

For the first time, Pretty Buffalo looked at the holy man. She placed the rattle that she had been holding onto the buffalo robe. And swiveled her head, taking in the image of the holy man.

In a flat, weak, voice she proclaimed; "Ahhh, He Who Speaks To Ghosts, I did not hear you enter. Please forgive my inattention."

"Pretty Buffalo Hair, Chief Old Wise One, as do all of those who sat at council, ask for your assistance."

****

Following, and as a result of, the tragic death of her beloved husband Running Eagle, son of Gray Wolf, Pretty Buffalo Hair, the beautiful, brilliant, vibrant daughter of the *"People"*, had become withdrawn… lost within herself.

Pretty Buffalo Hair, the name given to her by her adoptive Comanche father Gray Wolf, having lived, thrived and survived in three distinctly different cultures; black, white and red, had developed an innate chameleon-like ability, to successfully adjust, and to adapt to her physical and cultural environment.

After the passage of a mere four moons of living among the Comanche, *Mandy Billings*, her name before she came to the *"People"*, with the assistance of her adopted mother Little Flower, and her adopted sister Spring Blossom, had mastered and become fluent, in the language of the Comanche.

Little Flower, her adoptive mother, was genuinely impressed and had on numerous occasions, praised her adopted daughter, for her ability to so rapidly learn to understand and speak the words of the *"People."*

Pretty Buffalo Hair had humbly responded; "I thank you for your kind words my mother. However, as was pointed out to me by my sister Becky, my white-sister *who was captured with me, the one* given the name *Blue Wolf Eyes by the "People"*, thanks to you and to my red sister Spring Blossom's kindness and patience, I can now speak and understand, three languages."

"I speak the language of the *"People"*; the language of the of the white man; and the language of the black-man."

Shortly following the Comanche ceremony that had sanctified their union, an ancient ritual performed by the holy man He Who Speaks To Ghosts, Running Eagle, the son of Gray Wolf and Little Flower, had asked his wife, Pretty Buffalo Hair, to teach him "the white man talk."

For more than six of the happiest months of her life, the former black-slave Mandy Billings, now known as Pretty Buffalo Hair, the wife of the Comanche warrior Running Eagle, she and her husband had lived, apart from the village.

The newly weds *had given* as the reason for their seclusion; "that their removal from the many distractions of the village life, would aide Running Eagle in his efforts to learn the white-man talk, which could be of benefit to the *"People."*

A welcomed byproduct of the couples *"self imposed"* voluntary seclusion, was the alone time, the isolation, that the young couple shared.

Precious days of virtually total seclusion, which allowed the two young lovers to explore, share and exalt, physically, emotionally, and spiritually, in their complete and total love, for each other.

It had been remarked by all who saw them together, that the obvious genuine love between Running Eagle and Pretty Buffalo Hair, was both physically and spiritually deep, and real.

All who observed the couple together said of it, that the union of Running Eagle and Pretty Buffalo Hair, was truly a union brought about, and blessed, by the *"Great Spirit."*

Before Running Eagle's death, at the hands of Pretty Buffalo Hair; strong hands controlled and guided by the loud, shrill, vile, incessant, malignant, voices of the *"Evil-demons,* voices that continuously brought forth to her remnants, fragments, of memories, from the deepest recesses of her mind.

Pretty Buffalo Hair had sought to exorcise the voices, with the help, the ministrations of the Holy Man, He Who Speaks To Ghosts.

Her mind was fraught with memories of countless, heinous, depredations.

Memories stemming from atrocities and indignities, that *"Mahndee"* had witnessed, and endured, from her former life, the life of a black slave, on a Virginia cotton plantation.

The terrifying, recurring nightmarish, memories that had plagued her, memories of her having witnessed, the killing, and the savage butchering of her black birth-mother, and her white father, by barbaric, cannibalistic, heathen, red men.

The incessant, evil-pernicious, voices, spoke only to her. Shrill, strident voices, screaming the vitriolic words of Massa Jesse, sitting astride the back of her submissive brother Jason, when as children, they play-acted; *"The Adventures of Mountain Men and the Savage Indians.*

The incessant, evil-voices, that spoke to her of *the senseless whipping, by her white father, of "Pee-wee", the innocent stable boy, accused of being a "run-away", when he had been visiting his girlfriend, without permission.*

The evil spirits that flooded her mind, with images of her black birth mother, and her white father, being massacred and scalped by the Tonkawa warriors.

The evil voices, that had constantly trumpeted and repeated, malevolent instructions, directed at *Mandy Billings*—the person, the identity that she had so eagerly and willingly abandoned, when she had chosen to become a Comanche —, screaming odious instructions; *"To kill Running Eagle, who the voices labeled a heathen savage", her beloved husband, with whom, she* shared her sleeping-robes.

****

It had been at her husband Running Eagle's request, that Pretty Buffalo Hair had begun the process of teaching him, *"the white man's talk."*

Each day, Pretty Buffalo Hair would open their lessons, by quoting to her husband Running Eagle, her and her sister Rebecca's, favorite quote, a phrase emblazoned in their minds, by their young, Yankee tutor.

When they awoke, before leaving the warm intimacy of their sleeping robes, and before the commencement of his lessons, Pretty Buffalo Hair would tenderly kiss her husband's lips, then she would kiss his eyelids, then she would gently blow her sweet, warm, breathe into his ear, and lovingly whisper; "My husband, always remember;

"Knowledge Is Power."

The horror associated with the tragic death of her beloved husband Running Eagle, had to her psyche, the affect of erasing from Pretty Buffalo Hair's brain, all vestiges of her former life, her life, as a black slave in the
Antebellum South.

****

Pretty Buffalo Hair did not remember her life before she had chosen... had chosen to embrace, the life of a Comanche woman.

After the shaman, He Who Speaks To Ghosts, had told Pretty Buffalo Hair of the presence of the black-man in the village, the Shaman spoke of the headman Chief Old Wise One's many, frustrating, failed attempts, to communicate with the black-man.

The holy man told of Chief Thunder Cloud's suggestion, to have Pretty Buffalo Hair, who is known to speak the white man, and the black-man talk, tell the council the meaning of guttural sounds spewing forth from the mouth of the black-man.

He told of Chief Old Wise One's acknowledgement of the wisdom of Chief Thunder Cloud's suggestion, and the headman's unprecedented action, of inviting her, Pretty Buffalo Hair, a female, to attend a meeting of the tribal-council.

At first for some reason, a reason the holy man thought was known only to the *Great Spirit*, Pretty Buffalo Hair, had become petrified, frightened at the thought of speaking the black-man talk.

It was because of the intensity of her reaction, that he, with profound sadness, recalled that when he had been treating her, attempting to rid her of the voices, *the Evil Demons*, Pretty Buffalo Hair had said, that the voices of *the Evil Demons,* spoke to her in the tongue of the black-man.

After hours of measured, soothing talk, He Who Speaks To Ghosts, was finally able to calm the genuinely, mortified woman.

He explained to her that the council, especially the headman Old Wise One, and Chief Thunder Cloud, thought that the black-man might have important information—talk of *the white men, whose numbers were as many as the stars in the night sky, information*—that could help protect the "*People*."

Crucial information about the motives, and the movement, of the white men, and of the *tejanos,* as they continued to spread, like a plague of locust, across the *"People's"* hunting grounds, defiling and destroying the *COMANCHERÍA*.

He Who Speaks To Ghosts looked deeply into Pretty Buffalo Hair's frantic, terrified eyes. Slowly the shaman thought that he saw the terror, the horror, in her eyes, morph into what he perceived of as courageous, resolve.

Pretty Buffalo Hair wiped a tear from her eye, and in a calm voice spoke;
"I am not of the black-man's world, nor am I of the white man's world. I am Comanche! I live, breath, speak and think, Comanche."

"I no longer think or speak the white man, or the black-man's talk. I thank
He Who Speaks To Ghosts, for purging the *Evil Demon's*, words, the white man's and the black-man's words, from my mind."

"For the good of, and for the survival of our people, I will listen to, and I will try to understand the words of the black-man, the man who now sits among us."

****

Chapter 66

The Lodge of Chief Old Wise One
Reconvened Meeting of the Council

Britt Johnson, once again in less than four hours, as he had before, sat in front and apart from the two rows of assembled Comanche warriors.

During the past two hours, as he had sat alone in a small tepee, piled high with uncured buffalo hides, he had been racking his brain, trying to think of a way to communicate with these savages.

Johnson suspected that the only reason that he had not been, *"kilt* and *scalped"* by these godless savages, was because to them, he was most likely a novelty a curiosity.

Whether the novelty was because he was a black-man, or maybe it was due to the fact that he had rode-up, bold as you please, right up, unafraid to that "Injun-buck" guarding the pony-herd, whatever the reason, was to him of no importance.

What was important to him was, that because he was still alive, if *they* were still alive, he had a chance to find, and to rescue his family.

In order to accomplish that, Johnson knew that time was of the essence. He knew that it was imperative that somehow, someway, before they became bored and loss interest and killed him; he had to quickly the sooner the better, devise a way to communicate with these savages.

As long as he was alive, had his scalp, and had breath in his lungs, he still had hope; he had a chance to find, and to rescue his family.

******

For the second time that day, before the passing of a single sleep, the leaders of Chief Old Wise One's band, once again assembled in the spacious lodge of the band's venerable, headman, for the holding of a high-level council.

Britt Johnson's eyes scanned the two rows of warriors, seated across from him, separated by the stone fire-pit; He quickly came to the conclusion that nothing had changed.

Once again, the ancient ritual, the smoking of the ceremonial pipe by those assembled in council, was repeated.

While he apprehensively awaited his turn to "smoke-the-pipe"—a ritual that the black-man, had fleetingly thought, vaguely reminded him of the white man's practice of placing their hands on the bible, when they swore to tell the truth—, Johnson was beginning to suspect, that his time, as a harmless curiosity, was rapidly running out.

As before, the old man seated in the center of the first row, the man that he assumed was the leader, the "boss-man", lit the long-stemmed pipe, blew smoke in four directions, then passed the pipe to the distinguished warrior on his right.

When the pipe had been smoked in turn by each warrior, the pipe was presented to the black-man. As Johnson extended his hands to receive the pipe, for the first time, he became acutely aware of the fact, that something was different.

The short warrior standing before him, presenting him with the pipe, was a short man, a warrior — judging by the tremor of his hands —, and the streaks of gray in his scalp-lock, the warrior standing before him, was no longer in his physical-prime.

Something different was happening. This warrior who was now offering the pipe to him, was not the same man who had earlier handed him the ceremonial pipe.

That warrior at the first gathering of the council had been a strikingly imposing, extraordinarily well-muscled young warrior. A man who's every movement was that, of the cat-like grace, of a stalking, cougar.

That man, the warrior who had looked at him with the piercing, black, cold, eyes of a natural-killer, had struck Britt Johnson, as the most physically imposing, visage of a lethal warrior, that he had ever encountered.

To Johnson, the young warrior had exuded strength, grace and power. One look into the pupils of the man's intense, black eyes had convinced Britt Johnson, that the Comanche warrior was the embodiment of a lethal, natural-killer.

Johnson's eyes quickly surveyed the dimly lit lodge. The impressive, imposing young warrior, was not in attendance.

After the black-man had smoked the pipe, Chief Old Wise One raised his hand. The low murmur of conversation ceased.

The only sounds to be heard within the confines of the lodge were the crackling of the branches that were feeding the flames of the fire in the pit.

Chief Old Wise One, seated cross-legged, in the center of the first row of warriors, as he had done earlier, spoke; "Why do you, a member of the black tribe, travel through the land of the Comanche?"

Although he did not know their meaning, Johnson recognized the tone and the tenor of the old man's words.

Thinking that his words would result in the same bewildered look of confusion that they had received earlier, nonetheless, with a feeling of futility, once again, the black-man responded to what he assumed was a question.

Although he thought that his response, his here-to-fore, desperate attempts to be understood, would be futile, having no viable alternative, the black-man, began to speak.

As he spoke, he once again slowly, with the same deliberate, exaggerated, emphatic, motions, placed his right forearm, diagonally across his chest;

"Ise dun come here in peace."

"My name be Britt Johnson, da white mens dat da Comanches—he made a rapid backward wavy movement of the index finger of his right hand across his chest—, *da white mens dat Comanches calls tejanos, and dem mens dat dey calls tejanos-Rangers, dey calls me "Nigger Britt."*

He Who Speaks To Ghosts had informed Pretty Buffalo Hair that, the presence of a female at a council meeting was unprecedented.

When they entered Old Wise One's lodge, in an effort to avoid creating a distraction, the holy man had guided Pretty Buffalo Hair to the recess shadows, in the rear of the large tepee.

When the strange yet vaguely familiar words, began to spew forth from the black-man's mouth, Pretty Buffalo Hair began to experience an unsettling, queasy, sensation in the pit of her stomach.

Despite her nagging reticence, Pretty Buffalo Hair found herself straining to hear, and to make sense, of the words of the black-man.

"My name be Britt Johnson, da white mens dat Comanches calls tejanos, and dem mens dey calls tejanos-Rangers, dose mens, dey calls me "Nigger Britt."

At first, for her, his words held no real meaning. They were like the sounds of the chirping birds, everyday sounds that surround us. Ordinary sounds, without meaning.

Then toward the end of the black-man's talk, she heard the sound. The sound. That awful sound, the word, ***"NIGGER".***

That vile word ***"NIGGER"*** had exploded in her head.

Without her understanding, how and or why, it was happening, Pretty Buffalo Hair's mind, grudgingly, began to gradually recognize, and to once again understand the *"black-man talk."*

It was apparent to the holy man, He Who Speaks To Ghosts that the words of the black-man, continued to have no meaning for the council of warriors.

The holy man, now seated beside Chief Old Wise One, raised his hand; *"I would speak."* Old Wise One nodded his permission for the shaman to speak.

"As our war Chief Thunder Cloud suggested, and was agreed to by Chief Old Wise One, I spoke to our Comanche sister, the black woman."

"The woman who grew up in the black-tribe as *"Mahn-dee"*, and is now and will forever be, Pretty Buffalo Hair, a woman of the Comanche.

"I told Pretty Buffalo Hair of the presence of the black-man in our village."

"I spoke with her of the many important questions, we would ask the black-man. I told Pretty Buffalo Hair that it is possible that the man from the black-tribe, can answer our questions about the movements and the strengths of the white invaders, who are encroaching on our hunting-grounds."

"I told her of the council's inability to make talk with the black-man."

"I asked Pretty Buffalo Hair, for her help in making meaning for the council, the words of the black-man."

The warriors at council responded to the words of the Shaman, with a rustling of chatter, among themselves.

Chief Old Wise One raised his hand. The silence was immediate.

The chief turned; "What was Pretty Buffalo Hair's response?

In a swift horizontal motion, the holy man abruptly waved his arm.

"The black talk no longer resides in her mind, nor do the black-words flow from the lips of Pretty Buffalo Hair. The *Evil*-demons that, three winters past, seized and poisoned her mind, spoke to her in the tongue of the black-man."

"Our sister, Pretty Buffalo Hair fears that if she allows the black-man talk to return to her lips, she will once again be assailed by the voices of the wicked, "*Evil-demons*.""

"I assured Pretty Buffalo Hair, that my medicine is strong. That, as it did three winters past, if the wicked voices return, the medicine of He Who Speaks To Ghosts, will again defeat the *Evil-demons*.""

"Although Pretty Buffalo Hair fears the return of the voices of the *Evil-demons* to her head, in her heart, above all else, she loves the Comanche."

"Pretty Buffalo Hair stands there, he pointed to the rear of the lodge, beside me; listening."

****

Britt Johnson was becoming desperate. He instinctively sensed that his time was running out. He could see from the body language of the Indians, that they were losing patience, growing impatient, becoming increasingly, frustrated.

During the course of trying to understand, and keep up with the rapid flow of the strange alien words being spoken, Johnson's mind switched.

He abandoned hope of communicating with the savages and instead, began racking his brain, attempting to devise a plan of escape.

He realized that the odds of his escaping, thus saving his life, was highly unlikely.

E. Pluribus Unum

Britton Johnson was an intelligent, courageous man. He did not want to die. He wanted to live.

When he had entered the village, the Indians had confiscated his rifle, and his two pistols. With the exception of his hunting knife, he was unarmed.

"Nigger Britt Johnson was not afraid of dying. He was however afraid of dying without resisting. Afraid of dying like a helpless dumb animal. Afraid of being slaughtered like a helpless calf.

Johnson had gradually, reluctantly, come to conclude, that in all probability, he was a dead man.

Whether he lived or died, was no longer under his control. The only thing that he might be able to control was how he would die.

The fingers of his right hand gripped the hilt of his knife. His intent was to leap across the fire-pit, and before the others could react, kill the old man, the apparent leader of these savages.

Britt knew that the odds of him killing the Comanche leader were extremely small. Additionally, he also realized that the odds of his surviving an attack against the old man, was zero.

The black-man was resolute, determined, he had decided to act.

He did not want to die. But he decided, that if his death was inevitable, he at least, wanted his death to have had purpose. He wanted to have died for something.

He was determined that with his last breath, his dying breath, would be taken, expended, in if not saving, then in at least avenging, his wife Mary, and his two boys.

He would attempt to kill the chief, thus not only ensuring his certain death, but most likely, precipitating an agonizingly slow, excruciatingly, painful death, at the hands of these savages.

Slowly, as cunningly and carefully as he could manage, Johnson was able uncross his legs and to rise to his knees.

As he was gathering himself to lunge at the chief, he hesitated. The black-man had become aware of the increasing volume and the urgency of the various conversations, being held among the assembled Comanche.

Johnson had been so intent on executing his plan to kill the chief that he had failed to notice that one of the chief's advisors, the man who had been seated on the left of the old man, was no longer there.

The man, the only man at the council, that Johnson thought, did not have the look of a seasoned killer, the look of a savage, lethal, Comanche warrior, was now returning to his seat. An Indian woman was walking behind, the chief's advisor.

Despite the perilous situation that he was in, Johnson gasped at the sight of what he thought, was the most beautiful woman, black, white, yellow, or red that he had ever seen.

Although her posture and her demeanor were that of subservience— as one would expect from a female living in this primitive, male dominant, hunter- gatherer culture—, there was a distinctive aura of dignity, in the way that she held her head.

The stately, imposing Indian, holding the hand of the woman, stood in front of the black-man.

Johnson looked quizzically, first at the warrior, and then his gaze became locked on the face of the woman.

The first thing that he noticed was that the Indian woman was tall. She was at least two to three inches taller than the middle-aged, stately looking Indian, holding her hand.

The strikingly handsome woman was deeply tanned. The color of her skin, instead of having the faint copper red tone, of the warriors, was a deep brownish mahogany. While the eyes of all of the warriors, appeared to be black, this woman's eyes were light brown.

He Who Speaks To Ghosts gently nudged the woman, toward the black-man.

The holy man stood directly in front of the black-man; "I am He Who Speaks To Ghosts. Why have you journeyed to the land of the Comanche?"

Though he did not understand what he thought of as heathen *"gibberish"*, with a deep sigh of exasperation, the black-man for what he thought would be the last time, repeated the speech that he had so diligently, meticulously, practiced and memorized;

"My name be Britt Johnson. Da white men dat da Comanche—he made a swift backward, wiggling, movement of his index finger of his right hand, across his chest —, *da white mens dat Comanches calls tejanos, and dem mens dey calls tejanos-Rangers, dey calls me* **"Nigger Britt."**

This time, as he once again gave his recitation, Johnson was intently staring into the eyes of the Comanche squaw. Her doe-like, light brown eyes were dull, lifeless.

For the bulk of his speech, the Comanche squaw's facial expression had remained, passive, unreadable.

Just when the black-man was about to give up any hope of being understood, he saw in the squaw's eyes, a fleeting, flicker of recognition.

Towards the very tail-end, of his well-rehearsed—now to him monotonously dull and stupid—, little speech, Johnson thought he glimpsed a look of anguish, a fleeting look of pain, reflected in the dark Comanche-squaw's brown eyes.

E. Pluribus Unum

With a look of desperation, of renewed hope, *"Nigger"* Britt Johnson, looked pleadingly into the eyes of the Comanche Squaw.

The woman turned to face the warrior standing behind her, and with an anguished look in her eyes, she slowly nodded her head.

She placed her right hand beneath her left breast, and in a shaky but steady voice, began to speak the plantation-slave, black-man's tongue:

"I'se Pretty Buffalo Hair. Da Chief Ole Wise One, he be want'n ta know, wat fo you come ta da land of da Comanche?"

****

Chapter 67

"Nigger" Britt Johnson

Initially, the black-man was shocked. Then relief overtook his emotions. A wild surreal thought flashed through his mind; *"She's black, this Comanche squaw, is a black woman"!*

A satisfied, broad grin, spread across the face of the shaman. He Who Speaks To Ghosts was pleased.

As the black-man and Pretty Buffalo Hair exchanged the black-man talk, He Who Speaks To Ghosts turned and faced the council. Both Chief Old Wise One and Chief Thunder Cloud nodded their approval.

After five minutes of uninterrupted, continuous, animated talk, with the Comanche squaw, the black-man's initial feelings of exaltation were beginning to wane.

The black Comanche woman had sat, unmoving, showing absolutely no emotion, during his disclosure. He began to experience doubts.

Did this wild female creature, truly understand what he was saying?

As if she had been reading his mind, the Comanche woman, who when speaking to him, talked like a black slave, raised her head, and for a fleeting second, Britton Johnson, gazed into her eyes.

Pretty Buffalo Hair stood, turned and walked back to face the council.

The two rows of warriors, who had sat quietly, transfixed, while the black stranger spoke the alien words to Pretty Buffalo Hair, had all become engaged in conversation.

Chief Old Wise One raised his hand. Immediately the lodge fell silent.

Chief Old Wise One spoke; *"Pretty Buffalo Hair, who is this black-man, and why has he come to our village, why is he in the land of the Comanche?"*

"My chief, the black-man says that he has come in search of his family."

There was a brief flurry of puzzled conversation. Once again, Chief Old Wise One raised his hand. Again, there was immediate silence.

Pretty Buffalo Hair took a deep breath. Then she began to tell the words that the black-man had spoken.

"These are the words of the black-man. His name is Britt Johnson; he lives as a slave of the white man, in the tejanos village, across the Brazos River, in the village called by the tejanos, Elm Creek."

"Four moons past, while he was away, his home was attacked by many Comanche and Kiowa warriors. The raiding party was led by "Little Buffalo."

When Pretty Buffalo Hair mentioned the name "Little Buffalo", the name had evoked a rush of conversation between the two rows of warriors.

Each and every warrior in attendance at this council recalled the visit to their village, just six months past — during the moon of the falling leaves—, by Little Buffalo.

Little Buffalo, an ambitious young warrior, eager to gain honors and prestige, from exploits won on the-war-path, had sat at Old Wise One's council fire, attempting to recruit warriors to join his large raiding party.

After having raided up and down the Brazos country, Little Buffalo had remarked that the hair-mouth soldiers, who guarded the *tejano* villages, were gone, and that the *tejano* Rangers, who had hunted down, killed and scalped the Comanche, as they slept, were now, to few to matter.

Six young warriors from Old Wise Man's village had leapt at the chance to follow and to ride with Little Buffalo's, immense raiding-party.

Chief Old Wise One raised his hand. The lodge instantly, fell silent.

The venerable headman spoke; "Pretty Buffalo Hair…what other words did the black-man speak?"

"The black-man says that he comes in peace. He does not come seeking vengeance. He accepts the Comanche warrior's right to raid, to take scalps, to take horses from, and to make captives of, their enemies."

Following those conciliatory words, there was a universal utterance of agreement and acknowledgement, from the assembled warriors.

All of the men seated at council including the holy man, He Who Speaks To Ghosts, had on some occasion, stolen horses from, made captives of, and in combat, killed their enemies.

Chief Old Wise One, once again raised his hand. He looked at Pretty Buffalo Hair, and nodded his head, signifying his approval of the black-man's words.

Fragrant Lilly, Chief Old Wise One's granddaughter, stepped out of the shadows and offered the black Comanche woman, a gourd of water.

Pretty Buffalo Hair took a small sip of water…then continued; "the black-man has come to the land of the Comanche to trade for his wife and children…who he now believes belongs to the Comanche."

Chief Old Wise One gave a grunt of acceptance, and of approval at the black man's courage, and his initiative.

The two warriors, seated immediately to the left and to the right of the chief— the bands war Chief Thunder Cloud, and the shaman, He Who Speaks To Ghosts—, each simultaneously, added their grunts of approval.

Chief Old Wise One spoke; "Tell the black-man that the Comanche respect and admire men of courage. His actions and his words are honorable."

"Tell the black man that six moons past, a group of Comanche and Kiowa warriors, twenty times the fingers of both hands, warriors who had raided with Little Buffalo, entered our village."

"The warriors, rested for one sleep, on the edges of our village."

Again, Chief Old Wise One opened and spread the fingers of both hands.

"More than, ten times the fingers of both hands, of those warriors were Comanche warriors, our kinsmen who were returning home to their camp, the camp of Chief Milky Way."

"The Comanche warriors held as their captive, a white woman"

"The Kiowa warriors were returning to their hunting grounds, to lands north of the COMANCHERÍA.

"Those Kiowa warriors, friends of the Comanche, who traveled to their lands north of the COMANCHERÍA, hold three black captives, a woman and two boys."

"Tell the black man that when father sun rises, Crooked Eye, the young brave that brought him to us, will lead him to the camp of our Comanche brother, Chief Milky Way."

Pretty Buffalo Hair returned to sit in front of the black-man. As she was translating the words of Old Wise One, Pretty Buffalo Hair was acutely aware of the gradual change in the burly black-man's demeanor.

Where he had initially appeared to be a formidable, solid, determined, an obsidian rock, with each succeeding sentence, delivered by Pretty Buffalo Hair, his previous rock-like continence, was noticeably, gradually, softening.

It was obvious to Pretty Buffalo Hair that the black-man, who called himself Britt Johnson, upon hearing the news that his wife and sons might still be alive, was attempting to hide his emotions, to remain at least outwardly, stoically calm.

When Pretty Buffalo Hair stated that a white woman was being held captive by Comanche, in the village of Chief Milky Way — a kinsman of Old Wise One —, in a nearby encampment, the rate and the depth of the black-man's breathing, dramatically intensified.

By far, the most visibly detectable, reaction shown by the black-man occurred, when he was told that the Comanche's friends and allies the Kiowa, were holding captive, a black woman and two black boys.

As the black Comanche squaw continued to speak to him, to speak his language, "**Nigger**" Britt Johnson, fought to refrain from reacting.

As the dark Comanche squaw continued to speak to him, to speak his language, as her words penetrated his mind, "**Nigger**" Britt Johnson, bit down hard on his lip, drawing blood.

The black man was concentrating, trying to refrain from showing any outward emotion, lest these savages consider it, as a sign of weakness.

He fought his euphoria, attempting to not react, to maintain his self-control and composure.

"**Nigger**" Britt Johnson failed. Silent tears of joy and relief welded up, in the black man's eyes, and began to silently cascade down his cheeks.

For the first time in nine months, Britt Johnson actually believed that there was a real chance...that the possibility existed, that his wife Mary, and his two sons, might still be alive.

****

Chapter 68

The Lodge of He "Who Speaks To Ghosts"

He Who Speaks To Ghosts, and his apprentice, Pretty Buffalo Hair, sat eating buffalo stew, at the holy man's fire.

"Pretty Buffalo Hair, when you sat before the black-man, I at first, did not believe that you remembered the black-man talk. I am relieved to have been mistaken."

Pretty Buffalo Hair sighed. She looked at her mentor, He Who Speaks To Ghosts; "You were not mistaken."

Pretty Buffalo Hair picked-up, the Shaman's empty bowl. She walked to the rear of the lodge and retrieved He Who Speaks To Ghosts' bone-pipe.

She filled the pipe with sumac leaves, and handed it to her mentor. Pretty Buffalo Hair resumed her seat. "I at first did not understand the words of the black-man. The black-man's words were familiar, yet, to me they had no real meaning."

"It was when the black-man said the word *__Nigger__*", that the meaning of the black-man's words, all of the black-man talk, became clear to me."

He Who Speaks To Ghosts sat silently, lost in thought, puffing his pipe.
The holy man finally spoke; "What is the power of this word **"Neegah?"**

Of the many words put forth by the black-man, before he spoke the word **"Neegah"**, why did that word alone hold the key to your once again, understanding the meaning of the black-man talk?"

Now it was Pretty Buffalo Hair's time for contemplation. Seeing that his protégé was deep in thought, He Who Speaks To Ghosts remained silent.

Finally, after several moments of silence, Pretty Buffalo Hair spoke; "The word **"Nigger"**, is an especially vile and hateful word when spoken by the white man."

"It is a label used by the whites, to justify their treatment and their dehumanization, of the members of the black tribe."

"That disgusting word **"Nigger"**, was one of the words that the **"Evil-spirits"**, the demons that you holy-man...that you, He Who Speaks To Ghosts, chased from my mind."

"That ugly, loathsome word **"Nigger"**, was continuously being screamed at me by the demons, hollering in my head, during the time of the debilitating, crippling, illness of my mind.

That loathsome, vile, word **"Nigger...Nigger...Nigger"**, tortured and haunted me, and forced a part of me, to commit an unforgivable, evil act"

"Evil-demons, in the guise of senseless, blind prejudice...that I learned and witnessed as a child. Hateful thoughts that like a drum had been beaten into me my entire life.

Evil-White-Demons screaming at me; **"Nigger...Nigger...Nigger"**; they used me as an instrument to kill the love of my life, my husband Running Eagle."

"Now once again, that awful word *"Nigger"*, has returned to play an important role in my life. The word has acted as a key, which has unlocked the hiding place, and loosed a flood of memories, of my past."

"I remember having grown up as a black-slave, owned by a white man on a huge farm, far to the east of the **COMANCHERÍA**, a place called Virginia."

"I remember my white sister Rebecca…Becky, who was with me when we were both captured, taken prisoner by three Comanche warriors. Warriors led by my future husband Running Eagle, the son of Gray Wolf."

"I remember being a slave of, and then being the adopted daughter, of Little Flower, the wife of Gray Wolf. Little Flower the mother of Running Eagle, the mother of my sister Spring Blossom, my adoptive Comanche mother, who I grew to love and to cherish."

"I remember for the first time in my life, of living with a people, in a society where I was judged solely by my character, by my talents."

"A society that subsequently without reservation, accepted me and treated me, as a productive, welcomed, contributing member of that society."

"My heart rejoices and aches when I remember my life as the wife of Running Eagle. I remember the absolute love and devotion, that we felt for each other."

"I remember my life, as the wife of Running Eagle, as being the happiest time of my life."

"Also, I remember when my mind, and my will was being seized by the voices of the *Evil-White-Demons*."

"I remember how the *Evil-demons*, erased and removed, all of my happy memories, memories that I had accumulated by living with, and choosing to become Comanche."

"I remember fighting with all the strength that I possessed, the *Evil-White-Demons* that were inexorably infecting and taking over my mind.

"I remember the insidious Evil-demons that were replacing my joyous memories, with malignant reminders of past pain, injustices and hurts."

"I remembered the out-of-body experience that I, Pretty Buffalo Hair, experienced, watching helplessly in horror, unable to move, to intervene, as *"Mahn-dee*, killed my beloved husband Running Eagle."

****

Chapter 69

Stone Fist Remembers

Toward the conclusion of the morning council, when Chief Thunder Cloud had mentioned the name "Pretty Buffalo Hair, a name that to Stone Fist anyone, without speaking to either of his two wives, had leapt upon the back of his favorite pony, and had galloped out onto the open prairie.

Stone Fist stopped and sat beneath the sparse shade afforded by a scraggly juniper bush. He had a splitting headache. The blood vessels supplying blood to his temples were throbbing, for the first time in his life, Stone Fist felt faint.

To him the name "Pretty Buffalo Hair", was wicked, evil, taboo. It was understood by the *People,* that the name "Pretty Buffalo Hair", was not to be spoken in his presence.

Pretty Buffalo Hair, the black-captive woman, who Stone Fist had never fully trusted; Pretty Buffalo Hair, the beautiful black-spirit, the enchantress, who Stone Fist was convinced, had manipulated and stolen the heart and captured the soul and mind of his lifelong best friend, Running Eagle; Pretty Buffalo Hair, had once again come to taunt, and to haunt him.

Three winters past—during the time that the deer shed their antlers— Pretty Buffalo Hair, Running Eagle's woman, had violated one of *"the People's"* most sacred, tribal taboos.

Pretty Buffalo Hair had murdered a *"Nermernuh"*, one of *"the People"*, she a Comanche, had murdered a Comanche.

Pretty Buffalo Hair had slain Running Eagle, Stone Fist's life-long best friend.

She had slain Running Eagle, the man that she professed to have loved and respected, above all others.

Pretty Buffalo Hair had killed his life-long friend Running Eagle; the bravest, most loyal and trustworthy man, that Stone Fist had ever known.

Despite the Holy Man, He Who Speaks To Ghosts' pronouncements, his explanations, and platitudes that she, Pretty Buffalo Hair, had been chosen, had been touched by the *"Great Spirit"*, and having been touched by the *"Great Spirit"*, should therefore be protected, was something that Stone Fist could not, and would not, accept.

Instead of reverence, Stone Fist's heart had been filled with hate. His instinctive impulse was to kill the woman who had murdered his best friend.

Every fiber of his being had screamed at Stone Fist; *"slash, maim, kill"* the coward who had murdered, Running Eagle.

It had been the persistent words of He Who Speaks To Ghosts, and the blind acceptance of countless generations, of his innate adherence to ancient customs, taboos and beliefs, that had saved Pretty Buffalo Hair from the lethal, without mercy, wrath of Stone Fist.

Stone Fist eventually, had finally come to accept that the Great Spirit had completely removed from the mind of Pretty Buffalo Hair, all memories of her past.

As a mindless being with no memories, living under the protection of the Holy man, Pretty Buffalo Hair had given birth, to Running Eagle's son.

Stone Fist, the baby's adoptive father, had bestowed upon the baby the name "Never Still." Stone Fist chose the name, "Never Still"; because of the boy's proclivity of being always it seemed, in constant, accelerated motion.

These were the factors that had mitigated against, and had stilled from Pretty Buffalo Hair's skull, the lethal war club of Stone Fist.

These factors that had prevented Stone Fist from smashing open the head of the black-woman, the woman from the black-tribe, who had been accepted as Comanche, the woman who had murdered his best friend, his blood-brother, Running Eagle.

****

Chapter 70

Lodge of Gray Wolf – Pretty Buffalo Hair (Mahn-dee's) Comanche Father

After leaving Pretty Buffalo Hair, his brilliant apprentice, He Who Speaks To Ghosts had sought the companionship, the fellowship, and the wisdom, of his old friend Gray Wolf.

Gray Wolf, and He Who Speaks To Ghosts, were contemporaries; warriors of the same age.

The two elder leaders of this, the Kutsueka band of the Comanche, had played together, as small boys. They together, had learned to ride, to shot arrows, to wield and to defend, against, hand-to-hand combat, utilizing knife and tomahawk.

The two friends, of more than four decades, had grown up together.

As young teen-age braves, Gray Wolf, and He Who Speaks To Ghosts, had both, within the passage of two moon cycles, journeyed to the distant, sacred twin-peaked mountains, where each, on separate pilgrimages, had experienced inspirational visits by the spirits…visions that resulted in each young brave, obtaining his personal medicine, his *"Puha."*

It was the belief and the custom of the "People", that a young brave, not be elevated to the status of warrior, not be allowed to participate in the large, communal buffalo hunts; not be allowed to join raiding or war parties, until he possessed his own personal medicine.

It was the *People's* belief that the young man should obtain divine assistance, and have bestowed upon him an object, a talisman, which possessed supernatural, protective guiding forces.

These protective forces frequently came to the individual by way of a vision, a vision revealed to the young, aspiring, warrior, by the benevolent spirits, from the spirit world.

As youths Gray Wolf and He Who Speaks To Ghosts, had both, during the same moon-cycle, embarked upon their individual quest to obtain — from the spirit world — their own unique protective medicine, their *"Puha"*.

Gray Wolf had followed the path of the warrior, while his friend He Who Speaks To Ghosts; choose to devote his life to doing the bidding of the Great Spirit.

The holy man's lifelong friend Gray Wolf was the father of Running Eagle, the young warrior, killed at the hands of his wife, Pretty Buffalo Hair, the black-Comanche woman, who had been possessed and directed to do so, by malicious, *"Evil spirit-demons."*

He Who Speaks To Ghosts was anxious to inform his friend that at last, his adoptive daughter/daughter in-law, Pretty Buffalo Hair, had completely escaped, the influence, the words of the *"Evil demons" that* had killed his son.

He Who Speaks To Ghosts hesitated, then he gently, but firmly wrapped on the entrance flap of Gray Wolf's lodge.

From deep within the lodge, He Who Speaks To Ghosts heard the familiar voice of his old friend: *"Enter."*

Gray Wolf was seated, smoking his after-dinner pipe, sipping water from a buffalo-paunch, the vessel in which the "People" routinely carried their drinking water.

As he stepped inside the lodge of Gray Wolf, his old friend warmly greeted the holy man: "Aah my old friend, He Who Speaks To Ghosts, come in, come in. You are always welcome in the lodge of Gray Wolf."

Gray Wolf turned his head and spoke to his wife; "Little Flower, "please bring food and drink for our guest.

He Who Speaks To Ghosts sat next to his friend. Little Flower returned. She was holding a bowl of venison stew in her left hand, and a paunch filled with water, in her right.

When she extended the food, He Who Speaks To Ghosts' eyes were drawn to Little Flower's mutilated left hand. Little Flower was missing the index finger, and the middle finger of her left hand.

Among the "People", one of the most tragic events that could befall a village was the unexpected death, especially during times of peace, the death in the prime of his life, of a young hunter-warrior.

The extent of the mourning rituals that followed the unanticipated death of a young male was felt not only by the family of the deceased, it was felt by the entire village.

For the tribe, the devastating effect of the loss of strong, young, warrior-hunters and protectors, threatened the very survival of the "People."

Three winters past, when her son Running Eagle was murdered, Little Flower had been devastated.

Her grief, her mourning, had culminated, in her commission of several spontaneous acts of self-mutilation.

Little Flower caught in the throes of inconsolable grief, utilizing a knife that she used for skinning small animals, had severed two fingers from her left hand.

One finger was hacked-off to mourn the death of her son, Running Eagle; the second finger was for the loss of her adopted daughter/daughter-in-law, Pretty Buffalo Hair's mind, to the wicked, Evil spirit-demons.

Little Flower took solace and comfort, when He Who Speaks To Ghosts had explained to the band, that the "Evil spirits", not Pretty Buffalo Hair, were responsible for the murder of Little Flower's son Running Eagle.

That it was the *"Evil demons"*, who had captured and taken control of the mind of Running Eagle's wife, Little Flower and Gray Wolf's adopted daughter, Pretty Buffalo Hair.

Chapter 71

The Lodge of "He Who Speaks To Ghosts"

After He Who Speaks To Ghosts', departure from his lodge, Pretty Buffalo Hair sat alone, staring, transfixed, at the faint glow of the dying embers of the fire being feebly fueled, by the remnants of dried buffalo chips.

Pretty Buffalo Hair remembered!

She was now in possession of, and fully aware of her identity, of her past, as a slave of the white man, Henry Billings, her father.

She remembered that she and her white sister "Becky", having been captive slaves of the Comanche. She remembered her conversion, her decision to be a part of, and to embrace the life of the Comanche.

Pretty Buffalo Hair remembered the ecstatic, euphoric, joy of the happiest period of her life, her summer as the bride, the lover, the woman, …the wife of the Comanche warrior, Running Eagle.

She remembered the joy of being pregnant, as she and her husband Running Eagle, anxiously awaited the arrival of their baby.

Pretty Buffalo Hair now, after the passing of five winters, finally felt and mourned the tragic loss, of her husband Running Eagle.

Her grief was intensified by the knowledge that, Running Eagle's death was at her hands; her hands guided by the malignant powers of the malicious, Evil spirits.

Pretty Buffalo Hair remembered her recurring, episodic bouts of debilitating headaches; as the incessant, malevolent voices of the Evil Demons, incessantly screamed and infused into her mind, their hateful xenophobic filth.

She remembered watching helplessly, paralyzed, unable to intervene, as *"Mahn-dee"*, dressed in the clothing of Pretty Buffalo Hair, plunged the eight-inch knife, into the chest of the person that she, Pretty Buffalo Hair loved above all others, her husband, Running Eagle.

Pretty Buffalo Hair shuddered. She understood and accepted the words spoken by the holy man, He Who Speaks To Ghosts; *"Pretty Buffalo Hair, you are not at fault for the death of Running Eagle."*

"It was not you who killed Running Eagle. Running Eagle was slain by the *"Evil spirits"* that had ceased your mind, and forced you to plunge the knife into the chest of your sleeping husband."

Now after the passage of five winters, Pretty Buffalo Hair, in every fiber of her being, finally felt and mourned the tragic loss, of her warrior husband.

Although five winters had past since the death of her husband, to Pretty Buffalo Hair— due to the mind controlling powers of the *"Evil demons"*—, had loss the ensuing memories of five winters of her life.

Her husband Running Eagle's death was now, at that moment, in her mind, a new, heart-breaking, and very fresh event.

Pretty Buffalo Hair, who had been bereft of emotions, of feelings, for more than five winters, was instantly, overwhelmed with grief. She began to weep uncontrollably.

As would any woman of the "People", Pretty Buffalo Hair's reaction to the death of her husband, her lover, her provider, her protector, was that of uninhibited anguish, and sorrow.

At first her sobs of grief were barely audible whimpers. Silent tears cascading down her cheeks.

Pretty Buffalo Hair rose from the buffalo-hide couch, and picked-up one of the knives that she used to butcher, and to cut meat.

Her silent tears of mourning had changed. They were now piteous, audible, shrieks and wails, as she methodically used the sharp knife, to cut and chop at her hair. First the left, then the right braid, fell to the floor of the lodge.

Pretty Buffalo Hair thought of, and remembered the deliriously happy weeks, and months, that she and her beloved husband, Running Eagle had spent together alone, separated from the village, just days following their marriage.

She remembered the ecstatic time, the hours upon hours, that she and Running Eagle had spent exploring each other's bodies, as she taught him the white-man tongue, and he in-turn, taught her the essence and the joys, of becoming a woman.

Pretty Buffalo Hair, the butchering knife in hand, stepped over the two springy braids lying on the floor of the tepee. Blinded by tears, she left the holy man's lodge.

****

Chapter 72

Stone Fist

Toward the conclusion of the morning council, when Chief Thunder Cloud had mentioned the name *"Pretty Buffalo Hair"* a name that to Stone Fist, was repugnant and taboo, Stone Fist, without a word to anyone, to either of his wives, had leapt upon the back of his favorite pony, and had galloped out onto the open prairie.

Stone Fist sat beneath the sparse shade afforded by a scraggly juniper bush. He had a splitting headache. The blood vessels supplying blood to his temples, were throbbing, his vision was becoming blurred.

It had been almost five winters since he had heard the name, "Pretty Buffalo Hair", spoken.

Pretty Buffalo Hair, the black-captive woman, who Stone Fist had never fully trusted.

Pretty Buffalo Hair, the beautiful black-spirit, the enchantress, who Stone Fist was convinced, had manipulated and stolen the heart, captured the soul and mind of his lifelong best friend, Running Eagle.

Five winters past—during the time that the deer shed their antlers— Pretty Buffalo Hair, Running Eagles woman, had violated a sacred tribal taboo.

She had murdered a *"Nermernuh"*, one of the "People". She had killed, murdered, a Comanche.

She had slain Running Eagle, Stone Fist's life-long, best friend.

Pretty Buffalo Hair had slain Running Eagle, the man, the person that she claimed, to love and respect, above all others.

She had killed her husband, Stone Fist's life-long friend and confidant, Running Eagle.

Despite the holy man, He Who Speaks To Ghosts' pronouncements, the Shaman's explanations, and platitudes that she, Pretty Buffalo Hair, was special, and that the *"Great Spirit"* had touched her mind, and therefore, instead of her being punished, that she should be protected.

Stone Fist had resisted, he could not, and would never forgive, Pretty Buffalo Hair, for the murder of his friend.

Instead of reverence, and forgiveness, Stone Fist's heart had been filled with hate. His instinctive impulse had been to kill the woman who had murdered Running Eagle.

Every fiber of his being had screamed at Stone Fist; *"Slash, maim, kill* the woman who had murdered, Running Eagle, the brother of his wife Spring Blossom, the son of Gray Wolf, the best friend and confidant, of Stone Fist.

It had been the persistent words of the holy man, and Stone Fist's blind, unwavering, acceptance of countless generations, of adherence to ancient customs, taboos and beliefs, that had saved Pretty Buffalo Hair from the lethal, merciless, wrath of Stone Fist.

Eventually, Stone Fist had come to accept that the Great Spirit had, mercifully, completely removed from the mind of Pretty Buffalo Hair, all memories of her past.

As a mindless being, with no memories, living under the protection of the holy man, Pretty Buffalo Hair had given birth, to Running Eagle's son.

Stone Fist had come to realize, and to accept the fact, that had it not been for the words of the holy man, words that had stayed his war-club; if he had given vent to his overwhelming desire to kill Pretty Buffalo Hair, the boy, his boy…his son, who he loved and cherished, would not exist.

Stone Fist, the baby's adoptive father, gave the baby the name *"Never Still."*

Stone Fist chose the name, *"Never Still"*, because of the boy's—even when an infant—, proclivity of being in constant, accelerated motion.

These were the mitigating factors, which had stilled the lethal war club of Stone Fist. That had prevented Stone Fist from smashing open the head of the black-woman, the woman from the black-tribe that *"the People"*, had accepted as Comanche.

This woman who had come to them with the black name *Mahn-dee*, this Comanche woman, that Stone Fist would never… could never, forgive for murdering Running Eagle, Stone Fist's blood-brother, his best friend.

****

He Who Speaks To Ghosts, after leaving Pretty Buffalo Hair, had sought the companionship, the fellowship, and the wisdom, of his old friend Gray Wolf.

Gray Wolf, and He Who Speaks To Ghosts were contemporaries, warriors of the same age.

The two middle-age leaders of this, the Kutsueka band of the Comanche, had played together, as small boys. They together, had learned to ride, to shot arrows, to wield and to defend, against, hand-to-hand combat, utilizing the knife and the tomahawk.

The two friends, of more than four decades, had grown up together.

As young teen-age braves, Gray Wolf, and He Who Speaks To Ghosts, had both, within the passage of two moon cycles, journeyed to the distant, sacred twin-peaked mountains, where each, on separate pilgrimages, had experienced inspirational visits by the spirits…visions that had resulted in each young brave, obtaining his own personal medicine, his *"Puha."*

It was the belief and the custom of the *"People"*, that a young brave should not be elevated to the status of warrior, not be allowed to participate in the large, communal buffalo hunt; not be allowed to join raiding, or war parties, until he obtained ***"Puha"***.

His own personal medicine, often a talisman that possessed a supernatural, protective guiding force, that the young brave, had obtained through the guidance, usually in the form of a *"vision"*, revealed to the young man, after three or four days of ritualistic-fasting, by benevolent spirit(s), from the spirit world.

As youths Gray Wolf and He Who Speaks To Ghosts, had both, during the same moon-cycle, embarked upon their individual quest to obtain — from the spirit world — their own unique protective medicine, their ***"Puha"***.

The holy man's lifelong friend Gray Wolf was the father of Running Eagle, the young warrior, killed at the hands of his wife, Pretty Buffalo Hair, the black-Comanche woman, who had been possessed and directed to do so, by malicious, *"Evil spirits."*

He Who Speaks To Ghosts was anxious to inform his friend Gray Wolf, that at last, his adoptive daughter/daughter in-law, Pretty Buffalo Hair, the wife of Running Eagle, had completely escaped, the influence, the words of the *Evil demons* that had killed his son.

He Who Speaks To Ghosts hesitated, then he gently, but firmly wrapped on the entrance flap of Gray Wolf's lodge.

From deep within the lodge, He Who Speaks To Ghosts heard the familiar voice of his old friend: *"Enter."*

Gray Wolf was seated, smoking his after-dinner pipe, sipping water from a buffalo-paunch, one of the gifts from their animal-brother the buffalo, the vessel in which the *"People"* carried their drinking water.

As he stepped inside the lodge of Gray Wolf, his old friend warmly greeted the holy man: *"Ahh my friend "He Who Speaks To Ghosts", come in, come in. You are always welcome in the lodge of Gray Wolf."*

Gray Wolf turned his head and spoke to his wife; *"Little Flower, "please bring food and drink for our guest."*

He Who Speaks To Ghosts seated himself, next to his friend.

Little Flower returned. She was holding a bowl of venison stew in her left hand, and a buffalo-paunch filled with water, in her right.

When she extended the food, He Who Speaks To Ghosts' eyes fell upon her mutilated left hand. Little Flower was missing the index finger, and the middle finger of her left hand.

Among the "People", one of the most tragic events that could befall a family…a village was the unexpected death, especially during a time of peace, the death of a young hunter-warrior, in the prime of his life.

The extent of the mourning rituals that followed the unexpected death of a young male was felt not only by the family of the deceased, the tragedy was profoundly felt, by the entire village.

For the Comanche, the devastating effect of the loss of strong, young, warrior-hunters and protectors, threatened the very survival of the "People."

Five winters past, when her son Running Eagle was murdered, Little Flower had been devastated.

Little Flower's grief, her mourning was culminated on her part, by several acts of self-mutilation.

Little Flower caught in the throes of inconsolable grief, utilizing a knife used for butchering meat, had severed the middle and index fingers, from her left hand.

One finger was hacked-off to mourn the death of her son, Running Eagle; the second finger was for the loss of her adopted daughter/daughter-in-law, Pretty Buffalo Hair, whose mind had been loss, to the wicked, *Evil spirits*.

As He Who Speaks To Ghosts had explained to the band, and whose words Little Flower had readily accepted; *"Evil spirit-demons*, were responsible for the murder of Little Flower's son, Running Eagle.

Evil demons who had captured and taken control of the mind of Running Eagle's wife, Little Flower and Gray Wolf's adopted daughter, Pretty Buffalo Hair.

****

Chapter 73

Pretty Buffalo Hair – Mourns Running Eagle

The sounds of Pretty Buffalo Hair's piteous moans and wailings, faded, trailing in her wake, as she walked aimlessly, knife in hand, out onto the open-prairie.

With each step that she took, Pretty Buffalo Hair would slash her arms, her sides, and her breasts, with the knife. The vast majority of the multiple self-inflicted cuts were long, but superficial and shallow.

Pretty Buffalo Hair ceased her random meandering, and sat down beside a babbling brook, surrounded by a stand of Pecan Trees. The clear sparkling reservoir, served as the main source of water for the "People's" summer encampment.

The frequency and volume of her lamentations were gradually decreasing. Pretty Buffalo Hair absentmindedly, examined the multiple self-inflicted wounds that crisscrossed her body.

The bleeding from the superficial, shallow gashes, on her breasts and her flanks, were subsiding.

Bleary-eyed she could barely discern the outline of the "People", her people as they moved about in the village.

Pretty Buffalo Hair stared at—as if she were mesmerized—, at the bloody-butchering knife, that she held in her hand.

Slowly deliberately and methodically, she began to press the blade into the wrists of her left arm. A thin line of blood oozed from the wound.

Then, between heart-wrenching sobs, holding the knife with her left hand, she cut deeply into her right wrist. A bright red-stream of blood spurted from her wrist.

Pretty Buffalo Hair began to feel faint, light-headed. She glanced at her forearm and noticed that a long, deep gash, running from her elbow to her wrist, was gushing blood, in synchronized-rhythm, with the beating of her heart.

Weakly, in an instinctive act for self-preservation, Pretty Buffalo Hair attempted to stanch the pulsating loss of blood, spurting from her lacerated arm.

Pretty Buffalo Hair's vision was blurring, she was growing weaker and weaker.

With each beat of her broken-heart, blood gushed from the severed blood vessel in her right wrist, and began to pool in the fabric of her deerskin dress.

Realizing that she would not be able to stop the bleeding, Pretty Buffalo Hair became resigned, and calmly prepared herself to welcome death.

As she felt herself slowly drifting into the Shadow World, the land beyond father Sun, Pretty Buffalo Hair, who had chosen to live her life as a Comanche smiled, as she chose to end her life…to die a Comanche.

Pretty Buffalo Hair, growing weaker with each beat of her heart, *in her state of delirium, saw the sweet gentile face of her adoptive red-mother, Little Flower.*

Growing ever weaker, in a soft, muffled voice, *she began to chant, and then to sing, her death song:*

"Ta?ahpu tsahpunitu nuenapuu maai tu mukwo."

("*Great Spirit, show me the trail that leads to Running Eagle*").

Her eyelids were growing heavy. As Pretty Buffalo Hair began to drift toward unconsciousness, just as she was about to enter the "Spirit World", the image that had been with her, comforting her; the face of Little Flower, her red-mother, slowly blurred and morphed into the face of Ruth, her black-mother, Pretty Buffalo Hairs'… Mahn-dee's birth mother.

Pretty Buffalo Hair feebly, attempted to continue singing her death song.

Try as she would, her foggy brain would not give to her, the words, of her Comanche death song.

Inexplicably, as the light faded from her beautiful brown eyes, she instead, with her last breath, in a frail, weak trembling voice…she began to sing; to sing a song from her distant past, a song embedded in the deep recesses of her subconscious; a song from another life.

The last words that softly spewed forth from the lips of Pretty Buffalo Hair/Mandy Billings, were:

*"Swing low…sweet chariot
comin' fo to carry me home…*

*Swing low…sweet chariot
comin' fo to carry me home.*

****

Chapter 74

Lodge of Chief Old Wise One – May 1873

Old Wise One; He Who Speaks To Ghosts; **Chief** Thunder Cloud; and Gray Wolf, sat smoking and talking in the venerable, elderly chief's, lodge.

After Old Wise One's pipe had been passed and smoked by the four old friends, Old Wise One attempted to rise. The elderly chief's knees made a crackling sound, followed by the old man's groans, as he struggled to stand.

"My friends, it is time." As one, in unison, Old Wise One's three friends, looked quizzically, at their leader.

The Medicine Man, He Who Speaks To Ghosts, was the first to speak. "It is time? Of what do you speak, old friend?"

"I feel, and I accept the fact that my time…his eyes fell upon the face of Chief Thundercloud, that for some of us, our time has passed. And if we are to survive as a "People", it is time for our band to embrace new, young, leaders."

Chief Old Wise One's closest friends sat in silence. No one spoke. Instead they looked incredulously, as in disbelief, at one another.

The War Chief, Chief Thundercloud spoke. "Of what do you speak old friend? You are…"

Chief Old Wise One cut him off. "I am Old. The Great Spirit, in his wisdom, has with me, begun to hasten my inevitable journey, to join our ancestors in the Spirit World."

"Just as have my physical prowess…my strength, the clarity of my eyes has diminished over time, so too has the strength of my mind."

Gray Wolf opened his mouth to protest. Old Wise One lifted his hand. His hand began to tremble. Old Wise One sighed.

"As my hand trembles, as it shakes, as it is no longer steady, so too, has the quickness of my thoughts, the memory, and my judgment, has declined".

The lodge was silent.

Old Wise One picked up his pipe, inhaled and exhaled the pungent smoke. He passed the pipe to the Shaman, He Who Speaks To Ghosts.

After the pipe had once again, been passed among the four old friends, the band's War Chief, Thunder Cloud spoke; "I too have noticed that I, Thundercloud, War Chief of the Kutsueka Comanche, I am beginning to have difficulty keeping pace, with the stamina of our young warriors."

"For some time now, I have been preparing Stone Fist, to succeed me as War Chief."

Chief Thunder Cloud looked directly at Old Wise One; "Have you my chief, thought of, and prepared a worthy successor for yourself, our Headman?"

Old Wise One did not hesitate. "I have. I have for years been preparing my successor. A warrior of strong body and mind, a warrior who possesses, courage, wisdom, and sound judgment.   A warrior who can commune with the spirits, who can gain their assistance, as the "People" meet the ever-growing threat, of the encroachment of the white man."

Old Wise One held the Kutsueka Band's sacred ceremonial pipe in both of his hands. He thrust the pipe toward the man on his right, his trusted friend and spiritual advisor, the Shaman, He Who Speaks To Ghosts.

"I will recommend to the council, that He Who Speaks To Ghosts, be my successor."

****

Chapter 75

May 1876 – Chief He Who Speaks To Ghosts – Kutsueka-Comanche Encampment

At the first council, held in the lodge of the band's new headman, Chief He Who Speaks To Ghosts, the major topic of discussion, was that of the relentless proliferation, of the number of white settlers, invading the *Comancheria*.

Owl Face, a respected warrior, who had obtained many horses, and counted many coups, fighting the enemies of the Comanche, had recently returned from the northern reaches of the *Comancheria*.

Owl Face had been, for three moons, visiting his sister, who had married a member of the "People's *Yamparika* band.
Upon his return home, Owl Face had at first been surprised by, and then rejoiced and celebrated the news that his friend Stone Face, whom he had fought side by side with in many battles, now wore the eagle feathers of War Chief.

During his recent journey, covering hundreds of miles in their vast, formerly pristine, hunting grounds, Owl Face had been surprised, shocked, and dismayed by the number of whites who had invaded the homeland of the "*People*".

After he had exchanged pleasantries with his friend and comrade-in-arms, Stone Fist, Owl Face shared with Stone Fist, what he had observed during his recent journey to visit his sister, who now lives with her husband, in the Comanche *Yamparika* Village.

Stone Fist listened attentively, interrupting his friend, only to ask questions.

At Stone Fist's insistence, the two warriors together, went to visit the lodge of the Kutsueka band's Headman, Chief He Who Speaks To Ghosts.

After listening to Owl faces' narrative of the large number of whites into the land of the Comanche, the band's Headman, Chief He Who Speaks To Ghosts, had immediately called for a meeting of the Council.

The warriors in attendance at council were seated in two concentric semi-circles.

He Who Speaks To Ghosts, Stone Fist, Gray Wolf, Crooked Eye, and Thoughtful Man, occupied the inner circle.

Three feet behind, these tribal leaders, was the outer circle, which consisted of respected warriors who had, on many occasions, distinguished themselves in battle.

Seated on a plush buffalo robe, to the left, of the inner-circle was the band's former War Chief, Chief Thunder Cloud.

Following the ritual of each man in attendance, the smoking of "the-pipe", Chief He Who Speaks To Ghosts spoke; "After a journey of more than three moons to the north, through our hunting grounds, Owl Face has returned".

"He has told to me, and to Chief Stone Fist, of vast numbers of white invaders, brought into our land, by their "*Iron-Horse*", and the white-eyes desecration of our land".

There was a brief momentary, den of noise, as the assembled warriors conversed with each other.

He Who Speaks To Ghosts, raised his hand, the tepee became silent.

"Owl Face would now speak to the council".

"Chief He Who Speaks To Ghosts, these invaders are destroying our animal-brothers, the buffalo".

"The white invaders are shooting the buffalo, not to fed or to clothe their families, not to provide for their families shelter, they are shooting the buffalo for sport."

"The white hunters take from the slain buffalo, only the hides, the heads, and the tongues. They leave, to rot in the sun, the meat that would feed the *People*."

"In addition to the senseless killing of the buffalo for sport, the white-eyes, are driving the buffalo away by putting their cattle on the land, to graze and consume the sweet, long grass, that has forever, fed and fattened, the buffalo".

"The "*Iron-Horse*", brings many white hunters, many soldiers, and many farmers, to our lands."

"Our land is becoming ugly, scarred, by the *"Iron-Roads"* that the whites continue to build, and the endless long poles that hold the *"talking wires"*, that stretches beyond the sight of the eagle."

Owl Face sat.

Once again, the warriors began to, among themselves, share their thoughts, to exchange opinions, in response to Owl Face's words.

Buffalo Hump, a middle-age warrior, stood. Chief He Who Speaks To Ghosts, raised his hand. Almost immediately, the tepee was silent.

He Who Speaks To Ghosts' eyes met those of the veteran warrior. "Buffalo Hump would speak?"

"My chief, the words of Owl Face, tell of the white man's presence in the land of the Comanche. This is something that has been known to us for many summers."

There was a buzz of conversation, accompanied by the nodding of several heads, attesting to the veracity of Buffalo Hump's statement. He Who Speaks To Ghosts raised his hand. The murmuring chatter ceased. The tepee was once again silent.

Buffalo Hump, instead of sitting, had remained standing. He Who Speaks To Ghosts spoke; "Buffalo Hump, do you have more to speak?"

"Yes, my chief. I, as most of the warriors here, have heard tales of the *"Iron-Horse"*. "A few of us have either seen, or have had told to us, by distant family or visitors, the power of the *Iron-Horse*."

"To hear that this *"Iron-Horse"*, this beast is now in the land of the Comanche, a mere moon's ride from our encampment, is a threat that must be confronted and destroyed."

Buffalo Hump sat.

Gray Wolf, seated next to his friend—now his friend and his chief—, He Who Speaks To Ghosts, touched the buckskin sleeve of the chief's shirt.

He Who Speaks To Ghosts, looked quizzically at his friend, Gray Wolf, then the chief nodded his head.

 He Who Speaks To Ghosts stood. Once again, the tepee became quiet.
"Gray Wolf would speak."

"I too as is Owl Face, as is Buffalo Hump, as are all seated at this council, I too am alarmed by the presence of the *"Iron-Horse"*, in the land of the Comanche."

"The question that must be answered by this council—Gray Wolf looked directly at the young War Chief, Stone Fist—, is how do we kill, destroy, this monster, the *"Iron-Horse"*?"

Once again, the tepee resonated, with the voices of the agitated warriors.

Chief Stone Fist rose.

The War Chief stood, his obsidian-colored, black eyes, fell in-turn for a brief second, on each of the assembled warriors.

Although Chief He Who Speaks To Ghosts, had not lifted a finger; when the young War Chief stood, the tepee had immediately become silent.

"The path we must take is clear. We are Comanche! There is no question as to what we must do. We, as did our fathers, as did their fathers, fathers' fathers…we must fight for our hunting grounds".

"Our path must be the path of war. Our warriors must take to the "War-Path"."

The tepee erupted. Silence was replaced by a cacophony of the sound as the warriors, en masse, in unison, screamed the ancient war chant of the Comanche. ***"Aahe-hey! Aahe-hey!   Aahe-hey!   Aahe-hey!"***

Chief Stone Fist stood tall, stoic, silent, his arms folded across his chest, as the blood-curdling war cry of the *Nermernuh*, spewed forth from the throats of the warriors, the war chant filling every inch of space in the tepee, then rising and escaping through the tepee's smoke-hole. Bursting forth over the plains…interrupting the still, sultry air.

"Aahe-hey! Aahe-hey! Aahe-hey! Aahe-hey!" "Aahe-hey!

****

After a full five minutes, when the noise finally began to subside, Stone Fist raised his hand.

All noise in the tepee was abruptly silenced. In a low, authoritative, commanding voice, the young War Chief spoke; "Owl Face?"

The young warrior, Owl Face stood.

"Is it not true that the "*Iron-Horse*", as formidable as it seems to be, is completely dependant for its movement, upon having an "*Iron-road*", on which to travel?"

Owl Face nodded. "That is true. In my journey, the "*Iron-Horse*" was always sitting on, or in motion on, the "*Iron-Road*".

For a brief moment, Stone Fist appeared to be lost in thought.

The assembled warriors sat silently, waiting to hear his thoughts… the battle-plan, of their War Chief.

"How does this "*Iron-Road*", needed by the "*Iron-Horse*", come to be?"

Without hesitation, Owl Face answered; "My chief, little yellow men with slanted-eyes, short men, like the Mexicans, little yellow men, wearing on their heads, hats that look like inverted bowls... it is these yellow men, with axes, shovels and hammers, these are the men who make the "*Iron-Road*".

Gray Wolf spoke; "Tell us more, of these little yellow men. Are these slant-eyed men, warriors? Other than their tools, do they have weapons? Do the little yellow men with slanted-eyes, men, have long-fire sticks?"

Owl Face raised both of his hands, spreading his fingers. "The number of yellow men that I saw building the "*Iron-Road*", was as many as the fingers of my hands."

"The yellow men had only tools. Standing apart from the slant-eyed yellow men, were two white men. The two white men had long fire sticks."

"Around the white men's' waists, were the short hand-held, fire sticks."

"The white men were sitting, watching the yellow men, build the "*Iron-Road*".

A weak, trembling voice, from the left, of the inner-circle of tribal leaders, was heard. "My chief...I would speak"

The eyes of all of the warriors at council, almost as one, were focused on one of the Kutsueka's, most respected, venerable, leaders, Old Wise One.

With the aide of a sturdy tree branch, Old Wise One struggled to his feet.

He Who Speaks To Ghosts, friend and confidant of Old Wise One, and the man who had replaced him as the band's Headman, stood. "The council will hear the words of Old Wise One."

In deference to the old warrior, the former Headman who had led the band for more than three decades, both He Who Speaks To Ghosts, the band's new Headman, and Stone Fist, the new War Chief, sat.

All eyes were on the aged warrior, Old Wise One.

Old Wise One stood, bent-at-the waist. The knurled knuckles, of both of his arthritic hands, were curled around the walking stick that helped to support his weight.

His voice was weak, yet it seemed to strengthen, as his words resonated among the warriors, who set in complete silence, listening to the words of their former Headman.

"The appearance of the white man into our land is not new."

"My father, his father, and his father's, father, told of the coming of the white men. First were the helmeted white-soldiers, from Mexico, then the Texican-Tejanos came, now the hoards of white settlers, men women and children, protected by the blue-coat soldiers."

"The first of the white men said that they had come to trade. They claimed to have come in peace".

The white men brought many things. Things that are now familiar to us, that was at that time, unknown, to the "*People*".

"They brought to us metal pots, filled with beads. Our women now cook our food, in the metal pots, and are pleased the shiny beads. They brought the fire-sticks."

"The white men claimed to have come in peace, wishing only to trade, and to live in peace among us."

"It was because their metal pots helped our women; because their metal made the tips of our arrows stronger, and more effective; because their fire-sticks, helped our braves, hunt the buffalo; and because their number was barely noticeable in the vast lands of the Comanche, it is for those reasons that the "*People*", allowed the white man to come into our land."

The aged chief slowly removed his left hand from his walking stick. He raised his hand into the air, and spread his fingers.

"For these many summers, the number of fingers on my hand, when the white soldiers, the gray-coats, and the blue-coats, were at war, fighting each other, the number of whites in the land of the Comanche, had been as few, as there are trees on the prairie."

"Now that the big war between the white men, the gray-coats, and the blue-coats has ended, the white men have come into our hunting-grounds, like locust, during a time of plague."

"It seems that in addition to the "*Iron-Horse*" bringing these invaders into our land, the "*Iron-Horse*", and the "*Talking Wires*", seem to be needed, by the white settlers, for the survival of their villages."

"I have lived to see many winters. When I was a boy, I remember the people's joy upon hearing the deafening sound, of the herds of buffalo moving as one animal, covering the ground. The joyous sound of, as many buffalo moving on the prairie, as there are stars moving in the skies."

Before the white man came into the land of the Comanche, the wind blew free, the grass grew long and sweet, fattening the buffalo, that feed our women and children".

"At first I, —as did many of the "People" —, I did not oppose the presence of a few of the white men, those who traded, in the land of the Comanche."

"Now the white-hunters with their long, heavy, fire sticks…fire sticks, that sit on forked-sticks, these long, heavy, fire sticks that flash from a long distance, unheard by the buffalo, moments before the buffalo drops, are killing-off the herds."

"It is the "*Iron-Horse*" that bring these white men, in numbers too many to count, into the hunting grounds of the Comanche."

It is the "*Iron-Horse*" that brings the white settlers, with their plows that dig up the prairie; it the "*Iron-Horse*" that bring their cattle, and their sheep that eat the grass to the ground, leaving nothing for the buffalo; it is the "*Iron Horse*" that brings the Iron Guns on wheels, that spit forth the huge iron balls, that collapse our lodges.

"Now as our women and children hold their empty bellies, crying from hunger, as the women's babies suckle in vain at dry breasts. Dry breasts that shrivel and sag".

"Breasts that are dry because the hungry bodies of our women, our baby's mothers, can no longer make milk. This tells me that if we are to survive, we must drive the white man from our lands."

"It is now my belief that the white-man intends to take for themselves, the land of the Comanche. They must be stopped!"

"If we do not destroy the "*Iron-Horse*" that brings them, the white settlers will come in numbers that will overwhelm the red-man. They will take from us, the ancient land of the Comanche."

"We must destroy the "*Iron-Horse*", kill the men who build and protect, the "*Iron-Road*". "We must fight to survive."

Old Wise one sat.

****

Chapter 76

Silent Stalker

As a boy of ten summers, the boy then called *"Under-foot"* had been regarded by most in the encampment, as being a general pest.

His natural curiosity, and his penchant to somehow, blend-in, to infiltrate groups, and not be noticed, contributed to his being referred to as a child, as being always *"Under-foot"*.

The name "Under-foot", had been given to the boy, by his father Bear Claw.

Under-foot, as did all of the pre-pubescent Comanche boys, learned to hunt at an early age. His skills as a tracker, and his ability to approach game without being detected, set Under-foot apart from his contemporaries.

It was the custom, the tradition of the *"People"*, that a young man — prior his being elevated, being accepted, into the warrior society — that he should seek his medicine, by going forth cleansing himself, his body and mind, by fasting, and communicating with the spirit world, to experience a vision from a benevolent spirit.

The vision that he sought, would he hoped, bridge his communication with the spirit world. Under-foot was confident that a vision, sent to him by the spirit world, would lead him to acquire his ***"puha"***, his own unique medicine.

It was the *"People's"* belief that a warrior's personal medicine, would bestow upon him, protection, power, and wisdom.

This communion with the spirits, this ancient ritual, was a rite of passage into manhood, for the sons of the *"People"*.

Shortly following the passage of his fifteenth summer, as was the expectation for all of the sons of the *"People"*, Under-foot, on the threshold of manhood, made his obligatory, solitary pilgrimage, to commune with the spirits, in pursuit of his protective, medicine.

After his fourth night of fasting, without food and only cursory sips of water, after smoking his pipe packed with sumac leaves, Under-foot drifted off into an exhausted, restless, sleep.

His mind adrift in the spirit-world, Under-foot gazed down upon the flat, treeless, endless, prairie. A lone buffalo cow was grazing on the long stalks of lush, green, grass that carpeted the floor of the valley.

The tall grass was swaying in the wind. Down-wind, a mere fifteen feet from the buffalo, was a predator, a puma, his right leg lifted, frozen in time, when the buffalo cow lifted her head. When the cow lowered her head and resumed grazing, the puma bolted forward.

The predator sank his spear-like powerful fangs into the throat of the buffalo cow, as she wildly thrashed, before suffocating.

Under-foot, in his food deprived dream state of delirium, watched as the puma, with teeth and claws, ripped open the throat of the buffalo cow, and began to feed.

Suddenly, as if being disturbed by a sound, the puma's lifted his head.

Under-foot shuddered. He shook his head. The face of the Puma was his face. Not the face of the boy, Under-foot, but was his face to be…the mature face…the face of a Comanche Warrior, the face of *Silent Stalker*.

****

Chapter 77

Missouri, Kansas & Texas RR -
Line Camp - June 1873

The young warrior, Silent Stalker, had been honored when Chief Stone Fist had picked him, as one of the forty warriors to join the war party that would destroy the white man's "Iron-Road".

This would be the young warrior's third chance to prove himself in battle, to gain honors, fighting the enemies of the *"People"*.

His two earlier forays, facing an enemy of the *"People"*, had been raids into Mexico to steal horses and women.

Although he had acquitted himself well—he had twice, counted coup and had been awarded four stolen horses, actually three horses and one burro—, still Silent Stalker had not yet loosed an arrow, swung his war-club, or fired his rifle, at the enemies of the *"People"*.

Silent Stalker's two previous raids had been led by Swift Arrow, an experienced leader, known for his skill and accuracy, with the longbow.

When the mighty Stone Fist, War Chief of the Kutsueka Comanche, had asked him to join on this raid, this raid to destroy the white man's Iron Horse, to destroy the "talking-wires", and the Iron Road, Silent Stalker had been overwhelmed with pride.

Silent Stalker had acquired his name, shortly after he had been visited by a "vision", from the Spirit World. A vision that had identified the powerful, stealthy, big cat, the Puma, as being the young brave's guide, his animal protector.

The young warrior, Silent Stalker, lay prone, on his stomach; hidden, surrounded, by a sea of six-foot-high grass stalks, fifty yards from the bustling activity of the men lying track, for the Missouri, Kansas & Texas Rail Road.

The sun was at its zenith, directly overhead, in the South Western Sky.

The white man who was seated on one of two barrels, the barrel furthest from Silent Stalker, reached for, and looked down at his pocket watch.

He lightly tapped the barrel of his rifle, against the arm of his companion. "High noon, Luther. Time to feed the Chinks."

Silent Stalker watched as the man that he had heard being called Luther, place the thumb and forefinger of his right hand into his mouth, and blow.

A shrill, high-pitched sound filled the air.

As the white man was placing his pocket watch back into his pants, Silent Stalker's attention was diverted.

Silent Stalker's eyes immediately shifted from the white man, to the group of ten-chinamen who had been, since the sun had first made its appearance, in the eastern sky, working, steadily, diligently, nonstop, building the Iron Road, as the ten men in unison, together as one, dropped their tools.

As Owl Face had relayed when he spoke at council, the two white men, the men in charge, the two white men, who had been slouching, half asleep in the shade afforded by a makeshift lean-to, these two-armed white men, had stopped the work, of the ten, slant-eyed, little yellow men.

Two small, slant-eyed yellow men, who had been cooking food behind the makeshift lean-to, were approaching their ten-fellow yellow, tribesmen.

Silent Stalker admonished himself. During his reconnaissance of the work-site, he had not seen the two yellow men, who had appeared as if by magic, from behind the lean-to.

His missing those men, his failure to not report their presence to Chief Stone Fist, could have led to the injury, or even to the death of Comanche warriors.

Silent Stalker noticed, that while both of the men, where short, the yellow, slanted eyed, man in the rear was noticeably shorter, than the man that he was following.

Additionally, the long-braided hair, the plait that protruded from beneath the straw hats of the eleven other yellow, slanted eyed men, was for the man in the rear, missing.

The man in the rear, the shorter of the two men, was walking by taking a series of small steps.

Silent Stalker's thoughts were that the man appeared to be "prancing".

The lower half of the man's body was rigid, while his strides caused a swaying movement of his hips.

Both men wore around their necks, a wooden-collar that resembled the yoke that the white settlers placed around the necks of the hairless buffalo that they used to pull their wagons.

Two poles, equidistance from the center of the wooden-collar, that cradled the men's neck, protruded from the yoke; one pole on the left, the other on the right. From each pole was suspended a keg, which was filled with water.

Silent Stalker stared at the little man bringing up the rear. Something was strange. The little man in the rear's strides was noticeably, different from those of his tribesmen.

Instead of his not taking normal strides and despite, the obvious weight of his burden, the slant-eyed, little yellow man bringing up the rear, appeared to be taking half steps, three steps, to each step, of his companion.

Though obviously laboring under the weight of the barrels suspended on the poles, each step that the shorter man took, had a distinctly, dainty, feminine quality.

A sudden gust of wind caused the hat of man in the rear, to fly off of his head. A rope attached to the hat, tied under the man's chin, prevented the hat from falling to the ground.

Instead, the hat came to rest on the man's back, centered on a nest of long black, straight hair.

Silent Stalker was momentarily stunned, astonished, surprised. He forced his eyes to reexamine, and to reassess his earlier observation.

The woman's long, lustrous, beautiful, raven colored, straight black, hair which had been tucked under her hat, cascaded down her back to her hips, glistening in the noonday sun.

He rapidly concluded that, what he had thought to be a very short slant-eyed-yellow man, was not a man. He…she, was unmistakably, a beautiful, slant-eyed-yellow, woman.

****

Chapter 78

Foshan-China 1860

In 1860, after the death of his wife, *Mai-Ling's* mother, *Zeng-Zhong*, *Mai-Ling's* father, made the decision to leave their home, to leave his village in Foshan-China.

Zeng-Zhong left his three-year-old daughter with her aunt, his sister, when he, as did most of the Chinese who immigrated to America, left their homes and families, because of economic and political unrest in China.

Zeng-Zhong's plan was to work hard, to make lots of money in America, then as a wealthy man, return to his family, his village, in China.

One of the reasons that had contributed to *Zeng-Zhong's* decision to immigrate to America, had been his frustration in China, to accumulate sufficient funds necessary to fulfil his late wife's, wish to have their young daughter's feet, bound.

Zeng-Zhong's inability to enhance *Mai-Ling's* beauty, by transforming her pedestrian feet, into exotic "*Lotus*" feet, an obligation, which would thereby dramatically, enhance, and improve her opportunity, to later in life, marry-well, was an important reason for his having left China.

Zeng-Zhong, spent most of his life's-savings, booking steerage passage on a merchant ship which set sail from the Chinese port of Macau.

Unfortunately, contrary to what he had been led to believe, there was no "Golden Mountain", in America.

Gold nuggets were not everywhere, lying on the ground in the country's hills and streams. Gold nuggets were not, as *Zeng-Zhong* had been told, as plentiful as were, the grains of sand on a beach.

Chapter 79

Union Pacific RR Line Camp

In the summer of 1863 *Zeng-Zhong*, after two years, working as a cook in a Chinese take-out, was hired by the Union Pacific Rail Road, and assigned as a laborer, to a "gang" of Chinese railroad workers.

As a laborer, Zeng-Zhong was paid $31 dollars per month; he as was all of the chinamen, was responsible for paying for their own board and meals.

White men, mainly Irish and German, were being paid $30 dollars per month. However, the Central Pacific Rail Road provided at no cost to the white laborers, "Free" room and board.

Initially his work was that of a laborer. Clearing land, hauling away debris, and any menial task assigned by the foreman.

After three weeks of the same, monotonous, menial labor, Zeng-Zhong's fortune changed.

Zeng-Zhong had been randomly picked, to assist one of the blacksmiths who supported, the work of the men laying the tracks.

Ling's work consisted primarily, of manning the bellows, keeping the "forge-hot", by feeding oxygen to the never flagging flames.

That morning just before the noon meal, Terrance Flaherty, the work-gang's Irish "smithy", in the midst of performing his daily functions of repairing tools, shoeing horses and mules, let out a series of groans and suddenly doubled over, clutching his stomach.

Gritting his teeth, Terrance moaned; "Dammit ta hell, I knew I shouldn't have eaten that piece of smelly beef, last night".

Flaherty was experiencing, a severe case of dysentery.

With *Zeng-Zhong's* assistance, the two men just barely managed to get to the open prairie, before the smithy loss control of his anal sphincter, dousing his pants and the plains, with a copious amount of watery, "human-fertilizer".

The smithy doubled over and groaning and moaning, muttered; "*Aww shit*".

Zeng-Zhong, who had barely managed to avoid being doused, went over to the distressed, completely soiled, blacksmith.

Zeng-Zhong extended a handkerchief to the blacksmith. He smiled and in that melodious monotone, pidgin-English, that the Chinese used, spoke; *"Loo rittee Missa Smitty...plenty, plenty... aww shitty."*

The blacksmith ignored the handkerchief, in Zeng-Zhong's extended hand.

"Damn, I've gotta go wash-up and change these clothes. So far, I got three horses needing to be shod. And that busted wagon wheel, needs a new rim."

"The boss is gonna be fit-to-be- tied. That crazy "Mick", is gonna have my ass."

Zeng-Zhong, smiled; *"No woorly Missa Smitty...I plentee fixee."*

In less than an hour, the Irish immigrant blacksmith, returned. Terrance Flaherty knew that he was "under-the-gun".

Terrance as did everyone involved with the laying of the railroad tracks, knew that time was of the essence.

In fact, the entire country was aware of the competition between the Central Pacific Rail Road, whose route called for the laying of tracks leading eastward, originating from Sacramento California; and the Union Pacific Rail Road, whose laying of tracks leading westward, originated at Council bluffs, near Omaha Nebraska.

Both railroads, the Central Pacific and the Union Pacific, were given extensive land grants, by the government, to aid them in their race to be the first, to reach the hundredth meridian, at Promontory Summit, in the Utah Territory.

Terrance Flaherty's employer, the Central Pacific Rail Road, was racing to be the first Rail Road, to reach the two Rail Road's mutual objective, the link-up at Promontory Summit.

Thus, linking the nation by rail, from the Atlantic, to the Pacific, through the completion of the first, Transcontinental Rail Road.

When Terrance returned to the blacksmith shop, he was surprised, a bit stunned, to see that both of the unshod horses, had been shod and that the broken wagon wheel, had been repaired.

He heard the familiar sound of a hammer, pounding steel, on an anvil.

In the center of the shop, the Chinese laborer was holding with metal tongs, a red-hot, horseshoe, which he was about to dip, into a barrel of water.

When the Chinaman saw Terrance, he lifted the horseshoe from the water barrel, placed it on the anvil and bowed; *"Loo back...back. Soo solly"*.

Ling left the horseshoe on the anvil, and retrieved his broom. *"Want-chee me, back to work...chop, chop."*

Once it became known to the supervising foreman, that Zeng-Zhong was a skilled metallurgist, Zeng-Zhong, became permanently assigned, as a working-foreman, working and directing the work, in one of the construction crew's, three mobile-blacksmith shops.

Zeng-Zhong wages were increased. As a laborer he had been paid $30 dollars per month. Now in his position as a Foreman/Laborer, he was being paid $50 dollars per month, plus room and board.

The death of Zeng-Zhong's sister, coupled with his significant raise in pay, made it possible for Zeng-Zhong to bring his daughter Mai-Ling, to America and to fulfill his wife's wish, to have the feet of his daughter bound.

Creating for his daughter, the distinctive mark of beauty and femininity, the "*Lotus-Foot*".

****

Chapter 80

Kutsueka-Comanche Raiding Party Ten Miles South of MK&T-RR Line -Camp   June 1873

Silent Stalker returned to the main body of the war party, being led by Chief Stone Fist, which was camped, ten miles from the site of the railroad construction.

He leapt from the back of his pony and sought out the war-chief.

Chief Stone Fist sat smoking and talking with his friend Crooked Arrow, with a formidable warrior known as Bear Claw, and with Silent Stalker's father, Buffalo Hump.

Crooked Arrow, Buffalo Hump, and Bear Claw were Chief Stone Fist's most trusted warriors.

"Bear Claw turned his head; "Ah my son you have returned."

Crooked Arrow handed the out-of-breath young warrior, a strip of dried pemmican.

Buffalo Hump handed Silent Stalker, a waterproof-pouch that was filled with luke-warm water.

Chief Stone Fist sat on the ground, waiting patiently, to hear the details of the young warrior's findings.

After quenching his thirst with two sips of water, Silent Stalker spoke; "My chief, it is as Owl Face described."

"Last night during a half moon, after a two hours ride, I saw the camp of the men building the "Iron-Road".

I tied my pony to a scraggly bush, up-wind from their camp, and crept in the tall grass, to within ten strides of a white man sitting, half asleep, on a barrel.

The white man's long gun was at his side, leaning against the barrel, on which he sat."

"The edges of the grass that surrounded the clearing, was scorched. The builders of the Iron Road, had removed the prairie's tall grass, by fire."

"Sitting atop the arms of the Iron-Road, was a wagon with iron wheels, which was piled high with many unattached short and long, straight and curved, iron-arms, the tentacles of the Iron Road."

"The camp was quiet. There were but two tents. The sounds coming from one tent were the sleep-sounds, made by many men. The sounds from the other tent were the night sounds of sleep, made by one man."

"I crept back into the tall grass, and lay hidden from view, awaiting the rise of father sun."

Silent Stalker continued to recount what he had observed at the Railroad's Line-Camp.

Chief Stone Fist interrupted, only once, when he asked for clarification, further details about the small, slant-eyed, yellow men.

"Of these slant-eyed yellow men, and the yellow woman, tell us more. Are they warriors? Would you Silent Stalker, when we strike, would you consider the yellow men who build the Iron-Road, a threat to our attacking warriors?"

"The men, as do Comanche men, have hairless faces. While they are small like the Mexicans, their labor is efficient."

"The small slant-eyed yellow men work fast and well together. The only weapons that they appear to have are their small hands and the tools they use to build the Iron Road."

"While the yellow men's efficiency at work, speaks of team-work and discipline, there is no way of knowing if when attacked, if they would fight as a team."

Chief Stone Fist grunted. He looked to the faces of his three, most trusted warriors. No one responded. No one offered an opinion.

Once again, the War Chief grunted.

"It is time to plan the attack. Stay Silent Stalker. Listen to our talk. If you feel that our plan has faults, let us know. Among us, only you have seen the place where the Iron Road is built."

Silent Stalker, caught a glimpse of a smile of pride, on his father's face, as Chief Stone Fist, Buffalo Hump, Crooked Arrow, and his father, Bear Claw, began to plan the attack, the attack that would lead, to the beginning of the destruction of the *Iron Horse*, by destroying the *Iron-Road*, on which the *"Horse-of-Iron"*, travels.

After consulting with his three most trusted warriors, Chief Stone Fist decided upon his war plan.

"We will attack the builders of the Iron Road shortly after the sun is at its highest, and hottest spot in the sky. We will attack while the slant-eyed yellow men's muscles are tired from working, and while their bellies are full, from eating."

"Buffalo Hump, with four warriors, before we attack are to ride out, east and north, as scouts, to warn us, in the event of the coming, of soldiers."

"One mile before the work camp, we will dismount and leave our ponies. The ponies will be watched by six warriors."

"We will approach the camp on foot. We will be hidden by the prairie's tall grass, which surrounds the work camp. Our movement through the grass is to be as quiet as are the movements, of Silent Stalker."

"Crooked Arrow, with ten warriors, will kill all the white men. Today Silent Stalker saw two white men with long guns. Tomorrow, there could be more."

"With fifteen warriors, Bear Claw will kill the slant-eyed, yellow men."

"Silent Stalker, you are to take as slave, the slant-eyed, yellow woman, who wears the cloths of a man."

"Before we attack, Buffalo Hump with five warriors, will cut the talking wires, preventing the camp from calling for help."

****

E. Pluribus Unum

Chapter 81

MK&T RR - Line Camp June 1873

The Chinese laborer's mid-day meal, had consisted of dried oysters, sweet rice, crackers, dried bamboo, and salted cabbage.

Their nutritious meal had been augmented with, copious amounts of hot tea.

The Chinese laborers had consumed their meal, bunched together, seated at the work-site, on barrels filled with rail spikes and ties.

The two white men, Luther and Jethro, sat apart at the lean-to, next to the supply wagon.

Luther and Jethro were busy, mopping up from the edges of their tin-plates, what remained of their meal of beef, beans, bread, and potatoes.

The white men had washed down their meal, with liquid from two canteens. One canteen was filled with water; the other canteen was filled with cheap "rot-gut whiskey".

Unexpectedly, the chatter and banter from the men…the Chinese laborers and their white foremen, was interrupted by the sound of the heart stopping, blood-curdling war cry of the Comanche.

For a moment, the men, white and yellow, did not move. They stood in place, frozen, as two groups of Comanche warriors, one group lead by Crooked Arrow, the other by Bear Claw, burst forth from the tall grass, descending upon the two groups of railroad workers.

Luther was the first man to react. In a state of panic, Luther picked up his Henry rifle and aiming in the direction of the surging wave of warriors charging toward him, fired the round that he normally kept, chambered in his rifle.

Just prior to Luther pulling the trigger of his rifle, Crooked Arrow had loosed an arrow, an arrow aimed at the throat, of the panic-stricken white man.

The arrow bored into Luther's throat a fraction of a second, before his finger compulsively, squeezed the trigger of his rifle.

Luther's bullet grazed Crooked Arrow's left temple.

Luther was frantically attempting to lever a round into the chamber of his rifle, when Crooked Arrow, ignoring the superficial wound to his head, struck Luther, with his war club struck.

The force of the blow, caused Luther's skull to explode, to split open, spewing forth gray matter, like the fruit of a crushed, ripe, melon.

Jethro, with three arrows protruding from his chest, slumped to his knees onto the ground.

As he began to pitch forward in death, his momentum was abruptly halted, as the strong left hand of Stone Fist, became entwined in Jethro's long, dirty, blonde, hair, effectively stopping the mortally wounded, white man's descent.

With two quick swipes of his hunting knife, Stone Fist expertly, separated Jethro's bloody scalp, from his lifeless body.

As a unit, the unarmed slant-eyed yellow men, began to run toward the area where they had dropped their tools.

The eleven Comanche warriors, led by Crooked Arrow, overtook the fleeing railroad workers, as they were frantically, reaching for their tools.

With lethal precision, the warriors bludgeoned, stabbed, and hacked to death, eight members of the Chinese work-crew.

One of the slant-eyed men somehow, paradoxically the oldest of the workmen, eluded the charging warriors, and managed to grab a pickaxe which had been propped-up against one of the supply barrels.

Crooked Arrow swung his war club at the man's head. The slant-eyed, man raised the axe, shielding his face, and with the head of the pickaxe, successfully parried Crooked Arrow's blow.

The sound made, when the head of Crooked Arrow's stone war club, collided with the steel blade of the pickaxe, was heard above the war whoops of the Comanche warriors.

The little yellow man's, unexpected, unanticipated, parry, halted the deliverance of the intended deathblow, by Crooked Arrow's war-club.

The clashing of stone on metal caused the handle of Crooked Arrow's war-club, to vibrate in his hands.

Crooked Arrow was re-gripping his hold on his war club, when the little yellow man swung the pickaxe, burying half of the blade in Crooked Arrow's chest.

As the Chinese man frantically attempted to free the blade of the pickaxe from the red man's chest, the little yellow man's body was riddled with a volley of eight arrows, one in his throat, three in his chest, and four in his thighs.

The Chinese man died instantly. Collapsing, facedown, onto Crooked Arrow's body.

As the light was fading from the eyes of Crooked Arrow, the last sounds that he would ever hear were the plaintiff cries, the screams, of a women's voice; *"父亲帮助我"- "fù qīn bāng zhù wǒ" ("Father help me"!)*

When the Comanche warriors initiated their attack, Silent Stalker, as Chief Stone Fist had instructed, had immediately sought out, and located the slant-eyed, yellow woman.

Mai-Ling, the fourteen-year-old daughter of the Chinese foreman of the work crew, had been *busy working, behind the lean-to,* filling the workers' cups with hot tea, when she was startled by a high-pitched, *horrific* sound.

Her body went numb with terror, when the oppressive hot air, was shattered by the most chilling, terrifying, frightening sound, that she had ever heard, the battle cry of the Comanche.

As she was about to run to her father, her path was blocked by an aberration.

A wild man with two eagle feathers in his hair, stood before her.

His face was streaked with paint. One side of the demon's face was streaked with black paint; the other side was painted a vermilion-red.

Mai-Ling turned and with short, mincing, steps, attempted to run.

Silent Stalker hesitated. Instead of her running, the beautiful slant-eyed, woman's gait, to Silent Stalker, resembled that of a frightened, crippled animal, frantically trying to escape.

In two swift strides, Silent Stalker caught the hobbling woman. When he grabbed her by her arm, she screamed, *"父亲帮助我"- **"fù qīn bāng zhù wǒ" (Father help me!)**.*

Chief Stone Fist removed the pickaxe from the chest of his life-long friend, and confidant, Crooked Arrow.

With the tool in his strong hands—the pickaxe covered with the blood of Crooked Arrow—, Stone Fist walked over to the end of the Rail Road tracks, and ferociously began to swing the pickaxe.

No one dared speak, of the solitary tear that ran down the War Chief's cheeks, as he gave vent to his grief, the lose of his life-long friend, by savagely, digging, dislodging, and removing, the spikes that anchored the "*Iron Road*" to the ground.

****

Chapter 82

Kutsueka-Comanche Encampment- June 1873

News of the war party's return had been given to the village earlier, by two of the eight young boys who constantly tended the band's huge herd of ponies.

As the war party neared the village, one of the young boys that had been watching the pony herd rode ahead and alerted the village of the group's arrival.

The thirty-nine returning warriors of Chief Stone Fist's war party, whose faces now wore only the black paint of mourning, rode solemnly, into the village.

The inhabitants of the encampment, had been alerted to the fact, that the pony of one of the returning members of the expedition, had laid across its' back, the body of a fallen warrior.

The identity of the slain warrior, had not been given to the young boy who had earlier alerted the village, to the pending arrival of the war party.

Chief, He Who Speaks To Ghosts, and Old Wise One, stood at the head of the main path of the village.

Standing with the two chiefs were Gray Wolf and most of the members of the council.

When Fragrant Breeze, Crooked Arrow's wife, saw a body, wrapped in her husband's favorite blanket, draped across Crooked Arrow's war pony, a chorus of loud, piteous, mournful wails sprang from the very depths, of her being.

Fragrant Breeze's voice cracked as she began to spontaneously, shriek, and moan.

Swift Feet, the fifteen winters son of Crooked Arrow, and "Morning Dove", his daughter of eleven winters, attempted to comfort their mother.

Fragrant Breeze reached around her son's waist, and pulled Swift Feet's hunting knife, from its' sheath.

While continuing to shriek and moan, Fragrant Breeze, began to inflect a series of knife-cuts on her arms and legs.

Neither of her children, nor did any of the people, attempt to restrain the inconsolable, widow.

As the grieving woman continued to ritualistically cut her flesh, while shrieking and moaning, her arms and legs were becoming covered with her blood.

As she moved the knife toward two prominent blood vessels, that were visible in the croak of her left arm, the strong fingers of the Shaman, He Who Speaks To Ghosts, gently but firmly, took the knife from the hand of the grieving widow.

Chief Stone Fist was in front, leading the procession of warriors. Stone Fist held the reins of his pony in his left hand, and the reins of a large saddled, chestnut-mare on which sat a delicate, dainty, yellow-skinned, female.

Little Flower, the mother of Chief Stone Fist's wife, and the grandmother of Stone Fist's grandchildren, was standing beside her husband, the venerated warrior, Gray Wolf.

The young War Chief's return from battle, reminded Little Flower of a similar time, many winters past, when Stone Fist, and his best friend, her son Running Eagle, along with Crooked Arrow, had similarly, returned to their camp, bringing with them, the captive black girl, and her white sister.

Little Flower, shivered. The similarity between that time and now, was uncanny.

Little Flower's faltering eyes, studied the face of the female captive riding astride the horse, being led by Chief Stone Fist.

The girl's skin was neither red, white, nor was she black. Her complexion appeared to be yellow, the color of the kernels of ripe maze.

The yellow-skinned female's eyes were slanted. Curiously her eyes were of the same shape, as were the eyes of the People's, newborn infants.

For a brief moment, Little Flower wondered why was the female captive riding? Why, instead of being forced to walk, tethered to a rope, was she mounted?

Her inspection of the girl stopped, when she noticed the yellow-girl's feet.

The yellow-girl's feet were extremely small. Not at all the length, or the width, that one would expect that the "Great Spirit", would bestow on a nearly full-grown woman.

Was this slant-eyed, yellow-girl, a chosen-one? One whom the Great Spirit had selected as "Special"?

The answer to Little Flower's unspoken questions became apparent, when Stone Fist dismounted, and then pulled the girl from the saddled chestnut-mare. The yellow-skinned girl lay stunned on the ground, at the feet of the War Chief.

Mai-Ling was left alone, sitting, weeping, in the dirt.

After the warriors, their families, and friends, had slowly returned to their lodges, Mai-Ling attempted to stand, she could not.

Her ankles would not support her weight. She lay on the ground, where she had fallen.

Gradually, eventually, the Mai-Ling stopped crying. She lay whimpering in the dirt, waiting for the moment; that moment when these barbarians, as had happened to her father… when these barbarians, would kill her.

For hours, Mai-Ling lay in the dirt ignored by the People. She was hopeful that in time, the pain in her feet, in her ankles, and her legs, would subside.

When it did, she would be able to stand and to walk, …to walk away… to go where?

****

 E. Pluribus Unum

Chapter 83

Mai-Ling - In the Lodge of Little Flower and Gray Wolf

After she returned to the lodge of Gray Wolf, Little Flower while preparing her husband's evening meal, began to reflect on the similarities of the events that had transpired today, with those that had occurred—Little Flower spread the fingers of both hands in front of her face—, ten summers past.

It was then that oddly, *"out of the blue"*, words, white-man words, that her adopted daughter **Mahn-dee** (Pretty Buffalo Hair), had taught her, popped into her head.

Holding her hands before her eyes, she muttered aloud, the strange foreign word "Dee-cade", one of the words that her "Black-daughter", her adopted daughter that Gray Wolf had named, *Nananisuyake Ta? Si? Woo? Tso? Yaa (Pretty Buffalo Hair)*, had so many summers ago, taught her.

Dee-cade, the word "Dee-cade"…it meant these many. Little Flower held both of her hands; all ten fingers spread… in front of her face.

Little Flower spoke the word aloud *"Dee-cade"*. It had been nearly a *"Dee-cade"* since her black daughter, *Nananisuyake Ta? Si? Woo? Tso? Yaa, (Pretty Buffalo Hair)*, and Pretty Buffalo Hair's white sister, *Eebi Tseena Puis (Blue Wolf Eyes)*, had been brought as captive slaves, to the Kutsueka-Comanche Encampment of Chief Old Wise One.

On impulse, Little Flower left the lodge and returned to the spot where she had last seen the captive girl, lying on the ground.

The girl was gone. Although Little Flower was not a tracker, the trail left by Mai-Ling was incredibly easy to follow.

The girl had left a trail that consisted of a series of short, shallow imprints, disturbances in the grass, which led away from the village, out onto the open prairie.

Because the tracks, being of short intervals, the depth of the indentations of, every other step, was extremely shallow.

This fact led Little Flower to believe that the girl was not walking, or running, but was instead "*hopping*".

It was as if the tracks had been made, by a lame-animal, attempting to escape a pursuing predator.

A short distance from the village, well within sight of the encampment, Little Flower saw the girl, hobbling, limping towards her certain death on the prairie.

If not death by carnivores, then surely, death would come to her, from lack of water.

Little Flower called out to the girl; "Stop I have come to help." The girl upon hearing, what to her were the words of a "Barbarian", tried to run, where upon she took two faltering steps, and fell to the ground.

 "别烦我" - "bié fán wǒ" ("Leave me alone")!

Little Flower approached Mai-Ling, and gently placed her hands on the girl's shoulders. She looked into the girl's black, frightened, slanted-eyes and whispered; "I have come to help you."

Neither Mai-ling, nor did Little Flower comprehend the meaning of what to both of them, was the others, gibberish, meaningless sounds.

As they looked into each other's eyes, Little Flower saw in the slanted eyes of the yellow-girl, stark, naked, fear and terror.

Mai-Ling, when looking into the eyes of this red-skinned, female barbarian, to her surprise, saw only empathy and compassion.

****

Gray Wolf was sitting on his favorite buffalo robe, enjoying the taste and the smell of the aromatic smoke, as it wafted from his mouth and the bowl of his pipe, upward toward the tepee's smoke-hole.

Little Flower, supporting the weight of the yellow-girl on her shoulder, pushed aside the flap that covered the entrance to the Lodge of Gray Wolf.

Gray Wolf did not turn his head. Although he had been expecting, and had anticipated his wife's return, from washing their eating utensils, he was genuinely surprised by the commotion that she was making.

One of the things that he, over the years, had come to admire in Little Flower was her grace, and her agility.

Little Flower's noisy, clumsy; entrance into their lodge was most unusual.

When he saw his wife struggling under the weight of the yellow slave-girl, Gray Wolf still seated on his buffalo robe, slowly placed his pipe on one of the stones that surrounded the fire-pit.

"Little Flower why do you bring the yellow slave-girl, into our lodge? The girl is the property of our daughter, Spring Blossom's husband, Stone Fist."

Little Flower did not answer, instead straining under her burden, she lowered the limping girl, onto the three thick buffalo robes, that were neatly stacked, alongside the entrance to the tepee.

Gray Wolf still seated next to the fire, in a flat disinterested voice, asked; "Why does the yellow-one limp…is she hurt?"

Little Flower knelt on the buffalo robe and lifted Mae-Ling's foot.

While still holding the girl's foot in her hand, Little Flower removed the girl's oddly shaped, *"Stiff-Moccasin"*.

An involuntary moan, escaped from Mai- Ling's lips.

Little Flower turned toward Gray Wolf.

"My husband…come, you must see."

A huge bandage was wrapped around Mai-Ling's foot. The bandage was two inches in width, and ten feet long.

One end had been placed on the inside of the yellow-girl's instep. Then the bandage had been carried over her small toes, forcing them in and towards the sole of her foot, then wrapped under her foot.

Mai-Ling's large toe had been left, unbound. The bandage had then been wrapped around her heel, forcing her heel and toes, to be drawn closer together.

Each pass around her foot, with the figure-eight bandaging process, the bandage had been drawn tighter then was its predecessor.

The bandaging process had been repeated until the entire ten feet, of the restrictive bandage, had been exhausted.

Little Flower unwrapped the bandage. She flinched at the sight of the girl's foot.

The length of the yellow slave-girl's foot, from her heel to the tip of her large toe, was approximately three inches.

The light given off by the fire, as was the fire itself, was slowly dying. Gray Wolf stood, reached for a pole, which had been leaning against the tepee, and thrust the pole into the flame.

The end of the pole was wrapped in an animal hide, which had been saturated with flammable liquid. The tip of the pole flared-up, becoming a torch, a source of light.

The malformation of the yellow-girl's foot, was to Gray Wolf, grotesque.

Gray Wolf in his fifty-six winters and summers, had seen and had himself, inflected on the enemies of the Comanche, many tortured and mangled, bodies and body-parts.

Gray Wolf had seen the soles of the feet of captured warriors, the enemies of the People, burned, their toes, singularly, and en masse, sliced, cut-off, removed from the feet, of the enemies of the People.

The mangling of the feet, of the People's enemies, had purpose.

The enemy's foot mutilation, was intended to make it difficult, for the soon to be slain enemies of the Comanche, to in the after-life, not be able to walk the *DEATH??* Trail.

Gray Wolf, in his many years on the warpath fighting and killing the Pawnee, the Apache, the Tonkawa, the Wichita, and now the White-Man, he had never seen this type of foot-torture.

His curiosity aroused, and wishing to closely exam the girl's mangled feet, Gray Wolf held the torch, only inches from the slave-girl's foot.

Mai-Ling, who had been calm and trusting, when the barbarian-woman, unwrapped her foot, became terrified when the male-barbarian carrying a blazing-torch, held the torch but inches, from the mottled skin on her foot.

Mai-Ling, now panic-stricken, attempted to stand.

Little Flower seeing the panicky look in the girl's slanted-eyes extended her arm, halting Gray Wolf's forward motion.

"My husband, your approach with the flame, is frightening the girl."

Gray Wolf stopped, grunted, then spoke directly to the cowering girl; "What manner of torture is this? Your toes are mashed into the bottom of your foot. What enemy of the yellow tribe so deformed your feet?"

Mai-Ling stared in horror, as the male-barbarian's tongue, spewed forth, what to her, was a stream of unintelligible-gibberish.

Little Flower stood and patiently, ushered Gray Wolf back to his customary seat, in front of the dying fire.

"My husband, the slant-eyed girl, does not understand our talk." It is as it was, this many winters past she held up ten-fingers—, when *Mahn-dee...Pretty Buffalo Hair*, our black daughter first came to us."

"I will attempt to talk with the slant-eyed girl, using the language of sign, and the white man's talk, that was made known to me by our adopted black-daughter, Pretty Buffalo Hair."

Little Flower returned to the cringing, obviously frightened, slant-eyed girl.

Mai-Ling, who had other than the Chinese language, but a scant, rudimentary, understanding of English, was totally baffled by the barrage of strange sounds, coming from the mouths of these barbarians.

Little Flower gently tapped the shoulder of trembling girl. She spoke slowly, pointing her finger at her chest; "My name is Little Flower."

She then pointed her finger at Mai-Ling's chest. "What is your name?"

Mai-Ling, with a look of total bewilderment on her face, stared blankly at the female barbarian.

Little Flower repeated her question. This time, as she repeated the question, in addition to speaking the words, Little Flower, was rapidly gesturing with her hands, thus conveying her questions concurrently, in two mediums, in the spoken word, as well as in sign, the universal language of the plains.

Mai-Ling's, frustration at not being able to understand this strikingly handsome, middle-aged, barbarian woman's alien words, was now being exacerbated as she now, attempted to decipher the woman's obvious attempt to communicate with her, by using hand gestures.

Mai-Ling shook her head and slowly, in a wavering, soft voice, she whimpered: "我不明白你在说什么"; *(wǒ bù zhī dào nǐ xiǎng yào shén me)*
 ("I do not understand. What you are saying?")

"我不明白你在说什么" **ǒ;** (*"I do not know what you want."*)

Little Flower paused. To her, this exchange with the yellow-skinned, slant eyed girl, was eerily reminiscent of that time ten summers past—, when she first met the black girl Mandy, the black captive slave, who Little Flower and Gray Wolf had grown to love, and had subsequently adopted.

The name "*Mahn-dee*" had had no meaning in the language of the People.

Gray Wolf, because the black girl's hair resembled the wooly mane of their animal brother the buffalo, Gray Wolf had given his adopted daughter "*Mahn-dee*", the Comanche name, *"Pretty Buffalo Hair"*.

Little Flower clearly did not understand the "gibberish", the singsong noises that were coming from the yellow-girl's mouth. The words, if they were words, she thought must surely be, the words of some distant, yellow-tribe.

Little Flower walked over to the cringing, frightened girl. She sat, and then firmly placed her hands under the girl's elbows, and while lifting, she simultaneously issued a one-word command; "*Stand*".

Mai-Ling, with Little Flower's assistance, managed to rise to her full height of 4' feet 10" inches.

Little Flower, a full grown, mature woman of the People, stood 5' feet 5" inches, a full seven inches taller than the yellow-skinned-slant-eyed young girl, who stood demurely, before her.

The difference in height between the two, she and this strange diminutive, petite, yellow, slant-eyed, girl, contributed to Little Flower's thinking of, and treating Mai-Ling, as if she was a child.

Once again, Little Flower placed her hands onto Mai-ling's shoulder, and repeated in Comanche and in sign, her question.

Still frightened, the yellow-girl did not respond.

Little Flower, ever patient, tried again. This time she signed and spoke using the white-man's words. Words that her black-daughter, Pretty Buffalo Hair had taught her.

Again, pointing her finger at her chest, she spoke the white-man's words. *"My name is Little Flower."*

A flicker of recognition appeared in the girl's slanted-eyes. Mai-Ling recognized the sound of the white talk, the railroad-man's talk.

Mai-Ling hesitated. Then she pointed her finger inward, at her chest, and mumbled: "我叫梅玲 – *(wǒ jiào méi ling).* Then using the railroad-man talk, she mumbled; *"My name... Mai-Ling"*.

Little Flower smiled.

Mai-Ling then pointed her finger at Little Flower's chest. *"Wha-cee-loo name?"*

Little Flower had understood only, the white-man word *"name"*.

Little Flower once again pointed her finger inward toward her chest, and once again slowly repeated: *"My name is Little Flower."*

Mai-Ling concentrated, she pointed her finger at the barbarian woman and said; Little Flower's name. *"Loo?...Lilel Flowa"*.

Little Flower enthusiastically nodded her head. And once again pointed her finger at Mai-Ling.

Mae-ling, now beginning to understand, pointed her finger at her chest and in a subdued voice, softly mumbled: *"My name... Mai-ling"*.

Gray Wolf, who had been silently watching the two women, rose from his seat on his comfortable, buffalo robe. He walked over to the diminutive, frightened yellow-skinned girl.

Gray Wolf once again stared at her deformed foot. He pointed the stem of his pipe at his chest and exclaimed in an authoritative voice; "I am Gray Wolf". He then pointed the pipe stem at the cringing, slant-eyed girl...and declared *"Walks Oddly"!*

Gray Wolf returned to his seat by the fire.

Mai-Ling, confused, looked to the barbarian woman, whose name she now understood to be ***"Lilel Flowa"***

Little Flower smiled. She once again pointed her finger at Mai-Ling's chest.

Little Flower turned her head from side-to-side, the universal sign for *"No"* ... *"No Mai-Ling"*.

Little Flower then flexed her neck vertically, up and down, the universal sign for *"Yes"*.

Little Flower pointed her finger at the flustered girl and emphatically announced; *"Your name... "Walks Oddly"*.

****

Chapter 84

New-Rosewood - Cattle Ranch
[August 5th, 1875-11:00 AM]

Rebecca Billings McCloskey was seated on the veranda of her large, sprawling, five hundred sixty-six acre, cattle-ranch.

She sat relaxing, on a comfortable hand-made, green lounge-chair. The swinging lounge-chair, had been made for her by her adoring husband, thirty-five-year old, William (Billy) McCloskey.

Rebecca was slowly rocking back and forth, nursing her three-month-old, infant daughter, Mandy-Margaret McCloskey.

Rebecca and Billy had nicknamed the baby *'Three "M's".* The *'Three "M's",* referred to Rebecca's black-sister Mandy, her mother, Margaret, and the family's Scottish surname, McCloskey.

Rebecca was absent-mindedly humming a tune, a song that she vaguely remembered. A song that Ruth, her sister Mandy's mother, said that she had song to them, she and Mandy, when they were babies.

Rebecca was reminiscing about some of the many "girl-talks", that Mandy's mother Ruth, the ex-slave, she, and her sister Mandy would at night, share while just the three of them, sat talking around their camp-fire, during their ill-fated journey, across the country as members of Captain Samuel Smith's wagon train.

Rebecca, Ruth and Mandy, the three female members of the Billings' wagon, would frequently set after the evening meal, under a panoply of twinkling stars, talking of their former life, the lives that they had left behind.

Rebecca's life as the young Mistress, Mandy and her mother Ruth, as slaves, living in Richmond Virginia, on the Billings family's, Rosewood Plantation.

Rebecca smiled as she recalled Mandy's mother Ruth's, telling the girls of the times when they were babies… the times that she would bring the two hungry infants to her breasts, nursing both of them at the same time.

Rebecca chuckled as she recalled Ruth's words, reminiscing as they sat around the crackling campfire; *"I swears yall… dis here chile"* she nodded toward Rebecca, *"Good thing she dint have no teeth. She wooda bit off my nippy. She lik'd to suck on my left tit, more den she do on da rite one."*

"Now dis one," nodding her head toward Mandy, *"dis one, she won't par-tic-la.* Ruth would laugh as she said, *"dis one, she taks afta me, her momma. Eva one in dem slave cabins, dey noos dat when it cum ta food, ya cant be fussy. Lik my momma use ta say ta me an ta my sista Sadie... me an Sadie, we be her chilrens... momma usta said dat any food dat ain't got stuff movin in it, dat food, be good food."*

Ruth would chuckle before continuing; *"Well dere I'd be sittin' an ah rockin', wid ah white baby suckin away on my lef tit, an at dat same time, ah gots me ah black baby, ah suckin away on my rite tit.*

Ah'd be happy as ah pig in slob, justa rockin', an ah singin'.

Rebecca smiled as she remembered the words, to the tune that Ruth had been humming. Rebecca looked down at her daughter. Cradling baby Mandy in her left arm, she gently placed the index finger of her right hand on the baby's nose, and began to sing:

> *"Jesus loves the little children...*
> *all the little children of the world ...*
>
> *Be they red, brown, yellow, black,*
> *or white...they're all precious in his sight...*
>
> *Jesus loves the little children, of the world."*

Rebecca looked down, her eyes filled with love and adoration, as she looked at the face of her daughter.

For a brief second, the clear blue eyes of the little pink-faced infant, met those of her mother.

Rebecca smiled as she watched her daughter's lips, surround and suckle at the nipple of her left breast. As she was lovingly looking at her daughter's face, she was once again struck by the presence in baby Mandy's cheeks, of the familial, *"Billings' dimples"*.

The small indentations, depression, in both of the baby's cheeks, the dimples that she, her sister Mandy, her son, Hank, and her father Henry, had all inherited, passed down to them, from some distant, English ancestor.

When the baby's lips had stopped pulling on her nipple, Rebecca gently dislodged Mandy-Margaret's mouth, from her breast. With her left hand, she pulled up her smock, covering herself.

Rebecca then picked up the towel from her lap, placed it and the baby over her left shoulder, and began to gently pat the baby's back.

After a few light pats on the baby's back, Rebecca was rewarded by the sound of a *"burp"*.

Henry Billings II, Rebecca's twelve-year-old son, who two years earlier had finally shed the nick-name," Little-Hank"— for what he considered to be the more mature, name of just plain "Hank", burst onto the veranda, the screen door banging loudly shut, behind him.

Rebecca put her finger to her lips; "Shush, shush, Henry, you'll wake the baby. How often have I told you…begged you, not to slam the screen door?

As he bound down the three steps that led to the ground, Hank looked back over his shoulder, and shouted; "Sorry Mom. I'm late. I'm supposed to meet Ragged-Man at the cattle pens. Before he left, dad promised to let me help Ragged-Man, with the branding."

Ragged-Man was a reservation Indian, a fifty-seven-year-old Arapaho that Billy McCloskey, had hired as a ranch-hand.

The sound of the screen door banging shut caused the baby to stir. Baby Mandy-Margaret, began to whimper.

Rebecca cooed at, and eventually quieted the baby. She placed the baby in her cradle, pulled down the cloth netting that prevented flying insects from gaining access to Mandy-Margaret's sweet, little "dimpled" cheeks, and sat down on the lounge-chair.

Rebecca's thoughts turned to all of the things that had happened, since she and her then, four-year-old son," Little-Hank", back in the fall of 1867, had left the Richmond Virginia home of her Uncle Luis and her Aunt Delilah.

****

Chapter 85

Chicago Illinois, April 12th, 1869

Rebecca, with her seven-year-old son, *"Little Hank"* in toll, with the aide of the driver, carefully, cautiously, stepped down from the taxi.

The fetid smell of animal urine and feces permeated and filled the air. She could hear the constant sound of lowing cattle, the "bahhing" of sheep, and the grunts and squeals, of pigs.

Armed with a letter of introduction, given to her by her uncle, she approached the small house.

819 So. Baltimore Street

The sign hanging from Eve of the neatly whitewashed structure, read;

W.J. Westminster, Esq. - Wealth Management Consultant"

Rebecca carried with her, tightly clutched in her hand, her canvas-reticule-handbag, which in addition to her always present, nine-inch, serrated knife, contained a bank letter of credit, from "The Bank of Virginia, for the sum of $86,000 dollars.

Despite her being in possession of substantial wealth, Rebecca could not shake the feeling of being "destitute", of being alone in a strange, foreign, land.

Rebecca glanced at the address that she had written on a sheet of paper, before leaving their hotel-room.

Mr. Willard Westminster, Esq.
819 So. Baltimore Street, Chicago, Illinois

She and her Uncle Luis, had been diligently studying maps, reading newspapers, having discussion after discussion, trying to decide where she, a young white woman, a former captive of godless heathen, wild Indians, where she, and her five-year-old son of mixed-blood, should relocate.

Finally, the place that they chose was the city of Chicago, in the mid-western state of Illinois. Chicago was far, far, away from Richmond, … far, far, away from the South.

Their rationale for choosing Chicago was, that; In fact, they reasoned, although the state of Illinois had stayed in the Union, during what Luis now, euphemistically referred to as, "*The War of Northern Aggression*", the reason that they chose Chicago, was because of its' geographic location.

The city of Chicago, because of the network of railroad tracks linking North, South, East and West, had become the of the nation's "*Hub*" for the distribution of farm-produce, and meat across the continent.

And with the influx of thousands of migrants and immigrants, looking for work, Luis and Rebecca had concluded that Rebecca, and more importantly, that Little Hank would be surrounded by, and that he could grow up as a member of a heterogeneous, diverse, population.

Secondly, Luis in consultation with his vast network of business contacts, had become convinced, that with next year's anticipated, completion of the transcontinental railroad, tremendous opportunities, for those with vision and with the capital to invest, could realize huge profits.

Luis' exact words to his niece had been, "Chicago is the place, for making a financial killing".

It was for those two reasons— more so the former, than the latter, that Rebecca had agreed to relocate to Chicago.

Little Hank, with one hand tugging at her dress, and his other hand pinching together the nostrils of his nose, exclaimed; "*Pew-yew Mommy, this place stinks*".

A fleeting thought passed through her mind. Rebecca remembered one of the many cogent, phrases put forth by her's and her sister Mandy's former teacher, Miss Eleanor Leary; "*Out of the mouths of babes.*"

Rebecca reached into her handbag and removed her linen handkerchief, along with the knife, that she never traveled without.

Deftly, using both hands, she cut the handkerchief into two, almost equal pieces. She handed the slightly larger piece to her son.

With a quizzical look, Little Hank accepted the cloth.

Rebecca placed her piece of the cloth under her nostrils. "Breath through the handkerchief, like this. It will dilute, diminish, the smell."

Little Hank did as his mother had instructed. With his left-hand, he tightly gripped her right-hand. And with his right-hand, he placed her shredded kerchief, under his nose.

Rebecca made a fist and was preparing to rap on the door, when she noticed that the door had attached to it, a brass doorknocker.

E. Pluribus Unum

Rebecca lifted and dropped the hinged metal "knocker", against its' base. The volume of the sound, that resulted, startled both Rebecca, and Little Hank.

Rebecca was surprised. The man who answered the door, looked nothing like what she had imagined that, a *"Mr. Willard Westminster, Esq."*, would look like.

In her mind, Rebecca had envisioned Mr. Willard Westminster, Esq., as being a middle-aged man, with a receding hairline, a potbelly, and yellow, tobacco, stained teeth.

Instead, her first impression of the man who opened the door, and now stood before her, was that Mr. Willard Westminster, Esq., was a rather handsome man.

Rebecca noted that the man appeared to be slightly taller than was she, perhaps 5' 8". Though his physical stature was not by any means imposing, his smile and demeanor, was both warm, and engaging.

He was wearing a tailored suit of clothing. His open, double-breasted, black frock coat, contrasted well with his fawn colored brown trousers.

Willard's coat was buttoned at the top, displaying a ruby-red, quilted silk, double-breasted vest, which framed a black-silk cravat.

Willard Westminster's bearings, the way he carried himself, had the effect of making one feel that they were in the presence of a "Stately" man.

Rebecca's Uncle Luis had shared with her, a series of correspondence from Mr. Willard Westminster, Esq., in which Mr. Westminster had been effusively extolling his belief, that the imminent completion of the transcontinental railroad, in his words; "Will create Unimaginable Opportunities", to make lucrative investments in "Chicago's future".

Mr. Willard Westminster, Esq., had closed his correspondents with these interesting Predictions? Promises? Prophesies?

When discussing *"Will*'s" letters with her, Uncle Luis would laugh, and had said that some of Richmond's so-called business men, referred to Willard Westminster's, optimistic prose as being pure hyperbole.

Uncle Luis did not. He believed that if anything, "Will's Triple *"P's"*, actually fell short.

Uncle Luis' position, was that "Will's Triple *"P's"*, his **P**redictions, **P**romises, **P**rophesies, for Chicago's future, should, with the inclusion of yet another *"P"*, be expanded to be "Will's Quadruple *"P's"*.

The fourth *"P"* denoting for investors, enormous, **P**rofits.

Willard Westminster, Esq. was convinced, that within five years of the completion of the transcontinental railroad, Chicago would be known as:

"Hog Butcher For The World"

Willard's smiled, and looked deeply into the bright blue eyes, of the attractive young woman at the door.

Their brief, electric, eye contact, was almost immediately broken by the sound of a child's strident, voice.

"Hello mister, I'm, Henry…who are you?"

Willard's gaze shifted to the little boy, who was tightly holding the woman's hand.

He squatted down. And in a gentle, modulated, masculine, yet soothing voice, he answered.

"Well hello there son…Henry is it? My name is Will".

Rebecca stood still, motionless, momentarily mesmerized, staring at the neatly parted head of brown, wavy hair, that covered Mr. Willard Westminster, Esq.'s, very attractive head.

Rebecca's trance was broken by the sound of yet another child's voice; *"Who is it daddy… who's at the door?"*

Willard stood and grasped the hand of his son.

Trailing behind the little boy was an attractive red-haired woman.

Obviously annoyed and flustered, the woman was drying her hands on the hem of an apron, which was tied around her waist.

"Tony, you come back here this instant".

Still holding his son's hand, Willard stood. *"That's okay honey."*

He looked wistfully at Rebecca. He then put his arm around the shoulder of the woman. *"This is my wife Lucille, our son Anthony… and you are…?*

During their ride back to the hotel, Little-Hank talked incessantly about the "great-time", that he had had, playing with his new "best-friend", Tony.

After dinner, as she was tucking her son in for the night, Little Hank, with an imploring, pleading look in his obsidian eyes, pleaded with his mother, *"Mommy, can we go back tomorrow? Can I go play with Tony tomorrow?"*

"No not tomorrow baby. Tony and Mr. Westminster live way over, on the other side of town. We don't want to disturb Mr. Westminster".

"Mr. Westminster is a very busy man. Besides, don't you remember that awful smell?"

Little Hank responded; *"It didn't smell that awful-bad mommy…when can we go back? I want to go back and play with Tony."*

Rebecca pulled the sheet up, and tucked it under her son's chin. She kissed him on his forehead. *"We'll see honey…we'll see".*

Rebecca walked over to the chair, and wearily, sat down.

She sat thinking of the events of the day. Her mind inextricably, went to,

"That Moment".

"The moment", that electrifying moment, when their eyes first met. The moment, when she had been transfixed, staring into the gray-green eyes of Mr. Willard Westminster, Esq.

The last time that Rebecca had experienced that sensation, that fluttering feeling in the pit of her stomach, was when she was a fourteen-year-old, teenager, traveling with her father and her sister, in a wagon train, bound for Kansas.

At that time that now to her, seemed to have happened eons ago—, she and Bjorn Olsen, the eighteen year-old, handsome, young, blonde son of the Swedish emigrant family, traveling in the wagon just ahead of the Billings', had as the monotonous weeks dragged on, been increasingly sharing surreptitious, flirtatious, admiring, sidelong glances.

In a moment of frustration, and exasperation, Rebecca clapped her hand on to her forehead. She sluggishly shook her head and mumbled; *"What's wrong with me…what am I thinking? I'm acting like a swooning school girl, instead of a full-grown woman, with a six-year-old son."*

"Willard Westminster is a married man, a happily married man, with a lovely wife, and child."

Still, Rebecca was certain, that at *"The Moment"*, that moment when they had first made eye-contact, for a fleeting second, looking deeply into each other's eyes, she had seen in his…WHAT…what had she seen?"

As one of her slave's, Mandy's friend Lena, back on the Rosewood Plantation probably would have said had she been in this situation, *"Gal yuse bess gits a hole of yo self. Fo yu, dat dire man, means nuthin but tra-bull."*

Two weeks later Rebecca alone, without her son, returned to 819 So. Baltimore Street, to the home/office of; W.J. Westminster, Esq. - Wealth Management Consultant"

One of her neighbors, a matronly elderly lady, two doors from her room, for the sum of ten dollars, had agreed to watch Little Hank, for the day.

At Rebecca's second meeting with Willard (*"Please…call me Will"*) Westminster, Rebecca was all…strictly, all business.

After they had exchanged pleasantries, Rebecca handed the lawyer a two-page document.

Puzzled, Willard unfolded the first page, and began to read:

By these letters:

I, Rebecca Elizabeth Billings, hereby acknowledge, and authorize Willard Westminster, Esq., to act as my investment agent.

Subsequently on this date, April 26⁺, 1869, I have made available to Mr. Westminster, a bank draft, from the Richmond National Bank, made out in my name, Rebecca Elizabeth Billings, in the sum of eighty-six thousand dollars ($86,000).

In compliance with the below detailed instructions, and on my behalf, Mr. Willard Westminster, is directed to proceed as follows:

1.   Invest, on my name, (Rebecca Elizabeth Billings), twenty-five thousand dollars ($25,000), in Chicago's Union Stock Yards and Transit Company.

3.   2. Deposit at The First National Bank of Chicago, in my name (Rebecca Elizabeth Billings), the sum of fifty-three -thousand dollars ($53,000)

3. Wire to the Bank of Wichita Kansas, tin my name, (Rebecca Margaret Billings), a bank draft in the amount of four thousand dollars ($4,000).

4. Have delivered to my person (Rebecca Elizabeth Billings), at the Chicago Palmer House, a bank draft in the amount of two-thousand ($2,000) dollars.

As compensation for the provision of these services, Mr. Willard Westminster, Esq. is entitled to withdraw from my savings-account at "The First National Bank of Chicago", the sum of twenty-five ($25.00) dollars per month or, but not both, five-percent (5%), of the stock's value, excluding the principal, my initial investment of fifty-five thousand dollars ($55,000).

Signed: Rebecca Margaret Billings   Date: October 26⁺, 1869

                                                                Signed: Date:

With a studious, appreciative expression on his face, the lawyer looked at the second page. It was an exact duplicate of the first.

Willard walked over to his desk, sat down, and scribbled the same addendum, then his signature, to both sheets of paper.

He stood, then walked over and handed back to Rebecca, the two pages.

By these letters:

I, Rebecca Elizabeth Billings, hereby acknowledge, and authorize Willard Westminster, Esq., to act as my investment agent.

Subsequently on this date, April 26⁺, 1869, I have made available to Mr. Westminster, a bank draft, from the Richmond National Bank, made out in my name, Rebecca Elizabeth Billings, in the sum of eighty-six thousand dollars ($86,000).

In compliance with the below detailed instructions, and on my behalf, Mr. Willard Westminster, is directed to proceed as follows:

                                           E. Pluribus Unum

2.   *Invest, on my name, (Rebecca Elizabeth Billings), twenty-five thousand dollars ($25,000), in Chicago's Union Stock Yards and Transit Company.*

4.   *2. Deposit at The First National Bank of Chicago, in my name (Rebecca Elizabeth Billings), the sum of fifty-three -thousand dollars ($53,000)*

5.   *3. Wire to the Bank of Wichita Kansas, tin my name, (Rebecca Elizabeth Billings), a bank-draft in the amount of four thousand dollars ($4,000).*

6.   *4. Have delivered to my person (Rebecca Elizabeth Billings), at the Chicago Palmer House, a bank-draft in the amount of two-thousand ($2,000) dollars.*

As compensation for the provision of these services, Mr. Willard Westminster, Esq. is entitled to withdraw from my savings-account at "The First National Bank of Chicago", the sum of twenty-five ($25.00) dollars per month or, but not both, five-percent (5%), of the stock's value, excluding the principal, my initial investment of fifty-five thousand dollars ($55,000).

[The execution of this "contract", is conditional on the First National Bank of Chicago's honoring, the Richmond National Bank's $86,000 dollar bank draft, made payable to; Rebecca Elizabeth Billings.]

Signed: Rebecca Margaret Billings   Date: October 26th, 1869

Signed: Willard Westminster, Esq. *Date:* Oct. 26, 1869

Rebecca read Willard's addendum, in what he—in a strictly business tone of voice—, described as a *"Codicil"* to *"the contract"*.

After she finished reading, Rebecca nodded her approval.

She then handed the bank draft, to Willard, folded her copy of the "amended-contract", and placed it snuggly into her reticule, below her ever-present knife.

Rebecca extended her hand to Willard, and said; "Agreed".

Rebecca seated on the sofa, directly across from Willard, informed, her new Attorney-Wealth Manager, of her plans to within the next two weeks, be leaving Chicago.

The pleasant smile that had been on Willard's face, faded, replaced by a look of concern. It took him a few seconds to regain his composure. Then with a solicitous, but *"strictly business"* look on his face, he asked as to where, she planned to move.

Rebecca shared with Willard, her plans.

Rebecca told the Attorney/Wealth Manager, of her determined, fervent, desire, to fulfill her father's dream.

She told Willard of how, six-years earlier, during the war, with the imminent, impending collapse of the Confederacy, how her father had lost their home, Richmond Virginia's Rosewood Plantation. And how he had then arranged for, what remained of the Billings family, to relocate, to emigrate, from Virginia to Kansas.

Rebecca told Willard of her desire to finish what her father had started. She told of her wish to bring to fruition, her father's dream of building a new "Rosewood", in the mid-western state of Kansas.

She told of how she envisioned the "New Rosewood". Instead of it being a plantation, producing cotton, by breeding slaves, and perpetuating human bondage, Kansas' "New Rosewood" would instead be the "Rosewood Cattle Ranch".

A vast cattle ranch, that breed and shipped beef, to feed the world. Beef breed at the "Rosewood Cattle Ranch", transported by to the stock-pens of Chicago's Union Stock Yards and Transit Company.

****

Chapter 86

When Sgt. Major Jason Ruth—a fugitive from the law—, fled Richmond Virginia, he had hastily shied his uniform, as well as his former identity.

Jason knew that he had to change his name.

His criteria for choosing a new name was that the name be different, but to have the new name sound similar enough to his name Jason Ruth, that the sound of his new name would not be totally alien to his ears.

The pronounced emphasis on the *"Jay"* sound, in the name Justin, coupled with his choosing for his last name *"Gulliver"*, Maureen's pet name for him, he thought, was absolutely the right choice, … the perfect choice.

For nearly five years, Jason… *Justin Gulliver* had been aimlessly drifting westward, supporting himself, by sporadically performing a variety of mostly menial odd jobs.

While he had had no specific destination in mind, the geographic direction of his wandering was always in a southwesterly direction.

South, in the belief that the South, still smarting from its loss of the war, would be less interested in apprehending a *"Yankee-Nigger"*, deserter; And, west because he reasoned that, the further west that he traveled…traveling, into the *"Lawless West"*, the more likely that he would be able to distance himself, from *"The Long-Arm of the Law"*.

Usually, after finding work in a frontier town, Justin would strike a bargain with the owner of the local livery stable. In Exchange for allowing him to sleep in the stable, Justin would clean out the stalls, and would groom the horses.
Four years after his going AWOL, Justin had been forced to "put-down" his horse, when on a particularly dark, and moonless night, his U.S. Army horse, stepped into a prairie-dog hole, fracturing his left leg.

Justin's practice was to limit his time in towns. He made it a point to stay in towns, only long enough, to accumulate a little money, enough money for supplies, and if need be, enough to purchase a saddle horse, which invariably would be an old, practically decrepit, nag.

When he needed work, Justin's preference was to find work, at one of the small settlers' farms that were increasingly springing-up; on what for eons had been *"virgin-land"*, land that had never been touched by a hoe, or a plow.

Of the myriad chores that Justin performed to support himself, ironically the one task that he preferred above all others, a task that he actually enjoyed, was the menial task of caring for the horses.

While pitching hay and shoveling-out—ridding enumerable stables and corrals, of the ubiquitous piles of horse manure, that would invariably accumulate—, was tedious, mundane, dirty, work, those tasks for Justin, were more than offset, when he actually spent time, hands-on, caring for the horses.

Over the years, Jason Ruth (*"Justin Gulliver"*), had developed an uncanny ability, an affinity, to relate with… and to connect with, horses.

After many contemplative hours of pondering, as to where or why, he had come to possess this ability; Justin had come to believe that perhaps, his ability to relate to horses was due to his genuine empathy for, and with horses.

This empathy stemmed from his child-hood experiences. From when as a child, a seven-year-old black-boy, a black slave, he was actually, literally, saddled and ridden like a horse, by Jesse Billings, his ten-year- old, white *Massa.*

Justin remembered when before the war, his white Massa, Jesse Billings and he had together, gone off to college… to the Virginia Military Institute, Massa Jesse as a student, he as Massa Jesse Billing's manservant, the Massa's black slave.

Justin– *"Jason"*, remembered when *Massa* Jesse joined the Confederate Army. He had vivid memories of how he, a black man, was forced to serve, and to support the Confederate Cause, the continued enslavement of four million blacks—, by attending to the needs of his, *Massa*, Lieutenant Jesse Billings, and the needs of the *Massa's* horse.

The one task that he enjoyed doing in his service to the *Massa*, was the caring for, *"Charger"*, Lieutenant Jesse Billings' magnificent, war-horse.

Upon reflection, Justin smiled, as he recalled fond memories of the hundreds of hours that he had spent, currying, brushing, dust, dirt, and sweat from the *"Massa"*, Lieutenant Jesse Billings', huge black stallion.

On many sleepless nights, camped-out on the prairie, Justin would lay awake, gazing up at the stars, remembering the hours spent, brushing and currying *"Charger"*.

He remembered how he would gently, in a modulated, soft soothing voice, whisper speaking in slave dialect, comforting words to the horse:

"Eee-zy dere big fella, Massa he dun rode yu reel hard ta dey. I noos how yu be feelin. Wen we wuz chillin, da Massa an me, da Massa yusta ride me lik he do yu…ride me lik I was his hoss."
Justin remembered how his currying brush would slide over the stallion's flanks, Justin would remember the disquieting knot in his stomach, each time his brush-strokes encountered scar tissue, where Lieutenant Jesse Billings' spurs, had dug into *"Charger's"* flesh.

He remembered how he would, ease the pressure of his brush-strokes, while empathetically mumbling to the huge stallion; *"Ise still got dem same kinda scars, myself, on my own belly".*

Justin was convinced, that those sessions, grooming, cajoling, and comforting, that magnificent animal, "the *Massa's*" horse, had contributed to his acquiring his gift; his ability to control, and to communicate, with horses.

****

When Justin encountered one of the many, yet few and far between, small, frontier, cow towns, Justin usually had very little trouble finding some kind of work… work that was almost always, a variation of hard-labor, and/or, some sort of scut-work.
In order to sustain his life, to provide himself with the basic necessities; food, shelter, and an occasional new, or more often, a used, article of clothing, Justin would work in saloons, in brothels, or in saloon/brothels; sweeping and washing, creaky wooden saloon-floors, emptying and cleaning overflowing spittoons, and performing a multitude of any other, menial tasks.

Once and only once, did Justin unnecessarily prolong his stay in one of the cow towns.

It occurred during the summer of '72, in the small town of San Angelo, situated in the center, of the huge state of Texas.

It was six o'clock in the morning. Justin was mopping the floor in the town's, Silver Slipper Saloon.

He was rinsing his filthy mop, in a bucket of clear luke-warm water, attempting to wring the dirt, grime, and soap, from the heavy mop.

Justin's back was to the narrow staircase that led from the main floor, to the second floor of the saloon.

The 2nd floor contained six, closet-sized bedrooms.

Six transient rooms furnished each, with a bed, a table, on which stood a mirror, a pitcher of water, and a hand towel. The six small rooms provided a modicum of privacy, where the "working-girls", for the sum of three dollars, would entertain her customers.

At the conclusion of business, between the hours of 5am, and 6pm, the rooms served as *"home",* for the six "working-girls".

Perspiring profusely, Justin had removed his shirt, and was naked to the waist. With his long legs, straddling the mop's long wooden handle, he gripped the heavy mop head in both hands.

Gretchen Ehrlich, one of the establishment's more productive "working-girls", wearing a thin silk robe, stood on the landing, at the top of the stairs.

Her eyes were riveted on the tableau being innocently played-out before her.

Gretchen caught her breath. She stood motionless, transfixed, totally absorbed, as she watched the graceful, powerful movements, of the black man, as he squeezed dirty water from the head of the heavy mop.

The dim light from a single oil lamp, attached to the wall, served to highlight the tall black man's, glistening cooper-tone, and physique.

Each compression of the heavy mop-head resulted in an impressive outline of the man's muscles and tendons.

In the course of her time working in "the profession" the world's oldest "profession" —, Gretchen had on many occasions, seen men with much larger, possibly more impressive, muscle mass.

The thing that had intrigued Gretchen was not so much the man's mass of muscles, what had caused her to stop and to breathlessly gasp, was the definition, the symmetry, of the black man's, tall, lean, masculine body.

At the unexpected sound of glass breaking, Justin abruptly spun around, turning his head toward the stairs.

At the top of the stairs, he saw a slightly overweight, blonde white woman, who with one hand was attempting to hold together the folds of her thin robe, while bending over picking up shards of glass from the floor.

The woman, her eyes still on the black man, stumbled, and quickly grabbed for the wooden banister.

Justin dropped the mop and bolted up the staircase.

Gretchen panicked. She was momentarily startled when she saw the black man racing up the steps toward her.

She instinctively tightened her grip on the piece of jagged glass that she held in her free hand, and thrust it, as if it were a bayonet at the black man.

"Backup nigger…don't you take another step."

Justin stopped. He stretched out both hands, palms forward; *"Ezzy Missy…I ain't gonna hurt ya nun. Ise jus tryin ta help. Is ya alrite?"*

Gretchen, seeing the black man's hands moving toward her, slashed out with the jagged shard of glass. Justin reflexively, dropped both of his hands.

Gretchen's wild thrust, cut nothing but thin-air.

She looked at the piece of glass that she held, tightly clutched in her hand.

The glass was smeared with blood…her blood.

Gretchen dropped the jagged piece of glass. She felt light-headed, faint.

She began to fall forward. Justin instinctively caught her; supporting her weight, preventing her from falling down the flight of stairs.

With Gretchen in his arms, Justin stood momentarily confused. He mumbled; "Now what?" He quickly scanned the hallway.

Each side of the hall had three doors. Five of the six doors were closed.

The middle door on the left side of the hallway was open.
Justin hurried toward, and entered the open door, and with the heel of his left foot, kicked the door shut.

His eyes quickly scanned the room. The bed was the most prominent piece of furniture in the small room.

Justin gently placed the white-woman onto the crumbled bed-sheet. He surveyed the room, looking for something to use to stop the bleeding of the woman's injured hand.
Justin hastily tore off, a piece of the bed sheet. He made a two-fold bandage, and wrapped it around the woman's injured hand.
He then walked over to the table, picked-up the porcelain pitcher of water, and drenched the remaining piece of the torn bed sheet, with water.

Justin gently applied the cool, wet, compress, onto the brow of the unconscious white-woman.

Gretchen's pale blue eyes fluttered open. She groaned. Her gaze met the worried, dark-brown eyes, of the ruggedly, handsome, black-man.

Justin repeated his earlier question; *"Ezzy Missy...I ain't gonna hurt ya nun. Is ya alrite... is ya feelin' betta?"*

Gretchen slapped the black-man's hand from her forehead. The damp cloth fell to the floor.

In a low angry guttural, voice, she hissed; *"Hol deine dreckigen, schwarzen Hande von mir!"*

The black man, not understanding the woman, but clearly understanding the tone of her voice, recoiled, and stepped away from the clearly agitated white-woman.

By the confused blank, look on the black man's face; it had become obvious to Gretchen that the man did not understand.

Gretchen, realizing that she had been speaking German, her native language, quickly repeated her words, this time in English:

"Get your filthy, black hands, off of me!"

Without uttering a sound, Justin turned, opened the door, and left the room.

****

Justin finished mopping the floor. He put away his mop and bucket, and left the saloon.

He returned to his sleeping quarters at the livery stable. Justin climbed the ladder that led to the hayloft. He approached a haystack that consisted of three-bales of hay. Justin lifted the top two-bales, set them on the floor, and wedged his hand into the third bale.

He had previously, removed hay from the center of the bale, thereby effectively creating hollowed-out compartment, to hold his savings.

Justin withdrew his hand from the bale of hay. When his hand emerged, he held tightly, clutched in his fist, a faded red bandana that contained the sum-total, of his savings, twenty-three wrinkled, greenback, and dollar bills.

After his encounter with the white woman, Justin's initial survival instinct, had been to move on, or more precisely, as the black soldiers of the 54th, would have said, under similar circumstances; *"Time ta get your black-ass, "The Hell-Outta-Dodge".*

Justin *(Jason)* recalled, how when he was ten years old, how he had been given, by his mother Ruth, *"The Talk"*. The black survival talk, the talk that was dutifully given to every black boy, to every black, male, slave.

"Honey no matta what ya duz, ya dun't neva wanna-be by ya self, wit no white woman".
"It dun't mak a lik ah difrence, if she be da Mizztress, if she be the Mizztress' dawtah Beeka, or eben if she be one ah dem poo-white-trash, town-floozies".
"It dun't maks no matta, dem white mens'll hangs ya lik a dawg, iffin dey catches ya alone… eben jus talkin', wid a white woman!"

Justin felt that there was a good possibility based upon the angry, vile, accusatory words, that she had shouted at him—, that the woman whom he had helped…the white woman that, he had helped, just might have the law after him, or far worse, she may have accused him, a black man, of molesting her.

Although he was eager to put as much distance as possible, between himself and San Angelo, Justin knew that on foot, his chances of eluding, a pursuing posse, was at best, extremely slim.

Two months earlier, prior to his walking into the little town of San Angelo, looking for work, on a particularly dark, moonless, night on the prairie, his horse had stepped into a prairie-dog hole, fracturing the Navicular-bone of his left front-leg.

Justin had been forced to *"put-down"* his horse, the U.S. Army's mount that he had ridden and cared for, for five long years. The one living creature, that had been his companion during five long, lonely, years, of lonely days and nights, mostly devoid of human contact, alone on the prairie.

When he had negotiated his working/sleeping, arrangement with the proprietor of San Angelo's only livery stable, the owner of the stable, had for the sum of thirty dollars, agreed to sell Justin, a twenty-four-year-old mare.

Justin was seven dollars shy of the thirty dollars, which he needed to buy the horse.

After carefully weighing his options, Justin decided to risk it. He would go back to the saloon, and ask the owner to pay him… to pay him the nine dollars, owed him. The three days back wages, due him.
 He needed that horse!

****

Silver-Slipper Saloon – San Angelo, Texas August 6, 1872 - 11:10 AM

Justin entered the back door of the saloon. He knew that at this time of day— a little after eleven o'clock in the morning—, with the exception of the "working-ladies", asleep in their 2nd floor bedrooms, and Nicholas   Henshaw, the owner of the "Silver Slipper", who would most likely, be in his small office, counting last nights "take", the saloon would be deserted.

As he approached the office Justin hesitated, he thought that he had heard sounds of movement in the bar.

Instead of knocking on the owner's door, Justin cautiously entered the main room.

He stood in the shadows. Nothing. The room appeared to be empty.

Other than the five card tables, the floor was empty. All of the chairs were placed upside-down, on either the five-tables, or upside-down on the top of the bar.

Justin was about to retrace his steps. To go back to the office and to hopefully, collect his nine dollars, when he heard a noise.

The noise sounded to him, like the "clinking" sound made when glass touched glass.

Once again Justin's eyes scanned the room. Nothing. He stood perfectly still, immobile, holding his breath. He was certain that he had heard a noise.

There…there it was again, a rustling sound, and then suddenly between two upside-down chairs that sat on the bar-counter, a woman's head appeared.
It was the white-woman, the woman that earlier today, he had prevented from falling-down the stairs and breaking her neck.

When unexpectantly, their eyes met, the white-woman gasped, and her free hand, the one that was not holding a whiskey bottle, flew to her chest.

Justin was turning to leave, when, in what sounded to him as being a harsh accented voice, the woman spoke a single word; "Stop".

In response to her one word command, Justin muttered just one word, "Shit".

"Come here."

Justin instinctively, assumed his—when dealing with white folks—, "survival-posture", he hung his head and shuffled over to the bar.

"Yessum?"

"Where did you go? When I came to, I was lying on my bed, my hand bandaged, and a wet cloth on my forehead… you were gone."

"You had disappeared. You left before I had a chance to thank you for catching me, probably preventing me from breaking my neck".

Justin, who had been holding his breath, slowly exhaled and relaxed.

Obviously this middle-aged white-whore, had not raised the alarm, the all-to-often, false alarm, when a white woman found herself alone, with a black man.

She had not because he had, in the minds of so many white men, committed the ultimate capital crime, he had touched her—, and she had not "cried-out **RAPE**, thus labeling him… essentially, branding him, for all intents and purposes, a *"Dead-Nigger"!*

Justin raised his eyes and for the first time, actually looked at…really, looked at, the woman.

The white-woman had removed from her face, the layers of rouge and powder, the make-up, which to Justin, seemed to be the uniform, the mask that the "legions" of the whores plying their trade, in these western/frontier, saloon/brothels, wore.

Justin was struck by the transformation. While there was no way that the woman behind the bar, could be considered as being a young woman; lines radiating from the corners of her eyes, wrinkles that he had heard described as *"crows-feet"*, surrounded her pale blue-eyes.

Two lines, actually thin furrows, were etched into her forehead, above her eyebrows. Justin thought, that in spite of these age-related imperfections, that the woman somehow— in the more revealing, harsh light of day—, the woman was actually, quite attractive.

The women's imperfections to Justin, more then anything else, attested to the fact that the woman had, at sometime during her life, probably for most of her life, had not been a whore, but had instead worked with her hands.

Her hands were rough, calloused. The hands of a person who was use to performing hard, labor intensive, hard work. Her hands were definitely not, the hands of a woman whose sole profession in life had been that of lying on her back, performing the sexual acts, of a career-whore.

"My name is Gretchen. What is you name?"

Before responding…*Justin hesitated. He stared, studying the face of the woman.* Then he answered; *"My name bees, Jas…, he quickly caught himself, "My name bees Jus…, Justin".*

****

Justin was relieved. The fact that the white-woman had not sounded an alarm, a false alarm…had not falsely accused him of molestation, led to Justin altering his plans.

He decided, to instead of asking the owner of the saloon for the nine dollars owed him, he would continue working …at least finish out the week, and maybe stay a little longer…long enough to earn enough, to pay for the horse, and some supplies.

****

Gretchen was busy working the room, laughing and flirting with the dusty, dirty, cowboys.

Her job was to persuade the saloon's patrons to buy her drinks (water mixed with a splash of molasses-for color), drinks that the cowboys thought were whiskey, and paid full price. Gretchen received a dollar for every five drinks (water mixed with molasses-for color) that was purchased for her.

By far, Gretchen's primary source of income came from her frequent trips with the cowboys, to the rooms upstairs, where she and her sisterhood of Silver-Slipper whores, made their real money, charging their *"Johns"* three dollars for twenty minutes, five dollars for thirty minutes of "pleasuring".

The management of the "Silver-Slipper" kept two of the dollars from her "quickies", and three dollars for each of her half-hour sessions.

The vast number of Gretchen's clientele, mostly repeat customers, opted for the half-hour sessions.

While at the age of thirty-five, she was the oldest of the owner's "stable-of whores", she was without a doubt, the most talented and skilled, at her profession.

Nicholas Henshaw (Nasty Nick), the proprietor of the Silver-Slipper, considered Gretchen to be his most valuable employee...his most valuable asset.

Gretchen lay on the rumbled bed, her left-arm covering her eyes. Six times that evening, she had led a variety of six different—yet similar, in that they all smelled the same—dirty, drunken cowhands, "upstairs", to beds in four different rooms.

Following the end of the night's sixth, of a string of tedious *"upstairs"*, sessions, she muttered; *"Gott sei Dank."* She rolled over and repeated, this time in English; "Thank God…it's finished"

During working hours, any one of the six "working-girls", were allowed to use any one of the—at that time—unoccupied rooms on the second floor, to transact "business". It was only after the close of business, that the women would retire to—went to sleep in their own rooms… in their own beds.

Luckily for Gretchen, her last session of the night had been in her very own room, in her very own bed.

Gretchen lay in bed, tossing and turning, having difficulty falling asleep.
Unable to fall asleep, she sled her legs from under the sheet and sat-up on the side of the bed.

Gretchen reached over, and picked-up the whiskey bottle from the table.
She removed the cork from the bottle, poured four-fingers of the rotgut whiskey into the glass, and gulped it down.

Gretchen placed the half empty bottle of whiskey onto the table, and once again attempted to fall asleep.

Her mind numbed by the alcohol, Gretchen finally managed to drift off into an alcohol-assisted, anesthetized, fitful sleep.

****

CHAPTER 87

Goslar Germany 1862

In June of 1862, the Ehrlich family, twenty-six year old Gretchen, her husband Reinhold, and their twelve-year-old son Hermann, due to the combination of years of religious persecution, and a total crop-failure, that had made it impossible for the Ehrlich family, to pay several months of overdue rent on their small farm, located on the outskirts of Goslar Germany, the Ehrlich family was evicted.

For the first time in generations, the Ehrlich's were homeless.

Having had relatives… distant family and friends, who in the past, seeking a better life, had left Germany, to escape religious persecution, and having heard of large quantities of fertile land in America (sixty-five hectares), land free for the taking, because of the American president, Abraham Lincoln's signing something called the Homestead Act, Reinhold had decided to emigrate, to start over in the "New World".
Reinhold managed to arrange steerage-passage, for the family, on one of the rapidly dwindling, number of ships, propelled by wind and sail, that literally continued to, "set sail" to cross the Atlantic.

Although this was the family's first time at sea, Reinhold had non the less, signed a contract, that included as payment for their passage, he and his son Hermann would at the captain's discretion, assist the deck hands, when needed, throughout the voyage.

After a month at sea, both of the Erhlich men, had acquired their "sea-legs", and had adjusted well to performing simple tasks assigned them, by the ship's bosom.

The Ehrlich men—father and son, had adapted well to their role, as, as needed auxiliary *"crew-men"*, on a sailing ship.

Midway during the Atlantic crossing, on a day that started out as relatively sunny-slightly overcast, with the ship riding the waves nicely, in the semi-calm water, almost immediately, without warning, the wind began to picked-up. The gray, slightly overcast sky began to darken.

Brilliant flashes of lightning, followed by the deafening, rumbling of, explosive thunderclaps, filled the air.

Rain, first a sprinkle, then in torrents began to cascade down in sheets, from the skies.

The velocity of the wind increased. The howling wind gusts began to change the trajectory of the falling rain.

Torrential rain that had been falling vertically from the skies, had become, sheets of rain, driven horizontally, by the gale-like, gusting, southeasterly wind.

Within minutes a slightly overcast day, with moderately calm seas, had turned into pitch-black darkness, with fifteen-foot angry waves, threatening to swamp the ship.

Gretchen below deck clung to the metal frame of the bunk that she and Reinhold shared. She remembered how—following the storm—, how relieved she had been when she saw her husband, soaking wet, slowly descending down the ladder.

She remembered, how her heart sank, when she first saw Reinhold's face, how her emotions almost instantly changed from joy and relief, to dread and despair.

Gretchen would never forget, how she knew…how she knew from looking at Reinhold's grief-stricken face, Gretchen would never forget, how she at that instant, knew that their son Hermann…her baby-boy, was gone.

Reinhold too, had been devastated, at the loss of their only child, their son, Hermann.

As long as he lived, Reinhold knew that he would never forget the apprehension he had felt, when he and his son had emerged from below deck, and had been separated by the bosom to whom they had been assigned.

Reinhold had been detailed the task of lashing-down, the kegs of drinking water on the starboard side of the ship, while Hermann was given the task of securing the two barrels of salted-fish, directly opposite the water kegs, on the port-side of the ship.

Reinhold would never forget hearing… hearing, the bosom shouting, into the raging wind, screaming those two English words, which would forever haunt him:
"Man Overboard…Man Overboard!!"

Reinhold remembered the sickening, sinking, feeling in the pit of his stomach, while his eyes frantically searched for his son. How he had stood frozen in time, his eyes staring fixed on the spot, and then beyond, that he had last seen his son.

Both of the kegs of salted fish, that Hermann had been attempting to secure to the portside-bulkhead, as was his son, had vanished. Both his son, and two barrels, filled with salted fish, having been swept overboard, by a monstrous column of water.

Gretchen had been inconsolable. For the remainder of their time aboard ship, she remained in their cramped cabin, refusing to leave.

Reinhold managed to deal with his grief, by devoting his time and energy, to caring for his wife.

In mid July of 1862, as the ship neared its final destination, the port of New Orleans, the ship's captain gave the order that all passengers remain below, deck, as he and his crew prepared to attempt to "run" the Union Blockade.

Reinhold and Gretchen Ehrlich's stay in New Orleans was short. Reinhold was able to successfully contact a German-speaking organization that helped newly arrived German-speaking immigrants.

The German-speaking organization provided food, shelter and small sums of money to the newly arrived immigrants, to purchase passage, on steamships, traveling north, up the Mississippi River.

The Ehrlich's goal was to reach Pennsylvania or New York, states in this vast United States, that they knew, had large communities of German-speaking immigrants.

Reinhold, attempting to blend in, with his new countrymen, to as rapidly as possible assimilate, changed his name from Reinhold, to its anglicized equivalent, Reginald.

Despite his, and his now pregnant wife Gretchen's efforts; to clear the land; to plow the thirty acres; to plant the crops, and to then harvest the crop; proved to be too much for one man, and one pregnant woman.

Reginald and Gretchen were unable to pay-off the note on their thirty-acre piece of the American dream farm.
In addition to losing the farm, Gretchen's laboring in the fields during the fifth month of her pregnancy, had precipitated the onset of early labor.

Gretchen suffered a miscarriage, she loss the baby.

As had happened to the Ehrlich family in their native-homeland, and during their journey to the "New World", Reginald and Gretchen Ehrlich, had once again, in addition to losing their home had lost a child.

In October of 1863, four months after the Union Army's victory at Gettysburg Pennsylvania, three months after they had lost their farm; after a month of his being able to only find sporadic work, performing odd jobs, Reginald "Reggie" Ehrlich, in order to support himself and his wife, joined the Union Army.

Reggie enlisted in the 52nd, New York State Volunteers, an all-German immigrant, regiment.

Probably because of his aptitude for, and his ability to easily adjust to military life—at the age of sixteen, before his marriage to Gretchen, Reinhold had briefly served, as a soldier in the Prussian Army—, Pvt. Reginald "Reggie" Ehrlich, experienced rapid advancement in the 52nd, New York State Volunteer Regiment.

After having served just three months and undoubtedly due to the paucity of non-commissioned officer material in the 52nd, Pvt. Reginald *"Reggie"* Ehrlich was promoted to Corporal.
Corporal Reginald Ehrlich was in one of the companies of the 52nd, who while engaged in the battle of Spotsylvania Courthouse, had with "fixed" bayonets, charged across an open field toward the salient (a bulge in the rebels defensive-line), not stopping to reload their empty rifles, and had overwhelmed the "dug-in", entrenched confederate soldiers, at the juncture that the rebels referred to as ("The Mule-Shoe"), and in horrific hand to hand combat, broke the rebel lines.

For his courage and the leadership, he displayed, during the fighting at the Battle of Spotsylvania County, Corporal Reginald Ehrlich, was promoted to the rank of Sergeant.

To his surprise and astonishment, Reggie Erhlich discovered that he had found his niche in life. Reginald *"Reggie"* Erhlich was a natural *"Lifer"*. Reginald *"Reggie"* Erhlich enjoyed and excelled, at life in the army.
At the conclusion of the war, Sergeant Reginald Erhlich, made the decision to remain in the Army.

Sergeant Erhlich was assigned to the 6th Cavalry, at Fort Richardson Texas, a short distance from the north Texas frontier.

****

The indigenous population, the Comanche and Kiowa peoples, of the southwestern plains, met the return of federal troops, following the conclusion of the Civil War, to the north Texas frontier, with strong resistance.

The Comanche and Kiowa, during the five-year absence of soldiers in the Comencheria and in the land designated by the United States as, "Indian Territory", had managed to halt, and to actually reduce, the number of white settlers, and buffalo hunters, and subsequent white-settlements, within their Hunting Grounds.

The detachment, by the federal government, of increasing numbers of soldiers was not only to protect the settlers, the army's mission was also to protect, the rail-road construction crews; to ensure the safe passage of the mail; and to protect the white settlers from not only Indian raids, but also to protect them from the increasing numbers of outlaws and desperadoes, who were drifting into northwest Texas.

In November of 1868, Gretchen joined her husband as a military-dependent, at Fort Richardson, Texas.

Shortly after her arrival at the North Texas military installation, Gretchen became a widow.

Sgt. Reginald Erhlich and three of his men, were killed by Comanche warriors, when on patrol, they rode to lend assistance to the driver, and two passengers, of an overland, stagecoach, under attack by a dozen Comanche warriors.
Gretchen Erhlich, born and raised in Goslar Germany, who had immigrated with her family to the United States, was now, at the age of *32,* a widow, alone on the North Texas frontier.

While ostensibly the Army—the wives of the soldiers—, were sympathetic to Sgt Ehrlich's widow's plight, the Army regulations succinctly stipulated that, civilian housing at the fort was restricted to dependants of active-duty soldiers, stationed at Fort Richardson.

Alone in a foreign-country, bereft of family and friends, Gretchen had been allowed to move into a vacant shack on the fort's "Laundry Row", a conglomeration of government built "shanty-shacks", adjacent to, but outside of the gates of the fort.

In order to survive, Gretchen had begun to "take-in" laundry, to wash and iron clothing for the soldiers.

One evening, after a particularly exhausting day's work, one of her regular customers, Lieutenant Hayes, one the bachelor officers at Fort Richardson, instead of the two dollar payment, due her for washing his shirts and trousers, reached into his pocket, and threw onto the table, a wrinkled ten dollar 'greenback' bill.

Gretchen picked-up the bill and thrust it toward the officer. "I'm sorry Lieutenant, I can't change this."

Lieutenant Hayes shrugged his shoulders. "That's it Miss…that's all I've got." He extended his hand toward Gretchen…" Not to worry though. Tell you what, why don't you just keep it, and we can work-off the change."

As she was attempting to draw back her hand, the Lieutenant grabbed her by her wrist. Gretchen tried to extricate herself from his grip.

"Please Lieutenant, you're hurting me…let me go, let me go".
Instead of complying, the burly-soldier, tightened his grip, and began to drag Gretchen toward her bed.

Gretchen, to no avail, continued to struggle. As she frequently, unwittingly did when excited, she reverted to her native language; *"Lass mich gehen Du dreckiges Schwein…du Schwein!"* She repeated her demand, this time in English.

"Let me go you filthy pig…you pig!"

Lieutenant Hayes tightened his grip on Gretchen's arm; he dragged the thrashing, resisting, stumbling woman across the room, and threw her onto the bed.

Gretchen attempted to get off of the bed; she couldn't move. She was pinned down to the mattress by the weight of the burly soldier's body.

The Lieutenant grabbed the top of Gretchen's dress and twisted it in his fist. With one violent tug, the dress split apart.

Lieutenant Hayes, while still lying upon the squirming woman, placed his huge, callused, hand over her mouth, successfully muffling Gretchen's screams.

He maneuvered his body, and managed to rip from Gretchen's writhing buttocks, her coarse cotton underpants.

With one huge hand, the Lieutenant managed to hold Gretchen's arms above her head. With his free hand, the Lieutenant began to unbutton the fly of his trousers.

Lieutenant Hayes positioned his legs between Gretchen's, he then spread her thighs apart, he grasped his rock-hard throbbing penis with his free hand, positioned himself, and with one forceful thrust, he entered Gretchen's body.

Gretchen lay passive beneath the Lieutenant, as he continuously raised and lowered his hips, thrusting himself, over and over… again and again, into her placid body.

After five—or as Gretchen later thought, had been more like three minutes, Lieutenant Hayes ceased pumping, and instead collapsed upon her, burying his penis into Gretchen's now moist, well-lubricated, vagina.

The lieutenant, without uttering a word, quickly extricated himself and stood, buttoning his uniform trousers, not looking at the prostrate woman, who remained motionless on the bed, her right arm covering her eyes.

Lieutenant Hayes picked up his neatly packaged bundle of laundry, turned his back to Gretchen, and left the shack.
Gretchen, her arm still covering her eyes, lay unmoving, motionless, on the bed.

During the commission of the actual rape, inexplicably, Gretchen had felt nothing. Neither physical pain, nor oddly she thought, neither had she felt emotional shame, or revulsion.

Instead Gretchen had felt numb. It had been almost eight months since Reggie's death. Eight months of grieving, of living on handouts, and quite frankly, having on a few occasions, been practically on the verge of starvation.

Gretchen slowly placed one foot at a time, onto the floor, and stood. She reached down, and with a remarkably steady hand, picked up the crumbled ten- dollar "greenback", from the floor.

Gretchen stared at her hand holding the money, her rough, and dry, reddened hand. She dropped the paper money onto the bed. Then Gretchen held both of her hands together, in front of her face, rotating them, in and out, first intently examining the back of the hands, then her palms.

The hours, days, weeks, and months, that she had spent with her hands submerged in harsh alkaline soapy-water, had taken its toll.

Gretchen walked over to the table, that she used as a nightstand, picked up her hand mirror, and examined her face.

The face staring back at her was that of a stranger. The face that she saw was that of a pale, and haggard white, literally white-female.
Gretchen pinched her cheeks and was pleased to see a "little-color", return to her face.

She returned to the bed, picked up the ten-dollar bill and staring at the money, began to think, to concentrate, and to rationalize.

Her son Hermann; her unborn, unnamed infant; her husband Reinhold; even her beloved homeland, Germany, were gone; they were all gone, and she was left here…here alone in this destitute, and desolate, in this God forsaken country.

On numerous occasions, during moments of hopeless despair, Gretchen had, contemplated taking her own life…of committing suicide. It was only the deeply ingrained teachings of her faith; "That the taking of one's life was a Mortal Sin", a sin that would preclude her joining her love-ones, in the after-life, that had prevented her ending her life.

Gretchen's faith was anchored by her absolute belief in the redemption of sin, and the promised of the reuniting of loved ones, in the after-life.

As she stared at the ten-dollar bill in her hand, Gretchen whose *ciphering skills were limited* did a quick rudimentary numerical assessment.

She was being paid fifty-cents to wash and to press six shirts, and fifty-cents to wash and to press, three pairs of trousers. On average, working ten hours a day, six days per week, on a good week, Gretchen managed to earn, nine dollars.
Gretchen, seated on the bed, continued to stare at the ten-dollar bill. She had been paid ten dollars, for essentially three minutes of her time.

She carefully, meticulously, folded the money, stuffed it into a handkerchief, and placed the handkerchief under her mattress. It was at that moment, that Gretchen Ehrlich made a life altering decision.

Gretchen became a part-time, novice practitioner, of the World's Oldest Profession. She became a prostitute.
Gretchen was a quick learner. She brought to her new, far more lucrative means of supporting herself, the same work ethic that she had espoused and had adhered to, for her entire life.

Word spread quickly among the fort's officer corps. It spread by word-of-mouth, like a wildfire, after a lightning strike, during the hot, arid summer, on the South West's dry plains. Put crudely, as indeed it was, at the Officer's Mess; "That in addition to cleaning your clothes, that for a small additional fee, that lovely, petite, little blonde, Gretchen Ehrlich, would with that wonderfully sexy mouth of hers', she would thoroughly, expertly, "*CLEAN*" your cock, while "*Emptying*", your balls".

Within a month of the unsolicited "word-of-mouth" advertisement of the availability of Gretchen's, "*DELUXE*" laundry services, a hastily formed committee made up of officers' wives, forced the post commander, to issue an order proclaiming that:

The Gretchen Erhlich *"DELUXE"* Laundry Services,
Were now officially

"Off-Limits",

To Fort Richardson Personnel.

Since servicing the Fort Richardson soldiers, constituted more than 90% of her income, Gretchen was forced to move on.
Gretchen made arrangements with the first wagon-master, whose wagon train consisting of twelve families, traveling in Conestoga Wagons, stopped at Fort Richardson for supplies.
The wagon train's ultimate destination was San Antonio Texas. Gretchen joined as the "personal-guest", of the wagon-master.
The cost of her passage was paid, directly to the wagon-master, in the form of, "*Personal Services-Rendered*".

When the wagon train made camp on the outskirts of San Angela, a wide-open town, adjacent to bustling Fort Concho, Gretchen left the wagon train, and easily found employment at the town's largest, most profitable, Saloon/Brothel, the Silver Slipper.
It had been a little more than four years since the death of her husband. Four years since Gretchen had engaged in sex, with a man of her own, choosing.

****

CHAPTER 88

Gretchen awoke with a start. Once again, she had had the same old haunting, dream.

During that groggy, foggy, transitional period, between sleep and wakefulness, she had been dreaming, softly sobbing.

Her left hand was tweaking the nibble of her right breast, while the fingers of her right hand were stroking her vagina. Gretchen was once again reliving that night, the last time that she had slept with her beloved husband, Reinhold.

It had been four years since Reinhold's death.
During that time, those minds numbing three years…actually more precisely, the two years that followed her decision to prostitute her body, Gretchen had literally learned, perfected, and performed an extensive variety, of sexual acts.
Word had spread among the cowboys and the professional gamblers that, *"If she's gotta vacant hole, and you got the money, Gretchen'll let you use your "Johnson", ta plug it up."*

Gretchen had had intercourse, vaginal, anal, oral, with scores of men.

She had, for an additional— some might call, an—exorbitant extra fee, satisfied some of her client's more exotic and sometimes perverted, "special requests".

Gretchen Ehrlich, had earned the dubious distinction, the reputation from both her peers, as well as from her clients, of being, one, of the very best, most skilled whores, west of the Mississippi.

Despite the numbers, and the frequency of her sexual encounters after her husband's death, Gretchen was hard pressed to recall a single time that a sexual liaison had been for her, either physically, or emotionally, gratifying.
After Reinhold's death, Gretchen's only means of achieving her own, physical sexual release, was when, alone at night, reliving in her mind, either awake, or dreaming, of the last time that she lay in the arms of her massacred husband.

Gretchen had found that her only recourse, for obtaining sexual release, was to literally, to "take matters into her own hands".

Out of necessity, Gretchen had added to her plethora of sexual skills, and manipulations, the "Art" of masturbation. As with all things sexual, at this too, Gretchen considered herself, to have become expert.

****

Justin too, as had Gretchen, had been forced to resort to "self-gratification", for sexual release.

Since his sudden, unplanned, flight from Richmond Virginia, and the United States Army, Justin had spent the majority of his nights, alone on the vast, expansive-prairie, alone under the millions of stars that formed a panoply, over covering the western frontier's, dark lonely skies.

Justin was not only alone; Justin was depressed and lonely. He would spend endless hours staring at his campfire, a vacant, blank, expression on his face.

Justin had suffered bouts of deep depression, as he mourned and grieved, over the death of Maureen.

He would stare for hours, at the campfire, mesmerized by the crackling sparks it made, that mimicked an earthly version of the millions of twinkling stars.

Justin fantasized about the life that he and Maureen would have, and should have, shared.

At the age of 31, Justin's body was at the peak of its physical maturity.

While the death of Maureen had stunted his emotions, his body… his physiology, continued to function.
Endless lonely hours, alone sitting by his campfire, Justin would invariably, become consumed by thoughts and memories of the all to brief time, that he had shared with the love of his life, Miss Maureen Montgomery.

Inevitably his mind would fixate, and Justin would relive their last night together.

Vivid memories of their sexual union, inevitably, resulted in Justin's experiencing tremendous erections.

At first, during his first few months of isolation, of being alone with his thoughts on the prairie, if at night, his thoughts of Maureen lead to his becoming sexually aroused, Justin would wrap himself in his blanket, and eventually, he would fall asleep.

As his days and nights, alone on the prairie increased, Justin began to become aware of an, at first, annoying, sensation, a feeling of discomfort, of heaviness, in his scrotum.

One morning, following an intensely restless, night filled with vividly clear dreams. Dreams of his time with Maureen, Justin awoke to find that his drawers were "sticky", clinging to his body.

His immediate reaction was that of discuss with himself. This was the first time—since his teen years, a slave on the Virginia Plantation—, that Justin, had had a "wet-dream".

After removing and washing his underwear, Justin noticed that for the first time in weeks that the dull ache, that uncomfortable feeling of heaviness in his testicles had vanished.

Although Justin was by no means, and did not profess to be, a man of Medicine, as a professional soldier, a leader of men in combat, he was well aware of, and the significance of, "Cause and Effect".

Justin's analytical mind, almost instantly, made the connection.

Now instead, of feelings of melancholy and depression, Justin began to use his memories of his time with Maureen, as a readily accessible, necessary, therapeutic stimulus.

Justin would use his cherished thoughts and memories of "Maureen", his little *"Mo"*, as the need arose, to facilitate relief.

Relief for an ailment, a malady, that his barracks buddies in the Massachusetts 54th, had referred to as, the *"Blue Balls"*.

Justin had come to conclude, that the obvious, logical, solution for his problem would be for him to find a woman. Not find a woman to love—the last thing he wanted, or needed was a "commitment"—, Justin wanted to find a "working-woman", he needed a prostitute. When he was forced by circumstances, to look for work in towns, the chance likely-hood, that he would encounter a black woman, even a black whore was remote.

In one town, while mopping floors and cleaning spittoons in a brothel, in an establishment with the pretentious name, "The International Ladies Palace", Justin had been pleasantly surprised, when he noticed that, while the bulk of the prostitutes were white, two of the eight "working-ladies", were not.

One woman was, Asian, the other was a tall, buxomly, statuesque, black-as-coal woman, who went by the name, *"Black-Beauty"*.

Once and only once, when he happened to be in her presence, Justin had politely greeted the *"Black-Beauty"*, — *"Morning Mam"*—the black woman had contemptuously, rebuked Justin's attempt at civility.

"Dun't you come sniffin' round me boy, dis here black-ass ain't fo you."

When Justin just stood there, staring at her, with an unmistakable look of hurt in his eyes, the *"Black-Beauty"* softened her voice, and whispered; *"Nigger, as pretty as you is…if'n deese white boys gets word dat I been wid a "Nigger", dat be da end of me makin' any money in dis here town."*

Now whenever, the need *"arose"*, Justin would unabashedly, masturbate.

****

When her "sleep" had been interrupted, Gretchen remembered thinking that someone or something, was in the hallway.

She glanced at the gold-plated timepiece, on the table. A bauble, which had been given to her by one of her now anonymous, faceless, former clients.
Ten minutes past five.

Gretchen swung her legs to the side of the bed. She hastily put on and tied around her waist, her practically, translucent robe.

Barefoot, she plodded across the floor and opened the door.

E. Pluribus Unum

There he was, looking like some mythical "bronze" god, bent over at the waist, shirtless, his perspiring body glistening, reflecting the light from the wall-mounted, oil lamp.

Justin was at the top of the stairs, wringing out his heavy mop, when he sensed that he was being watched. He slowly turned, and there standing in her doorway, staring at him was the white woman…Justin remembered her name, Gretchen.

The light from the interior of her bedroom, passing through her thin robe, visually had the affect of separating, symmetrically, each of the white woman's long, shapely, legs.

Gretchen, who before being awakened by this *"bronze god"*, had been on the verge of physical release… of "climaxing", on an impulsive softly, whispered; "You their… boy. Bring that mop over here."

Justin straightened, lowered his head, and staring at his feet, mop-in-hand, slowly shuffled over to the white woman.

It had been more than three years, since the death of her husband, three years since Gretchen Ehrlich, had actually lain with a man…any man, of her own choosing.

Gretchen didn't know why. She hadn't given her spontaneous actions any pre-thought… out of all of the men readily available to her, Gretchen didn't really know why, she had chosen this man.

Then and there… at this moment in time, after two long years of sharing her bed with multiple partners, countless customers, having had multiple episodes of meaningless sex, Gretchen choose to have sex, with this man.

Justin instinctively assumed his "survival" posture, that of obsequious, servile, obedience.

"Yessum?"

Gretchen stood with her legs slightly spread apart. She nodded her head, toward the interior of her room. "I spilled a tub of face powder. It's all over the floor. I would be most appreciative if you would be so kind as to mop it up for me."

Justin— his mop in hand— stepped into the room. His eyes scanned the floor, looking for the spill.

Gretchen slowly closed the door, pushing it shut, and locking the door by lowering into place, the wooden bolt, which had been nailed to the wall.

At the sound of the door closing behind him, Justin spun around, facing the woman.

The white woman had opened her robe and with her left hand was cupping her right breast, while the two middle fingers of her left hand, had disappeared into the tuft of blonde hair, that shielded her vagina.

Justin's autonomic, physiologic reaction, to the sight of the beautiful, alluring woman, standing provocatively, invitingly, naked before him, resulted in his experiencing an instantaneous, pulsating, rock-hard, erection.

Despite his body's reflexive physical response, Justin's mental response, reinforced by more than two hundred years of slavery, depredation, and subjugation, including enumerable, lynchings—, was the complete opposite, the antithesis, of that of his lower body's, reaction. Initially, when Gretchen saw the black man's almost immediate, response to the sight of her nakedness, the unmistakable meaning of the bulge in his tight trousers, had resulted in the beginnings of a knowing smile, forming at the corners of her mouth.

Gretchen however, was momentarily perplexed and a bit confused and disappointed, when as rapidly as the "bulge", in the black man's trousers had appeared, it…the "bulge", was slowly, gradually, but most definitely, deflating.

Gretchen sat down on the bed. Still cupping her right breast with her left hand, she placed the index finger of her free hand into her mouth, and began to make slurping, sucking, sounds.

She removed her hand from her breast, her palm facing her, and made a fist. Her index finger, "sprung", extended from the fist, and with three rapid twitches, she beckoned Justin to join her on the bed.

Justin hesitated. While his initial reaction to the sight of, and the blatant invitation of the beautiful, practically, naked woman had been that of animal lust and desire... he hesitated.

Reality had set in, and he had managed to reverse his body's autonomic, natural, response, to Gretchen's sensual, provocations.

Hundreds of years of how to survive in the white-man's world, which had been incessantly, drummed into him since childhood, had counteracted, and had overcome his natural, biological, instincts.

Justin's rock-hard, throbbing, erection had been reduced to that, of at best, being described as an impressive, semi-erection.

More so than either of them knew, or could have imagined, Justin Gulliver and Gretchen Ehrlich, had much in common.

They had both, do to acts of violence, of having the "loves-of-their-lives", taken from them, "murdered", shared and had in common, a heart-wrenching, horrendous loss.
They had both, for years, been "alone".

Gretchen was "alone". She was "alone" even when, in order to survive, she had sold her body to a parade of hundreds, of faceless men.

Justin too was "alone" … a black man, an outlaw in a white man's world, "alone", staying alive by limiting and avoiding human-contact.

They were both "alone", living day-to-day, existing, and "alone".

The black man's hesitancy surprised and began to anger Gretchen.

This was the first time in her life that a man any man, had not immediately succumbed, to her "open-invitation", for sex.

Gretchen removed her robe and lay supine, down on the bed. With the same finger that she had been teasingly, thrusting into her vagina, she once again beckoned Justin.
Gretchen pointed to a spot on the bed, next to her.

When Justin hesitated, she whispered, "are you going to sit down here beside me, or I'm I going to have to wake-up the place, by screaming "*RAPE*".

Justin remembered thinking…" Oh shit, how am I going to get out of this?"

When Justin didn't move, Gretchen shrugged, "Okay, have it your way". She opened her mouth to scream, before she could make a sound, Justin's hand was clamped over her mouth.

Gretchen's eyes bulged in fear. She remembered thinking… "Have I gone too far, is this "Bronze Adonis", going to kill me"?

Justin slowly removed his hand from Gretchen's mouth, and slumped down next to her, onto the bed.

Gretchen stood, her eyes fixed, unblinking, upon his, began to deftly unbutton, Justin's shirt, then his pants.

Justin sat rigid, like a stone, not moving.   Gretchen, with her free hand, began to remove Justin's shirt.

Then she stood, kneeled on the floor, and began to tug on the black man's trousers. "Lay back and raise your hips." Justin complied.

As she slowly pulled down the black man's pants, Gretchen began to kiss the inside of his thighs, sucking at the taut muscular flesh, of his inner thighs.

The fingers of Gretchen's left hand, wrapped around Justin's semi-erect penis, while with her right hand, she gently caressed, cupped and then lifted Justin's testicles to her mouth.

Gretchen began to lightly plant kisses, in turn, onto each of Justin's testicles.

Justin shuddered. He knew that he was on the precipice; just seconds away from losing his battle, to remain passive.

Gretchen's mouth enveloped, first his right, then Justin's left testicle. She began to suck, creating a vacuum with her mouth.

She freed-up the hand that had been surrounding Justin's now fully erect, throbbing, penis, and used it to knead the taut muscles of Justin's upper-thigh.

Gretchen's tongue, as if it had a mind of its own, began to flick, licks, as her mouth slowly, tantalizingly, traveled up, the length of Justin's ever-expanding penis.

She kissed the head of his penis; she poked the tip of her tongue, into the "*eye*" of Justin's penis and then, she took his fully erect, throbbing penis, into his mouth.

Gretchen was surprised to discover, that in spite of all of her pre-coital foreplay, the black man's penis, was still expanding inside her mouth.

Gretchen, sensing that the pulsating, throbbing penis, now filling every inch of her mouth, was on the verge of exploding, hastily stood, disengaging, separating herself from this "*Bronze-god*".

Justin was indeed on the verge of exploding, when the white woman, abruptly removed her mouth from his penis.

Justin was disappointed. Disappointed that he had not climaxed, and disappointed even more so, that he had not had the ability to control his body.

Disappointed that despite his attempts to, he had not had the strength, the will power, to resist.

He struggled to regain control of his body. Though he did not know why, the white woman had stopped, she had in fact, stopped.

Justin knew that if she had not stopped, his penis—which he was now convinced, had a mind of its own—would have exploded, spewing forth "*gallons*", of pent-up semen.

Justin took a moment to attempt to refocus his mind. Trying to think benign thoughts, to concentrate on the admonishments, the sage wisdom of his mother… of all the mothers, passed down to him from generations of black mothers; mothers of black men, born into slavery:

"Honey no matta what ya duz, ya dun't neva wanna-be by ya self, wit no white woman".

"It dun't mak a lik ah difrence, if she be da Mizztress, if she be the Mizztress' dawtah Beeka, or eben if she be one ah dem poo-white-trash, town-floozies".

"It dun't maks no matta, dem white mens'll hangs ya lik a dawg, iffin dey catches ya alone… eben jus talkin', wid a white woman!"

Gretchen straddled Justin, wrapping her arms around his neck, and kissed him.

Her tongue, pushed against his clenched lips, finally darting into his mouth.

Jason moaned as without his guidance, his penis, like a moth to a flame, found its way, into Gretchen's welcoming vagina.

Gretchen, still impaled, astride the tall black man's penis, leaned over placing her hands onto the bed's headboard, and began to rapidly and rhythmically, move her hips, up and down, her vagina making sucking sounds, in sync with, and complimenting, her pelvic gyrations.

Justin gritted his teeth, attempting to control his body, to not give in to prolong the exquisite sensations, yet to somehow deny this white woman the satisfaction, and to forestall, and delay his rapidly approaching, inevitable, explosive ejaculation.

Losing control, and oblivious to the circumstances that had led to this moment, with both of his hands, Justin gripped each check of Gretchen's firm, glistening buttocks, slowing, then stilling, her now frantic gyrations.

Without their bodies breaking physical contact, Justin stood, supporting Gretchen's as though she were a feather.

Gretchen's legs were tightly wrapped, locked, around Justin's rib-cage, as the two of them as one, stumbled around the small room, bumping into and ricocheting from contact, with the walls, their mouths locked in a passionate kiss.

Still joined together by their loins, Justin's "key", firmly inserted and being massaged by the tumblers of Gretchen's "lock", Justin and Gretchen, with Justin on top, dropped to the bed.

Justin, covering Gretchen's mouth with his own, began to simultaneously thrust his rock-hard penis, and his exploring, searching, tongue, into Gretchen's two welcoming hot orifices, her hot, pulsating vagina, and her delicious mouth.

Gretchen, for the first time, since her husband's death three years ago, despite her having had to endure sex, with an endless parade of countless, faceless men, clung as hard as she could to this man.

Then as they exploded in ecstasy together, she cried out, oh, oh, oh… *"Gott im Himmel"*, *Reinhold, Mein Liebling*…I'm coming, I'm coming!"
Justin too, had reached his physical and emotional "peak".

With reckless, primordial, abandon, he buried his throbbing, rock-hard penis into Gretchen's, welcoming, moist, vagina, and he too exploded. A torrent of pent-up, semen, gushed forth from his loins.

Justin collapsed in Gretchen's arms, without realizing what he was saying, he began to moaning; *"Mo…Oh Mo…My Love… Mo"*.

Gretchen lay sprawled on the bed, spent, totally, physically drained, and exhausted.

Justin was berating himself; "What the hell have I done".
After his body's, having attained complete and total physical release and satisfaction, Justin's mind had crashed.

He had no illusions. If he were to be caught in this white woman's bed, she would turn on him…she most likely *points an accusatory finger at him, and scream, at the top of her lungs; "RAPE, that Nigger raped me"!*

In his mind, the same age-old thoughts, and alarms, were sounding.

His mother's words of warning, were repeating themselves in his mind, over and over again, a clarion, sounding the alarm: would

"No matta what ya duz, ya dun't neba wanna-be by ya self, wit no white woman". "Dat drives dem white mens crazy!"

"It dun't mak a lick ah difrence, if she be da Mizztress, if she be the Mizztress' dawtah, or eben ifin she be one ah dem poo-white-trash, floozies".

"It dun't maks no matta, dem white mens'll hangs ya… dem white mens'll hangs ya…, iffin dey catches ya, dem, white mens'll hangs ya… lik ya was a dawg.!"

Justin silently, picked-up his clothes—which had been haphazardly, strewn over the floor—, and dressed.

He glanced over his shoulder and looked at the "naked" white woman, lying on the bed. She was no longer naked.

While he had been gathering his clothes and dressing, the woman had pulled the bed sheet up over her body and appeared to be fast asleep.

In sleep, her face had softened. A tranquil look of peace, and serenity had smoothed out and replaced, the tiny, spider-web-like, lines around her eyes.

As quietly as he could, Justin walked over to the door, lifted its wooden bolt, opened the door, and left.

****

When he returned to the livery stable, Justin hurriedly climbed the ladder, that lead to the hayloft.

He brushed aside the two bales of hay that sat atop the "hollowed-out" bale, in which he hid his money.

Justin carefully disassembled the bale of hay, haphazardly adding to the accumulation of loose straw, which blanketed the floor of the hayloft.

Justin carefully, meticulously, advanced his hand through the bale of straw. He withdrew his hand. His fingers were clutching the faded red bandana that held his savings.

Justin counted the money, seventy-three, one-dollar bills.

Justin removed thirty-dollar bills, *folded the bills in half, and clenched the wad of money between his teeth.*
He then stuffed the remainder of the money into both of the front pockets, of his trousers.

Justin picked up his bedroll, in which he had carefully cushioned and wrapped, his Springfield rifle.

He threw the bedroll, from the hayloft, down to the floor of the stable.

With his left hand, he reached for his saddle. His hand automatically, went to the saddle's skirt, the area of the saddle where he had, painstakingly overtime, managed to remove the letters (*US*).

He then slid his hand into the open space, between the saddle horn, and the seat-rise.

Holding the saddle in his left hand, with his free hand gripping the top rung, he descended down the ladder.

When he reached the floor, Justin rummaged in, and removed an envelope from his saddlebags. He placed thirty-one-dollar bills, which had been clinched between his teeth, into the envelope, and shoved the envelope under the office door, of the owner of the livery stable.

Justin saddled, and mounted his bought and paid for, twelve-year-old mare. He removed his rifle from the scabbard, chambered a round, laid the weapon across his lap, and slowly, rode toward the edge of town.

When he reached the outskirts of town, he glanced over his shoulder and with his knees, applied pressure to the mare's sagging flanks.

The mare responded by increasing her pace, from a slow deliberate walk, to a canter, which was for her, a headlong gallop.

Justin, remembering the words often said by some of his Massachusetts's 54th, former comrades-in-arms, after a rowdy evening, spent in a town's seedy saloon, smiled and chuckled... "Now it's for damn sure as hell;

"Time ta get my black-ass, the Hell-Outta-Dodge".

****

It had been a little more than two months, since his rather hasty departure, from the town of San Angelo, when Justin now penniless, and practically out of supplies, was forced to look for work.

More so than in the past, especially after the potentially disastrous episode with the white woman, at the Silver Slipper Saloon/Brothel, Justin's preference for a place to work, was to if possible, find work at one of the scattered farms or ranches, that dotted the vast, expansive, Texas plains.

In an effort to conserve the steadily, dwindling, strength of his aging horse, Justin had resorted to a daily routine of riding *"Ole Girl"* for an hour, then walking an hour, while leading the laboring animal, by the reins.

It happened suddenly, while he was riding the mare. Apparently, a combination of age, dehydration, and weariness, had finally taken its toll.

The *"Ole Girl"* stumbled, and then collapsed. Justin, who had been dozing in the saddle, had managed to free his feet from the saddle's stirrups, barely avoiding injury, as the eight-hundred-pound animal, fell to ground.

Justin picked himself up, and pulling on the horse's reins, urged cajoled, and pleaded with the aged mare; "Come on "Ole-Girl", get up. You can do it…get up.

When the horse did not respond, Justin sighed, he removed his rifle from its scabbard, and chambered a round, …Sorry *"Ole Girl"*, guess it's just me now, who'll be doing the walking."

The old mare did not move. She just lay where she had fallen, her now dull unseeing eyes, staring into space. "Ole Girl", shuddered, and blew one last breath from her quivering nostrils, and dyed.

Once again, Justin was afoot. He looked around, surveying his surroundings. There was no sign, not a single wagon rut. Nothing to indicate that he was anywhere, near a town.
All that he saw was an endless sea of grass, interrupted only by a solitary juniper bush.

Justin removed his canteen and his saddlebags from the fallen horse. He left the heavy saddle, and with his saddlebags and rifle in hand, walked over to sit in the meager shade afforded by the near-by juniper tree.
He removed his canteen and his saddlebags, from the fallen horse. He left the heavy saddle, and trudged over to sit in the meager shade afforded by the near-by juniper tree.

Seated in the shade contemplating his options, Justin's chin had slumped down to rest on his chest. In the oppressive heat, he had momentarily, dozed-off.

He was awakened by the faint, distant, sound of horses…many horses.

Justin's immediate thought was, "Indians"! After five long, lonely years, most of it alone on the plains, his luck had finally, run out.

He knew that if he encountered Indians, multiple hostiles, he knew that a solitary man, on foot, without a horse, in this country, was in fact, a dead-man.

Justin ran over to the dead horse, frantically waving his rifle in the air, scattering the two buzzards that were busy feeding on the carcass of the dead animal.

Startled, the scavenging birds, spread their wings, and took flight.

Justin rested his rifle on the dead horse's rear legs, he lay prone, his face just inches away from the hole, oozing blood and intestines, that the vultures had torn the horses, rapidly putrefying, abdomen.

The outline of three men on horseback came into view. Justin sighted down the barrel of his rifle. As his finger touched the rifle's trigger, he stopped.

The men riding toward him were not Indians. The man at the front of the trio was white.

He was wearing a loose-fitting brown shirt. The white man's butternut gray trousers, reminded Justin of the uniform pants, which had been worn by the confederate rebels.
A wide brimmed, modified, Mexican sombrero type hat, with the front brim, turned-up, sat squarely on the white man's head.

The two mounted men, bringing up the rear, twenty yards behind the white man, wore the blue uniforms of Union Army soldiers.

Justin did a double take. The two uniformed soldiers were black. They were wearing light blue kersey trousers, with yellow strips running down the legs of the trousers, and light blue fatigue shirts, which identified them as United States Cavalry.

Justin stood, and holding his rifle by the barrel with both hands, as if it was a flagpole, without a flag, and began to vigorously wave the weapon over his head.

****

E. Pluribus Unum

"Well looka here, lookey here… a darky, all alone, by his-self, out here in Injun country."

"What you up to boy? What cha doing way out here, all by yourself, in this God forsaken country?

Justin immediately recognizing the man's distinctive, pronounced southern accent, and his condescending mannerism, automatically assumed the role of an emancipated, docile, freedman.

His mind was racing. *"Damn…just my luck. The two kinds of people that I lest wanted to see. A Southern Cracker, who's probably, still smarting from losing the war. And a detachment of army soldiers, who just might be on the look-out for deserters".*

Justin spoke, concocting his response, *"on-the-fly"*, while he was speaking.

"Morn'n Suh, name's Justin Gulliver. I'se on my way ta Fort Concho. Ridin' dere ta join-up wid da colored army, wen my hoss dun gone and died on me".

The two black troopers, Pvts. Anthony Jackson and Linwood Harvey reigned in their mounts.

They too were surprised to see a black man, a black civilian, alone in "Injun Country".

Justin pointed his finger at the black soldiers; *"Ise fixin' ta gits me one ah dem blue suits."*

Pvt. Jackson's horse's nostrils began to quiver, his eyes rolled in their sockets, as he smelled the blood and the entrails of the black man's dead horse.

Suddenly the horse reared on his hind legs, his front legs pawing at the air. When all four legs returned to the Earth, Jackson' horse began to violently buck, unseating his rider.

Pvt. Jackson falling awkwardly, in mid-air, instinctively extended his left hand in an attempt to cushion his fall. He landed with a thud, straining his left wrist.

Both the white man, as well as was Pvt. Harvey, was doubled over, laughing.

Pvt. Jackson managed to stand. He gingerly, with his right hand, examined his injured left-wrist.

Pvt. Harvey had regained his composure. He turned his horse's head, and trotted after Jackson's horse, grabbed the reins of the frightened animal, and walked him back, handing the horses' reins to Pvt. Jackson.

Humiliated at being the object of the two men's laughter, his left wrist throbbing, Jackson wrapped the reins around his injured wrist, and with his right hand, loosened his gun belt. He removed the colt revolver from its holster, and tucked the gun into the waistband of his trousers.

Pvt. Jackson, holding the horse's reins firmly, began to lash out at the horse with the gun belt.

His blows caused the horse to once again, rise up on his hind legs, his front legs seeking the skull of his antagonist.

The horse's ears were laid back. His whites of his eyes were red, bloodshot. Mucus was dripping from the animal's nostrils, and saliva from its' mouth.

Without thinking, Justin ran between horse and man.

"Cut dat out, stop beatin' on dat hoss. Da hoss was onlest afeared ah the smell of blood, ah death, comin' from my dead hoss."

Justin took the reins from the soldier, and in a tranquil, soothing voice, whispered to the agitated horse.

In a melodic, soothing voice, while he gently stroked the horse's muzzle, Justin began to talk to the frightened horse, to whisper in his ear; *"Eee-zy dere big fella; calm yourself down... it's alrite. I ain't gonna let him hurt you nun".*

"I noos how yu be feelin. Tain't eee-zy when yu smells blood an guts, is it? Specially wen da blood and guts be coming from yu own kind."

"Thar thar boy, yu jus calm yo self down. Eber thing be alrite."

The white man, and the two black soldiers, was silent. The stood, flabbergasted, staring in awe, and astonishment at the black stranger.

The white man was the first to speak; "Well I'll be damned…if that don't beat all. I've been 'roun horses, all my life. I've seen lots of men good at breaking and handling, horses. But I swear, I ain't never seed nothing, the likes of that."

"How'd you do that boy? I thought that horse's hoofs, was 'bout to split wide-open, the skull of that stupid-idiot."

"Tell you what boy, soons as Lieutenant Powell, and the rest of his "black-birds", them wannabe soldiers, herding those thirty-head of horses, catches up with us, I aims ta recommend ta the lieutenant, that he makes a "black-bird" soldier-boy, outta you."

****

Chapter 89

Bivouac location - Company "A" 10th Cavalry – Fort Concho Texas– 1873

Pvt. Justin Gulliver (*formerly, Sergeant Major Jason Ruth, [USA-AWOL]*, untied the dirty red bandana that had been loosely slung around his neck, and wiped the stinging sweat from eyes.

Although he had been born and lived all of his life in the South, Jason Ruth— who in order to avoid, the law, had changed his name, and was now known as Justin Gulliver—, had never experienced the intensity of the oppressive, relentless heat, of the west Texas sun.

Pvt. Gulliver was one of the four new, black recruits, that Sergeant Zachary Stevens had detailed the task, of digging a two-foot-deep, twenty-four-foot-long latrine-ditch, behind the Company A's, enlisted troops' barracks.

For this work-detail, Justin had been paired with a fellow member of his squad, Pvt. Vernon Munsford.

Pvts. Anthony Jackson, and Linwood Harvey were given the task of starting their excavation at the extreme end of the ditch, opposite the end from Pvts, Gulliver and Munsford.

Sgt. Stevens had planted stakes at the midpoint of the "new" latrine-ditch. He had promised a pass to the team that first reached, reached the stakes.

There was a steady synchronized movement, of the tools of the four laboring soldiers, as they attempted to loosen and remove the hard-packed earth from the ditch.

Following each swing of Pvt. Munsford's long handled pick-axe, Justin would scoop up onto the pan of his shovel, the pitifully sparse amount of dirty-white gravelly material, that the locals called caliche, and throw the debri over the lip of the ditch.

After digging out and lifting three large, heavy, rocks, with the pointed end of his shovel, Justin paused for a moment, and tentatively, gingerly examined his swollen left-hand.

A huge blister at the base of his middle finger had ruptured, and was oozing a pinkish mixture of blood and pus.

Justin placed his shovel between his legs, untied and removed the sweat and dirt saturated bandana from around his neck, balled it up, and used it as a cushion between his blistered left hand and the shovel.

Pvt. Munsford—seeing Justin attempting to, with his right hand and his teeth clamped to one end of the filthy bandana, trying to tie the scarf around his swollen left hand—, after two futile swings of his pick, attempting to bury the blade into the ground, stopped and let the pick fall to the ground.

Pvt. Munsford pulled a clean kerchief from the back pocket of his trousers, walked over to Justin, and stuffed the clean clothe between Justin's flesh and the filthy bandana. He then secured the impromptu, makeshift bandage, tying together the ends of the bandana.

Pvt. Munsford was an extraordinarily idealistic, naive, twenty-four-year-old, five-foot-nine inches tall, tan-complexioned, free born black man.

In addition to the fact that he was one of the few literate black soldiers in the company, a striking feature, an anomaly of Vernon Munsford's physical appearance, caused him to stand-out from the black-masses, thus preventing Pvt. Vernon Munsford from blending in; from just becoming another black face, in a sea of black faces, an anomaly that branded the young black man, as being different.

While the color of Pvt. Munsford 's skin was definitely a shade lighter than that of most of the soldiers of the 10th Cavalry—, the variety of skin tones from nature's palette, displayed by the *"Colored"* troops, ran the gamut from *"charcoal-black"*, to what had been described derisively y some, but more often in a jocular manner, by the white officers, and by the black troopers, as being *"damn near white"*—, Vernon's facial features, his broad flat nose, his *"kinky"* hair, were all consistent with that of the typical black soldier.

The one physical-phenotypic feature that set Vernon apart from his fellow black soldiers, was most definitely not, the color of his skin, nor was it the texture of his hair.

Vernon's unique distinguishing physical feature was most definitely the COLOR, not the texture… but was the natural COLOR, of his *"nappy-kinky"* hair.

Vernon Munsford had been blessed—he considered it, as having been cursed—, with a full head of tightly curled, *flaming red "nappy-kinky"* hair.

Pvt. Vernon Munsford, most definitely *"stood-out"*, in a crowd.

****

Vernon Munsford had lived an extraordinarily sheltered, insulated life. His parents had as best they could, protected and isolated, Vernon and his two younger sisters, from the societal cruelties of the real world.

Vernon's parents, John and Elsie Munsford, were, by any of the parameters used to measure a family's standing in the black community, John and Elsie Munsford, were a well to do, economically stable, educated black couple.

John and Elsie, Vernon's parents, and their circle of friends, were members of Philadelphia's elitist, black-bourgeois, community. A community that politically, tended to merely give token lip service, to the belief that the enslavement of their black brethren in the South, was "wicked and horrible".

Their apathy was undoubtedly fueled by the frequently mumbled liturgy, that was heard when a slave atrocity was reported in the northern press; "There but for the grace of God…"

The Munsford's social circle justified their selfish "look-the other-way" attitude, by feebly convincing one another that slavery in the United States, as had been the case in most of the civilized world, would eventually be abolished.

On numerous occasions, Vernon and his two younger sisters had been told by their parents, that in their encounters with white folks, that they should always be humble, courteous, and respectful. That they should thank God for his blessings, and that they should *"Not rock the boat"*.

The plight of the *"Black man" in America*, especially the plight of the four million enslaved black men, women, and children in the South, was rarely if ever, discussed, in the Munsford house.

"Rusty" Vernon's nickname, that had been thrust upon him due to the reddish-orange *rust-like* color of his hair, for his entire life, had lived in a segregated, protective cocoon.

His parents had provided for him, a safe sanguine, segregated, sheltered life, in the *"Colored"* upscale section, of the city of brotherly-love, Philadelphia Pennsylvania.

****

In 1863, when black men had been allowed to enlist in the Union Army, and to fight for their country… to fight for the abolition of slavery, Vernon had been an eager fourteen-year-old adolescent, chomping at the bit, raring to go, to join-up, and fight the enemy, the secessionist rebs.

Although the war had been over now for nearly a decade, and he had missed his opportunity to join-up, and to fight the rebs, Vernon was determined not to miss this opportunity to join-up and fight for his country, this time to protect his country from the savage, barbaric Indians.

In addition to his primary reason, that of patriotism, Vernon's reasons for enlisting in the army, included a strong secondary motivation. Vernon Munsford had a seemingly unquenchable thirst for adventure.

Vernon had convinced himself that his enlistment in one of the newly established, post Civil War "Colored" army regiments, was his chance to strike out on his own.

A chance for him to once and for all, get away from his boorish pedestrian life, as a member of the "Colored-Upper-class".

Vernon Munsford — Rusty was the nickname that he, for as long as he could remember, had preferred—, Vernon *"Rusty"* Munsford was a son of the *"Elitist Colored Folks"*, the preachers, teachers, the community shop-owners, the clerks, the upper echelon, Colored Aristocracy.

For most of his life, "Rusty" Munsford, had lived in an isolated fragile, pretentious 'colored" society, that either by design, or because of misguided contempt, had ignored the plight of the poor, illiterate black man, be he a southern slave, or what they considered a "shiftless" northern black nigger.

Young Vernon had been taught to love his country. As a kid he had believed in, the country's ultimate fulfillment, of its "Manifest Destiny", the country's expansion over the North American Continent.

Vernon's parents were aware of their son's idealistic, sense of patriotism.

After years of shielding, protecting their children— as best as they could—, from the harsh realities of being black in America, inexplicably*" Rusty"*, their twenty-four-year-old son Rusty, had done the unthinkable.

Vernon *"Rusty"* Munsford, an educated, literate, young black man, a *"Colored"* man of privilege, and social standing, in the black-community, had on an impulsive whim, enlisted in the United States Army's 10th Cavalry.

****

Sergeant Stevens, his arms folded across his chest, stood on the rim of the ditch, glaring down at two of the four recruits. The Sgt. cleared his throat, and spat into the excavation.

"You dere...you two Gulliva, an Moonsfuck. What's da matta boys, is dose smooth, soft, brown hands of yourn, dose hands dats as soft as a baby's ass, with nary a callous on um... is dose baby soft hands startin' ta blista?"

Justin, sensing that the rookie, Pvt. Munsford was about to probably earnestly answer, the Sergeant's leading rhetorical question… thus taking the bait, setting himself… setting them both up for further hazing, spoke-up;

"Jus gettin' a betta grip sarge…soos' I kin getta betta hold, a can shovel out dirt fasta frum dis here hole."

Sgt. Stevens was disappointed. He had been prepared and primed to delivery a real tongue-lashing, to what he had anticipated would be the recruits self-serving excuses.

Instead, the black non-com, once again "hawked-up" a ball of phlegm from the deep recesses of his chest, and spat into the ditch; *"Yu two ladies best ta quit holdin' hands, an get back to clearin' dat dere ditch".*

Sergeant Stevens spun on his heel and briskly walked away.

****

Sergeant Zachary Stevens was a thirty-five-year-old, semiliterate black man, who thanks to President Lincoln's Emancipation Proclamation, and the Union Army, was now legally, a freeman.

Zachary Stevens, was a civil war veteran, a black "contraband-soldier", who in 1864 as a member of the 4th Regiment U.S. Colored Infantry, had fought and been seriously wounded in the Battle of Chaffin's Farm, a battle that took place just south of Richmond Virginia. A battle that many believed was instrumental in precipitating the rebel army's, General Robert E. Lee's surrender to General Ulysses S. Grant.

Zachary Stevens had been born a slave on a rice plantation, located twenty miles north of the city of New Orleans.

At the age of twenty-eight, after having been *"swept-up"* after being read the soaring speeches of Frederick Douglas, and the abolitionist's writings of Horace Greeley, read to him by members of the "Underground Rail Road" —, Zachary Stevens had answered the call. He had joined the Union Army.

Zachary Stevens was but one of the tens of thousands of former slaves, who had escaped from slavery, and who, after President Lincoln's issuance of the Emancipation Proclamation, had joined the United States Armed Forces.

Sergeant Zachary Stevens was but one of the many *"colored"* soldiers, who had decided to remain in the army after the conclusion of their service during the *"War for the Black Man's Freedom"*.

At the conclusion of the Civil War, tens of thousands of black soldiers found themselves faced with a dilemma.

Many of these black men, veterans of the war, had known only two ways of life, the wretched, subservient, demeaning, life of a slave, or the life of a soldier in the Union Army.

They could either return to the place of their birth, and scratch out a living, most-likely as a "colored" man, a sharecropper, a defacto slave, in the white man's South; or they could possibly choose to live a life as a "colored" man in the North, competing with poor-white laborers, for a limited number of jobs, while being subjected to the more subtle, veiled, racist communities in the North; or they could choose, as thousands of black soldiers did, to remain as soldiers in the United States Army.

Despite the Army's policy of adhering to an inherently racists, all- white officer corps—, Sergeant Stevens, as did many of his fellow black-veterans, preferred the structured, racially segregated army-life, to the blatant, outspoken, overt racism facing the life of a *"colored"* man in the post Civil War, United States.

****

Chapter 90

Company "A" 10th Cavalry – Twenty-five Miles South of the "New" Rosewood - Cattle Ranch) August 4th 1875)

The air was still, hot and oppressive. Occasionally a sudden gust of dry air, would blow across the plains, causing the tails of the plodding horses to dance in the breeze.

Waves of shimmering stifling hot air, created mirages, illusions of distant, tranquil, cool silver lakes of water. Lakes that disappeared long before a man could reach them.

Captain Brian Griffin, Company Commander of the 10th Cavalry's Company "A", a veteran officer who during the civil war had attained the brevet rank of Lieutenant Colonel, was leading his first patrol in the west, tracking a Kiowa-Comanche hunting party, in territory known to be harboring militant, hostiles.
The former Lieutenant Colonel was anxious to reclaim what he felt he had earned leading Union forces, during the Civil War, the rank of Lieutenant Colonel.

It was well known throughout the Army, that a quick means for promotion was for an officer, especially a cavalry officer, to serve in one of the recently commissioned*" colored"* cavalry regiments, either the 9th, or the 10th United States Cavalry, who the Indians referred to as "*Buffalo Soldiers*".

Captain Griffin's patrol consisted of twenty-two troopers, of the 1st, platoon of the 10th's Cavalry's, Company "A".

Eighteen of the troopers rode, mostly in two columns, followed by a "chuck-wagon", that was manned by two of the company's cooks. Two troopers were detailed to provide security, by riding behind the wagon.

Sergeant Zachary Stevens, and Corporal Justin Gulliver, were two of the five non-coms, among the patrol's twenty enlisted men.

Additionally, the patrol had the services of an Indian scout. The scout appeared on the army's rosters as, Joe Light-Foot, Pawnee-Indian scout.

Joe Light-foot rode in advance of the patrol, sometimes as far out in front, as thirty miles, scouting, looking for Indian sign, ahead of the platoon.

The reason for the army's presence on the plains was to protect the white settlers, who thanks to the presence of the railroad, were now coming in droves, into the "Indian Territory.

Additionally, the Army's mission was to protect the travel routes, the mail, and the railroad crews from attacks by hostile Indians, and outlaws, and to explore and map the Great Plains.

For the past twenty miles, the men and their horses, had been plodding along, moving northeast, paralleling what appeared to the men to be, an endless extension of railroad tracks, that disappeared over the horizon.

The troopers were walking, leading their horses in columns of two's, less than a quarter of a mile, due east, of a line of low rolling hills.

Augmenting their regulation government issued summer uniforms, each of Captain Griffin's trooper's regulation trousers, had been reinforced with canvas patches on the seat and thighs.

The soldiers' McClellan saddles, carried a blanket-bedroll with an extra pair of breeches, tied behind the seat of his saddle.

Also attached to their saddles, were, a lariat, a picket pin, a canteen and a tin plate.

A saddle scabbard on the right side of the saddle, held the soldiers' Spencer Repeating Rifle.

Each trooper wore around his waist; a sheath knife on his left hip, and his holster with pistol butt forward, on the right hip.

All of the men had slung around their shoulders, bandoliers, brimming with cartridges.

As they trudged along under the hot sun, the brims of straw hats and the bills of a few kepi-caps shaded their eyes.

On the seventh day of their time in the field, the monotony of their trek across the plains had been briefly interrupted, by billows of black-smoke, rising from the chimney of the locomotive of a, westward bound, Union Pacific, passenger train.

As the train chugged by, each window facing the troopers, was filled with white civilians.

Men, women, and children, were all shouting and waving at the soldiers, from the windows of the train's three passenger cars.

It was obvious to even the most jaded of the black-troopers—the ex-slaves those soldiers whose backs would forever carry the crisscrossed scars from whips wielded by their former white owners—, that the train's white-passengers, alone in "Injun Country", were genuinely gratified and relieved at the sight of the heavily armed black-soldiers.

Shortly after the platoon crossed from the area designated by the government as "*Indian Territory*", into the state of Kansas, Joe Light-foot, the platoon's Pawnee scout, was spotted, leisurely riding his pinto-pony, riding back toward the advancing platoon.

Captain Griffin, rode ahead of the troop and slowed his horse, in order to match his horse's pace, with that of the Indian tracker's mount.

The Captain leaned across his saddle; "What's ahead Light-foot? Any sign of Kiowa or Comanche?

Joe Light-foot nodded his head; "Tracks, maybe three…maybe four days old."

He held his right hand up in front of his face four fingers, and the thumb extended, and flashed the five digits rapidly, three times.

"Tracks show this many unshod Indian-ponies…moving north."

The Captain turned his horse, and rode back to his troops. "Sgt. Stevens…Joe Light-foot says that about two miles northeast, is a little stand of bare trees, within spitting distance from a stream." "We'll camp there for the night."

Sergeant Stevens raised his hand to the brim of his straw hat, and snapped off a rapid salute. "Yes sir."

When the two columns of troopers dismounted and prepared to make camp at the stream, Sgt. Stevens motioned for Justin to join him.

"Corporal Gulliver, I want you to set up sentries around the perimeter."

Have a couple of the men string-out a picket line between those two trees, so's the men can tie their mounts, near that grove of scrawny trees. The horses can forage on the grass and old tree bark."

Justin spun his horse around and shouted to the troopers; "Dismount".

He then assigned three men, sentry duty, guarding the camp and the horses.

Mess Sergeant Clarence "*COOKIE*" Jones reined in the two mules that were pulling the "Chuck-wagon", approximately fifty yards from the edge of the small stream of water.

Sgt Stevens walked over to the wagon. "Cookie, how long before chow?"

Mess Sergeant Clarence "*COOKIE*" Jones, a short, slightly overweight man, with a dark-mahogany complexion, gingerly, carefully stepped down from the wagon.

"Be bout an hour…half dat time if you have some of your boys fetch us some wood from dem trees fo da fire, and some buckets a watta from dat creek, yonda."

Sgt Stevens leaned over his saddle horn, *"No problem"*. He was about to turn his horse's head, but instead asked the cook; *"What's for supper Cookie?"*

Mess Sergeant Clarence "*COOKIE*" Jones, smiled and shook his head; *"Same thing twas yesta day, and da day fore dat. We havin' the two "B's", beef and beans. Ony thing different ta nite, cause we got plenty watta, I'm gonna make us up, some biscuits."*

Cookie chuckled to himself; *"I reckon dem biscuits means dat to nite's special. Tonite we having three "B's, beef, beans, and biscuits."*

Sgt. Stevens smiled.

The men, who were not on sentry duty, were seated in small groups, around three fires.

Each man sat with his empty tin plate, and cup, awaiting the *"supper-call"*. Most of the troopers sat on the ground, a few sat on empty barrels.

Pvt. Garland Jones, Cookie's apprentice, in a high-pitched squawky voice, announced; *"Come an' get it!"*

The hungry soldiers, armed with their eating utensils, lined-up single file, at the rear apron, of the chuck wagon.

As each trooper walked by, Cookie placed a biscuit and a slab of beef on his plate.

After Cookie placed the obligatory biscuit and the slab of beef on his plate, Pvt. Linwood Harvey stopped in front of the corpulent Mess Sergeant, and asked, in a whinny, pleading, tone of voice;

"Sarge... can I have two of dem biscuits and two pieces of meat? I swear Sarge... I'm hungry nuff ta eat a bear".

"Cookie grunted. *"Move on boy... afta you finish whacha got on dat plate... you can come back fo more. As long as it lasts, you can have all you wants...just be damn sight sure, that you eats all dat you takes!"*

After the men passed through the line, they encountered a huge pot of beans, suspended on a tripod, over a fire. A long-handled ladle was submerged under the simmering beans.

Each man ladled beans onto his plate, and then returned to sit, in small groups, to eat, his evening meal.

Cpl. Justine "Gully" Gulliver, Pvts Vernon "Rusty' Munsford, Anthony "Tony" Jackson, and Linwood "Linny" Harvey, all members of the same squad, were all seated together, eating in silence, enjoying their meal.

The silence was suddenly broken, by a resounding sound... *"POOT"* immediately followed by a prolonged, elongated repeat of the sound... *"POOOOT"*.

Sheepishly, three of the four soldiers lifted their heads, and looked around at each other.

Pvt. Jackson did not lift his head. In his haste, for seconds, his haste to get back to the chow line, he continued to, uninterrupted, gulping-down his food.

Rusty Munsford was about to accuse Jackson, when before he could speak, the sounds of a series of *"POOTS"*, short, long, staccato, whispery; a symphony of gastric noises, as the sound of gas being expelled from a score of saddle-sore behinds, filled the air.

It was as if Jackson's flatulence, had unleashed a spontaneous barrage of *"fragrant"*, gastric explosions.

Sergeant Stevens, who was seated, eating next to *"Cookie"*, grinned and teased his old friend.

"Damn "Cookie", look what you've gone and done. Good thing Joe Light-foot said that there's no Injuns 'round. If there was, they sure as hell wouda heard them loud-ass, farts."

Cookie laughed. *"Come on Sarge, everybody knows dat fartings' good for ya. Dat it helps ta clean out your innards… gets ya ready for a good ole cleanin', dump."*

When I was a youngin' learnin' ta cook, I remember listning ta dis here ole song:

Beans, beans… dey good for your hearts
Da more you eats… da more you farts!

Da more you farts… da betta you feel
So let's have us some beans… fo evry meal!

****

Following the evening meal, as the perimeter-sentries were being relieved, Captain Griffin, wanting to get an early start, spoke to his six NCO's and instructed them to… "In the morning, have the platoon up before sunrise, to forego breakfast, and to be ready to move-out within a half hour of daylight".

The direction of the tracks of the fifteen or so, unshod Indian ponies, that Joe Light-foot had reported yesterday, had indicated that that group of Indians, was moving in a direction, that was devoid of any known white settlements or railroad construction crews.

Nor were there, as of the last reported army surveys, any isolated white farms or ranches in the Indians path.

Captain Griffin, did not think that catching-up with those fifteen Indians, was urgent. Certainly, the time elapsed before they intercepted the fifteen Indians, was not an issue, of life or death.

Just before day-break, the men were ordered to fill their canteens with water from the little stream, to saddle-up, and in columns of two's, be prepared to move out.

Sergeant Stevens told his troopers that as they rode, while on the trail in pursuit of the small hunting-party of Comanche, they should nibble on pieces of hardtack, and wash the dry-meat down with sips of water.

The Captain reasoned that if they traveled mostly keeping the horses' paces at a canter, they could close the distance between them and the Indians, without wearing-out their mounts.

Thus, giving the platoon ample time, to *"round-up"* the Indians, and to escort them to the reservation, at Fort Sill.

****

Chapter 91

Comanche Encampment
(Kutsueka Band) June, 1875

Silent Stalker's second wife, "Walks Oddly", the slant-eyed, yellow skinned-girl—who before she had been captured a little more than two summers past, and her assimilation into the world of the Comanche—, had been (*Mai-Ling*), was seated on the grass next to her "sister", Silent Stalker's first wife, Sleepy Woman.

The two women of Silent Stalker's lodge, had been seated for hours scrapping and curing, the animal hides, buffalo and deer, hides, that Silent Stalker had brought down during the summer's final hunt for meat, meat that would sustain and nourish the family through the cold, brutal plain's winter.

Sleepy Woman, and Walks Oddly, had finished, "butchering" the meat, cutting it into steaks, and slabs of ribs for roasting.

Additionally, much of the meat had been cut into strips, which were immersed in bowls that contained, a mixture of wild berries and chokecherries.

The saturated strips of meat were then hung on racks to dry in the sun.

The end result of the women's labor was a tasty, hardy, morsel that was resistant to spoilage, which the People called "pemmican".

During the winter-snows, when fresh meat was scarce, the pemmican would serve to nourish and sustain the family through the cold, brutal plain's winter.

Walks Oddly, her swollen belly, heavy with child, and Sleepy Woman, the two women of Silent Stalker's lodge, had for hours, been sitting, scrapping, and curing the nearly two dozen animal hides, buffalo and deer hides that Silent Stalker had slain, during the summer's final hunt for meat.

Silent Stalker's lodge was home for five, soon to be six, hungry mouths to be feed.

His first wife, Sleepy Woman, had borne for Silent Stalker, and ultimately for the Kutsueka Band, two healthy, fit, future young warriors.

Walks Oddly within two moons-time, was expected to be delivered of yet, for the Lodge of Silent Stalker, a third, healthy son, a third future warrior to defend, and to protect the People.

Among the many things that Sleepy Woman and Walks Oddly, fashioned from the finished hides for the family were, clothing, bedding, robes, rawhide utensils, carrying bags, and tepee covers.

Silent Stalker emerged from the lodge, following a young warrior who had been dispatched for him by the band's headman, Chief He Who Speaks To Ghosts.

The two warriors ignored the two women, Silent Stalker's wives, whose heads were bent in concentration, focusing on their work.

****

Chapter 92

Comanche Encampment (Kutsueka Band)
- Meeting of the Council June, 1875

Silent Stalker had been summoned, by Chief He Who Speaks to Ghost's, to the Chief's lodge. The leaders of the band had been summoned to attend, an urgent meeting of the council.

At the meeting of the council, the sole topic of discussion was the news of an event of major significance, to the *People*.

White Feather, an esteemed warrior of the *Quahadi* Comanche, a warrior who had counted many coup, and killed many of the enemies of the "*People*', had brought news to Chief He Who Speaks To Ghosts, of the recent disaster that had befallen the *Quahadi* Comanche.

White Feather told of how the blue coat chief, Colonel Ranald Mackenzie, with his white troopers, and his black "*buffalo soldiers*", had attacked the *Quahadi* Comanche, lead by the great War Chief, Quanah Parker, at their hidden encampment in the Palo Duro Canyon.

White Feather told of how the vast majority of Comanche women, children, and the warriors, had managed to escape—and that while only four of the encampment's inhabitants were killed—, Colonel Mackenzie's soldiers had captured and killed all— nearly fifteen hundred, Comanche ponies.

White Feather spoke of how Colonel Mackenzie had ordered, that every one of the hundreds of Comanche tepees, be put to the torch.

White Feather spoke to Chief He Who Speaks To Ghosts' Kutsueka council, telling them of how the white Soldier Chief Mackenzie's, bluecoat soldiers smashed and destroyed, crates of new rifles, and hundreds of rounds of ammunition.

To the warriors that sat silently listening to their visitor from the west, they as had Chief Quanah Parker, realized that a Comanche without a pony, unarmed, afoot on the Stake Plains, trying to allude capture or death at the hands of the relentless Colonel Mackenzie and his countless number of soldiers, was doomed.

White Feather spoke of his *Quahadi* Comanche band, having lost all of their ponies, the source and the symbol of their wealth; of their having lost their food supplies; and the loss of most of their rifles.

White Feather spoke of the words that his Chief, Quanah Parker had said at tribal council, following the disaster at Palo Duro Canyon.

The War Chief Quanah Parker, leader of the *Quahadi* Comanche, had spoken of the steady continuing extermination of the buffalo by the white hunters. Of how the *People* were losing or had lost, the buffalo the animals so vital for their existence, to the long guns of the white hunters.

White Feather spoke of how, without rifles, and more importantly without ponies, they would not be able to hunt the few buffalo that remained on the plains. He spoke of how the women and children would starve.

White Feather spoke of how Chief Quanah Parker had come to conclude, that further resistance against the power, the overwhelming numbers, and the powerful-medicine (*Technology*) of the white-man, was hopeless.

The mighty war chief, Quanah Parker, lead his proud band of *Quahadi*, Comanche, off of the Plains, to the Fort Sill Reservation.

White Feather was one of a few young warriors, of Quanah Parker's band, that had chosen not to follow their leader onto the reservation system at Fort Sill.

He and ten of his fellow warriors instead, had fled north, hoping to join their cousins, the Kutsueka Comanche and hopefully, with Chief Stone Fist, War Chief of the Kutsueka Comanche, they would continue to fight, and to kill the white-eyes.

Several times, during White Feather's oration, various warriors had reacted to his words, with shouts and chants, calling for vengeance.

On each of those occasions, He Who Speaks To Ghosts, the Kutsueka Band's Political/ Peace Chief, raised his hand, quieting the agitated warriors.

He Who Speaks To Ghosts, looked to his left toward his predecessor, his friend and mentor, the aged, venerable, wizened, aged, warrior, Old Wise One.

Old Wise One sat on a buffalo robe, apart from the rows of warriors.

White Feather, the visitor to the council, had noticed then, had ignored the presence of the old man seated alone, apart from the others, seated by himself.

The old man was leaning on a crooked-sturdy tree branch. His eyes were closed.

White Feather's eyes followed the eyes of Chief He Who Speaks To Ghosts, who was intently looking at the old man who appeared to be asleep.

He Who Speaks To Ghosts spoke. "Old Wise One, once again your people ask for your wisdom; would her your words."

White Feather noted, that all of the eyes of assembled warriors, were focused on what he had thought was a bent, senile, sleeping, old man.

The inside of the tepee, was eerily silent. The distant solitary howls of a coyote on the vast prairie, was the only sound that penetrated the silence.

E. Pluribus Unum

With his eyes still shut, as if he was talking to himself, in an at first weak trembling voice, that grew stronger with each word, Old Wise One began to speak.

"I, as did my father, and as did his father, and as did all Comanche fathers, back to the creation, have lived our lives free with the buffalo, under father son, on the prairie.

"I will say the words of Ten Bears, Chief of the *Yamparika* Comanche, when he put his mark on the white-man's paper, at Medicine Lodge Creek, nearly ten summers past."

"At that "Treaty" meeting, which was not attended by *Kutsueka,* or by *Quahadi* Comanche, Ten Bears spoke words from his heart, and the hearts of all Comanche."

"I, Old Wise One, will now speak to you, the words of Ten Bears. Words that Ten Bears spoke to the white chiefs, at Medicine Lodge Creek."

"My heart is filled with joy when I see you here, as the brooks fill with water when the snows melt in the spring; and I feel glad as the ponies do when the fresh grass starts in the beginning of the year…

My people have never first drawn a bow or fired a gun against the whites. There has been trouble between us…my young men have danced the war dance. But it was not begun by us. It was you who sent out the first soldier…

Two years ago, I came upon this road, following the buffalo, that my wives and children, might have their cheeks plump and their bodies warm. But the soldiers fired on us…and so it was upon the Canadian. Nor have we been made to cry once alone. The blue-dressed soldiers and the Utes came out from the night…and for campfires they lit our lodges. Instead of hunting game they killed my braves, and the warriors of the tribe cut short their hair for the dead.

So it was in Texas. They made sorrow in our camps, and we went out like the buffalo bulls when the cows are attacked. When we found them we killed them, and their scalps hang in our lodges. The Comanches are not weak and blind, like…pups…when seven sleeps old. They are strong and farsighted, like grown horses. We took their road and we went on it. The white women cried and our women laughed.

But there are things which you have said to me which I do not like. They were not sweet like sugar, but bitter like gourds. You have said that you want to put us on a reservation, to build us houses and make us medicine lodges. I do not want them. I was born under the prairie, where the wind blew free and there nothing to break the light of the sun. I was born where there were no enclosures and everything drew a free breath. I want to die there not within walls. I know every stream and every wood between the Rio Grande and the Arkansas. I have hunted and lived over that country. I live like my fathers before me and like them I lived happily.

When I was in Washington, the Great Father told me that all the Comanche land was ours, and that no one should hinder us in living on it. So, why do you ask us to leave the rivers, and the sun, and the wind, and live in houses? Do not of it more. I love to carry out the talk I get from the Great Father. When I get goods and presents, I and my people feel glad, since it shows that he keeps us in his eye.

If the Texans had kept out of my country, there might have been peace. But that which you now say we must live in, is too small. The Texans have taken away the places where the grass grew thickest and the timber was best. Had we kept that, we might have done the things you ask. But it is too late. The whites have the country which we loved, and we wish only to wander on the prairie until we die...

"Those the words of Ten Bears, have been burned into my heart, and into my mind."

"In just ten short summers, the world of the Comanche, our world, Ten Bears world, has changed. The buffalo, that had once covered the prairie, as thick as the blades of grass, are no more. Now the buffalo are as few as are trees on the prairie."

"The white man, unable to defeat the Comanche warrior in battle, have made war on the *People* by killing off the buffalo. Without the buffalo, our warriors cannot feed their families."

"Without the buffalo, our women and children starve, they have no clothes, blankets, or tepees to protect them from the freezing snow, and the soon to come, prairie-blizzards."

"Though their soldiers could not defeat the Comanche warrior in battle, the white man's extermination of the buffalo herds, is destroying the Comanche way of life."

"The whites' numbers are like those of a plague of locusts. The *Iron Horse*, brings the white men, women, and children, with their cattle, with their sheep, and the talking-wire, onto our lands."

"The white man has taken our land." The time has come."

"The *Kutsueka*, as have our brothers, the *Quahadi* Comanche, to survive, must attempt life, on the reservations."

At first, there was absolute silence in the lodge. Then a chorus of defiant chants filled the air; No! No! Never! We are Comanche Warriors we are not sheep. We must fight…we must kill the white-eyes!"

For a moment, Chief He Who Speaks To Ghosts stood in silence, while the warriors vented, giving voice to their emotions.

He Who Speaks To Ghosts raised his hand. Gradually the bedlam in the tepee dissipated.

He Who Speaks To Ghosts, the band's Political/Peace Chief, spoke: "For the past few moons each night, I have been visited by benevolent spirits."

"In each vision revealed to me, blue-coat soldiers were slaughtering the "*People*".

"Not only were they killing our warriors, they slaughtered our women, our children, and the old-ones."

"In my vision, I saw the guns of the blue-coat soldiers, ripping the "*People*" apart. Guns that spit-out bullets rapidly, and in large numbers, without the need of the soldiers to re-load."

E. Pluribus Unum

"Until now, I have told of these visions, to no one. Not even to Chief Old Wise One."

"White Feathers' news of the defeat at Palo Duro Canyon, of Chief, Quanah Parker's band of *Quahadi*, by blue-coat soldiers, by the white Soldier-Chief, Mackenzie, has removed from my mind, any doubts of the truth of my troubling visions."

"I hear and I agree, with the words of Chief Old Wise One."

"Although my heart, the heart of the Comanche, wants to fight, as Headman of the Kutsueka Comanche, my head tells me that it is, as Old Wise One has said; "It is Time.""

"I will, as has Chief Quanah Parker, lead the Quahadi…I, He Who Speaks To Ghosts, Headman of the Kutsueka, will take the Kutsueka Comanche to the Fort Sill Reservation."

Once again, the lodge was filled with sounds of grumbling warriors, as the warriors reacted to their Peace Chief, He Who Speaks To Ghosts, and their former Peace Chief, Old Wise One's, words.

The noise in the tepee abruptly, ceased, when Stone Fist, War Chief of the Kutsueka Comanche, rose.

Stone Fist stood motionless. He looked first at Old Wise One. The venerable old Chief sat, eyes shut, leaning forward on his walking stick.

Stone Fist shifted his eyes to those of the Headman, He Who Speaks To Ghosts.

Then in a clear resonant voice, filled with conviction, he spoke: "My Chief, I would speak"

"I have listened to, and I have heard the words of Ten Bears, the words of Old Wise One, and the words of He Who Speaks To Ghosts."

"Those words are the words of brave, courageous, and wise warriors. They are the words of true Comanche, leaders of the "*People*".

Their words…your words, are the words, that tell of the path that we, who now live free on the endless plains, must take, to ensure that we are not the last of the Comanche."

"I Stone Fist, as the head of my lodge—not as the War Chief of Kutsueka Comanche—, I Stone Fist have chosen for the family of Stone Fist, to live out our lives, as did our fathers, living free on the plains."

"The family of Stone Fist, will travel north, and we will join forces with, and fight alongside our neighbors, the Cheyenne, the Arapaho, and the Lakota, to kill the white invaders."

Chief Stone Fists' words of defiance, and resistance were followed by an eruption of war-whoops, from the assembled warriors.

After three minutes of bedlam, the holy man, Chief Who Speaks To Ghosts, raised his hand.

Silent Stalker, Bear Claw, and Crooked Eye, who had been seated next to each other, remained standing after the assemblage of warriors sat.

Crooked Eye, the oldest, of the three, spoke; "My Chief, our lodges would join that of Chief Stone Fist. We will travel north, and with our allies, the Cheyenne, the Arapaho, and the Lakota, we will fight to defeat the blue-coats".

As other warriors began to stand, He Who Speaks To Ghosts stood and extended both of arms, his hands raised, palms facing the warriors.

Dull Knife, who sat in council directly to the left of the Peace Chief, stood.

My Chief, I would speak. "I am a warrior of more than fifty-summers. I no longer possess the strength, the quickness, the eyes needed for me to ride the path of war."

"I have no illusions. While my heart and my head, tells me to kill the white invaders, my achy body tells me that that time for me, has passed.

"Though I can no longer ride the path of war, I would ask Chief Stone Fist, to allow me to travel with him North, to fight the white-eyes.

While Chief Stone Fist, Silent Stalker, Bear Claw, and Crooked Eye, ride the warpath with the Cheyenne, and the Arapaho, and the Lakota, I Dull Knife will remain with women and children of our warriors. I will protect and defend the families of our Comanche warriors, with my life.

He Who Speaks To Ghosts raised his hand. Gradually the noise in the tepee subsided.

He Who Speaks To Ghosts remained silent, his eyes swept over the two rows of assembled warriors.

Chief Stone Fist broke the awkward silence.

"My brothers, your desire to fight, and to kill the white devils, your wish to defend, and to protect the land given to the Comanche by the Great Spirit, is the spirit of the Comanche."

"Our only hope of defeating the blue-coats—who are as many as there are stars in the sky; the white-men who have guns that shot bullets, that kill our warriors at great distances, the white-men who have guns that spit-out bullets faster than can be counted—, our only hope of driving these devils from our lands, was if all of the bands of Comanche; the *Kutsueka*, the *Quahadi*, the *Tekapwai*, the *Yampariks*, the *Nokonis*… all of the bands of the Comanche, had united as one mighty force, then perhaps, we could have driven the white-eyes from our hunting-grounds."

"It is now too late. Without bullets, without ponies and rifles, fighting with just bows and arrows, with lances, and rocks, against the white devils, men who turn their guns on our women and children, as Chief He Who Speaks To Ghosts, says, would mean destruction. It would be the end of the "*People*."

As told to this council, by our brother, White Feather, Warrior of the *Quahadi* Comanche, Chief Quanah Parker, has left the plains. The Great War Chief has led his people, the *Quahadi* Comanche, to live on the reservation, at the white-man's Fort Sill."

E. Pluribus Unum

"If the white chiefs keep the promises that they made to Ten Bears at Medicine Lodge Creek, they will provide for the "*People*", lodges made of wood and sod, that they call houses; they will make still larger lodges-schools, for our children; a lodge for the sick that they call hospital".

"It is the white chiefs intent, to turn the Comanche, into "white", reservation Indians".

Though we may no longer, roam free on the prairie, hunting the buffalo, we will never be "white", reservation Indians".

In our hearts, we will always be Comanche!

His words were the most words that any could remember, the War Chief Stone Fist, ever speaking at council.

"For the survival of the Comanche as a people, as a people… we as a people, have no choice."

"We as a people must follow Chief, He Who Speaks To Ghosts, to life, on the Fort Sill Reservation"

"I have chosen to stay on the plains. I will fulfill Ten Bears' wish. I will die on the prairie, I will die living and fighting as a Comanche."

Stone Fist sat. He Who Speaks To Ghosts rose, and began to speak:

"I too, as would every warrior, every man here at council, would like to fight to the death. To die an honorable death in battle, fighting the enemies of the "*People*". That is the way of the Comanche."

"We, as have our fathers before us, have fought many battles. We have fought and defeated, the Utes, the Tonkawa, the Pawnee, the Apache and the first white men who wore the metal hats, who brought to the plains, the horse, the white men who came during my grandfather's, grandfather's, time."

"The Comanche have defeated all of these foes."

"The blue-coat soldiers, with their guns that shoot iron balls as huge as boulders; who carry hand-guns on their waist, that fire six bullets before needing to be reloaded; the blue-coat soldiers that now have guns that shoot bullets at a speed, more rapid than rain drops falling from the sky.

"Now we face the white Soldier Chief Mackenzie's', blue coat soldiers, who protect the white and yellow men, that build the *Iron Road*."

"The road on which, the *Iron Horse* travels, bringing the buffalo hunters with their rifles that slaughter, at great distances, the herds of buffalo, and kill our unsuspecting men, women, and children."

"Some of these soldiers, we can kill. But all of these white-men, who come into our land in numbers that rival the stars in the sky; all of these white-men and their magical weapons, all of these soldiers, we cannot defeat."

"If Chief Stone Fist agrees, his lodge and the lodges of Silent Stalker, Bear Claw, and Crooked Eye, will move north, and will for a short-time, join our friends, the Cheyenne, the Arapaho, and the Lakota, in their fight against the white-man."

"The remaining warriors…all Kutsueka-Comanche men, will travel with, and protect our women, children, and the elders, to the reservation at Fort Sill.

"There we will live, and with the help of the Great Spirit, we will have many papooses, thus insuring the survival of the Comanche."

Stone Fist rose, stood facing He Who Speaks To Ghosts. The two men clasped each other's arms.

"I, He Who Speaks To Ghosts, Headman of the Kutsueka-Comanche, have spoken."

****

Chapter 93

Dark Eagle - Eavesdropping, Listening to The Meeting of The Council

Dark Eagle, the eleven year-old adopted son of War Chief Stone Fist, and two of his friends, twelve-year-old Turtle's Pace, and Swift Feet, the fifteen-year-old son of the slain warrior, Crooked Arrow, Chief Stone Fists', and Dark Eagle's father, Running Eagle's boyhood friend, had been surreptitiously, listening, outside, the rear of Chief He Who Speaks To Ghosts' Lodge.

The three youths had lifted from the ground; the buffalo hides at the edge of the Peace Chief's tepee. They had been breathlessly listening, first to the words of White Feather, the *Quahda* warrior, and then to the impassioned responses, of their tribal leaders.

Dark Eagle, upon hearing the words of Stone Fist, the man who had adopted him, after the death of his father Running Eagle, had been bursting with pride.

While the warriors were solemnly solidifying the decisions of the council, by each warrior's smoking of the sacred pipe, Dark Eagle, Swift Feet, and Turtle's Pace, quietly left their place of concealment, and slipped out onto the prairie.

Swift Feet was the first to speak; "I will be riding with Chief Stone Fist, and my father, to drive the whites from the land of the Comanche."

Dark Eagle quickly added, as will I. We will ride with the Cheyenne, the Arapaho, and the Lakota. We will defeat the white-eyes, and drive them from our hunting grounds."

Turtle's Pace, caught up in the excitement of the moment, joined in;
"We three will be riding together. We will count many coup, and take many scalps.

Dark Eagle, though slightly younger than his friend Turtle's Pace, some- what pompously, interrupted his friend; "Turtle's Pace, did you not hear my father, Chief Stone Fist's words?"

"Chief Stone Fist will be taking north with our lodge, the lodges of Silent Stalker, Crooked Eye, and Bear Claw."

"The rest of our lodges, our families, our warriors, will be led by Chief He Who Speaks To Ghosts, to a life for our people, on the reservation, at Fort Sill."

Dark Eagle, speaking with exaggerated bravado, pronounced; "With Swift Feet at my side, along with Chief Stone Fist and the Cheyenne, we will drive the white-eyes from the plains."

Turtle's Pace, a young brave of a mere twelve summers, scuffed at the words of Dark Eagle, his "younger" friend.

"Dark Eagle, Chief Stone Fist will never take you and me, braves, of eleven and twelve summer; braves not yet warriors, to ride with him on the path-of-war."

"While there is no one with more skill when riding a war pony then Turtle's Pace, there is also, no one slower on the ground, afoot, then is Turtle's Pace."

Turtle's Pace remained silent. It is whispered by the young braves, that the only person in our village, that walks or runs slower then you, Turtle's Pace, is Walks Oddly, the slant eyed, yellow skinned wife, of Silent Stalker."

Swift Feet shrugged. "Turtle Walks, you and Dark Eagle are both to young to ride the war-path. I am a brave of fifteen summers. Soon to become a young warrior of the "People"

"It is my time, and the will of the spirits that I, Swift Feet, ride the war-path with Chief Stone Fist, Silent Stalker, Bear Claw, and Crooked Eye.

****

Chapter 94

New-Rosewood - Cattle Ranch
[August 5th, 1875] - 11:38AM

Rebecca's daydreaming was interrupted by the sound of her son Hank's voice.

"Mom…mom, wake-up mom." Hank was pointing at a small cloud of dust, rising in the distance. "Two riders coming. Riding hard, hell-bent-for -leather."

Rebecca smiled at her son's choice of the words, "Hell-bent-for leather".

Her son was turning into a real "cowboy".

She thought it remarkable, how her formerly withdrawn, introverted son, had emerged from his self-imposed solitude, into an effervescent, pre-teen.

Rebecca had been amazed at the steady, gradual, transformation of her son, as he was being exposed to the divergence of the "western" population, as they traveled south, through Kansas, on their way to Wichita.

At the various settlements and army forts, that they encountered, Hank saw for the first time, real-live people who actually looked like him.

He met and interacted with reservation Indians, and many mixed-blood men, women, and children.

He met and interacted with reservation Indians, and many mixed-blood men, women, and children.

Rebecca despite her long-held personal reluctance to go anywhere near the place where her father had been murdered, and she and her sister Mandy had been abducted, was more convinced then ever, that she had made the right decision.

The decision, to bring Hank out west, had been the right thing for her to do.

Her son had almost immediately, "fit-in".

Shading her eyes from the sun's glare, Rebeeca placed the open palm of her hand, on her forehead.

Immediately from a distance of about two-hundred-yards, she recognized the high-stepping gait of her husband's huge black stallion, and the tall figure of her husband, sitting in the saddle.

Trotting alongside his employer was Rosewood's top wrangler/cowpuncher, the ranch's foreman, Augustus (*Gus*) Thompkins.

In addition to his skill at handling cattle and horses, "*Guns-Ablazing-Gus*", was a great deal more than handy, with a rifle and a six-gun.

In fact, "*Guns-Ablazing, Gus*", had only abandoned his life as a gambler and gunslinger, when he unexpectantly, unceremoniously, "*met-his-match*".

It had happened during a poker game in Dodge City, when he, "*Guns-Ablazing-Gus*", had inadvertently, insulted a fellow gambler-shootist, by the name of J.B., Hickok.

On those few and far between occasions when Gus spoke of that particular encounter, he would invariably begin, by describing Mr. Hickok, as having been a "dandified" gent.

The "*dude*" —which was Gus' initial impression of the gambler—, had been wearing a fawn-colored, coat, a light-blue silk waistcoat, and a pair of costly tooled alligator-skin, boots.

The "*dude*" wore his long hair, shoulder-length. He had a full mustache, which covered a protruding, jutting-out, upper lip.

As the meticulously, well-dressed stranger was scooping-up his winnings, from the table, Gus had made the mistake of jokingly referring to the *"dude"* as "Duck-bill".

To Gus' astonishment and his complete surprise, before he could move, he found himself looking down the barrels of two cocked, 1851 Navy Model (.36 caliber) revolvers.

Gus, who had rightfully considered himself to be an above average *"Gunslinger"*, was flabbergasted.

The "*dude*" had seemingly without effort, drawn from his belt, two ivory grip, nickel-plated pistols.

The "*dudes*" formerly collegial, banal smile had changed. Instead of the passive, pale blue eyes of a *"Tender-foot-Dude"*, Gus found himself looking into the steely gray eyes of a killer.

Gus would never forget the words, or the ominous, matter-of-fact tone, of the man's voice. "My name Sir, is James, you can call me James, Jim, or even, JB.

"But…if you ever again refer to me as, or call me "*Duck-bill*", I will, … shoot you dead."

Gus' later learned, that that uncomfortable encounter, was with a fellow gambler-shootist, whose Christian, given name was, James Butler Hickok, better known by his well earned, nick-name; "Wild Bill Hickok".

****

Two months following that incident, after weeks of serious contemplation about his chosen life-style, Augustus (*Guns-Ablazing-Gus*) Thompkins, made a life changing decision.

Gus was hired by Billy McCloskey, as the top-hand, for the New-Rosewood - Cattle Ranch.

Rebecca, with her hand still shading her eyes, stepped down from the porch.

"Billy, I wasn't expecting you back for at least another week. Have you finished rounding-up, and branding the new calves?"

Then as if she had just noticed for the first time their absence, Rebecca asked; "Where are the rest of the hands?"

A week earlier Billy McCloskey, his foreman Gus, and five of his six ranch hands, had rode out, onto the open-range, to round up and to brand, the "Rosewood Ranch's", herd of calves.

Billy jumped down from his horse's back and swept his wife up into his arms. "Hi honey… did you miss me?"

Rebecca was momentarily flustered. She did not approve… had never, ever, approved, of public displays of affection.

As her husband bent down to kiss her, Rebecca averted his lips, by her turning her head. Instead of her lips, Billy's lips brushed her cheeks.

Her voice had a definite ring of surprise; "Billy, what in the world…I didn't expect you back for at least, another week."

"Neither did I. We were right, in predicting that it would take us a couple weeks to round-up all of the new calves."

"We took only three 'Double-R' branding irons. Turns out we needed at least one additional iron. Unfortunately, I ignored my own rule-of-thumb."

Gus gave his employer a quizzical look; "Your rule of thumb…what's that boss?"

Before Billy could open his mouth, his eleven-year-old, adopted son Hank, chimed in; "*Its far better to have it, and not need it*…Rebecca joined in, and mother and son, finished in unison; "*than to need it, and not have it!*"

Gus continued smiling. "Miss Rebecca, I offered to send a couple of the of the boys back for the branding irons, but the boss insisted, on coming back himself."

"Ask me I think he was just missing his two lovely gals, you Miss Rebecca,
and cute as all get-out, pretty little, *Missy Mandy*."

Billy playfully, put his arm around his wife and son. And with a huge grin on his face, confessed, "Alright…already, I'm guilty as charged."

Billy looked to his son. "Hank what are you doing here, I thought that you would be out looking for strays."

"I was Dad, I just got back a few minutes ago. I saw mom and the baby napping on the porch. I didn't wanna wake them."

Hank asked his father; "Dad, since when does it take two men to carry one branding iron."

Billy looked directly at Augustus. "That's the exact question that I put to Gus.

"Well Gus, how bout you explaining to Hank, why you felt that it was necessary to send two men, to fetch one branding iron".

"Sure nuff boss. Gus turned his attention to Hank. Well young fellow, I just told him that it's just common sense."

"Although we ain't seen none of them heathen red-skins, in these parts for some time now, it still ain't safe for a white man to be alone, by hisself, on the plains."

Rebecca saw the hurt look in her son's eyes, when Gus uttered the words, "*heathen red-skins*".

The boy's demeanor had instantly changed from that of enjoying cheerful banter, to that look, that she had last seen four years earlier, when "Little Hank", had come home from school, with a bloody-nose, from fighting with a boy who had called him a godless, red-skinned, half-breed.

Gus was confused. He too had noticed the abrupt change in the boy.

For the first time, Gus stared intently at the dark-complected boy; then at the boy's pretty, blonde, blue-eyed mother.

Gus recalled from conversations that he had had with the boss, that Miss Rebecca was from back east, and that she had been married and widowed, before they met, and got married.

That had been the extent of Gus' knowledge, about the history Wichita's McCloskey family.

Actually, thoughts as to who the kid's father might have been, was never of any interest to Gus.

Gus remembered once, his having a fleeting thought, that the boy's father had probably been one of them "*Dago-Eye-Talians*", or maybe one of "them greasy-swarthy-looking, "Greeks".

"One of them foorieners, that just keep coming over the ocean, to them Eastern cities, from them foreign countries over there in Europe".

What were his words, the exact words… his words, the words that had obviously upset the boy.

Gus racked his brain trying to remember what it was that he had said… oh yeah, something about not being caught alone on the plains, by "*heathen red-skins*".

As he was walking toward the barn, Gus stopped. His brow wrinkled as he concentrated.

For the first time, he pictured in his mind, the contours of Hank's face. The boy's high cheekbones, his straight, black hair, the blacker than black, color of his eyes.

Gus stopped walking, he shook his head, and whispered under his breath, "Well I'll be damn…the kid's a "*breed*".

As he approached the barn, Gus was mildly surprised, when he did not hear the ever-present whistling of Ragged-Man, the oldest member of Rosewood's crew of ranch-hands.

Although Ragged-Man at age fifty-seven, no longer participated in strenuous, "field-work", on the ranch, his skill as tanner-saddle maker, was an invaluable asset to the ranch.

Gus shouted Ragged-Man, Ragged-Man—the "old man's" hearing wasn't what it use to be—, Ragged-Man have you seen the spare branding-iron?

Gus stopped in mid-stride. The hairs on the back of his neck stood up. Something was wrong.

Gus opened the barn door. Ragged-Man was lying on the floor…two arrows were embedded, deep in his chest, the shaft of one arrow, protruded from each side of his throat.

Gus immediately crutched while simultaneously, drawing his revolver from its' holster.

****

Chapter 95

Company "A" 10th Cavalry – Eight Miles South of The Rosewood - Cattle Ranch [August 5th, 1875] - 1138 Hrs.

Captain Griffin raised his hand, halting the procession as Joe Light-Foot, their Pawnee scout, came racing toward him.

Sgt. Zachary Stevens and Cpl. Justin Gulliver spurred their mounts and rode forward to meet the rapidly approaching scout.

Joe Light-Foot ignored the two non-coms, and continued riding toward Captain Griffin.

Sgt. Stevens became alarmed at seeing this "wild-Injun", who only talked when spoken to, and then only in monosyllables, charging toward the captain.

The sergeant was pulling his rifle from its' scabbard, when Justin grabbed the reins of the sergeant's horse.

Justin had seen that Captain Griffin was shaking his head, and waving both of his arms in the air, attempting to stop Joe Light-Foot's charge, and/or to at least, stop Sgt. Stevens' from putting a rifle bullet in the Pawnee's chest.

The Pawnee-scout reigned in his pony, just inches from Captain Griffin, who had dismounted and was holding the reins of his horse, in his right hand.

The less than loquacious scout, and Captain Griffin, the company commander, were engaged in heated conversation.

Although Joe Light-Foot was an army scout and an essential member of the patrol, the Pawnee was known to be a loner, with a penchant for speaking, only, when in response, to direct questions.

Abruptly, Light-foot who had been kneeling, drawing figures in the dirt, rose to his feet, and leapt upon the back of his pony, and in a cloud of dust, rode off to the north.

Captain Griffin hastily instructed the trooper nearest him, to have the company non-coms, immediately report to him.

Within minutes, the six non-commissioned officers, four corporals and two sergeants, were huddled around the captain.

The captain spoke to the assembled men; "Light-Foot says that there's a pretty fair-size ranch, about twenty miles north of us, that wasn't there just three months ago."

"Except for a woman, her baby, a boy of maybe fourteen or fifteen years, and a middle-aged man, the ranch appears to be empty."

Sgt. Stevens spoke; "Captain, that don't sound right. Where are the men…the cowboys?"

"A spread of that size…couldn't be kept-up by a woman, a boy, and an old man?"

Captain Griffin had been nodding his head in agreement. "I had the same thoughts. "Light Foot says that he saw two, maybe three-day-old tracks of ten horses and a wagon leading out onto the prairie."

Corporal Gulliver, chimed in, "It's roundup and branding time, for these 'Free-range" ranchers. The men are probably out on the prairie, rounding-up their cattle, and branding the new calves."

The Captain nodded his head in agreement. "You're probably right corporal. Even though most of the tribes have gone to reservations, there are still a few stubborn militant hold-outs, running loose."

"Damn fool-hearted thing to do, leaving a woman, an old man, and a boy alone."

"Light-Foot says that the hunting party is from a small caravan of six renegade, Comanche families traveling north.

He saw their camp and counted six tepees, set in a quarter moon fashion, facing east."

"The Pawnee thought that what he saw, would suggest that the Comanche, mostly women and children in the camp, were hungry. That they looked to be in desperate need of provisions."

"Light-Foot believes that the hunting party that we've been tracking, are the warriors, of that Comanche Caravan, moving north.

"Light-Foot says that that uncharted ranch, twenty miles north of us, is right in the path of the Comanche hunting party, that we're tracking."

"He says that the hunting party is made up of about fifteen warriors".

"A boy of maybe thirteen summers rides at the rear of the hunters. The boy is holding the reins of three pack mules. There was no game, tied to the hunters' pack-mules".

"Light-Foot thinks, and I agree… that rather then return to their village, without meat, the hunters would more than likely, raid the ranch, take all the livestock, kill the old man and the boy, and take captive, the woman and her baby."

Before anyone could comment, Captain Griffin gave the order. "Have the trumpeter sound "Boots and Saddles"!

****

Chapter 96

Chief Stone Fist's Hunting Party – Three Miles, North of The Rosewood - Cattle Ranch) [August 5th, 1875] 11:50 AM

Silent Stalker had been riding well ahead of the hunting party. His search for sign of buffalo or deer had been unsuccessful.

The bodies of three jackrabbits, tied together by their hind legs, lay across the shoulder of his pony.

Silent Stalker dismounted and handed the rabbits to his wife, the slant-eyed, yellow-skinned girl, "Walks Oddly".

Chief Stone Fist's 2nd wife "Neetah", Silent Stalker's wife "Walks Oddly", and "Fragrant Breeze", Crooked Eyes' wife, had been brought by the hunting-party, to skin and to butcher the animals, that were anticipated to be brought-down, by the hunters.

Dark Eagle and Swift Feet, teen-age boys thought to be to young for the hunt, were brought along, to tend to the horses.

Silent Stalker hurried over to the fire of Chief Stone Fist. The fierce, battle-hardened, War Chief's turned his head, as the band's most skilled tracker, approached.

"Chief Stone Fist, I found no sign of large game. Only a few scrawny rabbits, felt the sting of my arrows. It is as if all of the buffalo, have been swallowed-up by Mother-Earth."

Silent Stalker turned his head and pointed south. Silent Stalker made a fist of his right hand, and rapidly extended his five fingers, three times.

"My Chief, there is a ranch, these many minutes distant. I saw many fenced-in horses, and many of the white-man's hairless buffalo, chickens and pigs. Enough food to feed our families through the winter"

Stone Fist gave a dismissive grunt. "A ranch of that size will have many white men with guns."

"We have but three rifles and twenty-two bullets. Our arrows and lances are no match for entrenched white-men with their many rifles, and their endless number of bullets."

"We come as visitors to the land of our friends, the Kiowa and the Cheyenne. We are not here to raid, and to plunder. We are here to join our friends, as they fight to rid our lands of the white-man."

Silent Stalker had remained silent, listening to the words of Chief Stone Fist. When the chief had finished speaking, Silent Stalker respectfully spoke:

"My chief, I would speak."

Stone Fist nodded his head.

"Forgive me my chief, I have not told you, of all that I have seen".

Stone Fist, with a slightly annoyed, and inquisitive look in his eyes, once again, nodded his head.

Silent Stalker, correctly interpreted the chief's gesture, he had been given permission, to continue speaking.

"As I turned my pony's head to return, I instead stopped. I had noticed that there were no men, at work on the ranch".

"Except for a white woman and her slave, a Mexican woman, a papoose, a boy of about thirteen summers, and an old man, the ranch was empty."

"The white woman, holding her papoose was seated on a platform that encircled the bottom part, of the huge, white tepee."

"I saw the tracks of many horses, and wagon-ruts leading away from the corral, out onto the prairie."

"There was but one old man, and a boy who looked to be perhaps, of the age of your son Dark Eagle. The boy was inside the smaller work-tepee. Other than the old man, there were no men at the ranch."

"The white-man's many hairless buffalo and the chickens and pigs that I saw, are enough food to quiet the rumblings of hunger, in the bellies of our women and children."

"There is enough meat to feed our families through the winter, and more to share with our friends, the Kiowa and Cheyenne."

After hearing this additional information, and his having complete faith and trust in Silent Stalker, Chief Stone Fist did not hesitate.

"We will attack, burn the ranch, and take the livestock, needed to feed our women and children."

****

Chapter 97

New-Rosewood - Cattle Ranch
[August 5th, 1875] - 12:01 PM

When the fifteen warriors of the Comanche hunting…now a raiding party, came within a mile of the ranch, Stone Fist, gave to Silent Stalker the task of killing what he perceived as, the only real threat to his warriors, the old man that Silent Stalker had seen in the barn.

While Stone Fist felt that based upon Silent Stalker's words—scouting words that he had always found to be accurate—, that this raid would be simple, he was fully cognizant of the fact, that if it were at all possible, that he not lose to death or to serious injury, any of his very limited number of warriors.

Within fifteen minutes of his departure, Silent Stalker, as his name implied, noiselessly returned to the raiding party.

"My chief, the ranch is as I said. With my arrows, I have killed the old man.

The woman and her papoose are in the large tepee. The Mexican woman is at work on the second platform of the tepee.

The boy of maybe thirteen summers is no longer at the ranch.

Chief Stone Fist…there are no men, at the ranch."

****

Chapter 98

New-Rosewood - Cattle Ranch -
[August 5th, 1875] - 12:30 PM

Billy McCloskey was seated on the porch swing. He was gently holding his daughter in the crook of his left arm, and was lovingly, looking into the baby Mandy's, bright blue eyes.

Billy never ceased to marvel and wonder as to, how he and… well not so much Rebecca, but how he could have, out of their love, created this beautiful, angelic being.

Billy, bursting with paternal pride smiled, and gently placed the tip of the index finger of his right-hand in turn, into the slight depressions, the dimples on each side of the baby's cheeks.

The touch of her father's calloused finger, resulted in Baby Mandy emitting a contented, cooing sound.

She responded to her father's touch, by wrapping the chubby little fingers of her right hand, firmly around Billy's finger.

Billy's tranquil father/daughter moment was shattered, when he spotted Gus—pistol-in-hand, running toward him.

Gus was shouting. *"Injuns! Injuns*!

Billy stood, with his right hand, scooped up the baby's bassinette. With the now startled baby in his arms, he rushed into the house, calling-out for his wife.

"Becky…Becky!

****

Rebecca, Hank, and the housekeeper, appeared at the top of the stairs.

The women were both holding towels, and bed linens in their arms; Hank was holding a bottle of linseed oil, a brush, and his disassembled Spencer Rifle.

Rebecca's heart was pounding in her chest. This was the first time, since she had met William McCloskey, that she had ever heard "panic", in his voice.

Her initial thought had been the baby, the baby… had something happened to the baby!

"Billy what's wrong?

The next word out of Billy's mouth, was the one word, that she had been dreading, the word that after the passage of a lifetime time… a dozen years since she and her sister Mandy's being taken captives by the Comanche, filled her with terror.

"Injuns!"

Rebecca ran down the steps toward her husband and child. She held out her arms reaching for the baby.

Baby Mandy's eyes shifted from her father's, face, which seconds ago had been smiling at her, to the frightened face, of her mother.

The baby began to cry.

Rebecca with her child securely held in her arms, shouted; "Lucinda…Lucinda."

Lucinda stood still, motionless, paralyzed with fear, at the head of the stairs.

Once again, this time in an urgent, but calm, authoritative voice, Rebecca spoke; "Lucinda, close the shutters!"

The commanding tone of her employer's voice penetrated, and galvanized Lucinda into action.

She dropped the linen that she held clutched to her bosum, and hurried into the master bedroom.

Lucinda, unlatched the shutters from the side of the house, and pulled them tightly together. She then placed a solid-oak, bar of wood into slots attached to each side of the window, on the interior walls of the room.

She then ran to close and shutter, the windows in the boy's…in Hank's, bedroom.

When their ranch house had been under construction, Rebecca had insisted that each shutter have cut into them, two ports, one that would allow you to see an approaching attacker; one below to accommodate the barrel of a defender's rifle.

Initially Billy had thought that the idea of "Making the ranch-house —his exact words—, "a fortress", was over-kill." In what Rebecca thought was a condescending, patronizing tone, Billy had then pointed out to Rebecca that; "Honey, this is 1876. In these parts…the Indian troubles, the raiding and the killing, is over."

Colonel Ranald McKenzie had defeated the Comanche, not on the field of battle, but had defeated the Comanche, by carrying out General Philip Sheridan's Doctrine of the Army's participating in, and encouraging the white hunters, to kill, and to nearly make extinct, the Comanche's food, supply, the buffalo.

The United States Army's strategy of destroying, what General Sheridan had proclaimed was the Plains Indians, "*Mobile Commissary*", the annihilation of the buffalo, by white hunters, was the strategic military tactic, that had succeeded, in forcing the Comanche to move onto the Fort Sill Reservation.

Billy, despite his belief in the truthfulness and the logic of his position, that the Indian troubles, were over, had decided to "give-in.

He reasoned that considering his wife's ordeal—her history of having been a captive of the Comanche—, the fact that she was being overcautious, was understandable.

Besides, Billy had to admit, the carpenter's "cuttings-carvings", of the slits into the shutters, had served to complement, the aesthetic look, of the windows.

As Gus, with one swift, athletic, stride leaped onto the porch. Billy swung open the front door, and breathlessly asked; "How many".

Gus shook his head, "don't know…I didn't see 'em".

Billy was momentarily confused, perplexed. Augustus Thompkins was not a man that was thought of, as being prone to overreacting to a perceived, threatening, or potentially dangerous situation.

"What do you mean…you don't know…! Exasperated, incredulously, Billy asked; "You didn't see them? Did you at least, see anything…any sign that made you think, that we're in danger of being attacked by Indians?"

Gus, checking the load of his revolver, in a flat matter-of-fact voice answered; "Oh sure…I saw sign alright…pert near certain sign that we in trouble."

"I saw Ragged Man lying dead as can be…in the barn. He had three arrows, in him. Sticking outta his body. Ragged Man been shoot thru and thru, with them arrow."

Billy was convinced.

He unleashed a barrage of questions at Gus; "How many Indians…when do you think they'll attack? Do you think we should make a run for Wichita?"

Gus satisfied that both his rifle and his handgun were fully loaded, holstered his revolver. "I reckon that there were no more than one or two Injuns…else they woudda overrun the place."

"Them bucks that kilt Ragged Man, most likely rode back to a raiding
or a hunting-party, to get the rest of them murdering savages."

Judging by the fact that weren't no flies round Ragged Man's body, and that his body still had its' hair, and depending on how far off thay is… most likely the main-pack's ten or more miles away, otherwise I reckon… they'd ah been all over us, by now."

"With the women and the baby, it don't make no sense ta run, and be run down, caught out in the open, by dem Injuns. Other than killing, riding their ponies is the best thing, them Comanches know how to do."

"One thing that works in our favor, is that them Indians that kilt Ragged Man, don't know that we, he pointed his finger at Billy, then to his own chest, that we two men with guns and rifles, are here."

Hank came bounding down the stairs and joined the men. He looked at Gus and then at his father…I'm here Dad, there are three men, he shook the rifle in his hands, there's three men with guns and rifles here."

"Gus turned to Hank, my mistake Hank…they's three men with guns here."

"Gus turned his attention to Billy; do you have any more guns and ammunition in the house?"

Billy nodded his head in the affirmative. "I've got four more rifles, two revolvers and plenty of ammunition. They're upstairs in my closet."

Without further conversation, Billy handed Gus a rifle, and three boxes of shells. Two of the boxes of shells were for the rifle, and a box of bullets, was for his six-shooter, his Colt-revolver.

Rebecca, with the baby in her arms, entered the room. She immediately went to Gus. Her voice cracking with emotion, she asked; "Gus, Hank, Hank… where is Hank?"

Hank, who had been closing and locking the door and the windows in the kitchen, ran over to his mother; "I'm right here Ma".

Relieved, Rebecca took a modicum of comfort and solace in the fact that her "Little Hank"— as she still in her mind thought of him—, had not been found in the barn, murdered along-side, Ragged Man.

Billy quickly overcame, the momentary shame he had felt for not thinking of his son…his son Hank's safety. He could only hope that Rebecca hadn't taken note of his apparent lack of concern for the boy's safety.

Billy wisely concluded that the saving of the life of his wife, the life of baby- Mandy, and Hank…saving his family, was his immediate concern.

****

Although Billy was Gus' employer, he wisely and seamlessly, deferred the leadership of their defenses to the ex-shootest, Augustus Thompson.

Billy asked; Gus, where do you want me and Hank?" "Do you think we can hold them off?

Gus again scratched his chin. "Depends on how many are coming at us."

"My guess is that they ain't spect'n much resistance."

"At most, if they did see your boy Hank, they'll be spect'n, maybe, a few wild-shots from a boy and maybe, from the woman."

"If the boy weren't here when they kilt Ragged Man, they won't be spect'n no resistance a-tall, from him."

"I think our best chance is to stay outta sight tell they's close enough for us not to miss."

"Then when I yell **<u>NOW</u>**, you and Hank upstairs, lets loose, shootin' thru the slots in the shutters, and me down here, doing the same, opens up on um."

"With most of their bucks gone ta reservation, them that's left won't be wantin' to lose too many warriors. We gotta make the price in Injun-lives, that they hav'ta pay for our scalps and the livestock, to big ah price to pay."

"That just might do it. Back during the war, when I rode with Quantrill's Raiders, Captain Quantrill, wouldda called it, "tactics us using on em, the element of surprise."

"I'm ganna need your house-keeper, the Mex-woman, down here with me, loading and handing me guns. Send her down-stairs, with two of them rifles."

"Miz. Rebecca can be doing the same loading, for you and the boy upstairs. If you get the chance, move ta anotha window and shoot. That way they might think that there's more of us…than there really is."

"Remember Mister Mac, don't start shooting till I yell, **NOW**. Surprise just might be our only chance ta come outta this with our hair still 'tached' to our heads."

****

Chapter 99

Comanche Raiding-Party 1,000 Yards - South-East of the Rosewood - Cattle Ranch - [August 5th, 1875] - 12:45 PM

Chief Stone Fist sent Bear Claw with three warriors, to the rear, on the western side of the ranch.

Bear Claw's instructions were to prevent escape by the women, but most importantly, in the event of the return of the ranch's white men, two of the four warriors were to swiftly, menacingly, ride toward the white men, but before coming in range of their rifles, to veer-off, toward the south.

This maneuver was intended to entice the white men to pursue the two warriors, who would be leading them away from the ranch.

In the event of the white men returning, Bear Claw was to ride back to the ranch to alert Stone Fist.

In his many battles over many years, Stone Fist had witnessed the panic, the fear in the eyes of the *People's* enemies, at the sound and the sight, of attacking Comanche warriors.

Chief Stone Fist's plan was simple. He and the remainder of his warriors, with the sun at their backs, in the eyes of the two women, would ride their ponies at full gallop, charging straight at the ranch house.

Silent Stalker sat upon the back of his favorite war-pony, beside Chief Stone Fist, eagerly awaiting the signal to attack.

His face, as were the faces of all of the warriors, was of two colors. The right side of Silent Stalkers face was painted black, and the left side, was painted a bright, vermilion, red.

Stone Fist raised his war lance. With his knees, the War Chief signaled his pony forward. First at a walk, that within a few strides, the walk became a gallop, a charge forward.

The chief took a deep breath, and screamed at the top of his lungs,
"Aahe-hey... Aahe-hey... Aahe-hey... Aahe-hey!".

Once again, the terrifying, primordial, blood-curdling war cry of the *Nermernuh*, rang-out...resonating, was reverberating, over the southern plains.

As the mounted warriors charged toward the ranch house, Silent Stalker experienced a sudden feeling of dread.

Something had changed… at that instant; Silent Stalker realized that the shutters surrounding the windows of the ranch house, the shutters that had before been open…were now closed.

****

E. Pluribus Unum

Chapter 100

New-Rosewood - Cattle Ranch -
[August 5th, 1875] - 12:38 PM

When she heard the to her, familiar words; "*Aahe-hey… Aahe-hey*", being screamed by the surge of charging Indian warriors, Rebecca knew that the thing that she had most feared and dreaded, when she had been wrestling with her decision to bring Little Hank, west, was occurring.

The nightmare was happening. Comanche warriors were attacking her and her family.

To her surprise, instead of being filled with, and consumed with fear, Rebecca was instead, filled and consumed with resolve.

As she stood next to Billy, ready to hand her husband, his second loaded rifle, Rebecca gritted her teeth, and under her breath muttered, "*Never again…Never, Never, again!*"

Billy, with his rifle cocked, was standing at one of the bedroom windows.

As instructed by Gus, the barrel of Billy's rifle was extended approximately an inch through the "cut-out" in the shutter.

At the sight of ten mounted screaming Indians boring down on the ranch house, it took all of Billy's will power, not to pull the trigger.

Following Gus' instructions, Billy sighted in on one specific target, on the imposing warrior, in front, leading the charging warriors.

Sweat was trickling down Billy's forehead, a few drops causing his eyes to sting. The tension was nearly unbearable.

Then he heard from downstairs, *NOW!* Followed by the crack, crack, crack, of Gus' rifle.

"Billy began to rapidly fire. Chambering round after round, into the chamber of his lever-action rifle.

At the precise moment that he heard the command *NOW!* A trickle of sweat in his eye caused Billy to blink. Instead of his initial shot striking Stone Fist in his chest, the bullet grazed the War Chief's shoulder.

Within seconds, five of Stone Fist's warriors had been blown from the backs of their ponies.

Under a blistering hale of bullets, Stone Fist and five of his warriors managed to safely reach the porch-veranda.

Stone Fist crutched below the opening in the shutter, the barrel of a rifle swept over his head. Stone Fist grabbed the hot barrel of the rifle and yanked the barrel down toward the floor of the porch.

Gus had loss sight of the warriors. Gus knew that he and the McCloskey family still faced a clear and present danger. Six of the ten warriors had escaped the volley of bullets that had met the Indian's initial assault.

Gus swiveled his rifle from side to side, attempting to acquire a target.

Suddenly the butt of the rifle, as though it had a life of its' own, was jerked upward, from his hands, hitting him in the face…dislodging a tooth, and splitting his upper-lip.

 As suddenly as it had started, the noise of rifle fire stopped.

Upstairs in the bedroom, Billy had run out of targets.

The five warriors that he and Gus had shot were lying in the dirt. Those five were dead, wounded, or dying.

Six of the warriors, presumably, those that made it to the porch, were attempting to gain entry into the house.

Billy heard the distinctive sound of pistol fire. He correctly attributed the pistol fire to having come from Gus' six-shooters.

Billy handed his rifle, and a handgun to Rebecca. "Becky if you hear anyone at the door trying to get in, don't wait…don't hesitate, shoot through the center of the door."

If you can… hide the baby in the closet. There are six bullets in the pistol.

If they get past me and Gus, that means that we're dead. Use the pistol.

Billy with six shot, revolvers in both of his hands, called out to his wife from the hall; "Rebecca, bolt the door! I'm going downstairs to help Gus."

****

The noise and commotion had upset, Baby-Mandy. Reflexively, in a desperate attempt to quite the baby, Rebecca unbuttoned the top three buttons of her dress, pulled her arm through the sleeve, exposing her breast.

She then brought the baby's lips in contact with her nipple.

Baby-Mandy, immediately began to, contently, suckle at her mother's breast.

Rebecca with the baby at her breast, she openened the door of the closet.

                                                     E. Pluribus Unum

With her free hand, she stuffed a wicker-basket with towels and bed linen.

Rebecca placed the baby in the basket and covered the basket with a blanket.

The baby, after having enjoyed her unexpected meal, despite the noise of the struggle downstairs, fell asleep.

Although Billy had not said how she should use the pistol, it was clear to Rebecca, what her husband had left unsaid, as to ho she should interpret his words.

Billy was giving her the option of taking her own life, rather than her being captured, and abused, by the warriors.

In the past, when speaking to her husband about her time as a captive, a slave of the Comanche, Rebecca had fervently repeated her heartfelt vow,
to Billy. Her vow; "Never again"; She had sworn to him that she would take her own life, rather than be taken prisoner again, by the Comanche.

When she placed her baby into the closet, covering her with the blanket, Rebecca had lovingly looked into baby-Mandy's innocent, sparkling blue eyes; at the prominent, "Billings-dimples" that were accented when the baby smiled.

It was then that Rebecca came to the conclusion; that her committing suicide, thus abandoning her daughter, would be by her, the ultimate act of betrayal, and of cowardness.

As Billy left her…probably for the last time, shutting the door, doing all that he could to protect her, and their child, Rebecca at that moment adamantly emphatically, decided against suicide.

She chose life. Rebecca chose to live. She silently vowed to Billy and to Baby-Mandy, to do anything, and everything, to now and if she and her child survived as captives of the Comanche, she would do all that she could, to protect their daughter.

****

Chapter 101

Creating a cloud of dust, Light Foot, the company's Pawnee scout, reined in his horse next to Captain Griffin.

Sgt. Zachary Stevens and Cpl. Justin Gulliver rode up to join the Company Commander, and the scout.

Light Foot jumped from the back of his pony; "Comanche raiders split". The scout held up his hand, folded the thumb over and extended four fingers, "Four warriors, rode west behind big white-man teepee."

Light Foot held up both hands, extending the fingers. "Ten warriors rode to attack the ranch."

The Captain pressed the scout for additional information. "What do mean …rode to attack?" Light Foot, your first report said that there was one woman, an old man, and a boy at the ranch. Are you telling me that a woman, an old man and a boy, put up any meaningful resistance?"

"Many gunshots from big teepee. Four Comanche warriors shot, fall from their ponies.

Light Foot grunted. "Only woman and boy, left to fight. Old man killed before Comanche attack".

Captain Griffin gave his two non-coms swift, crisp, concise orders. "Sgt. Stevens, take six troopers. Go after and neutralize, the four Comanche, who went west and flanked the ranch house."

"Cpl. Gulliver, you and I, with the rest of the troop, will ride double-time, to that ranch. "

"I pray to God that we get there in time to save that woman, her baby, and her boy."

* * * * * * * *

Chapter 102

New-Rosewood - Cattle Ranch
[August 5th, 1875] - 1:05 PM

When it became evident to Gus that at any moment, the warriors would break down the door, he pushed the housekeeper and Billy toward the stairs.

"Upstairs get up ta the high ground. I think we hit at least five of um. I counted six, that made it ta the porch."

"Gus was urgently, yet calmly, reloading his revolvers. "Mr. Mac, our best chance is if'n we can, shooting um down, when they try ta come up the stairs."

Gus gaze fell onto Lucinda, the obviously terrified housekeeper. He put a steadying hand on her shoulder.

"You did real good Lucy. You go on up them stairs now. You be with Miz. Rebecca."

Gus passed a half empty box of shells to Billy; "I ain't heared no gun fire from them devils, means they probly onlys got bows and arrows. And for in-fightin', got knifes and tomahawks".

"The two of us with these six-shooters, agins't six ah them with onlest knifes and tomahawks, gives us ah fightin' chance."

Suddenly Billy dropped the box of shells and yelling the housekeeper's name, bolted up the stairs. "Lucinda, stop!

As she was reaching for the doorknob, Billy lounged himself at the housekeeper, tackling her…knocking her aside, just as a rifle, from inside the room, discharged.

Billy lying on top of Lucinda looked over his shoulder, at the door. The door was splintered with a bullet-hole in the spot, that a second ago, was Lucinda's neck.

When Gus heard the wooden bolt across the front door cracking, he ran up the stairs, taking the twelve steps in three strides.

Stone Fist, followed by Silent Stalker, Crooked Eye, and Antelope Feet, rushed through the door.

Crouching low, the three warriors pushed through the barriers of furniture, sofas, tables, and chairs that Billy and Gus, had piled up against the bolted door.

Both War Chief Stone Fist and Silent Stalker, realized that, no matter the final out-come, this raid had been a catastrophic disaster.

Five of his warriors lay either dead, or dying sprawled, in the dirt.

During the heated battle, although the amount of rifle fire had been intense, Stone Fist had rapidly surmised, that based upon the fact that the heavy rifle-fire seemed to be coming from only two sites, there were but two individuals who had been effectively, firing, cutting-down, his warriors.

One rifle had been firing from a closed-shuttered window, on the second floor of the ranch house and the other, from a close-shuttered window on the ground floor.

****

If his hunting party had had any success in finding significant game, despite the scouting report given to him by Silent Stalker, Stone Fist would not have attacked the ranch.

Stone Fist and his small group of followers of *Kutsueka* Comanche, families, were visitors in the hunting grounds of their friends and allies, the Kiowa.

To initiate a raid, even a raid against the white-eyes, without the consent of the Kiowa, could easily have been construed by their Kiowa friends as being disrespectful...*bad medicine.*

This raid that had been meant to take from this ranch, enough food to sustain his people through, the harsh plains winter—this raid that he had initiated based upon now obviously, faulty information, that the ranch had but a woman and a boy, to defend it—this raid, had been a catastrophic failure, a disaster.

This raid had thus far cost the *"People"*, more specifically, his little group of *Kutsueka,* Comanches, dearly.

****

Silent Stalker had a heavy heart. He was mortified. He as well as his chief knew, that the information that he had given Chief Stone Fist, though accurate at the time, obviously did not reflect the ranch's defenses.

Silent Stalker knew that his favorable, enthusiastic, scouting report was at least, one of the reasons that Chief Stone Fist had attacked the ranch.

When the warriors had charged, what he had told Chief Stone Fist, was a defenseless ranch; their charge had been met with, concentrated, accurate, rifle-fire.

Chief Stone Fist and Silent Stalker knew that the amount, and the accuracy of the rifle fire that the warriors had encountered, could not have possibly come from just a woman, and a boy.

However, for both warriors, Chief Stone Fist, and Silent Stalker, now was not the time for second-guessing or recriminations.

Now was the time to make those in the ranch, whoever, they might be, pay with their lives, for the loss of life, of the fallen warriors.

****

Chapter 103

Before they saw the ranch, the troopers heard the distinctive sound of rapid firing from at least two, Spencer Repeating rifles. Each of the troopers, without having been told, gave extra spur to his mount, urging extra speed, as much speed as possible from their already galloping, horses.

Justin immediately took in the scene. Four Comanche warriors, lay motionlessly in the dirt, maybe fifteen feet, from the ranch house.

Three warriors were attempting forced entry, through the front door, of the ranch house. The physical stature of one of the three warriors, stood-him apart, from that of his two comrades.

The warrior's muscular physique, for just a fleeting instant, reminded Cpl. Justin Gulliver of one of those professional boxers, that he had seen, more than fifteen-years-ago, fighting in the ring, when he—, then Pvt. Jason Ruth, of the Massachusetts 54th, —had paid to see his first professional boxing exhibition, while he was on leave from the Union Army, in the city of Boston.

Four warriors, armed with battleaxes, had gone to the south side of the ranch house, smashed the glass in the windows, and were about to climb into the house.

Captain Griffin, his horse-matching stride for stride, Justin's mount, tapped Justin's arm with the broadside of his saber. He then pointed the saber at the warriors attempting to breech the front door.

Justin nodded his head, indicated that he understood the Captain's non-verbal order.

Captain Griffin and the column of troopers following him, veered off to the left.

Justin, leading his squad, continued straight for the Indians who had finally managed to break down the door and had gained entry, into the ranch house.

Before his horse could come to a complete stop, Justin his service revolver cocked, and in his right hand, leapt to the ground and ran up the steps that lead to the porch.

Justin nimbly jumped over the debri, which had been obstructing entry int the front door of the ranch house.

Pvts. Freddy Gilliam and Joseph Atkins were close behind.

A white man lay dead at the foot of the staircase. The blade of a tomahawk was still lodged in the white-man's chest. The man's torso was split wide-open.

The blade of the tomahawk had neatly, nearly, from his clavicle, to his naval, cut the man in half

The force of the blow had separated, cleaved apart, *as if done by a professional butcher,* the white man's rib cage.

On the floor at the top of the landing, yet another white-man lay, either dead or unconscientious.

Jason thought that he heard, what to him sounded like a woman's voice scream, *"Aahe-hey... Aahe-hey!"*.

There were a few seconds of silence, and then he heard the distinctive sound of a pistol being discharged.

Jason had been caught off guard. He did not remember seeing an Indian squaw with the war party.

For a fraction of a second, he hesitated, then he dove, headlong into the room, prepared to shoot and to kill, the murdering squaw.

****

When she heard the sound of someone running up the steps. Rebecca, tightly gripping the heavy pistol concentrated, straining, listening. The sound of someone approaching the door was not that made by a man wearing heavy boots.

She immediately thought of the sound that she had lived with, during the time that she was held captive by the Comanche. The sound that she was hearing was more akin to the sound made by moccasins worn on the feet of Comanche warriors

As her husband had instructed, Rebecca aimed and fired the pistol, at the center of the closed door.

Rebecca determined to protect her child, slipped into the closet, and closed the door. The baby began to stir.

Rebecca heard the sounds of a violent struggle in the hallway. Then she heard nothing... just quiet.

She heard the sound of the bedroom door opening. Rebecca picked up baby Mandy and attempted to quite her. In a muffled voice, Rebecca whispered," Shush, shush."

Suddenly the closet door was yanked open.

Rebecca gasped.

Standing before her was the embodiment of her nightmares…Stone Fist, his face painted, one side black, the other side red…the devil incarnate.

****

When Stone Fist, followed by Silent Stalker, and Croaked Eye, burst through the front door, Stone Fist sensing movement to his left, dove to the floor.

Silent Stalker, directly behind the War Chief, was struck in the chest, by two bullets, fired in rapid succession, by Gus Thompkins.

Silent Stalker was blown backwards. And was died before his body hit the floor.

Crooked Eye swerved, to avoid the lifeless body of his friend.

Stone Fist stood and charged directly toward the white-man at the foot of the staircase.

Gus leveled his revolver at the head of the oncoming, enraged warrior, and slowly deliberated, squeezed the trigger.

The last sound that the shootist/cowboy, Augustus Thompson would ever hear was hollow sound of the hammer of his revolver, striking an empty cylinder in his six-shooter.

With the unleashing of all of the strength and energy, bursting forth, from his adrenalin saturated, rock-hard, muscular body, with one ferocious swing of his tomahawk, Stone Fist ended the life of Augustus (*Guns-Ablazing-Gus*) Thompkins.

As Stone Fist turned to ascend the stairs, he suddenly felt a stinging sensation in his left shoulder. He had been shot.

Standing at the head of the steps was a white-man, frantically working the lever-action of his rifle.

Stone Fist raced up the stairs. As the white-man was raising the rifle, the head of Stone Fist's war-club made contact with the side of the white-man's head.

Stone Fist, his lethal hunting knife in his right hand, with his left hand, lifted the unconscious man's head by his hair.

As he was about to scalp the man, Stone Fist was thrown off balance, when someone or something knocked the knife from his hand.

"Don't hurt my father…leave my father alone."

Stone Fist turned. At first, he was confused. Standing behind the War Chief, with a chair lifted in the air was he thought… his son Dark Eagle.

During the attack, Stone Fist had been shot twice. He was slightly dizzy from the loss of blood.

"Why would his son Dark Eagle, strike him from behind…why was his son Dark Eagle, wearing white-men's clothes…what had happened to his son, Dark Eagle's long spongy, braids.

As the aberration, was about to swing the chair again, Stone Fist, deftly grabbed the chair with his left hand, and with his right hand, as his name suggested, delivered a resounding blow to who he thought was his son *"Dark Eagle's"*, chin.

Hank dropped to the floor, unconscious.

Still confused and slightly disoriented from blood loss, as he was about to go to the aide of the boy that he thought was his son, Stone Fist heard a muffled sound, coming from within the bedroom.

Stone Fist cautiously examined the bullet hole in the door. The exterior of the door was splintered.

Stone Fist deduced that the bullet that had made the hole in the door had been fired from inside the room.

Standing to the side of the door, with his left hand, Stone Fist turned the doorknob, and entered the room.

As he was surveying the room and about to open the door to the closet, Stone Fist heard, gunshots coming from downstairs.

He turned and was about to leave to investigate, when he heard, coming from the behind the closed door of the closet, a faint, shushing sound.

Stone Fist turned the closet's doorknob, and yanked open, the door.

On the floor, slumped over a papoose, was a white woman. Stone Fist reached down, intending to pull the woman to her feet.

His hand stopped in mid-air, when the woman looked up at him and screamed.

It was not the screaming of the woman that had stilled his hand. It was what she screamed, that had caused him to pause.

Aahe-hey… Aahe-hey!

While she was screaming, *Aahe-hey… Aahe-hey*, the woman repeatedly, five times in rapid succession, pulled the trigger of the six-shooter.

The blonde-haired white woman, continued screaming *Aahe-hey… Aahe-hey*; as the hammer of her revolver, continued to click, click, click, on the revolver's empty cylinders.

Holding his abdomen, Stone Fist slumped to the floor, in his state of intense pain and lingering confusion, the War Chief looked into the terrified eyes of the white woman.

Stone Fist's confused brain, managed to force from his lips, the words…the question… *Eebi Tseena Puis? (Blue Wolf Eyes?).*

****

The momentum of his dive into the bedroom carried Justin into the center of the room.

Justin rolled over to a standing position, sweeping his service revolver around the room, searching for a target.

Seated on the floor, slumped in the corner, his hand over his abdomen, blood seeping through his fingers, was the muscular warrior that he had seen, leading the assault on the ranch house.

Standing over the man was a white woman, she held a baby in crook of her left arm, and a smoking revolver in her right hand.

The Comanche warrior, with a surprised, a disbelieving look in his eyes, began to speak; "*Eebi tseena puis… (Pale Wolf Eyes…it is you?).*"

The wounded warrior coughed; a trickle of blood ran down his cheek. "*Eebi tseena puis… (Pale Wolf Eyes…you will take my family, my people, to the reservation.)*"

Justin did not understand a word of the gibberish spewing forth from the dying warrior's lips.

To his utter surprise, the white woman began to speak, what Justin believed to be the same non-sensical language.

"*Nananisuyake Ta?Si?Woo? Tso?Yaa…Pretty Buffalo Hair, where is my sister?*"

The warrior attempted to answer, but instead, he experienced a spasm of intense coughing, culminated with his coughing-up a stream of bloody-mucus.

The white woman yelled at the obviously dying warrior. *Nananisuyake Ta?Si?Woo? Tso?Yaa, Nananisuyake Ta?Si?Woo? Tso?Yaa,* Pretty Buffalo Hair, my black sister…*Mahn-dee, Mahn-dee,* is she with you?" Is Mahn-dee alive?

Try as he might, with the essence of life rapidly leaving his body, The War Chief of the Kutsueka Comanche, was unable to answer.

Stone Fist was dead.

Justin was fascinated. The white woman actually appeared to have understood what to him had sounded like, non-sensical gibberish.

Rebecca turned to face the black soldier, "The men, Billy and Gus…are they all right?"

When Justin did not immediately answer, Rebecca dropped the pistol, and grabbed the black soldier's sleeve. And pleadingly whispered, are they hurt…are they alive.

E. Pluribus Unum

Jason seeing the pleading in the woman's bright blue eyes, in a soft and caring tone, answered; one man is dead, I think the other man is not seriously injured. He's in the hall... gotta huge bump on his head.

Captain Griffin, his saber in his left hand and his service pistol in the right, stepped into the room.

The captain's eyes quickly surveyed the room. He saw the mortally wounded Indian slumped over dead, in the corner of the room.

His gaze took in the strikingly handsome, blonde white woman, with her infant held tightly in her arms, and he saw one of the company's corporals calmly holstering his side arm.

Before the captain could speak, the woman with her baby in her arms, bolted by him.

"Billy, Billy...thank God. Billy are you, all right? Hank, Hank...where's Hank?"

The teenage boy, rubbing his chin, walked into the room. I'm here mom, I'm okay."

The captain, wanting to give the family a moment's privacy, shut the door.

Captain Griffin concentrated, but for the life of him, he could not remember the corporal's name.

The captain made a mental note to himself, to learn the man's name, and to in recognition of Corporal...what's his name's valor, and his decisive action, to promote the corporal to the rank of sergeant.

Instead of addressing the trooper by name, which he could not recall, the captain remarked: "Well done corporal. It appears that the woman and her baby are unhurt."

Half listening to the captain Justin mumbled...yes sir. Justin saluted and left the room.

Rebecca, her fidgety baby, and the man that Justin presumed was her husband, where seated together, hugging each other, on the floor of the landing, at the top of the staircase

Justin decided not to interrupt the reunited family. As he stepped over the family, Rebecca lifted her head: "Thank you corporal.

Billy extended his hand, "Billy McCloskey, my family will forever be in your debt corporal. If there is ever anything, I can do for you, you've but to ask."

Justin touched the brim of his hat; he took one step, then turned and spoke to Rebecca. "I'm sorry mam, but I've just got to ask. When that Indian started spouting that mumble jumble, you seemed to understand what he was saying."

Rebecca lifted her head from her husband's shoulder. Half defiantly and half inquisitively, she responded. "I did...I did...I do understand a little bit of the Comanche language."

Justin blurted out, the reason I ask maam is because I didn't understand a word of the conversation, until I heard you say the word Mahn-dee."

Rebecca was startled. For what seemed like a full minute, she looked at… stared hard, at the ruggedly handsome face, of the tall black soldier.

 Justin was about to turn and walk away, when Rebecca calmly handed the baby to Billy, stood and asked; What's your name soldier?"

Justin, beginning to feel a little awkward answered, "My name is Justin Gulliver maam."

To Justin's surprise, he thought he saw a look of disappointment in the white woman's eyes."

Justin turned to continue down the steps, when the woman spoke in a hushed, muted voice; "I was hoping that you would say that your name is Jason Billings".

Corporal Justin Gulliver almost tripped, missing a step as he stumbled down the stairs.

****

Chapter 104

Campsite of Chief Stone Fist's Group of Kutsueka Comanches - [Two Days Later]

Antelope Feet, one of the four warriors that had been chased by the detachment, of Buffalo Soldiers, led by Sgt. Stevens, managed to elude capture, and was able to return to the Comanche encampment.

When the exhausted warrior rode into camp, he went directly to the lodge of Gray Wolf, who in the absence of Chief Stone Fist was the titular, transient leader, of the migrating small group of Comanche families.

Antelope Feet told Gray Wolf of what the hunting party— turned raiding party's—, disastrous raid on the white cattle ranch.

Antelope Feet told of the raid on the settler's ranch, to obtain food for the village. He told Gray Wolf of the sudden, unexpected arrival of the Buffalo Soldiers, and of his belief that, Chief Stone Fist and the entire hunting party, were either dead, or captives of the bluecoat soldiers

Gray Wolf's immediate thought was to convene a meeting of the council. Then the futility of that action, swept over him.

There were no warriors left to sit in council. There were no warriors left to hunt the buffalo, that now like his warriors, had seized to exist.

There were no warriors left to defend his now, defenseless group.

Gray Wolf was resolute. With sudden clarity, he reached the inevitable conclusion.

The time had come. It was time.

He, as had Chief Quanah Parker, and the other leaders of the many bands of Comanche, would prepare the followers Stone Fist, for the journey to the Fort Sill, Reservation.

****

Rebecca with baby-Mandy in her arms; her husband Billy, and her son Hank, were all seated on one of the four wagons, that Captain Griffin had given her permission to bring to the Comanche encampment.

Yesterday evening, as Rebecca was applying cold—actually luke-warm— compresses to Billy's head, Rebecca told her husband of her confrontation with the Comanche warrior who had killed Gus, bludgeoned him, and threatened her life, and the life of their child.

Billy was stunned, astonished, when Rebecca told him that the demonic warrior, that had attacked them was Stone Fist!

Stone Fist, the fiendish warrior that had repeatedly raped her. Stone Fist, who Rebecca had stressed to Billy, that although Stone Fist was the source of the sperm that resulted in the life of their son Hank, that Stone Fist was not Hank's father.

Billy hesitantly asked Rebecca if she intended to tell Hank, that the Indian that she had killed, was Stone Fist…that Stone Fist was his father.

Rebecca did not hesitate to respond. With tears streaming down her cheeks, she had loving held Billy's face in her hands.

She had looked deeply into her husband's eyes and emotionally, emphatically had stated; "No I won't. What good would it do? It would only establish in Hank's mind, that his being born, was because of the vicious act of a wild savage."

"Billy, you've often heard me speak of the influence in my life, of Eleanor Leary. Eleanor Leary was the Yankee school teacher that my father hired to teach me, and my brother the classics."

"Well one of the multitudes of wise statements, actually life-altering lessons, that Miss Leary taught Mandy and me was so simple, so obvious, yet so very, very, important to know, to appreciate, and to understand."

Rebecca paused and waited. When she was sure that she had Billy's full attention, she continued.

"No one, now living, or for that matter, no one who has ever lived, or will ever live… no one had, or will ever have, any control, as to who will be his or her biological-parents."

"For my sister Mandy, and to me, that was one of the most important precepts, that Miss Leary shared with the daughters of Henry Billings."

"And Billy, that is why you can damn-well be sure of, that I will tell…that I will teach that undeniable, universal fact, to our children."

"Billy you, William McCloskey, you… the man who taught him to ride a horse, to rope a calf, you, Billy, the man who when he was still a child, each night tucked him into bed, read to him, … Billy you, are Hank's father.

When the McCloskey family arrived at the Comanche encampment, Rebecca was once again, as she had been nearly a decade ago, instantly impressed by the efficiency of the Comanche women, as they dismantled the tepees, and packed their meager belongings, onto the travois', attached to their ponies.

It had been Rebecca's intent to assist the Comanche women, by making available to them four wagons, to transport their belongings, instead of their relying on as had their, mothers and their grandmother's, the use of the travois'.

Rebecca had reasoned that the Comanche braves, or perhaps, if need be, a few of the Buffalo Soldiers, could be assigned the task of driving the wagons ladened with the *"People's"* belongings, on the long journey, to the Fort Sill Reservation.

Hank was fascinated and impressed by the skill, and the industriousness of the Comanche women.

Hank's life-long suppressed prejudices, that he had been carrying since he was four years old, when his mother had reluctantly, with tears in her eyes, had told him the meaning of the slur, the pejorative term that his cousins, his mother's sister's children, continuously, called him, *"half-breed"*.

For two-thirds of his short life, Hank had been plagued with dormant, but real feelings of self-loathing, due to his "mixed-blood", due to his classification by society, as being a "half-breed".

The myth that Indians were lazy, indolent, people, a stereotype that had been reinforced in him, by the drunken, sloven Indian-beggars that he had frequently seen mulling around in towns, was being rapidly dissipated.

This was the first time that he had seen Indians, his father's people…his people, men women and children, living, working, in their natural environment.

****

Rebecca spotted her black-sister's brother, Sergeant Justin Gulliver. Sgt. Gulliver was riding, at the head of a column of Buffalo Soldiers.

Rebecca thought of the few words that she yesterday, had exchanged, with the impressive, buffalo soldier.

Rebecca had asked Captain Griffin for his permission…to allow her to "personally talk to and to thank… that corporal", who had so gallantly come to her assistance".
Rebecca had been seated, sipping a cup of coffee, at her kitchen table, when Justin, his United States Army's cavalry-men's Kepi Cap in-hand, knocked on the half-open door.

"Beg pardon mame…Cap'n said you wanted to see me?"

Rebecca picked up the coffe pot…filled a cup with the hot liquid. She pushed the cup of steaming coffee across the table…and pointed to a chair.

"Have a seat…she paused for a second. Then putting deliberate emphasis in her pronunciation of the name that the captain had provided…have a seat *Corporal Justin Gulliver*."

"No thanks you mame, I'm fine standing right here."

Rebecca was persistent. Please Corporal, again she addressed him as, Corporal Justin Gulliver. She then added, or should I say, please have a seat, Sergeant Major Jason Ruth."

> Following yesterday's action, Justin had had a lingering, a nagging sensation…a feeling that he had seen, this white-woman, Mrs. McCloskey before.

Rebecca seeing the confusion on the soldier's face, continued; "Richmond Virginia, 1867. "We were both dining at that trendy French Restaurant…oh yes I believe the name of the establishment was the *"Le Grand Vieux Manoir"*.

"I was there with a stuffed-shirt bore. When you in the dress blue uniform of a Sergeant Major, a row of glimmering medals pinned to your chest, entered the all-white restaurant, with a breath-takenly, gorgeous, beautiful black woman, clinging to your arm."

Justin walked over to the chair, sat and reached for the cup of coffee. Justin had thought; "Okay…this is it. My past has finally caught-up with me."

Before he could speak, Rebecca continued; "That night at the French Restaurant, when I passed by your table, I had this vague feeling that I had seen you before. Now that I've had time to think about that brief moment, I think that the reason that I did not recognize you, was that splendid uniform, with the shiny brass buttons, and the rows of medals, that distracted me."

"It was when I read that horrible news paper article—accusing the black-soldier, Sgt. Major Jason Ruth—, that the Gazette said was a runaway from Rosewood Plantation, that I fleetingly entertained the absurd thought, that that man Jason Ruth, may have been my former slave, Jason Billings, whose mother was my former slave, Ruth."

"I remember thinking it preposterous to think, that the man that I had seen at the restaurant, gazing oh so lovingly, into the eyes of his date, that that man, who I have come to believe was my sister's brother Jason, could be guilty of murdering that beautiful woman, that he so obviously loved."

"At that time, I dismissed, the accusation, as well as the vague feeling, that I had seen that soldier, before".

"Seeing the confusion in Justin's eyes, without giving him a chance to respond, Rebecca continued; "Jason, she stopped herself …I'm sorry, Justin. I apologize if I've upset you.

Justin, I too changed my name. Although its' not an alias…when I married William McCloskey, I took his name."

"Before my marriage, my name was Rebecca Billings."

"Henry Billings, my father, is your sister's…my sister, Mandy's father."

"I am your sister Mandy's, sister… I'm Becky, Mandy's sister."

                                         E. Pluribus Unum

For more than an hour, over several cups of coffee, Rebecca, and Justin sat talking.

Rebecca told of her and Mandy's, father's decision to sell the Rosewood Plantation, and to relocate in the west.

She told Justin of her and Mandy's father Henry Billings', death and of the death of his mother Ruth, when Tonkawa Indians, attacked their disabled wagon.

She told of how she and Mandy had been rescued, from the Tonkawa by the Tonkawa's archenemies, the Comanche. And then how she and Mandy had been made captive-slaves of the Comanche.

Rebecca told Justin of her's and Mandy's time living with the Comanche. Of Mandy's falling in love with and marrying, a Comanche warrior. And how together, Mandy and her husband, Running Eagle, helped her to escape.

Rebecca told Justin of Mandy's decision…Mandy's choosing not, to return with her to the white-man's "civilization".

She told Justin of Mandy's choice to become Comanche. She told of her…their sister's desire to stay with her husband, to live her life as a Comanche. How Mandy had made the choice to stay with her warrior husband, and to raise their unborn child, "*Free*".

Justin had sat quietly concentrating, while he listened, absorbing each and every word, as this stranger, this white woman, who as he studied her face he thought, looked like an adult, blue-eyed version of his sister Mandy.

As the woman continued to talk, Justin (*Jason*) stared at her mouth. Though her lips were not as full, as where Mandy's, on each side of her mouth, was an indentation, a dimple, identical to the two dimples, that he remembered highlighting, and enhancing his sister's radiant smile.

When Rebecca finished talking. There was a brief moment of silence, as Rebecca studied Justin's face, looking for his reaction, while he in turn, Justin continued to look at Rebecca's dimpled cheeks

Justin broke the silence. "Do you think that my…that our sister…is there a possibility that Mandy's alive and maybe with these Comanches?"

****

As she sat in the wagon, watching the Comanche women dismantle the teepees, in her peripheral vision, Rebecca thought that she saw among the Indian women, a group of three, working diligently. She noticed that one of the three women appeared to be walking oddly.

She walked as if her moccasins were too small, constricting her feet. Instead of walking, the woman appeared to be "prancing". Instead of a reddish-copper, skin-tone, the woman with the exceedingly, small feet, had a yellowish tinge to her skin, and It seemed to Rebecca, her eyes were nearly closed…slanted.

At first, she thought that two of the women, seemed familiar. Then with clarity, and certainty, the women's names, popped into her head.

Without preamble, with a ring of urgency in her voice, Rebecca shouted to her husband; "Billy, stop the wagon".

Rebecca handed baby-Mandy to her husband and jumped down from the wagon. She ran toward the three Comanche women. One woman appeared to be middle-aged, the other two, Rebecca, thought to be about her age.

Rebecca shouted; "Little Flower, Spring Blossom… is that you?"

****

The Indian women, turned. Spring Blossom, seeing the strange white woman running toward them, picked-up a stick, and stood defiantly in front of her mother.

When he saw the white woman, running at, the two Indian squaws, Sergeant Justin Gulliver, hastily reined in his horse.

Almost commensurate with his dismounting, from the corner of his eye, Justin saw the movement of a tall dark young, brave, movement toward the two squaws.

Justin nonchalantly, loosened the flap that secured his pistol, in its' holster.

This morning's orders, given to him by Captain Griffin, had been concise and precise: "Sergeant Gulliver, your squad is to observe, to supervise, and if need be, to assist the Indians preparation for their march to Fort Sill."

'You are to wait for my arrival with the entire company. At which time we will begin the journey, our original orders, to escort the Indians, to the Fort Sill reservation."

"I have granted the Rosewood ranch-owners request to—God only knows why— to provide wagons to help with the move. The entire company will join your squad at around 1300 hours."

"Those Sergeant, are your official orders. Unofficially Sgt. if anything…anything goes wrong and harm befalls that family, *the McCloskey family,* I'll have your ass."

"Yours' will be the shortest lived sergeantcy…if that's even a word…in the history of the United States Army."

Justin managed to get between the white woman, and the Indian Squaw, standing menacingly in front of the older woman. The two women had been joined by the tall, dark, brave.

                                                                E. Pluribus Unum

Rebecca's son Hank, in response to the tabloid unfolding in front of him, jumped down from the wagon, and ran to his mother's side.

Justin held his right arm, the palm of his hand facing the white woman, and his lift harm behind his back, palm facing the squaw with the stick in her hand.

"Whoa whoa, hang on there, Mrs. McCloskey."

Rebecca on her tiptoes, tried to see around Justin's 6'2" frame. Unable to do so, she pushed past Justin, followed by her son Hank, and this time instead of speaking English, she pointed to her chest and shouted; *"Eebi tseena puis, "Eebi tseena puis* (Pale Wolf Eyes, Pale Wolf Eyes).

Both Little Flower and her widowed daughter, Spring Blossom, in unison asked; "Pale Wolf Eyes, is that you?"

Justin, seeing the Indian squaws' reaction, primarily the younger woman throwing away the branch, and the relaxed posture assumed by the dark teenager, stepped aside.

Rebecca ran to Little Flower. Then speaking in long forgotten, broken Comanche, mixed with English, frantically asked; *"Nananisuyake Ta? Si? Woo? Tso? Yaa…*Pretty Buffalo Hair, where is my sister?
*Nananisuyake Ta? Si? Woo? Tso? Yaa…*Pretty Buffalo Hair, where is my sister Mahn-Dee?

Justin's demeanor abruptly changed, when he distinctly heard the word "***Mahn-Dee***".

Justin had become instantly, acutely, interested in the conversation, when he heard mixed in the potpourri of strange sounding words, Rebecca say the word "***Mahn-Dee***".

He experienced a queasy, nauseating, sensation in the pit of his stomach, when he watched the crest-fallen expression on Rebecca's face, when the older Indian answered Rebecca's question.

Little Flower reached out her hand, and placed on *Eebi tseena puis* (Pale Wolf Eyes' shoulder. Little Flower turned and beckoned the tall, dark, young brave who had obviously run to her defense.

With pride reflected in her eyes and her voice she spoke to Rebecca:
"This is my grandson Dark Eagle. He is the son, of my son, Running Eagle, and the son of your black sister Pretty Buffalo Hair, …*Mahn-Dee.*

Little Flower pointed at Rebecca and said, *"Dark Eagle is the nephew of Eebi tseena puis (Pale Wolf Eyes'). Dark Eagle is of your blood"*.

Rebecca sorrow had been instantly replaced with wonder. She looked into the black-obsidian eyes of the handsome, tall, young warrior.

Her eyes took in the in the texture of the youth's two glistening, curly, black braids, so reminiscent, of the way *Pretty Buffalo Hair's* (Mandy's), springy-braids, used to bounce off her chest, when she ran.

She looked at, and marveled at the young warriors' high cheekbones.

Cheekbones that, as she turned to look at the face of her son Hank, she reflected, had an uncanny, strikingly "familial" resemblance, to those of the young Comanche warrior, Dark Eagle.

Rebecca, noted that on each side of the young Comanche's face, were the two indentations, the "***Billings Dimples***".

They were, the same pair of dimples, that Rebecca, her sister Mandy, the dimples that Rebecca and Billy's daughter, Mandy Margaret McCloskey baby-Mandy, Rebecca's sister's namesake, and both of these boys, all shared.

As Rebecca critically, compared the faces of the two boys, her son Hank, and the young Comanche brave, who were now standing side-by-side, Rebecca was struck with the thought, the realization that; "Without his long braids, Dark Eagle, would be "the spitting image of my son… his cousin…Hank".

Spontaneously, out-of-the-blue, Rebecca to the confusion of all around her, inserted yet another language into the conversation, this time a French expression, that had been, taught to her and to her sister Mandy, by her former tutor, Miss Eleanor Leary.

Rebecca exclaimed, ***"Voila!" Le Coup-de Cras!"***

****

When mother and son…Rebecca and Hank returned to the wagon. Before Billy could ask, Hank, excitedly blurted-out; "Dad, you won't believe what just happened." Again, before his father could respond, Hank blurted out,
"I just met my cousin…my actual blood, cousin, a Comanche brave, Dark Eagle."

Billy looked first at his son, and then he gave an inquisitive, incredulous, look towards his wife.

Rebecca took baby-Mandy from, her husband's arms and whispered; "I'll tell you all about it, when we get home."

None of the Comanche women had opted to use the McCloskey's wagons.

They had instead, as Little Flower had explained to Rebecca; "The Comanche wished to, as the "People" had done forever, walk and ride their ponies, across the prairie to their new home, at the Fort Sills reservation."

The McCloskey family watched, as the small caravan, escorted by Buffalo Soldiers, led by her sister Mandy's brother, Jason, slowly moved across the prairie.

E. Pluribus Unum

While baby-Mandy, insistently nursed at the breast of her mother. Rebecca leaned against her husband's broad shoulders.

She was experiencing, mixed emotions. She remembered the sorrow, and the grief that she had felt when she first lost, her mother, then her father.

The grief that she felt now, more than a decade after she had last seen her sister, when she was told of her sister Mandy's death.

Mandy's death, more so than that of anyone that she had ever loved, hurt the most.

It hurt so...so…badly.

Not only had…had; No…not had, definitely not had.

Even after having been told of her death, the correct tense of the verb to express her feelings…, her emotions was, Did.

Rebecca even after hearing of the death of her beloved sister Mandy Billings... Pretty Buffalo Hair, Wife of Running Eagle, would always remember with love, her black-sister, Mandy.

As she looked out at the procession, slowly making its' way across the vast, seemingly endless plains, Rebecca's thoughts turned to Eleanor Leary.

Miss Eleanor O'Leary, the Irish Catholic woman, who had opened the eyes, and the hearts, of Henry Billing's two daughters, the privileged white girl, Rebecca, and the black slave-girl, Mandy.

Rebecca looked at the Indians, Little Flower, the three widowed wives of Stone Fist, Spring Blossom, his Mexican wife Juanita (Neetah), his Chinese wife Mai-Ling (*"Walks Oddly"*), Rebecca looked at the Buffalo soldiers, most of them ex-slaves, as had been, her beloved sister Mandy.

Baby-Mandy gurgled, signaling to her mom, that her little "tummy" was full.

Rebecca looked into the bright blue-eyes of her, beautiful white, Anglo-Saxon daughter. As she pulled her dress over her still moist, pink, nipple, she glanced at Hank, her mixed-blood son, now asleep in the rear of the wagon.

Rebecca glanced over at her husband, and in a muted voice, so as not to wake, baby Mandy, softly, under her breath, with reverence, muttered his name, William Anthony McCloskey.

As her thoughts once again, returned to the loss of her sister Mandy, Rebecca began to softly cry.

Billy placed his arms around his wife, the mother of his children.

He heard Rebecca mumbling. At first, he thought she was speaking Comanche. As he listened more closely, he decided that what his wife was speaking was neither English, nor was it, Comanche.

Rebecca sat up. Billy gave her his handkerchief; she wiped the tears from her cheeks.

"Honey what were you saying, what language were you speaking?"

Rebecca smiled. "I was thinking of Rosewood, not our ranch, I was thinking of the times that Miss Leary, Mandy and I had spent, down by the creek".

"I was thinking of one of our Latin lectures. I remember asking Miss Leary why was she wasting our time, teaching us an old, dead, language.

"Miss Leary had smiled and stared at me, then at Mandy, and finally, she had dramatically walked over to the creek, bent over and stared into the still, clear-water, looking at her own reflection."

Mandy and I watched—unbeknownst to Miss Leary, we had our own nickname for her, to each other, we had given her the nickname; "The Drama Queen", because of the intense emotion she had, when speaking about something that really mattered to her.

I will always remember Miss Leary's answer to my question, as to why she was "wasting-our-time", teaching us Latin, a dead language.

"Miss Leary had simply said that some of the wisest most sacred and most cherished thoughts and words, were put forth by men who spoke, and wrote Latin."

"Both Mandy and I stared at her, expecting from Miss Leary, a more detailed answer to my question".

Dramatically, as was her manner, Miss Leary, as if she was quoting from the "Dead-Sea-Scrolls, spoke:

"E. Pluribus Unum"
"Mandy had repeated the phrase; E. Pluribus Unum…and asked, what does it mean?"

"Miss Leary smiled and said, if you'll remember, before I spoke, I a gave you girls, three hints."

Billy was listening, hanging on to his wife's, every word.

Seeing that she had her husband's full attention, Rebecca continued.

"Once again, Miss Leary flashed that mischievous smile. Rebecca do you remember when I looked...stared at you; then I stared at Mandy, and finally I walked over to the creek, and looked at my reflection in the water."

"I had been looking at three different human-beings. First you Rebecca, a white girl, born into privilege, a daughter of the Southern Aristocracy."

"Then I looked at you Mandy, a black girl, born into a life of poverty, a life of slavery."

"Then I looked at myself, born the daughter of a poor Irish potato farmer".

"Born to parents who in order to stay alive and make, for their children a better life, immigrated to this still flawed, but wonderful country, the United States of America."

"The literal translation English translation of the Latin _**E. Pluribus Unum**_ is:

$$\textbf{\textit{E. Pluribus Unum}} = \textbf{\textit{"Out Of Many...One."}}$$

"Always teaching...Miss Leary went on to say; "That is what, I believe, is the key to America's greatness."

"Its' the diversity, its' our hetergeneousity, the cultural and intellectual contributions, made by the many divergent groups of people, that will make this country, some day, the greatest country on Earth."

Billy looked around at the slowly moving caravan of Comanche.

Its' population consisting of; Native Americans, Mexican-Americans, Asian Armericans, Americans of "Mixed-blood", and Americans of African descent, the (Buffalo Soldiers).

Billy shook his head and said; "That Miss Eleanor O'Leary must have been a helluva teacher!"

Rebecca with a huge smile on her face, affirmatively, nodded her head, as her Scottish born, immigrant husband, William "_Billy_" McCloskey, broke away from the caravan, turning the two mules' heads north, in the direction of their home.

The End

www.ingramcontent.com/pod-product-compliance
Lightning Source LLC
Chambersburg PA
CBHW030907300726
48970CB00001B/47